UNDER A HARD BLUE SKY

KIM MARTIN
MYKEL HAWKE

UNDER A HARD
BLUE SKY

A JAKE TYLER NOVEL

PIXEL DRAGON PRESS

For information, email: authors@martinandhawke.com.

First Pixel Dragon Press U.S. trade edition February 2021

Published and printed in the United States.

Book Design by Kim Martin
Cover Image: Marcel Kovacic

martinandhawke.com

ISBN: 978-0-9829316-3-9

PIXEL DRAGON
PRESS

ACKNOWLEDGMENTS

The intention was always to continue right on after the series launch. But...life happens...and brings challenging things. So it's been a few years. For the sake of continuity, and hopefully with the understanding of our readers, we have taken the liberty of a time blur. Obviously, much has happened in the years since the publication of *In the Dark of the Sun*, the first book in the Jake Tyler series; people have aged, technology has advanced, places have evolved, and then there was a pandemic. But in many ways a lot has not changed, most notably the good and the evils of the world.

With the interest of those new to our Jake Tyler series in mind, you should know that there are spoilers that reference the first book in the series. For this reason, while each book can be read as a stand-alone novel, you may want to read them in order.

An enormous amount of research and resources go into our thrillers, beginning long before the first word and continuing throughout the creative process. So, as with the first book, we have a great many wonderful people to thank...

Phillip Gonzales once again, for the initial facilitation that brought us together in this great endeavor.

Paul Jimenez and Jack Ewing for enduring friendship, support, and continued feedback. Special thanks, again, to *Hacienda Barú* and to Jack for his assistance and expertise in all things Dominical.

One of the earliest inspirations for this book was Nir Kalron of the Maisha Group. His organization is quite dynamic and diversified, but his work in countering the illegal trade of persons, wildlife, and natural resources is extraordinary, and we were most fortunate for his input.

Also early in gaining a foothold were some stellar organizations doing amazing things: Invisible Children, The Enough Project, The Resolve, The Sentry, The Leonardo DiCaprio Foundation, and The Eastern Congo Initiative with special thanks to Jason Russell, Sean Poole, Lisa Dougan, John Pendergast and, of course, George Clooney, Leonardo DiCaprio, and Ben Affleck. It is by your actions and advocacy many are heard and seen and given the means to better lives.

Additional thanks to Peter Eichstaedt and Ledio Cajak for the sharing of information based on their work.

In Costa Rica: The ever-enchanting Dominical, with special thanks to the owners of the beautiful Casa Serendipia for the use of their home; Alvaro Cedeño and Tara Tiedemann of the *Guardavidas* Costa Ballena who provide an invaluable service in protecting the beaches and those who enjoy them; additional thanks to Beth Sylver.

In Africa: Gaël Brose who shared his time at *Le Caf Conc* and much about his city and culture, as well as his friendship; respects to the memory of Noël Camillieri (RIP); Achille Diodio for his help with Garamba National Park and Alain Lushimba, Lobeke National Park; the ever-inspiring and dedicated personnel of African Parks.

Brother Roger Gumeagiti of Frères de l'Instruction Chrétienne for help with Dungu and insights into the Azande culture; Yegon Ephanitus for going above and beyond with his assistance in Nairobi, also Cyrus Tarei.

Martine Villeneuve, of the Danish Refuge Counsel for sharing the nature of her incredible work and Dr. Lanice Jones, Médecins Sans Frontières, for hers; both for a wealth of knowledge and friendship. Also from MSF, Dr. Alexander Nyman.

Nicholas V. Passalacqua, PhD, D-ABFA, Forensic Anthropology, Western Carolina University for lending his expertise in matters of the deceased; Dr. Sam Wasser, PhD, Endowed Chair In Conservation Biology, Director, Center for Conservation Biology, Research Professor, University of Washington, for the privilege of basing our Nairobi professor on his esteemed work in animal conservation.

For helping to guide us in the skies: esteemed pilots Barend de Klerk, Thomas Vander Velden, Jon Cadd of Mission Aviation Fellowship, Jean Deschênes of Aviation Sans Frontières, Simon Canning, and helicopter pilot Jay Brown. Also instrumental in aviation was the assistance of Darin Voyles of Paramount Business Jets, Nicole Wilke of Private Fly, Mary Beth Butler of Gulfstream; Luis Fernando Hernandez Bolaños for his assistance at Juan Santamaría International Airport.

On the seas: Benjamin Dinsmore for helping us navigate our way in container shipping; also, Jannik Fischer of Africa Container Shipping; Peter Kijzerwaard of Confeeder Shipping & Chartering; Demetrios Liaroutsos.

For the Tech: Eric Evenchick and Dennis Maldonado, black hats; Addie Ventris with Tactical/CORE; Joe Ailinger and Walter Patenaude at FLIR; Jordan Hassin and Iridium, Leslie Landers and Invisio. Special thanks and recognition to FLIR for providing so much of Jake's cool tech and to Lindsay Lyon of Ocean Guardian for the gracious use of their technology for Cyrus Keogh.

Michael Marriott of David Austin Roses for his suggestions on Callie's roses; Peter Wunderlin for help with flora.

Chris Chappel whose kindness and encouragement back in the day may very well have been the difference between continuing to seek the dream or not.

There are quite a few others whose help, information, and knowledge was key but who, for security reasons, wish to remain anonymous—they know who they are, and for their contributions, we are extremely grateful.

A band of brothers who, in one way or another, lent their spirit.

Finally, we thank our friends and families for their love and support.

AUHTORS' NOTE

While there are so many urgent and dire dilemmas ongoing in the world today—everything from wars to contagions to starvation and poverty to environmental disasters and climate change—the atrocities occurring every day in Africa are no less critical, but all too easily under-emphasized and over-shadowed. We salute the inspiring and diligent work of those who make it their mission to help the humans and the animals, often at their peril. To the tactical operators, the advocates and aid workers, the pilots and medical staff, the journalists and filmmakers, and the courageous park rangers…we can only hope our book enlightens and does justice to the wonderful souls that you are. THANK YOU.

UNDER A HARD BLUE SKY

PART ONE

THE DISAPPEARED

1

A HIGH-PITCHED, SUSTAINED whoosh and an enveloping weight-lessness, pressure building. Muffled sounds and movement lost in a white vortex. Spinning. Rising and falling, rising and falling…light peeling back layers of fog. The whooshing expanding, pressure bubbling and popping, building again. Light, lighter…air opening…and snuffed with a cloying mask that filled the senses. Drowning, air filling up with water and mud and darkness. Falling, falling, falling…into black.

Darkness without beginning or end. Heavy, dense, suffocating. Endless dark as high and wide and deep as the universe. Without boundaries, without direction, without dimension.

Moving through dark nothingness. No touch, no feel, no sensation.

And then, everything.

Cutting, biting, ripping, shredding, stabbing, pounding, rumbling, shrieking, roaring. Thick-bodied skeletons emerging from within the black void, massive and towering, solid as rock, rooted and alive. Limbs thrashing and whipping, tangling and binding. Flesh-impaling spikes soldering with searing intensity. Crawling, stinging tentacles and swarming clouds of white-hot embers. Slithering masses and groaning shadows that rose and fell.

Clambering through the gnarled labyrinth, moving deeper into the darkness, the ground by turns sucking and pulling then hardening and hammering bone. Sweltering liquid heat boiling the vapors and gluing to skin.

A granite fist of crushing weight, overwhelming and immobilizing. Hard, heavy, unyielding. Pulsing with excretions of musk-infused sweat. Hot, sour breath. Clawing fingers, clenching grips, and then the darkness was lifting…

The face and the body materializing in the purgatory haze, looming above and then sledgehammering down. Pummeling, relentless. Boring right through the core.

Screaming with no sound, no sound at all. Trapped air burning. Drowning. Paralyzed, pinned, nothing moving, a bubble pinned below glass. Arms and legs, body, all impotently deflated but their apparition floating above. Silently screaming, *move, move, move!*

Struggling to break free, helplessly frozen. Lungs aching, heart pumping, horror escalating. Screaming from the inside, nothing making it to the outside. Desperation surging like a running wildfire.

Can't move. No, no, no. Can't move, can't breathe…can't breathe…can't—

"—BREATHE, CALLIE."

She was twitching and moaning softly but her breathing was intensifying. His voice low and calm, he repeated, "Breathe, Callie. Slow, deep breaths." Jake had slipped his arm under her shoulders and could feel her pulse racing triple digits against his fingers on her neck. Her skin was warm, damp with perspiration. He leaned closer. "Callie."

Lightning lit up the room in a flash-bang, followed by an ear-splitting thunderclap and boom that shook the timbers to the floor.

She came awake in a panic, eyes wide, breathing hard, seizing up in his arms.

"It's okay, I'm right here. You're okay. But I need you to slow your breathing down. Slow…it down." He gently drew her to him and held her, speaking soothingly in her ear, "Relax…relax…relax."

Between the nightmare and raucous thunderstorm, she was shaking almost convulsively, heart thumping rapidly. He felt her tears and labored breaths on his bare chest as the big darkened bedroom windows steadily streamed with rain, thunder continuing to crack and rumble. A few yards from the foot of the bed, French doors rattled with the gusts of wind sweeping across the treetops. Branches whisked against wood and glass as the downpour pelted the roof in a timpani roll. Callie cringed and gasped with every amplified sound and vibration.

Jake continued to reassure her as the storm gradually lightened in volume and intensity, and when her shaking began to abate, said, "It's okay, angel. Mostly just rain now." He brushed a strand of pale blond hair back from her face, feeling the flush of heat on her cheek. A large wooden paddle fan snicked overhead, waving air around and shifting shadows over the walls and ceiling lightened by dusk-to-dawn LEDs plugged into evenly spaced electrical outlets. A small but significant gesture to allay her enhanced fear of the dark.

Close to an hour passed before the cadence of her breathing finally fell into the slow, deep rhythm of sleep, and by then Jake found himself restless. He carefully released Callie from his arms, replacing the covers, and stood over her for several minutes to make sure she did not reawaken. Then he padded across the cool tile floor, quietly unlatched the French doors, and stepped onto the terrace where rain still fell, sliding from the roofline and trickling through the trees. The summer storm had cooled the night air a few degrees but it was warm and humid, the breeze blowing in from the ocean mixing salted ozone with wood and floral scents from the drenched rainforest. Wind chimes tinkled below as he felt a broken palm frond skirt by his feet.

He stood at the terrace rail looking down at the pool's surface dimpled by dwindling raindrops, underwater lighting giving it an aqua luminance that seemed otherworldly. In the distance beyond, the lightning flashes and fading thunder moved farther out over the Pacific. It should have been a serene interval; for him it was anything but.

Only a few weeks had passed since Jake Tyler brought Callie Kane home to Costa Rica from the horrific ordeal in South America. They had not been together long, their paths initially crossing in San José when he'd helped her reclaim money stolen by a scam artist who took advantage of her naiveté. Jake was intrigued to discover that she had come to research and write, but he later learned that she'd also come to escape a stalker from her hometown in the States. Over the next week or so, Jake took Callie on a tour of the Costa Rican countryside he knew as the operator of an adventure tour business and loved as a peaceful retreat from his high-risk military contracts. But when the two worlds collided, forcing her into the mix, both of their lives had changed forever. In the short time since, he had been trying to provide comfort and understanding to help her recover while seeking some kind of settlement in their new life together.

As for their new life, that he was now the owner of a beautiful villa in paradise should have brought much joy. Instead, there was the heaviness of what Callie had been through—because of him. Compounding that was the sorrow he felt for the loss of the previous owner of the villa, his friend and business partner, Haskell Delaney, killed during the Colombian op. Jake was still surprised that Delaney had the foresight—or maybe foreboding—to draw up a will. He, himself, did not have one; he'd never had anything of value nor anyone to leave anything to.

That had all changed.

There was an instant spark of attraction when Jake first met Callie, but he immediately conceded that she was not his type. Even as they had traveled across Costa Rica and been swept up in the romance of its exotic natural beauty, he resisted. He spent an inordinate amount of time questioning his feelings, stacking all the reasons a relationship between them would not pan out. They could not have been more different, total opposites in fact. His adult life, which had been undeniably influenced and impacted by his years in the U.S. Army Special Forces, was one of hardcharging work and play; hers was one of diffidence and inexperience. He had even floated the idea that she stay at Delaney's villa for a while and then move on at her leisure. But in the end, he knew he had fallen for her even before he left Costa Rica. There was no longer any question or doubt. He was completely, profoundly, in love. And falling in love with her had come with a devastating cost.

While Jake was pursuing the drug cartel responsible for Delaney's death, Callie had been abducted from the villa and taken to Colombia where she was brutally and repeatedly assaulted while in captivity.

Jake stayed on the terrace for a while, listening to rain dripping from foliage, the guttural synthesis of frogs and insects, the swish of birds plundering about the canopy. A raindrop drizzled from his hairline, trailing down the side of his face. He reached up and combed his fingers across the top of his head, shaking out a few more beads of moisture. Flexed his neck from side to side to loosen small knots of tension.

Despite the tranquility left in the storm's wake, his thoughts remained uneasy. Callie's torturous dreams came almost every night and were taking a toll. He wished she could begin to bank the sound, restorative sleep needed to recover physically, because mentally, psychologically, and emotionally, the road was going to be a lot tougher, and a lot longer.

Peering into the surrounding blackness triggered his own flashbacks of the endless hours searching miles of Colombian jungle as dark and thick and hostile as any place he'd ever navigated—racing against a doomsday countdown to face a monster whose vileness defied all measure.

He sighed pensively and gazed at the dark sky whose moon was still obscured by clouds, offering up a silent prayer.

The resonance of night sounds eventually made him drowsy, and he returned to the bedroom, grabbing a towel to dry off. The king-size bed centered against the parallel wall was paneled at the head and foot with hand-carved tropical hardwoods that gleamed in the room's soft glow. He looked down at Callie, curled close to his empty pillow in what he hoped was peaceful sleep, and felt his heart flood with emotion. Slipping into bed next to her, he eased over until their bodies touched and placed his arm around her. Felt a tiny quiver and soft, even wisps of breath below his neck.

THE VIBRATION OF HIS phone woke him hours later. He rolled from the bed and slid the phone off the nightstand as quietly as he could, checking to make sure he hadn't awakened Callie. Relieved to see her still sleeping, he glanced at the iPhone's display and noted that it was just after five AM. The number shown was a lengthy one with a country code he did not recognize and normally wouldn't have answered, certainly not at this hour.

But there were four digits in the sequence that got his attention. 8816. The call was coming from an Iridium satellite phone.

2

TWENTY-EIGHT HOURS EARLIER, Eddie Falcone and Curran Niles stood together hunched over a table made from bamboo, covered with cameras and accessories, spiral notepads fanned with stained and wrinkled pages, some bananas, and a pair of plastic cups. Falcone lifted one of the cups to his mouth and took a sip of its contents, eyes squeezing shut and scowling as he worked the liquid through his mouth and down his throat. After swallowing, he stuck his tongue out and coughed. Across from him, Niles snickered.

"Christ, what I wouldn't give for a decent cup of coffee right now," Falcone lamented, gazing skyward as if somehow the heavens could deliver him a Starbucks dark roast. Regarding Niles, who was trying to stifle his mirth by sipping generously from his own cup, he leaned over and sniffed. "Hey, wait a freakin' minute. That smells like *real* coffee. Where'd you get that?"

Grinning, Niles replied, "Mmm, might have come from Cyrus' special stash."

"You sneaky little bastard." Falcone snatched the cup and took a swig. Closing his eyes in momentary reverie, he muttered, "Oh my God."

A collective titter of laughter that was almost musical came from around them as a hive of small brown heads the color of aged copper pennies bobbed in glee. Dozens of pairs of eyes, attentive and curious, honed in on every move and every utterance made by the two men—

one American and one British—captivated by their appearance and personality. Falcone, the American, was fit in a naturally athletic way, with textured and tapered dark brown hair that, despite its styling, always managed to look disheveled. His face, which had a distinctive Latin cast, was shadowed with stubble. Niles, the Brit, was male model-slender, dark blond-haired and gray-eyed. His fair skin was sunburned with patches of color over his forehead, nose, and cheeks, looking as if he'd hung his head over a pot of steaming pasta. A purple bandana was knotted under a stub of ponytail. Both wore jeans, t-shirts, and sneakers.

Surveying this morning's audience, all of whom would become part of a much larger entourage, vying for screen time with the zealous enthusiasm of a bundle of shelter puppies when the duo strolled the compound, Niles asked, "Still think we were a bit bonkers for doing this?"

"Nah," Falcone replied, grinning at the children as he reached for a Nikon 850 DSLR camera and began cleaning off the thin layer of dust already coating it. "But I'm never going to get used to third-world cuisine."

They were near the edge of an expansive courtyard centered by a field of grass and dirt where a battered soccer ball was being kicked around by another group of children. A tall blond man sprinted back and forth in their midst, gesticulating and clapping. Their excited shouts punctuated sounds of mooing cows and bleating goats, bells clinking against a ragged metal fence. Cooking smells drifted from another direction, blending oil and charcoal with the earthy green aroma of cassava leaves being boiled for stew. Morning sun, low and flat and veiled with clouds, was slowly draining the ground shadows and filling the sky with pale bands of gold and blue.

Niles, who had picked up a Canon video camera, was peering into the 405's LCD screen, playing back footage they'd shot. Beaming with pride, he watched as scenes and people came to life in vivid 4K resolution.

First was the reception center, crowded with new arrivals being registered and triaged for medical needs. The "welcoming committee" was comprised of a jovial young man in his twenties, Moise Ntoto, and a mongrel dog. Ntoto wore a faded yellow t-shirt sporting a vintage Beach Boys *Surfin' USA* logo, long gray pants, open-toe sandals, and a straw fedora with a red feather tucked in the band. The dog, which had been given the incongruous name of Thor, inspired by Ntoto's new obsession with Marvel comics, looked like a used hairbrush. A close-up zoomed in on the marquee-size message board filled with notices and photos, most of which related to displaced family members.

Beyond the open-air entrance, broader shots showed structures of varying composition ranging from mud and sticks, to bamboo and thatch, to rock and brick, to processed lumber. Just past reception was a wooden building with a mast of horizontal antennas overhead. Inside, the operator on duty explained the set up. "We have UHF, VHF, and HF," he said proudly. "It is very important that we communicate regularly with other villages."

On the other side of the camera, Falcone's Jersey-accented voice asked, "Why is that?"

The radio operator, named Paul Saliboko, replied, "Oh, we share information about rebel attacks or sickness…like the Ebola. Very deadly." He gestured to a man standing just inside the doorway watching them. "Antoine, hand to me the book there."

The man, who had not spoken, grabbed a red three-ring binder and, as he leaned toward Saliboko, exposed part of his midsection. Beneath his loose shirt, a long scar the color and texture of old chewing gum was visible from stomach to back, where the butt of a gun protruded from the waistband of his pants. The man quickly pulled the hem of his shirt down and handed the binder to Saliboko.

Flipping to a tabbed section, Saliboko said, "Our medical team gave this to us to tell people what to do and who to contact. Many of them do not have such services and we can give them information." Flashing a mouthful of gleaming teeth that resembled a wide-tooth comb, he added brightly, "And sometimes we have music!"

Saliboko's disposition became more expeditious as he announced, "Okay, now…*le rapport du matin.*" And took up the radio handset, depressing a sequence of buttons, greeting, *"Bonjour!"* What followed was a recitation of call signs for other operators and their voices crackling in response.

Next on screen were two men conversing in French as they walked past a span of bricked buildings. The taller one wore a brown suit jacket, matching trousers belted over a crisp white shirt. Adjusting a pair of wire-rimmed glasses that kept sliding down his nose, he pivoted and said into the camera, "Ah, yes, our esteemed guests. I am Yannick Libwatwani, and this"—he gestured to the shorter, stockier man standing beside him clad in khaki fatigues and strapped with a sidearm and two-way radio— "is Cédric Mbaya. I am the director and he is our security chief." Footage that followed surveyed on-site dormitories for children and thatched- roof housing for families in a village setting that stretched back toward gently sloping hills and high grass bordering clusters of palms, banana trees, and towering kapoks. The director led the way to a vocational workshop where men and women were learning carpentry, mechanics, sewing, and cooking. A ramshackle junker car that seemed beyond sav- ing sat in the middle of the area, parts spread around it like detritus from a meteor shower. But those working to bring it back to life had the ex- hilaration of children at a science museum allowed to fondle the bones in a dinosaur exhibit.

Libwatwani wrapped his sequence by showing them electric genera- tors, water pumping stations, solar panels, and a couple of satellite dishes that looked like extraterrestrial cyclopes gaping at the sky. "These re- sources," he explained, "are very recent additions and most out of the ordinary here."

Once more, Falcone's voice was heard, saying, "And sure helps keep us juiced for filming."

Another pan over the rudimentary delivery systems that supplied the essential elements of power, hydration, and communication transi- tioned to a waft of amber light, first in a mist rising from the ground and then in a whitening radiance that glimmered through trees and coated banks of grass with a chalky glaze. An indistinct sound of scraping, a plume of dust in sunlight, more clanking bells accompanied by intermit- tent lowing. Pulling back, the scene revealed a man and two women, clad in black and white garments, supervising a group of mixed age who were working in a vast garden, hoeing and raking rows of leaf clusters and curling vines and sprouting stalks, all the bright, healthy green of a field of spring clover. Father Jean Makuanza and Sisters Davina and Mireille took turns showing off their crops of beans, tomatoes, corn, peas, carrots, cassava, yams, cabbage, bananas, plantains, and peanuts while the gardeners weeded and fertilized with organic compost. Chickens picked and plucked around the edges as butterflies and bees circled lazily above.

Father Jean, wearing a black suit that had the umber sheen of fabric faded by sun, was a scrawny man with a patina of gray fuzz covering his head and a deeply lined face that chronicled his years. The two sisters, younger, but not by much, navigated with familiarity from one row to the next, lifting the hems of their black skirts. They wore white scarves fashioned into habits, silver crucifixes dangling from their necks. Three rust-covered bicycles with baskets woven from raffia were propped against the wire fence that ran the length of the field. A pair of giggling young boys chased a squawking chicken past the bikes, their peals of laughter lifting into the air like helium-filled balloons. They were barefooted and completely unmindful of the dirt caking in their toes or the rocks and sticks they trod over.

Through an opening in the fence, a dirt road wound past a giant acacia tree, its crown wide and domed against a sky the hue of forget-me-nots. At the end of the road, set back in a grove of palms, was a stone church. Constructed of stacked rock with a cross-engraved steeple, it appeared to have existed for many years, with sedimentary discolorations staining its sides with the crust and color of dried blood.

Back up the road and past the community garden, a large brick building came into view, painted white with red trim and identified by a sign that read: CLINIQUE MÉDICALE. Inside was a torrent of activity: men, women, and children in chairs, on tables and beds; white-coated staff attending to crying babies and expectant mothers; two doctors, one male and one female, trying to dole out their time by priority. Noah Goossens, a young Belgian with a shock of unruly brown hair, a nose that seemed too big for his face, and unflagging good humor, was known as "Doctor Goose," not only for his surname but for the quirky way he flapped his jacket to cool himself in the midday heat. His female counterpart, Dr. Julienne Baudin, with her tousled caramel-colored hair and a figure that formed prominent curves in her own white coat was, by contrast, the epitome of French reserve. But working together in tandem, they dispensed treatment with a proficiency that was nothing short of remarkable. Their clinic was subdivided into areas for waiting, assessment, treatment, and observation with a secured room for drugs and medical supplies.

Crossing the open courtyard where, once again, exclamations of boisterous play volleyed through the air, a grid of tables and chairs came into view—a dining hall for the many—and beyond that, a kitchen already in full preparation and assembly for those who would soon be filing in. Women stood in front of tin cauldrons, chattering and laughing as they stirred while others washed and sliced over sinks and tabletops. A circle of small children at their feet rattled spoons on inverted bowls, singing along in a language of their own creation.

"Walla walla eeyooo zing zing zing!" Bang, bang, bang with the spoons on the bowls. *"Yah yah oooyoo bamma bamma!"*

On the other side of the kitchen was a connecting outdoor path leading to a thatched-roof structure with window openings framed all around. Inside were rows of wooden desks, every one of the seats occupied by a child whose eyes were intently focused on the attractive young woman standing in front. Dressed in a pristine white blouse and a flowing skirt full of bold colors, Betty Ndongala wore her intricately braided hair twisted into an even more complex knot piled on her head. Ropes of wooden beads draped her neck and swung as she moved, a multitude of bracelets clinking and clacking up and down her arms. Behind her, blackboards were covered with words in French and English. As she pointed to each of the words, the roomful of voices repeated them in a singsong chant.

Rounding a corner into a more intimate space, the walls of which were papered with crayon and pencil drawings depicting birds and flowers and stick figure people, a redheaded woman sat encircled by a flock of toddlers mesmerized with her voice. She was reading from an oversize picture book, her diction soft and melodic, balancing a small child on one thigh—a girl of perhaps one and a half with the chocolatey smooth skin of a Hershey's Kiss, adorned in a frock the color of cotton candy and a daisy-dotted band around her head. The child's face was upturned to the woman's, little mouth open in an O of wonder. A tiny little hand reached up to the woman and grasped a fistful of the scarf around her neck, held it and became lost in it while the soothing voice coming from above it spoke. The child's eyes were pearls of light, lashes fine and black against cheeks that plumped with bubbles of precious baby breath. A haze of sunlight streamed in from an adjacent window, basking the woman and child in a golden aura as the words she read seemed to float through the air like tufts of dandelion seeds over a meadow.

"Once upon a blue sky day, a boy and girl set out to play…they walked along a river bed, and followed the flow to see where it led…climbed a hill in the great warm sun, where they danced and they sang and they had some fun. No worries, no troubles, just hope and much joy…stayed with them that day, this little girl and boy. Everything under that big blue sky, was joined together by the spirit up high…and when the sun finally set and faded its light, the blue sky day turned into a bright star night."

LOOKING AT THE CAMERA'S screen over Niles' shoulder, Falcone said, "Bud, I believe you have figured out how to work this thing."

Crooking his neck sideways, Niles smiled and replied, "Decent good start, yeah." He stretched his arms and rotated his head, massaging a neck already damp with sweat as the day's heat was building despite the cloud cast and early hour.

They both looked up as a voice called from across the courtyard. "You blokes going to be ready to dash? Get your kit together…wheels up in twenty!" The blond man who had been engaged in the soccer play was striding briskly toward the compound's administrative area.

"Right!" Niles shouted. To Falcone, he said, "I'll pack up all the gear here, can you go grab our bags?"

"Okay, meet you back in a few."

Falcone headed for the dormitories where he and Niles were sharing a corner they'd rigged into a somewhat private enclave by tacking up a canvas tarp. Ducking under the flap, he walked right into a body and was grabbed and flung against the building's outer wall. He tensed and extended his arms in defensive posture, hands balling into fists. Then, dropped them to his sides. He took a breath to curtail his adrenaline and grinned.

The woman pressed up against him was shorter, slim, and speed bag-fit. Without a word, she unbuttoned Falcone's 511 jeans, jerked at the zipper, and yanked the denim down his hips.

"Iris, what the—"

She muffled him with a kiss that covered his whole mouth, working her tongue inside. At the same time, she clamped his wrists and moved both of his hands to the back of her thighs, hopping up as he took her weight. Naked beneath her knee-length skirt, it took only seconds for Falcone's physical reaction. Hiking her thighs higher, he plunged inside her and they heaved into a quick and intense rhythm. Heat built and spread through him from loins to lungs as he sucked on her tongue and felt her own warmth expand all around him. The sexual current fired to its electrical apex and then drained as if a valve had been released in a high-pressure tank at the bottom of some deep sea.

Face to face, breath scissoring and skin blooming with perspiration, they broke their embrace and sat side by side on one of the cots.

Falcone studied Iris Margolis, his flushed face still registering astonishment. Watched as she straightened her sleeveless top, printed with crimson and brown paisleys, and fluffed her long, wavy brown hair. She slipped a hand in a pocket of her tan skirt and pulled out a pair of panties, put her ankle-booted feet through the openings, and pulled them over her shapely legs.

"I'm all for ambush sex, but Jesus, there's children everywhere! Why—"

"Because we're about to leave, Eddie." Iris peered at him through thick-rimmed cat-eye glasses that made her brown eyes look huge.

"Wait…what? I thought you weren't coming with us."

"We're not."

He stared at her, his thoughts not quite connecting. Her olive skin was glowing, full lips as naturally dark as Bordeaux—lips he wanted to keep kissing. Right now.

She fingered one of her earrings, a miniaturized dreamcatcher, trying to free an entangled lock of hair. "We're moving on to the next site."

His mouth opened, then closed, his throat swallowing dry air. "When?"

"We'll be gone by the time you get back."

"But we've only been here—"

She placed two fingers on his lips. "I know. I'm sorry. But everything is well in hand here, so it's time for us to go."

His eyes dropped to his lap, which was still tingling.

"Eddie," she said lightly, "I told you we wouldn't be here for long." Standing, she reached for his hand and gave it a squeeze. "You never know...there's a good chance we'll cross paths again."

"Yeah," Eddie said morosely. "Well, safe travels."

"You, too."

He watched her twist under the tarp, skirt swishing against her provocatively rounded ass, boot soles scuffling on the floorboards. And sat for several moments, listening to the sounds of children out in the courtyard.

3

IT WAS JUST PAST nine o'clock when Falcone and Niles strode across
the savanna, swinging duffel bags through waist-high grass to a clearing
where a crowd from the compound and village had gathered. They
could see Cédric Mbaya and several of his men walking the perimeter
and communicating with each other on radios, motioning the more enthusiastic observers to move back. Weaving their way between adults
and children, indulging a few with high fives along the way, they
reached the clearing—an area about the size of a football field—where a
silver Eurocopter AS365 Dauphin perched, a giant metal dragonfly with
its pointed nose and elongated body.

Standing within the line of onlookers were three Americans, one of
which was Iris Margolis. She was accompanied by two young men who
shared her millennial age—Neville Nias, short with sandy brown hair
and a toothy smile, and Drake Johanssen, lanky with a shaved head,
straggly goatee, and glasses. Spotting Falcone and Niles, Nias and Johanssen waved. Falcone saw Margolis also start to lift her arm in a wave,
then stop. He gave her a long look, forced a wan smile. Mentally, he was
trying to peel away everything he'd carnally felt only minutes ago; physically he was depleted. Niles watched him, eyes forming a question, but
Falcone shook his head in dismissal. His thoughts scattered like a flock
of scavenger birds in the highway path of an oncoming truck.

Five people were waiting by the helicopter, including the blond man
and redheaded woman. "Glad you could make it, mates," the blond man

quipped, holding up his watch. He signaled to the others and they began climbing aboard. Falcone and Niles took their seats behind the cockpit, the couple slipping in next to them. On the opposite row were a pair of security men, Wallace Pacheco and Beau Gabbitas, their combined bulk encroaching on the seat separating them from the final passenger, Cameron McNamara.

As they belted in, the blond man took note of Niles' t-shirt and cackled. *"Shark Week?* Really, mate?"

Niles glanced down at the Great White silhouetted against grungy font and grinned, his sunburned face coloring a little deeper. "Uh, never thought—well, you know, bit of a story, that."

"I reckon," said Cyrus Keogh, his voice distinctively accented Australian. In his early forties, his boyish looks and inquisitive blue eyes cast him younger by a decade or more. His styled, wavy hair was the color of a straw broom, tips lightened by years in the sun and, coupled with an even tan, further enhanced his youthful physique. He wore Tom Ford slacks, gray and pleated, with navy suspenders over a pale blue short-sleeved shirt, and charcoal suede Blundstone boots.

His wife Amelia, also Australian, was equally as tall, and slim. Her shoulder-length hair, a luminous shade of cognac, was worn in a high ponytail. She had an upturned nose and dimpled cheeks sprayed with freckles, lips and nails the robust berry of pomegranate. Clad in an abstract-printed tunic belted over a calf-length salmon-colored skirt, she could have walked out of a Coldwater Creek catalog. She carried her height with a confident grace, face reflecting the hopeful glow of one who believes in the world's better angels even as her jade green eyes suggested a fierceness of spirit ready to defend them.

Pacheco and Gabbitas were both bearded with close-cropped hair, dark blazers concealing their shoulder holsters, sunglasses concealing their vigilant eyes. McNamara, the Keogh's assistant, was dark-haired with the studious demeanor of an undergrad at an economics lecture. Wearing a blue Oxford shirt and navy slacks, he was dividing his attention between phone and tablet, the latter populated with schedules and briefs and emails, touching and swiping every few seconds.

As they waited for takeoff, Niles panned a GoPro HERO camera around the cabin, which was upholstered in beige leather and carpeting that rendered it noticeably quieter than the last helicopter he and Falcone had been in, not to mention eminently more comfortable. He swung around to film the cockpit where the two pilots were working through their checklist. He heard one of them say, "Engine one, start," followed by a clicking noise and a whoosh that sounded like a match dropped into a barrel of gasoline, and then the turbine's pitch began to increase before settling into an idle. The pilots continued their start-up regimen, checking instrumentation and monitors, repeating the process for the second engine. When both engines were powered up together, their whine merged with the whir of rotors slowly turning and then spinning faster from above and in the tail. At this point, all of them were jostled side to side and back and forth as wheels left the ground with a brief shudder, nose dipping slightly as the helicopter rose into the air and transitioned from hover to flight. Red dust billowed around them and then swirled in a vortex as the Dauphin climbed, building height hundreds of feet by the minute.

As they ascended, Niles aimed the GoPro out his window, capturing the entire compound and village. Before resuming the aerial filming, he turned the camera on the Keoghs, both looking out Amelia's window, husband leaning over wife and wife watching with an expression that was hard to gauge. Her typical benevolence was muted by a tinge of sadness that seemed to delve deeper, like the yaw of withdrawing from something that had become intrinsic. As height and distance shrunk the waving crowd below and then left them behind, Amelia Keogh's eyes misted and she turned away from the window, momentarily lost in her thoughts. Her husband kissed her neck and whispered something in her ear, causing a smile that spread warmth over her face. She brought her hand up to her mouth and nose, possibly covering a sniffle.

The Dauphin leveled into its cruising altitude of five thousand feet, heading south at 155 knots over a mix of open grassland and forest, variegated shades of green infused with tentacles of red earth and brown rivers—land without anything but dirt and grass and trees—a testament to the isolation of their site. The sky above was an ashen span of gauzy clouds filtering the sun's white light.

They had been flying for forty minutes when a reduction of engine and rotor noise indicated landing was imminent. The terrain began to delineate as the Dauphin descended to an altitude of three thousand feet—seven hundred feet above ground—and decreased speed. Trees and structures surrounding a river junction came into sharper detail, revealing a crumbling castle and a single-lane arched bridge, waters churning around rocky outcroppings. Three rivers met in the center of Dungu, a town of about fifty thousand; the castle, overgrown with vines, had once been a Belgian's château. Now, it was a neglected relic used as a hangout by local UN Peacekeepers. Following the Kibali River, which branched off the Uélé and Dungu, the helicopter banked south to the airport, but not before the passengers spotted the shiny brown masses of a hippo clan undulating through the water. They appeared to be having a family dispute as two adults thrashed into each other while a calf dashed ahead of them.

When the helicopter had navigated to the designated landing zone just off the airport's dirt strip, it lowered and set down next to a King Air 350.

THE DUNGU-UYE AIRPORT, like so many in the region, comprises one runway—a dirt strip lined by burgeoning banks of grass and weeds—just over three thousand feet in length. No tower, no air traffic controller, but managed by Avions Sans Frontières. Nearby are a few small metal-roofed buildings, scattered housing, a soccer field, and lots of trees. People from the town, children, and dogs, are often seen wandering about it as casually as those browsing a neighborhood market.

The group stepped from the helicopter onto a dusty clearing just off the airstrip. Sun was beginning to burn through the clouds, exposing sections of pale blue sky and simmering a pot of humidity. A pair of men stood waiting by the King Air, a white twin-engine turboprop with blue and red stripes swiped across the body. Both were uniformly clad in pressed black slacks and white shirts sporting striped insignias on the shoulders, four and three respectively, aviator shades shielding their eyes. The pilot, professional-dapper with short brown hair and a shadow of mustache and beard, stepped forward and extended his hand. "Good day, Mr. Keogh, I'm—"

"Captain Dubruyn, yes, good to meet you," Keogh greeted affably, shaking his hand. He tipped his head slightly to the side, face bright with a kind of inner affirmation that tended to convey a sense of goodwill and extemporization, as if any given moment or circumstance or relationship had limitless possibilities.

The pilot nodded and smiled. "Yes, Captain Bash Dubruyn, and this is my first officer, Niel Pietersen." He indicated the man beside him, tall and thin with dark hair graying above the ears.

"From South Africa, yes?" Keogh asked.

Impressed, Dubruyn replied, "Yes, indeed. You've done your homework. Okay, before we get underway, any special requests?"

"Not really, mate. Just get us all there in one piece."

"That's the plan," Dubruyn said and, with his first officer, began the boarding process. While Pietersen escorted them up the aft stair door and got them settled inside the aircraft, the captain met with the helicopter pilot to exchange notes and make sure all the baggage was transferred.

Inside the plane, Falcone and Niles took seats opposite the Keoghs in the rear section of two double-club arrangements. The interior was light and airy, facilitated by large round windows and pale gray leather. As the first officer gave an orientation of the aircraft's amenities and a safety briefing, Niles decided to temporarily occupy the one vacant seat just behind the cockpit on the co-pilot's side so he could film. Cameron McNamara remained fixated on his electronic devices, but the security men were both watching Niles, their jaws set and lips seamed, as if mentally processing his potential for mayhem and assigning some number on their havoc scale.

Captain Dubruyn came aboard and, after giving his passengers a final rundown on the flight plan, slipped into the cockpit as the first officer closed the stair door and joined him. The pre-flight checklist was quickly dispensed and start-up procedures followed as the plane taxied a short distance to the runway, directed erratically by a skinny man who had emerged from the hangar and looked barely old enough to shave. Lining up on the strip, the props building to a pitch that sent vibrations and sound rumbling through the aircraft, pilot and co-pilot commenced their departure dialogue. Fascinated, Niles watched and aimed the GoPro. He had no idea where, or if, this would fit in his film, but he was enjoying it, so at this moment relevance was of little importance to him.

"Set max takeoff power."

"Max takeoff power set."

"Auto feather armed. Brake release."

"Airspeed alive."

"Check."

"Rolling 10."

The aircraft accelerated down the strip, spewing salvos of red dust that colored the air pink as its wheels bumped roughly over the dirt surface, engines working up to a raucous roar.

"Passing eighty knots."

"Check."

As the plane shook and shimmied, gaining speed, the end of the strip rushed forward, tall grass and trees looming ahead. They grew closer, filling the windshield.

"V1, rotate."

The nose of the plane lifted fifteen degrees, then more, and land tilted away, the King Air using 2800 of the 3264 feet to clear. Niles felt air leave his lungs he hadn't been aware he was holding, hand gripping the camera clenched and damp. The pilot's facial expression, seen from the side, was as calm and composed as the surface of a lake on a windless day, his posture relaxed and movements unhurried, flipping switches, moving levers by rote.

"Positive to rate of climb"

"Gear up."

"V2…four hundred feet."

"Speed is good. Flap up, set climb power, yaw damper engage."

"Dungu traffic airborne, 10 left climbing 260."

Making the turn, the plane climbed steadily for the next fifteen minutes, leveling into a cruise of 250 knots at twenty-six thousand feet where a carpet of clouds rolled out below as white and thick as wool batting. The sky overhead was a gradient of blues that deepened to cobalt. Returning to his seat next to Falcone, Niles buckled in and said, "I think we're in good hands. Those blokes look like they know what they're doing."

Cyrus Keogh regarded him with mild amusement, thumbing the

bands of his suspenders. "Mate. I *also* know what I'm doing. Who do you think picked them?" Looking again at Niles' t-shirt, curiosity brimming in his eyes, he asked, "So, what's the story?"

With a little swagger in his shoulders, straightening against the seat back, Niles said, "Well, Eddie and I had leaped off this monster yacht, and we're thrashing about in the Caribbean…"

Fabric swished on leather as necks craned and heads turned from the forward club section, eyes all riveted on Niles.

"…and this massive bloody shark—"

Interrupting him with a cough and a roll of eyes, Falcone said, "Keep in mind, he's prone to exaggeration."

IT WAS CLOSING IN on two o'clock—which would actually become 1:00 PM on landing as they'd crossed a time zone during their flight southwest—when the King Air descended through the layer of cumulonimbus clouds into a dreamy diaphanous haze, bluish gray with an ambient glow of topaz. The sun cloaked within was like the flare of light on the tip of a match, an amber eye peering through whorls of smoke. As plane and ground closed the distance in between, green landscape began to give way to the tans and browns of urban colonization. Small squares became three-dimensional and sprawled in every direction below a horizon blurred by cloud cover as if an artist had smudged it with a wide brush. A change in cabin pressure and engine reduction signaled proximity to their destination, and within minutes the King Air was gliding smoothly on its trajectory toward N'djili Airport, tracing a curve of immense river before banking into a forty-five-degree angle eastward setting up the approach to runway 24. Wheels thumped lightly onto the tarmac and, after a short taxi, the plane turned left onto an apron stretching across a collection of terminal buildings and came to a stop next to the main one. It was painted an arresting canary yellow, matching the color of the cylindrical control tower on the left.

First Officer Pietersen escorted the group off the plane, where he stood by the stair door as Captain Dubruyn handed their baggage down. Walking aside Cyrus and Amelia Keogh, Dubruyn said, "Welcome to Kinshasa. It has been my pleasure."

Keogh said, "And ours, thank you. G'day, Captain. See you back here tomorrow."

Two drivers, wearing identical black suits and white shirts, stood by a pair of Mercedes GLS SUVs, gleaming with fresh wax. They were finished in obsidian black metallic with dark-tinted windows and chrome hubcaps as shiny and sharp as ninja throwing stars. Wallace Pacheco accompanied the Keoghs and Cameron McNamara in the first car; Beau Gabbitas took the second with Falcone and Niles.

With the security man seated next to the driver, Falcone and Niles climbed into the second row seats, stretching and looking out their windows as the vehicles exited the terminal and nosed into the mass of traffic on Boulevard Lumumba.

Almost immediately, the contrast with Dungu and points beyond was as dramatic as what they'd experienced only weeks prior, going from the primitive Amazon basin to Bogotá, a city of over eight million. It also quickly became obvious that the traffic, and those operating vehicles in it, was even worse. Their driver threaded his way in and out of the procession of cars, trucks, buses, motorbikes, and people amid a garish cacophony of horns, with as much regard for potential collision as a stuntman in a *Fast and Furious* movie. Lanes and traffic signals, where they existed, were universally ignored, vehicles merging with the pugnacity of a wildebeest herd; if there wasn't an opening or a path, one was created. People were packed in vehicles in every conceivable way: standing and swaying in the backs of flatbeds like cattle, jammed in blue-and-yellow taxi mini-buses with or without wooden bench seats, hanging from the openings of missing doors or trunk lids. Throngs of people swarmed along the roadside, many darting across without even a side-glance given to the motorists surging toward them. Street vendors stood in the midst hawking fruits, snacks, sunglasses, jewelry, and belts.

At this hour of the day, the flow of traffic was especially dense, and despite the luxury car's refreshingly cool air-conditioning, the stench of diesel and grease and compacted humanity was pervasive. Falcone and Niles helped themselves to bottles of water and drank, as much to ease their thirst as in an attempt to wash away the metallic taste developing in their mouths.

Remembering his camera, Niles raised the GoPro to the window just as a man lost his grip from the rear of a dilapidated van and bounced off the fender of the car behind it. The man got up and hopped back on the van just as a city bus with red, blue, and yellow swirls on the sides plowed past.

"Oh my God," Niles muttered.

Leaning forward, Falcone tapped the security man's arm to get his attention. Gabbitas, who had been sitting motionlessly in the passenger seat with his usual deadpan expression, twitched as if a rodent had dropped onto his shoulder. "You been here before?" Falcone asked him.

"Sure."

Falcone waited for more, and when it was clear nothing else was forthcoming, slid back into his seat, swigging from his bottle of water, plastic crackling as he drained every last drop.

The drive through the immense city took over an hour, frequently grinding to a halt in traffic gridlock. They passed through stretches that looked like any international city, with modern buildings made of heavy steel and reflective glass and distinctive architectural details. They also passed through larger expanses with the kind of soul-gnawing poverty that left the mind questioning the rudiments of dignity. And they passed through corridors that resembled an apocalyptic war zone, complete with rust-encrusted shells of eviscerated vehicles. At one point, a quartet of men in garishly spectacular suits paraded across the boulevard in front of them, as if inserted into a grunge music video for graphic effect. Taking notice of Niles gaping at them through his window, the men began swaying their hips and extending their arms in mock runway affectations.

"What are those blokes on about?" Niles asked, grinning.

Their driver chuckled and remarked, "Those men are *sapeurs*. You would call them influencers." He then pointed to an intersection they were approaching, exclaiming, "And look! See our traffic robot!"

"Your what?" Falcone asked, but his gaze found it, locking on the eight-foot-tall monstrosity anchored in the interchange that could have been some kind of dysfunctional Transformer action figure. The robot's chest rotated and flashed lights, but like its traditional counterparts, traffic directions were mostly met with disregard. *People out here are scavenging for food, for their survival*, Falcone thought, and here was a chunk of technology that probably cost tens of thousands that was little more than a ludicrous distraction.

Soon after, they came up on a monument their driver identified as L'échangeur, a four-columned tower that rose nearly seven hundred feet and, to Falcone and Niles, resembled an inverted spaceship with boosters at the top. Lumumba split, and the driver turned onto Boulevard Triomphal, passing Stade des Martyrs, a huge oval football stadium. On the other side of the intersection was the Palais de Peuple—People's Palace—a stately complex set back from the road by a stone esplanade and housing the National Assembly and Senate. Next to it was the National Museum. A turn took them onto Avenue Pierre Mulele which became Avenue Du 24 Novembre, passing a triangular golf course, a rare slice of green in the dense urban sprawl. A final series of turns took them into Gombe, an affluent area of the city's elite and main embassy district where commercial businesses and buildings were interspersed with blocks of residential real estate, quite a few mansions with swimming pools and tennis courts.

Niles had been continuously filming from the side windows, but Falcone had also cast occasional glimpses through the front windshield, leaning forward between the seats, and now he took notice of an older model SUV, a silver Toyota, passing them on the right. It had first snagged his attention when they'd made the last few turns; he'd seen it zigging and zagging through the knots of traffic but didn't give it a second thought until it stayed with them in the change of direction—not once, but three times—driving in tandem with the Keoghs' car ahead. He started to say something to Gabbitas and was surprised that it wasn't on the security man's radar, but decided to mind his own business. Neither of the security men had been the slightest bit friendly, even when Niles had been chattering away and engaging everyone else with his amusing banter.

They made the last turn, from Avenue De Lemera onto Avenue Des Nations Unies, where both Mercedes pulled up to the twenty-two-story Fleuve Congo Hotel, coppery glass panels glinting in sun that had emerged from the clouds and was heating up the afternoon with full tropical vigor. As the drivers transferred bags to bellhops and Pacheco and Gabbitas ushered the group into the hotel lobby, Falcone paused to look for the silver Toyota. When he didn't see it, he wiped his eyes as if they might have been conjuring imaginary drama, and went inside.

The five-star Fleuve's opulent lobby, with its gold-and-brown décor, is a mix of classic and modern styles: European furnishings and ornate crystal chandeliers with a geometrical front desk lit by a line of hanging pendant lights, the gilded open grid of squares and rectangles shining behind it. The marble floor glimmers like a pool of melted butter. While the Keoghs were personally escorted to the top-floor Presidential Suite by the Fleuve Congo's manager, Falcone and Niles headed for their suite a floor below.

Inside the elevator, alone for the first time since departure that morning, Niles nudged Falcone with his shoulder. "So, what happened with you and Iris?"

Falcone's brow furrowed and he hooked his thumbs in the belt loops of his jeans, tucked his chin. "Nothing. Really rather not talk about it."

"Eddie, just—"

"I said it was nothing," Falcone snapped, a little more testily than he'd intended.

The elevator door slid open and, after orienting themselves in the hallway, Falcone and Niles strode toward their suite.

"Hey, what do you say we head down to the pool?" Niles asked.

"I don't know, I might just grab a shower and crash."

"Come on," Niles urged, "I think there's probably a couple of beers with our names on 'em."

But Falcone was not listening. He couldn't pinpoint why, but a sense of unease had been building inside his chest, the way a drop in barometric pressure destabilizes the air and moves its molecules around and causes chemical changes to the brain's receptors. And now, as they stood before the door to their suite, Niles about to swipe the key card, a faint *bing* chimed from the second elevator. In that instant, Falcone felt his scalp tingle and tighten, a fizzing sound in his head like the burst of carbonation when a bottle cap was twisted on a soda. He reflexively looked back down the hallway, but did not see anyone get off.

Niles pushed the door open.

Stepping inside and seeing the luxurious accommodations, both gasped audibly. The smell and feel of the chilled room, after the sensory-jarring ride from the airport, elicited a response that was as much emotional as it was physical; the thought of an invigorating hot shower foamed and cologned by spa-collection shower gel, of sleep in a comfortable bed swaddled in Egyptian cotton sheets with four-digit thread counts, was nothing short of euphoric.

In tasteful hues of tan and brown and silver and gray, the design carried over the modern geometrics of the lobby with dotted circles patterned in the carpet and swirls on the lampshades. Fabric paneled the walls behind the beds in separate bedrooms, and the living area was full of comfortable seating, soft lighting, abstract wall and surface art. But the most incredible feature of their suite was the view.

They strolled to the floor-to-ceiling windows and looked down at the great Congo River.

4

THE TWO-STORY LOBBY was a cavern of golden light against an ink-blue night sky, chandeliers sparkling like icicle fountains. White letters spelling out the hotel's name glowed atop the overhang, vertical lines of LED illuminating the sides of the building in silvery stripes. Refreshed and rejuvenated by a dip in the pool followed by showers and naps, Falcone and Niles stood with the group as their cars were pulling up to the entrance.

Overhearing Cyrus Keogh instructing the driver of his Mercedes, Falcone said, "Hey, I thought we were going for pizza! You said there was a fantastic pizza restaurant here."

"I did say that," Keogh replied, "and we can have your car take you there."

Amelia Keogh played along, chiming in, "Oh, I could go for pizza!"

"We are not having pizza for our anniversary dinner," her husband chided, reaching for his wife's hand. Amelia Keogh was radiant in a sleeveless knee-length silhouette dress, dark olive with roses etched in silky fabric. Her hair was fashioned into a loose chignon with strands brushing her face, jade drop earrings dangling against her elegant neck. She chose flats over heels, the effect of which actually did little to minimize her statuesque height. Beside her, Cyrus Keogh wore a cream-colored Brunello suit made of linen, vested over a light blue shirt. His shoes were polished Oxfords, and a suede fedora was tipped over his brow.

Falcone and Niles had traded jeans for chinos, Falcone wearing navy with a royal blue plaid Madras shirt and Niles, beige, with a pink Cuban collar shirt covered in a riot of birds and vines. Niles' hair, damp from the shower, was down on his neck, pulled back from his forehead with a clip.

The evening air was still warm but more comfortable with a slight breeze blowing in from the river. A nearly full moon was on the rise, its incandescence shrouded by drifting clouds. Lightning like jellyfish tendrils veined the sky to the east, thunder buffered by distance. Filing into their cars in the same order as before, they headed east on Boulevard Colonel Tshatshi and Avenue Roi Beaudouin past the estates of the more prosperous, past government buildings and monuments, past banks and parks and Le Premier Shopping Mall with its signage backlit in purple over boxy glass storefronts.

Along the way, Falcone found himself peering out of the Mercedes windows, looking for the silver Toyota SUV. He was able to make out details of the vehicles around them, but colors morphed into varying shades of gray and black and he gave it up. The SUV following them earlier was probably just a fluke, he told himself, possibly someone else driving from the airport to their hotel. At this hour, shortly after seven, traffic and the chosen route was less congested, and they arrived at their destination in fifteen minutes.

Le Caf Conc, arguably the best fine dining in the region, is the gastronomic vision of a father and daughter who traveled from France some forty years ago and never left. Over that tenure it has seen a steady stream of dignitaries and celebrities, both revered and infamous. Its bright façade, as red as the feathers of a scarlet macaw, stands out in an otherwise stripped down neighborhood bordered by a city market at one end and the Belgian Embassy at the other.

The two Mercedes drew up to the restaurant's entrance where the doorman was waiting to usher them inside. On the other side of the frosted glass doors, they were met and greeted by a hostess who turned them over to the manager, a tall, tuxedoed man with a convivial manner who introduced himself as Gaël Brose. Passing the reception desk, he pointed to a round aquarium the size of a beach ball that sat on its corner. "This is Jean Jean," he said, indicating a vivid blue Siamese fighting fish fanning his tail as he swam. "Or, to you, John John."

Waitstaff, all formally dressed in black with starched white shirts, bustled by them as the restaurant began to fill with diners, the music of Charles Aznavour wafting from a lounge with the woodsy aroma of cigar smoke.

Brose led them to a room in the back, set up by prior arrangement for privacy and security. The restaurant's interior had the ambience of vintage French design with the smooth curves of art deco, the main dining area having the warmth of a bistro and carrying over the ecru, red, and brown of the exterior, with tables and dinettes sectioned by the C-monogrammed frosted glass from the entrance. By contrast, the back room had dark wood floors and furnishings upholstered in gold fabric, century-old paintings and photos on walls painted the color of mink.

They were seated around immaculately set tables covered in white linen and glistening with fine china and crystal glassware and polished silver. Rose petals clustered around white votive candles like crumpled red velvet on snow. Brose took drink orders—wine for the Keoghs and beer for Falcone and Niles—and retreated.

"Okay, well, this place will do," Niles said with an impish grin. For the moment, they were sharing the Keoghs' table; earlier Niles had requested a little screen time before the meal, and the couple had graciously agreed. Cameron McNamara was seated with the security men closer to the room's entrance, Pacheco and Gabbitas with as much animation as stone pillars. McNamara did not look particularly happy, examining his tie with an absorption that suggested its stripes might contain hidden anagrams.

Brose returned, accompanied by a waiter who poured from a bottle of Chateau Cheval Blanc 2007, allowing Cyrus Keogh to sample and approve before filling their glasses with the preeminent Saint-Emilion Bordeaux. A second waiter poured bottles of Heineken for Falcone and Niles and arranged an array of colorful appetizers, which included smoked salmon and duck. After reciting highlights and recommendations from the menu, Brose and the waiter left them to savor the first sips and tastes of the culinary experience. The Keoghs seemed as much in awe of the environment as a young newlywed couple splurging on a once-in-a-lifetime luxury destination—the antithesis of a couple whose capital worth joined the ranks of Forbes List tech wunderkinds and commercial czars and media moguls—Cyrus eagerly looking from face to face, his own happiness reflective of what he divined from the others.

Niles extracted the Canon video camera from his bag, flipping the touchscreen open and working his way through settings. When he was ready, Falcone asked, "Why don't you tell us how you met?"

Light spread over the faces of both Keoghs like sun coming across hills to vanquish shadow-filled valleys, color radiating in their cheeks. "As you like to say, Curran, there is a story," Cyrus Keogh said, his Australian tang sharpening as he launched into the narrative. Turning to look directly into the camera, he stroked his chin and pursed his lips and said, "It was summer and I was hanging at Yamba Beach, which is in New South Wales. On the surfing scene, beaches are ranked by level of difficulty, which is determined by a variety of factors. Geography, swells and wave height, tides and winds, breaks, like that. Yamba is a nice beach as far as they go, but it's really for beginners. So I'm hanging with some mates at a big barbie on the beach this particular evening and I hear some gals talking."

"And this is where *I* come in," Amelia Keogh said, drawing out the "I" and fluttering her eyelashes in an exaggerated fashion. Her hair had the sheen of brushed copper in the dining room's subdued lighting. "I was with a group of Bettys—that's surfer girls—and there was talk of a world-class champ in our midst. I said, 'that can't be right, nobody who surfs at that level would be *here*.'"

"What she didn't know, was I had been invited by a mate to help him kick off a surfing school—there's lots of them up and down the coasts of Australia, so having an appearance or endorsement by anyone notable in surfing circuits is key." Cyrus Keogh sipped his wine and continued, "I sought her out later, we had some drinks and dinner, but I never told her what I'd overheard. I went back to Melbourne, she went back to Sydney. A year later, I'm at a competition in Jeffreys Bay, South Africa— and this *is* one of the top-ranked surfing spots in the world, we call it J-Bay—in a restaurant after the first day, and I look around and there she is at the bar." He grinned. "No mistaking that red hair, right? I come up behind her and say, 'How about here? Would somebody who surfs at this level be *here*?'"

"That's classic," Niles said.

There was a pause, all of them taking a few moments to relish the lovely surroundings, studying the large framed oil paintings and historical photographs and ornate étagères, and then Falcone looked from Cyrus to Amelia, asking, "What got you here? Doing this?"

FOR THE NEXT FORTY minutes, the Keoghs now enjoying some dining intimacy, they feasted on a delectable menu that included lobster and citrus salad with grapefruit dressing, poached egg on potato with truffle cream, honey-glazed pastilla stuffed with foie gras and duck and sprinkled with toasted almonds. Each plate had the look of a cubist masterpiece, popping colors with dimensional shapes and clean lines. Midway through the meal, Chef Jean-Pierre Julien appeared to solicit their opinions. Judging from the soft moans of pleasure and flushed faces, he went away satisfied with his creations. They were on dessert— a decadent collaboration of strawberry cheesecake with a small pyramid of chocolate bordered by dollops of passion fruit and berry syrup dusted at the edge by pistachio—when owner Noël Camillieri joined them, an engaging man whose jocular face seemed to be the sum of his many storied years. Dressed in a suit that had, just minutes ago been covered by a white chef's jacket as he'd presided over the meticulously managed chaos of his kitchen, he stood between the tables, expanding his arms and then bringing them back together in the manner of an orchestral maestro.

"*Nous espérons que le repas est à la hauteur? Comment se passe votre soirée?*"

"A beauty!" Cyrus Keogh declared, kissing his fingers. "Simply superb." They carried on a short discussion of the food and then Gaël Brose slipped in to say something in Keogh's ear, gesturing toward a doorway on the other side of the room, getting a nod and a smile from Keogh.

At their table, after the dessert plates were cleared, Falcone said, "There was a silver Toyota SUV, maybe a 4Runner, following us from the airport."

Roused from the mild buzz of sated appetite, Niles swallowed the last of his third beer with a hiccup and said, "What?" His facial ruddiness had taken on the color of a ripe watermelon, a smudge of chocolate on his chin.

"I mean, I think it was." Falcone gazed at the fringe of foam clinging to the inside of his empty glass. "I didn't notice it until the last series of turns, when it made every one of them."

"Was it at the hotel, too?"

"I didn't see it, but it could have held back until we were inside." Falcone paused, sat back in his chair. "I don't know, maybe I was just doing what you always do."

"And what's that?"

"Dramatizing."

Niles rolled his eyes but didn't counter the claim. Both looked up to see Brose, accompanied by Camillieri, returning with a cake that sprouted a bouquet of sparklers spraying like a tiny fireworks festival. Somewhere behind them, a loud pop followed by a soft *shoosh* signaled champagne. Amelia Keogh gave a little squeal and clapped her hands as the cake was placed on the table between them and a waiter circulated, pouring from a frosty bottle of Dom Perignon. While Falcone and Niles dug into creamy mounds of cake, licking icing from their forks and chasing the sugary onslaught with swigs of champagne, they could hear the Keoghs trading affectionate banter from a few yards away.

Amelia Keogh was holding a large envelope up over the candlelight, angling it back and forth, jostling the contents. "I don't think there's any jewelry in there," she said playfully, "and definitely not perfume."

Cyrus Keogh just smiled and said nothing. Sipped and watched his wife over the rim of his glass as she opened the metal clasp and carefully slid her hand inside the envelope, extracting several papers. As she scanned their contents, her lips parted and her eyes grew wide, moisture filming their surface. Before she could say anything, Keogh asked, "Still prefer jewelry for your anniversary?"

"Cy, is this...does this mean...do we..." Her voice caught in her throat, mouth moving soundlessly as if someone had switched the volume off.

Keogh reached over and took her hand. "While you were shopping this afternoon, darling, I took some meetings at the consulate, the most important one with the lawyer who has been working on this. And while it's not quite all done—there are still a few i's to dot and t's to cross—we're there." His tanned face beamed with adoration, cheeks tightened by the breadth of his smile. He stood and pivoted toward the others, announcing, "Tonight we have much more to toast. Little Lula is about to be all ours!"

Falcone and Niles hopped up from their table, joining the Keoghs with congratulatory hugs. With that, the mood abruptly shifted from one of relaxed intimacy to festive celebration, and Cyrus Keogh had one more card in his deck of surprises. He led them into an adjoining room, another formal space with diamond-shaped wood parquet flooring and overhanging chandeliers. It was open, with tables and chairs grouped off to one side. On entering, music began to play and, over an elevated platform, a mirrored disco ball spun and sent glittering flashes strobing along the walls and windows.

"That's our song!" Amelia Keogh exclaimed with glee. The pop strains of *Angels Brought Me Here* filled the room. Cyrus Keogh began dancing with his wife to a ballad by Guy Sebastian that had topped the Australian charts the year they'd been married. With his arms encircling her slender waist and hers around his neck, foreheads touching each other's, they were the profile of perfectly mated swans in a lifelong union of love.

When the song ended, one of an entirely different genre started up, prompting a cackle from Amelia. "Oh my God, Cy!" The cackle turned into effusive laughter that escalated into a fit she could not stop. Cyrus was stepping and strutting along with reggae-hipster Shaggy to another hit from that year, singing, *"Hey sexy lady, I like your flow..."*

Wiping tears from her eyes as she tried to bring her hilarity under control, she said, "Keep your day job, mister!"

Niles joined in and, together with Keogh, warbled and swaggered. Falcone hooted and Amelia Keogh whistled through her fingers as joy took root and bloomed inside her like a field of sunflowers unfolding and opening to the sun. She went to her husband and he swirled her by the hand, fractals of light passing over them as they danced, both with indelible smiles.

Some twenty minutes later, they emerged from Le Caf Conc in a satiated haze, intoxicated with the jubilation of the evening. The Keoghs were looped together, arm in arm, Amelia's head lolling against Cyrus' shoulder. They were still talking and laughing as they waited for Pacheco and Gabbitas to check the cars and street. The air was balmy but the breeze had picked up, riffling leaves and fronds of potted plants by the entrance. Louder rumbles of thunder sounded from the north, and as they filed into the two Mercedes, raindrops were dotting the pavement. The cars pulled out and headed down Avenue de la Nation, initiating the route back to the Fleuve.

Across from the restaurant, an engine from another vehicle turned over, and embers from a discarded cigarette scattered and floated into the night.

FOUR AND A HALF hours after their departure from N'djili at 7 AM, they were in flight on the AS365 Dauphin. Thirty minutes earlier, they had changed from plane to helicopter in Dungu, bidding farewell to Captain Dubruyn and his first officer with some generous gifts from the Keoghs. Still lethargic from the previous night, most of them had dozed languidly on the King Air and were only now appreciating the beautiful day spread around them. It was virtually cloudless, the sky a ceramic blue that was hard to look at for more than a few seconds without squinting, with a sun that seemed to be right outside their windows, blazing white and nebulous. Most were keeping to themselves, the Keoghs exchanging quiet words, squeezing hands, and smiling contentedly. Next to them, Falcone and Niles felt strangely glad to be returning to the remote outpost, where possibly an even larger crowd than those who had seen them off would be gathered to greet them in the manner of triumphant conquerors from a treasure quest in some faraway land.

Ten minutes from their destination, as the helicopter began its descent, trees in the canopy below developing defined depths and edges, the luster of the day seemed to change. The sky was still shockingly blue and full of sun, but the landscape below had taken on a smoky gray cast that was hard to explain. As they neared approach, flying at fifteen hundred feet, pilot and co-pilot were conversing and gesturing with an earnestness that seemed unusual for a landing interchange. Looking out his window, Niles had already sensed something was wrong. "Hey," he said to no one in particular, "are we in the right place?"

For the past few minutes, he'd been seeing dark trails on the ground, blackened ruts snaking through the savanna. But more than what he was seeing, it was what he was *not* seeing that began to strike a chord of alarm; he was not seeing any people moving along the dirt road, no crowd gathering to meet them. The scene below was void of any activity at all. Across from him, he noticed for the first time that Wallace Pacheco had donned a headset and was apparently speaking with the pilots.

The helicopter banked away from the landing field and made a swift pass flying over the church, followed by a slower one from another direction. Everyone turned in their seats to look out the windows—like Niles, not sure of what they were seeing—the sound of the rotors above them amplified and yet somehow thropping in slow motion in a wall of white noise. Below, the church, the field, familiar but not.

From the corner of his eye, Niles caught a glimpse of the Keoghs. All color had drained from their faces, Amelia's an alabaster mask; neither seemed to be breathing. Looking through the window, not more than fifty feet in the air, he stared down at something his mind could not process.

Then it hit him all at once, like the circuit board in his brain had been yanked from its connectors.

They were in the right place, but the place was no longer there. The church was there, the landing field was there, but everything beyond had been reduced to a black mass of crumbled brick and scorched stone and melted metal. The helicopter set down in a light eddy of dust, its passengers in stunned silence. They disembarked and stood gazing numbly across the field. Unable to move or speak.

And then Amelia Keogh shrieked, loud and shrill and guttural, as if an electrical current had ripped through her body, jarring her to life. Her legs gave way and she collapsed to the ground, racked with heaving sobs. Cyrus knelt down and took her into his arms, lifting her up, holding her. His face was pale and stony with shock.

Wallace Pacheco and Beau Gabbitas were at the forefront, arms out, weapons in hand. Pacheco said, "Everybody stay here," and began walking.

That was when Amelia Keogh broke from her husband's embrace and ran, wailing from the center of her being. "Lula! No, no, no...*Lula!*"

Keogh took after her, Falcone and Niles running right behind him.

5

STANDING ON THE TERRACE, Jake swiped to answer his phone and held it to his ear. Before he could say anything, a familiar voice, garbled by static, launched into a string of sentences without breath or punctuation.

"Okay, slow down," he said, straining to sieve through the landslide of words to grasp any kind of thread. One did emerge from the babble. "Wait. You're *where?*" The sheer absurdity made him tilt his head back, as if to clear it of trapped air. "Fuck, Eddie."

He clamped a hand on his forehead, the stream of words overflowing like a river flooding its banks.

"Okay," he said, "stop, just stop. Start over, and tell me what's going on. Slowly."

He listened, and in a few minutes, the words and sentences began to assimilate, but he could not believe what he was hearing and more than once wondered if he was dreaming.

"Fuck," Jake repeated, this time more to himself. Inhaling deeply, he said, "All right, give me some time to think on this. Call me back...I don't know, maybe a couple of hours."

Holding the iPhone to his chest, Jake tried to think, but his muddled thoughts were in a disarray, due in part to the night and early-morning sleep interruptions but mostly to the emotional pulse that now fired on every awakening—and, probably, he realized, even long before. He stepped back through the French doors into the bedroom and stood gazing down at Callie, her face calm and still but for the shallow breaths of deep slumber. Sighing, he resisted the urge to stroke her hair, silvery-white in the blend of moon and nightlights. Moving away from the bed, he reached into a dresser drawer and extracted a pair of shorts and a t-shirt, found his running shoes in the closet, and went downstairs.

He left the villa, faced with an inconceivable and agonizing decision.

DAWN WAS A LITTLE less than an hour off as Jake made his way through the gardens covering the rear of the property, climbing the dozen-plus steps that led to a stone bridge crossing a stream brimming from the previous night's rain and trickling audibly over rocks as round and smooth as croquet balls. The encroaching foliage was lush and wet, brushing his skin as he passed, and by the time he'd traversed the bridge his clothing was damp and he was perspiring in the humidity. Navigating a path through rainforest echoing with pre-dawn birdsong and reptilian croaks and the throaty calls of monkeys, he hiked through the lower canopy dense with ferns, rhododendrons, and elephant ears, stepping over thick tree roots and dodging under twisting lianas. The ground was moist and spongy, smelling of decaying leaves, animal remains and droppings, moss and lichen. The waning moon filtered down through perforations in the lofty ceiling of guacimos and cecropias, beams slant-ing in conical spotlights of chalky luminance.

In less than ten minutes, the forest trail transitioned to tall palms, the sound and smell of ocean overtaking that of earthy compost. Stepping onto muddy silt and sand, he wound his way past the tall grass and dunes and stood on the beach. Felt and tasted the warm salted air. Listened to the somnolent hush of waves barely visible in the semi-dark. Over the Pacific, the sky was beginning to show thin layers of lavender above a glow of red and tangerine. Jake stretched his legs, winged his arms, and arched his back, loosening muscles. Then he took off down the beach, starting with a light sprint that gradually built to a rhythmic jog and fi-nally, a harder run in which he pushed his limits, arms and legs pumping as his heart and lungs worked to keep up. After thirty minutes, his foot-falls were being suctioned by wet sand as the tide advanced on the shore, surf sloshing around his ankles. He slowed back to a jog, stopping at the large flat rock he always used as his starting point. He hoisted himself up onto its surface and sat, enjoying the exhilaration of endorphin release and then found the bottle of water he'd wedged in a crevice and took a long swallow, peering out over the ocean.

The sky had lightened, purples fading, reds going pink, and oranges turning to bronze as the sun edged up and glimmered on the water like hammered metal. Sitting on the rock and watching the sunrise infusing gold into a sky that was incrementally bluing up right before his eyes, clouds wafting into place over the rising and falling waves, his thoughts turned to the stupefying phone call he could not wrap his head around.

Eddie Falcone and Curran Niles were in the Congo. *Congo.* How in the hell had they wound up there, of all places? Especially after everything they had just been through—what they'd *all* been through?

When Jake had first met them a little over two months ago, his initial impression was that they could not have been a quirkier couple of guys. But they had quickly grown on him, and during his time with them they not only earned his fondness, they also earned his respect. On parting ways a few weeks ago in South America, Falcone and Niles were only too happy to be returning to the relative civility of the States...so what, or who, had sent them to Africa? Were they on another scouting exposition for the asinine reality TV producer they'd been working for? Certainly, if they had called Jake to solicit his advice, he would have given them an emphatic *no*. And now they were asking—no, begging—him to come. What Falcone had blurted made no sense, but even over the patchy phone connection, the urgency in his voice was unmistakable.

Which brought him to the agonizing dilemma.

How could he think about leaving now, even for an instant? Callie needed him, and she had to come first. It was just too soon after the unimaginable trauma she'd suffered. The thought of leaving her made him physically sick and, with that, a rush of resentment for Falcone and Niles putting him in this position. But his ire just as quickly receded as he reflected on the bond they'd forged, Falcone and Niles risking their lives for him and her and almost losing their own in the process. Desperately grasping for any other options, he briefly considered recruiting from his network, multitudes of highly competent men he had worked and served with and, more importantly, who he trusted. He mentally tabulated some names, then rejected them all. No, Falcone and Niles, were *his* guys, his gratitude for their courage and loyalty and heroism incalculable, and they were his responsibility.

But so was Callie.

Jake gazed at the ocean, his head swimming with indecision and heart aching with the grief already splitting him apart like a seismic rupture in bedrock. He watched a brown pelican gliding a few feet above the water, suspended by gigantic wings as it scoured the surface for prey. Locking on a target, it soared high into the air and then dove straight down, long bill plucking its bounty from the sea. Following the bird's flight path toward the shoreline, Jake took in the sweep of palms hanging over sand the color of old burlap, masses of driftwood and outcroppings of rock awash with the incoming tide.

Sighing deeply, he hopped off the rock, and took a last look at the ocean, waves swelling and breaking in endless rolls, cascading and collapsing in lacy pools of foam. Turning away, he headed for the dunes, the trees behind them filled with mist.

THE BEDROOM BY MORNING, in contrast with the dark, stormy night before, was bright with emergent sunshine, as breezy as an island retreat. The rainforest glistened with green iridescence on one side, flowers and plants in reds and yellows and pinks bloomed from the gardens on the other, and the vast blue Pacific spanned the horizon from every open space in between.

Jake entered, finding the bed empty. He went to the terrace and opened the French doors to a warm breeze blowing in and the breathtaking view beyond. He left the doors open and stepped back into the bedroom. Furnished in guapinol and guanacaste woods, a herringbone panel of both behind the bed's headboard, the walls were the color of café au lait, hung with sea- and jungle-themed prints. Built-in bookcases and surface tops were decorated with hand-carved boxes, seashells, and pottery, end table lamps with palm leaves layering their bases. Teal was the predominant accent color, mixed with aqua and taupe in the bedding and pillows, and sparkling in glassware. He went around the other side of the bed to the adjoining bath suite. Tiled in big square travertine stone the color of copper, an oversize step-up spa tub with dark bronze fixtures was angled in a corner surrounded by high windows framing the tops of palms swaying in the sun. Arranged on the ledge were scented soaps and candles and a potted mix of yellow-veined crotons and fiery red lobster claw heliconias.

He rounded the corner to the massive walk-in shower, a continuation of tile on the floor and walls, and found Callie standing at the edge, swaddled in a big bath towel, shoulder-length curls tousled from sleep. Despite the warmth in the room, she was visibly shivering, arms crossed tightly over her chest, face as white as a bone china plate. Barefoot, Jake approached her carefully, stripping off his t-shirt, stepping out of his shorts and briefs. Standing behind her, he slipped his arms around her and said, "Come here, love…it's okay," and slowly drew her into the shower with him. He stood for a moment, just holding her, and then began to peel the towel away, taking his time. She was rigid, still shivering, but didn't resist. He could feel the anxiety emanating from her body with every breath she drew, so palpable it was like a living presence. When he had fully removed the towel, he hung it on a hook and, keeping his arms around her, reached up to turn the water on.

It had been a little more than three weeks ago when Callie was abducted from the villa, and though not from this bathroom—she had been taken from one in another bedroom—the memory would probably always be associated with any bathroom here. Since they had been back, knowing the therapeutic benefits, he'd made a point of spending time with her in water—the pool, the ocean—but the shower was still a challenge.

Jake turned on the rainhead nozzles and eased them both under the spray, the heat feeling good on his muscles after the strenuous run, but his focus was on Callie. He lifted her chin with his hand, looking into eyes haunted with distress, and asked, "Okay?" She gave a slight nod, and he said, "Yeah, it's okay," and began lathering soap on her neck and arms, his touch gentle but applying light pressure in specific points known to relieve anxiety and stress. A few minutes in, he could feel her starting to relax and continued lathering with his fingers, moving them along her back and hips. Even these weeks later, her face and body were covered with bruises, lacerations, and abrasions, discolorations in maroon and tan and yellow and green overlapping like a child's finger painting. With the residual soreness, they were constant reminders of not only the savage assaults but also the harrowing time in the jungle when she'd been bitten and stung and cut; multiple puncture marks were still visible around her waist where a spiked tree had impaled her. But the wounds and contusions were in the process of healing; the emotional and psychological trauma would, most likely, never fully leave her. And knowing that he was the reason she'd been brutalized was a heartache that would dwell in him for the rest of his days.

He turned her to face him, which caused her to draw up and seem even smaller than she already was, the weight that she'd lost in the past weeks more pronounced without the cover of clothing. With her body against his, he could feel her ribs on his chest, feel the nipples of her small breasts, feel breath moving in and out of her lungs. Massaging shampoo in her hair, he pressed his lips lightly on her forehead in a kiss, and lingered, his eyes closed, the water streaming down. The floral scent of soap and shampoo, mingled with the natural essence of her body, was intoxicating and generated an avalanche of emotional feelings and physical stirrings that he fought to control. Holding her close to him, feeling the touch of her skin, the beat of her heart, was torturous. More than anything, he wanted to show her that she could feel safe again, feel good again, feel the emotional joy and rapture and physical ecstasy of love. In the shower with her, in the ocean, in the pool, *was* therapeutic, but it also awakened memories of sensual experiences with her in the Costa Rican countryside when they had steeped in natural hot springs with steam perfumed by night-blooming flowers swirling around them and invigorated in the fresh, cool rush of waterfalls bursting from rocky jungle ledges into deep pools as blue and green as a peacock's feathers.

Watching the soap and shampoo dissolve in bubbles through the drain, Jake reached for the towel and draped it around her with a light hug. In her ear, he said, "Okay, angel, get dressed and we'll go downstairs for some breakfast." He nudged Callie gently out of the shower and then leaned into the spray, planting his hands in front of him, arms cabled with muscle. His coarse black hair was crow's head-slick under the stream, covering the back of his neck and dripping in a flap over his eyes. Several scars on his torso pinked up in the steam, a braided feather tattoo darkened around his bicep. Braced against the wall, he let the water run over his head and face, down his chest and legs, the ache in his loins as relentless as the one in his heart. He stood like that for a while, trying not to think about anything but the sound of water trickling on tile—trying, but not succeeding, not even a little bit.

JAKE CAME DOWNSTAIRS TO the appetizing aroma of sautéed peppers and onions, and found the housekeeper stirring some in a sizzling cast-iron skillet. The kitchen, through a wide stone arch, opened onto a capacious living and dining area with stone tile floors and stucco walls trimmed in wood and post beams, large paddle fans overhead. Furnishings, upholstered and accented in earth and oceanic tones, were grouped over jute area rugs and made of the same tropical hardwoods as the bedroom. On the back side of the villa, the wall of windows behind the kitchen sink overlooked the patio and pool.

Surveying the bowls and platters and pans assembled on the countertop and stove, Jake poured himself some coffee, sipped, and said, "*Buenos días*, Camilla. Got a small feast going here."

The housekeeper, a middle-aged *Tica*, gave him a pert smile and sprinkled some seasonings into a pot of rice and beans. She wore a red dress with yellow flowers, matching scarf around a head capped with dark curls. Her large eyes, plump cheeks, and broad forehead gave her a genuine and cheerful demeanor, her movements full of good energy. Waggling her fingers to shoo him from the kitchen, she said, "*Vaya y relájese, Señor* Jake."

Jake grinned, gave her a little bow of concession, and stepped out onto the patio, bathed in sunlight that shimmered across the pool surface like serrated pieces of sea glass. He was dressed in tan Tommy Bahama cargo shorts, a navy t-shirt imprinted with a beach graphic and the words *Palm Conditions,* and slip-on thong sandals.

Callie was seated at a chocolate brown dinette, table made of aluminum planks and chairs of resin-coated wicker with fabric cushions. It was set with round woven placemats and festively patterned plates, a big pitcher of freshly squeezed orange juice in the center. She was gripping a ceramic mug of coffee with both hands, as if a sudden gust of wind might rip it from her grasp. Wearing a mid-length white sundress with sweeps of violet and blue around the skirt, her gaze was captivated by a section of greenery near the patio where a troupe of birds fluttered among leaves and branches in a jewel heist of colors. Jake set his coffee mug on the table and took the chair next to her, kissing her on the neck. She shuddered, and the reaction sent an electrical tingle through his lips. Once again, he wanted badly, so badly, to turn her around and take her sweet face and kiss her petal-soft mouth, but reined himself in with self-restraint shredded to its core. It was a restraint, though, that he was determined to maintain until enough time had passed. Their hair was damp from the shower; his combed back with strands loose over his brow, hers hanging in gold coils that would turn champagne-pale when dry. It was still fragrant with the floral shampoo. He noted that a light blush had returned to her skin.

Leaning back in his chair and sipping his coffee, Jake watched a small striped lizard skitter along the pavement edge and drop into the foliage, but found his eyes gravitate to a spot not far from where he sat. Repeated power washing had reduced a stain the size of a watermelon to one almost undetectable, but in his mind, Jake could still see the liver-colored patch of dried blood where Pablo Luis Ayala's body had been the dreadful night he returned from Colombia, finding the young police officer dead and Callie gone.

His somber reflections were interrupted by Camilla, carrying a tray laden with platters of her *gallo pinto*: scrambled eggs, rice and beans, tomatoes, avocados, toast, and fresh fruit. Distributing them on the table, she looked pointedly at Callie and said, *"Tú, a comer."*

Jake chuckled and said, "You heard the woman, better eat up," the register of his voice low and soothing. He poured them some orange juice and began filling their plates. They ate and drank quietly for a few moments, Jake digging in hungrily, Callie much less so. Jake dredged a forkful of eggs through piquant sauce, spearing onions and peppers, and put the bite in his mouth, chewing with pleasure. He observed Callie sampling everything on her plate, happy to see that she appeared to be enjoying the food, even if the quantity of intake was negligible.

When he had polished off the last of his breakfast, Jake wiped his mouth with a cloth napkin and commented, "I really like this dress we got you the other day, very pretty."

"Thank you, I do, too," she replied with a shy smile that quickly dissolved as she added, "I know…I need to fill it out a little more. I'm…I'm trying." She glimpsed guiltily at the loose fabric, at sections that would be more flattering and form-fitting without the weight loss.

"It's okay, love. I know. Takes time." He touched her arm, saying, "And you're beautiful right now." That got the smile back, briefly.

He waited until she had eaten all she was going to, his chest tight with dread in anticipation of the conversation they were about to have, the weight constricting like a serpent had wrapped itself around his rib cage and was squeezing the breath out of him. Turning so that he faced her directly, legs on either side of her chair, he inhaled deeply and said, "Callie, I got a call this morning."

Looking at him, her brown eyes widened. They were dark and almond-shaped with naturally long and fine lashes that were flickering in new apprehension.

"Eddie, calling from Africa. He and Curran are over there doing God knows what, but they…" He stopped, searching for the right words, but somehow they evaded him. Despite what he'd gotten from the phone call, he was still having an impossible time reconciling it all.

"They're in trouble?" Callie asked.

He sighed. "Yeah, probably so." Watching her closely, he saw the dilation of her pupils, tiny dots of perspiration at her hairline, shallow breathing that quickened, and when he took her hands in his, they were trembling.

In the treetops beyond them, birds called to each other in whistles and trills, desolate in the sunny tranquility. A brown butterfly looped along the pool's edge, wings looking as though they'd been dipped in blue powder.

On the table next to him, his iPhone rang, the sound jarring in the quiet. Callie jumped.

Releasing her hands to reach for the phone, he saw the little bit of restored color blanch from her face, which was looking at him in that instant as if the support beams under every platform of her being had just collapsed.

6

AMELIA KEOGH'S WAILS WERE stridently feral and, without the buffer of structures, seemed to rend the air like the clarion calls of some shrill bird, expanding across the land. The wails eventually dwindled to retching sobs as Cyrus held her and tried his best to calm her, even as he was visibly overcome himself.

Falcone and Niles stood in the dome of brilliant sunlight, heat radiating with nuclear intensity from a sky empty of clouds, pure and blue and serene as a prayer. But on the ground below, a debris field of scorched and charred and burned matter stretched in every direction; wood was black and charcoal-glazed, metal was disfigured into garish aberrations, stone and brick were broken and scattered as if a wrecking ball had swung in big, arcing blows, pulverizing everything in its path. The air was acrid and smoky, the humidity causing it to shimmer in oily vapors that stung the eyes and nose. As they took tentative, uneven steps through the rubble, the ground snapped and crunched under their feet in a grating sound and sensation that made their jawbones thrum. Just ahead of them, the Keoghs and Cameron McNamara were taking the same cautious steps, while the security men in front were gnashing their way in thick-soled boots that insulated them from feeling whatever was underfoot.

Her voice still pitched and quavering, Amelia asked, "What's happened, Cyrus? What *is* this?" And then she started crying again, murmuring, "Lula," over and over.

Supporting her with his arms as they crossed what remained of their compound, Keogh looked around in a daze, his eyes vacuous, and said softly, "I don't know, sweetheart. I just can't imagine."

"God, I can't believe this," Niles muttered. "It looks like a bloody bomb site." He cast a glance at Falcone, who said nothing, his face as flat and gray as a gravestone.

As they traversed the grounds, random pieces of its former existence cropped up in the ruins, all incinerated, but a handful were just enough intact to be recognizable—a sandal, a schoolbook binding, a scorched pot, sooted photos and notes that had detached from the disintegrated message board, and a scrap of the tarp from Falcone and Niles' sleeping quarters. Seeing that, Falcone stopped and starred.

"Eddie?" When Falcone did not respond, Niles said, "Whatever happened...they were leaving, you know?"

Falcone did not speak for several moments, the Adam's apple in his throat bobbing as he tried to swallow, then he replied, "So, you think..." But the thought went unfinished because he could not think, because none of it made any sense.

Niles placed his hand on Falcone's shoulder and they stood somberly, gazing off toward the trees, where leaves and palm fronds at the compound's periphery were singed, not a single bird to be seen. There were large sections of burnt forest, limbs defoliated, branches and trunks charcoaled, but most of the destruction was confined to the compound and village, as if a laser sight had targeted them and sent a missile to their coordinates. Falcone and Niles were jolted by another agonizing wail from Amelia Keogh, and turned to see her holding something to her chest. Rushing to her side, they realized what it was almost immediately. She looked up at her husband's face, her lovely green eyes reddened and streaming tears, and held out her hands for him to see the crisped and blackened remnants of a book. It was coming apart, disintegrating into ash, but they all knew what it was, tiny bits of blue from the cover crumbling with the black cinders.

Wallace Pacheco and Beau Gabbitas approached, their faces devoid of expression. Pushing his sunglasses up above his forehead, Pacheco cleared his throat and addressed Cyrus Keogh. "Okay, we need to get you away from here, at least until we have a better handle on what's happened. We suspect there was an attack on the compound, but it appears that everybody fled. We haven't come across any"—he paused, aware of Amelia Keogh's frantic gaze fixated on him—"human remains."

Gabbitas took his lead and added, "We're going to keep investigating, but in the meantime, let's go to the church." He started walking, pointing off in the distance. "When we flew over, I noticed that it's still there."

They followed Gabbitas from the desecrated grounds, crossing the field toward the road. As they walked, Pacheco continued speaking to Cyrus Keogh, saying, "I've got a call in to my boss, to see what he wants to do, but most likely he's going to order an evac. We've still got the helo here, so—"

"No!" Amelia Keogh exclaimed, gripping her husband's arm. "No! I'm not leaving until...until we find them! Until we find Lula!" Tears started anew, cutting trails through the smudges of soot on her face. She was wearing sand-colored slacks and a matching gingham shirt that were smoked with ashy residue.

"What about that?" Keogh asked, hugging Amelia to him. "Could we conduct a search?"

Pacheco reached for his sunglasses and ran a hand over the bristle of his hair, his face creased in doubt. "I don't know. Truthfully, I don't think it's going to yield much, given where we are. But I'll ask. Right now, the best thing is for all of you to take shelter in that church, and we'll take it from there."

AS IT TURNED OUT, the church was, in fact, unscathed. It was also totally empty—Father Jean Makuanza and Sisters Davina and Mireille were gone, presumably among the missing.

The interior of the church was simple, walls and floor made of mud and stone, several rows of wooden benches arranged before a pulpit. Shaded by the surrounding grove of palms, it was cooler inside and the openings for windows allowed airflow that helped offset the mounting afternoon heat. Steering Amelia to one of the benches, Cyrus said, "There should be some bottled water in the living quarters."

While Niles went in search of the water, Wallace Pacheco and Beau

Gabbitas went back outside to make calls on their satellite phones. Niles returned and distributed water and some bananas he'd found, taking a seat next to Falcone. Insects buzzed in and out of the window openings as they ate and drank, the sound of plastic bottles popping and crinkling unusually loud in the musty gloom of the little church. They had been on the ground for nearly an hour, the harsh edges of an incomprehensible reality starting to close in as they rested and wrestled with their individual assessments of the situation. The emotional energy expended in Amelia Keogh's grief had left her faint and lifeless, laying across Cyrus's lap as he worked to keep his expression neutral; clearly, he was having a difficult time doing that, his blue eyes dulling to a shade of pewter and brimming with anguish. He looked up as Cameron McNamara entered the church, satellite phone in hand, but before he could try on a guise of hopefulness, his assistant was shaking his head in defeat.

Face florid and sweaty, he reached for a bottle of water and downed half before speaking. "I'm not really getting anybody, Cyrus. There's so much going on elsewhere, especially around Kivu with the Ebola outbreaks and the violence…"

"Did you try to reach Sanctuary?" Niles asked abruptly, referring to The Sanctuary Initiative, Iris Margolis' group. Falcone's head turned to him, then back to McNamara, eyes and mouth widening like a fish siphoning oxygen from water.

"I did. No response."

Falcone bowed his head, an elbow on his knee, fist pressed into his forehead. Then he stood and extended his arm to McNamara, reaching for the sat phone. "Let me have that for a minute, there's someone I want to call."

SHADOW FILLED THE DANK sanctum, the smell of earth and moss mixed with perspiration. The thin streaks of sunlight that had filtered in through the windows were all but gone, the interior cast in a deepening gray-brown haze. While the security men and the Keoghs' assistant had continued to work the sat phones outside the church, the Keoghs retreated to the living quarters where Cyrus convinced Amelia to rest. Falcone and Niles sat, slouched back-to-back on one of the wooden benches, listlessly gazing into the dimness, Niles watching a spider scuttle across the dusty floor.

"You think he'll come?" Niles asked.

"I don't know," Falcone sighed, adding, "and I woke him up."

"Oh, yeah, quite a big time difference."

"And it's a big ask right now."

"Right, Callie," Niles said morosely. Then, a few moments later, he blurted, "Iris is probably okay."

"What?"

"They probably left right after we did."

Falcone did not respond, just took in a breath and sucked in his cheek. His thoughts drifted to a day right after they had returned from South America, when he and Niles had found their way into a bar in Manhattan's Financial District, having just come from the Brooklyn offices of the TV producer they'd been working for.

The Dead Rabbit is an insanely popular pub-style establishment owned by a pair of young Irishmen from Belfast. The three-story brick tavern with sawdust on the floor and photographs depicting Northern Irish life teeming from the wood-beamed ceiling, had just reopened after a fire. Frequently at the top of national and international best-of lists, it was always packed, but Falcone and Niles found room at the ground-floor taproom bar this particular evening. They were deep into a second round of beers, reminiscing about their recent adventure, when a woman, twenty-something with an unruly mass of long brown hair and horn-rimmed eyeglasses sidled up beside Niles. She was sipping a cocktail the pinkish-red color of a Jolly Rancher candy, her big brown eyes riveted on Falcone. Indicating her drink, she said, "This is called *Bark at the Moon*, something I've been known to do on occasion." She cackled, her unabashed laugh causing a few heads to turn, but it was her provocative look that had every male head on a swivel. She was dressed in skin-tight jeans and a plunging leopard-print halter top stretched over copious breasts. Falcone was physically attracted to her instantaneously, but he found it odd that she wasn't hitting on Niles—all the women went bonkers over his English accent—and her overtly eccentric personality seemed more suited to his. But several rounds later, after moving upstairs to the parlor, conversation turned more serious and Falcone was intrigued by her wit and intelligence. The two young men in her consort, Neville Nias and Drake Johanssen, were equally impressive and the talk flowed as fluidly as the cocktails and beer.

Right after last call, the bewitching lady who had introduced herself as Iris Margolis turned to Falcone and Niles and asked, "How would you like to go to the Congo with us?"

The robust and beguiling images and thoughts from that evening, which had transcended into an exhilarating new endeavor, were now overwritten by the awful ruins of something terrible. What had happened? Where had they all gone? Were they still alive?

Cyrus Keogh returned, taking a seat across from them, the collar of his cotton shirt wrinkled and damp, top buttons undone. Like most of his couture, it was a fine piece, this one a blue micro print Zegna, but Keogh's style was anything but pretentious; more than a few souls at the compound had been the delighted beneficiaries of his shirts and trousers and jackets and shoes. But now, slumped on the bench, his impeccable tailoring, along with his perennial goodwill and confidence, had wilted. His tanned, youthful face had deflated to a puffy, pallid mask of despair. Hands clasped together in front of him, he said, "You know, things can be replaced, rebuilt. But the people here, and—" He stopped, gulping as if something was clotted in his throat. When he finally looked up, his eyes were wet. "This child...Lula...means everything to us."

Falcone and Niles twisted around to face him, planting their feet on the floor, hands folded, faces solemn.

"I'm not ashamed to say that I would have used any of my influence to cut through the considerable red tape," he said, rubbing the underside of his chin and then propping it on his knuckle. "But in the end, I did everything by the book, and truly, against all odds, she is finally..." He stopped again, this time unable to continue.

Wallace Pacheco entered and strode over to them, Beau Gabbitas and Cameron McNamara trailing behind. All of them wore grim expressions. Pacheco said, "I still don't know what happened here. A few sketchy reports, but not enough to put anything definitive together. I spoke with the boss. The rest of our team is currently deployed and spread out, but you are obviously our highest priority contract, so we can try to get some more guys down here to do a search."

"How long will it take for them to get here, for you to start?" Keogh asked.

Pacheco shrugged. "Hard to say, but several days at least."

"What about the UN?"

"Sorry, no help there so far." He crooked a thumb over his shoulder. "I need to go check on the helo and talk to the pilots."

When the security men had departed, Keogh stood and gave Falcone and Niles a long look, a decision being made. "Tell your guy, Jake Tyler, I'll get him here, cover everything and pay him whatever he wants."

Falcone took the sat phone outside and stood in the shade, tapping numbers on the Iridium, watching Pacheco and Gabbitas walking toward the field, handguns in their shoulder holsters, talking and smoking cigarettes. It was nearly 4:00 PM, sun high in the sky, the red dirt road baked the color of eroded rust. Falcone listened as the connection went through and dialing commenced. Listened as Jake answered and spoke.

The figures of Pacheco and Gabbitas grew small in the distance down the road.

And then the sound of automatic gunfire rattled from the far side of the field.

7

JAKE SNAGGED HIS IPHONE from the table, stood, and strode to the far side of the pool, hoping he was out of earshot. He attempted to keep his expression even as he put the phone to his ear and answered, but his eyes widened at the sounds he was hearing in the background. "Eddie, is that gunfire?" He listened intently as Falcone spoke for several moments, then said, "Okay, I'm coming. But get the hell out of there if it's not safe!" Falcone said something else, and Jake responded, "Well, if there's shooting, it's not safe, Eddie. You said there are security guys, where are they?"

After a few minutes, the call ended and Jake stood looking down at the pool sparkling in the sunlight, a bright pink confetti of bougainvillea petals floating across the surface. Trying to moderate his thoughts, which were already caroming around his head with the random disorder of billiard balls, he glanced over at Callie, who was no longer drinking coffee or watching the birds or looking at him; she sat with her hands clasped in her lap, gazing down at her dress. His chest hitched, filling with a draft of despondency as he recalled the day he had bought it.

He had been gauging her readiness to venture out of the villa and, after a week and a half had passed, thought it was worth a try. While he yearned to take her sailing—had, in fact, been thinking about taking her to the Bahamas where Delaney's boat, now his, was berthed—that was something for a much later time. He'd also considered a drive in the countryside; like sailing, it was something they had done before. But he knew he needed to take it slower, stay closer to home, and decided on a simple day in town. His suggestion elicited an involuntary reaction of panic, and when she finally agreed, he suspected it was only because she didn't want to disappoint him.

THE DAY HAD DAWNED in glorious tropical fashion, warm and sunny and full of paradisiacal promise. The short drive down from the villa took them through a verdant tunnel of rainforest to the Costanera Sur highway, everything lush and green from the regular rains of the season, coins of sunlight dappling the road. Monkeys could be heard howling and screeching from the trees, branches bouncing with their movements.

Dominical is a beachfront town located along Costa Ballena in the Puntarenas province of Costa Rica, populated by less than a thousand people. Many are artists or small business owners, some natives and some expats, and its laid-back retro hippie vibe is enthusiastically embraced by all, particularly the hundreds of surfers who patrol its beaches for the epic waves that often exceed ten feet in height.

On this morning, Jake had pulled his newly purchased charcoal-gray Jeep Rubicon onto a strip of gravel shaded by almond trees and coconut palms. On one side, tawny sand stretched into the ocean as it rose and rolled with surfers sprinting into the waves; on the other, a street market curved back toward the town. Jake took Callie's hand and they began to stroll the paver-covered road, moving from one vendor's booth to the next, perusing pottery, art, woodwork, jewelry, and apparel, lines of multicolored beach towels flapping in the breeze like a display of international flags. At first, she clung to him, easily startled when a kid on a bike reeled past in a sweaty blast or a couple of dogs scampered in front of them in pursuit of a squirrel. But it was the off season, the stream of people minimal, and Callie's anxiety slowly lessened as she became more at ease in the familiarity of a place they'd spent quite a few pleasant hours. Jake caught glimpses of the now-elusive smile that lifted his spirit, flashes of sun spangling through the canopy of palms overhead. They walked in a leisurely pace, her small hand secure in his, the breeze riffling her curls. He watched her closely, looking for signs of fatigue or physical discomfort, pausing often, reassuring frequently.

Nearing the end of the market, Jake saw Callie wistfully admiring the sundress but then quickly turn away. Earlier, he had purchased an art print for the villa, some shorts for himself, and a necklace for her. From behind her, he said, "Hey, that's pretty…you like it?"

"Yes, but…" Her voice fell off, an unknown emotion flickering in her eyes.

"But what? I like it." He reached for the hanger, held it up appraisingly, checked the size. A tiny number, and still looked like two of her might fit inside it.

Wearing pale yellow shorts and a sleeveless white eyelet top that covered a gapping waistband, Callie self-consciously dropped her arms over her midriff.

Jake handed a pair of *colones* notes to the vendor, one green and one blue, both engraved with images of Costa Rican wildlife. The vendor slipped the dress into a bag and they continued walking, Jake steering them to an open-air café at the road junction.

Café Mono Congo, just off the main highway entrance, resembles a jungle treehouse with dark wood planks and bamboo, surrounded by plants and trees. It overlooks the mouth of the Barú River, the flow of which feeds into the Pacific and plays an integral part in creating the big surf and beach regeneration. Inside, the café's tables and benches are also all wood, the stools around the deck bar made of tree cross sections. Hand-drawn doodles and art are everywhere, much of it colorfully chalked on blackboard surfaces with upbeat aphorisms such as: *Taste Love* and *No More War*.

Jake placed their order and selected a table on the deck, the Barú wide and deep blue green over the open rail, its far bank carpeted with a thick pelt of graduated forest. Settling into his seat, Jake said, "I'm starving," lifting his nose in the air to inhale the aroma of baked goods and strong, freshly roasted coffee. Other diners around them were conversing or immersed in phones and tablets connected to the café's Wi-Fi. The mellow indie folk of Xavier Rudd singing *Follow the Sun* was playing over the sound system, the river currents churning toward the ocean under a powder blue sky with billowing clouds that looked as though they had been airbrushed in place. Jake thought the day could not have been going any better.

Their server, a young man wearing a black t-shirt and ball cap imprinted with the Café Mono Congo curly-tailed monkey logo in white, set plates on the table—a Veggie Taco Salad for her and a Tico Burrito for him—and Jake rubbed his hands together in avid anticipation. He glanced at Callie, waited until she picked up her fork, and then took a healthy bite of his wrap. He chewed, swallowed, and sipped from a bottle of Mad Monkey cold-pressed Green Juice, watching as she began to eat. Nibbling, really, but eating, which made him happy. Even with the residual scratches and bruising on her face, skin around her eyes puffy from insufficient sleep, she was heartachingly beautiful, and when the light hit her at just the right angle—as it did now—flecks of gold speckled the deep brown of her irises. Her hair was like spun silk, swirls on top of swirls, coiled but flowing.

She looked up, saw him studying her, and color bloomed in her cheeks, head tilting down.

Jake was about to reach over, lift her chin and say something, when a tall man with a blond crew cut stopped by their table. He was deeply tanned, arms and legs sinewy from the vigorous workouts he got as a *guardavida*, identified by the tomato-red shirts and shorts they wore on duty.

"Hey, Jake," he said, "sorry to interrupt your lunch. I was just picking up an order for the guys and spotted you." Looking at Callie, his face flooded with sympathy, his carved cheeks drooping. He said her name softly, and then found himself at a loss for words.

Callie seemed to shrink in her skin, and Jake thought if she could have disappeared or slid under the table, she would have. He put his hand over hers, stroking with his fingers, and said, "Jerry, good to see you."

"Glad I ran into you, I was going to call." His eyes landed on Callie again, remembering her on the beach, hands sifting through the sand as she watched the tide advance and the seabirds circle overhead. And then, not long after, seeing a devastated Jake and hearing that she was missing.

Jerry Hadley was the head lifeguard of the first professional beach lifeguard service in Costa Rica, wholly funded by donations and patrolling the Dominical beaches seven days a week. Jake had known him for years and had contacted him just a few days prior with a request.

Hadley continued, "I've got the perfect guy for you. Jesse Segura. Fully vetted, but I'll get you his creds for your own scrutiny. He's been with us for several years, and he's looking for a new place and some side work. I talked to him about it and he'd really like to be considered."

Jake pondered for a moment, his face transitioning to recognition. "Yeah, I know who you're talking about. I've met him, nice guy. Send me his info."

"You got it," Hadley said, and went to retrieve his order.

On their way out of the restaurant, Jake picked up a bag of King Kong coffee and a couple of bottles of the cold-pressed juice, chatting with staff he knew. When they stepped outside, he saw Callie's unease fade, her gaze taking in clusters of little yellow flowers swarming with butterflies. They went next door to Mama Toucan's, a small grocery of natural and organic foods, where items were arranged so artfully and precisely they could have been the backdrop for a jigsaw puzzle, fresh produce popping with color and not a piece out of place. A young couple were ordering banana splits while their three-year-old twin boys, dressed in identical dungaree shorts and striped tops, played tag around them. Paying for fruits and vegetables they'd picked out, Jake saw Callie smiling as she gazed at the parents trying to subdue their frisky toddlers, and again felt he'd made the right choice in getting her out this day.

As they walked back to the Jeep, the sun warm on their skin, trees jittering with birds, Jake said, "It's still early, why don't we stop by Hacienda Barú and see Jack while we're down here?" He opened the passenger door and helped her in, waiting for a response. Her face was registering hints of an inner quandary, and when she didn't answer, he asked, "Are you getting tired? Hurting at all?"

She hesitated before finally saying, "No, I'm okay."

He would later realize that he should have known in that moment, by her expression and hesitation, anything more was crossing a bridge too far, but the day had been going so well he ignored his instincts. Hopping into the driver's seat, he cast another quick glance at Callie and, not seeing any discernible anxiety, started the Rubicon and headed toward the highway.

Hacienda Barú is 815 acres of tropical rainforest, wetlands, mangroves, river bank and beach front, designated a national wildlife refuge

in 1995 and developed into a renowned ecotourism landmark by Jack
Ewing and his partners. Its growth in recent years, adding guest
accommodations and a restaurant, among other amenities, have made
it a popular destination year-round, featuring nature hikes and zip lining.
Jake had become acquainted with Jack Ewing years ago, booking many
adventure packages for clients that included one or more days at the
conservatory; he'd also brought Callie here.

Entering the office, Jake spotted a gray-bearded man wearing a
brimmed canvas hat and tan polo shirt tucked into jeans. He was standing by the teak reception desk, surrounded by a group of tourists with
binoculars hanging from their necks, clutching notebooks and field
guides, listening with rapt attention to a story about the early days of
Hacienda Barú. Seeing Jake and Callie, the man nodded and wrapped up
his monologue.

Jake and Ewing clasped hands, Ewing eying Callie with affection and
concern. "I thought we'd get out for a little bit, in town," Jake explained,
"and since we were close…"

Giving Callie a light hug, Ewing said, "I'm so glad you came by." He
reflected briefly, then said, "Why don't you walk some of the Chirincoco
trail across from the office? You could just go a short way."

Once again, there seemed to be a glimmer of uncertainty in Callie's
eyes, but before Jake could adequately measure the depth, she looked
away. Slipping his arm around her waist, Jake asked, "What about it,
sweetie, feel up to that?"

"Okay," she said, but her voice was bereft of conviction.

Leaving the office, they started down the trail, moving in and out of
sunlight as a bare-throated tiger heron languidly picked its way on the
ground in front of them before flying into some mangos. They passed
an iguana sunning on a rock, the spines on its leathery back zebra-
striped, a noisy congregation of orange-chinned parakeets chattering in
a tree above. From a loftier perch, a mostly black chestnut-mandibled
toucan with its bright yellow throat and bicolored bill was yelping something that sounded like *yo-yip a-yip a-yip*. The trail, in its entirety, began
sparsely wooded with many open areas—ideal, Jake thought, for Callie's
level of comfort—but it eventually converged into a thickly forested
stretch along a small stream that paralleled the beach and ocean, which

he had no intention of entering. Already, he was noticing that her breathing was quickening, her hand tightening in his. Ironically, if Jake, who was normally hyper-aware of his surroundings at all times, had not been so focused on Callie, watching for the slightest trace of distress, he would have noticed the atmospheric changes a little sooner.

They were approaching a much denser stand of forest, Callie halting in her tracks with the branches beginning to obscure the light, when Jake picked up on a shift in the breeze with a more distinctively brackish tang, smelling of fish and seaweed and decaying matter. They retreated as the sky turned a greenish gray, clouds gathering into ashen bundles shaping and reshaping with building energy. And then something snapped directly overhead, like the break of a giant bone, crashing down in whacks and thunks as it dropped heavily to the ground. Simultaneously, the collective wings of dozens of birds shuddered in mass evacuation. Callie gasped and Jake pulled her into him, propelling them both forward. The severed branch, from a poró tree, landed just behind them, and Callie buried her head in Jake's chest, her whole body quaking. Before he could even say anything in reassurance, a crack of thunder detonated, loud and close, and shook the ground and everything around them.

"Okay, let's go, we're about to get wet," Jake said calmly, guiding her along the trail, keeping his arm around her until they got to the Jeep Rubicon. By then, rain was coming down in pea-size drops, the sky amassing smoky thunderheads nerved with lightning. When Jake turned onto the highway, the rain was sweeping across the road in white curtains, shimmering over the Jeep's windshield as the wipers thumped back and forth.

Beside him, Callie was curled into a fetal ball in her seat, shaking, her face blanched, eyes fixed and blinking rapidly. Gray dots of rain covered her white top, her face and hair dripping with moisture. Seeing her shivering, Jake reached over the dashboard and turned the heat on, despite the fact that the temperature outside was in the eighties. He drove slowly and cautiously back to the villa, feeling as if the buoyant air of the day had been sucked out in a backdraft.

He placed his hand lightly on her thigh, and she flinched. "It's okay, sweetheart," he soothed, "we'll be home in just a minute."

Later, she had tearfully apologized, to which he'd replied, "No, love, you did great," and felt a gulf of sadness wash over him.

PTSD was a horrible thing to experience, and over the course of his many military ops he'd seen a lot of it, had even endured brief episodes himself. But it was even more horrible to see it torture someone you loved.

Now, as he returned to his seat next to her at the table, she looked at him, her eyes plaintive. "You have to go?"

He said, "Yes, angel," and felt a jab like a railroad spike in his gut.

A FEW HOURS HAD passed since the second phone call, during which time Jake had been in constant motion: packing, making and receiving calls, logging onto his computer. Several minutes ago, a young, athletic man with dark skin and hair had met Jake on the patio. He was wearing jeans and a red t-shirt stenciled with the *Guardavidas* insignia. Callie sat at the kitchen bar, sipping from a tall glass filled with chunks of ice, slices of lime, and sparkling water, watching as Jake shook the young man's hand and began talking, his expression earnest and gestures emphatic. They strolled around the pool and then disappeared from view—below the patio area, Callie guessed, where a finished storage space had been converted into living quarters. Shortly after the return from South America, Jake had launched into a number of home projects, the conversion being one of them; his objective was to provide a non-invasive space for on-site security, and his request to Jerry Hadley resulted in a solid candidate. Jake spent hours on due diligence before inviting him over the first time and introducing him to Callie, who also remembered Jesse Segura from time on the beach.

She took her glass and moved into the living room, sitting on one of the mocha-colored sofas, leaning back into the comfortable cushions and looking around the beautiful room, another of Jake's ideas. The villa had been attractively appointed before, but he thoughtfully proposed some redecorating; in part to make it more personal to them, but also in a conscientious attempt to minimize any unpleasant memories that might be subliminally attached. So he had arranged for a decorator to bring catalogues and samples and computer-generated mock-ups, and in very short order, the vibrant Hispanic-style casa had been transformed into the idyllic oceanside retreat with its soothing turquoise and aqua accents and coastal art.

Hugging a pillow embossed with white coral, Callie sank down in the sofa and gazed up at the ceiling fan, wood blades carved into palm leaves. She stroked the pillow, and for just a moment, the slowly turning blades lulled her, and she closed her eyes. The air blowing down was cool on her face, and she felt her mind drifting to a place of calm. But the comfort was fleeting. The thought of Jake leaving filled her with such overwhelming dread that she felt as if an enormous cavern was yawing open below her, could feel the force of its vortex pulling her down. Fear serrated like a metal jaw clamping down across her chest, crushing bones and breath. She inhaled and exhaled deeply, sat forward and picked up her glass, coughing as she gulped a little too much of the sparkling water.

Going to the windows off the dining room, she peered out and saw Jake again, still talking to Segura—standing with his feet apart, hands on his hips, his trim, hard-bodied physique exuding absolute confidence— and felt a rush of emotion. Jake evoked feelings in her she'd never experienced before, a euphoria of mind and body and heart that was all-consuming, and she ached for his touch, his love, all of it. But thinking of that intimacy now made her tense up and feel a profound sense of shame, as if somehow she'd been stripped raw of everything that made her worthy of love or desire. And everything inside her still hurt, the twinges often triggering horrific memories of the brutalization. Tears welled in her eyes, trickling down her cheeks. She didn't want to be afraid, wanted to be okay, wanted to be brave in his absence so *he* wouldn't feel bad. But she was scared of the most basic things; scared of the night and its darkness, scared of the day and its glaring exposure— scared to go to sleep and scared to wake up. What got her through it was knowing that Jake would be there, on both sides.

And now, he was leaving.

The cavern inside her plunged like a sinkhole, gusts of panic rising up from the abyss.

AFTER A DAY FRAUGHT with the exigency of his ongoing travel

preparations, Jake had shut it all down for some time with Callie, unwinding with her in the pool. An hour later, he had poured them glasses of wine from a bottle of Chilean Pinot Noir while he cooked red snapper and vegetables on the patio grill, the villa emitting golden light behind them and the pool glimmering in aqua serenity beneath a navy blue sky studded with stars. Callie barely touched her dinner, and he'd found his own appetite less than robust as the gravity of his imminent departure cast a dismal pall over the evening.

Following dinner, they had ascended the stairs, Jake trailing Callie as she gripped the ornamental iron railing and slowly navigated to the second floor. She had tried to internalize her discomfort as she neared the top, but he heard the intakes of breath as she winced from the stretches.

Minutes later, they were in bed, Jake bare-chested and propped up by pillows with his MacBook open on his lap, Callie nestled against his side, wearing a silky white camisole. He'd brought the wine upstairs, hoping it would help her relax and, later, sleep. The windows were open, a warm breeze carrying the fragrance of jasmine and ginger and ylang ylang into the bedroom. Jake tapped keys, read, tapped more keys and scrolled, his dark eyes narrowed in concentration as he checked emails with last-minute confirmations. At one point, he tried the number for the sat phone, but the connection dropped, and after a few more unsuccessful attempts, he gave it up. Finally, he rubbed his eyes, closed the MacBook and set it on the bedside table. He switched off the lamp and turned to see Callie looking up at him, her eyes moist.

Gently, he lifted her over him and positioned her body between his legs, and began lightly massaging her neck and shoulders. Her hair and skin were luminous in the moonlight, her form feeling as delicate as a rose with petals that could break apart in a puff of air. He felt the ache of longing and despair of leaving sweep through him in a tidal wave as he lay his face against her neck.

"Jake," she said in a whisper, "I'm so sorry…" And then he felt and heard the soft sobs.

Slipping his arms around her waist, he said, "It's okay, angel." He turned her to face him, sliding her legs over his thighs, gazing into her eyes. Speaking softly, he said, "I love you, Callie. You just need time to heal." He paused, then continued, "None of us can ever really know if we're going to be okay or if everything is going to turn out okay. But if we have faith, we have to believe that the good Man Upstairs has a handle on things even if, or when, we don't. But what I can tell you, Callie, is that as long as I'm still on this earth, I will come back to you. That, I can promise."

He wiped her tears with his thumb, and she took a quivering breath. "Do you know how long you'll be gone?"

"I have no idea, love."

"Do you think Eddie and Curran will be okay until you get there?"

"I hope so," he said. He had actually been wondering the same thing, thinking how capricious and reckless they could be. Reaching for his wineglass, he handed Callie hers, and they each sipped quietly until the glasses were empty.

Outside the windows, the breeze was swishing through leaves and palm fronds, the chirr of insects faint in the background. Distantly, a paraque was calling *cuyeo cuyeo cuyeo*. It was as pristine as a summer night could be, but Jake felt a sense of gloom that was impossible to overcome.

He kissed Callie on the forehead and they both lay back. Drawing her close to him, he asked, "Think you can get some sleep?"

"I don't know…I am getting tired, but—"

"Well, try, love. I've got to push off pretty early in the morning."

Her voice small, she said, "I hope there won't be another storm tonight."

"Me, too. But if there is, I'll be right here," he said, and immediately regretted saying it, knowing she would make the leap that he would not be there after tonight. A well of anguish rose up inside him at the thought of her having to endure that panic alone. He kissed her tenderly on the lips and said again, "I love you, Callie."

"I love you, Jake," she replied, her voice hoarse with emotion.

"Try to sleep, baby."

But he suspected it would be him finding it hard to sleep tonight. Stroking her hair, he listened to her breathing as he watched the ceiling fan turn above them, praying for mercy from the nocturnal spirits.

8

AT THE SOUND OF the gunfire and Jake's fervent directive, Falcone hurriedly ended the call, looking up to see Wallace Pacheco and Beau Gabbitas coming back down the road in a trot. They both had their handguns out, Pacheco speaking breathlessly into his sat phone. Spotting Falcone standing outside the church, he barked, "Get inside!"

"What's going on?" Falcone asked.

"Nothing good. Get inside, now."

Falcone did as he was told, joining Niles, the Keoghs, and Cameron McNamara, who were grouped together just inside. Cyrus Keogh started, "Was that—"

Cutting him off, Pacheco wheezed, "Yeah, it was. It is." Pausing to catch his breath, he continued, "It's coming from over the hill and I don't know if it's advancing this way or not. With just handguns, we didn't stick around to find out."

McNamara gave Pacheco a bottle of water, and Pacheco guzzled half before passing the bottle to Gabbitas. Both of them were covered with red dust, pasted to their skin by perspiration and peppering their hair and beards. Their faces were as red as stewed tomatoes.

"What about our bird?" Keogh asked.

Gabbitas wiped his mouth on his sleeve and said, "It had to bail. Gunfire on the ground, that's a no-brainer." Gripping his handgun, a 9mm Beretta, he strode to the church entrance and peered out.

"The plan, for now, is to try to get the helo back in the morning,"

Pacheco said, "If all is quiet, we should be able to get out. It will be dark soon, so we'll have to shelter here. Gab and I will keep watch from the front. If there's any activity outside, we may have to evacuate from the rear into the woods."

Beside her husband, Amelia spoke up. "What do you mean 'get out'?" She had regained her composure after resting, her face pale but stoic, earlier emotions now held in check.

Pacheco seemed to gather himself before responding, a vein in his neck twitching. "We'll fly to Dungu, and from there—"

"No," Amelia said sharply, her jaw set. "We're not leaving here. I want to find out what happened."

Pacheco pursed his lips, crossing his big arms in front of him, still gripping his gun. "That's not safe, Mrs. Keogh. We can't allow you to put yourselves in danger." He quickly added, "On our watch."

Before his wife could respond, Cyrus Keogh said, "How about we fly to the next village instead of Dungu, maybe do an aerial search as we go?"

Pacheco hesitated as he considered the counterproposal, eying Gabbitas for input and only getting a noncommittal shrug. "Okay, we'll take that under advisement. In the meantime, why don't you all stay toward the back while we take sentry at the front." Without waiting for an answer, he turned and walked off to join his partner at the entrance.

Addressing the Keoghs, Falcone said, "He's right, we can't stay here. I got Jake on the phone and he *is* coming. When he heard the gunfire, he said we need to get out. Your guys can't protect us with handguns. Pretty sure that was automatic gunfire I heard."

"Right," Cyrus Keogh said. He looked at his wife. "Sorry, sweetheart, I reckon I've got to agree with them. There's probably not a lot of provisions here, either."

Niles put his hand on Amelia's shoulder. "Jake is coming, and I promise you he will find them."

Amelia Keogh did not respond but managed a wan smile.

Together, they all shuffled to the rear of the church where the late-day shadows had deepened to semi-darkness, for the moment the only audible sounds being those associated with their movements. Pacheco and Gabbitas stood at the front, flanking the entrance, guns in hand, smoking cigarettes and watching the road as the sun slipped below the horizon in a buttery melt that flamed dark orange across the sky and browned over the land.

FALCONE CHECKED HIS PHONE for the dozenth time, noting the hour and the dismal reality that its battery life was about to expire. After fortifying himself on sundries foraged from the church's modest living quarters, which included peanuts, bread, honey, and more bananas, he had joined Niles in a corner next to a window opening. Despite the cooler temperature, it was still uncomfortably warm, the humidity stifling in the stagnant air.

It was 9:15 PM, and they had been sitting on a makeshift bed for the past few hours. Pushing a couple of benches together and folding a blanket into a pillow, Falcone and Niles had the most austere sleeping arrangement, but the trade-off was a better position from which to monitor their situation. The Keoghs and McNamara were occupying the living quarters where there were two separate spaces, one for the priest and one for the nuns. Food and water had been shared, personal bags inventoried for useful contents. With the Kinshasa trip being an overnighter, clothing and toiletries were minimal, and the consensus was to hold off changing into something clean or previously worn until the next day. There were several gallons of water in a tin tub, sparingly used to freshen up.

Sniffing the sour odor emanating from his armpits, Falcone said, "God, I stink, even after putting on more deodorant."

Wrinkling his nose at the foulness of his own sweat, ringing the collar of his shirt and the waistband of his underwear, Niles replied, "At least it's mutual."

They sat quietly in the dark, both watching the silhouettes of Pacheco and Gabbitas, outlined by the scant moonlight in the church entrance, neither moving much.

"You shouldn't have promised her that," Falcone said.

"What?"

"That Jake would find them. He's not a superhero."

Niles scowled. "He is to me, mate. If anybody can find them, it's him."

"True enough," Falcone conceded, running fingers over the dark stubble on his jaws and chin. He reached for a handful of peanuts he'd set aside, shelling some and popping them into his mouth. In the stillness, crunching them between his molars sounded like he was chewing rocks.

"You think we got in over our heads here?"

Falcone gave a shallow laugh. "Uh, yeah."

"I can't stop wondering what happened to all the people," Niles ruminated, then, hearing Falcone blow out a breath, said, "I still think Iris and the boys left before…whatever happened."

Falcone had nothing to say.

Trying to lighten the mood, Niles pinched his thumb and forefinger together and quipped, "I was *this* close to snagging the French doc."

Falcone snorted, tossed some peanut shells at Niles. "Shit. In your dreams, buddy."

"I was! She flirted with me all the time."

"What are you talking about? She's so far out of your league you'd have to clear waivers just to get a seat in her waiting room."

A lengthy silence ensued as they hunkered down on the hard wooden bench and stared into the darkness, lost in their own thoughts. Abruptly, Niles asked, "You scared?"

"Nah," Falcone replied, a little too hastily. A few moments passed, and he admitted, "Yeah, little bit."

"Me, too. I just can't understand how there's nobody here. *Nobody.*" Niles suddenly rose halfway up, listening. "Do you hear that?"

"What?"

"It's the bloody chickens!"

Faintly, the muted sound of clucking could be heard from outside the window opening. It was so unexpected in the context of their circumstances, it seemed almost absurd. And then Falcone asked, "I wonder what happened to the cows?"

SHORTLY BEFORE DAYBREAK AT least one rooster made its presence known, crowing shrilly, jarring Falcone and Niles out of a spasmodic sleep. Minutes later, as they were blearily orienting themselves to time and place, their hair disheveled and clothing creased from tossing and rolling on the wooden benches, fingers of white sunlight began to creep through the window openings.

"God," Falcone groaned, squinting into the veil of light layering the damp air. "I feel like I slept in a cave."

"Kind of did, mate," Niles mumbled, clawing at the mess that was his hair.

The temperature had dropped during the night and, on waking, they found themselves awkwardly huddled together under the thin blanket, the smell of stale sweat and loam close around them.

From the front of the church, Gabbitas called out, "We're outta here as soon as it's light!"

The Keoghs emerged from the rear, groomed and wearing fresh clothes, McNamara hauling bags and gear. Assessing Falcone and Niles with a grin, Cyrus said, "We left you some water, mates, and I think you better use all of it. But you made it through the night, so good on ya." The waves in his hair were neatly combed, his face shaved. He was wearing a cream-colored shirt covered in palm fronds over khaki slacks, his eyes shaded by sunglasses.

"There should be some coffee on the helicopter," Amelia added. Her face was drawn, eyes lacking their usual clarity, but otherwise she was her normal lovely self, clad in a sleeveless cotton blouse printed with sunflowers and olive capris, red hair tied up with a yellow bow.

The prospect of coffee was enough to get Falcone and Niles moving, and within thirty minutes they were sprinting down the road toward the field where the helicopter waited, dressed in the jeans they'd worn to Kinshasa with fresh t-shirts. It was not quite 6:30 AM, the sun a diffuse peach glow, ascending below thick clouds limned with purple. Dew clung to the grass, a patina of mist suspended above the ground. A flock of gray parrots screeched and clattered overhead, flying into the forest, a smattering of other birds vocalizing from the trees within. They took that as an encouraging sign, most likely indicating safe clearance.

After boarding the helicopter—the same silver Dauphin that had taken them to and from Dungu, with the same pilots in the cockpit— seats were selected and everyone belted in. This time, Cyrus Keogh made sure he got a window seat, with Amelia between him and Falcone. Niles was again on the outside, GoPro in hand. Keogh, Niles, Pacheco, and Gabbitas wore headsets, prepared to communicate what they saw on the ground. As promised, a large thermal dispenser of coffee was in the cabin. When cardboard cups were filled and distributed, the Dauphin was cycled through its takeoff sequence and lifted into the morning haze.

For the first twenty minutes or so, not much was said, everyone sullenly drinking their coffee, heads turned toward the windows. The one exception was Amelia Keogh who could not bring herself to review the ruination below. Instead, she gazed hypnotically at some undefinable chasm of space in front of her, hands folded around her coffee container.

The helicopter climbed to five hundred feet and began a slow and steady sweep over the area, widening the distance with each pass. The vista had not changed, but it somehow looked even more blighted, as if the surface detritus had sunk deeper into the ground from the weight of its demise. Watching Cyrus Keogh, Falcone saw Keogh's smooth face tighten as he surveyed the ground below, and Falcone suspected that the eyes behind the sunglasses were fluid with emotion.

For the next hour, the pilots flew a circuitous route that had been pre-planned by the Keoghs, dropping down to three hundred feet when terrain allowed, rising up to a thousand when the vegetation grew taller and denser. Much of the way, mist blanketed the forest canopy like rolling smoke, the sky more gray than blue. By mid-morning, sun had broken through the clouds, the shadow of the Dauphin's elongated body and spinning blades crawling across the treetops and savanna. Three or four times during the flight, one of the four seated by a window reported movement on the ground, but in each case it turned out to be animals or birds. Flying over a large watering hole, they spotted a small herd of buffalo flush with cattle egrets, white as salt against the dark buffalo hides, diamonds of sunlight glinting from the water's surface. Crossing a wide savanna bisected by a river, they saw hippos. It was only as the helicopter began its downward descent, flying above a road leading into the destination village, that any people came into view; women balancing impossibly bulky cargo on their heads, children toting jugs as big as they were, men and boys pushing bicycles, most being wooden *chukudus* loaded down with sacks of food and other materials.

The sight and sound of the helicopter's approach brought the expected charge of villagers, emerging from out of nowhere with the vibrant enthusiasm of a flash mob, arms waving and cheering choruses of "*Mbote!*"

The pilots had to abort two landings to prevent contact with the advancing well-wishers, particularly mindful of the Fenestron tail, which was only four feet from the ground and could slice an arm off as heinously as a guillotine. When they were finally able to set down within an acceptable radius, Pacheco and Gabbitas were immediately dispatched for crowd control, using their limited indigenous vocabulary to meet and greet and attempt to curb the frenzied energy level. By the time the Keoghs, Cameron McNamara, and Falcone and Niles stepped off the helicopter, village elders had come forward to offer an official welcome, escorting the group to a communal area where midday cooking was already well underway, chicken and fish and goat being smoked over open fires. Women in brightly colored and patterned dresses were stirring massive pots of rice and cabbage, now with new fervor in anticipation of entertaining special guests.

The Keoghs were at ease in their midst and warmly embraced, able to speak and recognize some Zande or Lingala phrases and conversant in French. Children were drawn to Amelia like hummingbirds to nectar, her whimsical laugh casting a spell that had them clamoring around her in a giggling cluster. In the moment, she let herself be uplifted by their adoration, their guileless ebullience, and the touch of their small hands.

The chief elder, who introduced himself as Gali Nsabimana, and his wife, Bénie, sat at one end of the table with the Keoghs on their left, Falcone and Niles on their right; Pacheco, Gabbitas, and McNamara filled out the other end. Nsabimana wore a dashiki-style shirt, black with an intricately patterned V-shaped collar in vivid colors, his grizzled hair and beard cropped close, heavily lined face the texture of dark, grained leather. His wife was dressed in a full-length spotted black-and-yellow dress that had the look of a honeybee convention with a bow-tied yellow head wrap. The meal was incredibly good, especially after what had passed for dinner the previous night, and the conversation, though encumbered, was amicably received.

Watching Falcone scarf up the food on his plate, Niles smirked, "My, whatever happened to your discerning palate?"

Chewing hungrily, Falcone replied, "As long as I don't know what it is I'm eating, if it tastes good, I'm good."

Cyrus Keogh had chosen the village destination over Dungu with the hope that its closer proximity would yield information networked among other small communities and, as the table was being cleared, made the inquiry, piecing together various phrases he knew. When the chief finally seemed to understand, he shook his head. Trying, but not succeeding to conceal his frustration and disappointment, Keogh asked, "Can we stay and talk to your people?"

Nsabimana nodded vigorously, smiling, broad lips parting over large, gapped ivory teeth. "Stay, yes."

The afternoon sun was hot and oppressive, sending many if not most of the villagers inside their modest thatch dwellings, but the children, who had discovered Falcone and Niles and their cameras, were following them in an ever-lengthening conga line as the duo took an exploratory walk. Soon, they were met by a group of women, outfitted with drums covered in animal skins, pipes of bamboo, hollowed horns, and sticks. They broke out in song, dancing and raising their sticks high in the air, faces animated with joy. Niles, who normally loved to dance— though he did so quite ineptly—made no move to hand the camera to Falcone and join in. Looking over his shoulder, Falcone saw the Keoghs standing stiffly on the periphery.

Cyrus had donned his shades, staring straight ahead, his expression hidden; Amelia was struggling to keep a smile on her face, clapping spiritlessly, her eyes as hard and green as emeralds in the sunshine. All around, the voices rose in harmonious cadence, the colors of their garb flashing as their bodies moved in rhythm with the drumbeats. But Amelia's gaze kept drifting to the little ones, with their cherubic smiles and shy glances.

A pair of the women reached for Falcone, their arms outspread in invitation, but the last thing he felt like doing right now was dancing. He was watching Amelia Keogh, and he was pretty sure her heart was breaking.

9

DEPARTURE WAS EVEN MORE painful than Jake had expected.

He woke that morning well before dawn, too restless to even attempt falling back to sleep. Next to him, Callie was tucked small and warm against his side, slumbering now, but neither of them had slept much last night. Thank God there had been no storms, he thought, and from what he could tell, no particularly bad dreams for her. Even so, he'd spent many of the hours softly lulling her until she succumbed or lying awake as she squirmed, listening to her ragged breathing as she drifted in and out. It had been a long night.

Managing to roll off the bed without disturbing Callie, he headed for the shower, lingering under the hot spray. Not wanting the day to start. He dressed and went downstairs to make coffee, taking his mug out on the patio where he stood for a long while, alone with his thoughts. A full moon the color of French vanilla was descending behind streaks of indigo clouds, the sky above just beginning to lighten. The rainforest was relatively quiet this morning, with only an occasional birdcall over the low hum of insects, as if all of nature was granting him this last interlude of serenity before the turmoil that surely awaited. He felt a hollow expand in his stomach with the grievous memories of his last departure for a mission and the horrible consequence of grossly underestimating the means to which a motivated enemy with infinite resources would go to exact revenge. His entire time in the military, and subsequently as an independent operative, he had managed to remain emotionally untethered to anyone or anything that could become a point of weakness, a ransom of leverage. Once that changed, those who sought to take you out had all they needed to bring you to your knees. He now carried that liability, and it was something he would have to fiercely protect at all costs.

To that end, Jake had begun rectifying deficiencies within forty-eight hours of their return to Costa Rica, implementing multiple layers of protection. A state-of-the-art security system had been installed in the villa, but more importantly, there would be a constant human presence on the property. In addition to hiring Jesse Segura to live on-site, he had arranged for the two gardeners and pool man to work all day, at a minimum on overlapping days; Camilla had willingly agreed to twelve-hour shifts seven days a week until Jake's return. Like last time, he had notified the Dominical police department of his impending departure and, given the loss of one of their own who had been murdered by Callie's abductors, Jake had no doubt they would be taking patrols with a motivated and reinforced sense of duty.

Sipping from a second cup of coffee, he gazed up at the sky as it paled toward dawn, moon and stars dissolving with the spreading blush of light. From somewhere in the gardens, a single dove warbled forlornly, a reptile or small animal skittering in the brush. He heard a faint scuffle behind him and turned to find Callie in the doorway, looking like a lost child. She was dressed in a short spaghetti-strapped romper patterned with seashells in pastel pinks and peaches, standing with her feet pointed together, hands clasped in front of her, head tilted down. As was always the case, the sight of her took his breath away, but this morning it also sent a current of vulnerability rippling through him that all of his precautions put together could not mitigate. He extended his hand and she came to him, folding into the circle of his arm, into his hug, time suspending as he held on.

"Morning, angel," he said finally, kissing the top of her head. Then he turned and led her back through the French doors into the villa where he poured her some coffee and topped off his own before settling on the sofa. He cradled her in his arms, her shoulders and elbows and waist and hips as light and delicate as a tiny bird.

For him, departure for a mission had always been best executed in a quick and clinical ripping the Band-Aid off fashion, with a minimum of emotion and reflection to maintain total focus. But not now, not for him and certainly not for her. They both needed this time, this slowed-down syncopation, however torturous it might be. Tracing his fingers up and down the smooth skin of her legs, he said, "I had every reason to believe that I would have control over what I took on next and when. Obviously, I never saw this coming."

Swallowing hard, as if her throat was closing up, Callie rasped, "I know this is what you do...I understand."

"Well, *this* is not what I do, leaving you when I need to be here with you and for you. I expected that we would have time to talk about what happened before I took on anything else. Talking about it is a vital part of the healing process. But it has to be when you feel comfortable and safe and ready, and there just hasn't been enough time."

Her head was on his shoulder and he could feel the hitches in her breathing, knew she was crying. "I'm sorry, Jake," she murmured, tears touching his neck.

"Oh baby, nothing for you to be sorry about. Nothing at all."

He rocked her against him for several minutes, again letting himself slip outside the realm of elapsing time, inhaling the ambrosial scent of her and giving himself to the emotions and sensations, feeling the waterfall rush that was both warm and cool, fast and slow. His heart and mind went to a place of rapture where fields of night-blooming flowers opened to the beams of a pearlescent moon, where a pool of water deep in a gorge glowed green-blue and enveloped in wet warmth, where sand and sky stretched endlessly with a curling surf ribboned between and salted air was spiced with jasmine and ginger. It was a place he never wanted to leave, ever, and it was a place he was having to leave as soon as the time remaining on his departure clock ran out. Surrendering to these feelings now, just before taking off to face unknown combatants and hostilities was tantamount to exposing his neck to a predatory carnivore, but he did so with heedless abandon, filling his sensory memory with her smell, her feel, her taste, her touch, until the ache of need for more was so great he had to stop and reel himself in.

An incoming call ringing from his iPhone on the coffee table pulled him out of the reverie. Easing away from Callie, he retrieved the phone and walked back out on the patio.

*   *   *   *   *

CALLIE DREW HERSELF UP tighter on the couch and hugged her arms, heart fluttering. Her eyes followed Jake as he talked on the phone, meandering in a circle, the fingers of one hand in his back pocket. He was dressed in khaki cargo pants with a matching t-shirt and long-sleeved button-up shirt with pockets and epaulets, all designer-made by Armani, Banana Republic, and Calvin Klein. The attire, complete with Voodoo tactical boots, made him look both arrestingly handsome and intimidatingly no-nonsense. His jet-black hair was precisely combed, his face smooth-shaven.

Throughout the previous day she had watched in a combination of dread and awe as Jake prepped and packed in consummate proficiency: extracting a collection of "go bags" from a storage closet, meticulously layering clothing and personal items in duffels, arranging communications equipment in messenger bags, assembling camping gear and weapons. Jake had explained that he maintained a comprehensive collection of go bags that were pre-packed for different environments and situations, some of which were medical kits with enough equipment and supplies to stock a small clinic, but even though these were all ready to go, he inventoried them anyway. He also spent a considerable amount of time cleaning and oiling several handguns and sharpening a variety of knives. By dinnertime, everything had been loaded into the back of the Jeep Rubicon.

Callie gazed around the living room, as she did each time she was in it, or any of the other beautiful rooms in the villa, admiring all the elegant but comfortable furnishings, the rich wood tables displaying things that were pretty and interesting to look at, prints and paintings with sea turtles and other ocean life spaced along the walls. But what drew her attention again and again were the framed photographs on a wood shelf, pictures of them together—before South America. She quickly glanced away, her eyes filling with tears as memories of the day he'd left came flooding back, and of the profound desolation that followed. And then, the horror.

As brave as she was trying to be, anxiety and fear were rising to the surface, panic poised to spring like a wildcat. She looked up as she heard

Jake coming in from the patio, apparently concluding his phone call which seemed to have something to do with the airport. She saw him glance at his watch, and felt her stomach churn.

ENDING THE CALL, WHICH had been from an airport executive for final confirmations, Jake paused to exchange a few words with Camilla who had just arrived. Returning to the living room, he saw the glassy look in Callie's eyes, the tremor in her frame, and sat down beside her. Looping his arm around her shoulders, he cupped the side of her face with his free hand and, as if reading her thoughts said, "You don't have to be brave about this, love. I know you're scared."

Her eyes held desperately on his for a moment, a tear trailing down to her chin, and she took a shuddery breath.

"I do need you to promise me some things," he said gently. "So I'm going to lay a little guilt thing on you—you may not want to do it for *you*, but I need you to do it for *me*, okay? You have to promise me that you will eat. And don't stay inside, even if you just go out by the pool. Better, go to the beach." He managed a thin smile, adding, "Just be sure to put on lots of sunscreen. Okay?"

She sniffled and nodded, but he could see she was fighting to keep the tears from coming.

"There will be somebody here, day and night. And Jack and Jerry said they would stop by whenever they could." He continued, "I will try my best to call or text, but if you don't hear from me at times don't worry that something's happened. Communication in that part of the country is notoriously bad."

With his arm still around her, he flipped his wrist upward to glance at the face of his watch. It was larger than a silver dollar, attached to a wide black band with a titanium bezel and a multitude of functions. Made by Garmin, the tactix Charlie was one of several military watches he owned, but along with the Dakota Angler digital clipped to his belt, it was the one always on him. And now it rendered the sobering edict he'd been dreading for the past twenty-four hours.

Sighing from the depths of his diaphragm, Jake rose, bringing Callie to her feet with him. In a voice that sounded steadier than he felt, he said, "Time for me to go, sweetie," and wrapped her in a prolonged hug. When he released her, he brought his hands up to fondle her face, wet with the tears she could no longer hold back.

"Breakfast?" she asked hoarsely, her eyes filled with the futile entreaty of a last-ditch appeal.

He gave her a sad but whimsical look. "You going to eat?" When she could not respond, he said lightly, "Didn't think so," and kissed her, with tenderness and unrestrained longing, feeling it in his lips and throat and chest and everywhere beyond. He felt her weight collapse and dropped his arms to hold her, burrowing her face against him, one hand clasping her head as if it were the most breakable thing on earth. "I love you, Callie," he murmured, his voice catching.

He could hear her trying to say the words, but they were lost in a deluge of emotion.

"I know, angel...I know."

Camilla handed him a travel cup filled with coffee, and he walked Callie to the foyer where the big wooden entry doors loomed like the hatchway to some harsh primeval territory. She leaned shakily against the wall, clearly struggling. Standing close to her, he could feel her chest heaving, her whole body shaking, and everything inside him was screaming at him to just go now, but his feet would not move. Her espresso-colored eyes were wide and pleading, her pale skin flushed from the stirrings of their intimacy. Every molecule of his resolve evaporated, a sound like breaking waves rushing through his head, his pulse racing, and he could not stop himself from kissing her again, their lips melting together in a sensation that was a fusion of utter bliss and excruciating pain—rapids surging over a cliff, wet and warm and flowing, and then crashing down into a rocky basin below where the currents broke and streamed away—and he knew he was going to pay for this on the long drive to the airport.

He stepped back and opened the front door. Placed his hand over his pounding heart as he looked at her one final time, turned, and pulled the door closed behind him, walking leadenly out to the Rubicon, his boots crunching over the crushed-shell drive. A pair of doves burst from the grasses, their wings flapping with the emptiness of a white sheet snapping on a clothesline in the breeze. Jake got behind the wheel of his

Jeep, keyed the ignition, and felt like something deep inside him had ripped loose and shredded and drained all of the air from his lungs.

SECONDS AFTER THE DOOR closed, all pretenses of a brave front crumbled. Callie emitted a strangled cry, her legs going limp, back sliding down the wall until her haunches rested on the tile floor, knees drawn up in front of her. Everything around her seemed to blur and spin, as if there were no edges or foundation or ceiling. She felt her empty stomach heave, her heart and respiration convulse, so immersed in distress that she wasn't even aware of Camilla's strong arms lifting her up and then embracing her. *"Oh, mi querida niña…todo estará bien,"* the housekeeper uttered, clutching Callie to her broad bosom.

Sometime later Callie found herself lying on top of the bed, propped up on the nest of pillows, a warm breeze drifting in from the open French doors. She had no idea how she'd gotten upstairs but saw Camilla hovering nearby.

"Estás bien?" the housekeeper asked, her eyes ripe with concern.

When Callie nodded, Camilla showed her a pitcher of iced water and a glass on the bedside table, observed for a few more moments, and then retreated.

Callie's eyes roamed around the room, slatted with early-morning shadow, and one of the first things she noticed was her phone by the water pitcher. A yellow Post-it was attached to the front. Taking the phone in her hand, she saw a simple smiley on the note, penned in Jake's scrawl. When the iPhone's screen icons appeared, she saw a voicemail and tapped it. Lifting the phone to her ear, she heard his husky voice calmly speaking to her: *"Hey sweetie, I just thought I'd leave this for you. Maybe it'll help when you're feeling anxious or scared or when there's a storm. Just know that everything's going to be okay and I'm right there with you in spirit, okay? It's just rain and dreams. Light and day will be there on the other side. I love you, angel."*

The message seemed to end in an instant, and she replayed it numerous times before putting the phone down, tears pooling. She lay back on the bed and rolled onto her side, eyes squeezed shut, something soft and feathery touching her tear-streaked cheek. Eyelashes blinking open, she saw what had been carefully placed below the pile of pillows—an exquisite orchid bloom, just as Jake had left for her the last time. She gingerly picked up the pale lavender flower and touched it to her face, hearing his voice in her head and feeling everything else of him in her heart. Outside, chimes twinkled faintly in the breeze, as if a tiny fairy were playing a secret song of solace meant only for her.

JAKE PULLED AWAY FROM the villa and maneuvered slowly to the end of the drive where he braked to a stop, breathing heavily, every nerve in his body on fire, aching all over—an ache so intense that the slightest move set off a series of agonizing pulses that reminded him of a Taser. He knew he had let himself go too far but had been powerless to abstain. Clamping the tops of his thighs with his hands, he groaned and clenched his teeth. Took bracing breaths and, as if there were ever any doubt, said to no one, "God, I love you." Unless God was actually listening, and he truly hoped He was, thinking of the last time, when his parting words to Callie had been: *You'll be okay. And I will be back.* And she had not been okay—and was still not okay. Foreboding clawed up his throat like bile and he fought to suppress it, steering onto the road that led to the highway.

Crossing the Barú River bridge, he headed north along the Costanera Sur, a pale yellow sun behind him, the sky bruised in cast and scudded with clouds that resembled snowy tire treads. He powered the Jeep's windows down, the fresh air bracing. His usual access to the San José airport was via regional carriers from nearby Quepos, which cut the commute by more than half, but the local airport had been closed for a much-needed overhaul and the alternate airstrip was questionable on short notice, so it would be the lengthy drive instead. Traffic from this end was fairly light and he made good time, passing long stretches of trees and coastline and palm oil plantations with old timbered structures surrounded by African palm trees and housing settlements. North of Quepos and through Parrita, the land was flat and green with farms and small burgs, the highway veering west to hug the coast around Jacó, a popular beach town where traffic grew denser with the morning rush-hour. Clearing that, the route turned north again, running parallel to the forested expanse of the Carara Biological Reserve and traversing the Tárcoles River, its bridge lined with tourists gaping down at gargantuan crocodiles lounging on its muddy banks. Here, the highway took a final northeast trajectory into the interior countryside, the elevation beginning to steepen with coffee plantations tucked amidst rolling valleys and set back on its slopes. The Autopista del Sol toll road intersected just outside of Coyolar and headed east through Ortina, roadsides dotted with fruit stands. The grade continued to climb as the route wound toward the southern end of the Cordillera de Tilarán, its peaks like jagged slate against the light blue sky.

As he drove from the coast through the flatlands and the valleys, the hills and plateaus, Jake tried to keep his mind void of what he'd left behind with Callie or what lay ahead with the mission. For the latter, there would be plenty of time during the marathon transoceanic flight; he found it a lot more difficult to evade thoughts of the former.

After navigating a winding sweep of road above the Tárcoles River valley and passing through Atenas, where large poultry farms were interspersed with more populated areas, he exited to the Radial El Coyol which bisected a sprawl of industrial and commercial development as it led to the Inter American Highway, snarled city traffic, and the San José airport, northwest in Alajuela. Exiting from the highway, he followed the directions to turn right, away from the main airport, circling an oval parking lot and pulling up to the new domestic terminal for regional and private flights. Checking his watch, he saw that he had made the trip in just over three hours, arriving at 10:38 AM.

Jake had been instructed to look for a handler who would be meeting him. He had barely pulled up to the curb when a young man pounced to his door, causing Jake to posture defensively until he realized there were actually three handlers waiting for him; the one at his door asking for keys to valet his vehicle, a second one, wearing a bright yellow safety vest with a luggage cart for his bags, and the third, a suit-clad agent who would be escorting him directly to the plane. After explaining that he required the baggage handler to keep his bags close, Jake accompanied the agent and porter inside.

Juan Santamaría, small by international standards, is the country's second busiest airport, processing around five million passengers a year.

The interior has the modern elements characterizing most inter-continental hubs: high, airy ceilings spanned with industrial metal; glass-paneled walls overlooking the airfield; polished floors that seemed almost liquid in the reflective light; a collection of splashy shops teeming with tourists wearing backpacks and trundling wheeled carry-ons. However, unlike his previous departures, Jake saw none of that and was spared comingling with passengers milling about or scuttling from point to point or queued up at the airline counters and security screening. Instead, he was taken straight through this smaller, self-contained terminal where his passport was given a cursory review to confirm his identity; the rest of his travel documentation had already been processed. From there, he was put into an airport car and driven a short distance to the airfield.

Though they moved quickly and seamlessly from inside to outside in a matter of minutes, heads turned as they went. Jake, who preferred to stay under the radar in most situations, had a tendency to attract attention despite his best efforts to blend in. At five-foot-ten and 165 pounds, he was hardly an imposing figure at first glance, but his chiseled features with the lustrous black hair and piercing eyes, his deep natural tan with the muscular physique, trim waist, sculpt chest and flat stomach, suggested otherwise; his confident countenance and air of self-possession confirmed it.

The car came to an abrupt stop on the tarmac and the agent popped out to open Jake's door. During the few calls with the Keoghs' travel coordinator, he had been told the flight would be on a private jet and he'd not really thought much about it, so when he stepped from the car and saw the plane, he was momentarily taken aback. In an almost cinematic reveal, sunlight gleamed off the ultra-white finish of a Gulfstream, light and dark blue stripes swirled across the body, auxiliary power hissing quietly. Lettering on the tail identified it as a G650ER, the largest and fastest in the fleet and, more importantly, the one with the most extended range.

"You sure this is my ride?" he asked the agent beside him.

"Yes, sir, Mr. Tyler."

For Jake, who had flown in everything from mammoth, bone-numbing military cargo planes to helicopters with bullets whizzing past and, in many cases, into their open doors, this would be a wholly new experience. He strode to the airstair, sliding his Outlaw Fugitive TAC sunglasses to the top of his head as he mounted the steps and was met at the threshold by a cabin attendant and pilot, both flashing dazzling smiles and crisply uniformed in black and light blue: skirt and vest with a striped scarf for the attendant, slacks and blazer with matching striped tie for the pilot. Two other pilots were going through their pre-flight checklist in the cockpit. Jake had been briefed on the crew during one of the preliminary calls, and now it made sense; an extra pilot had been added to ensure the entire crew was well-rested during the fifteen-hour flight. He'd also been told the three pilots, all in their thirties and forties, had a combined twenty-four thousand flight hours. The aircraft and crew had been appropriated from St. Maarten in the Caribbean, having completed a charter for a wealthy family vacationing in St. Barts.

The cabin attendant introduced herself as Bettina Paloma, speaking in an accent that seemed vaguely British, tall and slim with dark hair tucked into a bun. She spent a few minutes giving Jake an overview of the immaculately appointed cabin as he settled into a club chair that was possibly the most comfortable he'd ever sat in, soft leather the color of latte cream. Oval windows the size of a bathroom vanity mirror filled the craft with bright light, sixteen of them spaced along the sides, fresh air flowing as if they were all vented from the outside. Taking in the opulent interior in a daze—the wide reclining chairs and long sofa, the exotic wood surfaces and cabinetry, the handwoven and –stitched materials, the high-end electronics, the decorative accents throughout—Jake thought, *I must be dreaming.* But minutes later it became very real as the aircraft powered up and, after a short taxi, raced down the runway, twin Rolls-Royce engines roaring like the supersonic thoroughbred it was, 33,800 pounds of thrust launching it smoothly into the sky, commencing a flight of over eight thousand miles, Jake the sole passenger.

10

FALCONE AND NILES AWOKE in a village church for the second day in a row, this time by shafts of daylight breaking through collapsed holes in the thatch overhead. If one or more of the roosters here had crowed, they'd slept through it. Looking around, they discovered everyone else was already up and out, the musty hut laden with dust and particles of straw, smelling of dried dirt and animal odors. Stumbling over each other, they collected their belongings—which now included some bedding brought by the helicopter—and emerged into the sunlight, vapid and unkempt, shielding their eyes against the unexpected brightness.

"Jesus, what time is it? We really overslept," Falcone grumbled.

"Well, it's not like we had anywhere to be," Niles replied wryly.

They headed for the communal area where they'd dined the day before, irrationally hankering for coffee and breakfast. To their surprise, they actually saw a pot of something that smelled like coffee steaming over the fire. The Keoghs were seated at the table, drinking whatever it was from tin cups.

"Glad you could join us, mates!" Cyrus Keogh scoffed, raising his cup.

Grinning, Amelia Keogh said in a coddling voice, "Needed their beauty sleep."

"Something like that," Falcone slurred, the inside of his eyelids feeling like sandpaper.

"Help yourself to some brew," Keogh said. "They apparently keep some on hand for special occasions. Not sure where they get it, and it's a bit strong, but better than none at all, yeah?"

Falcone and Niles found cups and dipped up some of the pungent liquid that had the color and viscosity of crude oil. The contortions twisting their faces as they tasted it had both Keoghs doubled over with laughter. Falcone and Niles could not help but smile at the Keoghs' mirth, something that had been completely stripped away in the aftermath of tragedy. Helping themselves to bread and honey, they listened as Cyrus Keogh outlined the plan going forward. The village, known as Nakalé, was small, populated by perhaps five hundred and, unlike their compound prior to its demise, had no electricity and only the most basic life sustenance. Keogh had therefore decided that they would stay at least one more day and have the helicopter return with provisions for their hosts. The sat phones had been recharged by solar power the day before, and Cameron McNamara had been tasked with contacting sources in Dungu to order whatever could be loaded onto the Dauphin. Once the goods were dispensed, the group would depart.

The Keoghs this morning seemed to be somehow functioning outside of themselves, their faces waxy, both looking a little too animated. Amelia's gaze kept drifting to the children frolicking nearby, her lips parted as she idly fidgeted with the wedding ring on her finger. Cyrus, watching her watch them, was unreadable, but his hands were splayed on his thighs, elbows out, as if he was on the verge of making some decisive pronouncement that would resolve everything, his blue eyes a little too vivid.

Cleansing the acrid aftertaste of the coffee with some cut up mangos, Falcone and Niles hoisted their bags of camera equipment and set off to wander through the village. Glancing over his shoulder as they walked, Falcone saw Cyrus Keogh trying to communicate with a man who had brought him parts of an HF radio set. Keogh, wearing tan slacks with brown suspenders over a blue shirt, rolled up his sleeves, and began an assessment. Amelia Keogh, dressed in khaki pants and a carnation-pink blouse, was scribbling on a notepad as she followed several women and a bevy of youngsters, undoubtedly compiling a list of things to procure for them. She had to pause every few steps to respond to the kids tugging at her pants leg.

It was a beautiful day, but the air was hot and stagnant, and it wasn't long before Falcone and Niles were sweating and swatting at flies and mosquitos as they strolled. Spotting a plank bench beneath some banana trees, they sat in the shade and cooled off, a gaggle of children surrounding them. Niles took out his Nikon camera and began photographing, to the delight of his enthralled subjects who obliged him by cavorting and making comedic faces in front of his lens. After a few minutes he realized the low battery indicator was blinking and stuck the camera back in his bag. They commenced walking, sticking close to the trees, passing men building fishing traps, circles of young girls braiding each other's hair, women weaving baskets and mats, children laughing and running everywhere. Scrawny goats scampered about chewing grass, their ears and tails flicking. But the complacency that this little village waypoint embodied could not dispel the miasma of gloom that clung to Falcone as the hours passed. He found himself wondering if whatever had happened to the Keoghs' compound was going to happen to these people.

They had paused for another respite, leaning against the girth of a sycamore fig tree with its erratic array of branches, when Falcone said, "Being who they are, you would expect them to just pack it in, maybe start over somewhere else. Instead, they're digging in like this is the last frontier." He gestured toward Cyrus Keogh, some fifty yards away, scaling a tree with rope lassoed over his shoulder.

"Which is why I know Jake is going to like them as much as we do," Niles replied. "What is Cyrus bloody doing in that tree?"

Falcone tilted a water bottle up and drank, not bothering to wipe the moisture from his mouth or chin. When he looked down, a little girl was standing in front of him, her round face upturned and dimpled with a pixie smile. She wore a white cotton shirt printed with multicolored butterflies and yellow shorts, plastic thongs on her feet. Her head sprouted coils of hair tied off with ribbons.

"Well, hello there," Falcone said, smiling at her. In response, the little girl giggled and darted away.

"That little vixen, what a tease," Niles chided. Blowing loose strands of hair hanging over his forehead, he said, "I bet me and the doc would make some lovely babies."

Falcone did not take the bait this time, but after a contemplative silence, he said, "We should have been able to get them on the sat phone."

"Iris and the guys?" Niles asked.

"Yeah. And now I almost don't want to keep trying because each time I don't reach anybody, it becomes more real that something bad has happened."

"You really like her."

Falcone lifted his head, gazing up at the craggy limbs of the fig tree, its leaves turned lime green in the sunlight. A pair of pigeons were pecking at fruit that hung like bunches of grapes, bits pelleting the ground. He brushed some from his shoulder. "I don't know…I mean, yeah, it was fun, casual, but—"

"But you *like* her."

"It was fast. I don't know. Maybe."

They pushed off the big tree and resumed their stroll as women swept out huts, washed clothing in buckets, ground cassava flour, and tended to babies. Many of the men and boys had departed to fish in a river some miles away, but a large mixed group had assembled toward the back end of the village to mud the woven hollow walls of a newly framed structure, women ferrying water in every available container and children gleefully stomping around a vast pit of reddish-brown sludge being mixed to the requisite consistency.

Niles was watching in fascination as handfuls of the mixture were slung and slathered into every gap, some being pitched overhand by youngsters as if firing a baseball into the glove of a Little League catcher, when he became aware of Falcone nudging him.

"What?"

Falcone pointed to the road leading out of the village where two men were having what looked to be a heated exchange, one astride a motorbike, the other standing beside it. "That guy on the bike look familiar to you?" he asked.

Cupping his hand over his eyes against the sun's glare, Niles squinted at the two figures in the distance. "You know, I think so," he said sharply, and they started walking briskly down the road.

Both men spotted Falcone and Niles and immediately stopped talking. They wore loose dark shirts and pants tucked into dust-covered rubber boots. The man on the motorbike, an old Chinese-made Haojiang with a red finish pitted and faded nearly pink, locked eyes with Falcone and raised his boot to kick off. When he twisted around and grasped the handlebars, the back of his shirt lifted just for a second, revealing a bulge in his waistband below a pucker of discolored flesh.

"Wait!" Falcone called out. "We want to talk to you!"

But the man clearly had other ideas, and revved the bike's engine, gray smoke curdling from the exhaust. He held up a hand in deflection, but Niles had reached him and clamped onto the rear fender. For a moment, the tires spun, clouds of dirt filling the air and mixing with diesel fumes, causing them to cough and wave it out of their eyes and faces. Niles' hands came off the fender and the man on the bike tore down the road in a trail of red dust.

"Shit," Falcone spat angrily, still hacking to clear his throat and lungs.

They looked around to find that the biker's companion had also disappeared. Addressing a scattering of nonplused onlookers, Falcone asked, "Does anybody know that guy? Where did the other one go?" His query, whether understood or not, was met with silence and blank stares. He turned to Niles. "Hey, what about our footage? Maybe he's in it."

Niles started to dig through his camera bag, then stopped, dropped his head. "Bloody hell. Dead battery, and it's my last spare."

"Damn. Well, let's find the Keoghs and tell them."

"Tell them what?"

"That we just saw a possible witness—or maybe something more—go flying down the road like a bat out of hell."

WALLACE PACHECO AND BEAU Gabbitas were not happy with the new development. They stood stone-like, arms crossed, their expressions bland as they listened to Falcone and Niles telling the Keoghs about what they had witnessed. The afternoon sun was as hot and moist as a sauna, the air lacking even the slightest breeze, Falcone and Niles sweating heavily and coated in dust from head to toe.

Amelia Keogh exclaimed, "This is good news!" Green eyes as round and lucid as marbles, she panned the assembled faces for endorsement. Perspiration dampened her hairline, the freckles on her skin florid in the heat. "Isn't it?"

"Hard to say," Pacheco replied tersely, his head angling toward Falcone and Niles, a scowl tugging at his mouth.

"Maybe we should stay another day, in case he comes back," she gushed hopefully. "Cy, what do you think?"

Before Keogh could respond, Pacheco dug in, his patience gone. "No, out of the question. When that helo gets here, we're heading to Dungu. We went along with a stop here to see if there was any word among the locals. From what I've been able to tell, there's not. Our instructions from the boss were to get you all to Dungu as quickly as possible."

"But if this fella is from our village, he could know what happened," Cyrus Keogh countered. Turning to Falcone and Niles, he asked, "Guys, what did he look like? How did you recognize him?"

Falcone and Niles exchanged ambivalent glances, the foundation for their premise beginning to weaken. "Uh…not sure we can describe him in a definitive way," Falcone said uncertainly, "but there was something about him that struck me. Just can't put my finger on what it was."

"If our camera batteries hadn't died, we could find him in the footage," Niles supplied. "Pretty sure he's there."

"We get you to Dungu, you can get those batteries recharged," Gabbitas said, swiping the toe of a boot across the dirt as if drawing a line of containment.

"And you sure as hell stand a lot better chance acquiring intel there," Pacheco added.

The Keoghs went quiet, Cyrus deep in thought, Amelia visibly deflated. Several yards away, children had formed a circle and were singing as they sashayed one way and then the other, each child taking a turn flailing backwards and then rebounding, their linked fold like a rudimentary mosh pit.

"Way to get their fucking hopes up," Gabbitas muttered under his breath as he shouldered past Falcone and Niles.

"You know, you're supposed to be working *for* them, not against them," Falcone said sourly, looking directly at Pacheco.

"We're supposed to be protecting them," Pacheco replied, a flinty edge to his voice, "which is what our boss pays us to do."

Falcone badly wanted to say: *Your boss answers to, and is paid by, the Keoghs.* But wisely, his brain overruled his mouth, and he said nothing more.

Pacheco moved off with an angry snap of his lighter, expelling cigarette smoke over his head in an exasperated huff.

11

THE ROLLING GREEN LANDSCAPE of the San José central valley was drifting away, forests and rivers and mountains and city clusters shrinking down to Google Earth dimensions as the Gulfstream made its climb, accelerating to three hundred knots before hitting Mach 0.85 at thirty thousand feet. Twenty minutes after takeoff, it was cruising at forty-one thousand, the world below overlaid with a foam of clouds, the sky surround so fiercely blue it seemed the white blaze of sun might shatter it.

Watching the celestial vistas float by the wide oval window next to his seat, for the first time since the flurry of calls to put arrangements in motion, Jake thought about the relative absurdity of the flight and path he was now on; extracted from a place over eight thousand miles away and installed in a seventy-million-dollar jet that cost six figures for a trip of this scope, charged with an unimaginable mission almost certainly doomed to fail if, for no other reason, the geography. Even more incredible, the man footing this staggering tab did not know Jake and had only contracted him at the behest of Falcone and Niles, having known them for less than two weeks.

The cabin attendant approached to inquire about lunch, and Jake realized that he'd had almost nothing to eat since the day before, his stomach rumbling at the very suggestion. When she retreated to prepare his meal in a pristine gallery that would have satisfied the requirements of any elite chef, the relief pilot, Captain Matt Cortez, took a seat across from him. He was swarthy-skinned with dark hair buzzed on the sides, lightly cologned and manicured. Holding an iPad so Jake could see the screen, Cortez said, "I thought I'd show you our flight plan, Mr. Tyler," and spent the next few minutes going over the route, the weather forecast, and other details. He explained that although the flight length was at the high end of the aircraft's range, it was within comfortable limits so there would be no need to stop for refueling. The typical point of entry to the DRC was Kampala or Entebbe, Uganda, but Jake had chosen Kenya instead. Since he had been actually working a contract when everything went down in Colombia, he'd had contacts and connections for gear, logistics, intel, and support. This was not the case in the Congo. But he did have a contact—a good one—in Nairobi, which was therefore the destination and his launch point in Africa.

When Cortez finished going over the plan, he said, "I'd just like to say, on behalf of the crew and myself, it's a privilege to be flying with you, and we thank you for your service."

Momentarily taken aback, Jake replied, "Thank you."

Reading his bemused expression, Cortez said, "We were thoroughly briefed and instructed to take the utmost care of you, which I assure you will be the case. You're actually in very capable hands, all of us coming from some branch of the service ourselves. Captain Sandoval, who is currently at the controls, comes from the U.S. Air Force, First Officer Graham Hyberts from the British RAF, and me, U.S. Coast Guard."

"Well then," Jake said, smiling, "thank you for *your* service."

"You're in for a treat if you like seafood. We picked up some fresh lobster in St. Maarten."

"I sure do," Jake replied, "I'll order that up for dinner."

Cortez tapped his forehead in a mini-salute and returned to the forward compartment.

Minutes later, the electronic console table in front of Jake had been set with a spread worthy of a Michelin-star restaurant: linens, gleaming china and silver and glassware; a colorful fruit tray; a deli platter layered with meats and cheeses and artisanal breads; a bowl of chicken tortilla soup; a bottle of imported sparkling water and a pot of freshly brewed coffee. Jake scarfed up the soup and then built a sandwich and devoured it. Hunger abated, he poured some coffee and took out his MacBook, a notepad, and folders of information he had printed out, and settled in to bring himself up to speed on the Keoghs, what little he knew of the situation, and the current state of affairs in the Congo.

Prior to that first phone call, Jake had never heard of the couple, and seriously doubted Falcone and Niles had, either, but the more he did the deep dive for intel, the more he realized he should have known who they were. Reading articles from the mainstream media, as well as delving into financial and business resources, their illustrious profile began to take shape.

Cyrus and Amelia Keogh were in their early forties, both born and raised in Australia. At first glance, particularly in images from their early years together, they could have been prototypes for an Aussie Ken and Barbie: tall and slender, tanned, beautiful hair and eyes, radiant smiles. But over the years, even as they seemed not to age at all visually, their maturity into intelligent and inspiring individuals was undeniable. Cyrus Keogh had attended the University of Melbourne, where he had excelled both academically and athletically, competing in everything from track and soccer to fencing and tennis to boating, swimming, and surfing. It was surfing that proved to be his calling and the springboard for his future success. After graduation from law school, Keogh had worked at his father's prestigious firm for a year or so before setting off on a "surfing vacation," from which he never returned. He rose to near-celebrity status in the circuit, capturing numerous tournament titles and landing mega endorsement deals in the process. When he met Amelia, first in New South Wales and then again in Jeffreys Bay, South Africa, he had declared she was the one and would have followed her around the globe. As it turned out, that was not necessary; the stunning redhead, a teacher with a psychology degree from Sydney, was also smitten and accepted his marriage proposal under an Australian night sky glowing with a rare blue-green aurora borealis. Keogh's company and foundation would ultimately take its name from that ethereal event.

Keogh, who had represented some young techies while lawyering, was struck with an idea and developed a then-cutting edge surfing app and "smart" board. When his best friend and surfing buddy from college survived a close call with a shark, losing a leg in the ordeal, Keogh was driven to take the technology further and, collaborating with another friend from college who had gone on to pursue engineering and software development with Bosch, the innovative app and surfboard design turned the industry on its head. Keogh's *Big Bluey*, with its aerodynamic shape, weight, and recyclable material had made him a multimillionaire, the brand and company name, Blue Aurora, as iconic to surfing as Bass Pro was to fishing or Calloway and Titlest was to golf.

The app, in addition to vital forecasting information from sensors integrated into the board, relayed real-time data about waves, wind, and the surfer's performance along with that of other surfers in the area. Utilizing reported sightings and sonar, it also broadcast shark warnings. Keogh eventually sold the technology to Shark Shield who took it to the next level and revolutionized ocean safety when their company became Ocean Guardian.

Blue Aurora's line of surfboards and surfing products were manufactured and distributed worldwide, Keogh's warehouses and shipping operations—the inaugural and primary ones being located in Australia, South Africa, and the Seychelles—lauded for their environmentally green rankings. The foundation arm of his enterprises included programs devoted to oceanic ecology, revitalization, and preservation.

Talk about your six degrees of separation, Jake thought, and wondered if Falcone and Niles realized that the seed of technology originating with Keogh had most certainly saved their lives when they'd been targeted by a shark in the Caribbean.

The consensus of financial data Jake studied indicated that Keogh's current worth was said to be just shy of a billion. Curious about what had led the couple to their philanthropy in the DRC, he searched until he found references linking to a website for an advocacy group known as The Sanctuary Initiative. It was founded by millennials from Seattle and San Francisco who had been inspired by the Kony 2012 movement, propelled to historically viral proportions by Invisible Children, another advocacy organization formed to raise awareness of the atrocities perpetuated by the Lord's Resistance Army and its leader, Joseph Kony. The LRA mention spiked Jake's attention and he put a mental pushpin in it for later follow-up. Scanning Sanctuary's website, he saw a blog entry chronicling their efforts to lobby various high-profile people to elevate or endow their cause which was described in their mission statement as:

"Providing a path to sanctuary and subsistence for those afflicted by the ongoing conflicts in Central Africa." After years of persistence, they caught the eyes and ears and, ultimately, the hearts, of the Keoghs. Last year, the Keoghs had accompanied the group to the Congo, visiting a handful of villages that had been the benefactors of Sanctuary's various initiatives, which included continuing the work of Invisible Children and The Enough Project in places that had fallen through the gap, helping them connect to early warning networks and setting up sources for clean water. Seeing the dire needs of so many and the potential for dramatic life improvement by fortifying infrastructure, the Keoghs were inspired and excited to get involved—but only if they could put their own hands on and boots on the ground.

Opening a file Jake had transferred from his phone to his laptop, a video played. It was a collection of snippets that Falcone and Niles had managed to send shortly after the second call, showing scenes from the Keoghs' compound before it had been destroyed; children playing and learning, adults being productive and attending vocational workshops. There was another video, this one a short clip of the Keoghs. It opened with Cyrus Keogh bounding across a field of kids kicking a soccer ball back and forth, his face suffused with joy, so much so that, had it not been for his tall, lanky frame and his glaring whiteness, he might have been mistaken for one of them. The scene dissolved to him speaking directly to the camera, saying, "I've always had anything, everything, I ever wanted or needed in life. To see other humans without even the basics, when I have so much, was a call to action. We know they're out there, we *know* that. But when you see them, when you're there amongst them, you're one of them. We may not be able to fix the whole world of people who are in need, but we can fix the ones we find, take the responsibility to foster them and give them what they need to be self-sustaining and safe and happy."

The last sentence sent a ripple through Jake that felt like a flock of broad-winged birds had lifted from his chest, the words reaching into the very core of his humanity and stirring the embers of passionate feelings from the Africa he'd experienced years ago.

Amelia Keogh came into frame, a small child cradled in her lap. Husband just over her shoulder, both were gazing at the child with illuminating smiles that set their skin aglow. When she spoke, Amelia's voice had a lilting quality that blossomed with emotion, exclaiming, "Oh my God, the first time I saw this little girl, I was in love!"

Jake now knew why Falcone and Niles were so enamored of the Keoghs. An essential part of his military training centered around knowing how to read people—being an effective interrogator depended on it—and there was no doubt in his mind that the Keoghs were completely free of guile; he saw no hidden motive or agenda, no subterfuge or fraud or gimmickry of any kind, just compassion at its simplest, most honest, most profound—and a commitment to people, and a child, that they had lost.

Looking back at the screen of his MacBook, Jake swiped through a series of still images Falcone and Niles had also sent. The first few, like the video, had been taken before the destruction, showing various parts of the compound and village. Nearly all of them featured smiling faces of men and women and children, most appearing to be in good health and adequately fed. He noted the structures, newer ones made of sturdy materials, older ones reinforced, all of them set in an efficiently organized layout. The implementation of communications and energy were visible, decent security measures in place. Of course, the technical upgrades—electric generators, solar panels, satellite dishes—would have made them a tempting target, as would their extensive garden, food and medical supplies. The last images were grim and graphic, everything he'd just viewed reduced to rubble and looking exactly like the destruction of combat and wars Jake had witnessed countless times before.

Giving his eyes a rest from the screen, Jake poured more coffee and sipped from his cup, but even after several minutes had passed, his mind was still imprinted with the grisly images and the barbaric fate they suggested.

Shifting his focus to the region itself, he went back to poring over online information and private intel his military security clearance gave him access to, much of which he already knew. The harsh reality was that the Democratic Republic of Congo, embroiled in war for decades, remained one of the most lawless and bloody hotspots in the world. In ten years' time, over five million people had been killed in conflicts that spilled over every one of its borders, making it the deadliest human disaster since World War II. A country the size of Western Europe, the DRC was a powder keg of volatility with an estimated $24 trillion in untapped natural resources and minerals, including coal, oil, diamonds, gold and, arguably the most contentious, coltan, which was used in the production of cell phones and virtually all other electronics. Corruption and competition over these resources fueled the fighting, with mineral trades providing the financial means for militias to operate and buy arms. On a humanitarian scale, displacement was so widespread and catastrophic—thirteen million plus—that the UN had declared an L3 Emergency, the highest level recognized. Added to that was the influx of refugees from South Sudan's own conflicts. It was utter bedlam.

The Keoghs' compound was within the tri-border nexus of the DRC, the Central African Republic, and South Sudan which, Jake suspected, was why they had selected the location in the first place. Government agencies and NGOs had all but abandoned the area, extremely vulnerable to the exploitation of violent armed groups taking advantage of the porous borders and lack of governance. Poaching and wildlife tracking was rampant, atrocities involving abductions, child soldiering, brutal rapes, mutilations and murders, were massive.

Circling back to the LRA, Jake knew they were very much still in play, and even though they were only one of more than forty armed groups known to operate in the eastern DRC, he felt there was a strong possibility they were behind the destruction.

Joseph Kony's Lord's Resistance Army had plagued the region for decades, beginning in the 1980s when they originated as a rebel group waging a relentless insurgency against the Ugandan government that went on through the nineties, pillaging northern villages and forcibly recruiting young boys as soldiers and young girls as sex slaves, both being made to commit horrendous acts against their families and villages. Jake had seen manifestations of the horror firsthand while working a contract to train Ugandan military, so the possible involvement of the LRA here struck a portentous chord in him. Their ranks were greatly diminished; at the height of power they numbered in the thousands, but after years of multinational offensives, they were said to be reduced to low hundreds. Even so, their egregious leader Joseph Kony continued to elude being captured or killed, and the LRA's reign of terror continued to this day from splintered groups mobilized across the tri-border area.

While the U.S. had also been involved in the pursuit of Joseph Kony, who had been indicted for war crimes by the International Criminal Court, most of the world did not know he existed until Invisible Children reviled him in their Kony 2012 YouTube video, which became the most viral in history at the time, garnering over one hundred million views within days of its posting. The purpose was to "make Kony famous," and that, it did. But the sensational social and media tsunami that followed resulted in Invisible Children's young co-founder Jason Russell's infamous mental breakdown, and the fervor soon burnt out like a Fourth-of-July sparkler. Jake remembered the empathy he'd felt for Russell, at best criticized for over-simplifying the conflict and, at worst, condemned for exploitation and having "white savior complex." Jake had believed Russell's intentions were sincere and that he not only accomplished his goal of raising awareness, but also spurred more U.S. military involvement. That involvement had since wound down with troops of advisors being withdrawn, but it had been a significant factor in reducing Kony's strength and reach. Jake was not sure to what extent The Sanctuary Initiative had entrenched itself into the status quo, but it had inadvertently resulted in Falcone and Niles being thrust into the fray.

He snapped the lid of his wafer-thin laptop shut, unable to digest any more for a while. All of it was an emotional minefield for him, churning thoughts of what had happened to Callie, and those of his past in the continent emerging like an underground vapor released by stepping across a recessed pool.

OUTSIDE HIS WINDOW, EVENING was darkening the atmosphere, the cloud pillow glowing with an aura that was the intense blue of a deep-ocean dive, bleeding to a blue-black ceiling of moon and stars. The moon, missing a minute sliver of its full form from the previous night, seemed translucent in its ghostly pale, stars scattered like silver glitter on satin. Earlier, he had watched the sun's melt turn everything gold before flatlining to bronze and ceding to twilight. Crossing multiple time zones at Mach speed made it feel as though he was chasing the night on an accelerated time-lapse reel.

The dinner of lobster had lived up to expectation and then some; served with a jumbo shrimp salad, teriyaki rice and vegetables, it had been phenomenal, and the gin and tonic mixed with Bombay Sapphire that he was now enjoying provided the perfect balm to quiet the torrent of thoughts in his head. It was cold and refreshing and blurred the jagged edges, ice clinking softly against the glass. His boots were off, legs outstretched to the raised footrest. Gazing out the window, he was relaxing with his drink and listening to music through Bose earbuds, when Tom Petty began his poignant serenade *Into the Great Wide Open,* an artist and song that had an acutely sentimental significance for Jake. The first few notes triggered an immediate emotional swell that filmed his eyes as he saw, and felt, Haskell Delaney, followed by the enduring image of his best friend being blown apart from his plane. The loss still evoked great pain and, he was sure, would for a long time to come.

Petty was gone, too, he realized, maybe jamming for Delaney somewhere in that great wide open. *Be free, my brother...be free.* Maybe not among the wildflowers Petty also sang about, but in a boat out at sea, most definitely.

Leaning his head back as the song played out, Jake was suddenly overtaken by exhaustion. He left his seat, stretched, and padded in sock feet across the smooth carpet, past the sofa where, for a while, he had attempted to distract himself with a movie on the large-screen television. Tropical flowers overflowed a crystal vase in a burst of island gingers and heliconias and birds of paradise. Coffee-table books were also displayed on the polished wood surface of the credenza, titles including R.G. Grant's *Warrior* and Sun Tzu's *Art of War,* the latter a classic from which he read often, prompting him to wonder if the selection had been made for him specifically. The cabin attendant caught up to him as he reached the VIP berth, outfitted with a full bed and bathroom suite. She had another Bombay and tonic for him, some heated towels. After making sure he had everything else he needed, she retreated, sliding the doors closed.

He washed up, stripped down to his briefs, and slid into the cool pocket of sheets, sighing as his head came to rest on the pillows. But as tired as he was, his thoughts would not shut off so easily. The images he'd viewed earlier kept fading in and out of focus, Keogh's words playing a refrain in his mind: *We can fix the ones we find.* That pledge went to the heart of what his Special Forces background had indoctrinated in him, and it now morally connected him to the Keoghs' mission.

Flying in the Gulfstream, probably close to forty-eight or forty-nine thousand feet at this point, the bed felt weightless and he had the sensation of floating, soothed by the whisper-quiet hum of the plane's engines and infused fresh air. He savored his drink, luxuriating in the silky softness of the bed linens, knowing it would be a while before he could indulge in this kind of pampering. His last thoughts before succumbing to sleep were of Callie, the familiar ache permeating his chest as he reached for his iPhone and navigated to the picture he most cherished, taken on the deck of a forty-six-foot sailboat before he'd left for South America. In the image, one arm was around Callie's waist, her head tilted on his shoulder, a cascade of morning sunlight shimmering behind them, their faces flushed in sensual bloom. The night before, he had made love to her for the first time as the boat gently swayed in the currents of the Pacific. He mourned the loss of buoyant light in the feelings from the moment that photo commemorated, a light that could very well be a long time coming again. He fought the urge to call her, noting that it was still early enough in Costa Rica, but set the phone aside. Closed his eyes, and fell asleep.

His dreams were steeped in the duress he'd been feeling all afternoon as memories from years ago in Africa resurfaced and what he'd just experienced with Callie—what *she* had experienced—struck him like a rockslide of boulders tumbling out of the darkness, rolling down a steep incline. Running from the sound and vibration, running and then stopping in the middle of the din, on a dusty strip, helicopter blades swirling dust, red dust and raindrops…no, not raindrops, blood…dust and blood. He turned and saw a sea of small beings, hollow eyes staring with gaunt desperation, none of them speaking. But others, adult men and women, began to scream: *Take me, Mr. Jake! Take me!* Arms waving frantically. Behind him, the rotors spun, he was swept up into the chopper, and the screaming faded as the bodies vanished in the wake of red dust.

Then, disjointedly, he was carrying Callie through dense jungle. Artillery clattered from every direction, punctuated by the explosions of overhead shelling, jet aircraft engines coming closer. She was lifeless in his arms, barely alive. He pushed on, searching for a way out, finally emerging into a clearing. In front of him was a wide gorge, spanned by a rickety bridge of wood planks. Securing Callie, holding her tightly, he began to cross, the scaffold swinging wildly. And then he felt her slip from his grasp, plunging below him into the cavern of darkness. His lungs were bellowing, *nooooooooooooooo!*

Jake was awakened by shimmying that, at first, felt like part of the dream. Then, more pronounced bumps and thumps. Sitting up in the bed, he remembered where he was, and realized that the aircraft was hitting some turbulence. He looked through the compartment windows, and saw flashes of white-gold lighting up in the clouds in a sky gone sapphire on the other side of midnight, somewhere just off the western coast. Flying at this elevation, the plane was minimally impacted, what was sure to be boisterous thunder muted by the engines, but the light show all around it increased in mass and frequency for a while, streaks of lightning sizzling like lit fuses.

He watched the storm, thinking of Callie, and prayed the skies over her were calm.

JAKE WOKE TO LIGHT beaming through the oval windows—he had purposefully left the shades open so he would be up with the sun and best able to acclimate in real time. But the bed was so incredibly comfortable, the cabin air so fresh and cool, he draped an arm over his eyes and dozed for another thirty minutes before finally rising. After dressing, cabin attendant Bettina Paloma greeted him with coffee, and he made his way to the cockpit to chat with the pilots. All were amiable and seemed well-rested as they relaxed over their breakfast, informing him that they had just passed into DRC airspace, putting them right on course for arrival in Nairobi in a few hours. Jake settled in the mid cabin, taking a seat on the sofa and watching news on television as he drank his coffee. Then he returned to his seat for what turned out to be another remarkable meal consisting of a breakfast quiche, baked apples, sliced melons, and orange juice. When he was done, he refilled his coffee and watched the mostly green landscape drift below.

Roughly thirty minutes from destination, the cobalt blue of Lake Victoria's northern edge came into view and, soon after, they crossed the border from Uganda to Kenya. The flatlands began to crinkle into the swells and troughs of ridged escarpments and deep valleys, many with lakes and huge volcanoes. Just beyond that, the terrain transitioned to a mottled tan-and-olive canvas that resembled a lunarscape, rising up to the pocked peak of Mount Suswa and then rolling down over ripples of green that thinned into settlements and towns.

Minutes later, the Gulfstream banked northeast over Nairobi National Park and made its final approach toward runway 6 of the wheel-shaped Jomo Kenyatta International Airport, touching down, and then taxiing in to Terminal 2, newer and separate from the main airport.

Jake exchanged parting words with the flight crew and descended the airstair, stepping onto the tarmac. He stood in the bright midday sunshine, peering through the Outlaw TAC sunglasses contoured around his head, his feet back on African soil and about to find out what he had really let himself in for.

12

NAIROBI TEMPERATURES ARE AT their lowest in the summer months, typically topping out in the sixties or seventies, and today was no exception. As Jake walked from the apron into the terminal, the air was pleasantly cool and dry, a light breeze rifling his hair and open shirt collar. His handlers moved him quickly and effortlessly through an expedited clearance, then escorted him out. Prior to landing, he had received a text from his friend letting him know that a driver would be waiting and, just as described, a man stood leaning against a sage-colored Range Rover that was road-seasoned with dings and dents and dirt. His skinny frame was neatly dressed in tan slacks and a navy button-front shirt printed with gold and tan leaves, hair shaved close on his head and a thin mustache lining his lip. The identifier was a pale Stetson cupped to his chest, brown feathers tucked in its band.

When he spotted Jake, the man stepped forward and extended his hand, gripping Jake's with surprising vitality. "Welcome, welcome!" He then added the second identifier, which was, "I bring greetings from Mr. Remington."

Veteran travelers were frequently met with signs announcing their names for all the world to see; veteran military implemented layers of subtle security, necessary or not.

"Thank you, my man," Jake said, and tossed his bags in the back seat, climbing into the passenger side of the front.

"Jimiyu Chilemba," the man said, fitting the Stetson on his head, "but everyone calls me Chile, like the hot peppers." He nudged the hat brim up, his grin full of teeth white as chalk against his dark skin.

Jake buckled in and Chilemba pulled away from the terminal, heading south along Airport Road. A silver charm engraved with *Hakuna Matata*—Swahili for "no worries"—swung from the rearview mirror, the windshield filmed with a patina of dust. Open savanna stretched out to the left with industrial complexes past the airport on the right. Approaching lunchtime, even with three lanes, traffic was beginning to build as they took the northwestern turn onto Mombasa Road.

"I looked on my map," Jake commented. "Seems about a forty-five-minute commute?"

Chilemba laughed, thumping the heels of his hands on the steering wheel, the whites of his eyes and teeth gleaming. "For this time of day, that is optimistic, my friend!"

Mombasa Road rolled through Embakasi, east of the Central Business District, where factories and warehouses bordered residential enclaves housing many of the most notable Kenyans. Largely unused footbridges snaked above the roadway, while below pedestrians ambled in and out of traffic as if right-of-way was theirs by sanction. Buses lined up on one side, a small herd of cattle grazed in the grassy median on the other. Heading west into Imara Daima, they passed business parks anchored with low- and mid-rise buildings, glass panels reflecting blue-green in the sunlight. Chilemba turned out to be a loquacious driver, one hand on the steering wheel as he pointed out things of interest with the other, all the while executing fast and loose maneuvers from lane to lane to maintain the maximum speed. Despite many a daredevil turn in vehicles of every axel, and death-defying spins in just as many craft of air and sea, Jake found himself bracing against the dashboard more than once.

Less than ten minutes in, the volume of cars and trucks and buses had grown considerably, and when they came to a span containing distinctive commercial properties, the flow slowed. They idled past several architecturally striking structures that took up vast acreage including the Sameer Business Park, Tulip House, 2000 Mombasa, The Panari Hotel, and Vision Plaza. When they reached another glassy building occupied by a furniture retailer, Chilemba exited to a cloverleaf that broke them from the snarl of city traffic to a modern dual carriageway.

The Southern Bypass is an eighteen-mile four-lane split by a lighted median that navigates through the southwestern neighborhoods around the north and western perimeter of Nairobi National Park. Built by the Chinese, it was designed to allow travelers from Mombasa destined for western Kenya or Uganda to bypass the notorious inner-city congestion.

The change was dramatic, going from wall-to-wall traffic stalled in slower and slower moving strings to an expanse of smoothly paved highway with vehicles more widely dispersed and streaming at a brisk pace. The immensity of the wildlife park on the left swept by in a blur of tans and greens, dotted with scrub and acacia trees, blocks of residential settlements on the right. Jake felt himself relaxing as Chilemba tuned in to a radio station playing a mixture of upbeat music and drove in a more uniform fashion, weaving back and forth across the dual lanes to circumvent vehicles at or below the 100-kph speed limit. They passed the estates of the west, built up with complexes of houses and rows of apartments and, as they began to travel more south and west, crossed the national park for a few miles. Heading north, overhead signs indicated options for the city center, including Ngong Road coming up from the left lane, which was the route they took, passing through more residential development in Uhuru Gardens and Southland Estates. And then, as the route neared the Nairobi River, the highway seemed to split between worlds; the left with tidy stacks of newly constructed apartments and houses surrounded by tracts of land staked for development; the right, below the overpass, sprawled with the blight of Africa's largest urban slum. Seen from the air, the diversity is even more shocking: on one side, geometric squares and rectangles align in precise blocks of bright terracotta roofs and green patches of lawn, seamed by pristine new road and shouldered by emerald golf courses; on the other, fractal and faded wood and metal cram together like a river logjam of oxidized and decaying barges.

Every continent has one or more epically indigent burgs: Maharashtra and Dharavi in Mumbai, India; Neza in Mexico City, Mexico; Orangi Town in Karachi, Pakistan. Nairobi's Kibera, briefly humanized as the backdrop for the film *The Constant Gardener*, is estimated to contain up to two million people within a three square kilometer area, living in twelve-by-twelve shanties immersed in extreme squalor. It was founded in the early 1900s by Nubian soldiers who, upon returning from service in the British army, were granted plots of land. Over time, other tribes moved in and became tenants of the Nubians, and with the Uganda Railway running through, even more piled on in search of work. Descendants of the original settlers were eventually given titles to their land, but the legally deeded area represents only a small percentage of what is occupied.

As the patchwork of rusted metal roofs flashed by his window, Jake caught Chilemba watching him thoughtfully. Finally, his driver said, "They take tourists through there. They actually pay to see the slums. It has become a big attraction."

Jake did not know what to say to that. Just beyond the miles of shantytown, skyscrapers rose empirically on the horizon, sparkling modern city beacons. Juxtaposed with the slum, it was a stark reminder of the ever-widening disparity between classes, and to think of well-fed and - dressed tourists traipsing through their impoverished environs, gaping and snapping pictures as if its inhabitants were animals on a safari, was a dour commentary.

Jake looked away, focusing on the road ahead where the grade was becoming steeper, banks of red dirt topped with trees lining the section known as Ngong Forest Road. Trucks and gasoline tankers chugged up a third "climbing" lane. They drove in silence for a while, Kiss FM playing Cardi B and Maroon 5 and Ariana Grande as highway unfurled below a robin's-egg blue sky clotted with cottony clouds. The incline flattened out as the direction turned southwest, a pleasant rustic stretch leading into Jamhuri and running parallel to the Ngong Forest, a sanctuary of almost fifteen-hundred acres stocked with hundreds of species of wildlife, trees, and plants. Small towns came and went on the side to the left, with open stretches in between. Consulting his watch, which told him it was 11:40, Jake realized it had taken them about forty minutes to go little more than fifteen miles.

As Chilemba moved into the right-hand lane and floored the accelerator to pass a sluggish panel truck hauling logs that extended well out the back of its bed, Jake asked, "Have you always lived in Nairobi?"

"Yes. I used to live not far from Kibera, actually." He paused, compressing his lips, his cheeks sunken. "Mr. Remington saw me one day. I was working as a *makanga*—you know, they are the ones who get the passengers on the buses—but I wanted to become a driver, so I could go other places. He put me through driving school and now I get to live in the country." Chilemba looked at Jake with undisguised veneration. "You travel the world like Mr. Remington?"

"I do," Jake said, and could not imagine what it was like to be confined to one place and culture with limited enlightenment of the world at large.

They were making better time now, traveling the forested span which, in places, looked as if the road had been carved through, tree roots dangling from the eroded edge of earth and scrub trailing down the side. Soon the directional sign for Karen appeared overhead, indicating they were three kilometers away. Remembering that it was close to their destination, Jake thought maybe they would arrive in under an hour, after all. But emerging on the other side of the Karen roundabout onto Ngong Road, all hopes for a quick finish evaporated.

Traffic was nearly at a stand-still, vehicles inching along a narrow two-lane with no median, dozens of nursery vendors displaying arrays of plants, and others, hodgepodge collections of baskets and clay pots and animal carvings. There were also the ever-present elements of ongoing road construction—earth-moving equipment lining the roadsides and piles of cleared wood and stone rubble. They advanced slowly past clusters of markets and schools and churches, the road margins wider than the road itself, often furrowed with trenches from the previous rainy season. The route finally reverted to four lanes, and the flow picked up, but only slightly as they were now entrenched in the town commerce of Karen with more construction vehicles and transport trucks competing with cars and buses for road space. Colorful *matatu* buses were also prevalent in the mix, their shells painted in Marvelesque graffiti, exhaust puffing and speakers blaring. Motorbikes and people moved up and down and in and out of the procession, a number of them parked haphazardly on the periphery. Rounding the Ngong intersection of Dagoretti and Langata Roads, another influx of traffic added to the congestion. After that, a return to dual- and then single-lane road passing through the outskirts with more nurseries occupying the edges, grassy fields extending beyond. For several miles, the drive curved through a corridor thick with shrubbery and trees—particularly the blue gums sprawled atop the wide crowns of wattles—a welcome hiatus from the dusty and busy town junctures. Rolling through more pastoral country-side, once again the components of village aggregate began to appear in the form of scattered groupings of small businesses. Unsurprisingly, given the amount of dust and dirt everywhere, car washes were found in abundance, many next to tire dealers.

Chilemba continued his verbose commentary on the people and scenery, mentioning that the town Karen was known for Karen Blixen, the Danish author of *Out of Africa*. In between snippets of locality and trivia, he would interject questions about Jake's background. Jake fielded the inquiries, meant to be conversational, with the polished ease of a baseball player scooping up a soft fly and lobbing it back to the mound; he appreciated the interest and admiration of his persona and skills and service, but he was unwaveringly tight-lipped about his military biography with civilians. He listened politely, answering in generalities and with a dry humor that Chilemba seemed to find both manly and scintillating.

Transitioning to the township of Ngong, shamrock-green signage for Safaricom telecommunications seemed to be plastered or painted on every other surface from its suburbia to city center. Multistoried build-ings hosting colonies of mom-and-pop shops, known locally as *dukas*, joined single-level strips and stalls and open-air peddling as, again, the progression of traffic slowed with drivers turning in and out of busi-nesses. They had crossed into Kajiado County in the Rift Valley province, which extended to the Tanzania border further south and, glancing at his watch again, Jake said, "I'm beginning to think I should have hired a chopper."

"No, no," Chilemba laughed, "we will get there, I promise!"

They came up on a crowded street market, a sea of umbrellas shading merchants plying clothing from tall heaps, crates of produce, and housewares, a bright red cart selling Farmer's Choice smoked sausages next to a pickup truck with pineapples tumbling from a pyramid in its back. Traffic came to a stop next to a large bricked platform teeming with *mikokoteni* carts and *matatus*. Mostly made of truck parts welded together, each *matatu* was structurally pimped up and splashed with provocative graphics depicting a cultural gumbo of themes including hip-hop artists and pop stars, athletes and politicians, historical events and religious leaders. Chilemba slammed on the brakes, propelling Jake almost into the dashboard, as an eye-searing pink bus surged from the lot, strident horn warbling, a young man clad in jeans and an orange silk shirt swinging from the doorway. It had panels that looked like Hello Kitty had exploded in a field of jellybeans.

"That is what I was doing when I met Mr. Remington!" Chilemba exclaimed, a proud grin creasing his face. He pointed to the man clamped to the bus and they watched as he leapt to the ground, jogging alongside it, drumming his fists on the panels when he had snagged one or more passengers. Even with the windows of the Range Rover rolled up, Drake could be heard all up in his feelings from a multitude of speakers.

Chilemba took a left turn onto Forest Line Road—the Ngong-Kiserian Road—driving through a run-down sector of matchstick buildings and dirty single-lane road where cars and trucks wormed around each other, parked vehicles, people, and animals. Minutes later, after passing a large field edged by a painted blue fence with signs proposing the future presence of an eight-thousand-seat stadium, the terrain opened up again with rolling pastures, hills, and valleys. Vivid sprays of red and fuchsia bougainvillea and pockets of diminutive yellow Mexican sunflowers grew wild and abundantly amidst banks of greenery, much of the roadsides wooded or bordered by dairy and livestock farms. Chilemba informed Jake that Kiserian was about five miles away but, with two hours logged, Jake was not sure he believed it. They passed a scattering of small businesses and a modern multistory building containing the Institute of Applied Technology on the right, followed by Naspepa Gardens on the left, a fun park known for the scenic views of Ngong Hills it offered destination events. Another college and a recreational center went by, a wooden cart towed by a pair of haggard gray donkeys clicking along a row of *dukas* that led into the next township where goats wandered around markets, motorbikes congregated at the curbside, and kids clad in red school garb played in fields.

The final stretch into the environs of Kiserian was enjoyable, traffic moving at a breezy pace. The sky had taken on a more baby blue intensity, the clouds more massive and shadowed with gray. A slight sway in the treetops further suggested an afternoon shower might not be far off. Approaching town, they were enveloped in a grimy swarm of pedestrians, motorbikes, cars, trucks, and *matatus*, maneuvering amidst outdoor merchants and a mix of old and new buildings. Abruptly, Chilemba turned off the road, nosing into what looked like a narrow alley. Jake had not seen a signpost anywhere, but the passage widened into a dusty road that ran west, away from town.

"We are now on the Kiserian-Kamuranga Road," Chilemba informed him, and after ten minutes of driving through increasingly rural farmland randomly interspersed with residential parcels, he made a series of turns into what could only be described as spectacularly panoramic landscape. Verdant hills climbed in every direction, greens ranging from lime to pine against the satiny dome of sky and clouds.

Chilemba made one last turn down a dirt track and drove through the arched gate of a vast estate surrounded by wood rail fencing. A half-dozen horses roamed and bowed their necks over the grass of an immense paddock, their manes lifting in the breeze, and in the distance behind them, a generous herd of cattle gathered. The Range Rover pulled up to a ranch house made of timber and chipped stone, fronted by a veranda with thick columns. Iron lanterns were spaced across the length, a pair of oversize carved wood doors in the center.

Jake realized that Chilemba had gotten out of the vehicle and come around to open his door. With a wide sweep of his arm, he triumphantly announced, "We have arrived!"

JAKE WAS MET AT the door by a young man in his early twenties, dressed in belted tan chino slacks and a white polo shirt. Introducing himself as Issa Lusalah, he waited until Jake had set his bags down, then led him through the house.

With no foyer, the great room encompassed living and dining areas under an exposed beam ceiling that rose to a peak of twenty-five feet, paneled and floored in honey-hued wood. One wall was dominated by a fieldstone fireplace with a hand-hewn beam mantle that looked like it might have come from a century-old saloon, a pair of eye-shaped Maasai warrior shields and spears mounted above. Around it were a tobacco-colored leather sofa, chairs upholstered in patterned russet suede, and a heavy square coffee table made of reclaimed wormwood with aged iron hinges, all arranged over an Oriental rug. The other wall backed a modern kitchen with commercial-grade appliances, separated by a granite-topped island and nailhead-studded barstools. Iron-and-wood wagon wheel chandeliers hung from the ceiling, French doors and full-length windows across the back let in natural light that gave the wood surfaces a liquid shine. Given the bucolic tone of the house, conspicuously missing were any kind of animal furs or hides or antlers.

Lusalah took Jake past the wall of windows, down some steps, and through a mud room door. Pointing to a cypress-timbered barn about fifty feet away, he said, "Mr. Remington is in there, expecting you."

Thanking him, Jake walked along a flagstone path edged with bright rows of purple asters and yellow black-eyed Susans, backed by sprays of fountain grass, noticing that the barn was one of several in view; two more were set much farther back amidst the spread of green-gold pastureland. This one also had antennas and a satellite dish on its roof. He raised his fist to knock on the door but, feeling the thudding bass vibration of music, he gripped the handle and swung it open, immediately blasted with the high-octane exultations of Bon Jovi. The tall, broad-shouldered figure standing with his back to the door was accompanying them on air guitar, left hand working imaginary chords and right hand strumming. He was also singing, loudly.

"Whoa-oh, we're halfway there-ere...whoa-oh, livin' on a prayer..."

Clapping expansively, Jake called out, "Right on, brother!"

The man's singing stopped abruptly as he turned, grinned, and strode over to greet him. The two clasped hands and embraced.

Nash Remington said, "The years have been good to you, man. How long has it been?" A subtle twang could be heard in his voice, an inkling to his native Tennessee. Wearing jeans and a light blue t-shirt that were snug against the contours of his muscular body, tattoos on Remington's arms seemed to profile his past and present; his left was inked with the Special Forces crossed arrows crest, his right, an outline of Africa inset with an elephant. His auburn hair was faded on the sides to a short textured top, trimmed mustache and beard circling his mouth and chin.

"It's been a minute," Jake replied, eyes roving past his friend and taking in the surrounding interior, which looked nothing like that of a barn. Obviously soundproofed, built-in cabinetry and shelves lined the perimeter, large workspaces set up in between. Desktop and laptop computers were distributed throughout, each screen displaying something different; multiple radio stations and scanners were wired in and operational; maps and images and diagrams took up nearly every open space on the walls. A large oval table in the center was covered with stacks of printed material and photographs, folders and binders, tabs and Post-its, pencils and pens and highlighters, and ruled pads filled with copious notes.

Following his gaze, Remington said, "If you haven't guessed, this is my war room."

"Impressive," Jake mused, exploring the room and, as he did, noticed for the first time a pair of Belgian Malinois dogs, holding court at one end of the oval table. They were clearly on high alert, postures erect and eyes riveted on him, nostrils quivering with sensory perception, but as motionless as statues. Their coats were fawn-haired, faces like sooty masks.

"*Vrij*," Remington commanded, and the two canines rose in unison and approached Jake, who slowly offered his hand for them to smell. Satisfied with his body language and scent, their tails wagged approval. Kneeling, Jake massaged the scruffs of their necks, prompting both to lean into him. After allowing them a few moments indulgence, Remington said, "*Loslaten*," and the dogs retreated to their prior position.

"Amazing."

"Luna and Solis, my bodyguards," he laughed. "They're my pets, and I spoil them shamelessly, but they are actually fully trained as tactical assets."

"I believe it."

"They didn't bark or rush you when you entered because I had them in stay."

"Thanks for that," Jake quipped.

Adjusting the volume on his CD player, Remington took a seat at the table and asked, "Want some coffee? Water? Something stronger?"

"Water's good, need to hydrate."

Remington rolled in his swivel chair to a mini fridge and extracted two bottles, tossing one to Jake. "So…a G-stream? How was *that?*"

Jake took a long drink of water, wiping his mouth with the back of his hand, and chuckled. "It did not suck."

Placing his hands flat on the table top, Remington said, "I am really glad you reached out, brother. Sorry I couldn't pick you up myself, but I wanted to put as much time into intel as possible. Also juggling several jobs."

"No sweat, just grateful for your help, and glad business is good. It's certainly beautiful out here in the country, but that city traffic…"

"Oh, it's a bitch. Just be glad you didn't arrive during morning or evening rush hour. That would have added at least another hour to the drive. But that's why I have Chile, so I don't have to deal with it."

Remington reached for a notepad and was shuffling through several pages when a computer behind him issued a notification chime. He rolled over and studied the screen.

"What's up, Remy?" Jake asked.

"Shit. Well, this is not good." He returned to the table, looked grimly at Jake. "You still meeting your guys and the group in Dungu?"

"Last message I had, yeah. Why? What's going on?"

"Dungu is being overrun."

"What? By who? Militia?"

"By South Sudanese refugees, thousands of them, and the town is rebelling."

13

SEATED ACROSS FROM REMINGTON, Jake looked into the gray-green eyes of his friend for several moments without speaking. Even though it had been quite a few years since they'd last engaged, as with most of his military comrades, there was an abiding kinship built on mutual respect for their combat collective and shared valor. Jake had first met Nash Remington at Fort Bragg where they were both completing a course for Advanced Special Operations Techniques. Years later, they crossed paths again as contractors, working at different times in Sierra Leone and Uganda—Sierra Leone, to support the country's government and army in its effort to prevent a coup and later as security consultants; Uganda, as part of a UN peacekeeping mission to provide progressive military training for the Uganda People's Defense Force soldiers.

"Have you gotten a recent sitrep from them?" Remington asked.

Jake blew out a breath. "Not exactly. Commo has been minimal. If I had to guess, it's probably because the sat phones are out of juice."

"Or—"

"Yeah, or something else," Jake finished. "But I've got to go on the assumption that they'll still be in Dungu to link up with me. I'll try to call or text them in a bit."

"You know this is a fool's errand with bad outcome written all over it. Uprising aside, you are about to sail into one gigantic shitstorm, my friend."

Jake sighed, leaned back, and laced his fingers behind his neck. "I know."

"Okay, let's talk territorial situation." With his finger, Remington drew a circle around an area on a Military Grid map in the center of the table. "There is heavy fighting ongoing in the central and southern areas of the region, most volatile in North and South Kivu. Mineral conflicts, refugees, political protests, and widespread disease. I'm sure you know about the Ebola outbreaks."

Jake nodded.

"All that plays into the isolation of the north. Much of the humanitarian efforts, NGOs, peacekeepers, and military have been deployed to the south. Haut Uélé and Bas Uélé have almost none, and the few there are pretty useless as they have poor supplies, capabilities, or support. Non-existent infrastructure."

"Remy, who do you think did this?"

Remington drummed a pencil eraser-end on the table. "I know you're thinking LRA, and it could very well be. Conflict trackers show increased LRA activity in the area where their compound was." He pointed out clusters of symbols on the map. "We know that Kony has ordered more abductions to repopulate his ranks. The latest intel on his location still has him in a safe haven in the Sudanese-controlled border of northeastern CAR, Kafia Kingi, but his soldiers are all over northern DRC. The compound would certainly have been on their radar as a prime target. The only thing that gives me pause is the way it was executed. Most of these attacks are vicious and messy, lots of blood and bodies. This almost seems like a professionally planned operation."

"Yeah, I had that thought, too," Jake said. "If there were killings, there would be bodies. They would not have removed them. Also, some would probably have escaped and still be in the vicinity. If you want to know the truth, the whole thing has a creepy vibe."

"It does." Remington handed Jake several sheets of paper clipped together. "Here's a printout of all the reported incidents from a fifty-mile radius over the past couple of days. You'll see that none of them bear much resemblance to what happened at the compound. Assaults, abductions, looting, and even some killing, but on a much smaller scale and, as you noted, plenty left behind to make reports."

They exchanged prescient looks. Jake said, "Something is really off here."

MUCH OF THE AFTERNOON was spent reviewing intel and monitoring the tense situation in Dungu, also discussing gear and supplies for Jake's expedition. Jake had twice tried to make contact with Falcone and Niles but was unsuccessful. After a couple of hours in Remington's tactical barn, they took a much-needed break, stretching their legs over some of the acreage surrounding the ranch. The sky had turned overcast, pale lavender with drifting ashen clouds, a cool breeze stirring the treetops and swishing the field grasses. They watched as ranch hands fed and watered the horses and cows and goats and chickens, Remington telling Jake about his home and business as they walked around the pastures and through orchards of olive and tamarind trees, the Belgian Malinois pair playing a spirited game of tag-and-run ahead of them. Gray crowned cranes with their golden mohawks plodded at the edge of a large pond rimmed by reeds and sedge and covered with lily pads and hyacinths, sandpipers and dragonflies skimming the surface.

Like Jake, Remington had served a dozen-plus years of active duty in the army Special Forces and again as many as a reservist and contractor. He told Jake that while they'd been working in Uganda he'd become fond of the place and people and decided to stay in the region, settling in the more stable Kenya. With the financial backing of several investors, he found and purchased the property, built the ranch, and set up *Habari*, Swahili for intelligence and information. He characterized his services as security logistics, which ran the gamut of brokering and implementing security systems to high-tech surveillance and ground operations, working for government officials and agencies, foreign diplomats and dignitaries, wealthy individuals and executives. But he described himself as more of a niche player in the market, opting for challenging jobs that appealed to his ethics rather than those in the militaristic mainstream.

"I'm sorry that I won't be able to accompany you tomorrow," Remington said as they were later relaxing on his rear patio.

He stood in front of the large drum of a grill, aromatic smoke from wood chips and crackling coals wafting through the crisp air that smelled of hay and manure and pine. Steaks as thick as law books were sizzling next to aluminum-wrapped potatoes and skewers of onions and peppers. Beyond them, a fine green carpet of Arabic grass extended to a mixed line of trees stenciled against the breathtaking backdrop of the Ngong Hills, their undulating silhouette an opaque shadow the color of eucalyptus. Pinks and purples were bleeding from the horizon rim as daylight waned, the sun's diminishing flare still muted by cloud.

Seated in an acacia wood chair, Jake was giving his arm a workout, pitching tennis balls across the lawn for the dogs to chase and retrieve. "I understand, and I didn't expect that you'd be able to just drop everything for something like this." In between throws, he sipped from a glass of iced tea sprigged with fresh mint, the cool air enhancing its chill in his throat.

Repositioning the meat on the grill, Remington said, "I've got security for that multinational environmental summit at the UN compound, which is a huge event. Then I have a meeting for an heirloom jewels exhibition. I might be able to join you after that."

"I hope to have it wrapped by then," Jake said.

Remington turned, waved at the smoke curling around his face. "Surely you don't expect to have everything resolved that quickly."

The dogs had finally expelled their energy and were panting at Jake's feet, tongues lolling. He stroked the tops of their heads, surveying the spectacular view, a pair of ibises squalling as they passed overhead. The sky was fired with bronze, the clouds massing in thunderheads taking on the gray of tarnished pewter. Hearing a low rumble off toward the hills, Jake's thoughts immediately gravitated to Callie. Glancing at his watch and calculating the nine-hour time difference, he decided it would be a good time to call her. He was about to excuse himself when Issa Lusalah emerged from the house with plates and a bowl of salad, arranging them on the table. Bulbs strung across the wooden pergola illuminated as it grew darker, a fire pit lit for warmth as the temperature began to drop.

Remington handed Lusalah a dish of grilled meat for the dogs, and they trailed him back inside the house, noses sniffing at his elbow. Placing steaks, potatoes, and skewers on their own plates, Remington asked, "So you had the whole freaking Gulfstream to yourself?"

"Well, yeah, with the pilots and hostess." Jake carved a slice of steak, juices oozing as he extracted it with his fork and placed it in his mouth. "Oh, brother," he said, eyes closing in pleasure as he chewed, "this is perfection."

Remington regarded him with a salacious smirk. "You and the hostess do any mile-high clubbing?"

Jake chuckled around a mouthful of salad, shook his head.

When there was no further comment, Remington goaded, "Really?" His expression suggested an alternative belief based on a dossier of past dalliances.

Swirling butter and sour cream in his potato, Jake shook his head again but did not reply.

Still not buying it, Remington said, "Oh, what, you're all on-mission? Is that it?"

"Yes, but no," Jake said, and changed the subject. "I heard stories about all the VIPs they've flown...rock stars and celebrities, world-class athletes, the uber-wealthy."

"And you are now employed by one of those uber-wealthy."

"This is not about the money at all. Sure, it's great, but the only reason I'm doing this right now is my guys."

For the next few minutes, Remington listened without interruption as Jake told him about South America, his eyes honed in on Jake's, trying to mine a nuance in his demeanor that was eluding him.

"I was wrapping up my contract in Colombia and the next gig I had lined up was to advise and strategize for these two TV guys," Jake explained. "But when I was in-country with them, things went sideways and, as a consequence of one of our last missions, when we took out a cartel kingpin, I had a price put on my head. These guys risked their lives for me."

Jake purposefully left out any reference to Callie in his account.

When he had finished, Remington said, "I did hear about Delaney. That was fucked up. I'm so sorry."

Jake felt his throat tighten, took a long sip from his tea, and gazed pensively into the mauve dusk settling across the land, the grass and trees darkening to indigo as the molten lava of sun flamed out in a liquid swell over the hills. Birds flying in circles above resembled black embers floating in the twilight.

"You have a wonderful place here," he said.

Dragging his chair closer to Jake's, Remington sat back down and replied, "Yeah, I love it. The killer view, the serenity. It's special."

Flames from the fire pit snapped in the breeze, the chitters and croaks of insects and frogs rising as the daylight continued to fade. The horses could be heard whinnying close by as their restlessness grew with the grumbling thunder from the hills.

"The only thing missing here, bro, is a woman." Jake looked at his friend's face, auburn mustache and beard shining like copper wire in the firelight.

Remington gave a bawdy laugh. "Haven't found one who could handle me! You know how that is. Doesn't mean I haven't had fun trying. The Nairobi club scene is off the chain." He lifted his eyebrows suggestively, peering at Jake. Then, seeing something, staring inquisitively. "Oh...*there* it is."

"There what is?"

"You...there's somebody now, isn't there?"

Jake said nothing, and Remington rose from his chair. "I think it's time for some Tennessee whiskey." Before he made it off the patio, his phone rang.

Remington had been making and taking calls sporadically all afternoon, but this one seemed to spring a hair-trigger. Jake watched him pace off as he held the phone to his ear, running a hand agitatedly through the blunt crop of hair on top of his head. When the call ended, it took him a minute to return to Jake.

"Son of a bitch," Remington fumed.

"What's wrong?"

"I just got a tip from one of my sources. About an ivory trafficker—low-hanging fruit, really—but I've been tracking him and his network for quite a while. My source just told me that a communication was intercepted indicating the guy has a meeting set, tonight in the city, with a major broker who is on an Interpol Red Notice, Bái Zhuang." Remington paced again, spouting, "Shit timing."

"Forget that. What do you want to do?"

"I mean, I'm pretty skeptical that the meeting's really with Zhuang. The guy's a freaking ghost. But...if it is...I want the guy. Bad." His face had filled with color, eyes glimmering with fervor. The fingers of his hands were clenching and unclenching, his t-shirt stretched taut over his broad chest.

"Okay, what do you need?"

"No, look," Remington said, distractedly weighing options in his head, "you stay here, kick back, get some rest. You're going to need it, brother."

"You've been working for me ever since I called you. I'm here, I can rest later. You might not get this chance again."

Remington's eyes locked on Jake's. "You sure?"

"Let's go get the bastard."

They left the patio and headed for Remington's tactical barn, lightning stitching the sky like gold thread, droplets of rain misting the air.

14

BEHIND THE WHEEL OF a different vehicle, this one a new black Rubicon, Nash Remington had left a visibly dejected Chilemba standing in his ranch drive as he and Jake headed back into the city, pavement grinding under knobby thirty-three-inch off-road tires. The rain was behind them as they sped north, but clumps of storm clouds were migrating into the eastern skies, edges singed like cigarette ash. It was now Boston whanging from the Alpine stereo system's nine speakers, the Jeep's crisp LED headlamps blazing a blue-white path on the road ahead of them. The evening rush hour was on the wane, inbound traffic significantly lighter than the flow egressing from the city center.

Taking in the Rubicon's sleek, stitched leather interior with all its digital tech, Jake said, "So this is the one *you* drive."

Remington laughed and winced. "Chile is begging me to drive it. I just haven't been able to bring myself to give him the reins yet. But I'll have to give in pretty soon, the whole idea being a classier appearance at the higher-profile gigs. I don't bring him on field ops, so he wouldn't have driven tonight anyway."

"I just got one, too. Love it."

"Did some off-roading in Maasai Mara and the Serengeti last week. It's a beast."

Jake looked down at Remington's laptop which was propped on his left arm and open to a site he'd found after googling their destination. The location where the meeting was said to be taking place was a high-rise building sandwiched between the affluent Milimani and Upper Hill districts, just outside the CBD and surrounded by upscale neighborhoods, embassies, medical facilities, premier banking, and international businesses. Scrolling through the site's content, Jake asked, "You sure you got the right address?"

"Angani Place. Why?"

"It says here that it's still under construction, currently leasing but not ready for occupancy until next month."

"Huh. Interesting…but maybe even a smart choice."

Reading from the laptop screen, Jake said, "It's a luxury condo, forty-seven floors, fully furnished units with balconies…ten thousand square feet of garden space, a supermarket, shops and restaurants, gym and spa, heated indoor pool, rooftop club with lounge and dining. My goodness…even shows a helo pad."

Remington glanced at the dash touchscreen and saw that it was coming up on 7:30 PM. Approaching the Southern Bypass, they were making good time, but it was going to be close, he thought. Looking sideways at Jake, he said, "Thanks for coming."

"Of course. Any other guys?"

"I wasn't able to scramble a team tonight, but I've got one guy meeting us. I'm sending him with you to DRC. I think you'll like him. Former COS, 1st Marine Infantry, which is French Special Forces. He's worked with me on a number of anti-poaching ops over the years, something I am really committed to."

"Near and dear to me as well," Jake said.

"Bái Zhuang is high up in the largest ivory smuggling syndicate in the country, maybe even the world." He looped onto the Bypass and built speed along the dark stretch of Ngong Forest, the Jeep's engine working through the upper range of its transmission. "The Chinese ban last year has seen the demand decrease—officially—but banning it legally has only served to boost the illegal trade and a raging black market. There are also countries where it's still legal, like Japan, Philippines, Thailand, and Vietnam. The poachers don't make much, about two hundred dollars a pound, but on the market-end two tusks go for upwards of two hundred thousand. As you know, it's a big part of the funding for militias, terrorist groups, the LRA. Most of the ivory comes from DRC and

CAR, but much of the dealing is done here in Kenya. A lot of Chinese nationals have moved into African countries and established lucrative side businesses to front their illicit operations, most in Tanzania and Mozambique behind timber and fishing. They have complicit clearing agents in all the ports, shipping tusks in batches that are bundled as coffee berries, charcoal, tea leaves, sugar, just about anything."

After passing the diametric divide of Kibera and the south estates, Remington merged onto Langata Road, the skyways over Wilson Airport pulsing with the red and white beacons of planes taking off and landing.

"The Kenyan trafficker is a Somali by the name of Daahir Aljabarti," Remington continued, "and if Zuang is, in fact, meeting with him, it is probably to place an order for ivory, by the tons. The price will be negotiated and then Aljabarti will coordinate with smaller brokers to set a timetable for delivery. Those brokers will contact the poachers in DRC and CAR, maybe South Sudan, and the cycle begins." His grip on the steering wheel tightened. "From the animal slaughters in the countryside to the smugglers to the ports and points of passage and delivery in the East."

They lapsed into quiet, Remington maneuvering a roundabout in an acute angle onto Mbagathi Way, Jake monitoring the Jeep's navigation screen. As they drove north on the smoothly paved four-lane, shorter rows of housing began to give way to the taller heights of residential and commercial real estate. Another roundabout took them briefly back onto Ngong Road, past the Kenyatta National Hospital, and then a left turn onto Ralph Bunche Road put them on a stretch with a Java House coffee shop and a few small boutique hotels. Remington took the right turn indicated by the GPS mapping and advanced slowly down a tree-lined corridor.

Checking his phone, he said, "Got a text from my guy. He's here... parked just past the building's sign."

They rolled forward, both looking and then spotting the big billboard anchored on the corner, enveloped by gum and jacaranda trees. It was emblazoned with an artist's rendering of the high-rise, along with the words: NOW LEASING THE LUXURY YOU DESERVE. Thirty yards beyond, the pinnacle of Angani Place rose 775 feet skyward, some of its glass gleaming from illuminated spaces, a wash of amber lighting glowing from the grounds below. A short distance past the sign, a pair of head-lights flashed twice in the darkness.

Remington pulled off the road and parked in the trees. Come fall, the jacarandas—which were planted throughout the city—would be burst-ing with orchid-colored blooms, but the mass of fernlike leaves now covering them made for good concealment. He and Jake got out of the Jeep, went around to the rear and retrieved their gear bags from the cargo storage. They walked toward a blue Isuzu D-MAX pickup, where a man was leaning against the side. He was barely visible, wearing all black. Prior to departure from the ranch, Remington and Jake had also changed into black, tactical pants with long-sleeved shirts over tees.

"Hey, man," Remington said, and turned to Jake to proffer an intro-duction. "Luther, this is Jake Tyler. Jake, Luther Baladur."

Reaching for the man's hand, Jake said, "Nice to meet you." As his eyes adjusted to the gloom, he could make out Baladur's French and Congolese features: blue-gray eyes set in topaz-hued skin, flawless but for a two-inch scar curved over one brow, a fine stubble of dark hair on his head and face. He was slender with the bone and muscle sinew of a field athlete, his expression a mix of composure and acuity.

"Likewise," Baladur replied in an accent that was slightly more Euro-pean than African, clasping Jake's hand with easy geniality.

"Sitrep?" Remington asked.

"Yes," Baladur replied. "I got a quick look before you arrived, and I think there is a good chance the intel is solid. There is a building security guard in the lobby. I suspect he has been bought, because I spotted an-other man standing around who was not in uniform, and it looked like he was armed. He went back toward the lifts a couple of times, talking to someone I could not see, so possibly there is a second one."

"Okay, what about other access points?" Remington asked.

In response, Baladur held out his phone and thumbed through a se-ries of images. "There is a service lift down from the entrance, in the parking bay, and I did not see anyone there. But evidently it requires a card."

"It has a card reader?"

"Yes. Oh, and of course there are security cameras, but I managed to stay out of range."

"Good precaution, though it's possible that the building security guard being on the take might have disabled any surveillance that would compromise those guys. Go back to that last picture," Remington said, and pinched and spread his thumb and forefinger on the phone's image to zoom in. When it came into legible focus, he smiled. "Okay, good."

Remington thought about the scenario for a few moments, scanning the building from top to bottom, the contours and edges in deep shadow. The balconies that extended from the sides, with the random bits of interior light, gave it the look of a giant honeycomb. Gusts of wind wisped through the trees around them, the air smelling of freshly poured cement, topsoil, and peat. "Lots of floors, lots of units," he said, "so first thing we need to do is make sure it's actually them and try to pinpoint where in the building they are. I have just the thing to accomplish that."

Both Jake and Baladur looked at him curiously.

Remington knelt and unzipped his gear bag, removing and opening a canvas pouch. One side encased a video screen, the other held what resembled a game controller and two miniature helicopters.

Recognition broke over Jake's face and he emitted a hearty but audibly restrained laugh. "Brother…how the hell did you come to possess these bad boys? This is top-level proprietary military shit." He reached into a pocket compartment, took one of the gadgets in his hand, and gazed at Remington in nonplussed wonder.

"I have my pipelines," Remington said with a sly grin. "It's actually a prototype of what's currently being used, but works just the same."

"That looks like a toy," Baladur mused, his face animated with fascination. "Is it what I think it is?"

"A FLIR Black Hornet drone," Remington said. "Light as a feather, fits in the palm of your hand, sensors with EO and IR cameras. And yes, I am an authorized operator…drone laws in Kenya are complicated. But we will be technically breaking a few restrictions." He handed the pouch to Jake. "If I give you a quick how-to, think you can operate it?"

"Oh yeah."

"Good, because I have another task for Luther and me."

✳   ✳   ✳   ✳   ✳

IN MINUTES, JAKE WAS up to speed and deploying one of the two drones, using the joystick controller to manipulate its covert recon mission of the building. Developed for the military and used by the armed forces of several nations in Afghanistan, the six-inch-long Black Hornet weighed just over an ounce and flew up to thirteen miles per hour. As it disappeared into the night, Jake monitored the video display, studying the views of its three cameras.

Next to him, Remington had taken out a messenger bag containing a black, inch-thick twelve-by-twelve square device, which he activated by flipping a missile switch. It beeped, and Remington closed it up in the bag. He also took out a black-and-purple windbreaker and ball cap, both branded with an authentic FEDEX logo. After Baladur had slipped those on, Remington handed him the messenger bag, a lanyard clipped with a plastic FedEx card, and a computer tablet. He took a minute to pull up the template of a shipping document, typed in a generic address on the same street, and handed the tablet to Baladur.

"All you have to do," Remington instructed, "is go into the lobby—if it's locked, knock on the glass—and get within a few feet of the security guard. You can show him the tablet display if you want, tell him you have a delivery for that address. He will probably say you're in the wrong place, and of course he won't know where it is and will want to get rid of you, so just say sorry and retreat."

"That's it?"

"Yep, short and sweet, quick in and out." He reached into his gear bag and came up with another case, this one containing Invisio X5 comm sets. He gave one to Baladur, tossed another to Jake, and waited for them to fit the buds in and around ears and connect to their radios and control units. "Commo check?"

"Copy," Jake said, repeated by Baladur.

"Engagement?" Baladur queried, lifting the hem of the FedEx windbreaker to show Remington the handgun that was tucked in the back of his pants.

Looking to both Jake and Baladur, Remington replied, "Obviously, we don't want a shootout here in the city on an unsanctioned op. If I'd received this intel much earlier I could have gotten a green light and assembled a full team. But if it's them or us, do what you have to do. Luther, if anybody other than the security guard approaches, if it looks like they might pat you down, say: 'Isn't there a Java House around here?' Then back your way out of there, smiling and watching them, and we'll be right on you."

"Got it," Baladur said. He slipped the messenger bag's strap over his shoulder, adjusted his cap, and headed for the front of the building.

They watched him walk beside a rough-graded strip at the edge of the grounds, stepping in and out of yellow ellipses of light and around mounds of topsoil and wooden pallets, then corner and enter the overhang of entryway. Remington set up next to Jake, opening his laptop on the hood of Baladur's truck and plugging in a device the size of a playing card, circuitry exposed, a CD-like disk antenna connected to it.

Jake returned his full attention to the drone's video display, alternating between the fluorescent greens of night vision and the fiery rainbow of infrared. The wind was continuing to pick up, blowing through his hair, pellets of rain beginning to flick against his face. "What's the weather tolerance on this thing?"

"It's rated for light rain, wind to fifteen knots sustained, gusts to twenty, so we should be fine."

As Jake sent the drone higher and higher up the side of the building, maneuvering it in a circle at each level and analyzing the images, he asked Remington, "So what exactly *is* the plan if we get a visual?"

"I'm still wrestling with that. As much as I want to take him down now, I would also love to track him and see how far into the syndicate he might take us. Just not sure we'll have either option. But getting eyes on will be a major accomplishment."

"Okay, I'm all the way up to what's probably the penthouse level and I haven't—oh, hel-lo—"

Remington came over and looked at the display. Jake toggled the imagery, showing him the green ghosts of two men seated together, then the reds and oranges of their heat signatures. "Goddamn," Remington muttered, "there they are." A little dumbfounded by what he was seeing, he said, "Be sure you get screen captures. Hey, I don't see anybody else in the room, do you? No security?"

"No, I don't. Maybe in the hallway. Maybe they were foolish enough to only have coverage at ground level. Wouldn't that be nice?"

"Only one way to find out."

They both looked up at the sound of Baladur's approach, his feet scratching softly on the soil and then shuffling over grass. The audio of his foray into the building's lobby had been transmitted through their comms and, hearing everything progress without any obvious duress, Jake and Remington had concentrated on confirmation of their target. Now, Baladur asked, "Did I get what you needed?"

"We'll know in a minute," Remington said, taking the messenger bag from him. "Everything go okay?"

Baladur smiled, shedding the FedEx jacket and cap. "Perfectly. The guards watched but did not approach me."

Remington slid the square device—which was a long-range RFID reader—from the bag, turned a thumbscrew on the front, and lifted the lid. A covered circuit board took up half of the interior, the other half rigged with two rows of AA Duracells, a smaller open-sided circuit board, and an LCD panel. From the small circuit board, he removed a micro SD card, which he then plugged into his laptop. Tapping keys and reviewing the windows that opened on the screen, he pointed to a line of code that appeared. "That, my friend, is what you got," he said triumphantly. "The hexadecimal code for a 26-bit HID card."

Baladur eyed Remington hazily and then caught on. "Ah! We copied the access card."

"Exactly." He placed a blank card on the disk antenna of the connected Proxmark device and typed: LF HID clone. Pasted the code and watched as it was successfully copied to the new card. Looking to Jake, he asked, "They still there?"

"Affirmative."

"All right, go time. Luther, hold it down right here. Let us know if you see anything going on, anybody in or out."

Baladur nodded and reached into his truck, coming up with a night vision monocular, and jogged down the road to get a better vantage point for the entrance.

Jake brought the drone down and replaced it in the pouch while

Remington put the RFID capture and clone electronics back in his gear bag. He took out a larger tactical messenger bag and loaded it up with a CORE camera kit and an assortment of GPS trackers, bugging devices, detectors and jammers, and the computer tablet. He also added a handful of zip-tie restraints and extra cartridges for their Glocks. He draped the messenger bag across his chest, nodded to Jake, and the two of them walked toward the immensity of Angani Place.

THE PARKING BAY WAS dimly lit and vacant. As Baladur had reported, not a soul or vehicle was anywhere to be seen; it was just late enough for any lingering workers to have cleared out. Adjacent to what would be an elaborate lobby porte cochere—with a full-length marble fountain, a Mediterranean-tiled drive incorporating the Angani caligraphy logo, ventilated metal columns that splayed into a ceiling with rings of light—was the space designated for valet service that ramped down to the lower parking level. Littered with boxes of the driveway tile, either broken or yet to be placed, buckets of concrete grout, metal scaffolding and plastic sheeting, spools of cabling and cut pieces, the air was heavy with cement dust dampened by the elevated humidity of imminent rain.

They advanced cautiously past the valet platform, staying close to the wall, Glock 17s held out by their sides. The echo created by low concrete ceiling and cavernous space amplified the sounds of their movements as they continued into the garage area, Remington's eyes immediately roved upward, seeking the locations of surveillance cameras. Finding them, he signaled Jake to halt while he determined the type and manufacturer, training a Steiner miniscope on one of the fixtures until he made out the brand name.

Talking just above a whisper, he said, "These are Wi-Fi. Let's see if they're online."

He took out the tablet, attached a network adaptor, swiped and brought up an app. In a few seconds, he said, "Got 'em." He tapped and scrolled, tapped some more, waited. "Okay, we're good to go."

"What?" Jake asked, incredulous.

"Basically, the network adapter detected all the wireless traffic in our proximity, and then software pared it down in a way that I could find the brand name of the cameras and the MAC address. With the name and Wi-Fi address the network is broadcasting on and the address of the cameras themselves, I targeted the channel with the traffic and sent a command to take them offline via denial-of-service. Best of all, if the security guy even notices, he'll probably think it's a Wi-Fi outage, which it is."

"Okay, don't understand anything you just said, but that's just badass," Jake said, shaking his head.

Stuffing the tablet back in the messenger bag, Remington said, "Now for the payoff from Luther's bit of skullduggery."

They proceeded to the service elevator, fingered the UP indicator, and stepped inside when the doors parted. It was tall and wide and gleaming in chrome all the way around, trimmed with thick metal railings and lit by low-watt LED panels in the ceiling. Remington waved the cloned access card in front of the reader on the digital touchscreen. It beeped, red light turning to green. After evaluating the floor selection, he tapped 43, and the elevator ascended with a soft whir. Jake did not have to ask; they would take the stairs from the floor below the forty-fourth.

Which was what they did, climbing to the penthouse level, Remington in the lead with his Glock aimed in front of him, Jake covering from the rear, aiming behind and below them. The stairwell was gray with shadow and ripe with unfinished drywall, tape and compound crisscrossing the seams, capped electrical wires dangling from outlet openings. They stopped on the landing, careful to avoid a metal trough filled with scrapers and sanding materials next to the hallway door. It was reinforced metal, inset with a narrow slat of glass that emitted just enough light to cast a flickering reflection, generated by movement on the other side.

Standing back and away from the window pane, Jake trained his Glock on the upper middle of the door while Remington crouched just to the side of it, sliding his CORE Under Door camera across the threshold. The insertion panel was not much thicker than a ruler, connected by an elongated neck to a handheld grip. He viewed live video on the five-inch monitor attached to his arm by a Velcro strap, moving the camera slowly across the width of the doorway, then backed away to where

Jake was standing and straightened up, gesturing for Jake to move closer to the stairs so they could talk.

He expelled a breath. "Well, good news and bad news," he said, running his thumb around the camera's flap. "Good news…there's certainly something going down, and my gut tells me it's exactly what I think." He paused, pressing his lips together, nostrils flaring. "Bad news…not one or two, but at least three armed guys in the hallway. We didn't see any inside, and of course that doesn't mean there aren't any, but to me, looks like all the security is standing guard on the outside."

Jake said nothing, pondering tactical options.

"A distraction would be too risky, probably alert and spook them inside, not to mention the time it would take to strategize and execute. I don't think we have that kind of time with this."

"Agreed," Jake said.

"Given their relative positions, we can't take them out quietly, and as I said before, gunplay has to be a last resort."

"Fall back and wait for their exit on the ground, follow them?"

"I don't think so. That would really be hit and miss. Since there were no vehicles in the parking area and none in front of the lobby, there's no way to know for certain where they will exfil…Luther, you copy?"

Baladur replied, "Copy, boss."

"Anything happening down there?"

"Everything is the same."

Remington paced, played back the video on the monitor attached to his arm, and shook his head in frustration.

They stood in silence for several minutes, the stairwell seeming to swell and condense at the same time, and then Remington said, "I have an idea…but it's pretty extreme."

Jake could not imagine what, in this instance, could be more extreme than a military drone, hacking access, and disabling surveillance, but said, "You know me, brother. In for a penny, in for a pound." He grinned. "Bring it."

"You got a flight suit in your gear bag?"

15

STANDING AT THE EDGE of the roof looking forty-seven stories down, Jake said, "Okay, bro…this *is* extreme. But I'm game if it's what you really want to do here."

"To be fair, I'll make it totally your call, no disrespect from me." Even in the darkness, Jake could see the laser intensity of his eyes, could feel the ardent appeal.

After only a brief pause, Jake replied, "I'll grant you, it is a solid plan. Let's do it."

Minutes ago, Remington had given Jake the cloned access card, instructing him to take the service elevator back down and retrieve another gear bag from the Jeep while he remained in the stairwell staking out the penthouse hallway with his CORE Under Door camera. During that time, nothing had changed in the hallway or, per Baladur's latest update, in the lobby. When Jake rejoined Remington in the stairwell of the forty-fourth floor, they had climbed the three levels up to the roof and begun looking for anchor points. The two floors directly below were taken up entirely by the club lounge and restaurant, but a quick look around at the crates of kitchen equipment and stacks of furnishings and islands of construction debris had ruled it out.

In the middle of the roof, scaffolding surrounded the helipad being built two stories above and set back from the club, the top level of which was open-aired with chest-high safety glass. But construction on it had only just started. Steel beams that trellised overhead and plunged down the side to the top of the lobby base would be a risky choice without knowing if they had been inspected for structural integrity. The beams were also only on the front of the building, not close enough to the penthouse unit with the two targets inside. The most "bombproof" anchors, when they had located them, were the obvious choice.

Rooftop tieback anchors are installed on most high-rise buildings for use by window washers and structural inspectors, and are also a go-to for emergency responders. OSHA compliant, they are made of steel capable of sustaining five thousand pounds, typically riser posts one to three feet in height with a cast loop top and set in a square baseplate bolted into concrete. Best of all, there are usually many of them, equally spaced around a roof's perimeter. As was the case with Angani, so after testing them to make sure they were fully set, Jake and Remington had quickly laid out the equipment from the bag Remington sent Jake to retrieve and gone to work.

Now they stood side by side in zip-up Nomex flight suits, Petzl harnesses snug around their groins and waists, Glocks tucked into snapped on holsters. They were strapped to two anchors each with two girth-hitched slings to each of those, redundancy being key for safety. Those were joined together with two locking screw gate carabiners, again, for redundancy. The girth hitches would self-tighten on the anchor points; the screw gate carabiners would lock down and tighten rather than loosen gates if they were somehow flipped upside down. "Screw down so you don't screw up" was the mnemonic instructors often used to drive home this practice.

"Ready?" Remington asked.

"Let's go hot," Jake said, and straddled the four-foot concrete parapet surrounding the rooftop.

They faced each other briefly, eyes meeting before swinging both of their legs over. Perched on the wall ledge, rain blowing into their faces, they slipped off and swung around to the building. And began their descent from over seven hundred feet, leaning back into space, held by ropes and anchors and links and the rigging of all, peering down into blackness and walking against the structure, easing the double rope through belays, one arm extended out for braking. At this height, the wind was more pronounced, causing them to veer back and forth and sometimes slam against the side as they descended. Thunder cracked and rain shelled their heads and faces, feeling like slivers of ice and streaking the window glass.

"Seriously?" Jake heard Remington say through his comm. "It *never* rains here this time of year!"

Jake grinned in the darkness.

They had roughly fifty feet to rappel which, under ideal conditions, wouldn't have taken more than a few minutes, but with the wind and the rain, they were forced to slow their rate of descent for the swaying ropes and wet surfaces. The plan was to enter the penthouse unit through the balcony, which extended from the master bedroom suite to the living area, and go in from the bedroom. They had discussed the contingencies and decided to play it fluidly; if they could take the targets without the hall guards being alerted, a call would be made for support, but if that was not possible, at the very least they could get a visual of Bái Zhuang and maybe even plant bugs or tracking devices. Either way, it would be a win. If the targets or hall guards got the draw on them, well, the luxury condo would probably need some drywall repairs.

A hefty gust of wind swung Jake halfway around and for a moment as he dangled, the lights of the city skyline shimmered through the mist, slashes of lightning casting electric spotlights that outlined other buildings from afar and the blackened landscape below, giving perspective to how high above the ground they were. From half a mile away the spired Britam Towers sparkled like a multicolored Christmas tree, a year prior heralded as the city's tallest at 656 feet. Angani Place was only one of several skyscrapers currently under construction that would significantly eclipse its height. He twisted back into position, the chilled air chaffing his nose and cheeks, fed more rope and continued down, the tips of his boots eventually touching the top edge of safety glass rimming the penthouse balcony. He tied off, looping the rope several times around his leg. Glancing to his left, he saw that Remington had reached the same point.

"On three," Jake said, got a nod from Remington, and on the count, they eased themselves over the glass panel, untied and unclipped, and stood on the balcony. Rain dripped from their hair and faces and trailed down their flight suits, puddling on the ceramic tile. Both removed gloves and drew their Glocks. Gazing at Remington, Jake could see the muscles in his neck rippling with anticipation, lines creased over his brow.

The interior lighting was dim and filtered through sheer white curtain panels partially drawn across the sliding glass entry doors to the living area and master bedroom suite. Remington stepped past Jake and tried the handle on the bedroom slider. When it held firm, he reached into a pocket and took out a small sleeve of lock picks, slipping a shove knife into the jamb and working the latch, then kneeling to spring another lock at the bottom. In seconds, he had both released and slid the door open. Jake followed him inside.

Given the overall unfinished state of the building, what they saw on entering was a surprise. Not only were the walls painted, the floors covered in hardwood, subdued lighting originating from recessed ceiling orbs—the room was fully furnished with a king-size bed, elegant furnishings, and art. But more surprising, in a vaguely disconcerting way, was the lack of any sound coming from the next room. It was absolutely quiet, no TV or music, no talk, no shuffle of movement.

They both froze, listening, but hearing nothing.

Remington took an articulating scope camera he had selected from his CORE kit when he'd been packing his pockets on the roof, attached it to the grip, and crept across the floor, new hardwoods creaking faintly with each tread. Jake was right behind him, eyes sweeping from side to side, arms extended and gun aimed along his sight line. Remington's breath seemed to be coming quicker and quicker as he positioned and repositioned the scope, and within a few moments he slowly advanced through the doorway, stopped, and let the hand holding camera and grip drop to his side. Coming up beside him, Jake saw what he saw—an empty room. Also fully finished and furnished, but empty.

Wordlessly, they entered the living and dining area, Jake moving out in front to canvas. He went swiftly from room to room, and returned to where Remington was standing with an expression as dazed and aghast as if he'd been slapped, his cheeks filling with color. He looked to Jake for confirmation of what he already knew.

"All clear," Jake said, adding, "hallway, too."

"What the hell?" His mouth went slack, his eyes full of conflicted thought, and then he spoke through his comm, again checking in with Baladur. "You're not seeing any movement in or outside of the lobby? No vehicles pull up or take off?"

"Negative," Baladur responded. "I do not see how they got out of there. I have been watching the entire time. Do you want me to drive around the building?"

Remington let out a frustrated groan. "No...no. Just stay put. We'll be down shortly." He glanced abstractedly around the condo. "Goddammit."

"Sorry, Remy," Jake said. "But let's at least give it a quick going over."

"Yeah, yeah," Remington muttered in disgust, and began a patrol through the living area, nothing seeming to be out of place or even touched, not a scrap of paper or pen or cigarette butt in an ashtray. No obvious sign of anyone having been there. Like the bedroom, the outfitters had spared no expense, top-tier European designers and high-end fabrics and finishes, original paintings and sculptures. The furniture was contemporary, Ikea-stylized with sectional sofa and cubed tables, scooped chairs, area rugs and pillows and art in grays and browns. "I know we didn't both imagine their presence in here."

"No, we didn't, and look—" Jake was in the kitchen, holding up a cardboard beverage container, dark orange with a brown lid and logo graphic of a smiling sun face. From Java House.

Remington came over and peered into the shiny stainless steel sink where another beverage container and a bag had been left. "Okay," he said, the corners of his mouth crinkling slightly. "That's something."

Jake stuffed the two containers in the bag and took it, following Remington back to the bedroom and watching as he glanced inside the walk-in closet and bath suite. "No clothes or personal items," he observed as Remington opened drawers and cabinets.

"Just for shit and giggles, I'm going to place a few bugs and then let's get out of here."

Jake waited while Remington implanted a half-dozen pea-size devices around the unit and then they returned to the balcony, reconnected to their ropes, reversing for the upward rappel to the rooftop. The wind had died down, the rain diminished to a random spray of sprinkles, as if the sky were wringing out the last of its aberrant shower.

*   *   *   *   *

AN HOUR AND A half later, around eleven o'clock, Jake sat in Remington's great room, freshly showered in Under Armour joggers and a cotton t-shirt, his feet bare, hair damp and combed back from his forehead. His eyes landed and lingered on a painting of elephants grouped around a watering hole, the textures created by brush and paint so tactile that he found himself immersed on an almost spiritual level.

Coming into the room, Remington commented, "I'm not much for art, but I love that piece more than I can say." He had also showered and changed into sweats.

"It's beautiful," Jake replied.

"Time for that Tennessee whiskey, my man. More than earned." He went to an antique mahogany sideboard, plucked Jack Daniel's from a collection of bottles and poured generous shots into two crystal tumblers. Handing one to Jake, he slumped into the suede chair next to him and raised his glass. "To less fucked up outcomes."

Jake acknowledged the toast and took a bracing first sip. The whiskey curled through him like a sun-heated wave over a storm-thrashed island, and suddenly he felt drained and exhausted, the jet lag catching up.

"Sorry for dragging you into all this tonight," Remington said.

"Nothing to apologize for, good to flush some adrenaline after all those hours on the plane. Just sorry it didn't go down like we hoped. We couldn't have missed them by much."

"Yeah, that was unbelievable. I'm thinking the lobby security guys might have told them about Luther coming in, and even though they seemed to accept his pretense, it could have caused the meeting to wrap up quickly. They clearly had a secure back way out. I guess that's why he's been a ghost...he's careful and cautious." Remington drank his whiskey down in one gulp, mouth rounding as it expanded through him. "Tonight does give me new leads to pursue. I doubt if the images we got are clear enough for good facial rec, but it's more than anyone has had. I'll do a deep dive on that condo, also on the building security guy, see if he's connected in any way or just facilitated for a nice chunk of change. If Zhuang was spooked, he'll most likely go back to ground, but if the condo turns out to be tied to him or Aljabarti, maybe I'll get something from those bugs."

Jake finished his drink and set the tumbler on the table between them. Remington got up, poured them another, and returned to his chair, leaning back to extend his arms and legs.

"About that," Jake said, his eyes lit with intrigue. "Where did all that black hat shit come from? I don't remember you as being particularly techie."

Remington smirked. "Oh, I'm not. But I have a guy working for me who is. He's brilliant and I'm glad he uses his powers for good, for me. His whole job is procurement of tech, weaponry, systems, everything available and a whole lot more that's not—like my Hornet drones. In fact, he's the one I gave our grocery list for your expedition."

"And he taught you all that hacking?"

Remington chuckled. "He did, and I have to say it's shameful how much I enjoy it. Security penetration is a substantial part of what I do, and most of the time, like tonight, it's ridiculously easy. Here's this ultra-modern, luxury building with supposedly state-of-the-art security, but in actuality, it's all old gen. There are much more impenetrable devices and systems, but most continue to opt for legacy technology which, as you saw, is easily breached by those with the tools and skills."

Jake stifled a yawn, glancing at his watch.

"Go...call her," Remington said. "Then get some rack, bud. I'll be dragging our asses out of bed at o-dark-thirty to head out."

A COOL BREEZE, SCENTED with the rain-moistened nectar of jasmine and aromatic oils of pine, drifted through a partially open window, ruffling the gauzy white fabric draped over the four-poster bed. The room was large but cozy in an old-world traveler kind of way, with a wooden chest trimmed in leather and tarnished brass, a vintage dresser with a porcelain pitcher of white calla lilies, and a carved French writing desk with an antique globe and cloth-bound volumes of a half-dozen books by early African explorers. Stripped to briefs and t-shirt, Jake sat cross-legged in the middle of the big bed, his iPhone in hand as it dialed and displayed *calling Callie...*

After several ring cycles, a motion-blurred image appeared, as if flipped or dropped or both, before finally revealing her flustered face. Gasping, she said, "Sorry, Jake…I haven't done this before."

He smiled, feeling his chest constrict at the first sight and sound of her. "It's okay, love, you'll get the hang of it, although it might be a while before I can do FaceTime again. It's late here, got in this morning but I've been busy with Remy all day. I just wanted to call and let you know that I got here safe and sound."

"I'm glad to know that," she said, self-consciously brushing at her hair, dropping her head.

"Is everything okay? Has it been a good day? It's what, about two-thirty there?"

There was a hesitation as she was clearly trying to conjure something encouraging to tell him. "Yes, good," was all she could manage. Strained, he thought, manifesting the brave front.

When she looked shakily into the phone, her cheekbones seemed more gaunt than he recalled from the day before. She was wearing a white top with yellow and pink flowers, ruffled sleeves and collar loose around her arms and neck. Her skin had the pallor of rice paper, and earlier he'd read a text from Camilla saying: *Callie no está comiendo, qué quieres que haga?* Not eating. He noticed that she was sitting on the bed.

"Hey," he said lightly, "go outside and enjoy the sunshine for a little while, okay? I promise it will make you feel better."

"I…yes, okay…I was just a little tired today."

"Understand. Put on plenty of sunscreen and rest by the pool with one of those big umbrellas. I asked Camilla to make you some smoothies."

"Okay."

In an effort to keep it light, he spent a few minutes telling her about the Gulfstream and Remy's ranch and his dogs, but he found it hard to stay the course. The little tremble of her lip, the quick flick of her eyelashes, the intake of breath, all caught in his throat like a bubble that could not escape. He heaved a sigh that seemed to drain the well of his emotions in one pull of a plug, wanting to hold onto the connection, however tenuous, but knowing he had to end it quickly or he would not sleep.

"I love you, Callie."

"I love you, Jake," she said, her words struggling through a breaking damn of tears. "Be safe."

"I will, sweetie." He touched his fingers to his lips.

Disconnecting, he set an alarm on his phone and placed it on the nightstand, turned off the lamp, and stretched out beneath the bed covers. The mattress was comfortable, the breeze refreshing, the sonata of night sounds outside his window soothing. But sleep did not come right away. Thoughts of Callie would not leave him easily, but as the minutes ticked away and fatigue settled in, he found his mind circling back to the airspace he was now occupying. Ever since the initial call from Falcone and Niles—and especially during the subsequent call with gunfire in the background—he'd had the feeling he was at the edge of a tripwire. Tomorrow he would be stepping over it, thrust into the vortex of whatever it was, his gut already telling him it was far more than the mission he had taken on.

16

CALLIE SAT ON THE bed, gripping her phone tightly, breath finally slowing some five minutes or so after the call from Jake. She had been laying on the bed, hovering on the edge of sleep when the ringing iPhone jolted her up in disoriented alarm. A scramble to get the phone off the nightstand sent it flying in the air before she had it in hand and found the button to tap, framing Jake's smiling face. Seeing him, hearing his voice, brought a surge of emotion that was an equal blend of joy and sorrow, and the entirety of the brief call was wrought with the struggle to maintain composure, to not come apart.

Now that it had ended, the tears came in a torrent, streaming until her eyes were cried out, her lungs raw. The reality of Jake being gone burrowed deeper, the grim possibility that he might not return sinking in. She could not imagine a world without him in it, without him making everything all right.

After Jake's departure the previous day, the remainder of the morning and afternoon had passed in a dizzying blur. Camilla left her to rest until dinnertime, when she implored Callie to come downstairs for supper. Too nauseated to eat, Callie sat at the table looking forlornly at a plate of salad as Jesse Segura checked in, his lifeguard shift done. He told them he was going to shower and eat and then take a walk around the grounds, reminding Callie to call him if she needed anything. The pool man, whose name was Ramón Cárdenas, also looked in, offering to hang around a little while longer if Callie wanted to come out for an early-evening swim. Like Segura, he was young and fit and happily purpose-ful, his head always bobbing to some tune playing through his Beats earbuds. She had thanked him but politely declined. Camilla cleared the dishes, gazing dispiritedly at Callie's untouched plate, and offered to stay the night or at least until Callie felt comfortably tucked in. Callie thanked her also, and said she'd be fine. The housekeeper gave her a long hug, collected her things, and departed.

And then Callie was alone in the villa, again.

Ascending the stairs, she felt anxiety gnawing its way from the pit of her stomach into her chest, felt her pulse and heartbeat accelerating, hands quivering, gait unsteady. After undressing and putting on pajama shorts and tank top, she opened the French doors to the terrace and stood listening to the somnolence of the waves in the growing darkness, the distance of their reach softened to a whisper on the breeze. A waning gibbous moon cast silver-white light over the water, winking in the swells. She heard the chimes' sweet melody and the hush of air flowing through the palms and trees. Slowly, she began to relax. She climbed into bed and watched the blades of the ceiling fan wind in rhythmic ro-tations, followed the flicker of their shadows across the walls, something that, ironically, soothed her before falling asleep but often frightened her on waking before daylight.

But without Jake, she could not close her eyes. The now primal fear of all things nocturnal cloaked every thought, stirring the brew of wor-ries about storms and nightmares and unfathomable horrors. So she lay awake, gazing at the space unoccupied by Jake, trying to hold him in the forefront of her mind as sentry against the night terrors. When she felt a spike of panic from a shadow or a sound—a swishing in the treetops near the windows or a rush of wind across the terrace—she'd reach for her iPhone and play Jake's message, often multiple times, and his voice calmed her. As terrified as she was of falling asleep, the days and weeks of cumulative exhaustion were thickening around her like layers of con-crete, the heaviness of her eyes and dull ache in her head drawing her into a hallucinatory haze.

But she fought it with everything she had…because of the dreams, afraid that one of them might not let her escape.

They were all unimaginably horrible, horrifically real, invaded with hundreds of crawling things on every inch of her flesh, biting and sting-ing, of tunnels into blackness with a surround of shrieks and growls and grunts. But it was the monster who lurked in the darkest recesses of her nights, his evil anvil eyes and vile sneering mouth and all the violation he'd inflicted, a frenzied battering ram inside her, that she most feared in her dreams.

The hours of darkness seemed endless, but eventually the pale creep of dawn began and the air was still, the sounds of nature muffled in tran-sition. And it had not stormed. It was a new day.

Callie had wearily gotten out of bed and headed for the bath suite, stopped in front of the shower. It was open and inviting, the coppery travertine tile gleaming in the early-morning sun that beamed through the high window. There was no reason, no reason at all, that she couldn't just turn the water on and step right in, feel the cascade over her, the warmth, the steam, the suds of the bodywash that smelled like freshly cut flowers. But just putting one foot tentatively over the edge sent a peal of panic rippling from head to toe, and she quickly withdrew it. She stood for a long time, trying to work up the courage to try again, rush in and turn the water on before she could think about it. Tears welled and slid down her face—why couldn't she do this?

It was not the same bathroom, not the one in the bedroom she'd first occupied in the villa; it was *their* bathroom, where only the two of them had been. But she still experienced flashes of what had happened in the other one: the sudden presence of men in black, their rough hands on her, jabbing something sharp into her neck, and then, some undefinable time later, she was gone from the villa, gone from Costa Rica, with every terrible thing that followed.

She sat on the top ledge of the step-up tub and splashed water from the bronze faucet over herself, lathering soap and rinsing it off, sham-pooing and conditioning and rinsing her hair. By the time she had finished, toweling off and dressing, she was drained with the effort, but she knew if she didn't go downstairs for breakfast, Camilla would come get her. She scrunched fingers through her damp curls and left the bedroom.

As expected, Camilla greeted her cheerily with coffee and a plate of eggs with fruit and toast. Callie drank the coffee, which momentarily

rejuvenated but then soured in her stomach. Over Camilla's docile protests, she made her way back upstairs and, for a while, watched the
gardeners and pool man from the terrace, feeling fatigued and queasy.
The first day and night had passed interminably, and Jake was probably
going to be gone for a long time, she thought dismally. She would have
to find a way to get through the nights and navigate the days. She'd done
it the last time, reading, writing, walking along the beach. But the sense
of normalcy and ease that had eventually settled into those days did not
seem remotely possible now. She looked down at the aqua brilliance of
the pool, Ramón Cárdenas sweeping a long-handled skimmer through
the water. He glanced up and gave her a wave, the action causing the
pair of gardeners, Estabon Mina and Mauricio Leguizano, to look up and
wave also. They all smiled and went back to work, Cárdenas bopping to
an upbeat song as he dredged flower petals and leaves and bits of grass
from the pool, Mina and Leguizano wiping perspiration from their faces
as they weeded and raked around vegetation.

She went back to the bed, sitting and then dropping onto it, so over-
whelmingly tired, thinking that if she closed her eyes in the daytime,
maybe that wasn't really sleeping.

And then Jake had called.

CAMILLA TAPPED LIGHTLY ON the door before entering. "Miss
Callie," she called, her voice soft and songful. She peered around the
corner of the bedroom foyer and saw Callie curled up on top of the bed,
sound asleep. *"Ay mi dulce niña."* She glanced at the tall glass in her
hands, filled to the brim with frosty pink froth, and said, "Okay…*hasta
luego.*"

Before retreating, she strolled to the terrace, debating whether to
close the French doors. The surf was pacifying, but the breeze seemed
to be picking up, the chimes clanging below. She looked out over the
ocean, noting the capping waves and gunmetal clouds gathering on the
horizon, the sky behind them an ominous oyster-gray.

17

JAKE STOOD ON THE patio, watching the sun come up over the Ngong Hills, the dark outlines of trees and slopes backlit by sky the color of a blood orange. As it crested the peaks, yellow-gold light washed over the valleys, the air filled with amber mist and birdsong that trilled and twittered like a flautist's scale. The moment had the serenity of an impressionist painting or a Debussy composition, until the Belgian Malinois dogs exploded through the doors behind him, their toenails scraping stone as they cleared the patio and hit the yard at a full gallop, exuberant barks sharp in the crisp cool air. Dew and moisture from the previous evening's rain sprang from the grass in their wake.

Remington laughed. "Obedience pretty much goes off the rails first outing of the morning."

Extending his arm, Jake said, "With that out there, don't blame 'em." He was dressed in fresh khakis, shaved and groomed, sipping coffee from a tan mug etched with the brown graphic of an elephant head that was the *Habari* logo.

Filling his own mug from the pot of coffee Issa Lusalah had put on the patio table, Remington came abreast of Jake and shared his appreciation of the view. They were quiet for several minutes, absorbed in thought, and then Remington asked, "What's her name?"

Jake held his silence for a long moment, as if the query required a certain permission be granted, and then his countenance tempered. "Callie," he replied.

"Short for…?"

Again, a brief hesitation. "Caledonia."

Remington studied his face, saw the latent protectiveness and guarded emotion. Jake slipped his phone from a pocket in his cargo pants, tapped and swiped to the photo taken on the deck of the sailboat. Remington smiled, eyes soft with reverence. "Oh, man."

Jake put his phone away but said nothing.

Remington's smile flattened, his expression sobering. "Did you leave an envelope for me?"

Jake peered into his empty coffee mug, sucked in a gritty breath. "Yeah." The envelope to which Remington referred had been prepared back in Dominical, the night before Jake had left. It contained a letter along with specific information, including instructions for making contact with, and notification to, Callie.

Coffee was refilled and they watched the dogs romping across the vast span of grass, vividly green and glistening, dew and rain beaded like tiny rhinestones. Eventually, Remington gave a shrill whistle and the frolicking dogs froze as if a wizard's wand had zapped them with a spell, heads raising on their necks. "Luna, Solis…*hier,*" he commanded, and his canines came trotting back to the patio.

AFTER BREAKFAST, REMINGTON AND Jake walked about thirty yards past the barn housing his war room, to a second one where, Jake noticed Chilemba had parked the sage-colored Range Rover. Like the first, this barn was heavily reinforced and secured by multiple layers of security, the most obvious being a biometric scanner by the entrance. But it had already been accessed, the wide double doors propped open. Just inside, Chilemba was avidly watching another man who was looking over a meticulously packed pallet of gear that resembled an interlocking Chinese block puzzle.

"Good morning, boss!" Chilemba said, his face bright with anticipation. He wore a collared red shirt printed with big blue flowers and navy slacks, his smile broad and unrelenting.

Jake's gaze went past Chilemba and the other man, to the interior of the barn, his eyes riveted, mouth open in astonishment. "Holy shit,

Remy."

Like the first barn, every wall had built-in shelves and storage, but this was of a specialized kind, made of heavy-gauge steel with perforated panels encasing row upon row of modular racks and slots and drawers. Secured in the lockers, in mass quantities, were arms and ammunitions of every conceivable category and make: pistols and revolvers and shotguns, sniper rifles and carbines, submachine guns and launchers. There was also every manner of tactical gear: vests and armor; holsters and belts; packs and supplies; optics and communications; parachutes and tents; knives and tools. The rear of the barn took it to a whole other dimension. It was a hybrid of research lab, mechanic's garage, engineering test ground, and Silicon Valley server room, with tables full of circuitry and wiring, nuts and bolts, wrenches and screwdrivers and drills, gadgets and components in varying states of build. There was a ballistics lab and a welding bench and a shatterproof simulator space. The shelves in this rear area housed equipment both familiar and technologically avant-garde. Jake had never seen anything quite like it, certainly not outside of high-caliber military installations.

The man overseeing the stacked gear stood, clipboard in hand. He was slender, with neat brown hair and lightly tinted glasses, dressed in jeans and a *Habari* t-shirt. There was a technological vibe about him, but his deportment was anything but demure.

Remington said, "Jake, this is my black hat guy, Efron Kipnis."

Extending his hand to Jake, he said, "Hey, good to meet you."

"Efron was recruited from the Israeli Defense Force by the Mossad for his *special* skills…and then he was recruited from Mossad for me." He smiled slyly. "I have sources everywhere." He looked at Kipnis. "We good to go?"

"You are. Everything on the list." A trace of a smile crinkled at the corners of his mouth. "Plus a few other things I thought might come in handy."

"Okay, then. Chile, let's load up and hit the road."

In short order, the gear and Jake's bags were packed into the Range Rover's rear cargo and they were off to Wilson Airport, taking the same route they had the previous night Magadi and Langata roads—which were quickly becoming congested with morning commuter traffic, something Remington had intended to avoid with a pre-dawn departure from the ranch. While they had both been up and ready to go, a series of calls problem-solving his upcoming UN summit gig kept Remington embroiled just long enough to push breakfast and the drive to the airport past daybreak. Despite the setback, Chilemba's frequent use of the opposing lane and road shoulders to bypass slower moving vehicles got them through the rural section fairly quickly; when there was no oncoming traffic, he simply drove in their lane. With the commercial proliferation in Ongata Rongai and the stream of *matatus* joining the flow, they hit several grinding snarls, but as they approached the southwestern edge of Nairobi National Park, traffic began to move again—particularly when Chilemba took the Range Rover hurtling along the dirt track parallel to much of the road.

Jake watched the roadside scenery sweep by his window, merchants opening markets and shops, donkey carts clopping down the sideways, mothers and fathers scuttling small children off to school. Low clouds clumped a pale, stonewashed-blue sky, the banks of trees edging the park tall and dense. He tried to keep his mind in a neutral space as Remington made and fielded calls, making on-the-fly adjustments to surveillance and security for the summit, but found himself unusually preoccupied with speculation about what lay ahead. He had never been especially anxious about deploying for an op of any kind, did not feel apprehensive about the risks or perils, or about death. With his contentious childhood, time in the military, and work as a contractor which—in many ways, was more inherently dangerous—he had long come to terms with the prospect and heightened odds of his mortality. Came with the territory he'd signed up for. But for the first time, if he was being honest with himself, he did feel an undertow of anxiety. Because for the first time in his life, he had someone he could not imagine leaving his skin or the earth for.

They merged onto the multilane stretch of Langata and crossed over the Southern Bypass, going through Uhuru Garden and Nairobi Dam Estate, the most crowded span of the drive, and wound their way to the airport entrance.

Consulting the screen of his phone, Remington said, "Forty-five minutes in rush hour, not bad. Crushed it, Chile!"

Beaming with pride, Chilemba continued to the airfield.

Wilson Airport, though primarily a regional hub with an emphasis on private charters for tourists and businesses and aid organizations, also handles international flights, and as they drove past the mélange of hangars—some brightly painted and graphically detailed, others bare and ramshackle and sagging—planes of every size and variety crowded the tarmac, looking like a flock of seabirds posturing for feeding territory. Pulling up beside a single-engine Cessna, Chilemba hopped out and opened the Range Rover's passenger doors for Remington and Jake. Luther Baladur was already there, standing next to the plane in conversation with a man wearing olive-green slacks and a khaki shirt. Had it not been for the captain's stripes on his shoulders, the man could have been mistaken for a musician in a reggae band. He was lean with a carefree demeanor, hair braided into dreadlocks and beaded on the ends. As he spoke, his hands moved as if he were orchestrating a soundtrack for the meaning behind his words.

Remington introduced him as Keanjaho Dmello and had already briefed Jake on his background which, like Baladur's, included time in the military. Dmello was Kenyan and had served in their Air Force, where he'd flown everything from Cessnas for reconnaissance to Bombadiers for transport and even Bell and Airbus helicopters. Greetings dispensed, Dmello informed them the plane was fueled and ready to go, and went to help Chilemba load their gear.

Before boarding, Jake drew Remington aside and gave him an emphatic embrace. "Thank you for everything, brother. I don't know anyone else who could have put all this together for me so quickly and completely."

"Hey, it's what I do," he replied blithely, "but of course I would be at your disposal. Just wish I was free to accompany you, but hopefully I'll be available in a few days if you need me, and you might. The intel that Kipnis got this morning indicates that nothing has changed on the ground in Dungu. I've instructed these guys to have your six."

"Thanks, Remy," Jake said, and smiled at his friend as he backpedaled a few steps, adding "give those good doggies an extra treat tonight." Turning, he boarded the Cessna and strapped in beside Baladur, flashing a thumbs-up to Remington through his window.

Dmello completed his pre-flight and, with clearance from the control tower, they were lined up for takeoff from runway 32, Pratt & Whitney turboprop whistling as it rose in pitch and power. On the nose, a three-blade McCauley propeller spun into a shadowy blur. Soon they were rolling and lifting and climbing through the clouds, a white radiance of sun emerging on the other side.

CAMILLA HAD BEEN FOLDING clothes in the laundry room downstairs when she thought she heard thunder. The room was just below the kitchen and dining area, on the other side of the space Jesse Segura now occupied, and one of the only places in the residence without windows. The dryer was still running, tumbling a load of towels, which muffled most extraneous sound.

Her mind was on Callie who, physically, mentally, and emotionally, was hanging by a thread, and her concern was growing by the hour. Camilla cared for her immensely, as she would have a child or sister, of which she had neither, and she considered Jake family. She had known him and Haskell Delaney for many years, tending the villa for Delaney from the first day he'd taken ownership, and now, for Jake. Working for Delaney had been a gratifying experience and he was wonderful to her, but she could not even begin to quantify how blessed she felt with Jake. It was a much deeper connection, a blend of fondness, respect, and trust. He regarded her and the rest of the staff not as servants, but as members of the household, and for that and many other reasons, she was pretty sure any of them would walk on hot coals for him; she knew she would.

And then there was Callie. She had watched Jake become infatuated with her, and then smitten, and finally swept past the point of no return. Shy, sweet, beautiful Callie had never had a chance, and Jake, Camilla thought, was the man God created for her. She loved them both unconditionally, so when Jake had asked if she would consider working every day until he returned, she had not even hesitated and took the enormous responsibility he had entrusted in her with the utmost gravity.

Camilla Orellana Márquez's life outside the villa was mostly one of modest independence. A widow for more than a decade, she had lost her husband to a brain aneurysm, and though she'd dated a few men in recent years, she remained uncommitted. This place, these two, were her primary focus.

At first, she thought the rumble was the dryer, and she continued sorting and folding, her mind knotted with the dilemma of what to fix for dinner that Callie might eat. But when she opened the dryer door, its steady thrum stopping, she heard the percussive sounds more distinctly and hurriedly stuffed the towels into her laundry basket. Thumping up the steps to the kitchen, she was alarmed to find it and the connected living area immersed in blue darkness. A strident clap of thunder seemed to crack right over the roof, followed by a sequence of lightning flashes that strobed the interior with flare-like intensity and then a resonating boom. She dropped the laundry basket and ran to the stairway, chest heaving as she clambered to the top.

She went straight to the master bedroom, where she'd left Callie sleeping not more than an hour earlier. In the moment, it did not even occur to her that the door had been only slightly ajar and now it was all the way open. "Miss Callie?" she called as she entered, the room steeped in the same deep blue light, her eyes going immediately to the bed.

Callie was not on it.

Thunder rolled in a drumbeat with regular crashing crescendos and she could hear wind and rain from the open terrace doors. She strode to them, stuck her head out and looked in all directions. The terrace was empty, rain splattering and pooling on the tile. She pulled the doors closed, latched them, and continued into the bath suite, but did not find Callie there, either. Her alarm began to escalate as she explored every part of the room, even kneeling to look under the bed, thinking of Callie's terror of storms. She checked the large walk-in closet, poking around clothes hanging from the racks.

"Callie?"

Heart thudding, Camilla took her search to the rest of the upstairs, canvassing the two other bedrooms and another bathroom. Looking under beds, looking in closets, looking everywhere. Still no sign of Callie, she raced back down the stairs and combed the entire floor. Now on the verge of hysteria, she peered through the kitchen windows and saw the pool man and gardeners watching the rain from under a patio umbrella. She opened one of the French doors.

"Has visto a la señorita Callie? No la encuentro en casa!"

All three turned at the sound of her voice, which had gone shrill with panic.

"Qué? No esta ahi?"

They darted over, their heads ducked against the downpour, Ramón Cárdenas telling Camilla that they had all just returned to the patio after getting their tools and supplies out of the rain, into storage around the side of the villa. She asked how long they'd been away from the pool area and the grounds beyond it. Maybe fifteen or twenty minutes was their response.

The thunder was getting louder, wind gnashing through the trees and whipping palm fronds back and forth. Rain swept across the patio like an oscillating sprinkler, coming from one direction and then collapsing back upon itself in the other.

Camilla's hands clutched her head at the temples, eyes wide and distraught. *"Oh Dios mío! Oh Dios mío!"*

The gardeners, Estabon Mina and Mauricio Leguizano, tried to console her, Cárdenas saying they would search every inch of the property. Before she could ask or say anything else, they took off in a sprint, each in a different direction. Camilla stood in the doorway for a moment, unsure of what to do, and then she stepped back into the villa and began going room to room again, upstairs and downstairs, calling Callie's name. This could not have happened again, she told herself frantically, it just could not.

She returned to hold vigil by the French doors, hugging herself and murmuring a litany of prayers, tears filling her eyes.

WHEN THE SUN ROSE over Nakalé on the morning of their second day in the village, Falcone and Niles had been more than ready to move on and really ready to reunite with Jake. Had, in fact, been packed up and waiting in the field when the helicopter set down in the haze of dust and golden light, running to help unload the goods procured for their hosts. Excited villagers swarmed the landing zone, accepting and carrying off bags of rice and soya beans, containers of cooking oil and utensils, bed mats and blankets, gardening tools and crates of medical supplies, many of them taking up a celebratory musical chant.

Falcone and Niles delivered a last box to an eager young man who gushed his thanks. Even in his Lingala or Zande language, the translation was clear by the huge smile on his face. They returned his smile, shook his hand, watched him trot gleefully toward the village's communal area, and picked up their bags.

They turned to each other and Niles asked, "What should we do?"

Twenty yards in front of them, the Dauphin's engines had powered up, the rotors were turning, the pilots looking in their direction, waiting.

"Our last message to Jake was we'd be in Dungu today," Falcone said. "We have no way to tell him otherwise, so I say we go."

Niles thought about it for a moment, his gray eyes clouded with fretful equivocation, then nodded in agreement.

They headed for the helicopter, eddy from the spinning blades sending specks of dirt into their perspiring faces, hair blown back, clothing pressed flat against their skin.

Minutes later, hundreds of arms raised in jubilant farewell, waving as the Dauphin lifted into a sky with the pert blue of emergent day, banking toward the southeast. Crowns of the trees rolled like waves of a deep green sea in the downdraft as it passed over, and then, from somewhere within them, a blast. Instantly, perhaps six hundred feet above, another, the silver bird canting sideways, clouds of gray and then black smoke puffing and billowing as it spun in a kind of slow-motion unwinding. Rotors still spinning, the Dauphin spiral-floated back to the ground, and exploded.

THE FLIGHT TO THE Congo aboard the Cessna took much of the same trajectory as the Gulfstream in reverse, even if with dramatically less flair, passing over Mount Suswa and the northern edge of Lake Victoria. On the latter, however, the small plane was able to do something the high-powered jet was not; about 150 miles out, pilot Keanjaho Dmello momentarily dropped from his ten-thousand-mile altitude to one low enough to showcase a spectacular sight, saying, "I know we are on a serious mission, but I could not let you miss this." As they had approached the airspace over Homa Bay County, another pilot radioed the heads-up and Dmello adjusted his course to go directly over a small crater lake a few kilometers off the large one. A thousand feet below, the eastern shore of Lake Simbi Nyaima was awash with a fluttery pink tide, thousands of flamingos flocking together in a perfect outline of the land. It was as if a flotilla of rose petals were clinging to the banks, moving with the currents of air and sea.

Captivated, Jake took several pictures with his iPhone as Baladur told him about the legend of the lake, its name meaning "the village that sank." According to local folklore, residents refused to shelter an unsightly old woman who sought food and refuge from a storm, the consequence of which was monumental flooding that formed the lake and eradicated the village. "They also believe the lake has healing powers," Baladur recounted, "and it is one of only a few places in the world you can see these beautiful birds, and only a few times a year. It is truly incredible that we are seeing them right now. With the ways we have changed the environment, they are appearing less and less."

The rest of the flight took them three hundred miles over Uganda and Lake Albert into the DRC, where they put down briefly in Bunia to clear customs and top off fuel. Like the Keoghs, Remington had also facilitated clearances, though through very different channels, so they were able to continue on with minimal delay. Flying over vast expanses of forested terrain, Jake was reminded of the inconceivable gauntlet he would face in this mission and, admittedly, he was not optimistic. Even so, he intended to give it his all, as he did with each and every mission he took on. What did give him a measure of reassurance was the level of professionalism and expertise both of Remington's guys possessed. Conversing with them during the flight, he learned that their military backgrounds were impressive, that both had served in Afghanistan, among other theaters, and both made it to officer ranks in their respective branches. They knew weapons and equipment, they knew methods and maneuvers, and they were multilingual.

On final approach to the Dungu airport, Dmello was engaged in what Jake interpreted as intense conversation about the ground situation. He heard Dmello, speaking in French, tell someone that diverting was not an option. Turning to Jake, Dmello said, "I am speaking to another pilot who is telling me we might want to divert, but I told him we must land in Dungu. He said he could not say whether there is conflict at the airport itself, but when he flew over the city, there were mobs with rioting and some areas on fire."

"Okay, do what you have to do," Jake said grimly, "but I have to get in there to get my guys and the clients."

"Then that is the plan," Dmello replied, "we will be landing momentarily." He began the descent, lining up with the dirt strip runway, dividing his attention between the Garmin avionics and the landscape below.

Jake and Baladur kept watch through opposite windows, searching the ground for any sign of trouble. So far, it appeared that they were clear for landing. Both had retrieved their handguns from the rear cargo and handed Dmello his. The Cessna coasted over treetops and set down on the strip with a jarring bounce, slowing and rolling bumpily to the end. Dmello turned the plane and taxied back to the airport access point, pulling up in front of a hangar. All three checked their weapons, tucked them in at their waists, and prepared to exit the plane. Jake glanced at his watch as he stepped off, noting that it was just past 12:30.

AS SOON AS THEY emerged from the plane, a man puttered over on a motorbike, welcoming them and introducing himself; he was with Frères de l'Instruction Chrétienne, Brothers of Christian Instruction. He wore dark slacks, a lemon-and-lime floral shirt, scholarly glasses, and a benevolent smile. He shook hands with Jake, then Baladur and Dmello, and some small talk was exchanged between them in French. The man, Brother Lucien Gauthier, waited while another man appeared from within the open-front hangar, clipboard in hand, and talked briefly with Dmello who signed some documents and paid the landing fee.

Dmello said, "We are under the impression that there are tensions in the city."

"This is true," Gauthier admitted, "but things are peaceful around our compound. Is there anything we can assist you with?"

"Actually, yes," Jake replied. He looked to the man from the hangar. "We're here to pick up some folks. Do you know of any waiting, where we might find them?"

The man from the hangar shook his head. "I have been here all morning and yours is the first plane to land today."

"Okay, maybe yesterday? Would have been a helicopter."

"Sorry, no. But we can go inside, make some inquiries on the radio."

Jake, Baladur, and Dmello went with him into the A-framed bricked hangar which was the operating base for Avions Sans Frontières, going into a small office where a young man sat at a desk. They spent the next few minutes listening as he made contact with the UN airport on an HF radio, about six miles northeast of town. After some back-and-forth transmissions, the UN airport could only report that they were not aware of any civilian air traffic at their base. Gauthier, who had been standing by just inside the hangar entrance, motioned to them.

Stepping outside, they followed him to his motorbike, which he straddled and started. It was an older Senke, red paint dulled with age, but it had been well cared for and its engine had a healthy rumble. "Please, make yourselves welcome in our midst. If we may be of any further assistance, we are happy to help." He pointed past the exterior of a large bricked complex across from the hangar, which he identified as Institut Wando, a secondary school of the seminary.

"*Merci beaucoup, Frère* Gauthier," Jake said.

Gauthier waved and rode off through the trees from which he'd come, rounding the corner at the end of the school and disappearing from view. Walking the same way, they found a grassy soccer field edged by trees. Fronting the mission compound, it stood vacant, the narrow dirt road around it devoid of people or vehicles.

"Well, it is certainly peaceful here," Baladur observed.

They had strolled the length of the soccer field when Jake's sat phone rang. He stopped to answer, Baladur and Dmello seeking shade from the sweltering sun under a cluster of palm trees. Recognizing Remington's number, Jake pushed the button to connect, uncapping the bottle of water he'd brought from the plane, upturning it to drink, his head tilted back. Above, the sky was hard and flat, as intensely blue in the midday heat as a propane flame. For a moment, it was oddly quiet.

"Hey Remy," Jake said, "we just landed, and—"

He listened, his face going rigid and draining of color. Then he removed the Iridium from his ear and just stood, his gaze fixed on some indeterminate point in space.

"Jake? What is it?" Baladur asked. Sensing something wrong, both he and Dmello had come up beside him.

Jake could not say anything, his head roaring with a noise like grinding gears. Baladur asked again, but it was as if the words were formed in a soundless vacuum, coming from a shapeless face with lips opening and closing.

Finally, still as expressionless as a stone, Jake said, "A helicopter was shot down in a village about sixty kilometers from here." He swallowed, his throat tight.

In an instant, he felt an exhumation of his recent past, what he had just lived, felt and saw Delaney before him—his enchanting and fraudulently smiling face— there and then blowing up, taking everything of him and their friendship to some forever place. Saw Falcone and Niles, living and laughing, fighting alongside him, trusting him and giving him everything of themselves.

The vacuum was loud and raw and wrapped him in a shroud of live wires.

He said, "Remy says it was a Eurocopter."

PART TWO

IN A FIELD OF MUD AND BONE

18

MINUTES PASSED WITHOUT ANYONE uttering a word; Baladur and Dmello didn't know Jake well enough to know how to react, what to say or do after hearing such potentially devastating news. Jake finally moved, turning in one direction and then another, his face a blank slate. But a determination was brimming in his dark eyes, and when he spoke his voice had regained its authoritative timbre. He swigged the remainder of his water, twisted the cap back on the bottle, and crushed it in his hand.

"Remy said he was trying to get specific intel, so until we know more, let's keep going."

Baladur and Dmello exchanged dubious looks, Baladur replying, "Okay, Jake. Why don't we go to the mission, see what other calls we can make."

"Yes, let's do that." Jake was eying the road on the other side of the soccer field. "Then maybe we'll head into town."

As they reversed direction, Jake's mind was beginning to thaw out a jumbled block of frozen thoughts and emotions. The incredulity that it could have happened again, that he could lose someone—two people— to whom he'd grown close; the trickle of an anguish that he could not yet allow himself to feel. Part of him was taking a defiant stand on the side of pragmatic reservation, of waiting for fully confirmed facts. But another part of him, one that was threatening to override that hidden hope in abeyance, was reeling with the pending reality. Pausing near the corner, Jake gazed at the mission building, debating his next course of action and thinking there really wasn't an obvious one.

Grappling with his thoughts, he became aware of a familiar buzzing overhead, looked up and spotted a plane, another Cessna, bright white against the brilliant blue sky, sun winking off the wings as it descended on a trajectory toward the airport. No one had to say anything, their feet shuffling into a synchronized gait back to the hangar, where they stood and watched the single-engine Cessna bounce onto the airstrip and roll to a stop in a spume of dust. It turned and taxied to the grass apron, just as they had done less than an hour ago. A young pilot emerged from the cockpit and strode to the other side of the plane, glancing curiously at their Cessna parked near the hangar.

Jake's eyes followed the pilot, half-expecting him to open the airstair door and then see Falcone and Niles spring out and bound around the back of the plane with the Keoghs on their heels. But of course that did not happen. Instead, the pilot unloaded and stacked boxes that took up every cubic inch of the cargo space. He heard the man from the hangar call out, *"Bonjour,* Laurent! *Avez-vous fait un bon vol?"*

They conversed briefly, and at one point both looked in Jake's direction. The pilot nodded and walked over to Jake, Baladur, and Dmello. He was in his late-thirties, slim and fit, wavy brown hair lightened by the sun, wearing a traditional pilot's uniform with captain's epaulets on the shoulders of his white shirt. Grasping Jake's hand, he said, "I'm Laurent Pelletier, *Avions Sans Frontières.* I hear that you're looking for people who should have already arrived in Dungu?"

Jake said, "Yes, but"—his voice dropped as if the breath forming it had evaporated—"things are not looking good." He conveyed the report they had received, adding that they intended to pursue every possibility until they had final confirmation.

"I understand," Pelletier replied, "and I would do the same." He paused thoughtfully. "You know, with everything going on in the city, it's entirely possible your group could have slipped by at the UN airport. I don't want to get your hopes up, but it's something to consider at least."

While they were talking, a Toyota LandCruiser drove up, white turned nearly tan by road dust, the green TSF crest barely visible on the side. The tall, broad-limbed man who extricated himself from the tight space behind the wheel saw Jake studying the logo and said, "I almost taped it over this morning. We're not exactly popular at the moment."

"So I've heard," Jake replied.

Introductions were once again exchanged, and Laurent Pelletier filled the driver in on Jake's situation. The man, whose name was Santu Bilenga, said, "While it is not the best time for a drive through the city, you are welcome to come along. Once I drop these supplies off at the clinic, I can take you up to the UN airport for a look around, then bring you back here."

"That would be great, and much appreciated," Jake replied, and thought, *certainly better than just hanging out and hoping.*

AFTER HELPING BILENGA LOAD up his vehicle, they all piled in, maneuvering around the soccer field to the road going into town. Heading west and adjacent to the Kibali River, passing through grass and scrub and strings of palm trees, Bilenga told them about *Avions Sans Frontières*. He explained that they were often mistaken for the more widely known Aviation Sans Frontières, the French-founded equivalent of *Médecins Sans Frontières*—Doctors Without Borders—but were, in fact, established by the Brothers of Christian Instruction to help the underserved region of Haut-Uélé in the DRC.

"As you probably know, Dungu has been ravaged by the LRA for years, and while it has gotten better recently, allowing the town to build up and prosper, they continue to come under attack. But the presence of the brotherhood and other missions, like the MAF, Mission Aviation Fellowship, has been a game-changer in their survival of the LRA and subsequent restoration. And our pilots," he said, face full of pride, "keep the people here from being cut off from the rest of the world."

Passing a boarded up roadside market, he went on, "The Sudanese refugee crisis has also been ongoing over the years, and this latest influx has pushed many to the brink. They have taken entire families into their homes, given them food and shelter to the point that their own are now in need. With the UN being drawn down here and NGOs deploying to other regions where Ebola and war is escalating, at the moment it is feeling a lot less stable."

Even as Bilenga made that statement, evidence of the volatility they'd been hearing about but not yet seen began to materialize in front of them. They were approaching a star of intersecting roads, anchored by a church and several other brick buildings. The center of the interchange was swelling with people shouting with raised fists, the level of noise growing as the mass continued to expand from all sides. A uniformed policeman came up beside the LandCruiser, gesturing for Bilenga to roll his window down. Trying to be heard over the din, he gave directions in French, pointing toward a side road. Nodding, Bilenga reversed and turned off, working his way around the commotion by taking passages that were barely wide enough for the vehicle to clear, eventually getting back on route. They drove on past settlements of mud-bricked and thatched housing, past men and women and children walking along the roadside or riding bicycles, past empty, tree-shaded stretches, until they came to the intersection of the town's main road.

The RN4, or *Route Quatre* as it is known locally, connects Dungu to Faradje, 147 kilometers to the north. Cut and smoothed by Indonesian military engineers under the supervision of MONUSCO, it crosses the river bridging the south and south-center sections of Dungu. But before they reached the bridge, they hit another roadblock, this one even larger and more tempestuous than the first. Bodies thumped up against the LandCruiser, rocking it on its suspension as Bilenga attempted to plow through. Angry faces filled the windshield and passenger windows, fists beating on the glass. On the scale of similar vehicular assaults Jake had encountered during his years in volatile war zones, this one was negligible, but you could never underestimate the potential of the passions in a rancorous crowd to escalate to the point of flashover, when suddenly the aggression of a few became the amalgamated force of many with glass being shattered and doors being ripped from their hinges and flaming objects being tossed and engulfing the whole frame in one big whoosh. So he and Baladur and Dmello braced themselves, handguns clutched in their laps, just in case. Finally, with a sustained blast of his horn, Bilenga got just enough of an opening to break free of the throng and continue toward the river where, fortunately, a police contingency had prevented protestors from occupying the bridge. After trundling over the churning brown waters, Bilenga drove to the clinic and quickly dispensed with his delivery.

There was minimal talk during the five-mile drive across increasingly uninhabited and tree-covered acreage, sun following overhead like a hot yellow laser beam. On approach to the UN airport, they passed several parked trucks with FARDC—soldiers of the Congolese army—camouflage-clad with green bowl helmets and black rubber boots, the red, blue, and yellow country flag appliqued on their shoulders, assault rifles strapped across their chests. Twice they were stopped for identification checks, both times waved on without incident when Bilenga showed his NGO paperwork. The third time was a different matter.

Slowing for a checkpoint with the end of the airport runway in view, they were waved off. Bilenga stuck his arm out the window and gestured for the soldier to approach. *"Ne sommes-nous pas autorisés à nous rendre à l'aéroport?"* he asked. The vague response was that only UN personnel were being allowed due to a security emergency. Turning the Land-Cruiser around, Bilenga said, "That probably means there is a peacekeeping defensive at the northern side. There is a South Sudanese refugee camp close by, and my guess is they have a clash going on with the townspeople or they are trying to keep its refugees from migrating further into town. But there may be another way in."

Driving back to a fork in the road, he turned and headed up a corridor mixed with rondavel huts and markets, populated with foot traffic, motorbikes, bicycles, and an occasional car or truck. Things appeared to be calm and routine for most of the way, but after a mile of forest-lined road curving to the far end of the airport compound, that all changed. A barricade of UN and FARDC vehicles, including one Abrams tank, painted white with UN lettering stenciled on the rear, were holding off hundreds of people in a procession that stretched as far as they could see.

"Yes," Bilenga said, "it is as I suspected." Seeing a blue-helmeted UN soldier striding toward the LandCruiser, he added, "I am afraid this is probably as far as we will get."

"Okay," Jake replied, "let us out here and maybe we can slip in on foot. Go back a ways if you have to, stay with your vehicle. If you don't feel secure or if they run you off, just go and we'll find a way back."

Bilenga gave him a speculative look. "Are you sure?"

Baladur and Dmello were already getting out of the LandCruiser. Opening his door, Jake said, "Yes, I'm sure. Wait for us if you can, go if you have to." He tapped the roof of the LandCruiser with the palm of his hand. "Thank you, Santu."

Jake motioned for Baladur and Dmello to follow him, and the three of them ducked into the trees along the road.

ABOUT A HUNDRED YARDS through the wooded swath, they came out on the frontage road and walked with purpose toward an entry point to what was otherwise hedged and hemmed by concertina wire. But where a couple of armed sentries should have been stationed, wearing UN-blue helmets and vests and military camouflage, they saw no one.

"What the hell?" Dmello muttered.

"Yeah, this is not necessarily a good thing," Jake commented, looking around the vacated guard post. "We're not supposed to enter a UN compound carrying. A couple of guys should be here, not only to check our IDs but our weapons as well."

They all heard an outburst of raised voices just beyond the tree line at the north border, and waited for base personnel to emerge. After a few minutes, Baladur said, "They must be fending off some of those people we saw on the road."

Mildly dumbfounded, Jake shook his head. "Okay, well, let's proceed carefully."

They walked along a path leading to the airfield, spotting a white UN Mi-17 helicopter sitting idle on the apron, no other aircraft incoming or outgoing on the adjacent runway. Like the ASF strip, it was made of red dirt but was vastly wider and more than twice as long. They turned into an enclosed subsection centered by a large hangar and surrounded by smaller outbuildings. Before Jake had a chance to seek out anyone, they were flanked by a pair of dark-skinned soldiers, clutching M16 rifles and scowling with distrust. They were not wearing any obvious UN garb, but having served with many different peacekeeping units, Jake recognized the green-starred red flag patch on their sleeves as Moroccan.

"*Pas un geste,*" one commanded.

Jake held out his hands, Baladur and Dmello doing the same.

"Qui êtes-vous?"

Pointing to his cargo pants, Jake said, "ID," and when the soldier nodded, he slowly reached into a pocket and withdrew a leather case containing his passport and military credentials. With the other soldier holding his rifle barrel at a downward angle toward them, finger looped in the trigger guard, the inquisitor thumbed through Jake's portfolio and studied the contents. He unholstered a two-way radio from his belt and spoke into it, the volume of his voice too low to make out what he was saying.

"Et le vôtre?" the other soldier asked, tipping his chin at Baladur and Dmello. They complied wordlessly, handing over their credentials, and waited.

Speaking in French, Jake said, "There were no guards at the entrance, and we have handguns we need to—"

Before he could finish, both soldiers stepped back and raised their rifles, one repeating, *"Pas un geste,"* only this time the demand was riddled with nerves. Jake, Baladur, and Dmello all held their arms out from their bodies and froze as one soldier kept his M16 trained on them from the front and the other went behind, extracting handguns from each of their waistbands.

Apparently summoned by the radio relay, a third soldier appeared, clearly outranking the first two. His camouflage was starched, his boots shiny, a light blue felt beret with a gold UN crest slanted on his head. His demeanor, by contrast, was unperturbed, his expression neutral. Standing in front of Jake, in accented English he said, "Mr. Tyler, I am Lieutenant Colonel Brahim Hadji. I apologize for what I am sure must be some kind of misunderstanding. What is the purpose of your visit?"

"Pleased to meet you, Lieutenant Colonel," Jake said evenly. "I was about to explain that we waited at the guard station to present our identification and check our weapons, but no one was there. We're here to see if some friends of mine and their party might have landed yesterday or today."

"I see." Hadji was basketball player-tall and spindly with a mustache the color and sheen of shoe polish brushed over his upper lip. "Let us inquire inside here." He led the way into the hangar, his soldiers bringing up the rear, and they all stopped before a counter where another dark-complected man in black slacks and a white shirt was typing on a laptop computer. A widescreen monitor on the wall behind him displayed a grid of information that updated every few seconds. There were notebooks lined along a workstation below and folders stacked on the desktop. Regional and aeronautical maps were affixed to the walls.

Jake stepped up without waiting for invitation, asking, "Have you had any civilian flights come in, helicopter or plane, yesterday or today?"

The man looked up, momentarily taken aback by the assemblage before him, then flipped through a few pages in a notebook at his elbow. "Not that I can see," he replied, adding, "other than a few NGOs, all UN and military traffic, and that is the usual."

"What about VIPs? The group I'm looking for would be two guys and a VIP husband and wife with a security detail." Jake watched his eyes and face for any flicker of elevated interest but found none.

"Nobody like that, and we would all be informed of such an arrival."

"Even if it was unplanned?"

The man behind the counter frowned, suspicion creasing his forehead. "What are you trying to say happened?"

His frustration beginning to show, Jake shifted his weight from foot to foot, one hand on his hip, the other on the counter. He took a breath to center himself. "I'm not trying to say anything happened, I was just asking if it *could* have happened."

"No. No, I do not think so," the man said, and resumed typing on his laptop. He paused, something occurring to him. "Did the Dungu airport call earlier about this?"

"Yes, they did, but we wanted to check in person."

"It was very busy this morning, lots of traffic in and out, but as I said, all of it was UN or UN sanctioned."

The Moroccan officer came up beside Jake. "Let me make some calls around the base for you, just to settle your mind."

THEY MADE THEIR WAY off the base thirty minutes later and were surprised and relieved to find Santu Bilenga waiting in the LandCruiser, but Jake's mind was anything but settled. With each passing hour, it was becoming more and more inevitable that he was chasing a fiber of hope that was rapidly disintegrating.

Bilenga drove back down the settlement road, pulling off at a few of the markets so inquiries could be made. Jake had left his cell and sat phone number with Lieutenant Colonel Hadji and let him know that he would be returning to the Dungu airport; he gave the Dungu airport contact to others wherever they stopped. After crossing over the Uélé, they checked a few spots where food or lodging was available, and did the same on the other side of the Kibali, finding many of the places closed or cleared out in anticipation of looting. Avoiding the hotspots they'd run into earlier limited the scope of their canvas, but Jake already knew there was nothing out there to find.

When they arrived back at the hangar, Jake, Baladur, and Dmello graciously thanked Bilenga and lumbered out of the LandCruiser, fatigued and defeated. Stood in the gathering shadows of late afternoon sun. The air was still, the only sound a faint tinking coming from within the hangar where the ASF plane was now parked.

The metallic noise stopped and Laurent Pelletier emerged, holding a wrench and wiping his hands on a towel. "Nothing?" he asked. When he got no reply, he said, "Come to my house, rest, have some dinner." He flashed a winsome smile. "Maybe they will fly in yet and you will be right here to greet them. My house is only about a hundred meters just through the trees." He pointed to a path off to his left.

"That's very kind of you," Jake said, and realized that none of them had eaten anything all day, Baladur and Dmello looking at him expectantly.

Pelletier spoke with the hangar attendant and led them to his house nestled in the woods.

THE RED-ROOFED DWELLING was surprisingly large, bricked and surrounded by mixed trees and palms. While they freshened up, Pelletier began preparing dinner, which consisted of the ubiquitous chicken and rice cooked on an ancient wood stove piped through the roof, firewood stacked beside it. But as they took seats around the dining room table, it became clear the young pilot was a more than proficient chef, taking those mundane staples to a much higher level. He moved fluidly between sink and stove and cabinets, a towel draped over his shoulder, humming as he hand-sprinkled ingredients into the bubbling and steaming pots. At one point, he splashed some wine into the mix, stirred, and cupped his hand to draw the aroma to his nose for appraisal, then sipped from a wooden spoon and smiled to himself.

When he brought the platters from the kitchen, Luther Baladur beamed, gushing, "Ah, *coq au vin*, something my mother used to make!"

"It looks wonderful," Jake agreed, but his voice was devoid of Baladur's enthusiasm, and despite an empty stomach and the appealing assortment of food—which Baladur and Dmello were eagerly digging into—he found it hard to embrace the culinary gratification. Not wanting to insult their gracious host, he ate, but the process was mechanical at best as his mind and heart were finally edging into the somber borderlands of despair. The tender and succulent food in his mouth might as well have been silt from the pithy roots of a riparian bog.

Pelletier had removed their plates and served coffee, engaged in animated conversation about the confluence of French culture in the Congo with Baladur and about African aviation with Dmello, when Jake's sat phone rang. The room went as abruptly and completely silent as a courthouse gallery awaiting the reading of a verdict. Without seeing the display, they somehow all knew it was Remington.

Jake stood and walked outside, standing in the backyard of the house. Clouds had moved across the sky veiling the sun, but even with the slight breeze that came with them, the humidity was high and stifling. His skin was clammy, his mouth and throat dry, and his heartbeat sounded like a bass drum in his head.

"Remy?"

He listened, his face going numb. Finally, in a voice that seemed to come from the other side of some faraway canyon, he heard himself say, "So, that's it." Then, "Yes, first thing tomorrow."

The last bastion of his fortitude crumbled and he felt the same raw gust of grief rip through him as when he'd lost Delaney. He and Delaney had been friends for years; he'd only known Falcone and Niles for months. But the connection was every bit as strong. He wasn't sure why, it just was. He became aware of Pelletier, Baladur, and Dmello standing behind him. He tried to hold himself together. His eyes leaking tears, voice struggling to keep from breaking, he said, "Remy got confirmation. It was their bird. No survivors." The last came out in a gulp, and his shoulders slumped forward, chest hitching.

After letting a considerable amount of time pass, Baladur quietly asked, "What do you want us to do?"

Drawing in a deep breath, pulling it from some unknown reservoir of inner strength, Jake said, "We're flying to the crash site. First thing in the morning. To…" He broke off, his voice catching on a shard of emotion. "To recover the remains and take them home."

19

WHEN THE ADRENALINE SURGE from Jake's call had drained away, so did every ounce of threadbare resistance to hold off the all-encompassing exhaustion. Callie had sagged back on the bed and let her eyes close, and before she could remind herself it was only for a second or two, she was gone. Floating helplessly away like an untethered rope in a fathomless sea. Waiting for her on the other side was the dreaded chamber of horrors in one of the worst dreams she'd had since the return to Costa Rica. She was in the throes of its terror when the storm blew in.

Two things happened.

The explosive thunder ripped her from the dream's murky depths into the twilight-blue darkness of a room her disoriented brain could not assimilate, and the suddenness of her ascent back to the surface pulled much of what she had been experiencing out with her; she was still wrapped in layers of the dream, her mind unable to separate the waking world from the subconscious one. And, in the limbo levitating between the two, someone or something omnipotently evil was coming for her, and a disembodied voice was yelling *RUN*.

Callie clambered off the bed and staggered blindly from the room, grappling her way down stairs that somehow found her feet, and plunged through the villa's front door into a torrential downpour that overwhelmed her dazed senses even more. The rain pummeled her head, blinding her sight and filling her ears. She careened along a scattered course on wobbly legs, stumbling through brush and stepping over rock and thatch and roots, pain deadened by the stun of deafening thunder and accompanying pyrotechnics all around her.

RUN, run, run…

Callie lurched and wallowed through curtains of soaked palm fronds and leaves, gravity pulling her down and down, and finally to a landing place that was hard and soft, shallow and deep, but dark and wet and like a tunnel where she could see, and not see, anything familiar.

The rain came down, the dome of lightning and thunder converged, and Callie drew herself into a fetal ball, trying to become invisible to whatever was coming after her.

JESSE SEGURA WAS SLOGGING up the hill, wearing a windbreaker over his *Guardavidas* shorts and t-shirt, the traffic-light colors of his work attire bright in the lush, liquid greenness of the rain-drenched landscape. The treads of his Reef flip-flop sandals slipped in the rivulets of rainwater sluicing along the path to the villa as thunder clamored overhead, the heavy downpour shuddering through the forest canopy, streams of it cascading between the gaps. Afternoon showers this time of year were pretty much a daily occurrence, usually brief, lasting thirty minutes to an hour. But even before Segura had checked the weather app on his phone, masses of cumulonimbus clouds roiling and spreading over the ocean as thick and dark as volcanic ash told him this was not going to be one of the quick or moderate ones.

Normally, he would still be at the tower—lifeguards had to remain on the beach for the duration of their shifts, even in a storm—but with this being the first day after Jake's departure, Segura wanted to check on things at the villa. His days on shift were always busy, from the moment he and one or two colleagues set up the tower and rescue equipment at eight in the morning until five o'clock when they closed it down. Their hours were filled with continual monitoring of ocean conditions and watching for hazards, flagging for rip currents, physical fitness and training. This had been an especially hectic day in which he'd participated in several rescues and preventions, constantly moving people in the water from one area to another due to especially strong rip currents. An imprudent group of *pollos* from Canada kept him on his toes, ignoring admonitions to keep their brand new surfboards out of the larger swells, so it was something of a relief when he was finally able to pull them out as lightning began prickling through the clouds.

Costa Ballena *Guardavidas* Captain, Alvaro Cedeño, strictly enforced the rule of staying on the beach, so as the weather worsened, pitching whitecaps exploding into mammoth waves, Segura was grateful when an off-duty lifeguard who had been surfing and hanging out at the tower offered to cover for him.

Segura was elated when Jake engaged him for on-site security, not only for the job and beautiful place to live, but to be part of his household. He had known Jake casually prior to the proposal, their paths crossing on the beach and in town, and Jake's reputation in the area was stellar, but it was the way the rest of his staff spoke about him—all of whom Segura knew well—that sent Segura practically begging Jerry Hadley for a recommendation. He really wanted to be part of *that*. Now that he had the position, he intended to do everything he could to keep the household secure and Callie as comfortable as possible, so Jake could concentrate on his mission without worrying about what was going on at home. The rapidly intensifying storm made Segura feel uneasily defensive in a way he was not accustomed because now he was responsible, not just for those randomly having fun on the beach, but for the safety and well-being of those whose home he shared—and, more crucially, for someone who was everything to Jake.

A crash of thunder that rattled the trees and rang in his ears caused him to almost lose his footing, a gust of wind sending a spray of rain into his face. Wiping his eyes, he heard a mewling sound, like that of a small, frightened animal. As he came to the stone bridge, he spotted slight movement amidst the thick grass and plantings at the edge. Bending closer, through the layers of rain, he saw white fabric with bits of pink and yellow. Then, movement again, and whimpering. He dropped his gear bag and knelt down. Saw the wet blond hair.

"Ay, ay, ay...chica, qué estás haciendo aquí?"

Callie drew up even tighter, shaking under the dripping leaves of a ti plant. Her blouse was torn, leaves stuck to her skin and clothing, pieces of vine broken off in her hair. She was soaked and muddied, her arms and legs scratched and scraped. He could not see her face.

"Come, Callie…we go inside, okay?"

Segura removed his windbreaker and draped it over Callie while try-ing to coax her up. She shook and sobbed but would not respond, so he slung the gear bag over his shoulder, scooped her into his arms and walked briskly across the bridge, rain sounding like the staccato march of heavy boots on the stone. When he got to the other side, he could see Ramón Cárdenas, Estabon Mina, and Mauricio Leguizano thrashing through the gardens and trees around the villa and heard them calling Callie's name. They all looked up as he approached and, seeing Callie in his arms, rushed over to accompany him inside.

At the sight of Segura with Callie, Camilla's hand went to her throat, eyes popping with consternation, and she wailed, *"Dios mío! Qué?"*

Segura's emergency medical training kicked in as he issued instruc-tions, asking for towels and a blanket. Cárdenas got an armful of towels from a downstairs linen closet and Camilla sat on the couch, draping a blanket over her lap. Segura lay Callie on it, and Camilla began gently wiping her face, then drying her with the towels, tears spilling from her eyes as she murmured, *"Oh, mija!"* She hugged Callie close, felt the trem-ors of her small form, teeth chattering against her neck. *"Jesse, dónde? Que pasó?"*

"No sé, but we need to get her dry, keep her warm." He looked to Mina and Leguizano who had been anxiously watching from behind them and said, *"Agua."* They hustled off to the kitchen for water, and he then noticed that Callie's bare feet were cut up and bleeding. While he tended to the lacerations with antiseptic and bandages from his first aid kit, Segura thought about his conversation with Jake the day before Jake's departure. Without going into specific detail, Jake had told him about Callie's PTSD, and while Segura did not know too much about it, he was fairly certain today's incident was caused by it.

Camilla cooed soothingly, plucking the bits of leaves and vines from Callie's hair as she dabbed at it with a towel. She took a bottle of water from Leguizano and, after insistent pleas, got Callie to take some sips. The ghostly white pallor of Callie's skin slowly began to look less translucent, her lips changing from blue to something closer to pink.

When Segura had finished his aid, he put in a call to Jerry Hadley, explaining what was going on and letting him know another lifeguard was covering. Hadley immediately offered to come over but Segura told him he had everything under control. Not more than ten minutes after disconnecting, Hadley was seated with Segura at the kitchen bar. Having been in action on all of the Costa Ballena beaches, he wore the same red and yellow, but his tanned gringo blondness was quite a contrast with Segura's dark skin and hair.

"I know you've got it, but I just wanted to give my support," Hadley said, casting a concerned look to the living room where Camilla remained with Callie's head and shoulders in her lap. She had sent Segura to the bedroom to fetch dry clothes, and the men stepped aside while Camilla peeled the wet garments off, slipping an oversize t-shirt and knit boxers on Callie's still-shivering frame.

"I appreciate it, man," Segura said. "I'm guessing this is the PTSD Jake told me about."

"No doubt," Hadley said.

"Camilla said she was asleep when she checked on her before the storm, and then when she went up later, she was gone."

"I think it must have been like what sometimes happens with animals when fireworks go off…they are so traumatized, they bolt."

HOURS LATER, EVERYONE WAS gone but Camilla and Segura. Camilla had not moved from the sofa, Callie drifting restlessly in and out of sleep on her lap—making forlorn little sounds, stirring and then going still, her skin damp and warm, breathing raggedly. Segura sat in one of the chairs, his hands clasped between his knees. The storm had passed and all was tranquil again, lights dimmed in the villa, the aqua glow of the pool shimmering through the kitchen and dining room windows.

"I have got to figure something out," Segura said.

"I should have…" Camilla shook her head, misery drawn in her face.

"You are not to blame. We will figure this out together."

"What can we do?" Camilla asked, stroking Callie's hair and forehead. "We cannot let anything happen—" Her voice broke, and she lowered her head, a hand on her temple. "*Dios mío, ayúdame.*"

"I know, and we won't. I am thinking maybe some motion detectors inside the house that we activate at night. I could monitor them. During the day, we would just have to—"

"I will have her during the day," Camilla said fervently. "This I promise." She met his gaze, her eyes glistening.

"I know," Segura said. "I know. We all will."

"Do we tell Jake?"

Segura thought for a moment, then shook his head. Jake had emphasized that he wanted to know everything that happened, had looked adamantly into Segura's eyes when he'd said it, but Segura knew that telling Jake about this might derail him and he did not want that. He sensed that Jake was a man who put mission above everything, but when it came to Callie, she was the big exception to that. "No. We will tell him when he comes back. For now, we will just handle this."

20

JAKE HAD NO IDEA how long he'd been standing outside the pilot's house, but it was semi-dark and mostly quiet, leaving him alone with his grief. Leaving him alone to think about why he had come here, and what it had cost. He'd left Callie at a time when she desperately needed him, only to get here too late. If he'd somehow arrived more quickly, could he have prevented the loss of Falcone and Niles? Or might he have been taken, too, leaving Callie to be served that envelope with the depth of his feelings for her circumscribed to words on pages that included the notification of his own demise? He just could not believe he was going through such a profound loss again, especially so soon after losing Delaney. But that was the nature of the world in which he operated; the rewards were unlike anything a bank vault could bestow, the risks as prolific and escalatory as nuclear fallout, and the losses, cruel and unfair and epically devastating.

In his mind, he saw Falcone and Niles, meeting them for the first time, the yin and yang of their unlikely friendship, their grumbling and blundering offset by the unexpected ardor of their convictions. He saw them bravely waiting for him on the other side of that hill in South America, in defiance of his order to leave, artillery firing all around them and raining down from above.

The breeze had picked up, the plum-colored sky draped with black clouds interspersed with the paler ones of departing day, heat lightning flickering inside them. Somewhere in the trees a hawk screeched and then flew off in a crackling of branches. Jake stood in the deepening darkness, as alone as a man could feel in a place that seemed, in that moment, like the middle of nowhere and at the edge of everything bad. Listening to the rustling leaves and the empty air moving them, he let his grief consume him.

THE MORNING WAS SHROUDED in a humid vapor from the night's rain, moisture clinging to surfaces and coating the dirt turned to mud. Doves warbled softly from the woods beyond the hangar, light rising with the languid waft of steam over a hot spring. Jake sipped from a mug of coffee, sullenly watching as Pelletier assisted Dmello with his pre-flight checks of their Cessna. Pelletier had been the consummate host, putting them up for the night in his two spare bedrooms and packing a cooler full of food and water, a large thermos of coffee.

Despite the short distance to the crash site, driving on a road that was not much more than a footpath, especially after rain, would have taken hours if not the better part of a day; getting there in the Cessna would take about ten minutes, so the mode of transportation had been an easy decision. They thanked Pelletier for his hospitality, climbed aboard the plane, and rolled to the airstrip for a bumpy takeoff.

Their course took them north over patches of savanna ringed with forest, all of it skimmed in mist, the sky a washed out gray. After taking the plane up for a short cruise at several thousand feet, Dmello announced, "We are approaching the coordinates Remy gave us, but I have no idea if we can land close, so let's try to get a sighting first and then hopefully I can find a clearing with enough room to land."

"What do you need, about five hundred meters?" Jake asked.

"I have done a little over four hundred, but that is really tight and, in these conditions, can be more than a little…exciting," Dmello replied, beaded dreadlocks clicking against the earpieces of his headset as he twisted to look at Jake, flashing a mischievous grin that seemed to indicate he had experienced a few of those "exciting" events.

They were over mixed terrain when Baladur called out, "There, is that it?"

Dmello banked and made another pass, and Jake saw it, too—the blackened cavity half in and out of the trees, a single silver fragment gleaming like a dislodged tooth filling. Numbers and letters were clearly visible on the piece of tail, and now Jake knew how Remington was able to get irrefutable confirmation from the broadcasted report of a pilot whose flight path had taken him over the crash site; a quick lookup of registry would yield everything about its identity, from aircraft type to country of origin and ownership. It would have taken someone with the intelligence procurement prowess of Efron Kipnis less than five minutes to obtain all that and more, including the last filed flight plan and passenger manifest.

"There's a 5Y in the tail number," Dmello pointed out, "that's a Kenyan registration."

Jake said nothing. Hearing it from Remington had been one thing, but seeing it with his own eyes made it undeniably real. He looked away from the window for a moment, the imagine seared into his brain.

"There is not enough area here to land," Dmello said, "but I might be able to use the road past it."

In the next few minutes, Dmello took the plane low alongside the narrow dirt road, assessing its viability. Though empty of people or any kind of transport, there were a few goats wandering around and more than a few rutted stretches puddled with rainwater. There were also scattered palms on both sides, but the width between was adequate. After a couple of passes, he was confident enough to take it on. He climbed back to a thousand feet, circled and, after lining up with his extemporized runway, reduced power, decreased altitude and speed, approaching at seventy-five knots. Down another ten knots, he adjusted the flaps to twenty degrees and focused intently on the road stretching out below and in front of him. When he was sure of his threshold, he brought the flaps all the way down for the safest landing speed given the less than ideal surface conditions.

"Here we go!" he called out. "Better brace, might be a bit rough."

The Cessna's nose tipped up as the landing gear hit the road with a hard thump, then lowered as Dmello braked and brought the flaps all the way back up, dirt splattering the windows. Jake and Luther Baladur were each clutching their seats with one hand, sides of the plane with the other. Both released an audible breath when the Cessna slowed and came to a stop. About a dozen yards up the road, the goats stood gazing vapidly in their direction.

HIKING THE DISTANCE FROM the plane to the crash site took them just over thirty minutes, pausing once to hydrate in the rising heat radiating from a floe of sun the color of eggnog. They wore backpacks and carried automatic rifles which they swept in all directions as they advanced, keeping close to or inside the trees for cover. Birds jabbered overhead and monkeys squeaked from within the brush, a good indication that the path was clear, but an attack could come from well beyond the limits of their scope and had to always be taken into the spectrum of contingencies even when there was no reason to expect one. But the downing of the Eurocopter sent the needle of possibility ticking well into the probability range, so baseline vigilance was heightened, their eyes scanning the trail up close and distant.

Jake studied the GPS and TOPO mapping on his Garmin tactix watch to make sure they were on track to the site coordinates, and a few minutes later, he knew they had arrived before anything from the debris field came into view.

It was the smell.

The distinctive odor of burnt jet fuel scorched into earth and grass and woods was unmistakable, but there was another just as unmistakable—not only for the smell associated but for the visual and visceral memories it evoked in anyone who had experienced it as much as he had—and Jake did not have to look at Baladur or Dmello to know that they recognized it, too. The smell of burned human flesh is unlike any other and not one you ever forgot; charred and smoky, yes, but both rancid and sweet in a way that defied description. It permeated the sinuses and taste buds in the way a mesquite fire fogged the hair and skin, but it could not be washed away in the shower because it embedded in a place deep below the surface.

Beside him, Baladur cleared his throat and Dmello made a snuffling sound. Jake felt a steely shiv in his gut, straightened his spine and lifted his chin, his heart pulsing in his ears. None of them said anything as they continued through the trees and emerged into a clearing that had been a mix of grass and scrub with another stretch of forest on the other side; it was now a pit of incineration from the point of implosion to the ground scored with black lines running out and into the trees as if gun powder had been ignited, charcoaling bark and cremating leaves. The diameter was strewn with pieces fractured and crushed like a bed of composted eggshells, twisted strips of metal, melted plastic, and gnarled wires still smoking from electrical fires despite the rain overnight.

A trio of vultures broke away from their morbid huddle in a blur of gray-brown, hissing in protest.

Jake removed his Voodoo Tactical backpack, filled to its squared thickness with items that represented both hope and resignation: tools such as an axe and folding shovel, first aid equipment and supplies, Kevlar blanket and extra water—tools that could extricate and treat survivors, but could also extract and transport remains. Taking in the scraps ground into the blackened mud crater, he knew those tools would be used for the latter, and began a solemn assessment, stepping carefully around the perimeter. When he came to the only part of the helicopter that had remained intact enough to provide identification—the silver tail boom—he stooped to examine the seared edges of a missing chunk, running his gloved hands over the opening and, just inside, finding an olive-colored shard of metal the size of a quarter.

Eying what he recognized as a piece of RPG warhead, Jake felt fury bloom in his chest and closed a fist around it. After a moment, he stuck it in a pants pocket and resumed his survey of the site. Close to the middle of the pit, he came across what he'd been dreading.

Squatting down, he gingerly brushed back the rubble and fingered mud away from the outline of human bone, a femur—incredibly with some fabric and bodily tissue clinging to the surface—and all sight and sound and thought siphoned into a blinding white void. His head dropped, a balloon of anguish exploding in his lungs. He finally stood, aware of Baladur and Dmello silent behind him, respectful and reverent, their faces grim.

Wordlessly, Baladur handed Jake the shovel tool, and Jake knelt back down to dig lightly around the bone, the sounds of Baladur's and Dmello's boots crunching over the graveled wreckage as they searched. Jake's eyes burned with tears acrid from the caustic and sickening odors, and from the expanding pond of grief in his soul, thoughts hazily tumbling in his mind as though wrapped in cotton…*Too much, it's just too much…too much to see, to feel, to know. Too damn much.*

There was not a lot more to be found. Mixed in the mud were some other bone fragments and splinters and congealing matter, all of it saturated with a greasy film of fuel and oil and caked in dampened ash. Finding so little did not surprise him; he'd seen crashes where whole bodies had been discovered, held together by their skin, innards reduced to a gelatinous puree, and others where the remnants of an entire team of soldiers could be removed in one helmet.

When he was convinced there were no other human remains to recover, Jake got the Kevlar blanket from his backpack and unfolded it over the leg bone from possibly one of his two friends, or possibly one of the others, but their disintegrated bones were here somewhere. The blanket's silver surface sparkled in the sun like a shattered mirror. Kneeling with one hand on his heart and the other covering his eyes, Jake began a silent prayer. Breathing through his mouth, he felt a wave of nausea, a gulf of profound sorrow, perspiration dampening his hairline and neck.

From behind him, he heard a scraping of feet, and, "Oh God, Jake, I'm so sorry."

THE NEURONS AND RECEPTORS in Jake's brain were in overload, emotions and thoughts and physical reactions all scrambling in chaotic circuits looking frantically for purchase. When he moved, everything seemed to slow down and speed up at the same time, creating a vertiginous sensation.

Jake turned to the voice and stared into the face of Eddie Falcone.

Before he could even form articulate thoughts from the tumult going on in his head or manufacture corresponding words, Curran Niles stumbled past Falcone and clamped Jake in a breath-choking embrace.

"Oh my God, oh my God," Niles blubbered, "Jesus bloody Christ, we're so glad to see you!" His face looked feverish in the heat, cheeks like ripened crabapples. Loose strands of wheat-colored hair hung from a red bandana, turned gray with dust and sweat. Releasing Jake, he took a step back, caught his dazed expression, glanced at Falcone whose comprehension had been more immediate. In a softer voice, Niles said again, "Oh my *God*. You thought we were…"

Beginning to recover from his shock, Jake shook his head mutely, planted his hands on his hips, looked away to collect himself, mumbled and then more forcefully said, "Motherfuck…mother*fuck*."

Looking past Jake at the wreckage he and Niles had seen the day before, Falcone licked his dry lips and said, "We didn't know how you could know and had no way to contact you. The village has a radio but it's not working, and—"

Jake cut him off with a look they knew all too well, coal black eyes that bore right through you with inscrutable emotion until he spoke or scowled or smiled, and sometimes even then you could not be sure. Finally, Jake said, "I can't believe this," and drew Falcone into an impassioned embrace. Did the same with Niles, who sniffled witheringly against his shoulder.

By now, Baladur and Dmello had approached, their expressions cautiously happy. Jake made introductions and smiles flowed from one to another as hands were clasped, Niles blurting, "We're the undead!" Beside him, Jake made a grunting noise in his throat. "What? Too soon?"

Noting the raw-meat flush in both of their faces, Jake got bottles of water from his backpack for Falcone and Niles who flicked off the caps and drank as if they'd just come off a trek across the Sahara. Slurping the last mouthful from his bottle, Falcone panted, "Ran out of our water last night."

There was a ponderous interval in which they all seemed to be making mental recalculations to the here-and-now reality; Falcone and Niles, scruffy and sweaty in yesterday's jeans and t-shirts, gazing at Jake and his new comrades clad in tidily functional tactical wear and strapped with assault rifles, and Jake glancing over his shoulder at the shiny square of Kevlar covering the bone of someone who had perished in a helicopter that Falcone and Niles were supposed to be on.

Responding to Jake's unspoken question, Falcone looked at the ground and said, "Just the two pilots."

Villagers had been slowly appearing along the far side of the clearing, adults holding back inquisitive children who wanted to dash across the field of grass separating them from the crash site. A puzzled expression was forming on Jake's face as he tried to clarify a picture with more than a few missing pieces. A fatigue drawn from the restless night before and the emotionally draining revelation etched lines in his forehead and formed a band of pressure over his temples. Crossing his arms, his gaze shifted from Falcone to Niles, eyes narrowing. "Okay, so…you came from the village, which I saw on the map…"

"Yeah," Falcone replied, avoiding Jake's probing eyes.

Jake continued to study the pair of them, his intuition telling him they were holding something back, and in the next exchange his suspicion was confirmed. Retrieving his backpack and shifting his rifle around to his side, he said, "All right, let's go meet up with the Keoghs and see where we go from here."

He started off in the direction of the village, Baladur and Dmello falling in behind him. The sun was higher in the sky, steeping the fetid stench of death that hung in the air and turning the brown mud back to red dirt. Jake realized that Falcone and Niles had not moved. He stopped, looked over his shoulder.

Falcone said, "Uh…about that…"

ON AWAKENING IN NAKALÉ the day before, Falcone and Niles had sensed something amiss almost immediately. Even though they tended to be the last ones up—and sure enough, everyone else's belongings had been cleared out of the church—there was an intangible emptiness that went beyond spatial, and one that felt more than minutes old. The thatched dwelling stank of the same organic musk, denser after the night's rain, but conspicuously absent were hints of any human smells, like the cigarette smoke from Pacheco and Gabbitas or the subtle trace of Amelia Keogh's lavender-scented sunscreen or the genteel aura of Cyrus Keogh's Creed aftershave.

When they stepped into the pale morning light, village activity was stirring in its normal, modest manner, men preparing to venture out and provide and women preparing to make the most of those provisions. Fishing apparatus was being assembled; fires were smoking under pots. Children in various stages of undress scampered amidst domesticated animals that clucked or bleated or brayed. But some of the villagers had stopped what they were doing, looking pointedly at Falcone and Niles.

Falcone and Niles peered uncertainly back at them, at the same time seeking out the Keoghs. They strolled around the communal area, then traversed the length of the settlement. Nowhere did they see any sign of the Keoghs, McNamara, or Pacheco and Gabbitas.

On return to the village center, the chieftain, Gali Nsabimana, had approached them wearing his native dashiki shirt and an intent expression that seemed to indicate he had something of importance to convey. The only problem was, he spoke very limited English, which was the case with the rest of the villagers. Despite the language impediment, the chief vocalized at length, punctuating his chronicle with increasingly effusive hand gestures in an attempt to convey the key points of his message. Falcone and Niles watched him dimly but with a growing sense of unease. In between Nsabimana's bursts of babble, they tried to ask questions, inanely simplifying their words and also pantomiming as if playing some third-world version of charades, but this only triggered a renewed string of indecipherable vernacular.

Falcone gave Nsabimana a charitable smile for his efforts, turned to Niles and said, "It's early, let's just go wait on the chopper."

"I'm with you, mate!"

Which was when they'd heard the helicopter's rotors sputtering in the distance and, accompanied by a flock of villagers, eagerly jogged to the landing zone. When they reached the Dauphin, the two pilots were offloading the supplies that had been appropriated for the village, so they pitched in, fully expecting to see the Keoghs materialize at some point during the process.

When the last of the supplies had been dispensed, Falcone and Niles scanned the group of spectators that remained to see them off. Heard the shrill windup of the helicopter's engines, saw the pilot at the controls motion to them. Torn between staying and going—letting the chopper go and staying for the Keoghs, or boarding it without them and making it to Jake—the choice seemed clear. They had told Jake they would be in Dungu today.

They sprinted for the Dauphin and were perhaps a half-dozen yards away when both halted in their tracks as if some overriding logic had prevailed like an unexpected detour sign between road and washed out bridge. After a brief exchange, their voices shouting over the high-pitched whine of the Dauphin, they had pivoted and walked away, pausing at the line of villagers waving to the departing helicopter as it ascended into the sky.

And got blown up.

JAKE STOOD, ONE HAND resting on his AK-47, the thumb of his other tucked under a strap of his backpack, his face unreadable, but his eyes popped like hot tar. He did not speak for nearly a full minute after Falcone had finished their recount. They fidgeted visibly, awaiting a reaction, Niles flicking at the loose strands of his hair, Falcone plucking at his damp t-shirt. The air felt as thick and sticky as glue.

Jake's face, his stance, never so much as twitched, but his voice rose in cadence. "You're telling me the Keoghs are *gone?*"

Both nodded bleakly.

Jake's eyes rolled upward and he bent back on his heels.

Niles blathered, "We couldn't believe they'd bloody leave us, something must have happened. I guess. I mean, like Eddie said, when we woke, everyone and all the gear except ours was gone. We looked all over the village and we tried to talk to the people, but none of them speak English."

"Lingala or Zande," Baladur said. "Zande, more likely. I know Lingala and a little Zande."

"All right," Jake said, his jaw tight. "As long as we're here, let's see if we can find out what they know."

Crossing the field and following a trail that led back to the village, Niles leaned into Falcone and mumbled, "He looks pissed."

"That's pretty much his normal look," Falcone quipped.

The chief and his wife were waiting for them in the communal area, extending ready greetings of welcome, Bénie Nsabimana setting out cassava bread with honey and a paste made from peanuts. Sampling the fare and proffering warm smiles, they gathered around the table.

"*Sene fu roni,*" Baladur said amiably, and then got right to the point, asking, "*Pisi aboro?*"

As he had earlier, Gali Nsabimana broke into a demonstrative narrative, gesticulating with his hands. They all listened, Falcone and Niles still uncomprehending anything being spoken or manually illustrated, but Jake, Baladur, and Dmello seemed to be culling some information, Baladur interjecting two- or three-word phrases, Jake and Dmello both glimpsing off toward the far end of the settlement.

"From what I could interpret," Baladur said, "I believe he is saying that a vehicle came with two men and spoke to the three Keoghs. They were excited, got in the truck, and drove down the road out of the village. He said something about two more going after them."

"Three, that would be the Keoghs with their assistant," Falcone said.

"The two more after had to be the security guys," Niles added, his mouth puckering as if he had just tasted something sour.

Taking note of his expression, Jake said, "Tell me about them."

It was Falcone who answered, "Military background, tough guys…but if you ask me, they're a couple of self-righteous pricks."

"Well, in fairness to them, they were right to insist on getting all of you to Dungu, as I did, which didn't happen."

They were all quiet for a moment, processing that, knowing the outcome would have been very different—everyone present and accounted for, the search underway, and most importantly of all, no dead pilots.

"I guess this is a bit of a bloody mess, isn't it?" Niles remarked glumly, picking at his fingernails.

"No shit," Jake snipped. "Do you have any idea just what kind of a mess you guys have inserted yourselves into? I mean, really, *do* you?" There was a caustic edge creeping into his voice, his face beginning to show glints of emotion. With the revelation of the Keoghs' disappearance, Jake's gut reaction had been to abort, to pack it in and just get them all home. But even as his exasperation of the now exponentially complicated situation began to fester, he was loath to concede. The Keoghs had already paid him a shitload of money, wired into his Bahamian account before the Gulfstream had even left the ground, but for him, it was not about the money. It was the value of his commitment, something he'd never shirked. But this development changed the mission he had agreed to. He found himself more conflicted than ever.

He twisted away from the table, observing the children nearby, little girls and boys dressed in stretched and tattered clothing that had time-traveled through missionaries and NGOs, some with graphics from sports teams and cartoons and universities—entities and animations and places they'd never heard of—color and print faded by sun, soil, and constant wear. One boy, standing off to the side, gaunt and skittish, wore a t-shirt that appeared almost new and which fell past his knees. The image, against a red-and-white-striped background, was of a young and energized Bruce Springsteen, upraised arm about to swing down over the strings of his electric guitar. Jake knew where that t-shirt had come from, and felt a disarming tug of sentiment.

He turned back around and looked at Eddie Falcone, then at Curran Niles. Took a deep breath and exhaled. Smacking his hands on his thighs, he said, "Let's go, gents. We'll talk about this on the plane."

They all stood, shook hands with the chief and his wife, and moved away from the table. Glancing over his shoulder to make sure everyone was with him, Jake saw the boy in the Springsteen shirt raise his hand in a meager wave. And saw Eddie Falcone pause, back up, and stoop down to give the boy a quick fist-bump.

21

HIKING BACK TO THE plane, Jake had advised Falcone and Niles to avoid talking, a precaution underscored by his placement of Luther Baladur and Keanjaho Dmello to the front and rear of them, on pivot with weapons ready. Even in the shade of the trees, the heat was an invasive voyeur draining perspiration and energy, so when Jake diverted them through the woods, he knew they all probably thought it was as a respite from the sun, but in actuality his detour had another objective; he was taking them around the crash site to prevent anyone from seeing it again—once was more than enough. Before leaving the village, he'd called Nash Remington to let him know what had happened and Remington assured Jake he would initiate recovery of the deceased and monitor any developments.

When they reached the plane, Dmello paced off six hundred meters of road, while all of them worked to remove large rocks, tree limbs, and other obstructions from the path. Falcone and Niles took turns filling holes with the shovel tool, Jake slashing overhanging branches with his Condor Golok machete. Dmello gave the stretch a final inspection, deemed it viable, and began his outward check of the plane.

Baladur took the co-pilot's seat, Falcone and Niles filed into the rear, and Jake took one of the two in front. The heat trapped inside the plane had the shocking sear of stepping barefoot onto sand that had been under the sun's broiler for hours, hands and arms scorched by the leather upholstery. Jake dug into the cooler and handed everyone a chilled bottle of water and, for the next few minutes, the cabin was filled with the sounds of gulps and gurgles and crinkling plastic. Dmello climbed aboard, took a bottle for himself, and in between swigs asked Jake where he wanted to go.

Still at odds with his intentions, Jake was wrestling with where to draw the line in the altered shape of his original commitment. If he decided to continue, time was of the essence as the Keoghs had already been gone for almost half a day. He could feel Falcone and Niles tense up behind him, their whole cause and effect hanging in the balance. "For now, let's fly over the road going away from the village. Maybe we'll get lucky and spot the truck."

"Roger, and off we go," Dmello said, and got the Cessna rolling forward, jittering over the lumps and bumps but accelerating quickly to forty and then fifty knots before lifting off and clearing the treetops.

When they had leveled off to two thousand feet, Jake turned in his seat and looked at Falcone and Niles, who were leaning against the cabin and peering anxiously through their windows. When they realized he was waiting to speak, they scooted closer for the conversation neither were eager to have. Over the past few days they had been anticipating Jake's arrival with the kind of quavering expectancy of errant children awaiting the inevitable wrath and relief of a parent coming to spring them from whatever brand of trouble they'd ensnared themselves in. The joy and exuberance they'd felt on catching the first glimpse of him standing at the crash site instantly evaporated when they had seen the mask of profound grief and devastation on his face.

"I gotta tell you, I'm not too keen right now to pursue this," Jake said sharply. Filtered through the headsets they wore, the plane's engine had the distant sonorous hum of a neighborhood lawn mower, but it was subdued enough for the edge of Jake's voice to cut through. "It's one thing to conduct a search for the people of their compound—"

"And their child," Niles injected.

"Yes. But now that mission—a pretty damned daunting one to begin with—has been further compromised because the *clients* are missing. All they had to do was wait just a few more hours for me to get here."

Falcone and Niles exchanged wilted looks, taken aback by the level of Jake's frustration.

Checking his tone, Jake said, "I don't think you guys realize what I had to sacrifice to be here."

Though spoken more evenly, those words had the sting of an open-handed slap, their faces blanching and then swelling with color.

Niles bit his lip, eyes suddenly bright with moisture. In a small voice, he rasped, "God...how...how is Callie?"

"Not good," Jake said tersely, and glanced away.

"Jake, we—" Falcone began.

Jake stopped him with a shake of his head. "I'm here now. I made a commitment which I will do my best to honor." He took a minute to reshuffle his thoughts, gazing through the window across from him, the ground below an unending mosaic of forests and grasslands and pocks of reddish brown. "How could they just leave you like that, without telling you?"

"We've been wondering the same thing," Falcone replied. "Maybe they thought they'd be back before we woke up. I don't know."

"That's a possibility," Jake said, "and maybe it's why the chopper still showed up when it did, because they didn't notify the pilots of a change in plan." He paused, a splinter breaking off from his speculation and lodging in a mental sidewall, something more to it but not quite salient.

Falcone said, "I still don't know what stopped us. The helicopter was there, ready to take us to Dungu and you. We were one hundred percent coming to you, figured the Keoghs would call the pilots and they would go back for them or pick them up wherever they went...something. And then we were about to board and both of us just stopped, like somebody had closed the departure gate."

"God did," Niles murmured.

"I mean, it was just this sudden gut feeling...I don't know how to explain it."

"When something like that happens, there's no telling why," Jake mused, again glimpsing out the window, the road they were following looping in and out of woodland, not a vehicle or village to be seen. "All you can do is thank your maker and live to fight another day."

"How did you know about the crash?" Falcone asked.

"The pilot of a plane flew over not long after it happened. He reported it by radio, gave the tail number, and also relayed seeing a flatbed truck with armed militia speeding off." Jake dug into one of the pockets in his cargo pants, extracting the RPG fragment. Palming it, he showed them. "This is a piece of a rocket-propelled grenade I found at the crash site."

"Jesus," Falcone said. The skin around his mouth and jaws was shadowed with dark stubble, gray smudges beneath his brown eyes. His hair was spiked like a porcupine.

Jake put the fragment back in his pocket and repositioned himself in his seat so he could scan the road. Falcone and Niles sat slumped against their windows, silent and morose and looking shrunken within themselves, eyes cast downward over the sun-swept, barren landscape.

SEVERAL HOURS OF FLYING had yielded little more on the move than a buffalo herd and some grazing bongo, chestnut-colored antelope encircled with distinctive white stripes. They saw no people walking or biking along the road, and no truck of any kind. Dmello informed them that they would have to either return to Dungu or land at a strip farther north in order to refuel—aviation gas could be scarce in remote regions of DRC—so, after listening to Baladur make radio contact with Nakalé and hearing nothing about the Keoghs, Jake instructed Dmello to take them back to Dungu. Just before leaving the village that morning Jake had repaired their HF radio and given the chief Dungu Airport's call sign, asking him to make contact if the Keoghs came back. On landing in Dungu, they saw that the ASF plane was gone, but the hangar attendant gave Jake an envelope from Laurent Pelletier. In it was a key to the pilot's house and a note indicating he would be gone overnight and letting them know they were welcomed to stay.

They were now relaxing on Pelletier's patio, late-afternoon shadow slatted through trellised panels of the porch beside it. All was quiet for a while, each absorbed in their own thoughts as they sat listening to birds warbling and scratching around the grounds, flittering and calling from the trees. Finishing cans of soda they'd found in the refrigerator, Dmello and Baladur excused themselves for a walk to give Jake some time alone with Falcone and Niles.

Jake leaned back in his chair, flexing his neck to loosen the tension, eying them with weary resignation. "All right, so why are you guys here instead of having a cold one in some New York bar?"

Niles started to snicker but a reproachful look from Falcone subdued him. "The bloody pub was actually how we wound up here," he said, unable to suppress a grin. "You know what they say, either incredibly brilliant or incredibly stupid ideas come from—"

Falcone interrupted, saying, "Crazy as it sounds, after being back a few days, even after everything we went through in Colombia, I dunno…it was like a big letdown. I mean, it's not like we wanted to go right back into the fire, but just feel that edge."

Jake nodded. "I get that. I do. It's something I often experience after a mission." He waited for them to continue.

Falcone told him about meeting the trio from The Sanctuary Initiative and the invitation to accompany them to the Congo. "We'd already been shitcanned by our boss for, you know, going off the reservation. Then when we heard about the group's work in Africa and the Keoghs, it sounded like an amazing gig."

"But did they tell you anything about what's going on here?"

Falcone and Niles glanced uncertainly at each other, Falcone replying, "Well, yeah. They told us about the millions of displaced people, about their efforts to raise awareness and get funding for programs to provide safe sanctuaries—as the name of their organization implies—about getting the Keoghs on board. Really impressive causes and work, we thought."

"Sure, but I think they gave you a nice highlight reel with some upbeat spin-doctoring," Jake said bluntly. "Did they tell *why* there are so many displaced people? Did they tell you about all the conflicts raging over here? About the militias and rebels and the LRA attacking villages, murdering and kidnapping, raping and trafficking women and children for sex and soldiering? Did they tell you about that?" Color had risen in his face, dark eyes flaring.

Jake's harsh characterization hung in the air for several moments, as though a word jumble of their circumstances had been placed before them. Neither could summon a coherent response because the truth was, they could not recall much if any of that being included in the glibly inebriant hours spent at the New York bar in the company of Iris

Margolis and Neville Nias and Drake Johanssen. Did not, in fact, recall hearing more than fleeting and ambiguous references to those issues at any point during the flights over. They had, however, been subsequently enlightened by stories from the compound's people they'd interviewed on film and by the informed dialogue of the Keoghs.

Falcone crossed his arms stiffly while Niles flexed his fingers against the fabric of his jeans, asking, "Do you think that's what's happened here? The compound was attacked and the people abducted?"

"I don't know," Jake said. "Maybe. But there are some things that don't quite add up."

Something suddenly occurring to him, Niles lurched from his seat and said, "Hey, this place has electricity!"

Jake regarded him with dull bemusement, but Falcone, who had developed a mental shorthand with Niles from the amount of time they spent together, instantly connected the dots. "The cameras!"

The three of them went inside the house and Niles dug through his camera bags, extracting an AC adaptor which he connected to the Canon video camera. They found an outlet and plugged in the power supply. Standing over them, Jake watched mutely as Niles flipped the LCD panel open and began panning through footage. A few moments later, Niles exclaimed triumphantly, "There! Bloody hell, there he is! I knew we had that bloke on film somewhere!"

Falcone clapped him on the back and the two of them turned to show Jake the image they'd frozen on pause. "We saw him in Nakalé!"

When they saw Jake trying to process that, Niles explained, "Eddie and I were walking around the village that first day and we saw him. We were pretty sure we recognized him and were going to review our footage from the compound to confirm it, but all the bloody batteries were dead."

"He was on a motorbike," Falcone continued, "and we yelled at him to wait so we could talk to him...find out why he was in the village, see if he knew anything about what had happened at the compound...and he just took off. That was the reason the Keoghs decided to stay an extra day in the village, in case the guy came back."

"He might also have something to do with them being gone," Jake commented, unsettling thoughts beginning to stir like a precursory breeze ahead of a storm front.

BALADUR AND DMELLO READILY volunteered to make dinner, both being familiar with the workings of wood cookstoves, creating a savory stew from the leftovers of the prior evening. To the chicken and rice, they added chopped cabbage and carrots, setting the big pot in the middle of the table with a loaf of bread. Devouring the meal with the appetites of a pair of ravenous ranch hands, Falcone and Niles had reverted to their mischievously titillating selves, regaling tales of everything from mayhem in muscle cars to bedlam on the Atlantic City boardwalk. Jake listened and observed with a thin smile ghosting his lips, slipping quietly away from the table amidst the clatter of dishes and volleys of laughter.

Strolling outside the house, he stood watching the light change in the sky, a drama of deep blues inflamed with the sun's last blood. Stars began to freckle the darkening ceiling and air curled through the leaves of the trees around him, atomizing the citrus of lemon with the floral of the pink frangipani. He leaned against a palm, feathery fronds swaying above, inhaling the scents and embracing the coolness. He twitched and turned at the sound of footfalls, finding Falcone and Niles coming to join him, their faces flush from the consummation of good food and fellowship and the bottles of Nile Special beer Pelletier had left for them.

"Oh man," Falcone said, "feel that breeze."

Niles tipped his nose into the air and closed his eyes with the contentment of a dog framed by the open window of a car driving along a winding country road, locks of hair blowing back from his forehead and cheeks.

When Jake said nothing, Falcone came up beside him and studied his profile, trying to take measure of his disposition, noting the stubborn set of his jaw, the hard glint in his eye. He shifted his focus to the space in front of them where the trees were etched against the ambient glow of sundown and said, "We're really sorry for dragging you into all this."

Jake sighed and said, "I'm not mad at you. I'm just not happy with the situation. It's not a good time for me to be away from home."

On the other side of him, Niles attempted another inquiry, asking,

"Callie's having a really hard go of it?"

Jake tensed and for a long moment, did not reply. When he did, it was not in answer to the question. Instead, he said, "I noticed some people in your footage are not natives. European?"

"Oh," Niles said, "you mean the doctors, yeah." A spur of sensation heated beneath his skin at the reference, the vision of Dr. Julienne Baudin hovering in a disconnected aura.

"Anybody else?"

"Uh… no," Falcone replied. "Other than us, the Keoghs, the security guys, and the Sanctuary. Why?"

"Just trying to get a bead on things. You said the Sanctuary group were about to leave right after you did, but you haven't been able to get in touch them?"

"No. I just hope they got out." He cast a sideways glance at Jake, sensing a worm of suspicion. "What are you thinking?"

"Again, just trying to get a read," Jake said evenly.

"There *was* something else," Niles remarked. "Eddie thought we were being followed in Kinshasa."

Falcone recounted his observations of the vehicle he believed had tailed them through the city, from the airport to the hotel and then from the hotel to the restaurant.

"By itself, maybe nothing," Jake said, "but when you put that together with the guy materializing—on the footage you showed me, I heard the name Antoine—it starts to suggest things."

"Like what?" Falcone asked.

"Like this was not random."

Jake's words evoked a lapse of heavy silence, the breeze wisping through the trees as lightly as rustling tissue paper. The sky had emptied of color and gone blue-black, stars as bright as fireflies.

Jake cupped his hands on the backs of their necks, the touch conveying a warmth and reassurance both had been craving. "Let's try to get some sleep as it's likely the last comfortable sleep you'll get anytime soon." As they returned to the house, he added, "I want to go to the site of the compound first thing tomorrow, see if I can figure out what really happened there. Then maybe I can get a real starting point."

22

NO ONE WAS STIRRING in the pilot's house when Jake stepped out into the pre-dawn air, moon and stars fading in the sky. The blend of sweet and piney scents were overlaid with the earthiness of dew-laden grass and ground, the night's coolness beginning to cede to the yawning warmth of approaching day. He made his way through the trees behind the house to a path that led to the soccer field where he did a series of head-to-toe stretches followed by isometric presses, planks, and squats, building and releasing tension in each muscle group until he felt the invigorating thrum of boosted circulation. He stretched again and took off in a light sprint along the circuit of the field. The spring and impact of each footfall fired a release of endorphin-spiked energy, stimulating his senses to experience whatever was outside the realm of fundamental elements. He increased his tempo, pushed himself, and then pushed some more, pores opening, lungs expanding.

He was trying to keep his mind empty, a clean slate on which to sketch out thoughts and map strategies, but the fog of troubling factors made clarity elusive. He'd been feeling it almost from the beginning, something really off, and his gut told him there was something bigger at play. He hoped the answer, or at least a clue, was somewhere in the ashes of the Keoghs' compound.

After a couple of laps, he cooled down with another set of exercises, muscles prickling from the vigorous workout, skin damp with perspiration and the humidity that was already on the rise. He drained a bottle of water and took his iPhone from a pocket in his shorts, thought about trying to call Callie with his Iridium sat phone, wished more than anything that he could see and hear her right now—and it might be the last time he could for a while—but it was late in Costa Rica. He slipped the phone back in his pocket and walked to the house, peering up at the paling wedge of moon and listening to the dwindling insect tremolo. He stood, head bent, breathing it all in, and then went inside the house. Baladur and Dmello were dressed and moving about the kitchen with coffee and breakfast production underway, connected in an upbeat and familiar rapport.

"Where are the guys?" Jake asked them, reaching for a hand towel to mop his face.

Baladur said nothing, but his grin provided the answer as he cocked his head away from the dining area.

Jake thumped down the hallway and thrust their bedroom door open, giving it a solid smack with his hand that caused the two inert and snoring bodies huddled under covers to pop up like bread ejecting from a toaster. They gaped at him, faces creased and misshapen with sleep, blinking in the semi-darkness, hair chaotically bouffant.

"Let's go, gents!" Jake barked. "Get your asses up!"

"Shit," Falcone grumbled, but he was already scrambling out of bed. Across from him, Niles moaned something unintelligible and followed suit.

Thirty minutes later, they appeared in the kitchen, still groggy but groomed and shaved, got coffee, and joined the others at the dining room table. Anticipating that Falcone and Niles would need more bush-appropriate clothes, Jake had brought them khakis in drab shades of tan and green made from fast-drying, ripstop fabrics, as well as Palladium boots that resembled high-top Converse sneakers with chunkier tread. Baladur and Dmello were dressed similarly, Jake clad in a long-sleeved tactical shirt over a silk tee tucked into Crye Precision cargo pants. He had on a pair of camel-colored Rocky S2V boots that looked like they could kick some serious ass.

They loaded their plates with scrambled eggs, bread, and fruit, sun beginning to cast pools of light into the house. The interior was a throw-back to earlier decades with simple wood furniture and accents, colors in reds and greens. Jake glanced at his iPhone several times while they ate but found no messages. Earlier, he'd gone back outside with his sat phone and tried to contact Remington for an update. A few minutes later he had received a call from Efron Kipnis, explaining that his boss was already at a job site and letting Jake know they were still seeking intel and would pass along anything of importance. Turning to Dmello, Jake asked, "Have you looked at the maps to see if we can land anywhere near the compound area?"

Collecting empty plates from the table, Dmello said, "I have, and no, we will definitely have to do some hiking. There are not even any roads."

"How far?"

"A couple of kilometers at least."

"That's what I figured since the Keoghs took the helo to and from there." He swallowed the last of his coffee and said, "Okay, gear up and get ready to go. Time to do some jungle CSI."

THE CLOSEST SAVANNA WITH enough continuous space in which to land the Cessna turned out to be six kilometers from the compound site, but termite mounds, obscured by grass and as hard as concrete, were a concern, so Dmello had to fly a little farther to find a completely flattened stretch worn down enough to fully visualize the surface. After a breathlessly rugged touchdown that kicked up clouds of red dirt and grit that riddled the windows, they collected their gear and deplaned.

"This is really remote," Jake said. "You want us to gather some brush to partially camouflage the plane?"

"No worries," Dmello said, flashing a sly grin that revealed a spec of gold in the gleaming white of his teeth.

"Oh…what, you've got some kind of security tech?"

"Yes. Kip has it covered, *mon*." He winked.

"So like if some dodgy character comes along and tries to make a go for it, he'd get zapped or something?" Niles quipped.

Jake waited for him to explain, but Dmello just continued to smile.

Backpacks strapped on, they set off on a hike that took them through staggered grassland and forest thick with vegetation and humidity and swarming insects. Without knowing what threats might be ahead, Jake had once again warned everyone to be as quiet as possible as he led the way, AK-47 slung against his hip, hand comfortable but ready over the trigger guard.

Stopping for refreshment a few times, they reached the site in just over an hour, traversing the last hundred or so yards through apocalyptical landscape with trees burnt bare and black, limbs reaching to the sky like craggy skeletal talons, scorched soil still smelling of the fire that had raged nearly a week ago. Leaves turned to crepe paper cinders crackled as they tread, the absence of insect and animal sounds stark in their silence.

It looked exactly the same as Falcone and Niles remembered, their emotions every bit as ripe, but they could no longer conjure any apparitions of the life that had existed here, of the adults finding a way back to stability, of the happy children laughing at play. They stood at the edge of what could have been the widespread and devastating destruction of a tornado were it not for the charred blackness that permeated everything. Jake gave them some time, watching solemnly as they tentatively picked their way around the remains of the compound, prodding bits of brick and other random pieces with the toes of their new boots. And, just as he had done when they'd walked it with the Keoghs that day, Falcone stopped by the scrap of tarp, plastered in place by a plod of dried mud. He glanced back at Jake, his face collapsed with despondency and bewilderment.

"We slept here," he said, his voice strained.

Jake went to him, put his hand on Falcone's shoulder and gave it a light squeeze.

Falcone dropped his head, shoulders hunched, and swallowed a sob that came out of nowhere. When he looked up again, clearing his throat, he asked, "What the hell happened here?"

"Let's see if we can find out," Jake replied, and moved on ahead of him. "Show me what was where."

Baladur and Dmello flanked the three of them as they patrolled, alert for any movement from the perimeter. While Falcone pointed out each area, Niles showed Jake correlating images on his cameras. Jake stopped often to sift through debris, studying the underlying ground and fragmented objects and materials. He spent a considerable amount of time in the garden, prodding the soil with his shovel tool, raking his gloved fingers across the tops of what had been rows of vegetables. They proceeded slowly across the entire site, Jake methodically evaluating but not saying much. Standing at the back end of the compound where the village housing once sprawled, he gazed off in the direction of the grass and hills and trees, grayed from smoke and ash. His expression, partially hidden behind the shades of his Outlaw TAC sunglasses, was unreadable, but the hands planted on his hips suggested a readiness to put something to action. He walked to the edge of the village tract and stopped, a glint of metal from the ground catching his eye, the size and shape and appearance very familiar to him. He stooped to pick it up, turning it over in his hand, holding it close to scrutinize figures etched on one end. Glanced around and picked up a few more that were close by. When he was satisfied he'd found all that were scattered in a radius of a half-dozen feet, he put them in a pocket of his cargo pants and rejoined Falcone and Niles who had been watching him curiously.

The sun was starting to climb and, without the protection of trees or dwellings, so was the heat. Jake started back toward the gutted garden where he'd seen the road that led to the village church.

As they walked, Falcone asked, "What did you find?"

"Let's get out of this heat for a bit while we can," Jake said, his head tilting up at the unexpected sound of birds sweeping en masse overhead, black and tight in formation until they suddenly broke like cracked peppercorns across the sky.

INSIDE THE CHURCH, EVERYONE took a few minutes to cool down, wiping their faces and drinking water. Then, after a short conversation with Jake, Baladur and Dmello took up sentry duty at the entrance, Falcone and Niles taking seats on one of the wooden benches, peeling wrappers off protein bars made of nuts and fruit. Jake removed his backpack and rifle and sat across from them. Biting into their snacks, Falcone and Niles peered expectantly at him from under the brims of their baseball caps.

"Okay," Jake began, one hand on his thigh, the other draped across his knee gripping the wide-brim boonie hat he had been wearing. "Here are my thoughts. First of all, as I have already said, I don't believe this was a random strike, and what I've observed supports that." He ticked points off on his fingers. "The commodities—electric generators, water pumps, solar panels, satellites—have all been removed in entirety. The garden was not just destroyed, it was excavated, even root plants like carrots and potatoes pulled up. Food and cooking utensils, gone. Medical supplies, gone. Like the people, the animals are gone. No bodies, and as far as I can tell, not a bit of blood."

"So, it was like a raid?" Falcone asked.

"In a sense," Jake replied. "But there's more to this. From everything you told me and showed me, the Keoghs did everything right. They had armed security in place and a pretty solid communications setup tied into early warning networks that broadcast reports of violent groups and incidents. I suspect their communications were compromised…security probably was also. To me, this at least suggests that there were individuals at the compound that had a hand in it."

"Like that Antoine bloke," Niles said, licking salt from his fingertips.

"Yes. But the scope of what happened here would have taken at least a handful of people collaborating." He paused, a shadow of some dark thought still in process passing over his face. "This attack was well-planned, executed with precision and, to me, it also feels…vengeful."

"Vengeful? What do you mean?" Falcone asked.

"Everything was not just trampled, structures were demolished, everything was burned to the ground. In a word, it was overkill."

Jake glanced out a window opening where a buzzard was perched on a decaying tree stump, brown-backed and white-chested, its head swiveling in quest of prey.

Turning back to Falcone and Niles, Jake said, "I'm not sure it was a coincidence that the Keoghs were away from the compound when it was hit. In fact, I think it may have been planned that way."

"What?" Falcone coughed around the nougat of protein bar he was chewing, swallowing roughly.

"You might have been right about being followed in Kinshasa, maybe by someone tapped to keep tabs on where they were when it went down. I also think it's possible that *you*—not the Keoghs—were the intended target on the bird."

"*What?*" Falcone asked again, his eyes bugging.

"The Keoghs were lured or forcibly taken away, so if all this was orchestrated, there would have been no other reason to shoot down the helo."

"Fuck," Falcone muttered. Beside him, Niles was speechless, breathing shallowly, twisting and untwisting the empty wrapper of his protein bar.

"And then there's this," Jake said, digging into the pocket of his pants where he'd put his findings. Unfolding his fist, he revealed four brass objects, cylindrical and just over an inch in length. "Bullet casings from an AK-47. Which might or might not be relevant here. For all we know, these could have been laying around for a while. But something tells me they *are* significant, and here's why."

Falcone and Niles moved closer as Jake prodded one of the casings to show them the etchings.

"Ammunition almost always has numeric or logo markings called headstamps, which identify the origin of manufacture and year."

"So they can be traced?" Falcone asked, squinting at the engraved figures on the ends of the casings.

"Yes, but here's the thing. These are like nothing I've seen before. They're certainly not local. I'm going to see if Kipnis can make an identification."

He reached into his backpack for his iPhone and Iridium GO and went outside. After snapping several images of the casings, he synced his phone to the sat com device and sent an email to Remington and Kipnis. He asked Baladur and Dmello to join him back inside. When they were all together, Jake said, "Luther, let's see the pictures you got while we were flying."

Baladur handed over his phone and everyone looked on as Jake thumbed through the images. He stopped on one and expanded it to zoom. Over his shoulder, Baladur said, "I did not see that before…it looks like a smaller road or path of some kind."

"It does," Jake agreed. He took out one of his maps and studied the topography between the compound site and Nakalé and then along the road they had overflown, comparing satellite imagery from Kipnis. He deliberated what he considered the most likely routes: northwest toward CAR, northeast to South Sudan, and east into Garamba National Park. Finally, he pointed to a spot and addressed Dmello, saying, "Let's fly to this strip."

"By Garamba," Dmello said.

"Yeah. It's not far from that other road. As good a place as any to start looking."

Baladur nodded. "I know what you are thinking. Into the jungle, that is how they would go."

Falcone and Niles both looked confused. "How who would go?"

Jake explained, "If the LRA or any other armed group is behind this, they would ultimately move captives through jungle, and Garamba is a known haunt." To Falcone and Niles, he said, "You guys sure you're up for this so soon after our Amazon ordeal?"

Wariness was pulling at their faces, throats working dryly, but Niles answered before either could really think about it. "Right, then, let's do it, yeah? Eddie?"

Falcone nodded, facial muscles twitching.

Outside the window opening, Jake watched as the buzzard sprang from the stump and dropped onto the ground, wings arched, claws spiking something in the grass. When it lifted in flight, the body of some furry rodent was clamped in its beak, wriggling as the bird flapped away.

Everyone slipped on their backpacks and stepped outside into the hot sun, Jake glancing over his shoulder at the little stone church set amidst the grove of palm trees, fronds hanging limp in the airless heat. They headed back down the road, past the giant acacia tree and the expanse of eviscerated garden, past the ravaged grounds of crushed and crumbled brick and carbonized debris that tumbled into the hills like a trash-polluted oil field flowing blackly across and defiling a diminished green sea.

23

THE AIRSTRIP THEY LANDED on was the roughest one yet, carved out of dense woodland and clearly long-abandoned from any kind of maintenance, so when Dmello lined up over the seemingly unbroken span of corrugated green, everyone drew in a breath and prepared for a gut-pummeling impact. And then the narrow strip of dirt appeared, like a sudden incision from a surgeon's scalpel, grooved from years of rain and latticed with weeds, and Dmello deftly dropped the plane into the opening. The Cessna's wheels came down hard, rolling over clods of dirt and spidering patches of grass before scudding to a stop.

Dmello went through his checks and shutdown flow as Jake issued instructions on what gear to bring. "We'll probably be covering a lot of ground this afternoon," he told them, "and quite possibly setting up camp somewhere before nightfall."

Falcone and Niles looked up from their packing, faces peaked with nervous anticipation. It was all happening again, this time from something *they* had initiated. They watched stiffly as Jake and Baladur selected additional weapons and ammunition from the cache Efron Kipnis had put together, listening to them discuss objectives and worst-case scenarios, the prevailing logic being to go as light as possible and still have enough to handle most situations, favoring gear and weaponry that was known to the region and would not scream operator.

For everyday carry, Jake opted to stick with what he considered his gold standard, the Glocks and AKs, but he also added some additional rifles and ammunitions along with various suppressors and scopes and an assortment of grenades and charges. Turning to Falcone and Niles, he asked, "Do you guys feel comfortable enough to carry a semi-automatic rifle? I trained you, but I know you didn't really do much shooting."

Falcone opened his mouth and then closed it, unsure of what to respond, but in typical fashion, Niles spontaneously blurted, "Hell yeah, mate!"

Jake's eyes narrowed, his lips compressed in stern reproof. "Okay, I need to feel confident that you can handle any weapon I give you, that you won't be either intimidated or trigger-happy." His gaze shifted to Falcone, more concerned about his reluctance than Niles' eagerness. "Eddie?"

"Uh, yeah, sure," Falcone said, but his reply and facial expression were uncharacteristically light on conviction. "Maybe give us a refresher?"

"Of course," Jake said, and reached first for a pair of Glocks, then two AR-15s. "These are lighter than the AKs and arguably a little bit easier to shoot." He demonstrated, propping one of the rifles high and tight against his shoulder. He moved over so Falcone could see better. "You want to hold the grip firmly and pull it back to you, in the stance I showed you, feet shoulder-width apart, knees slightly bent and weight forward. Tuck your elbows, keep the rifle snug to your body. Put your firing hand high up on the grip with your thumb beneath the safety. Hold the handguard with your other hand. Bring the gun up to eye level and plant it against your cheek, line up the sights, disengage the safety with your thumb, and move your finger to the trigger. Press it evenly, and bang." He passed the rifle to Falcone and concluded, "The spent shell will eject and a new round will be loaded into the chamber. You stop or keep going until you're out of ammo, depending on the situation."

He looked pointedly at both of them. "Think you can manage? We can work on it some more later."

They nodded mutely.

"Okay then," Jake said crisply, evaluating the transference of cognition that passed between their eyes. "Luther, make sure they've got everything else and set up with comms."

"Got it, boss," Baladur replied.

Jake finished organizing his supplies and gear and stepped away from the plane, slipping on his sunglasses and hat. Even in the border of trees, the sun's heat was steeped into the ground and air above it. He took a long draw from his pack's Nalgene water bottle and checked GPS and navigational data on his Garmin watch. When the others had joined him, he asked, "All set?"

With a collective affirmation, Jake started off, threading a path cut through the forest. Fifteen minutes later they were emerging onto the far end of the road out of Nakalé.

THEY WALKED FOR SEVERAL hours, covering close to ten miles. Limbs from the massive evergreens entrenched along both sides intertwined overhead, filtering out all but occasional sprinkles and sprays of sun. The shade made the trek more tolerable, but Falcone and Niles still struggled. They plodded leadenly, their weapons initially held awkwardly in front of them and then, after the first hour, bumping against their hips. They panted and swiped at the perspiration drizzling from beneath their caps, faces bloated with heat.

From time to time, Jake would crouch down to look for tire imprints in the dirt, but the only tracks he found were the paw and hoof indents of animal crossings. As they walked he kept thinking about the stillness—too much stillness. There were bird sounds and the swishing of monkeys doing acrobatics in the tree branches, but mostly it was quiet, with only the soft rasp of their clothing, the scuff of their boots, the inhale and exhale of their breaths. He had expected it at the compound grounds; fire left a tableau of stark exodus that would be a long time refilling with life of any kind. But there were villages and people beyond these trees, people that traversed this road. Where were they? The feeling of something intangibly wrong continued to build, creating a tension inside him that was like rubber stretched almost to the point of snapping. He took a deep breath and slowed his stride, noting the subtle downward drift of the sun, and began to search the roadsides for potential campsites.

A few minutes later, he honed in on a spot. He could see a semi-cleared area set just far back enough from the road for them to hear a vehicle but with some concealment they could reinforce. "Let's stop here, guys," he said.

Falcone and Niles exhaled in relief, bending over to catch their breaths.

Jake led them through lofty hardwoods and palms that edged the road to a transition of compact brush with an opening surrounded by more of the taller trees. Baladur and Dmello immediately went about the task of gathering limbs and leafy stalks to fill in the gaps while Jake dispatched Falcone and Niles to collect wood and rocks for a fire pit. He conducted a brief perimeter survey, checking for animal tracks or scat, human footprints or debris, thrashing the vegetation for snakes or other hazards. At the farthermost point of his venture, he thought he detected a loamy, riparian tinge to the air, which could be both good and bad; good as a source of water for their refreshment and replenishment— although they were not quite in need yet—but bad as it would provide the same for predatory animals. He debated moving to another spot, but after hiking for several more minutes and still not catching a glimpse of a pond or stream or river through the foliage or feeling the ground become spongier underfoot, he reversed course and returned to their campsite.

He was pleased to see the progress everyone had made and joined Falcone and Niles in the construction of the fire pit, arranging the tinder, lighting it, and helping them build the teepee of kindling until he was confident the fire would hold. Next, he pointed out placements for their hammocks and assisted them with tying up and draping mosquito nets and ponchos. Falcone and Niles both saw Jake's gaze lift as they finished, scanning the openings in the canopy, which had begun to fill with the golden undertones of impending sunset, and for a moment he seemed to go somewhere else, his expression opaque.

Aware of their scrutiny, Jake said, "We're in the rainy season, so there's always a good chance. Hopefully we'll get lucky and not have a downpour. Believe me when I tell you, you've never seen a thunderstorm with torrential rain like an African one."

"We haven't had any like that so far," Niles said, his nose crinkling as a fly or mosquito buzzed his nostrils. He waved a hand in front of his sweaty face and blew out his breath, neither of which deterred the insect.

"Get some more repellant on you before we eat," Jake said, and left them to find a spot to set up his Goal Zero solar panels for recharging phones and devices while there was still some daylight. He wanted to check in with Remington or Kipnis, but the more persistent inclination, feeding like the flames of their fire lapping briskly at the sap-infused air, was to call Callie.

BY THE TIME THEY assembled around the pit to eat, the sun had saturated the woods with bright red light that inflamed the limbs and leaves before being extinguished by the blue-green aura of dusk. The heat of the day had only barely abated, the air mixed with the scents of ebony and mahogany and humus and spoor.

Baladur and Dmello leaned against each other chuckling as they watched Falcone and Niles plunder through the contents of their MREs with the voracity of children digging for the prize in a McDonald's Happy Meal. Beef stew entrées were heating in their packets, propped up against the rocks forming the outer ring of the pit. Falcone was munching pretzels while Niles squeezed peanut butter and jelly on a wafer. Both looked up, caught the other's amusement, and glanced at Jake as if to consult him for the rules of MRE etiquette.

Smacking the PB&J conglomeration around his tongue and cheeks, Niles responded with typical ingenuousness. "What? It's good!"

That only made Baladur and Dmello laugh harder, Dmello telling Jake, "I love these guys."

Jake shook his head, but the corners of his mouth ticked up in a wry grin. "They're a pain in my ass." He reached for his food pouch and emptied the chunks of beef and potatoes and carrots into the entrée section of his MRE platter, mindful of the steam. Next to him, Falcone and Niles were already slurping stew into their mouths, wincing and cursing as it burned their tongues.

"How did that get so bloody hot?" Niles exclaimed, almost dumping the food from his lap.

"Let's talk situational awareness," Jake said, hoisting a spoonful to cool as he spoke. He looked at Baladur and Dmello but quickly cut his eyes to Falcone and Niles, letting the two former soldiers know who the briefing was primarily for. Baladur and Dmello nodded imperceptibly in comprehension. In between bites of his meal, Jake continued. "First and foremost, buddy system always. Even when you go for a piss, you better have the other one on your six. Obviously, be aware of everything around you, including overhead and on the ground. One of the deadliest snakes in the world, the black mamba, is common here. It is hard to see, aggressive, and fast."

Falcone and Niles stopped eating, utensils clenched in front of their faces which had gone slack.

"Their bites are fatal, usually within twenty minutes. They're more active during the day and usually burrow at night, but if you disturb them—"

"Shit," Falcone muttered, and dropped his spoon onto his tray, glaring at Jake.

"Hey, Africa is every bit as dangerous as South America," Jake said. "Maybe even more so. We are right in the middle of a wild kingdom and very far down on the food chain."

Dmello added anecdotally, "Many of the animals can outrun you."

Jake set his tray down, leaning forward with his hands clasped between his knees. His black hair gleamed in the firelight, skin bronzed the color of aged whiskey. Speaking in an even, measured tone and gazing candidly from Falcone to Niles, he said, "Just have respect, be careful and aware." He expanded his focus to include Baladur and Dmello. "We'll alternate rack and watch between us and keep a fire going. We obviously don't need it for heat, and rain might put it out during the night, but animals tend to be afraid of fire, so it makes a good deterrent. We need to keep it moderate, though, so we don't attract attention. In everything we do, we want to keep a low profile." Directing his speech again to Falcone and Niles, he added, "This is a different scenario than Colombia. Always be prepared to go hot but as a last resort."

Falcone and Niles were listening avidly but clearly fading, their faces gaunt with fatigue. They stood, gaits unsteady, glancing warily around them.

"Why don't you two get some rest," Jake suggested. "It's been a long day."

"That it has, mate," Niles said, and shuffled listlessly off to his hammock, Falcone right behind him.

Jake walked over to the spot where he'd set up the solar panels and retrieved his Iridium sat phone. The evening sky was now hedging into night-dark, stars bright and defined. He took the clarity as an incentive, and when the phone's network connected, scrolled to Callie's number and made the call. As he listened to the dial tone, he checked his watch and factored the time difference, already knowing it was midday in Costa Rica; it was coming up on 7:30 PM, making it 11:30 AM there. Should be an ideal time, he thought.

Three dial tones burred and the call was answered, but not by Callie.

"Camilla? *Está todo bien?*" He immediately tensed, felt his heartbeat quicken, his grip on the sat phone handset tighten, and strained to listen as the housekeeper spoke in a lowered voice. She explained that Callie was still not sleeping at night but sometimes would doze for brief periods during the day, on the living room couch. Camilla told him she would put soothing music on for Callie and do her cooking and cleaning and laundry in the vicinity to keep an eye on her.

"*No ha pasado nada? Está todo bien?*" he asked again. There was a brief pause, and he heard a soft intake of breath before Camilla replied that everything was fine. Responding to the housekeeper's hesitant inquiry about waking Callie for him, Jake quickly declined, requesting that she just tell Callie he had called, not to be upset that she'd missed it, and that he would call again when he could.

After disconnecting, he tried but did not get Remington.

He put the solar panels and sat phone in his backpack and strolled back to the fire pit. Baladur and Dmello had cleared everything from dinner and were talking quietly. When they looked up at him, despite his own tiredness, he said, "I'll take first watch, you guys get some rest, too."

Jake inspected the ground below a mahogany tree closest to the fire and sat in between two of its thick, spreading buttress roots. It towered at least a hundred feet overhead, the gray-brown bark smooth and warm against his back. Peering up at the stars twinkling through the oblong, pinnate leaves forming the tree's massive crown, he thought about the day, about his plan for tomorrow, about the evolving quest before him, but his mind kept replaying the call with Camilla. It troubled him, not so much because of what she had said, but because he couldn't shake the feeling that she was holding something back. He was instinctively astute in reading people—eyes and facial expressions, gestures and movements, word selection and vocal inflections, body language—but even over the phone he'd elicited a protective deception. He deliberated calling Jesse Segura, and would at some point anyway, but told himself for now he needed to uphold the trust he had staked in his domestic gatekeepers. He slid his iPhone from a pocket in his pants, powered it on, and navigated to his favorite picture of Callie. Smiling, a flutter rippling inside him, he sighed and put the phone away. He picked up his rifle and, holding it across his lap, listened to the quietness of the day give way to the audible stirring of night denizens.

SOME HOURS LATER, NILES was trying to get Falcone's attention, calling over to him in a stage whisper. "Psst! Eddie…Eddie, wake up!"

Falcone raised his head, disoriented in the darkness. "Wha—Curran? What?"

"I've got to hit the loo, mate."

Remembering where he was, Falcone replied, "Now? Really?" But at the mention of it, he realized his own big boy was amenable to the suggestion.

"Yes, now," Niles said insistently.

Falcone groaned, even as he felt the urge himself. "Can't you…you know…"

"What?"

"Go from there."

"From the hammock? No! Are you daft? You know what Jake said!"

"All right, all right," Falcone muttered irritably, extricating himself from the netting and hung bedding with considerable effort, wrestling with it until he was standing on the ground.

Despite a ten- to fifteen-degree drop in temperature since sundown, the air was uncomfortably moist with humidity, their clothing clinging to their skin like wet tissue. No longer still, the forest was a cacophonous mashup of owls hooting and frogs croaking and insects clicking and vibrating. They took the path Jake had cut earlier, pulses pounding, pointing their small flashlights in every direction, so worried about snakes that they did not immediately notice movement in the bush ahead. Their boots crunched over desiccated leaves and twigs, low-hanging branches skimming their heads and shoulders. When they reached the designated spot, both lined up, straddled their legs, unzipped, and began to urinate into the trough they had helped to dig, exhaling with relief as they emptied their bladders.

A peculiar and shrill garble close by startled them in mid-stream.

"Shit!" Niles hissed. "What the bloody hell is *that*?"

They now saw and heard the rustling in the brush and stood paralyzed, gripping their penises, faces masked with terror. There was a series of whoops farther off that seemed to be coming closer. And then, a hair-raising low snarl followed by a growl that sounded demonic.

"Oh God," Falcone murmured, floundering to stuff himself into his pants. His fingers were inept, his throat dry. He bounced on his feet and shook, desperately trying to get tucked in and zippered up.

Beside him, Niles had paled white as soap, his face stunned and motionless in the moonlight. His lips moved but produced no words, loose hair damp on his cheeks and forehead.

Falcone nudged him urgently in an effort to instigate action, but Niles stood transfixed, as if lit up by the beacon of an alien mothership. "Curran! Finish and let's go!"

The beam of Falcone's flashlight, clamped between his teeth, caught the red glare of eyes just a few feet away. The growl connected to the eyes expanded into a chorus of several as Falcone and Niles stood visibly shaking. Rustling turned into vigorous gnashing, a feral odor flaring.

Finding his voice, Niles whimpered, "Oh, f-f-fuck, Eddie," and cringed, ducking his head away.

And then something swept from behind them, thrust in the direction the growls were coming from, and they hobbled backwards, not sure if they were falling into or out of the abomination. Jake lunged by, brandishing his spear stick, a bloom of fire on the point, jabbing it aggressively toward the brush until the growling was replaced by strident whoops in retreat. The last vocalization, from a distance, sounded absurdly like hysterical cackling.

Still badly rattled, Niles blew out a shaky breath and said, "Jake, thank God."

"What was that?" Falcone panted. "Lions? Wild cats?"

"Hyenas," Jake replied. He looked astoundingly calm and intrepid in the flickering flame from his spear.

"Oh." Lines of tension creasing Falcone's face began to ease, the stiffness in his shoulders relaxing. He turned, draping an arm over Niles' neck, and began walking away.

Jake caught up and leaned close to his ear. "Make no mistake. They would have ripped your asses to shreds."

DRINKING STRONG COFFEE THAT had been boiled over the fire, they watched the early morning light change from its dark blues to the silvery glow of false dawn and finally to a surly gray from the mist that filled the woods with a smoky haze. For a while, no one spoke much, but Jake, Baladur, and Dmello moved efficiently around camp, packing and cleaning up and tending to their weapons. Falcone and Niles, neither of whom had slept after the incident in the night, sat in a stupor, slouched and lethargic, the skin under their eyes pouched and sallow.

Jake approached and stood over them, hands on his hips. Somehow, even wearing mostly the same clothing as the day before, he looked and smelled fresh. His hair was neatly combed, face scrubbed clean, skin smooth beneath the sheen of stubble. When he got no acknowledgment of his presence, he crouched down and waited until their heads came up. Lightly, he said, "All right, so you didn't have the best first night on the trail."

Neither Falcone or Niles said anything.

"Learn from it, as you should with everything you encounter, and hit reset."

"What should we have done?" Falcone asked, gazing glumly at the sludge of coffee grounds in the bottom of his cup.

"Well, you did the buddy thing as we discussed. You had your flashlights...but where were your spear sticks?" He was referring to the sturdy limbs they had all selected and sharpened with their pocket knives, like the one he'd used in their defense. "As I said, we're in Africa, we're going to have to deal with animals. You need to be ready. Most of the time, they're as scared of us as we are of them."

"You didn't seem scared," Falcone said, a hint of petulance in his voice.

"Being calm in those situations only comes with experience," Jake replied evenly, overlooking Falcone's demeanor.

"Why didn't you just shoot 'em?" Niles asked.

"Remember what I said about keeping a low profile? Gunfire may deter animals, but it also alerts people—potentially unfriendlies—of our presence and position. We always have weapons at hand but avoid using them unless it's necessary." He stood up. "You going to be ready to move in a few minutes?"

Falcone and Niles nodded morosely and watched him stride over to confer with Baladur and Dmello. Groaning, they rose and began organizing their gear. A few minutes later, Jake gave the campsite a final inspection to make sure it had been returned to its prior appearance, all traces of their inhabitation erased, and led them back to the road.

The clouds populating the sky began to group into thick clusters, opening pockets of blue that became wider and wider expanses emblazoned with the yellow brilliance of sun. Again, they hiked in the shade of the palms and trees lining the road but perspired heavily in the building heat. They still had not seen a single human soul, which continued to perplex and bother Jake. In contrast, the wildlife along the roadsides was increasingly active, with primates pillaging and squabbling among mango and banana trees and grunting hogs plowing through low brush. The forest was filled with the flashes of bright plumage and the lively twittering of kingfishers and weavers and sunbirds and bee-eaters. The cinnamon-colored road stretched on before them, yielding nothing but more and more of the same. Trees and dirt and slices of sky, sun and heat and sweat.

Monitoring their levels of fatigue as the day progressed, Jake had decided it was time for an extended break when the dense woodlands began to thin into a savanna of tall green and gold grasses. The satellite imagery loaded into his phone and the mapping on his watch confirmed that they were approaching a small river, an ideal waypoint where they could take respite and also top off their water supply. It came into view a few minutes later, flowing through tree-covered banks and spilling across an oasis of mudflats edged with papyrus and reeds and water lettuce, slate-green surface dimpled with the slow-moving currents. The protruding tops of rounded rocks scattered in the middle had the smooth warm buff of bread dough in the sunlight. There was no shortage of aquatic birds in or around the *bai*—flocks of Egyptian geese in flight, clouds of egrets lifting in and out, storks and cranes and ibises wading, a few fish eagles soaring and diving into the river—but oddly, no grazing animals.

They found a spot shaded by bushwillows, stretched and slipped off their backpacks and weapons. Encouraging the others to rest, Jake took out the Katadyn water filtration kit he used, which included a ten-liter gravity bag. He walked to the streambed, stooped down, and filled the bag. As he was rolling and clipping the top for carry, he became aware of a tremendous stork nearby, four to five feet tall, bending on stilted white legs to pick at the remains of some kind of prey. He watched in morbid fascination as the bird's head came up, pink gular sac and white chest streaked with blood and pulp, bits of inorganic matter hanging from its long beak. When Jake stood, the stork flexed its enormous black wings and flapped off, the sound like that of wind whipping into the headsail of a boat. His eyes followed the stork's flight over the river and distant trees where other carrion birds were circling.

Jake hung the gravity bag on a tree limb and filled all of his bottles and Ziploc pouches and tucked them in his backpack. Behind him, Falcone and Niles were once again generating hilarity from Baladur and Dmello.

Niles was saying, "Actually, what happened last night was kind of exciting."

"What?" Falcone blustered. "Almost getting eaten up?"

"Well, not that part, mate. But it felt like, you know, riding a rollercoaster and trying not to piss your pants, and then when you're done you can't wait to do it again."

Falcone shook his head. "You're not right."

Addressing them all and indicating the filtration kit, Jake said, "Come on, replenish your water supply. When it's empty, just scoop up some more from the river, fold the top, hang it and fill." He smiled, watching their astonished reactions to the clear, purified water flowing from the bag's hose. He gazed back over the *bai* swarming with birds and, even though he suspected he knew why, heard himself say, in the way a disappointed child might lament a zoo animal hibernating out of view in its enclosure, "I thought maybe we'd see some elephants."

Baladur shook his head pensively. "I cannot say I am surprised. This whole area is known for poaching. Gone are the days when you could see hundreds. Now you are lucky if you see a few. Garamba has been hit especially hard."

Jake frowned, a deep-seated animus stirring inside. The day was full of abundant sunshine and deep green trees and tranquil blue skies, and the slow and steady ebb of river to stream, but somehow the beauty around him only made his thoughts more abject. And maybe it was the redness of the soil or the omnipresent smokiness from wood fires throughout the country or the irrepressible heat, or maybe it was simply in the DNA of Africa itself, but no matter how bright the sun or how verdant the trees or how vivid the sky, the landscape always seemed to have a heavy aged cast, as if everything were being viewed through the sepia filter of a lens muddied and bloodied by decades of war and death.

THEY RESTED FOR A half hour before resuming their trek and had not gone far before they finally came across what they'd been looking for—and then, something they had not seen coming.

As they approached the junction of the secondary road in Baladur's images, a set of tire tracks appeared in the dirt on the other side, turning and continuing down the narrower route. The imprinted treads led them into denser forest, at times the tree limbs so close overhead or on the sides that it was hard to envision a truck making clearance, but the trail of ongoing tracks and broken branches confirmed that it had. Humidity simmered through the woods, flies and mosquitoes amassing in furious whorls, the soil's compost emitting a pungent stench.

As they walked on, each of them began to gasp and cough at the intensifying odor, which had the ripe, fecund rot of spoiled food and raw waste, arms over their mouths and noses, eyes tearing.

Swatting frantically at the insects blitzing his face, Falcone wheezed,

"God Almighty, what is that smell?"

Hacking and spitting, Dmello said, "I would say the remains of a large animal."

A finger of light drew Jake's eyes upward to a porthole of sky in the canopy where he saw what was possibly the same formation of birds he'd observed earlier and, a moment later, heard the heavy drop of one or more of them. Grimacing inwardly and wiping perspiration from his brow, he took a few steps forward, already knowing that they were not about to discover the carcass of an animal. He stopped and felt a premonitory twinge in his rib cage, and also knew in that moment everything was about to change again. He took another step, breathing through his mouth, and caught a glimpse of black-and-white feathers flicking through the bush. When Jake moved again, the vast wings whapped, taking the bird off in a noisy thrash, the strip of fabric that had been caught in its beak fluttering to the ground. The buzz of thousands of insects cut the air like an electric saw.

Jake poked the end of his rifle into the vegetation where the bird had been, releasing a backdraft of frenzied flies, and looked down at the two bodies sprawled in the mulch.

Behind him, he heard choked inhalations from Falcone and Niles.

"Jesus…oh God," Falcone uttered, bile crawling up his throat.

"Is that…bloody Christ…" Niles' hand flew to his mouth, retching and then vomiting. When he got himself somewhat under control, he turned and forced another glance at the forms ravaged beyond recognition.

But everyone knew who they were.

24

JAKE BACKED THEM AWAY, momentarily turning his attention to Falcone and Niles. Both were dry heaving, their faces splotchy and oozing perspiration, and he knew they would quickly become dehydrated in this heat. He sat Niles down and gestured for Falcone to do the same, splashed them with water and encouraged them to take small sips. After a few minutes, he asked, "You guys okay?"

Niles nodded weakly and blotted his face with his shirt sleeve, but every time he swallowed, his stomach hitched and his facial muscles spasmed.

Jake said, "It's okay if you're not. That's tough stuff."

Reclaiming some of his bravado, Falcone straightened his posture, lifted his ball cap and ran an agitated hand through his damp hair. "Yeah, yeah, we're fine." He replaced the cap on his head and started to stand.

Jake put a hand on Falcone's shoulder to stop him and got no resistance. To Dmello, he said, "Kean, stay with them…Luther, will you come with me?" He dug into his backpack, taking out several pairs of nitrile gloves and a cravat, which he tied around his head to cover his nose and mouth.

Baladur followed him back to the spot, battling the flies as he stepped around in the brush taking pictures with his phone. Even predisposed as they were to all kinds of death, the sight and smell was still overpowering. The noxious stench of putrefaction condensed in the stagnant air like the vapors of a hazmat contamination, stinging their eyes and constricting their throats.

Focusing on his mouth breathing, Jake moved in to take a closer look. Both bodies were face up, blowflies swirling and beetles and ants crawling in and out of every opening and orifice. Maggots were wriggling in slimy fissures created by gaseous expansion and the feeding of scavengers. Brush and soil were spattered with corporeal matter and leached fluids.

Cause of death was indisputable.

There were a couple of bullet wounds in each of the torsos, jagged blackened holes that bore through lots of vital life-sustaining organs and blood vessels, some of which might have been survivable with immediate treatment and quick evacuation. But the tops of their heads had also been blown out, almost as if the brains inside had erupted in volcanic fashion, shards of bone mixed with the pulp clabbered in the dirt. There was no surviving that.

Below the head shots, jaws were distorted and slack, tongues protruding from swollen lips. Dark brown blood was dried in smears from nostrils. What eyeballs remained intact were bulging from the sockets, dulled with a milky glaze. Flesh was grossly bloated and mottled gray-green, abdomens distended. Jake gingerly ran his gloved hands over both bodies, trying not to cause further dissolution, searching for anything from pockets and finding nothing. He looked over at Baladur, who had been combing the ground for bullet casings, and got a shake of the head.

The two of them rejoined Dmello, Falcone, and Niles. Jake tugged the cravat off his face, blowing upward at the hair fringed over his brow. With the cravat now looped around his neck and the boonie hat, skin ruddy in the heat, he had the look of a cowboy after a grueling roundup. He pulled off the nitrile gloves, ran water over his hands, and drank thirstily from his Nalgene bottle. Wiping his mouth, he took a seat on the ground at the road's edge, next to Falcone and Niles. They were sitting with hands clasped between bent knees, heads lowered.

"You okay?" Jake asked again. When they nodded, he said, "The security detail." Stated, without a question in his voice; Falcone and Niles had obviously known it was them, but his identity came from the build and look of the bodies. Despite decomposition, the military cues were there: beards, boots, and physique—though significantly altered post mortem—and they were Caucasian.

Niles said, "They were bloody arseholes, really, but my God…"

"I'll never be able to unsee that," Falcone said hoarsely. "It's seared into my brain." He pressed his fingers into his temples.

"I'm sure," Jake replied. He took another drink of water, the sourness of decay lingering in his mouth. "I can't be sure how long they've been dead, and this environment escalates decomp, but my guess is about two days. From what we heard in Nakalé, they took off after the Keoghs, and they've been gone three days. The bodies are past what's called the fresh stage and into active decomp…" He heard gulps from Falcone and Niles, but continued in clinical detachment. "The bloating, color and marbling of skin, the type of insect activity are all indications. They were most likely shot with an AK. We didn't find any casings, but the bullet wounds support that. Fairly close range, so they were probably caught off guard. I didn't find any personal effects and their weapons are missing." He paused thoughtfully. "Since we can't spare anything to cover them, we could at least further conceal them in the bush, and I'll send the GPS coordinates to Kipnis. What are their names?"

Falcone and Niles looked at each other, mouths parted in dumbfounded incapacity. "Shit," Falcone finally said. "I don't know. They used nicknames…Patch and Gab. I don't remember ever hearing their full names. Do you, Curran?"

Niles shook his head.

"So I guess you have no idea who they worked for?" Jake asked. When he got no response, he stood and gazed down the road and then up to the sky where buzzards and vultures and at least one stork hovered, waiting to return.

AFTER COVERING THE BODIES with some mulch and a lot of brush, they resumed following the tire tracks down the road. Falcone and Niles were nauseated and lightheaded, clutching their rifles tensely and twitching at every new sound, Baladur and Dmello silently on their flank. Jake's right hand was on the pistol grip of his AK, finger by the trigger as his eyes did a continual sweep of the road front and sides.

Tactically, he was running through countermoves in the event they were ambushed, something he'd told them was now a real possibility. Whoever had killed the security detail might be long gone, but they might also be holed up somewhere along the trail, and although the Keoghs' guys could have been a random target of opportunity for their weapons and personal effects, Jake was inclined to believe otherwise. So before setting off, he had delivered a briefing which included instructing Falcone and Baladur to walk close to one side of the road, Dmello and Niles on the opposite side; if they were attacked, they would pair off accordingly. He had reviewed gun operation and engagement with Falcone and Niles to ensure they were prepared, hoping there would be no need for them to fire the weapons, but with each passing mile he felt the swell of forewarning expanding in his gut.

They hiked on into the afternoon, the sun shining in bright white starbursts through the trees, sporadic birdsong lilting with the whimsy of a childhood summer's day, but the underlying tension kept their anxiety crackling like low-frequency static. Several times, a swishing of grasses or a thrashing of tree branches set off a reactionary sequence of defensive stances and head swivels and clicks of weapons' safeties, but for hours the trail remained unassailed.

The gallery forest began to thin and open up to scrubby savanna and, with less cover, Jake slowed their pace and became all the more vigilant, pausing frequently to scan the distance through a pair of Steiner binoculars. They had resumed walking after a refreshment break when a small structure came into view about two hundred yards ahead. It was made of mud and thatch, framed and reinforced by heavy limbs. Jake raised a closed fist, signaling everyone to halt, and focused his binoculars on it. An instant later, he waved an arm down and they all crouched in the waist-high grass.

A man emerged from the far side of the shack and stood in front, arm slung across an automatic rifle.

"Whoa," Falcone said, a little too audibly. "Maybe that's—"

Jake quickly silenced him with a zip-it pantomime over his lips.

They all watched as a second man crossed from a sparsely wooded copse, rifle clenched in an armpit, adjusting his pants and then fishing in a pocket for a cigarette, which he lit and stuck in his mouth. He joined the other man, the two talking with the slouched postures and lax gestures suggestive of a long and uneventful day. But they were clearly on some kind of sentry duty, remaining close to the front of the shack.

In a low voice, Jake said, "Those guys are guarding something—might not be people, could be supplies, could be contraband, could be anything—but I want to check it out. It's too open for us to surprise them and I don't want to take them out unless or until there's a reason, so I think the best option is to get them away from the hooch long enough for me to get over there and take a look. I can't tell if the vehicle tracks continue, but they went as far as the transition from dirt and there are worn ruts through here."

He put the Steiners back to his eyes and, through laser-sharp 10x magnification, studied the expanse of savanna around them, noting the dispersion of trees, thickets of brush, the edge of another forest off to the west, and the footage between all. Gazed again at the two men stationed by the shack. And then turned in his crouch, facing into their huddle, and told them what he had in mind.

THE RELATIVE PLACIDITY OF the afternoon was displaced by a mellifluous chorus of voices crooning in layers of harmony, emanating from somewhere beyond the wooded edge of the field.

"Ooh-Ooh...Ooh-Ooh..."

The chorus gave way to the rhythmic beat and airy pop vocalizing of Sauti Sol's Bien-Aimé Baraza, singing, "I think we fell in love too fast...African nights and a cool rush..."

Hunkered down past a grouping of sausage trees with their salami-size fruit hanging from ropey vines, Dmello and Niles passed binoculars back and forth, watching as both men in front of the shack reacted to what they were hearing. The men exchanged words, their expressions reflecting cagey curiosity. Predictably, their hesitation was short-lived, hours of ennui weakening the yoke of duty. With a precautionary look in all directions, the pair sauntered across the span, rifles pointed toward the trees. Following the waft of music, they sought out the source, searching at eye level until almost on top of it and then realizing it was coming from somewhere on the ground.

As soon as the two men entered the woods, Jake's voice broadcasted through comms, "Moving," and Dmello and Niles saw him trot briskly toward the shack.

The song continued on repeat, the men using the barrels of their rifles to rake through brush, occasionally kneeling for a closer look—a pair of AK-wielding guys on a musical Easter egg hunt.

"Hapo ulipokamata nafeel so sweet…"

"Voici!" one exclaimed victoriously, stooping to pick up an mp3 player Dmello had planted and concealed under a pile of leaves. The man's face creased with confusion as he worked to extract the thin rectangular device which seemed to be stuck in the dirt. He managed to free it, straightened up and held it in the air for the other man to see. But the player was dropped almost instantly when a long hiss from the ground was followed by a thrash overhead several yards away—a thick vine stretched taut zipping back to the tree branch it was tied to, whipping into the tree's crown and swaying limbs and leaves as if something or someone were moving about. Both men jerked defensively, turning in a circle with their rifles extended. They saw nothing to question, the shack mostly obscured from their view by the network of vines and fruits and limbs surrounding them, and were about to retreat when they heard the thwack of something hitting a tree trunk farther off. They stood undecided, looking and listening, glancing back and then moving warily forward.

Dmello threw another rock, this one striking bark a few yards beyond the first. This time, the two men did not advance, apparently grasping the distance they had wandered from their post.

Baladur and Falcone, who remained in place to cover Jake, had heard the music start and, like the two men guarding the shack, could only just make out the sound at their distance. They had watched as the men took the bait and headed for the woods to investigate, Jake waiting for his opening and then swiftly advancing on the structure. They listened as the upbeat tune continued playing, the stirrings of a light breeze riffling the grass around them, clouds scattered in the sky above, and then saw the movement in the upper limbs of a tree when Dmello's rigged vine retracted like a yo-yo string and released the tethered bough.

Jake's voice broadcast through the comms again.

Baladur and Falcone sprang to their feet as rounds of automatic fire popped across the savanna.

Somewhere on the ground, Bien-Aimé Baraza was still singing from the mp3 player.

25

CROSSING TO THE HUT, Jake had taken a quick look to make sure the two guards were in the trees, and then focused on the door, which was made of wood planks and secured by a simple hasp lock. Doors were by no means a standard on these structures, even the more well-made ones, and metal closures certainly were not. Unsurprisingly, the hardware was eroded from age and the elements, but the staple loop had twisted upright easily enough. He'd pushed it through the hinged strap and felt a slight release from the planked door. Then, slowly nudging it open, heedful of possible booby traps, he'd peered into the dim interior, his eyes adjusting to the changing dimensions as daylight invaded. The trapped air had hit his nose, rank with the odor of animal hides and hair and entrails, and he'd realized the structure was, or had been, a hunting shack. He picked up another smell, similarly musky but fresher—that of human perspiration.

The instant he'd made the association and discovered the source, semi-automatic gunfire clattered from the woods.

"Go hot now!" he had commanded and, from the bush closest to the shack, he heard the reaction from Baladur and Falcone as they fired their weapons, Dmello and Niles joining in from across the field.

Inside the shack, on the other side of a wood worktable stained dark with old blood, Jake saw two men and a woman, seated on the thatch-covered dirt floor, cloth gags in their mouths, hands zip-tied behind their backs. He slipped his Spartan Horkos knife from its hip sheath and pulled each of them up, slicing the plastic restraints from their wrists. Then he moved to the doorway with the stock of his AK propped against his shoulder. He flipped the safety lever down, racked the charging handle, and aimed into the open savanna, sighting on the guards running toward him across the field. Bullets were coming at them from multiple angles, causing the guards to turn and shoot as they ran, but they were still making a beeline for the shack.

The three freed captives were gasping and coughing as they removed gags, scuffling to retrieve duffle bags that had been piled into a corner. When Jake felt them at his back, he said, "Get ready...on my go, to the bush off from the rear, fast as you can." He took a step forward to give them room to exit and began firing at the oncoming men, shouting, "Go, go, go!"

With the woman between them, the two men fled from the shack while Jake gave directions through his comms, instructing Falcone to intercept the threesome as he joined Baladur in laying down fire to give cover for Dmello and Niles to retreat. In the field, one guard hopped up and then collapsed as if he were attached to a puppeteer's string. Seconds afterward, the other sprang backwards and dropped into the grass. Neither moved, so Jake called for a cease-fire, waiting while Dmello searched the guards.

Niles at his side, Dmello jogged to Jake and Baladur and said, "Nothing but cigarettes, a few franc notes. No kind of identification. But I got their extra ammo and a radio."

"Good, you can monitor it, see if there's any chatter," Jake said. He checked his watch and added, "Much as I'd like to search that hooch, this time of day it probably won't be long before others come to relieve them, so we need to get out of here." He looked at Niles, whose breath was coming in puffs, skin flushed, the pupils in his gray eyes like ink blots. "Curran?"

An aftershock of adrenaline rippling through him, Niles cracked a nervous grin. "What? I'm good." Turning to Dmello, he said, "Quite like that tune, bloomin' earworm...who is it?"

The brush extending behind the shack abutted another forest, thick with a mix of medium to tall trees. They hurried into the widest opening and moved briskly along a trail of trampled undergrowth until closing in on a line of swaying vegetation. Jake stopped and watched, saw swatches of clothing, the top of Falcone's ball cap, and a flash of the woman's hair.

Niles also saw it and broke from their formation, bolting forward before Jake could stop him. "Bloody hell! It *is* you!" he exclaimed, pouncing on the woman and wrapping his arms around her.

Amelia Keogh gave a soft squeal and said, "Oh, Curran." And then pulled back in embarrassment, her striking red hair frayed and loose in a ponytail tie and dulled with dust. The skin around her eyes was pale and sagging with fatigue, the green irises tinged with yellow. "Sorry, we smell bad."

"Ah, we all do," Niles retorted. He looked to Cyrus Keogh, standing beside his wife, then to Cameron McNamara, both equally wan and disheveled, their clothing grayed with dirt and sweat and grooved with wrinkles. "So what happened?" Niles asked. "Why did you—"

All eyes snapped abruptly to Jake, who was now standing next to Niles. He offered a brief smile but his voice left no opening for social niceties. "Let's save the warm and fuzzy reunion for later, and if you want a *live* reunion, we need to get some quick distance from here." Extending his hand to Cyrus Keogh, he said, "Jake Tyler."

Keogh clasped his hand with a disarming grin full of his patent charm and congeniality, as if nothing remotely unpleasant had happened and meeting Jake was part of a normal afternoon in a composed and civilized setting. "G'day, mate," he said, gesturing to his wife and assistant with an open palm. "Amelia and Cameron."

Jake nodded politely but his patience was rapidly diminishing. His head tilted to the treetops, where the breeze was rustling leaves and tugging at the ends of branches, the canopy gaps covering over with clouds the color of etched tin. "We're going to need to find a secure spot for shelter, and soon, so let's beat feet."

AFTER ISSUING A STERN reminder to proceed quietly and without talking, Jake found their spot an hour and not quite two miles away in a forest mixed with sycamore figs, marula, and natal mahogany trees, all wide-crowned and densely leafed with a network of sturdy lower limbs and forked junctions which would provide the ideal framework for the shelter they needed. He would have liked to get even more distance from the shack and the men they'd killed, but everyone was visibly tired and it was getting dark. The sun's presence had been totally obscured by thick clouds for a while now, the backdrop of sky turning like ripening berries, going purple to blue-black. The uptick in the breeze would have been refreshing were it not for the humidity rising with it, seeping into the ground and tree bark and filling the air with the alluvial odor of sphagnum spiced by a composite of living and dead things.

The Keoghs and Cameron McNamara had rain ponchos and mosquito nets but no hammocks, so Jake's first priority was constructing several sleep shelters in the trees, making platforms by wedging and lashing limbs in the nests of two or more trunks and then laying parallel rows of smaller branches for a base. On top of this he piled leafy bows, fronds, grass, and leaves of big-eared plants, repeating the process in limbs above to form a roof.

When he was done, Jake made a circuit to inspect his work and the efforts of the rest, enjoining everyone to start on fire making next. No one was really speaking yet; the Keoghs were outwardly maintaining stoic equanimity but Jake caught the vaguely disconsolate glimpses between them and held Falcone and Niles at bay by keeping them busy.

The pit got built, the fire lit and established, and the group settled in around it.

While the Keoghs freshened up as best they could, Jake, Baladur, and Dmello disassembled their rifles for cleaning. Falcone and Niles sat next to Jake with their weapons and tried to follow along, watching as he removed the magazine, opened the takedown pin to separate the upper and lower receivers, and extracted the bolt carrier group. All of it with the quick and nimble fingers of one who had done it innumerable times over the years, in every conceivable—or inconceivable—combat situation, in every element of weather, in daylight or dead of night. He dabbed cleaning solution on a microfiber cloth and began wiping down each of the parts, following up with silicone lubricant. When he was done, he reassembled his AK-47, which was actually the Czech VZ58 folding stock version he favored, and reloaded the thirty-round magazine with 7.62 x 39 bullets.

The evening air had become more infused with the metallic-tinged moisture of coming rain, birds flittering agitatedly in the trees. Though still some miles away, thunder was percussing in increasingly resonant runs, lightning flashing from within the clouds like the flare of a vintage camera lamp, and Jake no longer suspected they were in for one of those epic storms—he knew it. MREs were distributed and heated, freeze-dried coffee stirred into water boiled over the fire. Jake opened and arranged the components of his meal, squeezing Buffalo hot sauce and cheese on chicken chunks and folding the mix into two tortillas. As usual, Falcone and Niles were enthusiastically diving into theirs, munching on the pretzel balls and assorted nuts of Recovery Trail Mix as they emptied packets of M&Ms, First Strike energy bars, accessories, and the main course onto their trays. Jake did not share their fondness for the all-too-familiar rations, but he embraced the nutritional value of calories in fat and protein and the psychological boost of a well-rounded meal comprised from familiar menus.

With food heated and consumption underway, all eyes gravitated to the Keoghs. Both had cleaned their faces and tidied their hair—Amelia Keogh's pulled into a neater and tighter ponytail—and dusted off their clothing, Cyrus in relaxed-fit gray-brown Norfolk pants and a dark blue Ralph Lauren Polo shirt, Amelia wearing oatmeal-colored linen pants with a lavender cotton jersey t-shirt. Cameron McNamara sat beside them, hunched and withdrawn, self-consciously tugging at his damp clothing.

Taking a bite of his chicken tortilla and chewing hungrily, Cyrus Keogh looked to Jake.

"Okay, let's hear what happened," Jake said.

Keogh took another bite, sipped some coffee, and sighed, his expression contemplative as if he were conjuring a sequence of events other than those that had transpired. Finally, he said, "First of all, we are both *so* sorry." He glanced at Falcone and Niles, his face sincere with regret. "Especially to you, mates. We never intended to leave you like that."

"We really thought we were coming back," Amelia Keogh interrupted emphatically, her green eyes glistening in the firelight.

"Eddie told us about the chopper being shot down and our pilots…" Keogh's voice broke off, his gaze dropping to the tray on his lap. When he looked up, his skin tone had gone pallid. "It all happened very fast and abruptly as we were sound asleep, or else I'd like to think we'd have been much more cautious. We were awakened in our hut by a couple of blokes and told to gather our bags and go with them to a truck that was waiting. They told us some of our people had turned up at a refugee camp to the north, but we needed to hurry because the camp was so overcrowded many were being sent away. Amelia was about to rouse Eddie and Curran when the blokes hustled us out, saying they only had room for the three of us. I looked around for our security, and I remember thinking it strange that I didn't see them right outside the hut, but I also knew they would probably prevent us from going. So we all got in the back of this truck and they drove us a good long way, into the morning, and stopped at that god-awful hunting shack where you found us. The driver said he was almost out of fuel but knew where he could get some nearby, that we should get out of the sun, rest inside, and when he came back we'd resume the trip. The other one stayed behind, and just as soon as we were in the shack he pulled a gun out and tossed the ties to me, ordered me to secure Amelia and Cam, then zipped me up. He went out, got our bags, tossed them in, and that was that. I started asking him what was going on and he gagged us."

Amelia Keogh leaned against her husband, squeezing his arm.

Keogh continued, "He left, too, and from that point on we only saw the blokes that must have been rotating guard duty. They'd escort us out from time to time, you know, for a piss. And then you showed up." His face beamed with the winsome smile that came so easily to him, skin crinkling at the corners of his eyes. "I must say, Eddie and Curran did not overstate your badassery."

Still processing their story, Jake did not react to the comment. "What kind of truck was it?"

"An old Toyota pickup like every other one you see in these parts," Keogh replied.

"Where was it?"

"You mean, was it right outside? Actually, we had to walk a little bit…oh, I see what you're thinking. They were just far away enough that our security wouldn't see or hear it."

"Right. And while it's possible those guys could have been on a smoke break, if they were competent they wouldn't have wandered too far off. It's more likely they were drawn away to investigate something. A distraction of some kind, like we did." Jake paused, his lips pressed into a tight line. "We found them on the road. From what we were told by the village chief, they saw the truck drive off and went after it."

The Keoghs stared at him, Cyrus comprehending but Amelia blinking in puzzlement. "You found them?" she asked.

"We found them dead," Jake said. "Ambushed and shot."

Her hand went to her mouth. "Oh my God!"

"We had to leave them, of course, so I'd like to notify whoever they worked for, relay the coordinates. Eddie and Curran didn't know their full names."

Cameron McNamara spoke up, as if stirring from a trance, and seemed grateful to be able to contribute. "I can get that information from my tablet, but it will need to be charged up."

"That brings me to something I find odd," Jake said. "Those guys didn't take anything? They told you to bring your bags and then stashed them in the hooch with you?"

Keogh nodded. "They took our sat phone, but I think that was it."

"It's also significant that they didn't harm or kill you. Could be, this was going to be a kidnap for ransom thing." Jake paused again, this time delving down into the more latent layers of his thoughts, fragments tucked away from earlier observations and events—things that did not make sense then but were beginning to now.

They were all watching him intently, his gaze detached but focused on something unspooling in his mind.

From the start, sparks of speculation had been floating weightlessly, like fireflies flickering in the dark, but those beads of light were beginning to string together and Jake was coming to the realization that all of it had been unfolding long before he—or possibly even the Keoghs—had set foot in Africa. "Consider this," he said. "Your compound was destroyed after you left for Kinshasa. The helo was taken down when Eddie and Curran were expected to be on it, not you, as you had been taken from the village by those guys. Your security detail was killed when they tried to catch up to you."

Jake glanced at Cyrus Keogh to see if he was making the connection, but Keogh's face was blank. He went on, saying, "I believe the attack on the compound was timed to occur when you were away, and I think people connected to you have been targeted to make it easier to control you."

"Control us…why?" Keogh asked.

"I don't know," Jake said, "it might be because of who you are or something else entirely, but I don't think any of this is random."

Wind was blowing the flames of the fire sideways, embers popping off and disintegrating in the damp air. Thunder and lightning were close now, the trees shuddering blackly against the sky's electrical pulses. Falcone and Niles were hastening to finish everything on their trays before the wind swept them clean, prompting chuckles from Baladur and Dmello.

"Hey, this food might as well be Le Caf Conc when you're starving, eh mates?" Keogh said. "Beats the bananas and bread those blokes gave us."

"It also beats eating chickens you've named and watched in the garden," Amelia Keogh added, and then glanced away, as if to conceal a linked emotion.

"Or monkey," Niles said, stuffing a handful of M&Ms into his mouth.

"You've eaten monkey? Crikey!" Amelia exclaimed.

"Under duress," Falcone said, casting a sarcastic look Jake's way.

"Tell me about the two guys who came for you," Jake said.

Cyrus Keogh's eyes widened expressively. "Oh, I meant to say at some point that one of them was from our compound! I reckon he was the bloke Eddie and Curran had seen earlier in the village."

"What?" Niles gasped. "Was it Antoine? We had a chance to review our footage and identified him as one of guys we saw."

"Yes," Keogh replied. "It was the other bloke with him that did most of the talking, so I'm not sure if Antoine was a part of it or just going along."

"Now I really want to find this guy," Jake remarked.

"I just want to say again how sorry we are for mucking things up even more by being sucked in to that ruse," Keogh said. "But I have to do everything I can to find our little girl…"

Amelia Keogh bit her lip, tears welling and then rolling down her cheeks.

Keogh continued, "And even if we don't find her, I want to find any of our people that we can. We made them a promise from the outset that we would keep them safe, and I feel like we broke the promise. We took a night to celebrate us, away from them, and it might have cost them their lives."

"I understand and respect that," Jake said. "And it's possible there may be some truth in the ruse. I'll check with Kipnis in the morning, see if he can get some intel on refugee camps in our vicinity." He looked squarely at both Keoghs, hands on his thighs. "I will do my very best. But…going forward…this is my op, my rules."

Keogh smiled, tapped his forehead with two fingers in salute. "You got it, mate."

Jake was not totally convinced, recognizing a bit of a roguish streak in Keogh, but he found himself liking the couple and appreciating their integrity and determination. He stood, glancing upward as drops of rain began to fall, spritzing his face. "Well, folks, not gonna lie. We're in for a rough night."

That turned out to be quite the understatement.

AFTER A THIRTY-MINUTE prelude of light to moderate rain orchestrated by rumbling thunder and an ambient lightshow, the heavens seemed to rip open like a dark cloth that could no longer hold the great valley of water straining against it, shelling everything below in an unrelenting fusillade. With the intensified onslaught came ground-shaking booms that detonated with the magnitude of battleship cannons and blitzes of lightning that twisted in long, sizzling threads and then blasted the forest in blinding white incandescence. Wind whipped forcefully through the treetops, sending shredded leaves and shattered limbs to the ground in a hail of flying shrapnel.

It felt like the end of days.

Their shelters held—for the most part—but in this kind of storm, even the most expertly constructed coverage and military-spec rain gear could only go so far in countering the force of the wind and water coming at them. Jake had framed the shelters and tied them off based on the predominant direction of wind, but even so, rain was assailing from all sides. His quick-release knots kept joints secure, and much of the thatched awnings did exactly as he intended, diverting water away and cascading over the edges, and their ponchos kept them mostly dry. But after hours of the incessant barrage, the wet began to penetrate and, despite the warm temperature, chill them to the bone. They huddled and shivered, teeth chattering, flinching every time thunder cracked or a branch came crashing down. Below, the forest floor had turned into a flash of rapids rushing over everything, rising and swelling and breaking off in churning eddies. Rain banked in towering waves, immersing all ground and space in water.

Jake, Baladur, and Dmello had given their hammocks to the Keoghs and McNamara, putting them in the center, Falcone and Niles on either side; Jake and the others were staked at the triangular outposts, Jake's point facing the way they'd come. He sat back against the thick trunk of the sycamore fig tree that anchored his shelter and listened to the miserable murmurings of his group trying to find an elusive pocket of comfort in conditions that were only going to get worse before they got better.

After a few minutes, he sighed wearily and said, "All right, guys, let's just get through the night."

Eventually everyone went quiet and Jake's thoughts drifted to Callie, the desire to call her becoming a familiar default in his private moments, the ache of absence as intrinsic as muscle memory. Every time thunder exploded, he could almost feel her burrowing into his body, her small frame quavering against him, her heartbeat next to his, her warmth on his skin. His loins felt weak, remembering, the overwhelming craving and need stanched by the pain of hurt and wanting to heal it. He drew a deep, clearing breath, held it in his lungs, and exhaled. But the essence of her was still with him. Around him, the woods were a basin for the sky's waterfall and a battlefield of nature's tempestuous uproar. It was raining, amplified by the lightning and thunder, as if there were no end.

He was keeping watch through a FLIR Recon thermal imaging monocular, even though the weather all but guaranteed that no one was going to be in pursuit of them tonight. So when moving dabs morphed into the ghostly grayscale framed in the scope's lens, he was momentarily taken aback.

"What the hell?" he muttered under his breath.

The dabs multiplied.

Toggling between color and polarity palettes, he studied the heat signatures in motion and quickly realized they belonged not to animals but
to humans—incredibly, even in this torrential storm, humans were on
the move toward them, and they were armed. The Recon's range was
about twelve hundred yards in the best of conditions, so by the time the
shapeless blots clarified into individual profiles he estimated their proximity to be half that. The force of wind and rain and the flooded ground
was slowing advancement, but the figures were almost within firing
distance.

Grabbing his rifle, Jake used the tree to climb down from his platform, carefully navigating the splayed roots submerged by water and
viscous with mud. "We've got incoming!" he shouted. "Everybody get
to ground, now! Eddie and Curran, stay back behind trees, cover the
Keoghs and Cameron. Luther, Kean, with me." Boots splashed and then
trudged heavily as Falcone and Niles fought streaming currents and the
mire beneath to get to the Keoghs, Baladur and Dmello clambering their
way to Jake's side.

"What have we got?" Baladur asked, blinking against the rain blowing into his face, water dripping from the hood drawn around his head.

"Looks like five or six tangos at about—"

Before he could finish, gunfire rattled through the whitewash of wind
and water, muddled by the ongoing volleys of thunder, but muzzle
flashes popping in the darkness revealed their opponents' position less
than four hundred yards away.

"Fuck," Jake said, his mud-encased boots slipping and then sinking as
he set his stance, aiming his rifle at the line of fire, selector set on full
auto. Rain spit into his face.

The three of them clamored through one magazine and reloaded,
continuing the assault. Rounds from their aggressors were returned
with equal persistence and, in spite of the weather's disruption, passed
increasingly close, the air saturated with the acrid odor of wet gunpowder. Bullets smashed into tree trunks, sliced and severed branches,
plopped heavily into the ground streams. Jake felt the hot buzz of rounds

just missing his face, the wisp of rounds skirting the ripstop nylon of his poncho. "Everybody okay?" he called out a couple of times as he continued firing, but if any of them responded he didn't hear. He did see Dmello go down, but it turned out to be from misplaced footing as Dmello slid in the mud and temporarily jammed his AK in the process. When the Kenyan raised his hand to signal he was all right, Jake pulled him up and resumed shooting.

Without being able to stop and sight on their assailants, they were firing blind, and it was impossible to know if they were hitting anybody. At one point shots began to come from wide angles to the far right and left, and they were forced to defend themselves, turning away from the middle. Immediately, they were targeted with a closer, more direct assault. Jake thought, *Oh shit, we're done.* And: *How are they seeing us so accurately?* Tucking further into the trees, they timed their retaliation and, on Jake's signal, opened up into what they hoped was the center charge, pivoting to strike the corners again afterward.

Twenty minutes later and three spent magazines apiece, it appeared to be over.

Jake took the Recon monocular from its belt holster beneath his poncho and looked into the eyepiece, adjusting the zoom and alternating modes as he scanned in all directions. Finding no heat signatures, he gave the all clear and made his way back to the interior of their flooded camp, water sloshing around his shins and seeping over the tops of his Rocky S2V boots. The density of the rain had begun to slacken the slightest bit but was still driving hard, thunder and lightning loud and electric and lingering. Glancing at his watch, Jake saw that it was coming up on midnight.

"Goddamn," Falcone proclaimed, eyes round with stupefaction.

"You reckon that was for us?" Cyrus Keogh asked, clutching his wife's hand. Both were opening and closing their mouths in an attempt to clear the ringing in their ears brought on by the concussively loud gunfire, not having the noise protection that was integrated into the rest of the group's Invisio comms.

"Don't know," Jake replied, half-turning and peering again through his scope. "But whoever it was had to be mighty motivated to be out at night and in this weather. And they were not playing." Looking into the tense faces of those assembled around him—Amelia Keogh and Cameron McNamara's both chalky pale—he queried, "Everybody okay? Anybody hurt or hit?"

After a few moments of group canvassing, he got a gaggle of affirmative responses followed by a collective expiration of relief. Niles approached, squinting at him in the rainy darkness. "Mate…you're bleeding."

Jake touched the side of his face, drew his hand back and studied the blood on his fingers. "I'm all right," he said dismissively, "just a graze."

Baladur stepped over, inspected the burn-rash and red drizzle by Jake's ear, and said, "Whoa…close, brother, but not bad. I will get you some gauze."

A lapse of dazed silence hung over them and then Niles asked, "What do we do now?"

"We don't have much choice," Jake said, frowning. "It's a risk to stay put, but it's more dangerous to go anywhere around here in the dark and especially in this mess. So let's shore up our shelters and try to rest. I'll keep watch."

"You think they'll be back?" Falcone asked, wiping his wet face and gazing anxiously off into the watery depths from which the attack had come. Rain was streaming from hoods to capes of every poncho.

Jake did not reply. Even though he had not spied any heat signatures after the assault ended, he'd also not seen any bodies on the ground. It was entirely possible the unit was reloading and even recruiting more men, depending on their intent, and if that was, in fact, to recapture the Keoghs and kill anybody in their way, they had gone to great lengths to do so.

Everyone was all still watching him, so he deflected, remarking, "I think the rain's almost over."

Which was not the case for another hour or so, but nobody was thinking much about it anymore.

26

JAKE WAS RIGHT ON both counts. The conditions got worse before they got better, and their attackers had been highly motivated. But possibly not for the reason he had assumed.

When the rain finally stopped altogether sometime before dawn, the suffocating humidity returned. What parts of themselves they had been able to keep somewhat dry were now moist with sweat. Mosquitoes and tsetse flies and other bloodthirsty species buzzed and clung to the netting draped around their shelters, waiting to feast. The forest swelled with the croaks of frogs, thrum of insects, grunts and yowls of primates and other mammals. Hearts leapt at any sound, any movement, immediately expectant of another assault. Nobody slept much, if at all.

In the morning, the sky glowed with a spectrum of red and pink and orange so intense it seemed painted in neon. The vivid rainbow melted beyond the trees and slid off the savanna, leaving a blue in its wake that was the washed out color of bleach-faded denim, seamless and without a single cloud. It was as if the sky's infinite canvas had been purged by the storm of all shapes and shadows, every flaw or impurity, blown pristine for the new day. Water dripped through the forest layers in a rhythmic trickle, dimpling puddles and pools spread across the ground, mist rising into the trees.

Each of them stirred with groans of soreness and exhaustion, moving stiffly and unsteadily as they took cautious inventory of themselves and their environment in much the same way one would in the fog of hangover, mentally backpedaling to fit the loose pegs in place and re-connect all the tangled wiring.

Jake, who had disassembled his shelter and been patrolling the camp since dawn, managed to start a small fire, much to everyone's amazement. Given the amount of rain, no one would have thought such a feat remotely possible, but he had done so by procuring kindling and tinder from the most naturally concealed spots within the trees and then shaving wet bark from larger limbs. He stood next to the pit, drinking coffee, his face as drawn with fatigue as the rest, but the caffeine was starting to stimulate blood flow to his cheeks and restore the luster in his dark eyes. He had cleaned up and dressed in a spare shirt and cargo pants, hair neatly combed, a small Band-Aid covering the abraded laceration by his ear.

The others waddled their way through swaths of mud and over trenches of standing water to join him for coffee. Baladur and Dmello had chopped several logs into pieces and set them around the fire pit, so each took a seat and sipped in sullen silence. Kingfishers whistled blithely from the trees as the first laggard glints of sun needled through the foliage.

Jake pulled a ragged smile and said, "Morning. Rough night, I know."

No one responded, just regarded him with numb, glazed expressions.

"Needless to say, the sooner we get out of here the better. Whoever took us on last night will almost certainly return, and probably more of them. We need to get back to the plane to resupply before we do anything else."

"But what about the refugee camp?" Amelia Keogh asked. Her hair hung down, face pale with a scattering of red splotches.

"We will pursue that," Jake replied. "But we need to resupply first. Let's clean up, pack up, and hit the trail pronto."

In answer, coffee was begrudgingly finished and perches abandoned. Disjointed murmurings drifted off as they went about the process of erasing their footprint in the woods; the rain and mud had already done a lot of that for them. Jake strolled to an opening in the trees, powered up his Iridium sat phone, got a good signal, and selected the pro-grammed number for Efron Kipnis. The call was answered before a full ring had even completed.

He caught Kipnis up to speed, telling him about finding the Keoghs, gunplay with the men guarding them, and last night's engagement with unknown hostiles. Explaining how the Keoghs' captors had lured them from the village, Jake inquired about refugee camps in the area. Kipnis did a quick check and told him there was, in fact, a large one north of them, close to the South Sudanese border. "Okay then, that's where we'll be heading next, so get whatever intel you can." Kipnis asked if he had gotten the identities of the security detail and the company they'd worked for, and Jake said, "The Keoghs' assistant has all that on his tablet, but it needs charging, so I'll try to get it to you later today."

Before the conversation ended, Kipnis related his findings on the bullet casings from the Keoghs' compound. Jake listened in bafflement as he learned that the etchings on the headstamps were Persian, the initials of the Iranian Defense Industries Organization, which was associated with the Revolutionary Guards. These particular bullets, Kipnis elaborated, dated back to the end of an Iranian war in the late 1980s and had been smuggled into Sudan, arming rebel forces and militias, including the LRA and Janjaweed, as well as several others of local notoriety.

"How the hell does that figure into what happened with the compound?" Jake wanted to know. Kipnis said he had no idea but was still investigating.

Again, something was blipping on Jake's mental radar.

The call completed, he calculated the time in Costa Rica and knew it was too late to try Callie. Here, now, the sky was lightening with the beginning of day, but there she would be tucked in for the night, hopefully sleeping. Hopefully peaceful. *God, please, let her have some peace*, he prayed.

CALLIE WOKE, AND THE villa was full of daylight. She had apparently dozed off on the living room sofa. She sat up and looked around the open space, through the stone archway and into the kitchen, turned to check the foyer and dining room behind her. She seemed to remember Camilla busy in the kitchen, chopping vegetables, stirring in pots, washing dishes, humming, and gazing out the windows. She did not see or hear her now, and felt a tiny prickle of unease.

She stood, barefooted, and padded to the kitchen, her movements having the weightless sensation of floating above ground. The space was empty, nothing cooking on the stove, no food prep in sight. Sunlight streamed in through the wall of windows behind the sink, gleaming on the clean granite countertops and the spotlessly polished stainless appliances. She continued to the dining room, the dark wooden table simplistically elegant with high-backed rattan chairs and a modern blown glass vase of vivid red flora freshly cut from the gardens. An antiqued brass globe chandelier hung overhead, the painting of a lone sailboat against a sunset-steeped horizon centered on the wall. She peered through the French doors, taking in the patio and pool and ocean beyond. She saw no one, not Jesse Segura or pool man Ramón Cárdenas, not the gardeners, Estabon Mina and Mauricio Leguizano.

She opened the doors and stepped outside, looked and listened. Distantly, she could hear the soft break of waves, the squeaks and caws of seabirds and the squawks of jungle parrots. She did not hear the sound of yard maintenance equipment. The bright green grass that extended in a smooth plateau just below the pool's edge, ringed in variegated liriope, had been recently mowed. Below, rainforest rolled down to the shore and ocean. The sky was a placid, cloudless blue, the sun's warmth like an invisible embrace. She walked slowly from one side of the patio to the other, peeking around the corners of the villa, gazing across the gardens and into the plants and palms. Still, she saw no one.

Going back inside, an accordion of panic squeezed her chest. Again, she looked around, and again, found no one. Standing in the living room, the stucco walls seemed detached and unreachable, the tile floor without foundation. And, once again, she could feel the foreboding of that dark and malevolent presence coming for her—formless and faceless now, but hovering from behind in a dense black shadow, from above, from everywhere.

She felt a tug that drew her up and out, like a separation of inner and outer self, and then a light touch.

"Miss Callie? *Estás bien, mija?*"

Callie's eyes flicked open, lashes blinking rapidly. For a moment, she could not grasp context. The time and place seemed exactly the same, but as her focus began to sharpen, she realized that it was the *real* time and place and not the one that preyed on her from the ethers. She sat up on the sofa with a dizzying rush of relief. Camilla stood in front of her, watching with concern as Callie put first one foot and then the other on the handwoven area rug, wiggling her toes to feel the texture as if to make sure it was tangible.

Pleasant indie folk music played at a modest volume from Bose speakers on the wood beam shelf across the room, acoustic guitar strumming an uplifting sequence of notes that ran a scale reminiscent of bumblebees flitting from flower to flower in a shower of sunshine.

Camilla let Callie listen for a few minutes, the music appearing to clear her mind of the fog and calming the transition to clarity. Even so, tears brimmed, distress taking hold. "Come," Camilla said, extending her hand until Callie took it and left the sofa, limping and wincing inwardly. The housekeeper gave her a smile of encouragement and strolled toward the French doors to the patio. She wore a full red-and-blue gingham skirt that swished around her hips as she walked and a white peasant blouse embroidered with a matching yoke, blue bandana tied around her thick, wavy hair.

Callie slipped on her thong sandals and they stepped onto the patio where Camilla had set the table with a glass pitcher of lemonade, tacos and tortillas, and a platter of fruit. The housekeeper poured from the pitcher, loaded with ice and lemon slices, and handed a glass to Callie, which she accepted and sipped from. The sun was high and hot, shimmering in white rivulets across the pool's surface.

The absentee players from Callie's dream were all present and accounted for with the exception of Jesse Segura, who was on duty at the beach. Ramón Cárdenas, in navy swim trunks, tan *Envision Festival* tank top, and sunglasses, was kneeling by the pool with his test kit, head moving to the music broadcasting through his earbuds. Even as Cárdenas was totally absorbed in the audio, his attention was focused on the plastic receptacles and chemicals he added by droplets to his water sample to evaluate the levels of chlorine, ph, alkalinity, and acid demand. When he caught sight of Camilla and Callie, he set the kit down and reached for the phone in his pocket, tapping on the screen. A second later, the tune that had been in his ears came out of a Bluetooth speaker nearby, the breezy strains of Matt Simons's *Catch and Release* filling the air. That got a shy smile from Callie, and Camilla gave him a nod of appreciation. Estabon Mina and Mauricio Leguizano, dressed in cargo shorts, button-up cotton shirts, and straw sun hats, were seated at a concrete table on the grass just beyond the pool, finishing their lunch and drinking from tall melamine glasses.

Leading Callie toward the pair of gardeners, Camilla said, "They have a surprise for you, *mija.*"

Both stood, beaming broadly at Callie. Mauricio Leguizano said, "*Ven, mira lo que tenemos,* Miss Callie."

Callie looked questioningly to Camilla, who gestured for her to follow them. The two men walked around the side of the villa to one of the garden areas. Surrounded by tall palms and a lower breadth of tropical plants, it was a location that provided an optimum balance of morning and afternoon sun while providing enough shade to protect against the harshest heat of the day. There were sacks of manure and potting soil, an array of gardening tools, a rope of hose and, most prominently, rows of pots.

What was growing in the pots made Callie's eyes go wide with amazement. "*Roses?* You got roses? Where...how?"

Callie loved roses and had sought some to plant after coming to Costa Rica—first from local sources and then from anywhere in the region. She'd found a few possibilities but was consistently discouraged by every vendor she'd contacted. Although roses were associated with a deeply disturbing incident before she'd come to Costa Rica, they also harkened back to beloved childhood memories of her mother's and grandmother's flower gardens. The positive far outweighed the negative.

While grouped among the world's top wholesale flower-producing countries, Costa Rica's tropical climate, particularly that of the southern coast, is anything but hospitable to roses, which thrive in more temperate conditions; even as some varieties have been known to fare reasonably well in a range of hardiness zones from cold to hot, the pervasive humidity and rainy season of the tropics are extreme deterrents.

Knowing this from the many discouraging inquiries she had made previously, Callie was astounded to see the collection of at least a dozen varieties, already fragrantly blooming in ice cream colors, their petals layered like crushed tissue paper. She looked back and forth between the gardeners, the potted roses, and Camilla, at a loss for words.

"They come from Señor Jake," Estabon Mina said. He was the youngest of the two thirty-something gardeners and, as was the case with the even younger pool man who had come to join them, neatly groomed in spite of the heat. They were all smiling with unrestrained delight.

Callie's mouth parted in awe and confusion.

"He order them for you," Mina explained.

"But where? How? I tried and never could."

"*Señor* Jake," Mina grinned, waggling a hand and clicking his tongue.

Callie gingerly knelt in front of the pots, fingering the tags banded around the canes, reading names that revealed mostly antique or old garden tea roses, such as Archduke Charles and Le Vesuve and Monsieur Tillier and Mamam Cochet and Marchessa Boccella. She sat back on her calves, sighing happily and almost forgetting her soreness, a flurry of emotion coursing through her, overwhelmed by Jake's incredible insight and thoughtfulness. Brushing tears from the corners of her eyes, she stood, dusting soil from her legs.

"*Nos ayudas a sembrar?*" Leguizano asked. "Help to plant?"

Callie looked down at the strapped romper she was wearing, the cotton fabric light and clean, gathered at the waist and top, white with pale pink stripes. "I...well, I'm not..."

Camilla nudged her with an elbow. "You get dirty, I will wash it up. Okay?"

Callie eyed the roses longingly, a hesitant giddiness tickling from within. She cast a glance toward a section the gardeners had already cleared and prepared for planting, holes dug a foot wide, foot and a half deep, spaced three feet apart—precisely the recommended dimensions. A smile tugged at her mouth. "Okay," she said finally, and carefully squatted in front of the first hole, running a hand over the dirt. The gardeners had broken it up and added manure and enriched potting soil. Mina and Leguizano were standing on either side of her, one with the rim of a pot clamped in a canvas-gloved hand, the other leaning on a shovel handle, granting her time to savor the activity.

Callie's expression slackened, her thoughts seeming to trail off to a place neither could guess. The soil was warm in her hand, the palms overhead shading and abating the heat of the sun. And then suddenly, she cried out, slipping backwards as she lost her balance scrambling to get up.

As she had moved her fingers through the rim of dirt excavated from the hole, a familiar sensation memory fired off in her brain instants before the conjoined feeling triggered the physical reaction. Adrenaline surged through her blood, pain circulating like liquid flame. She saw without seeing, inner hysteria blinding, a frenzied stream of ants running from her fingers and hand up to her arm, an eruption on the ground spilling over her bare feet and invading the crevices of her toes and trundling along the leather straps of her thong sandals. Circling her ankles and ascending upward.

Callie could feel her heartbeat escalating uncontrollably even as her mind began to shut down, the pain dispersing in fuzzy electrical coils, the air becoming heavy and smelling of freshly turned earth and floral sweetness.

Camilla grabbed her by the arms as Mina dropped the potted rose he was holding and reached for the hose, spraying water on Callie's legs and feet. Leguizano was wiping her arms with a wet towel, Callie's body limp against Camilla. Behind her, Ramón Cárdenas was on his iPhone, talking in Spanish. Pausing, he addressed Camilla, who was trying to rouse Callie. "Jesse says get her inside and give her some Benadryl…and ice." Phone still at his ear, he listened for another minute, ended the call, and said, "Jesse is coming."

Head bowed in dejection, Camilla helped Callie back to the villa, both of them dripping wet from the hose.

IN SOME WAYS, IT seemed like what had happened earlier was part of one of the awful dreams she was always having. But as Callie sat in one of the two cane-woven swivel chairs on the bedroom terrace and looked at her hands, then at her feet, all covered in swollen red bites, she knew it had been real. There were still scratches and healing lacerations from days before, the result of some kind of episode she only half-remembered. She felt a renewed sense of anguish for being unable to quell the deeply entrenched anxieties or to dissolve the images or stifle the sounds, for not having any control over what would unleash the hounds of horror at any given moment; for not being able to replace the despair with joy from something as simple and pleasurable as planting a rose-bush. Anything and everything could rip the hinges off the trapdoor and bring the terror screaming back—a drop of rain, the crackle of a tree branch, ants in the garden. She recoiled, quivering, and swiped involuntarily at her arms and legs. The deep, physical hurting inside was bad tonight.

Jake kept telling her it would take time…but how much time? Would she ever feel okay again?

The landscape below the semi-circle of balcony was dark, the ocean and sky a merging of sapphire realms. The wedge of half-moon and its court of stars gleamed distantly, a thin sheen of light limning the horizon. A gentle breeze was blowing, just barely stirring the chimes and perfuming the air with the intoxicating scents of plumeria and ylang ylang. The soothing roll of the ocean's waves always drew her into a safe, serene place, and however fleeting that serenity was, she embraced it and imagined Jake feeling it with her. Imagined his arms around her, both of them together at the wrought iron railing, gazing down at the illuminated pool or out to the moonlit ocean.

She slipped through the open French doors into the bedroom where lamps were on to dispel the night, providing a warm and comforting ambience. She crossed to the bed, climbed on top and sat amongst the pillows, still able to view the ocean past the terrace until it grew too dark. Reaching to the bedside table, she picked up her iPhone and looked at the blank screen. Then she navigated to the message she had listened to countless times, a lump forming in her throat at the sound of Jake's voice.

"Light and day will be there on the other side. I love you, angel."

AFTER THE CALL TO Kipnis, Jake took his Katadyn water filtration kit and sought out spots where the rain had ponded, finding one that was deep enough for him to easily fill the gravity bag. He was about to stand when something in the muddy crater of rainwater caught his eye. It was hard and rounded and had the sallow color of a yellowing tooth.

Then he noticed another just like it a few feet away. And another next to that one.

He ran his gloved fingers over the first one, which was about three to four inches wide and appeared to have a much greater length than what was exposed. He dug around the pit and snagged on bits of burlap. Digging further, he realized what he'd found.

The heavy downpour that had pummeled for hours overnight had uprooted a burial site.

Baladur and Dmello had come up behind him with water bottles and bags to fill. Baladur asked, "Have you found something?"

Kneeling by the partially exhumed pieces, Jake handed the Katadyn gravity bag up to Baladur. "Yeah, I have, and I think it might be the actual reason and motivation behind what took place last night."

27

FALCONE AND NILES, THE Keoghs, and Cameron McNamara had joined Baladur and Dmello, watching Jake as he carefully worked his shovel tool around the edges of the most protrusive piece. With each jab and scrape, more of its enormous dimensions were revealed, the length nearing six feet. After fifteen minutes of digging, Jake stopped, set the shovel aside, and wiped his sweating forehead on a shirt sleeve.

Baladur handed him a bottle of water, and said, "That is from a male, probably between fifty and sixty years old."

Swigging thirstily from the bottle, Jake let the water dribble down his chin and neck, head tilted back in Baladur's direction. When he paused for a breath, he said, "Looks like at least a hundred pounds." Then, "Damn."

Kneeling beside him, Baladur ran his fingers over the long curvature of the elephant tusk. "This one here would probably get seventy to a hundred American dollars per pound...a minimum of seven hundred dollars per kilogram on the higher end of the chain, possibly as much as fourteen hundred."

"That makes it worth ten thousand or more dollars now, ten times that down the line," Jake replied, "and a hell of a compelling reason to come after us at night in a storm like that. You can see parts of a few others...that makes for some haul."

Baladur said, "There are most likely quite a few more below them. Poachers typically clean the tusks and either consume or sell the meat and fat, then they bury them for safekeeping until they are ready to move. They bury and retrieve them at night."

Jake thought about that and eyed the Keoghs. "This tracks for me. I expected your captors to take up pursuit as soon as those sentries were found…at daybreak, today. But a cache like this would be plenty of incentive for them or another unrelated group to come for us at night and in that storm. Especially if they were worried the amount and intensity of the rain would expose it, which it did."

"Poachers are not usually as active during the rainy season, which we are in," Baladur explained, "but it has been dryer than usual." When Jake didn't say anything, he added unnecessarily, "These groups are very dangerous."

"Then we probably shouldn't muck about," Cyrus Keogh commented. He distributed bottles of water he'd refilled from the Katadyn gravity bag, his wife taking a couple and passing around the rest.

"Nope," Jake said bluntly. He stood and scanned the periphery.

"Are we just going to leave this here?" Falcone asked.

"Sadly, yes," Jake replied. "As much as I hate to let these bastards have it—and believe me, I do—it would take too much time and effort to dig it all up, not to mention the weight of hauling it. I'd be inclined to rebury it somewhere else, just to keep them from profiting off it, but that would just make us more of a target."

All eyes stayed on him as he looked down at the dredged pit, let out a frustrated breath, and then stooped down to retrieve his shovel. "Let's just cover this back up as quickly as we can and get moving."

Some helped Jake fill in the mud pit, some brought armfuls of wet leaves to scatter on top, and then they all rinsed off, gathered their gear, and set off.

IN THE COURSE OF hiking from the plane to the road junction, then to the location where the Keoghs were being held and on to the campsite overnight, they had almost come full circle, now north going south. Jake estimated a full day's travel would get them back to the plane, but he knew that was going to be a tall order given the physical and mental exhaustion from the previous day and night, not to mention the unknown factor of the Keoghs and McNamara. But as they stacked hours on the road, much to his surprise, the couple and their assistant proved not only to be fit and adaptable, but also pleasantly disposed. They kept up without complaint and conducted themselves with disciplined comportment. As the group moved along a trail that took them through woods and across open savanna, Amelia Keogh engaged in cheerful small talk while pointing out various birds grouped in the branches or strutting amongst the grasses and Cyrus Keogh conversed with Jake in measured increments, in a way that was both self-assured and deferential. Jake found himself taken by their humility, intelligence, and compassion.

At one point, he asked, "If we should find your people, do you have a plan in mind?"

Without hesitation, Cyrus Keogh replied, "We'd like to start over. Our goal, after seeing how well it was going—before this, anyway—was to replicate it throughout the country, maybe throughout the continent, in similarly under-served and vulnerable spots."

Jake regarded him, brows arched. "That's mighty ambitious, but if you can do it..." He didn't know how to finish the thought, hovering somewhere between awe and incredulity.

"Oh, we can do it, but I reckon we'll have to rethink some things." Keogh's gaze was fixed on an imprecise point in the distance, his mind seeming to go briefly adrift before regaining focus. "We already had one of our cargo ships loaded up and ready to head for Mombasa with the materials and supplies to get a second place going. My best bud who runs all that for me is coming himself to oversee the logistics from sea to shore to air and overland. I was actually supposed to give him a call when we got back from Kinshasa."

"Okay, well, let's hope we can get all that back on track."

Cyrus Keogh glanced over his shoulder, his wife walking a few feet behind him, blowing at a loose strand of hair that had slipped beneath her sunglasses. His head turned, eyes meeting Jake's. "I would go to the moon for her. I would do anything, whatever it takes. Those people are everything to us, but that little girl...that little girl is the moon."

Jake felt something twist inside him, a clot of emotion strangling in his throat. It took him a few moments, and then he said, his voice low,

"I understand. I really do."

It was now early evening, clouds high and wispy and widely dispersed in the still-bright sky, a check of coordinates on his Garmin tactix watch confirming they were almost to the plane. Their pace, painstakingly sluggish for the first part of the day as they slogged through mud and saturated woods—in many places ankle- and shin-high in water—had slowed even more in the afternoon, the heat bearing down with unyielding fervor over fields of sprawling grassland, and Jake could hear the others heaving and scuffling behind him.

Fortunately, the thick stretch of forest that encompassed the airstrip was just ahead. On entering the arbor of its shade, there was an audible exhale of reprieve, the vaulted boughs above a rich avocado-green against the sun's blaze, ground exuding an effluvium of moist earth underfoot.

Throughout the day, Dmello and Baladur had alternated scout duty, one or the other venturing ahead to surveil the path before them. Dmello, who was currently on point, dropped back and came abreast of Jake, binoculars in hand. He said, "We might have some trouble, boss."

Jake took the Steiners and peered in the direction Dmello had come from. Through the lenses, about eight hundred yards ahead, he could just make out the tail of their Cessna, the rest of the plane still obscured by trees. He could also see what Dmello saw—the splintered optics of moving heads and booted feet, uniformed figures next to the plane. Raising his fist, he halted the group, and watched. The men staked out by the plane, three or four of them, were clad in what appeared to be Congolese military garb, camouflage fatigues with shoulder epaulets. But they were not wearing the customary berets; one had on a camo cap, another a plain flop hat, at least one more no hat at all. They were, however, all armed with AK-47s.

Jake drew everyone close and said, "There are some military-looking guys hanging around our plane. I can't tell if they are legit military or not. Either way, I don't want all of us exposed. I'm going to confront them with Kean and Luther." He looked at Falcone and Niles. "You guys stay in the trees, and be ready in case things don't go smoothly. Okay?"

Falcone and Niles nodded, hands clutching their rifles uneasily, and followed Jake on through the forest until they were within a hundred

yards of the airstrip, finding a position where they had good concealment and a view of the plane. Making sure the Keoghs and McNamara
were well behind them, they took up a shooting stance and pointed their
rifles toward the strip.

Advancing with Dmello and Baladur, Jake said, "Let's approach them
casually, see what their play is. Kean, up front with me...Luther hang
back and be fluid." They proceeded quietly along the tree line, emerging
when they were almost adjacent to the plane.

Affecting a countenance meant to convey a reasonable mixture of
concern and affability, Jake strolled toward the Cessna, the grip on his
rifle reflecting calm confidence. He nudged the brim of his boonie hat
up with a knuckle but did not remove his sunglasses. "Hello, gents," he
said with a thin smile. "Is there a problem with our plane?"

The men all swung their focus on him, guns held across their torsos.
They were not immediately hostile, nor were they welcoming, and no
personal introductions were offered.

When no one answered him, Jake said, *"Bonjour, messieurs. Y a-t-il un
problème avec notre avion?"*

The soldier wearing the cap approached Jake rigidly, taking note of
both Dmello and Baladur, his face full of questions. He stared at Jake but
addressed Dmello, replying, *"Est-ce votre avion?"*

Jake deferred to Dmello, who said, *"Oui, ça l'est. Nous pouvons vous
fournir une preuve."*

The soldier continued to stare flagrantly at Jake, the man next to him
in the flop hat flexing his fingers open and closed on the pistol grip of his
AK. Two other men stood on either side of them, cued for the alpha
soldier's lead.

Dmello waited him out, offering a slightly more restrained version of
his normally effusive smile, and the camo-capped soldier finally moved
his eyes off Jake. He extended a hand, palm up, and crooked his fingers.
Dmello reached into a side pocket and produced a small waterproof document pouch which included his passport and visa, government-issued
photo ID, and an assortment of licenses and certificates. There were also
documents for the Cessna, including a copy of its registration and own-
crship information.

Before Dmello could present anything, Jake put a hand out to stop him. *"Que voulez-vous?"* Without knowing who these guys really were, he was going to make them say what they wanted. Sizing them up, he could not be sure they were authentic military; with their slightly mismatched attire, they were most likely paramilitary, but they could also be militia posers. It was common practice for rebels to steal and clothe themselves in illicitly acquired uniforms, which gave them an advantage in staging attacks or abductions. He also had to wonder if they were connected in any way to the poachers or to the Keoghs' abductors. Had they just incidentally happened on the plane or had they been tipped off? There were a lot of possibilities to consider.

The soldier glared at Jake, his eyes narrowing as he deliberated his response. He was close to Jake's height and weight, his head shaped like a rounded cube, hair shaved beneath his cap. His cheeks and lips were thick, a sparse mustache that resembled etched charcoal below his wide-bridged nose.

He said, *"Vos documents d'identification, maintenant."*

Dmello glimpsed at Jake, got a slight nod, and unzipped his document pouch, sliding out the passport and visa. He handed them to the soldier, who scrutinized the pages for an unduly length of time.

The soldier's gaze went again to Jake. *"Que faites-vous ici?"* he asked in a manner that suggested he had every right to know.

"What are we doing here?" Jake repeated. *"Commission géologique."* He knew identifying themselves as surveyors was a credibility stretch, but he was not about to reveal their real mission which would raise more questions in the least and, possibly, red flags. Their heavily soiled clothing might help to sell it, their weapons not so much.

As he suspected, camo cap was not buying it. *"Pour qui?"*

Still speaking in French, Jake told him that they were contracted by a private company for research purposes. The soldier's face remained inscrutable, his eyes shifting from Dmello to Jake. Bending his neck to see past them, he cast a wary look at Baladur, standing several yards behind.

Dmello let his smile expand and reached for his passport and visa, but the soldier made no move to return them. *"Y a-t-il un problème ici?"* he asked.

The soldier scratched the side of his nose, puckering his lips, and flicked a glance at the plane. In French, he said, "You owe a tariff for the occupation of the plane."

Jake's temple creased but he kept his temperament even. *"Pour l'occupation? Expliquez, s'il vous plait."*

The soldier bristled, replying that there was no explanation necessary, and hitched up his rifle, Dmello's passport and visa pinched between his thumb and forefinger.

Dmello drew Jake aside and said quietly, "Do not make too much of this, it happens all the time here and is mostly bluster, but we will have to pay him something."

"I get that," Jake said, "it's a standard the world over, but if we pay anything it opens the door for more. Not only with this guy, but word will get around, and we'll be everybody's money pit. I know there will be times we can't avoid it, but we should whenever we can. This strip hasn't seen another plane in probably six months, maybe longer."

"So what do you want to do?" Dmello asked.

"For one thing, patience is key. The longer we hold firm and don't let them fluster us, the more likely they are to back down."

The soldier cleared his throat loudly in an attempt to break up their side conversation, announcing that the fee was five hundred. Looking squarely at Jake, he added, "U.S. dollars." Jake looked back at the soldier but did not respond, keeping his face neutral. After a few minutes had passed, the soldier brandished Dmello's passport and visa in the air as if they were a winning hand of cards. *"Trois cents!"*

Again, Jake said nothing, his expression unchanged.

The soldier countered one more time, coming down from his reduction of three hundred to two, informing them adamantly that it was his final pass. When Jake did not bite, the other three soldiers racked their rifles and tensed, trigger fingers primed. He stared them down, unable to keep a dismissive scoff from escaping his lips.

That seemed to elicit a shift in the alpha soldier's perspective as his gaze extended to the trees beyond Jake, Dmello, and Baladur, panning left to right.

Watching him, Jake wondered again, *Did they have advance intel about us? Do they know about the Keoghs?* Time to wrap this up. Conferring with Dmello once more, he said, "I have an idea. We'll give them something, just not money."

"Something like a material bribe?"

"No, I'm thinking we give them something that may satisfy their greed and get them off our case."

TWENTY MINUTES LATER, HUDDLED with everyone by the plane, Jake explained how he had successfully dispensed with the soldiers.

"What did you do?" Falcone wanted to know.

"I told them about the ivory," Jake said simply.

"What?" Falcone asked, slack-jawed. "I can't believe you'd give them that."

"Well...I really didn't."

"What do you mean?"

"I gave them some coordinates, but not the correct ones. I also told them our offer came with the caveat that we could not be held responsible if, by the time they got to the site, the poachers had returned and retrieved their bounty."

Falcone was still perplexed, but Dmello and Baladur laughed, Baladur expounding, "What Jake did was give them the possibility of a big reward over a minimal payoff, and going after it got them away from us."

Jake grinned. "Exactly. It was a gamble. Either they were legit military with a corrupt streak who would jump at the opportunity to round up some poachers or, for all I know, they could be part of a poaching network themselves, but I figured either way, they couldn't afford to turn their backs on that bounty." He eyed the Cessna, sides spattered with dried dirt, tires rutted in mud, and said, "Okay, time to get out of here in case they return with buyer's remorse."

28

THE EVENING SKY WAS a clear, deep blue, stars as sharp as ice chips, for the moment not a hint of rain in the atmosphere. Camp was set in a glade near a small stream, enclosed by trees of mixed heights and densities that afforded a good balance of coverage and visibility.

After making a flight twenty miles to the north, filling in the remaining seats with the Keoghs and their assistant, Keanjaho Dmello had secured the Cessna at another unmanaged airstrip just as isolated as the last. There was also no fuel depot, but because of the short distances they were flying, he was still in good shape. Best of all, the strip was close to their camp. They had loaded up on MREs, fresh water, changes of clothing, supplies, and ammunition and were now arranged around the fire pit, eating and drinking in measured contentment. While everyone else was coddling each component of their meal packs, Jake finished his chili and macaroni with quick efficiency, set the rest aside, and excused himself.

He took his coffee and walked several yards away to have some privacy, finding a large flat-topped rock to sit on. Through the brush he could hear the faint gurgle of the stream, openings in the treetops bright with moonlight. He drained his cup and checked his watch. It was a quarter past seven, 11:15 AM in Costa Rica. He took his Iridium sat phone from a side pocket in his pants and made the call he'd been intensely craving since Nairobi, five days ago.

When Callie answered, in a soft, breathless rush of disbelief and exhilaration, he felt his heart bounce, a wide smile spreading across his face. "Hey, sweetie," he said, warmth flooding his cheeks. He could hear her swallowing to collect herself, so he continued. "I have a little time and thought I would call you while I could. You doing okay?" He listened as she thanked him for the roses, gushing over the beautiful blooms and colors and exquisite fragrances. "I am so happy that you like them. Estabon and Mauricio got them planted?"

She told him they had, but there was a subtle reticence in her response; she was leaving something out and he wanted to know what it was, but not at the cost of making her uncomfortable or, worse, shutting her down. He remembered feeling the same way talking to Camilla, but he would just have to trust for now. Being so far away, the loss of control was maddening.

He quizzed her lightly about eating and sleeping, knowing she was being anything but forthcoming as she assured him she was doing better, praising Camilla's cooking and expressing how comfortable the bed was. He let her tell him, let her believe he believed, and told her he was glad to hear it. He offered reassurance and encouragement, told her it would continue to get better, heard a tiny hitch in her voice, and said, "It will be okay, love…it will." He inhaled, held the breath, and let it out. "Okay, I have to go, but I will call you again when I can. Be good, baby. I love you." He clenched the phone in his hand, not wanting to let go of the connection, already feeling the chasm of separation.

He sat on the rock, listening to the stream and gazing at the stars, his mind in a free fall of sentiments, his heart aching. *I should be with her, not here*, he thought. He let his feelings hold court for a while and then cinched up his composure, hopped off the rock, and walked back to the fire pit to rejoin the others.

Fed and hydrated, their collective mood was one of relaxed conviviality, the conversation purposefully veering wide of the clamorous center lane like a car avoiding an obstacle course of potholes. When Jake took his place in the circle, they were somehow simultaneously debating the best cheeseburgers, coolest scenes from Marvel Cinematic Universe movies, and rock concerts for the ages—all of which Baladur and Dmello seemed to know more about than he would have guessed, Remy's influence no doubt. Or maybe they were all just trying to keep up with Niles' pinball-velocity talking points. The words ricocheted emptily around him as scanned the assembled faces, shiny in the fire's reflection, each laden with the stress and fatigue they were trying to manage. His gaze landed on Amelia Keogh, who was seated near him with her husband, and found her observing him thoughtfully.

Leaning sideways toward Jake, she asked softly, "Talk to your girl?"

Unaccustomed to being read so easily, Jake was caught a little off-guard. He nodded, dark eyes glazed with emotion he could not fully repress.

"Is she okay?"

Jake did not respond for a moment, then said, "As much as she can be." He gave her a weak smile and looked away.

Amelia tucked the last piece of MRE shortcake into her mouth, catching crumbs with her fingertips, declaring, "This is really delicious!" She reached for her bottle of water and drank, sighing with satisfaction. Her eyes on Jake, she said, "The guys told us what you all went through, and honestly, we would never have sought your help if we had known beforehand. It has got to be really hard being away from her right now."

Jake continued to look away, not trusting his face. He was glad to be diverted by Falcone, coming up behind him. "Hey, can I use the sat phone?" he asked.

"For?"

"I want to see if I can reach Iris or anybody from Sanctuary."

Jake handed him the Iridium and watched him walk off. A few minutes later, Falcone came back and returned the phone without comment, his expression dismal. He strode over to Niles, said something to him, and the two of them left the fire pit.

Jake asked Amelia, "Is there something more to that?"

She laughed lightly, the highlights in her coppery hair gleaming in the firelight. "Oh, they were quite an item, Eddie and Iris."

"Huh," Jake said, "well, good for him."

"I don't know about that. Eddie definitely had a thing...I just didn't see it from her. She was in it for the minute, you know? Poor bloke, he's going to wind up with his heart broken, I'm afraid." Nodding toward Falcone and Niles, she said, "Those two are special."

"They are," Jake agreed, and grinned. "Just don't tell them I said so."

"We have given them access to us no one else has had, and I must say we've really grown fond of them."

"What are your thoughts about Sanctuary?"

"Oh, I think they are doing good work as advocates and activists. If it weren't for their persistence to enlist us, we might never have become involved…certainly not to this extent. Why? Do you have some concerns about them?"

"Not necessarily," Jake said, "but they were, or are, part of the big picture."

He started to get up, but Amelia touched his arm, causing him to pause, look at her. "Jake, do you really think there's a chance our people are still alive…that we'll find them?" Her eyes held on his, imploring truth.

"There is always a chance," he replied, trying his best to exude optimism. "Look, I'm sure you realize that it's a long shot, but we hope and move forward as long as there is cause for hope." He gave her wrist a squeeze.

She smiled. "Thank you."

WHILE THE OTHERS TIDIED up camp, Jake straddled a log and opened his Toughbook laptop, which he had brought from the plane. Booting up, he navigated to a folder with the intel provided by Remington and Kipnis, reviewing documents and toggling through a series of maps and satellite images. As he skimmed the data, he was mentally analyzing the timeline. It had been nine days since the Keoghs' compound had been destroyed, six since he'd arrived. On one of the maps, he calculated the mileage that could be walked or driven in the time that had elapsed, input the variables, and saw a circle appear defining the probable area. Within the circumference, he set markers for Nakalé, the location of the dead security detail, and the site where the Keoghs had been held. Next, he zoomed in and studied the villages and uninhabited terrain, the hunting grounds and known poaching zones, Garamba National Park and the borders. He pulled up the tracking reports for incidents of all kinds: abductions, lootings, assaults, killings. Noted the groups involved or suspected. So much, so many. Then he went through the information on the refugee camps, particularly the one that had been floated to the Keoghs. Was it a credible lead or just a ruse? He continued to weigh whether that incident, perhaps every incident, was part of a larger scheme or merely a string of random occurrences. He was still leaning toward the former, and his default setting for coincidences was that of skepticism. If it was a coordinated scheme, that would suggest the Keoghs were specifically targeted.

By whom?

Which brought him to Antoine who, at this point, appeared to be something of an inside man and someone Jake really wanted to find.

He became aware of a presence next to him, in buffed Blundstone boots, and glanced up to find Cyrus Keogh. Without the benefit of extra clothing from the plane, Keogh's change of outfit had been rinsed and dried from a previous wear, and yet he somehow managed to appear unwrinkled and stylishly groomed in his blue shirt and tan slacks, a pair of Oliver Peoples reading glasses propped in his sandy blond locks. The irrepressible smile was there, the candid blue eyes and easygoing disposition, hands in his pants pockets as if he were out for a leisurely evening stroll.

"Hey, mate," Keogh said. "Mind if I join?"

"Pull up a log," Watching as Keogh swatted ineffectually at the insects swarming around his head, Jake said, "The color blue attracts tsetse flies."

"Well, I wondered why the Mosi-Guard wasn't working as well," Keogh chuckled. Dragging a log from the fire pit, he sat, slipped his glasses on, and looked over Jake's shoulder.

"Here is the refugee camp," Jake said, and tapped the screen of his Toughbook, "and this is where your compound was."

Keogh studied in silence.

"It's conceivable that your people could have made it there in the time that has passed." Jake looked at Keogh, gauging his reaction, which was neutral. "There are many possibilities, but I have to admit, this is a good one, if Antoine was giving you a real lead."

Keogh lifted his eyes and ran a hand through his hair. "I don't know what to believe. But we should check it out." Returning his focus to Jake, he said, "Thank you for letting us borrow your extra sat phone. I spoke with my bud. Our ship is en route."

"That's good." Jake was quiet for a minute, then said soberly, "It's not the best idea for you and your wife, your assistant, to go with us. I can have Kean fly you back to Dungu or Nakalé, even Kinshasa. That's what I would advise."

"No, no, we have to go," Keogh said insistently. "How else would you know who you were looking for? No, we have to go so we can identify them."

Jake mulled that, and said, "Eddie and Curran would most likely be able to identify some of them."

Keogh shook his head. "We really need to go."

Jake nodded begrudgingly. "Okay then."

They both looked up to find Cameron McNamara with the sat phone and his tablet. His face was blotchy with insect bites, hair astray and glasses fogged by the humidity. Unlike Keogh, his clothing appeared to have been subjected to a suitcase battered from airline hell, the fabric both stretched and puckered from hand-washing.

"I have everything you need," he said, and squatted down by them.

Jake scanned the screen of McNamara's tablet. Indicating his Iridium GO sat connect, he asked, "Can you sync and send all that to me?"

When the transfer was complete, Jake opened the file and gave it a quick overview. "I've heard of them. Seem to be a respectable outfit. What made you choose them?"

"Actually, they are our first major security contract," Keogh remarked. "I spent a lot of time vetting, lots of calls and meetings. I wanted a company that had international reach, a good history with no black marks, but not one so huge they couldn't give us their priority."

"Okay, solid choice."

He went on, "We knew we would have to keep a low profile in-country because having a large security detail in the bush just isn't practical. We felt we had good protection in place at the compound that was capable and, at the same time, homogeneous enough within our order to blend. The two guys assigned to us personally were the exception and we felt confident with them."

"You did it right," Jake assured him. "Anything on a grander scale would have drawn much more attention and scrutiny." He started to say, *But things happen.* And something had, he just did not know what.

"I'm going to get in touch now, let them know what's happened." He moved off with McNamara, waiting as his assistant placed the call.

Jake read over the information McNamara had shared in the form of a dossier on Machai, ranked among the top thirty private security companies in the world. It had been established in the early 2000s by Shane Joost, former South African Special Forces, or the Recces as they were colloquially known. Based in Johannesburg, Machai had offices in London, Dubai, the Dominican Republic, and Mclean, Virginia. Their profile contained all the usual services and specialties demanded in a modern militaristic world, discreetly characterized in corporate-friendly euphemisms; their contractual background was replete with a healthy portfolio of Iraq and Afghanistan military support as well as governmental and private-sector assignments around the globe.

Not seeing anything unusual, he closed the file. McNamara had included a few administrative documents, but Jake decided to review them later. He used the Iridium GO to send a text to Kipnis with the contractor's name and then packed everything up and headed for his hammock. He stopped beside Cyrus Keogh, who appeared to be wrapping up his conversation on the sat phone.

Looking pointedly at Jake as he spoke, Keogh was saying, "Again, really sorry about the loss of your guys...appreciate it, mate, but I think we're good for the moment." Holding Jake's eyes, he said, "Yes, I'm sure."

THERE HAD BEEN SOME rain overnight, just enough to re-muddy ground that had begun to dry in the previous day's sun, making for another cloyingly humid morning. After taking advantage of the stream to freshen up, guzzling coffee and munching on bananas and protein bars, insect repellent was slathered on, gear packed, and camp sanitized. The ascendant sun skulked below the horizon in a milky filament and then bobbed up with a rotund yoke of butterscotch yellow. Heat bloomed in the dampness like a fevered breath.

After discussing options with Dmello, it had been decided to hike to the refugee camp; studying their intel, it was unclear whether a viable landing zone was proximal, and an actual airstrip to accommodate humanitarian aid and workers was still under construction.

They set off heading farther northeast through forested swaths in what is known as *Domaine de Chasse des* Azande, territorial hunting grounds west of Garamba National Park, following a footpath worn by both man and animal. Barely an hour into the trek, across an opening in the bush, something caught Jake's attention. On the far side of a line of doka trees, a swatch of maroon-colored fabric was sticking out from behind one of the trunks. The air was heavy and hot and lacking any kind of breeze, the fabric unmoving. Before he could say anything, Amelia Keogh gasped from behind him.

"That's Antoine's shirt!" She jockeyed next to Jake to get a better look and exclaimed, "Yes, I'm sure that's his shirt! Isn't it, Cy?"

Jake swung his arm out in front of her, Cyrus Keogh tugging her back beside him at the same time. "Whoa, whoa," Jake cautioned. "I want everybody to stay right here. Luther, let's approach."

Jake and Baladur advanced slowly, watching for movement in the brush. Not detecting any, they paused just short of the tree and, in a non-threatening tone, Jake called out, "Antoine, *c'est toi?*" Receiving no answer, they stepped closer, able to see an arm and then legs, extended straight out on the ground. "Antoine," Jake said again, and took another step. Looked down, stooped, and peered into the man's face.

A moment later, Jake gave everyone the okay to come forward. When they were all standing by the tree, faces blanched and mouths pinched in reflexive revulsion. The man named Antoine sat with his back against the trunk, head slumped to his chest. His cropped black hair was gray with dust, flies looping and landing in buzzing clusters. A gunshot wound to his midriff had shredded and soaked the maroon material of his shirt with blood, turning it a very dark brown, big droplets redder in color pattered on the ground beside his hip.

"Jesus Christ," Falcone muttered. "is he alive?"

Jake knelt down and felt for a pulse in the side of the man's neck. Without answering, he lifted Antoine's chin and fingered the lids of his eyes, studying the pupils, which were the size of BBs. Next, he prodded the gut wound, deducing that the gunshot had hit the liver or spleen. Jake thought he might have five or ten minutes to live.

"Hey, Antoine…hey." Jake lifted the man's chin again, jostling it a little, but the eyes were closed, parted mouth barely drawing breath. "Antoine! Talk to me…*parle moi!* Tell me who…*qui…*"

Antoine's eyelids flicked slightly and for just a moment, his lips appeared to be moving, but no sound was coming out. Then nothing. He was gone.

"Goddammit," Jake said, and stood, looking up the road, then back and forth across the tree line.

"How long?" Baladur asked, following his gaze.

"This kind of wound, could have been an hour ago, could have been minutes ago." He twisted his rifle around from behind him and took off past the left side of the road. "Take the right, Luther. Kean, everybody else, stay here."

Jake dashed in a zigzag pattern through the trees, searching for any sign of disturbance—snapped branches, bent limbs, depressions in the ground—but found none. The crowns of the dokas were tall and wide, without much beneath, green umbrellas covering but not concealing; if anything or anyone had been on the retreat, they could have been seen from a good distance. When Jake returned to the road fifteen minutes later, Baladur was waiting for him with nothing to report.

"Bloody hell," Niles remarked. "Everybody keeps winding up dead."

"Yeah, they do," Jake said dryly.

Cyrus Keogh said, "I don't know what to make of this."

Jake shook his head in frustration. Antoine had been taken out for any number of reasons; possibly because he'd lost the Keoghs, possibly because he was a loose end, and certainly because he knew things Jake really wanted to find out.

Baladur snapped some pictures on his phone and checked Antoine's pockets, coming up empty.

Jake blew out a breath, fanned flies away from his face, and started walking. There was no longer any doubt in his mind that much more was at play here. He'd been feeling it all along, and now his nerves were twanging like high tensile wire.

CHECKING THE COORDINATES ON his watch, Jake determined

they were within a mile or so of the refugee camp and, as they walked on, the terrain began to change. The flatlands elevated, rising gradually into hills, woods thinning to palm-dotted savanna with scattered clumps of trees. The trail became a red-dirt road, widening and stretching interminably. And, almost as if a cinematic set had changed, people began to appear in sporadic dribbles; men pushing bikes piled high and stout with bedding and belongings, women balancing bundles of firewood and containers of grain on their heads, children with babies hoisted on their small hips or hung from their necks in sling wraps. A few bony goats tagged along in their wake. They all marched silently toward some unknown destination, arms and legs moving in a kind of resigned cadence.

Amelia Keogh broke out in a tentative sequence of smiles, her nose and cheeks roseate from the sun's concentrated rays. "I'm getting a good feeling," she said. "I think maybe they're here."

"I'm hopeful, too," Cyrus Keogh said, "but let's stay grounded."

Jake did not comment, but his expression echoed Keogh's cautionary note. He aimed his binoculars on the inclining road before them, sides once again thickening with trees. The sky's blue had become subdued by a thin haze of clouds brushed with gray, though the heat had not diminished at all. He dabbed at the sheen of sweat on his face, chugged from his Nalgene water bottle, and resumed walking.

They continued up the hill and the staggered strings of people began to drop out of sight, as if sliding over an infinity edge. The slope leveled out briefly and then gradually descended, rolling into a shallow valley where the trees gave way to mostly grassland. They hiked up another long incline and came to the crest, stopped and looked out over a view spread below that rendered them all dumbfounded.

Finally, Amelia Keogh gulped and said in a withering voice, "Oh my God."

29

SPRAWLED FROM THE BASE of the valley, side to side to seam of the overcast sky, was a massive jigsaw of blue and white misshapen pieces, earthen outlines crawling with people. Tens of thousands of people, moving like ants in a labyrinthine colony, the sounds of their activity rising and falling from indeterminate points throughout the landscape. Beyond the tarp-draped thatched huts was more permanent housing, grids of framed structures with attached roofs, palms and straggly trees sprouting up in their midst. Some were constructed in the Sudanese style of *tukuls*, rounded and conical and fortified with mud. A road splitting the settlement teemed with an influx of even more people loaded down with everything they could carry, appearing at the top of the incline and descending in an endless procession. Big Iveco trucks, canvas-covered flatbeds crammed with passengers, rambled alongside, dust billowing around them.

"Oh my God," Amelia Keogh repeated numbly.

Jake, who had seen his share of such places, found himself somewhat stunned at the enormity, and thought, *God help us*. Clearing dust from his throat, he said, "All right, let's get in there and find someone who can help us navigate, but first we'll need to break down our rifles and conceal."

"What?" Falcone asked, confused.

"Weapons are not allowed in refugee camps," Jake said, and stepped over to show him how to do it in a way that would allow for quick reassembly, leaving the mag in and lower receiver pins open.

When all the guns were secured in their backpacks—with the exception of the Glock Jake had stuck in the back of his cargo pants—they made their way toward the camp's perimeter, which was partially cordoned by orange plastic fencing, sagging and split and re-rolled in much the same way tape was strung at crime scenes in an attempt to maintain some kind of decorum. The effort was largely futile to contain the swell of people moving about, only to bottleneck at intersecting points. The entirety of the camp was enclosed with barbed wire, and Jake found an opening and maneuvered through the jostling throngs to an unoccupied space below a cluster of banana trees.

"There must be, what, ten thousand people here?" Niles asked incredibly.

"At least," Jake concurred. "Okay, listen up. I want us to stay together and move as a unit." He glanced at the sky, the clouds beginning to curdle. "We don't have a lot of daylight left, and it looks like rain might shorten that."

They set off walking, the lighter skins of all but Baladur and Dmello drawing some attention, but for the most part they seemed to be inconsequential in the masses of tired and hungry and unsettled. The air was filled with bodily odors and the smoke of cooking fires. A generic reek of waste came and went like swirls of incense. Lines buckled from food and supply stations, comprised of mostly women in patterned *kitenge* dresses that were fashionable in spite of the layers of soil clinging to them, and barefooted children wearing a mismatched assortment of shorts and threadbare shirts in stripes and plaids and faded colors imprinted with Batman and Dora the Explorer and other icons from the civilized world. There were fewer boys than girls, and even fewer men.

Ever since achieving independence, South Sudan has been one of the most unstable places in the world, civil wars erupting over government coups and ethnic conflicts, resulting in an exodus and internal displacement of millions, widespread disease, and famine. The DRC is one of a half-dozen bordering countries absorbing the fleeing refugees, even as it struggles to take care of its own IDP population. From the intel Jake had, this particular camp had been established only a few months ago and was already pushing past capacity.

Their inconspicuousness was soon upended as a flock of curious children assembled around them, exclaiming, *"Kawaja! Kawaja!"* and drawing them further into the camp, laughingly tugging their clothing to direct them one way or another.

"I believe that's a registration site," Amelia Keogh said, pointing up ahead to a long table sheltered by the awning of a white tent with a blue UNHCR logo. It was impossible to tell where the line in front began or ended, but the two men and two women seated at the table seemed to be working efficiently, typing on laptop computers, filling out cards, and dispensing information. Some wore white UNHCR-branded t-shirts with lanyards around their necks, others a bright blue smock-vest with the logo for IOM—International Organization for Migration—and, as a group, appeared to be multinational. As Jake got closer, taking care not to cross any of the people in line, he noticed a couple of the registrars eying them with interest, one staring with what might have been a look of vague recognition.

Halting several yards away, Jake addressed the Keoghs. "If any of your people are here, they should be in the camp's database."

"Exactly!" Amelia bubbled, her perspiring face beaming with expectation. "Cam's got a list on his tablet." She asked their assistant, "Is it still charged up?"

McNamara shook his head with a frown. "I tried to power it on earlier."

To the Keoghs, Jake said, "Yes, well, I think you two need to stay off the radar, so"—he turned to Falcone and Niles—"do you guys know some names you can have them look up?"

"We do," Niles replied, removing his ball cap to wipe sweat from his forehead.

"Okay," Jake said, "Luther and Kean, stay back with Cameron and the Keoghs." He led Falcone and Niles to one side of the table and stood by politely until the woman seated at that end gave him her attention. Removing his sunglasses, he smiled graciously.

The woman was African, though of what descent was hard to tell. She was in her early thirties, hair worn in a braid past her shoulders. Returning Jake's smile, she asked in accented English, *"Anglais ou Français?"* When Jake waggled his hand to indicate either, she continued,

"How can I help you?"

"My name is Jake Tyler and I'm here with some folks who ran an IDP site west of here. It was destroyed by some kind of violent incident and we're trying to locate the people."

"I am sorry to hear that. These people are from DRC then?"

"Yes. We got a tip some of them might be here."

The woman, whose lanyard identified her as Ketia Makamba, craned her neck, her gaze angled toward the Keoghs. "The couple back there— the beautiful lady with the red hair—they are the ones who had the IDP?"

"They are," Jake said, keeping his voice casual.

"I took notice of them because they seem familiar to me," Ketia Makamba mused thoughtfully, staring a moment longer before returning her focus to Jake. When he didn't offer any affirmation, she said, "I can search our registration if you have names," and tapped a few keys on her laptop.

Falcone and Niles stepped forward and began to rattle off as many as they could think of. Ketia Makamba typed each name, trying spelling variations or feasible derivatives, but each query got no results. Finally she said, "I am so sorry."

"Is it possible they just aren't registered?" Jake inquired, watching as the man next to her used a biometric scanner to input the fingerprints of a woman and the small children latched onto her skirt, issuing ID cards and wrist bracelets.

"We have registered close to fifty thousand, so it is possible," Makamba replied, "but they must register to have access to food, supplies, housing, medical services." She paused, adding, "I will say this...many are afraid of who and what they have fled. We suspect some register under other names, sometimes under one surname, so there is that possibility."

"We also heard that some people were being turned away."

"Hmm...I don't think so. When a camp becomes overfull, we usually find placement with other camps or set things in motion to expand or establish a new camp. We are definitely close to that point, but I haven't heard of any being turned away."

Jake put his hands on his hips and glanced around, unable to see beyond the crush of people. He shook his head dolefully. "There's a lot of ground to cover, any suggestions?"

"I will call the camp manager. She may be able to give you more help." She picked up a two-way radio, spoke into it in French and, after a prolonged pause, got a response and said, "Actually, the country director is in the camp now and she will be here directly."

Jake thanked her and walked with Falcone and Niles back to the others. When he shared the negative outcome, the hopeful elasticity in Amelia Keogh's face deflated like a days-old party balloon.

"Not a single name? How many did you try?" She eyed Falcone and Niles desperately.

"Amelia, we tried a lot," Falcone said gently.

"Honestly, I was surprised by how many we remembered," Niles supplied helpfully.

"What about the doctors or the teachers or the father and the sisters? Or—" Her eyes were moistening with tears.

Cyrus Keogh took his wife by the shoulders, pulled her close. "Sweetheart, it's okay. We're just getting started."

"That's right," Falcone said, and gave her arm a reassuring touch. Turning to Jake, he asked, "What do we do next?"

As if in answer, thunder grumbled overhead, a breeze blowing through the superheated legion of desperate souls pressed together around them. The sky had darkened to the color of flint, lightning rippling within the amassing clouds.

"Pretty sure we're done for today," Jake said, "but there is someone coming who may be able to help us."

SHE CAME WITH AN umbrella, an exuberant smile on her face as rain thrummed over its contours, dripping down as it pounded everywhere else. Ducking under the shelter of the UNHCR tent, she collapsed the umbrella, tossed it aside, and shook. "Ah, these African rains!" she proclaimed. Wiping her face, she held her hand out to Jake. "Hello, pleasure to meet you...Simone Duvall."

He took her hand, smiled, and introduced himself and everyone else as she gestured for them to join her inside the tent.

"How did you get here?" she asked.

Jake looked at her blankly, unsure of the question.

"I mean, where is your vehicle?"

"We came on foot," Jake replied.

"On foot? From where?"

"We hiked from south of here. We have a plane, but we couldn't see where we could land it."

"Your information must be outdated. Our airstrip, it is still a work in progress, but it would have worked for you." Her accent was faintly French, nuanced with international acclimation.

Simone Duvall was a vibrant personality packed into a petite figure. Her dark blond hair was ponytailed and pulled through the opening of the black cap on her head, which had the same DRC logo as the gray vest she wore over a burgundy-colored shirt. Loose-fitting white pants were cinched with a beaded leather belt and tucked into western-style boots. The lanyard around her neck endorsed her as *Directrice pays, République Démocratique du Congo: Conseil Danois Pour Les Réfugés*. The radio clipped to her belt squawked, *"Charlie Delta 1, état du rapport, s'il vous plaît."*

Jake said, "I apologize for taking you away from your work."

She responded to the radio with a touch of exasperation and stuck it back on her belt. "It is fine, really. Actually, I am just here for few days to check on progress. I was with the camp manager when she got the call and wanted to meet with you myself. So, tell me about your inquiry and I will do what I can to help."

Deciding to trust her, Jake explained who the Keoghs were and summarized their story and predicament. As he spoke, Simone Duvall eyed the couple with growing interest, her face by turns registering admiration and dismay. When he was done, she said to the Keoghs, "I am in awe of your accomplishments and devotion to the people you were caring for. I am certainly familiar with who you are and know about some of the work you have done, but I had no idea how much you were doing here. I understand the need for discretion and will do everything I can to maintain that. I don't think it will be a problem for the most part." She paused, thinking. "With the rain and the time of day, maybe you want to rest for the night?"

Duvall took them through the tent and, sharing her umbrella with

Amelia Keogh, strode along a path leading to a dilapidated brick structure that once could have been a school or meeting place. On either side of the path, children splashed in the rain and mud, momentarily blissful and oblivious to the depravity of their circumstances. While Jake and the others walked, now draped in their rain ponchos, Duvall filled them in on the camp and her role with it; with more than fifteen years working in humanitarian aid organizations, most of them in Africa, she was clearly a force of nature and knew her field from the roots up. In her position as country director for the Danish Refugee Council, she oversaw operations of every camp as well as local communities, working in alliance with numerous NGOs in assisting the entire displacement process, from arrival and protective sheltering to the supply of essential needs and services and, ultimately, to the process of rebuilding new lives or returning to improved ones. The South Sudanese crisis, she informed them, had been ongoing for many years but was escalating, this latest evacuation exacerbated by a combination of famine, ethnic clashes, and a cease-fire breach, and with the newer conflicts breaking out in Kivu, she was obviously spread pretty thin.

Inside the dwelling, crates and boxes were stacked to the roof, the back wall crumbled around an opening covered with tarps, but on one side there were folded cots and enough space in which to arrange them. Duvall spread her arms. "As you can see, we are converting this into a warehouse. Not much, but you are welcome to stay here. I will get you some food and supplies. There is a latrine and shower area just behind."

"Thank you, this is great," Jake replied. And thought: *Tonight, we will have some comfort while on the outside, so many are living in a world of misery having escaped an infinitely worse misery*...and wondered if, indeed, some of the Keoghs' people were amongst them, huddled together under some of those tarps.

WITHIN THE HOUR, SIMONE Duvall had returned with blankets, water, a couple of solar lanterns, and a big pot of rice with goat meat in a tomato sauce, which was gratefully consumed and followed up with a succession of trips to the shower. Even a bucket of tepid water to wash away sweat and grime was refreshing and, with full bellies and a change of dry clothes from their packs, a quiet repose settled over the group.

With the exception of Jake, whose mind would not wind down.

He lay on his cot, staring up at the tin roof, hands behind his head, listening to the rain plinking as it diminished and thinking about the convoluted trail of death and destruction behind them: the compound and village that had been destroyed and burnt to the ground; the slain security detail; the armed sentries they had killed to free the Keoghs; the militia that had attacked them at night in a horrendous thunderstorm; and today, the discovery of a dying Antoine who had played some unknown role in the sequence. He was hoping that there really wasn't anything sinister afoot, hoping they would find at least some of the Keoghs' people here and get them all out so they could begin again, and he was especially hoping that he would soon be on his way back home to Callie. It was always Callie in his last moments before sleep. But as the others around him slipped off to slumber with relative ease in a shelter that was not ensconced in the forest, he lay awake for a while, alert for any sound or change in the light, his Glock moved from the back of his pants to the front, its hard squared barrel snug against his stomach.

STANDING OUTSIDE IN THE pre-dawn, Jake sipped coffee he had made with an MRE heater packet, absorbed in his thoughts and wondering if today would bring something, anything good. He swallowed the freeze-dried mixture, scowled, and looked up to find Simone Duvall, in jeans and a tank top beneath the DRC vest, Panama-style hat on her head, hair down, glasses framing her lively eyes.

"Nescafé?" she asked, indicating his cup.

"Yep."

"Would you like some real coffee?" She held up a large thermos.

Jake smiled broadly. "Hell, yeah."

"I have an Italian coffeemaker."

His brows arched. "Now we're talking."

Jake emptied what remained in his cup and waited as she opened the top of the thermos and poured from the rich, black contents. He took a sip, leaned back, closed his eyes, and sighed. "Oh my God, woman."

She handed him the thermos and a canvas sack. "Also some boiled eggs, fruit, and bread that came in yesterday. Enjoy." She gave him a piece of paper with a hand-drawn diagram of the camp. On it, she had scrawled notes with a few names. "These are community representatives, and most of them speak some English. I also suggest visiting the places where there is the most gathering…food and water, medical, like that. Honestly, if they are here, they should be in our rolls somewhere. Even before newcomers are fully processed in, they are typically on our NFI list—that means non-food items. When they first arrive they get basic things like a tarp, buckets, soap." She shrugged. "But you never know. This camp is huge and it is still getting organized, it's possible they are here and as yet unaccounted for. I will be asking around myself and will check in with you later. I hope you find them."

Jake bowed his head in thanks, his own hope tempered.

As the rest woke and made their way to join him, he filled their cups and watched the sun's light emerge, heard the distant clatter of pans, smelled fire on wood and charcoal, the rhythm of life in the camp slowly initiating. Chickens clucked, goats bleated, babies cried.

They left their overnight accommodation to begin searching the camp, trying to be as respectful as they could strolling by the tarp-covered stick frames, some more evolved in their construction than others, passing women outside them, cooking or washing. Grain mixtures as thick as wet cement were being churned in wide pans with long sticks, clothes scrubbed and pounded and laid out or hung on lines. Naked children were dunked in basins of murky water, dabbed dry, and swaddled in *lapa* wraps. Though the camp was muddy from the previous evening's rain, the insides of shelters were fastidiously whisked with hand brooms made of lashed thatch. Everything done with the order of normalcy, tended with discipline and dignity, essential everyday routines placidly conducted as if nothing was amiss—even as everything of their lives had been torn apart. But there was no mistaking the hollowness in their faces, the harrowed glossiness in their eyes that foretold the tragedies secreted within.

Weaving their way through the vast sea of blue and white, they stopped wherever anyone seemed approachable or receptive, Luther Baladur doing most of the talking in Swahili or Arabic, Zande in some cases, or going through a community representative when the indigenous languages of Dinka and Nuer were spoken. By mid-morning, they had covered only a small portion of the camp with no promising leads. The few men were stony and laconic in their replies, the women warily reticent; children were either shy or unabashedly inquisitive, again calling out, *"Kawaja,"* which was the South Sudanese version of "white person," some tagging along in a happy cortege, clapping their hands and chanting or singing.

But when the occasional man or woman did speak more freely, what they shared was heart-wrenching and horrific.

They came across a young woman in her early twenties, bouncing a toddler in her lap. She had been watching them approach, her expression unreadable.

Amelia Keogh walked over slowly and knelt in front of her. "Your dress is absolutely beautiful!" she declared, her melodic Australian accent and charming smile eliciting a brief flicker of cheer. The woman was clothed in a variation of the traditional Sudanese *toub*, typically a long dress, the fabric of which wrapped the head and draped the shoulders and arms; hers was an ornately patterned turquoise and fuchsia, shortened and worn over a t-shirt, her plaited hair uncovered. She had fashioned the baby's top from some of the same fabric. Encouraged, Amelia ticked the baby's chin and was rewarded with a gleeful gurgle. She cooed, "What a beautiful baby," flashed her luminous green eyes, and the young woman's defenses fell away.

Her name was Emmeline Balandiya and, like so many others, she was a widow. In addition to her baby, she had two children under the age of five, both playing on the dirt floor of their shelter. Her husband and mother had been killed by rebel soldiers who descended on their village one night, going house to house, looting, cutting, raping, and slaying. Balandiya raised each arm, the material of her *toub* sliding back to reveal pink wormlike scars inscribed from wrist to elbow. Her voice lowering, she told them she had witnessed the attacks on her husband and mother before being raped herself and left for dead. The instinct to save her children gave her the fortitude to flee. She recounted days and nights of running and hiding in the forest, fearfully alone with her children, until she finally found a group of others traveling together and ultimately made it with them to the refugee camp.

Still kneeling as she listened intently to Emmeline Balandiya's story, Amelia managed to keep her face free of emotion, but her eyes were glistening as she looked at the children behind their mother, thinking of the things they had seen and experienced that no children ever should. It took every ounce of self-control she could muster to keep from staring at the baby, her heart fluttering. After wishing the young woman good fortune in the coming days, Amelia made a silent vow to find her again before they left, a compulsion she would feel with many more in the camp.

When they had started walking again, Cyrus Keogh took his wife's hand and leaned close with a few quiet words. She nodded, and they continued their quest.

Not long after the interchange with Emmeline Balandiya, Amelia noticed Jake, his shoulders stiff, gait mechanical. She came up beside him, peering into his face. His eyes were locked forward, not on the continual roam. "You okay?" she asked.

He broke from his trance, looked at her. "What? Yeah, sure. Why?"

She didn't respond, but he knew what she was thinking and let it hover for a while. Finally, he sighed deeply and gazed off, something hard and heavy in his chest. "Hearing that from her…it…" He could not finish. The feeling in that moment was breaking him in ways that he could not elucidate. He was thinking of what Callie had gone through, the innumerable violations and then her terror in the jungle as she fled, the strangling dread she must have felt when she'd been recaptured.

"I'm so sorry, Jake," she said softly. "I can't even imagine."

A sentient look passed between them, and Jake said, "You, too."

As hot as it had been hiking in the bush and savannas, the heat here felt as though it could blister paint, sucking breath from the lungs and broiling perspiration like steam from a boiler room. In an attempt to minimize attention, Amelia Keogh had swept her hair into an olive-colored scarf, but as the noon hour approached and sweat was seeping through her clothing, she unknotted it and shook her tresses loose, fluffing with her fingers and exhaling in relief.

Reestablishing his group vigilance, Jake glanced around and saw everyone with him except Falcone and Niles. "Goddammit," he bristled "Where the hell did those two go? I told them not to wander off."

*   *   *   *   *

SHORTLY BEFORE THE GROUP had approached Emmeline Balandiya, Eddie Falcone and Curran Niles had spotted a man with a
camera. He was young and slim with neck-length brown hair, clad in
faded jeans and a blue t-shirt, and he was shooting prolifically from a
Canon EOS Mark III.

Niles nudged Falcone and said enviously, "Look at that bloke...I wish
we could have brought our camera gear."

"Me, too, but our packs are a hell of a lot lighter without it."

They continued to watch the man as he lined up his shots, clicked,
and moved. Aiming up and down, twisting right and left, making adjustments, checking the results in his monitor. But when he was targeting
people, he was also crouching and leaning invasively into his subjects,
crawling without invitation inside their shelters.

"Whoa," Falcone said, halting in his tracks. "This guy is really pissing
me off...not cool, asshole." Though Niles was usually the impulsive one,
Falcone's outrage over the blatant breach of privacy set him in motion.
He began striding toward the man, who was now squatting with his
camera inches from the bewildered face of a little girl not more than
two. The child was holding her crying infant sister in her skinny little
arms. Falcone was within six feet of the photographer when Niles
grabbed him.

"Eddie, no!" Niles hissed, yanking him back.

Falcone pulled free and the momentum got him almost on top of the
guy, but half-turned in Niles' direction he was suddenly reminded of the
reason they were supposed to be discreet. They had drifted a dozen or
so yards from Jake and the others, and as he looked, Amelia Keogh had
just released her hair. Cyrus Keogh stood in full view beside her.

"Oh shit," he muttered, and at the same time caught the attention of
the photographer.

Niles reached for his arm again, but Falcone was already moving. The
two of them took off, the photographer now jogging in pursuit. They
could hear his feet thumping on the ground, the intake of his breath.

"Fuck," Falcone huffed, and ran into the Keoghs and Cameron
McNamara, his arms outspread like a giant bird. "Go, go, go!" he

shouted.

Startled, they looked around, saw the man running behind Falcone and Niles, his camera raised in the air. "Eddie, what on earth…?" Amelia Keogh asked as Falcone pushed them forward.

"What the hell?" Jake demanded and, quickly grasping the situation unfolding, sprang for the Keoghs and hustled them down a narrow gap between shelters. "They've snagged a fucking journalist," he growled, "and I'm pretty sure he's recognized you." Urging them on in front of him, he checked over his shoulder, saw the others right behind him, and picked up the pace, guiding the Keoghs and McNamara in and out of openings wherever he saw them.

After dashing a gauntlet through the breaks between shelters, veering off in varying directions, Jake stopped and gathered everyone together. He gave Falcone and Niles a stern look but did not say anything right away.

"Jesus, I'm sorry, Jake," Falcone said. "But the guy was being totally disrespectful."

"Okay, I get it. I probably would have done the same thing…in other circumstances. You've got to remember the priority here, which is to provide cover and protection for the Keoghs."

"Understood."

"We've still got a hell of a way to go," Jake said. "Kean, can you take the rear and keep a look out for that guy?"

"You got it," Dmello said.

Amelia Keogh pulled her hair up and rewrapped it in the scarf, which she tied behind her neck, and they began walking again.

They had all been so focused on evading the journalist, no one took notice of another man who had been watching them since before they'd awakened that morning.

30

IN MANY WAYS, SEEING the camp in the full wattage of sun was more stark and somber than the darkening cast of the clouds and rain of yesterday's arrival. Today the sun had risen quickly and grandly and continued to reign supreme in a clear sky, its heat never wavering. Activity was robust with people in various phases of settlement, humbly accepting what help they were offered while trying to redefine the dignity of their existence. The NGO presence was robust and included the likes of CARE, the ICRC, and Save the Children, all on maximum implementation. As Jake, Falcone and Niles, Baladur and Dmello, the Keoghs and McNamara walked on into the afternoon, speaking with everyone they could, they heard many more stories of the besieged and their desperate escapes, of those in their circles who survived and of those who had not.

They watched as aid trucks struggled down the mud-caked road, often getting stuck in the process until being pushed by a contingent eager to line up for whatever food items or supplies were on board. There were always crowds of people left over when the last of the cargo was dispersed. They passed a water station with a borehole, from which a line of yellow jerrycans curled out of sight. Elsewhere in the camp, a water truck was being mobbed by others, while children also scooped dirty water from drainage trenches. Sacks of maize and beans and jugs of cooking oil vanished as quickly as they touched the ground.

But there were heartening stories and scenes of aspiration. They heard the hopes of those who wanted to start or resume livelihoods—seamstresses and tailors, barbers and beauticians, farmers and shopkeepers, mechanics and musicians—and children who yearned to go to school. In the more permanent section of the camp, an education center was under construction, and there were teachers already holding sessions in open-air tents. A street-length market was being set up and stocked for merchants to work and refugees with cash vouchers to choose and purchase goods for themselves.

Still, hours in, it became hard to listen and hard to watch, especially when they had yet to find a single soul who knew anything about a displaced group from the DRC. And the sheer magnitude of the place and the volume of the aggrieved was overwhelming.

They managed to successfully evade the journalist the rest of the day, but not without a few close encounters. Though Jake had assigned Dmello lookout duty, he made a regular patrol around the group himself and almost came face to face with the man near a handful of children rolling an old bicycle tire back and forth. The man had been photographing them and straightened up to preview his shots when Jake turned and spotted him. Jake steered the group in another direction, voicing, "Move," in his comms, and they did, putting enough distance behind them to lose the journalist once more.

Not long after that, Jake caught a glimpse of the other man, his premonitory senses twitching. He thought he had seen him somewhere else in the camp, but wasn't sure. Seeing him now, just a flash of his profile—tall, dark-haired, khaki clothing—there one second and then ducking out of sight the next, pinned him on Jake's radar.

The sun's yellow had deepened to gold and was low in the sky by the time they reached the medical compound, which was separated from the inhabited part of the camp by a fairly wide dirt road. Occupying another old brick building roofed in tin with several large white tents framed in metal on either side, the entire complex was enclosed by a combination of bamboo and metal fencing. The red logo for *Médecins Sans Frontières* was printed on banners and signs, red-and-white-striped tape strung outside one of the tents corralling a line of people waiting for vaccinations.

Jake was guiding his group toward the fence when a mud-blasted white Toyota LandCruiser pulled up, Simone Duvall hopping out of the passenger side. She was speaking in rapid French, her voice elevating as she concluded the exchange.

"Sorry, sorry," she said, striding briskly to them, "I had every intention of catching up with you before now. Just so much going on all day."

"Nothing to apologize for," Jake assured her. "Your plate is quite full here."

"Any luck?" she asked, searching their faces for a sign of good news.

"Afraid not."

"Okay, well, let's go into the clinic. There is a lot of staff and they are as knowledgeable as any who work around the camp. They also have an outreach team who go from shelter to shelter to seek out those who are in need of medical attention. And they go to nearby communities. Maybe they have come across some of the people."

Both Keoghs, who had become increasingly dispirited over the passing hours, visibly brightened, exchanging hopeful looks.

Founded in 1971 by a group of journalists and doctors, *Médecins Sans Frontières*—Doctors Without Borders—is a self-governed non-profit with a presence in over seventy countries, providing medical care in conflicts, epidemics, disasters, and for those without access to health services. Their tightly integrated teams consist of professionals of every capacity: doctors and nurses, administrative and support staff, logisticians and technicians, and water and sanitation specialists. Comprising international expats from a mix of countries, they are joined by skilled locals to serve as a unit, all ethically dedicated and politically neutral. Their supply chain for vehicles, equipment, building materials, medical apparatus and medicines is considered one of the most expedient of all aid organizations in the world.

Duvall spoke briefly to a security guard stationed at the metal gate and they were allowed admission. She led them through a tent with wooden benches and chairs filled with haggard men and women, scared children and listlessly silent or bawling babies, and entered the clinic. They were met by the medical team leader, a fair-haired Canadian doctor clad in an MSF t-shirt and vividly colored and patterned pants made of *panga* fabric. She had bright eyes framed in collegiate-looking glasses

and a ready smile, introducing herself as Nora Caron. The expat personnel, clad in the t-shirts and vests and rumpled slacks, many thumping
around in yellow gumboots, attended to a full house of patients. The
national support staff, by contrast, were more fastidiously dressed, the
men in pressed shirts and trousers, the women in dresses or skirts and
elaborately braided hairpieces.

In the general treatment area, screenings were being conducted for
common regional afflictions, notably the three M's—measles, malaria,
and malnutrition—physical examinations conducted, blood drawn, the
weighing and measuring of youngsters by hanging satchel and a flat
board. In the Therapeutic Feeding ward, mothers were counseled and a
multitude of RUTFs—ready-to-use therapeutic foods—were being dispensed in the form of milk-based F-75 in colored plastic cups and packets
of peanut-buttery Plumpy'Nut. As they continued the initial tour, they
passed doctors and nurses checking vital signs, treating infections and
wounds and broken bones, hanging IV drips and consulting each other
over charts, their accents a blend of African, Nordic, Slavic, Hispanic,
French, Canadian, Australian, and British. The building swelled with the
babble of conversation and the hum of generators, punctuated by
coughs and cries, moans and groans, and calls from one colleague to another. The pungent smell of chlorine masked stomach-turning odors of
bodily fluids and excrement and vomit, but only at first. Moths swarmed
as overhead lighting was flickering on, dusk casting dark shadow
through the windows. Lighting came on outside, blinding and obliterat-
ing everything beyond it.

Strolling between Pediatrics and Maternity, Internal and Emergency
Medicine, Cyrus Keogh commented, "Our clinic was great, but this is so
bloody impressive." He watched with interest as a logistician picked his
way through a thick nest of cabling in one corner while, in another, several nurses were drawing blood from members of a family in an effort
to get a transfusion for a critically anemic child.

While the Keoghs were talking to a couple of nurses, Dmello came
up to Jake and said, "That journalist was outside just now, and I think
he was going to come in here." His face creased with perplexity. "But
then some other guy appeared and grabbed him and dragged him
away."

"Some other guy?" Jake asked, and already had an inkling who it was. "Tall, dark hair, dressed like us?"

Dmello looked at him narrowly. "Yes, that is him. Who is the guy?"

"I don't know," Jake said tersely. "But I noticed him before, so now we need to keep an eye out for him, too."

Dr. Caron was about to introduce them to a mustached Swedish doctor with long, dark blond hair twisted into a man bun when both of their radios crackled: "Emergency! Incoming knife and gunshot wounds! *Urgence! Blessures au couteau et par balle!*" Heads swiveled and tension rippled through staff and patients like the voltage of an electronic shock.

THE MSF LANDCRUISER TRANSPORT vehicle pulled in through the gate and up to the tented receiving area, not far from where they were standing. It was the traditional road-dusty white with red MSF logos on the hood and sides, a huge black Codan HF antenna mounted at the bumper and a no-weapons symbol prominent on a rear window panel. Everyone backed away except Jake, whose instinct was to assess and then react accordingly. As several victims were helped from or taken out of the back of the vehicle, he heard one of the medical attendants saying that the wounded were refugees who had been attacked by militants on the road to the camp. The MSF team had been returning from conducting a mobile clinic when they were waved down. The injuries Jake could see appeared to be pretty serious, deep knife or possibly machete cuts on arms and legs, one bleeding profusely from a gunshot to the stomach, another with cuts on the neck and face. Some were wailing from pain, others were silenced by shock.

Dr. Caron took charge, clearing out other patients and non-essentials and issuing instructions to nurses as she triaged each of the five victims; two were designated red and taken straight into the trauma treatment area while the other three were graded yellow. One of the doctors, a dark-featured Czech surgeon who was working to staunch the flow of blood from the gunshot wound, shouted, "Does anyone know if there were family members with this group? We are going to need blood!"

His appeal sent support staff off to canvas the occupants of the clinic and waiting areas.

Standing in the yellow zone—designated by a large colored rectangle on the tarp underfoot—Jake's medically informed mind processed the range of wounds by urgency and severity and honed in on a skinny adolescent boy of perhaps fifteen or sixteen who sat slumped in a chair, a small, dark patch of blood seeping from his thigh through the fabric of his pants. Three of the five others had been more obviously exigent in their bleeding, but Jake was noticing the overall lethargy of the boy, his face drooping, a bluish tinge to his lips.

Reaching into a pocket for his Swiss Army knife, Jake went to him and knelt down, flicking the blade out and slicing the boy's pants from above the bloody spot all the way down. As he had suspected, the thigh inside was swollen to a grotesque size for such an emaciated frame—he was bleeding out from the inside and needed immediate intervention; the leg would need to be cut open to find the bleeder and tie it off. The Czech surgeon had been watching from the next tent, which was the air-conditioned and higher-equipped and -functioning red zone, and called over, "Medic?"

"Yes, U.S. Army, Special Forces," Jake replied.

"Go ahead, see what we've got."

Jake flipped his backpack around and dug in for his aid kit, extracting a scalpel and QuikClot gauze. He snapped on nitrile gloves and cut a line over the wound, which elicited only the slightest moan from the boy and expelled blood in a bloom of crimson. Pressing the gauze into the wound, Jake saw the source of the bleeding, and reported, "Got an arterial bleed." He started with an Israeli bandage, but when it became evident the IBD was not working to stop the bleed, he reluctantly took a R.A.T.S. tourniquet from his bag—a last resort, but at this point the best chance to save the limb. He held the cleat and configured the three-finger loop, worked the strap around the leg and into place, and firmly wound the wrap.

The boy was transported from the chair to a table, Jake getting a respectful nod from the surgeon.

While he had been working on the boy, Jake had also fleetingly noticed the fifth victim, a vague sense of something not quite right but nothing ticking his medical cognizance. The man was in his twenties, clad in a long-sleeved gray shirt, loose and open over a t-shirt, brown pants stuffed into dirty lace-up boots missing the laces. He was pacing around agitatedly, his eyes darting as if he were looking for a means of escape. There was blood spattered on his clothing, but Jake could not see an obvious wound. Before he had a chance to investigate, his back turned while the boy he'd been attending was moved, there was a muffled cry of distress.

Jake pivoted and saw the fidgety man, a young nurse clenched in front of him, arms pinned helplessly to her chest. She had long brown hair and dark eyes that were popping with panic, a seven-inch bush knife held across her throat. The nurse, one the Keoghs had met and been speaking with earlier, was an Australian named Sophie Whelan, and Jake's first move was to keep her calm. "Hey Sophie," he said evenly, "look at me. Just look directly at me, okay?"

She could not nod, but her eyes held desperately on him.

"Go limp," Jake told her.

She looked at him, uncomprehending.

"Like a ragdoll. Dead weight…will make you harder to handle."

Getting it, the nurse went slack, her body becoming lifeless and heavy, the would-be assailant momentarily flustered and handicapped. Jake took the moment and lunged forward. As anticipated, the man's grasp on the woman loosened and then let go, his defensive instinct taking over. He slashed out at Jake and, when he was close enough, Jake grabbed his wrist with one hand and shoved his other into the man's face, smashing his nose. Blood spurted and the man yowled. But the knife hand, immobilized by Jake, was still in play. With a quick foot sweep, the man went down, and the knife clattered away. Falcone stepped forward and stooped to confiscate it.

The medical staff continued working on their patients but were stealing incredulous glimpses of Jake. Glancing at the blood on his shirt and pants, and at the astonished faces around him, he thought: *So much for keeping a low profile.*

IT HAD BEEN NEARLY full dark by the time order was restored to its normally frenetic level so, at Simone Duvall's invitation, they decided to spend a second night at the camp. After eating and cleaning up, everyone was exhausted and retired to their cots with minimal preamble, crawled beneath mosquito netting, and eventually fell asleep to the scratches and screeches of bats in the termite-riddled wood beams precariously supporting the tin roof.

The next morning, Baladur and Dmello did a preliminary scout, looking for the journalist or the other man of dubious intent. Not seeing either, they reported back to Jake and the group set off for the medical center. Since they'd not had a chance to talk to many the previous night, it would be their first stop. Amelia Keogh had donned Cyrus' beige bush hat and both Keoghs wore sunglasses, but as they had discovered yesterday, any attempt to downplay appearances was mostly for naught, their posse attracting copious attention as they walked.

With her delivery of coffee and breakfast earlier, Simone Duvall had said she'd meet them and was standing by the immunization tent, chatting with staff and making demonstrative exclamations to the gaggles of children who gleefully held out black-polished fingernails for her inspection, an indication of having been vaccinated.

"Yes, I see, I see! Excellent!"

Amelia Keogh watched, her expression obscured behind the sunglasses, but the compression of her lips and dip of her head hinted at the emotional struggle.

Greeting the group, Duvall asked Jake, "Have you still been seeing that journalist?"

"Some, but now there's another guy." He gave her a description and related what Dmello had seen outside the clinic compound.

She shook her head. "Does not sound familiar, but yes, that is certainly strange. I will ask around."

They went inside the main building, where activity was no less hectic than before, chairs filled with the sick and suffering, the walking wounded, the starved children, the pregnant women. They shuffled through Therapeutic Treatment, nurses measuring tiny little arms no bigger in circumference than a garden hose with MUAC strips color-coded from green to yellow to red showing the degree of malnutrition. The room and its waiting area were packed with children whose faces and bodies were cruelly shriveled and bereft of all the soft curves molded by baby fat. They continued past the array of other patients with festering sores and abscesses and infected limbs, the feverish and anemic, the bleakly diseased. One little girl caught Jake's eye and he grimaced inwardly, noting the necrotic foot below a wad of foul-smelling and fluid-stained bandaging wrapped around her shin. Probably a snakebite, he thought, knowing that, sadly, she was going to lose the foot and maybe even much of the leg.

Entering the in-patient ward with its barrack-style bedding, they found the Czech surgeon making rounds. Tall and hulking with striking blue eyes and a dimpled smile, he stood up from the bed of a patient he'd been checking and looped his stethoscope around his neck. He reached for Jake's hand, clasped it firmly, and said, "Jaromír Dobrovolný…call me Jaro. Good work on the assist last night. Thank you."

Jake smiled modestly. "Glad to help out."

"Turns out, he was one of the rebels. Let us transport him, maybe to get medical attention, but also probably to get into camp and see what he could take. We treat, no matter who, of course. Have not had that happen since I am here. Some police came and got him."

"I must say, Jaro," Cyrus Keogh said, face light with his easy smile, "the work you are all doing here is quite inspiring." He paused, his expression shifting to one of seriousness which, given the magnetism of his charm, had an even more arresting effect and got the doctor's full concentration. "We had an IDP compound in a village west of here, not nearly so large as this, but with medical facilities, a couple of doctors and staff."

Dr. Dobrovolný was nodding vaguely, holding his chin, his brow knitting. "Yes, Dr. Caron told us about it yesterday. You are looking for the people."

"That's right," Amelia Keogh said, the pitch of her voice rising with anticipation.

"I am afraid none of us think we have seen any from here, just the Sudanese," he replied and, noticing the way her shoulders sank with his answer, added, "but of course that does not necessarily mean they are not here. Is a huge camp."

Drawing herself up with a stabilizing breath, Amelia said, "Our doctors…Noah Goossens and Julienne Baudin…they are missing with everyone else." She faltered. "Have you…?"

The Czech doctor shook his head, but a dark look passed over his face. "I do not want to say this, but we have heard about some doctors being held."

"Being held? What do you mean?" She looked stricken, as if she'd been slapped.

Cyrus Keogh intervened, asking, "You mean in captivity, possibly to treat some group?"

"Unfortunately, it happens," Dr. Dobrovolný said glumly. "But again, that does not mean what we hear is true or if it is your doctors. Just maybe something to look into."

On the rest of their way through the building, people they spoke with and things they saw were equally discouraging and often profoundly disturbing. A male nurse reviewing a tableful of Paracheck rapid tests, all of which displayed the two red lines indicating positive results, was writing up orders for antimalarials. In a bed nearby, a young mother was cradling her infant who was far beyond the salvation of medical remedies as his chest heaved weakly until it stopped and she cried out in grief. Amelia Keogh was already edging into a dark place when they passed a series of signs painted with a single pink flower and then came to a tent with the same flower painted on the entrance, which was closed. She was puzzling over what the flower could signify, thinking perhaps a gathering place for children, when a stream of downcast women emerged and slowly shuffled by, accompanied by several MSF advocates, and Amelia knew immediately what kind of space this was, and looked away, slipping her sunglasses back on and hastening her step toward the exit.

Jake knew, too, and felt as though his gut had been split open and everything inside caving like quicksand, the urge to be with Callie in that moment crushing him.

FALCONE AND NILES HAD opted to wait outside the compound and were scuffling aimlessly back and forth. Both of them were hot and cranky, their clothing already soaked with sweat, water bottles empty.

"God, this place is depressing," Falcone remarked. "And the smells are making me sick."

"Not wrong there, mate," Niles replied, scowling.

Falcone whipped the cap off his head and waved it in front of his face. "Shit. Goddamned bugs are eating me alive." He scratched viciously at his neck, further irritating the swollen welts.

"I thought you darker blokes didn't attract those buggers. Jake sure doesn't seem to."

"Yeah, well, nothing dares mess with him," Falcone scoffed.

"You're putting on the repellant aren't you?"

"Yeah, yeah…but you know it just runs right off."

They lapsed into silence and watched the children watching them, unable to summon the energy to engage or animate in their typical way. At one point, Niles poked Falcone and asked, "Hey, isn't that the dodgy wanker?"

"What? The frickin' journalist? Where?"

"No, that other guy Jake mentioned." He crooked his head, and Falcone looked in the direction Niles was indicating.

Leaning up against the side of some kind of storage shack was a man with dark hair cut short and combed sideways on top, wearing khaki pants and shirt over a black tee. He had on wraparound sunglasses and was smoking a cigarette, his head angled away from them. He did not look like a journalist or anyone working in a refugee camp, not with a sat phone sticking out of a pants pocket, tattoos inked on his arms, and a fancy tactical watch on his wrist like the one Jake wore.

"We need to go tell Jake," Falcone said.

"Maybe we should stay here and keep an eye on him or follow him or—"

Falcone grabbed Niles by the shirt and pulled him back behind a tree next to the compound. "Shit! I think he just saw us."

When they stepped cautiously around to take another peek at him, the man was gone.

WALKING WITH SIMONE DUVALL, they passed an area that had been cleared since the day before, a new tent being erected. There was a flurry of activity that included men thrusting shovels into the ground and heaving up hunks of red dirt, others hammering timber into framework, and several more trying on protective gear that resembled spacesuits: canary yellow hooded Microgard, facemasks and goggles, aprons and gloves and boots. An MSF watsan—water and sanitation specialist—was supervising the installation of latrines and showers.

"You've got Ebola here?" Cyrus Keogh asked, his brows hitching in surprise.

"No, no," Duvall said quickly, "but there are outbreaks to the south, so we want to be ready. Just in case."

"Dear God," Amelia said, "let's pray it never comes your way."

"Yes, it is really horrible. Fortunately, they have started screening for it at the borders."

Jake was listening, but he had been distracted by the news Falcone and Niles had brought him moments ago, checking every space between shelters and around every corner. So far, he'd not spied either the journalist or the other man in question.

They walked on into the morning, talking to everyone they could, Amelia noticing a group of a dozen or more women that seemed to be making the same circuit they were. Finally, she asked, "What's going on with them?"

Simone Duvall hesitated before replying. "This is a common thing in the camps, in these situations. You have probably noticed that most of the people here are women and children, yes?"

Amelia nodded.

"That is because most of these women are widows, and many of them have been separated from their children…so they are searching, hoping their children will turn up in the care of others."

The words had barely been spoken when the despair Amelia Keogh had been holding in check for the past few days broke apart. Tears streamed from behind her sunglasses, rolling down her flushed face, her body racked with breathless sobs. Cyrus took her into his arms and held her.

Between gasps, Amelia said, "They're not here, Cy. We're not going to find them. They're gone, they're just gone!" She cried into his chest, the others drawing in around the two of them.

She stayed like that for a while, no one knowing what to say because deep down, they'd all started to expect such an outcome.

And then, just above her knee, she felt a light tug on her linen pants. Removing her sunglasses, she wiped her eyes and looked around, her head tilting down. The grinning brown face of a youngster peered up at her, a six- or seven-year-old girl with meticulously cornrowed hair, dressed in a red-white-and-blue t-shirt speckled with stars and elastic-waisted blue jeans.

"Miss Amelia," the little girl said, her grin breaking into a smile.

At first Amelia Keogh could not speak, and then she exclaimed, "Georgette! Oh God, oh God, Georgette!" She bent over and swept the girl up in her arms, swinging her as she hugged and cried and murmured incoherently. When she finally put the girl down, she asked, *"D'où viens-tu? Où sont les autres?"*

The little girl named Georgette led her by the hand, striding toward the rear of the camp, turning down the one path they had not traversed. It was close to the road, along the rows of more permanent housing. They were taken to a shelter of overlapping tarps, beneath which was a conclave numbering about thirty, nearly all women and children, several toddlers and babies. Many hands flew to mouths, some arms were raised jubilantly in the air, utterings of exhilaration were voiced.

But Amelia Keogh was dumbfounded. Her eyes were darting wildly left to right, her mind disjointed from exactly what she was seeing. Her mouth was frozen in a dazed smile, as if it didn't quite fit her lips. "Is this…where are…" And then the smile collapsed, her jaws quivering. "Where are the rest?"

Jake and Cyrus Keogh were on either side of her. They both knew in that awful moment what was coming next.

One of the women shook her head slowly.

"L-L-Lula…" Amelia stammered. "Where is she?" She lurched forward, the congregation parting as she moved through the shelter. Woven mats and a few bedrolls were arranged over the dirt floor, jerrycans of water and cooking oil sat next to a small collection of pots and pans. Nothing else.

Amelia turned, asking again, her voice smothered in emotion, "Where is Lula?"

The woman reached out and took Amelia's hands, looked into her liquid green eyes. Again, shook her head somberly.

Whispering now, Amelia asked, "Where is Lula? Where are the rest?"

The woman, named Beatrice, wearing a full-length *pagne* dress, pink with a leopard design, was as tall as Amelia, and a beauty. She continued to gaze into Amelia's imploring eyes.

And said: "I pray they are with God."

31

AMELIA STOOD GAZING AT the woman named Beatrice Tshisungu, her mouth open, the words just spoken pulsing through her head in numb bursts, like water alternately clogging and clearing the ears.

"What...what do you mean?" she stammered.

"Let us sit," Beatrice said, unable to look directly into Amelia's eyes.

The two took a spot and lowered to the ground, the rest of the assembly following suit. Simone Duvall had been on her radio, requesting additional water and food and some mats, and within minutes camp staff had appeared to distribute the goods. Cyrus Keogh took a seat next to his wife, Falcone and Niles behind them with Cameron McNamara. Jake remained standing while Baladur and Dmello stationed themselves by the structure's openings.

Water was poured into cups that were passed around among the clan, each drinking with a fervor that suggested such hydration had been spare for quite a while. Several of the children had scampered over to Falcone and Niles and McNamara in recognition and were already climbing over them and trying to get into their backpacks.

Amelia Keogh took a long drink from her water bottle, wiped her mouth, and inhaled shakily. Then she looked at Beatrice and asked hoarsely, "What happened?"

Tshisungu smoothed the fabric of her brightly colored dress, folded her hands together in her lap, and began, speaking in proficient English. "We were having such a good day. The sun was shining, the children

were playing. Then a nice evening. We had a big fire, ate well, and celebrated our blessings, celebrated you, celebrated us. We sang, we danced,
we were so happy. We cleaned everything up, we said our good nights,
we went to sleep." She paused, swallowing. "And then in the night we
were awakened by gunfire."

Jake had been listening intently, but now he was rapt, thinking of the
bullet casings he'd found at the site.

The Keoghs were also holding onto every word, but their faces had
gone pale, their eyes glassy with an agony that was just beginning to
register.

"So much gunfire," Tshisungu said, clasping her arms. "We were so
afraid, but we went out to see what was happening. There were men
with guns and more men with torches. They were setting fire to our
homes, to everything!" She shuddered at the memory, tears forming in
her eyes. "Everything was burning up. We all ran away as fast as we
could. The fire was everywhere. We fled into the woods and ran for our
lives." She stopped, head bent low, crying quietly. Those around her
were eerily silent, but their faces reflected the anguish of their ordeal.
When she was able to continue, she said, "I heard screams—so many
screams—but I just kept running. I knew if I stopped, it would be me
screaming. But—"

Amelia leaned over and embraced her, murmuring, "Oh, Beatrice, I
am so sorry…"

Within Amelia Keogh's embrace, Beatrice sobbed more audibly,
"There were children screaming…*children*…and the animals…I still hear
it in my dreams." She withdrew from Amelia, twisting her hands in her
lap, and went on. "We kept running as long as we could, into the night
and the next day. Then we just walked all day, every day, staying in the
forest. We were so scared and then so hungry and thirsty. I think it was
eight days of footings until we made it here," she said, referring to the
term that was universally used to indicate distances walked.

Simone Duvall, who was standing next to the Keoghs, asked, "Beatrice, when did you all arrive here in the camp? How long have you
been here?"

"We only just arrived last night."

"You did not get registered anywhere?" asked Duvall.

The woman dropped her head contritely. "We were...no, I am sorry."

"That is okay," Duvall told her. "I will have medical visit you." She stepped back and got on her radio again.

Cyrus Keogh knew what his wife wanted to ask, saw the struggle in her face, and reached for one of Tshisungu's hands, patting it comfortingly, his blue eyes soft with empathy. "Beatrice, do you know what happened to the others?"

She sniffled and shook her head. "No, not for sure."

"So they could still be alive?" Amelia asserted, her spine straightening. "They could be out there somewhere?"

"I hope with all my heart," Tshisungu said, "but the men were after them. They chased them."

At this point, Jake had come closer and was squatting down in front of Tshisungu, sunglasses propped on his head, hands on his thighs. He gave her a reassuring smile. "Beatrice, I'd like to ask you some questions...is that okay?"

She eyed him uncertainly, glanced at Amelia and got a nod.

"Do you have any idea how many men there were?"

"It seemed like a lot, but I do not know."

"Do you remember if they were dressed like soldiers? With green or brown shirts and pants, boots?"

She pondered that and said, "They might have been."

"You said there was a lot of gunfire...did it all sound about the same? Like maybe the same kind of guns?"

"I think so, I really do not know. It just happened all at once." She paused, remembering something. "They were shooting up in the air with their guns."

"So they weren't aiming at people?"

"Oh yes," she replied quickly, adding, "but shooting in the air."

Jake thought about that; no bodies left behind, just the few casings he'd recovered. What was their intention?

"I'm seeing only a couple of men here and also not many boys," he said carefully. "Were they targeted?"

She looked at him, her expression troubled. "Targeted?"

Jake lowered his head, grappling with how to frame what he was

going to say next. Finally, he explained, "When there are deliberate attacks—and it's becoming clear to me that this was deliberate—often the
attackers have a motive, and sometimes that is to take boys and men."
His eyes scanned the others seated around her. There was another sub-
group he was not seeing proportionately represented in this mix:
teenaged girls. He could not bring himself to point this out, but he didn't
have to.

Tshisungu said, "I know what you are saying. They take the boys and
men to make them fight, and they take the girls to…" She broke off, a
choked sound issuing from her throat. "That is why I said I pray they are
with God."

Jake stood, his face grim, and waited until the Keoghs looked up at
him. "We need to talk," he said.

THEY WERE GATHERED IN one of the camp's office quarters, a tent
with a combination of wood and plastic tables and chairs, powered by
solar panels and generators that allowed Wi-Fi connectivity for laptop
computers and, to their delight, a couple of electric fans. There were
bottles of cold water and sodas in a small cold box and a collection of
snacks, including things like Pringles, Nutella and crackers, fruit and
cheese and chocolate. There were wood planks stacked for storage,
whiteboards scrawled with to-do directives and personnel schedules,
maps and charts affixed to the sides of the tent. Desks were set up on
several of the tables, a grouping in the middle apparently for meetings
or breaks. A few staff members sat at the desks, laptops open, sipping
cold drinks and chatting as they worked, cords and cabling coiled at their
feet like sleeping snakes.

Jake and the Keoghs were seated together at one of the free tables,
the others pulling up chairs around them. Heads tilted back and eyes
closed as they reveled in the breezes of the oscillating fans, even if they
were only moving hot air. Falcone and Niles guzzled from cans of orange Fanta, McNamara cleaned sweat and dirt from his glasses, and
Baladur and Dmello sat with their chairs facing outward, keeping watch.

Before Jake could begin talking, Amelia Keogh asked, "What are we
going to do? We need to get them out of here!"

It had taken over ten minutes to convince her to leave the people behind, even if momentarily. She'd wanted to stay with them, sweating in their cramped shelter, not let them out of her sight now that they had been found, and no matter what her husband had said, or how reasonably he'd said it, she was adamant. Jake had ultimately prevailed, firmly but mildly saying, "Let's leave them for now, let them be attended to, and then we will come back."

Now, looking across the table at the Keoghs, Jake said, "We have some decisions to make. Yes, we can get your people out of here. Logistically, no doubt it's going to present some challenges, but I think we can make it happen. Where do you want to take them?"

"I've already given that some thought," Cyrus Keogh said, "and the most logical place would be Nakalé"—he glanced at his wife—"don't you agree, love?"

"Yes," she replied, "yes, please, let's do that."

Jake glanced upward to gather his thoughts, and then said, "You've got to know that at this point, finding any of the rest is practically untenable."

The Keoghs were both looking fixedly at him but neither spoke.

"I know this has been the mission, and only finding some of them is a huge letdown...I know that. But look, it's been ten days or so. We're a very long way from your compound site. From what we've heard, they were fleeing in all directions, and separated from the get-go. The others could have gone in any direction, could in fact be way farther to the west...or north or south. And, if we're being honest—"

Amelia Keogh leaned forward, her face drawing taut with an intensity that was almost angry. "No...no, no, no. Jake, don't you say it. Don't." She balled her hands into fists and placed them on the table. "If this was Callie, you'd—"

Falcone and Niles were frozen in place, their eyes moving anxiously between Jake and the Keoghs, breathing shallowly.

Jake felt as if a red-hot poker had been thrust into his gut. His eyes held on her, throat closing, the skin over his temple tightening. The sound of the fans whisking seemed to fill all time and space for several moments. He inhaled deeply, exhaled, and tried to push every reaction into a dead zone.

Amelia's face was like a shattered alabaster plate, pale, broken, devastated. Her voice came out in a disembodied whimper. "Oh God, Jake...I—"

He put out his hand vaguely, looked away.

After taking a minute to recollect himself, he said, "I understand...believe me, I do. As I have said before, I always hope for the best...but I also have to accept realities and make adjustments. I wouldn't be serving you well if I wasn't totally honest and straight with you."

Amelia had gone still, but her eyes were bright with renewed desperation. "Jake, please. You have to find our little girl. You have to. *Please.*"

Cyrus Keogh placed his hands over hers, bent and kissed her neck. Gazing at Jake, he said, "We obviously have the means to keep the search going as long as it takes, but we will respect and abide by your decision." Amelia shifted restlessly next to him, turning her head to conceal the volatile emotions wrestling in her face.

"Okay, let's do this..." Jake said. "Cyrus, you and I will work on getting the transport, see what our options are and hopefully get that going. Then we'll revisit the rest."

"Fair enough," Keogh said.

WHILE JAKE, CYRUS, AND Cameron McNamara remained in the camp's office tent, the rest headed back out to rejoin the Keoghs' people. McNamara took advantage of the Wi-Fi to catch up on Keogh's business via phone and Internet, and Keogh and Jake worked their phones trying to make arrangements for available transportation. They had quickly realized that a truck was going to be their only viable option, but finding one for hire proved to be an onerous task. After nearly an hour of unsuccessful inquiries, Jake suggested they return to the medical compound, remembering something Dr. Caron had mentioned about their logistician being the "go-to guy" for everything from rubber bands and lightbulbs to centrifuges and cargo planes.

Outside, the sun was flat and white in the sky, relentlessly hot, the air thick with the stench of wood fires. Each exposure to the tableau was more harsh than the last, the sights and smells more invasive, the feeling infinitely more deflating.

The guards at the gate for the medical compound, on seeing Jake, gave them quick admittance and affected martial arts poses in homage of his feat the previous night. He smiled and they reacted as though a Hollywood action hero had graced their presence, chuckling and punching each other in the arm.

Inside, Dr. Caron spotted them and came over. "Hello, handsome ones."

"G'day, doctor," Keogh said. "Has anyone checked on our folks?"

"As a matter of fact, I just got back. I went with a team to assess them. They're like most, significantly traumatized. Dehydrated, as you would suspect, also a few infections…nothing too severe, thankfully. It's evident they were doing quite well under your care. They are lucky, though, being able to escape. They were obviously a very tight knit community and are grieving what might have happened to the rest of them. I understand from Simone Duvall that you want to relocate them from camp?"

"Yes, to a village where we stayed called Nakalé," Keogh replied. "Do you know it?"

"I do," Dr. Caron said. "We've done some outreach there. It's quite pleasant, but small and without much in the way of subsistence."

"We had some goods brought in for them," Keogh told her, "and we're prepared to do more."

"Well, that plan would get my blessing as long as there's no violence currently in the area."

"We're trying to hire a transport vehicle, but not having any luck," Jake said.

"Talk to Geoffrey," Dr. Caron said. "He's around here somewhere. He can probably help you with that."

They thanked her and moved off to hunt down the logistician, finding him crouched down working on a generator, talking on a cell phone via earbud at the same time, saying, "I need to know what happened to our ceftriaxone. It was left off the shipment we got today. What? No, we need it now. Right, ring me back." He appeared to be MacGyvering several parts from another unit while a mechanic handed him tools. Noticing Jake and Cyrus Keogh, he stood to greet them.

Geoffrey Edgecombe was a young Brit, tall and wiry, clean-shaven with neatly combed brown hair. His clothing was another story entirely; jeans worn shapeless and threadbare at the knees, MSF t-shirt soiled with stains of both biologic and prefabricated origin.

Jake said, "Dr. Caron thought you might be able to help us. We're trying to hire a truck."

The mechanic assisting him took over and Edgecombe led them to an administrative area where they all sat. Twirling a pencil on his desktop, he asked, "A truck for...?"

"To transport about thirty people to a village about a hundred kilometers from here," Jake said.

"What's the name of the village?"

"Nakalé."

"I know it, yeah. For when?"

"As soon as possible. Tomorrow."

Edgecombe let out a little whistle. "Well, that might be tough, but let me make some calls."

"Appreciate it, mate," Keogh said.

An older Congolese man was hunched over a radio logbook, scribbling notes. He was dapperly dressed in a print button-front shirt and sharply creased brown slacks, the tight frizz on his scalp drizzled with gray. He seemed to be paying attention to the conversation but was humming to himself and focusing on his writing, a pair of wire-framed glasses low on his nose.

As Edgecombe began making calls, Jake looked at Keogh and said, "I've been thinking about it and there is something that might be worth looking into. It sounds to me like the men and boys were culled, which means they were taken for a purpose...soldiers or slaves, maybe both."

"What about the others? The other women and girls, our staff, our doctors?"

"I don't know. It could be they simply scattered and went another way. Or they could be being held somewhere near the men and boys. I can see what intel there is for this area, groups, rebels, militias, their territories. I just have a gut feeling...we only found a handful of bullet casings, and Beatrice said she thought they were shooting in the air. When we were investigating the site, we didn't see any blood or find any bodies. I am more convinced than ever that this was a planned and precisely executed attack, that they purposefully did not shoot *at* people. The shooting was to scare them, get them moving, while the fire destroyed everything." He paused, frowning, the skin around his eyes drawn from fatigue. "My theories are one thing, but having actionable intel is another, and right now we're just about out of it."

Keogh's face was flat, his ever-present smile absent. "I know, mate."

The elder man on the other side of Edgecombe looked up from his logbook, slid around in his chair, and said, "I can help you."

HE WAS KNOWN AS Papa B, his actual name being Salomon Bijou, and he was the pillar of wisdom and regional knowledge base for the camp. He came from a large Zande clan and, with his wife of thirty-five years, had eight children and innumerable grandchildren. His ties to surrounding communities and familiarity with aid work had made him a treasured asset, but his broad network, which extended throughout the country, made him indispensable. His designation was administrative support, but his responsibilities were as endless as his energy to carry them out.

He now held Jake and Keogh's full attention.

"Hearing your dilemma," he said, speaking in remarkably enunciated English, "I have some ideas." He brought his hands together in his lap and looked from one to the other, gauging their interest. There was a large gold ring inset with a black onyx showing above one of his thick knuckles.

Jake did not hesitate. "I'm all ears."

"In the area we are in and north to the borders, there are always a lot of armed conflicts and many active groups, including LRA. I have heard some reports recently of large abductions."

"Do you know locations?" Jake asked.

Bijou nodded. "A few. Let me do some connecting." He turned back to his work, made a few additional entries, and reached for a notebook. Then he stood, excused himself, and carried his substantial bulk into the adjoining communications room.

Geoffrey Edgecombe watched Bijou amble through the doorway and remarked, "Papa B is our human Google. If anyone can get you a lead, he's your man. All right, I have found you a proper lorry. It's not going to be cheap, but I understand that won't be an issue." His eyes flicked to Keogh, who gave him a subtle nod. "Weather and roads willing, it can be here in the morning."

"Wonderful," Jake said. He glanced at his watch, the Garmin display revealing the late afternoon hour. To Keogh, he said, "We should get back to the others, make a plan for tomorrow, maybe get something to eat."

Edgecombe smiled. "Dr. Nora has asked me to extend an invitation for your group to join us for dinner tonight in the expat compound."

"That would be lovely," Cyrus Keogh said.

IN A SMALL CLEARING, Falcone and Niles were booting a ball amongst a growing horde of cackling children who jockeyed for the chance to kick it. None of the youngsters understood more than a word or two the pair uttered in enthusiastic ovation, but the joy of fun and games more than compensated for the language barrier. For almost an hour after returning with Amelia Keogh to the people from their compound, the two had stayed with her inside the stagnant confines of the stick-and-tarp shelter. Finally, they had to stretch their legs and get some air. They had to remove themselves from the gloom.

Now, as they ran around with the kids, seeing the glee in their faces and hearing the excitement in their voices, they felt their own spirits lifting for really the first time since arriving at the camp.

Stopping to clear the sweat from his eyes, Niles noticed that they had once again managed to distance themselves from the others. McNamara was inside the shelter with Amelia, Baladur and Dmello stationed just outside, all of them about a dozen or so yards away. "Think we should get back?" he asked.

"Yeah, I guess so," Falcone sighed, picking up the duct-taped ball and tossing it to one of the children, who snatched it and dashed off. The little boy tripped and lost possession, the ball rolling away from him down a passageway between tents.

Niles went after it, retrieved it at the end of the gap and threw it to the boy. He was standing on the far side of a parallel row of shelters and was about to rejoin Falcone when a movement nearby drew his gaze.

"What is it?" Falcone asked, walking toward him.

"It's that bloke again," Niles said incredibly.

"The journalist?"

"No, the other one."

Falcone came up beside him, looked, and saw the man they'd seen the night before loitering outside the medical compound. He was wearing the same khaki clothing, the sunglasses concealing his eyes, which seemed to be focused directly on the shelter where Amelia was. Without saying another word, Falcone and Niles approached the man who was facing away from them.

"Hey," Niles said, and the man whirled around, his arm up and elbow jutting out, striking Niles in the face and simultaneously bringing a knee up to his stomach. It all happened so quickly that Niles was too stunned to cry out, blood spouting from his nose and oozing from his face, knees buckling beneath him. Falcone grabbed him around the waist, and in the few seconds it took for them to regain their balance, the man had taken off.

"Son of a bitch!" Falcone sputtered, his head jerking in every direction and then back to Niles. "Goddamn, Curran, are you okay?"

Spitting blood from his mouth, Niles blubbered, "I dunno…yeah, I think. Where did the fucker go?" Everything in front of him was swimming, the ground uneven under his feet.

Falcone looked around again, longer this time, casting a wider scope, and shook his head. "Gone." He continued to scan in the direction he thought the man had fled, and several minutes later, caught sight of him moving swiftly up an incline just beyond the camp, disappearing through the brush.

"Come on," Falcone said, "we need to get you looked at." He draped Niles' arm over his neck and they trudged slowly back to the parallel footpath.

Jake and Cyrus Keogh were coming down the path and, at the sight of them, ran over. "What the hell happened?" Jake demanded. He slipped off his backpack and took Niles' face in his hands. "Cyrus, my aid kit, get me gauze."

"Bastard clocked me good," Niles slurred, the right side of his face puffing up with redness and swelling, blood from his nose and mouth and a gash across his cheek smeared and dripping.

"Who?"

"Not the journalist," Falcone said, "the other guy."

"What happened?"

"We walked up on him, he just reacted."

"Where did he go?"

Falcone crooked his head and said, "Out of here."

Noticing Niles' other hand cradling his midriff, Jake asked, "You get hit in the stomach?"

"Kneed," Falcone told him.

Jake gave Niles' face a thorough exam, palpating the orbital bones around his eyes, his cheek and jaw bones, and poking at his nose, which he already knew was broken. He looked inside his mouth, checked his ears and neck, and went back to the task of tending to his nose, manipulating the bone and cartilage with his fingers to realign it.

"Ow, ow, owww!" Niles bemoaned, his hands clenching and unclenching at his sides as Jake gently pulled and pushed and then pressed gauze into his nostrils. He did a quick neurological assessment and then prodded Niles' ribs and stomach. Niles winced and recoiled but assured Jake he could walk.

They retreated to the shelter, Jake glancing over his shoulder, his eyes on the woods outside the camp.

32

OGLING CURRAN NILES' BRUISED and bloated face, Cyrus Keogh remarked, "That's a beauty, mate," and took a healthy swig of Primus, the bottle's glass sweating in the heat.

His wife poked him. "Cy."

"I reckon it'll only give that pretty mug a bit more character...aye, mate? Whaddya think, Eddie?" He grinned at Falcone and reached over to Niles, lightly touching his bandaged nose.

Niles pulled back, brooding. After returning to the shelter, Jake had checked his rhinoplasty fieldwork and, finding it up to his standards, taped Niles up and given him some Tylenol 3 for pain. Slurping gingerly from his beer, Niles was not altogether sure the pain reliever was working, and the metallic taste of blood mingling with the stringent tang of antiseptic in his mouth and sinuses had dismantled his appetite.

They were seated on benches at a picnic-style wood table, one of many arranged in rows inside a framed structure draped on all sides by mosquito netting and covered with tarps. In one corner, a couple of *babula* stoves and portable grills were filling the air with charcoal smoke, and in another, a small refrigerator was packed with beer and sodas. The structure was in the common area of the *Médecins Sans Frontières* segregated compound, staff beginning to shuffle in as their shifts ended for the day.

Jake reached into the fridge, plucked a bottle of water, and took a seat at the table. Looking at Niles, who held a cold pack over his nose, he asked, "Any trouble breathing?"

Niles shook his head wordlessly.

Turning to face the Keoghs, Jake said, "I spoke with Simone and she's going to clear us to take them out of the camp."

Amelia Keogh took a swallow of beer and said, "I don't understand."

"On entering the camp, your people automatically fell under the protection of their charter, of the UN humanitarian coordination. Normally, for anyone to leave, the council and all the associated entities—like MSF—have to be in approval, meaning that they have ascertained the people are going somewhere safe and free of known conflict. Usually they have to meet and discuss it, investigate. It can be a lengthy process."

"But they've got to know that we—" Amelia started.

"Yes, yes, they know," Jake assured her. "I'm just explaining what their standard procedure is. Actually, I respect that a lot."

Cyrus Keogh said, "I do as well. But we're good to go, yes?"

"Yes. They know who you are and there are absolutely no issues. As for tomorrow, I've gone over the route and, if the truck gets here early enough, we might be able to make it in one day. But that's if the weather cooperates and we don't get stuck or if we don't get detained. We'll stop at the plane, Kean will fly it on to Nakalé, and we'll keep driving." He looked from Cyrus to Amelia. "I want you two on that plane."

"What?" Amelia asked. "Why? No, Jake. I want to stay with them, all the way."

"I know you do," Jake said. "But there are a lot of things that can happen on the road. It's my responsibility to keep you safe. You'll be safer on the plane."

"I'm not leaving them," she said defiantly.

Jake held her gaze, looked to Cyrus. Keogh tilted his head slightly to indicate the decision was hers to make. "Okay," Jake said. "I'll take it under advisement."

A tableful of young female staffers nearby were stealing looks at them and giggling. Keogh grinned and leaned toward Jake. "They're talking about you, mate."

Jake looked at him. "What?"

"I heard 'em when I went to get my coldie." In exaggerated falsetto, he said, "'I didn't see a ring on him...But I heard they're leaving soon…So what difference does that make?'" He laughed, and quickly lapped the beer that he'd nearly spilled from the bottle.

Geoffrey Edgecombe appeared, brushing through the mosquito netting, radio in hand. He came directly to their table.

Addressing Jake, he said, "Papa B wants to know if you can meet him."

"Where?"

"There's a bar just about a kilometer down the road from the camp. It's where some of us go, usually right before dinner since we have a six o'clock curfew."

"An actual bar? Around here?"

Edgecombe laughed. "Um, yeah, mate. Anywhere there's expats like us with money to spend, you'll have a local pop up!"

Jake hesitated as he considered, and immediately there was a chorus, both male and female staffers, asserting, "We'll go!" Several hopped up from their tables.

"Uh, okay," Jake replied, standing. He looked at his group, all just settling in comfortably. "You guys stay here, I won't be long."

Baladur stood. "Boss?"

Jake waved him down. "Naw…I'm good. Relax."

His female admirers were eager to escort him. Keogh smirked.

Jake gave him a flippant look and joined the bunch heading out.

THE BAR WAS A basic wood shack with a tin roof that could have been anything, but inside it looked like a typical dive joint in any banana republic, complete with a counter, rickety wood tables and plastic chairs, straw on the plank floor, and a generator-powered blade fan hanging crookedly from a roof beam through the middle. It was windowless and dark, the only sources of light coming from the front and back doors— left open for air flow—and strings of Christmas lights strung haphazardly around the interior. The yeasty smell of spilled beer mingled with human perspiration was steeped into the walls from many days and nights of close congregation. Music emanated from a large pair of speakers, conical drivers exposed by their missing covers, positioned on either side of an elevated stand that might have been capable of holding eight or ten bodies, depending on the degree of extravagance in their dance moves. The platform was currently empty.

A pair of men behind the counter began extracting brown bottles of Primus from an old refrigerator, popping caps and placing them, dripping foam, in front of the familiar faces filing in.

Jake spotted Papa B at a table toward the back, sipping from an actual glass. Seeing Jake, he stood and held his hand up in greeting. They both sat, and Salomon Bijou, aka Papa B, asked, "What will you have?" He tapped his glass. "Some whiskey?"

"Ah, yes, that works," Jake replied.

Bijou signaled one of the bartenders, and two glasses were brought over. Bijou finished the one he'd been drinking with a satisfied exhale and Jake sampled his, pleasantly surprised to find that it was, in fact, whiskey and not some local moonshine with the taste and burn of lighter fluid.

"How long have you been working with MSF?" Jake asked.

"I have been at this camp since it was set up a few months ago," Bijou replied, "but I was recruited from one of their established hospitals in Faradji. There, I worked for a long time, but I like the challenge here. Every day brings something different. Like you." He lifted his glass and smiled.

Jake returned the toast and helped himself to a dish of peanuts on the table, cracking and tossing aside the shells, which were strewn throughout the straw beneath his feet.

Bijou was wearing a suit jacket over his starched print shirt, precisely tailored to fit his wide shoulders and walrus-stout chest. He reached to an inside pocket and withdrew several sheets of folded papers. It was at that moment the dance platform filled up, the volume of the music increasing with, of all things, the very Anglo Calvin Harris clubbing it with Dua Lipa over the possibilities of *One Kiss* and significantly impeding normal conversation. Bijou rose from his chair, took his drink, and gestured for Jake to follow him. They went out the back door and stepped into a dusty courtyard, the enclosing bamboo fence strung with more of the Christmas lights, a plastic table and chairs off to one side, shaded by a mango tree. Fruit ranging in color and ripeness from pale yellow-green to blushing red to rotting brown lay scattered around the base. To the rear of the space was a three-by-three outhouse with a back-sloping vented roof, banana trees growing behind it.

The pre-dusk sun cast a butterscotch haze over the courtyard, shadows absorbing some of its heat. Bijou had pulled the rear door closed as they'd stepped outside, the music's bass and drums thumping through the wood frame. Taking a seat, he set his drink down and put the papers he'd extracted from his jacket on the table, flattening them with his hand.

"I have a good bit of information for you," he said.

In the chair across from Bijou, Jake listened with heightened interest. Overhead, the branches of the mango tree were flush with gray parrots, warbling and squawking as they scrabbled through the leaves.

Bijou said, "I think some of your people are here." He tapped a place on the top page of his papers.

Jake studied a map imprinted on the sheet. "That's close to South Sudan. What's there?"

"A mining operation," said Bijou. "From what I have been told, it is under the control of the LRA."

Jake felt the skin over his scalp constrict, his neck crawl as if insects were skittering there. "LRA? Are you sure? They're pretty diminished these days."

Bijou met his eyes. "That is what I am hearing, and believe me, they are still very much around. But not only that."

Jake waited.

"This mining operation has recently added to its workers from people that were taken. From an IDP compound. The timing, the number, makes me think it could be your people." He reached for his glass, put it to his lips, tipped it back and swallowed the last of his whiskey. Deposited the glass back on the table.

Jake glanced off, hearing the buffered music and laughter from the bar, but his mind was drifting to another place, back to Uganda when he'd been training soldiers and first learned about Joseph Kony and the LRA. That seemed a lifetime ago, and a near-impossible mission. In many ways, like the one he was pursuing now. A massive country, virtually no ghost of a trail.

"Something else you need to know," Bijou said. "There is also an

American team operating there."

"What do you mean? An American company?"

"No. An American security contactor."

THE LAST WORDS SPOKEN by Papa B were still resonating long after Jake had gone back inside. He stood at the bar, distractedly counting out some franc notes to cover their tab, noting the addition of many more nationals from the MSF staff and, at the same time, a sudden scramble amongst the expats to pay up and hit the road. Glancing at his watch, he saw that it was almost 6:00 PM, and remembered their curfew. As the batch of them hustled for the front door, he heard one of the nurses remark, "Damn, we're almost late!" Followed by, "And I was hoping to get a dance with Mr. Dark and Sexy." Jake paid no particular heed to the comment, but then the nurse turned, her eyes landing on him. He ducked his head, his face empty of expression.

Before Salomon Bijou had made his departure from the courtyard, he'd given Jake his paperwork with the map and his notes, but as much information as Bijou had imparted, Jake found himself questioning what to do with it. A mining operation, illicit or not, was certainly credible, and he already knew from his initial intel that there were plenty in the region; reports that a recent influx of slave workers thought to be from an IDP camp, on the other hand, was much more auspicious. And, if an American security contractor was active in the area, that could potentially provide a huge abetment. Or could it? Dealing with private security contractors could also be a slippery slope into murky territory.

In any case, he told himself, this was the lead that gave him a reason to keep the mission going.

But as he strolled along the road leading back to the refugee camp, the sky going from gold to orange to mauve, amorphous thoughts bounced around his head that never took lucid shape, something vaguely unsettling inside him about this latest development.

By the time he reached the MSF compound, just a few minutes shy of the curfew, dinner was being served, so he got a plate and rejoined his table. The national staff employed as domestics had prepared the usual meat *du jour*, rice, and tomato sauce, but on this occasion, in honor of their esteemed guests, they had roasted a chicken—*choma*—spiced up the sauce with garlic and herbs, and added beans to the rice. The beer had apparently revived Niles' appetite, but he was having a hard time chewing, so Falcone fixed him a bowl with just beans and rice.

"Here you go, bud," he said, "eat this. It won't hurt so much."

Niles gave him a lopsided smile and dipped a spoon into the bowl. And chugged some more beer, which was beginning to make him feel buzzy, but it was also making him forget his throbbing nose.

Dr. Caron came by their table and, having heard about the scuffle, quipped, "I'm beginning to think you guys attract trouble."

"Like a magnet," Jake said around a mouthful of chicken.

She slipped a finger under Niles' chin, inspecting his nose and the stitched gash on his cheek, and nodded to Jake. "You do excellent work. If you ever think about leaving whatever it is you do, you should come work with us."

Jake smiled.

Amelia Keogh's eyes had been fixed on him since he returned and now she asked, "Did you get any leads?" When they had freshened up before dinner, she had applied a scant amount of makeup and brushed her hair, the dim lighting giving it a satiny luster. She tucked a strand behind one ear and tilted her head inquisitively.

Having already decided to keep the new information to himself for a while, and especially from Amelia to keep her expectations reined in, he simply said, "Possibly."

"Like what?"

"I need to check with Kipnis, see if there's anything worth following up."

Reading his response as a way of downplaying whatever he'd heard during the meeting with Papa B, her face clouded and she poked at the remains of her dinner.

Cyrus Keogh had also been watching Jake closely, but came to a different conclusion and flashed Jake a look to let him know it. Wiping his mouth with a paper napkin, Keogh stood with his plate in hand and asked brightly, "Anyone else want some more chicken from the barbie?"

*   *   *   *   *

WHILE EVERYONE ELSE WAS bedding down, Jake stood outside the old building accommodating them and made a call to Kipnis. He actually got Nash Remington and began sharing the information he'd received from Salomon Bijou. Remington listened without comment until Jake got to the part about an American contractor, letting him know that he was unaware of any working in their vicinity, adding for emphasis that he knew them all and kept current with their operations as part of his own business. Jake heard Remington say something to Kipnis about checking into it and continued, relaying his plan to get the Keoghs and the people they'd found to Nakalé with the footnote that he'd be leaving them when he headed back out to pursue the mining lead. Remington immediately offered up another one of his guys who would be flown into the village, which was a great relief to Jake because he'd been struggling with the notion of being short Baladur or Dmello or both, and he was not about to leave the Keoghs without security. The call wrapped up with Remington saying Kipnis would get back to him with updated intel on mining activity.

Next, he called Callie. As he waited for the connection, he felt a pinch of anxiety coupled with the tingle of anticipation, and then, when the call went to voicemail, a well of disappointment. He left her a short message and tapped the entry for Camilla's number. The housekeeper answered promptly and excitedly told him that Callie had let Jesse Segura persuade her to accompany him to the beach.

Jake's eyes widened in astonishment. "The beach? Really?"

Camilla explained that Segura had taken his usual mid-shift break to check on things at the villa and had encouraged her to go back down with him for a little while. She told Jake that Segura did that all the time, but Callie always declined. Today he managed to convince her to give it a try, assuring she could return to the villa anytime she wanted.

"And how long has she been gone?" Jake asked, noting by his watch that it was close to one o'clock in the afternoon, Costa Rica time. "Almost an hour? That's wonderful!"

He ended the exchange, and briefly considered calling Segura but decided not to bother him while he was on duty. He slipped the sat phone in his pocket, smiling happily, his heart lightened. He'd been troubled after the previous call several days ago, sensing something amiss, but now he was thinking it was just his protective instinct, which went into overdrive where Callie was concerned.

Inside the building where everyone was asleep, Jake nodded to Baladur who was taking first watch, and strolled through the space, pausing to check on Niles. He was breathing mostly through his mouth and his poor face looked like a battered puffer fish, more swollen than it had been earlier and coloring up in a whole palette of blues and purples.

"Damn," Jake muttered to himself.

He went to his cot, slipped his backpack off and sat down, the cot's metal frame creaking beneath him. Looked around in the dimness. Lay down, arranged his mosquito netting, and stared at the beams and roof. Ten minutes later, he was up, telling Baladur he was going for a walk.

"Want me to get Kean to take my watch or go with you?" Baladur asked.

Jake shook his head and said, "I'm good. I'll call on comms if need be."

He stepped outside, walking along a path between shelters dotted with small fires and the flicker of oil and solar lanterns. It was quiet and mostly still, the populace bedded down inside their rickety housing, no doubt still hungry and haunted, but grateful for the sanctuary. With only a sliver of moon in the sky, it became increasingly dark as he made his way past the inhabited interior of the camp, finding a section of fencing missing enough slats for a person to slip through.

Which he did.

HE HAD ENTERED THE woods fifteen minutes ago, illuminating the way with his Nitecore tactical flashlight, Glock aimed alongside it. The terrain gradually inclined as he got farther away from the camp, and several times he stopped, turned, and gazed down to analyze the view by height and angle and range. There were good vantages and, with a decent pair of binoculars or scope, a person could see a lot from up here; could, in fact, see the building where Jake and his group were staying. The temperature was cooler, and a breeze had begun to riffle through the trees, a hint of coming rain. Other rustling, closer and crisper, kept him swiveling, pointing his light—on a lowered setting—in the direction of origin. Small animals skittered away from the beams while insects converged in hari-kari frenzies as he pushed forward.

He was hiking a narrow trail, combing the brush for bent or broken limbs, depressions or disturbed ground, but so far had seen nothing of significance. His light washed over a small clearing and he pulled it quickly away, waiting for his eyes to adjust in the darkness, listening. He heard nothing, detected no movement. Edging forward, he slowly raised the Nitecore and swept it from side to side. Panned it through the boughs and branches of the trees overhead. Waited, and swept it all again. Doused the light and stepped cautiously into the opening.

He sensed a presence, with a kind of static prickle that he almost always experienced, though whether it was a current or recent presence he could not be sure. He remained still for several moments, his eyes roving, and saw a patch of dirt that looked like it had been scuffed over, so subtle most anyone else would have missed it.

He knelt down, dragged a gloved hand across the dirt, and pinched some, holding it to his nose. It smelled faintly of burnt wood. But any remnants of a fire had been scraped away. Still, there was another kind of smokiness that lingered despite the breeze, the stale kind from cigarettes.

It had all been cleaned. Not a single butt littered the ground. There were no traces of food, not so much as a pile of crumbs. He wasn't picking up any whiff of buried waste. But he was still fairly certain he'd found what had been a campsite. Who *was* this guy? Was he watching them as a group, or the Keoghs, or himself? How long had he been on them? Jake had to believe he would have picked him up before now if he'd been tailing them at any earlier point. And goddammit, he'd wanted to catch up to this guy, if for no other reason to show him the consequence of his actions, for what he had done to Niles.

Whoever you are, he thought, *you're good…*and maybe a pro.

He poked through the surrounding grass, and saw something he recognized almost immediately. *Maybe not as good as you think, you son of a bitch.*

Because probably in his haste to clear camp after the assault on Niles, the guy had missed it. He had been remarkably thorough in his bug out, but he had missed this one thing. Jake plucked a piece of cloth from the grass. It was a two-inch cotton square, and he was familiar with it because he used such pieces himself. They came in bags or boxes in various sizes, some round, some square. They could be used by anyone, but usually were not. Usually, cut scraps from t-shirts or just paper towels were used, and probably not nearly as regularly as they should be.

Looking at the gun cleaning patch in the palm of his glove, he thought, *this guy just might be military.*

33

CALLIE HAD BEEN SITTING in a wooden Adirondack-style chair, painted a bright shade of aqua, when Jesse Segura came up on a break to check on things at the villa. She was sipping from a tall acrylic tumbler with iced fruit juice or, as Camilla referred to it, *agua fresca*—fresh local fruit with a touch of lime and agave, blended together with water and poured over ice. She wasn't sure what was in this one, possibly pineapple, mango, and something else because of its slightly pink color, but it was really good. After the usual nighttime vigil and battle with nocturnal demons, she had dozed intermittently, listening to the musical bird chatter of dawn and the soft roll of surf below the hills. When she got up, she had dressed in an off-the-shoulder white cotton romper patterned with lilac-colored roses and dark green leaves, drank some coffee, and gone out to her newly planted rose garden. Despite their aversion to the tropics, the fledgling bushes were doing quite well and already putting out new shoots.

As the gardeners worked their way around the grounds and into the gardens, they encouraged Callie to do whatever she wanted toward the maintenance of the roses, but after the ant attack, she was admiring their beauty from a safe distance.

"*Ay, pequeña señorita,*" Jesse Segura called out as he padded over to her, clad in his red Bermuda shorts and yellow long-sleeved Spandex shirt. "Is a beautiful day," he remarked, smiling broadly. "Come back with me to the beach."

She had given him the same sad smile of regret that was her response each time he asked, her eyes dropping to peer into the tumbler of fruit juices, sides shimmering with the chill of melting ice.

But today he had seemed especially determined. *"Tu vienes…for a little while. Stay or no, but I think you stay."* He kept smiling, his skin burnished nearly the color of brick with his many days in the sun.

Callie had felt an unexpected pull of temptation, maybe because lately she'd been yearning to somehow find a way to push herself past all the fear, to be better by the time Jake returned. She wanted that more than anything. A whizzing sound and ripple in the air made her look up, just in time to see a small squadron of rufous-tailed hummingbirds swirl around the roses, their iridescent green heads and backs gleaming in the sun. They hovered in a blur of synchronization for a few moments and then zipped off, drawing Callie's eyes toward the serene blue sky and then to the lush green hills that led to the ocean below. The call to that magnificence was an enchantress almost impossible to deny.

To Segura's astonishment, she had risen from the chair and said, "Okay, Jesse, I'll go."

NOW SHE SAT IN A wooden sling beach chair just below the *Guardavidas* tower, a structure made from a metal shipping container that was painted in vibrant red with their big white cross on the sides, raised off the ground and supported by concrete posts and framed with wood beams, all covered by a slanted corrugated roof with a wide overhang. Segura was joined by two other lifeguards, a younger Tico named Javier and an American expat named Tara. Javier was scrawny and looked like he might have trouble making it from one side to the other in a kiddie pool, and Tara was blond and built like a Nordic cross-country skier; both could bust ass on the beach or in the water. Spotify was streaming a playlist from one of their cell phones, the reggae vibes of Sigala's *Feels Like Home* filling the air. Below the tower, in the shade of the trees, several off-duty lifeguards were doing pull-ups on metal bars or squats against a wood platform, physical fitness they did every day to stay in top condition for the demanding rescues they performed.

Segura had just distributed lunches provided gratis by the *Feed a*

Lifeguard program, today's benefactor restaurant being Tortilla Flats. There were burgers and subs with fries and sodas, Segura plowing into a Ripken Club, honey Dijon sauce dripping down his chin. Callie had shyly accepted a California Chicken and even taken a few bites.

Segura had been right, it was a beautiful day. The beach, normally crowded with European tourists this time of year, was not as populated today, and though the temperature was in the high eighties, humidity was moderated by a light easterly wind blowing at about ten miles per hour with eight- to ten-foot swells. The tide had been going out since peaking mid-morning, and the majority of surfers had retreated to hangouts on the beach road to await the more productive and less dangerous waves associated with higher, incoming tides.

Taking a small bite of her sub, Callie thought that Jake would be proud of her, and felt an emotional surge that lapped at joy, looking out at the beach and ocean and sky spread before her and, in that moment, feeling as if she were back to the beginning of it all. Back before anything bad had happened…back when it had just been she and Jake on this beach, strolling along the sand with the tide washing over their feet, the sun rising or setting or shining as brilliantly as the afterburn of a rocket ship blasting to a faraway universe. The two of them as intimately together as a whisper in a big, wide world that did not exist beyond the moments they shared.

For a little while, she actually seemed to drift off into the atmosphere that she loved so much, watching the ocean waves rolling in, sparkling sapphire blue and frothed with caps like bubble bath soap suds, the frigate birds with their forked tails and long, pointed wings sailing the air currents overhead, billowy white clouds scattered across the bright sky. She lay her head back, closed her eyes, and listened to the blowing wind and rumbling surf, the sound and embrace of both drawing her into a cocoon of drowsy whiteness. Nothing beyond it, just the somnolent rhythm, the haze of a safe place outside of everything else.

She was not sure how long she'd been suspended in that soothing hollow, but a shadow cut through the light and stirred her from it with a jolt of disorientation.

"Miss Callie."

She blinked and saw Segura standing over her, a pleased look on his face.

"You see? This is good for you," he said. "I am going on beach patrol. You want to stay here? Is okay…" He tipped his head toward the top of the tower where the blond female lifeguard stood smiling down at them. "Tara say she will keep an eye out."

Callie sat up in the chair, glancing between the two, unsure of whether to stay or go. Segura decided for her, extending his hand to help her up. "Okay, *ven conmigo*."

Segura waited while Callie applied some more sunscreen and put on her sunglasses, grabbed his rescue torpedo, and they began walking south along the beach.

Segura was mostly shin-deep in the water, his eyes panning the waders and swimmers and surfers, looking for any sign of distress or reckless behavior or veering off into treacherous rip currents, Callie padding barefoot just close enough for the surf to brush her ankles, the tawny sand warm beneath the soles of her feet. She held flip-flops in one hand, the other plucking flaxen strands of hair from her face as the wind blew down from the line of trees and coconut palms and out to the ocean. Whimbrels and willets stalked through the tide in front of them, long bills poking the sand in search of crabs and small fish. A rainbow-colored paraglider sailed high above on a course that would take it down to the mouth of the Barú River. Families were picnicking in the shade of the trees fronting the beach; a group of twenty-somethings were punching and spiking a volleyball back and forth over a net; parents watched young children playing in the sand; a fit-looking man in red swim trunks walked alongside a curvaceous woman in a white string bikini who had one hand clamped over the crown of her straw hat to keep it from blowing off her head, both looking out to the waves and pointing.

Callie stopped and followed their gaze, and thought she saw the dark gray upper side and stubby dorsal fin of a humpback whale, pods of which migrated here seasonally in large numbers, coming from Alaska and California in the north and Antarctica in the south. Watching the man and woman together, Callie felt an acute pang of longing for Jake, wondering how close he was to coming home. She continued to watch the couple and the swath of ocean where she thought she'd seen the whale, and several minutes later was startled to realize that Jesse Segura had moved farther away. Her pulse spiked as a surge of anxiety coursed through her.

Up ahead, Segura glanced over his shoulder, saw her lagging, and waved her forward as he headed for the big rocky outcroppings near the Roca Verde hotel beach access. Callie caught up to him, saw him speak with a group of teenage surfers and then wait until they retreated, the teens looking downtrodden as they disappeared around the bend leading back to the hotel.

"Is much too dangerous, the surfing conditions right now," Segura explained when he rejoined Callie. "Especially for the *turistas*."

They reversed direction to return to the *Guardavidas* tower and, as they approached the Main Street frontage, Callie noticed that the beach was becoming much more crowded than it had been earlier. She picked up her pace, anxious to get back to her chair, thinking that she was ready to go home. Her skin radiated with sunburn, her nerves jittering from a sudden feeling of having pushed herself too far too fast. Behind her, Segura called out for her to hold up as he took off running for a pair of swimmers who were approaching a rip current, thrashing as it pulled them out to sea. He splashed into the water, arms outstretched over his head, and dove in, flotation torpedo trailing behind him. Another lifeguard who had not been at the tower went out to assist, both reaching the swimmers and starting to bring them in to shore in a smooth, steady parallel course.

Callie had not heard Segura call out.

Shakily making her way through the people milling along the beach, she came to an abrupt stop, her heart seizing up in her chest. Directly in front of her, only a few feet away, a man stood with his back to her. But the profile of his posture, the set of his shoulders, the proportions of his body and the swarthy tone of his skin were immediately identifiable to the core of her limbic cerebrum, forever embedded there. As was the dark hair, greased and shiny, drawn tightly into a short ponytail.

As if sensing someone behind him, the man started to turn, the ponytail brushing across his neck, a flash of gold at his ear.

Callie ran.

* * * * *

SHE WAS RUNNING TO escape, running for her life, a tortured, horrified voice shrilling in her head: *How could he be here?* And answering, *He can't, he can't, he can't be here...it can't be him!*

She staggered through the trees that lined the beach, stumbling over rocks and pieces of driftwood, clambering up and cutting through parked SUVs and vans and campers, angling away from people who stared at her as she fled. Kids on skateboards and bikes peeled off to avoid colliding with her, dogs scattered. She got entangled by a hammock strung between two palm trees, fought for release, and kept going, her insides ablaze with pain. Looking back, she was sure she saw the strong legs pumping, heard the thud of footfalls, and turned, running headlong into a flotilla of flapping oversize beach towels hung from a network of clotheslines—a crazy quilt of abstract and tropical designs in a kaleidoscope of brilliant colors—throwing her off-kilter and into an even more panicked state.

The voice came from within the twist of terrycloth, the swirl of color. *Muñequita*...the menacing growl that pulverized her mind in the same physical way he had, the overpowering reek of cologne mixed with the sour secretion of testosterone-infused sweat.

Now she could not get her breath, everything was spinning, the ground collapsing, her chest tightening and aching for air. *Oh God, oh God, he's coming...*

JERRY HADLEY HAD JUST come to check on his lifeguards, as he had earlier when he'd covered for Jesse Segura to go to the villa. He was up on the platform, reviewing the activity log, when he heard Segura calling Callie's name and caught sight of him running into the trees behind the tower. Handing the log to Tara, he dropped to the ground and ran in the direction Segura was headed.

Both whipped their way through the maze of beach towels and reached Callie at about the same time. Segura was doubled over from the exertion of his back-to-back sea rescue and sprint into the trees.

Hadley asked, "What's going on, Jesse?"

Still puffing, Segura said, *"No lo sé*...I look up...she is running."

Steering Callie to a bench and sitting her down, Hadley said, "We've got you, Callie. Catch your breath for me, okay?"

Callie was gasping, but she was drawing air into her lungs again, shaking and looking around the two of them.

Hadley knelt in front of her. "Look at me, darlin'. What's wrong? Somebody bothering you?"

"He's here," Callie rasped, her chest heaving, tears breaking from her terrified eyes. She clutched her abdomen in anguish.

"Who's here?" Hadley and Segura both glanced around, seeing only concerned onlookers. "Who's here, Callie?" Hadley asked again.

She could not say his name.

Hadley and Segura studied her for several moments, exchanging puzzled looks, but both had a general understanding of what was going on even if they did not know what—or who—specifically, had sent her into the spiral.

"Take her home, Jesse," Hadley said finally. "I'll cover you the rest of the afternoon."

CALLIE LAY ON THE bed, cleaned up and wearing a cotton sleep shirt. After Segura had brought her back to the villa, Camilla had helped her rinse off—showering was still a struggle—and, after both tried to get her to talk to them about what had happened, left her alone to rest.

What she had experienced at the beach flashed back numerous times, each recall sending her heart into a gallop that she fought to control. She kept seeing his profile, his head, his hair. Heard the voice and smelled the scent. Felt the vileness slide through her in serpentine quickness, penetrating every inner fold. Several times, she lurched from the bed and made it to one of the bath basins just in time to heave until her insides had nothing to expel; there was almost nothing in her stomach, so she waited until the urges subsided, splashed water on her face, and returned to the bed.

She wanted Jake to be here so badly, wanted to be nestled in his arms, hear his voice softly in her ear, feel his skin against hers, know that he had her and nothing, no one, could hurt her.

At some point, she absently picked up her iPhone, and the screen materialized. There was a missed call and voicemail. Now her heart jumped in desperation but then sank, knowing it could only be Jake. And it was. Tapping to play the voicemail, she heard the deep, low cadence of his voice say: *"Hi Love. Just wanted to see how you're doing, let you know I'm thinking about you. Hope all's well…and…I'll try to talk to you soon. Love you, Callie."*

Tears came in a torrent as she lay back in the pillows, phone in her hand, the well of deprivation and need overflowing. Why had she gone to the beach? If she'd just stayed here, she would have gotten Jake's call. She wished he was here right now more than anything she'd ever wished for in her life.

After a long while, after replaying his message too many times to count, she gazed out across the balcony. The sky was darkening, clouds multiplying upon themselves in thick, gray masses, thunder shuddering. Another storm coming, another endless night.

In her mind, she saw the man turning. Buried her head in the pillows, trying to blot out the image.

Who had she seen? It couldn't be *him*, she told herself. He was dead. Jake had killed him, hadn't he? And yet, he seemed to continually resurrect himself in the nightmares, so maybe he was not dead.

Oh God.

The sky lit up and darkened again, thunder crashed. Rain pattered and then pounded. She drew up in a ball on the bed, arms covering her head, sobbing from the depths of her soul. He was going to get to her again. She knew it. Deep into the bowels of an unimaginable hell.

JERRY HADLEY PATROLLED THE length of their beach, accompanied by Tara Tiedemann. She wore an abbreviated version of the red swim trunks and a black sports halter, her hair straight and collar-length. The two blonds were deeply tanned and muscular, confident in their environment and comfortable in their friendship, two Gringo expats in a Tico world.

"What do you think happened?" Tara asked.

"Could have been anything," Hadley replied. "With everything she's been through, it doesn't take much."

"She was saying 'he's here'?"

"Yeah. Somebody out here apparently triggered a memory. Jesse did good getting her out, getting her to the beach. It's what Jake would want, and he trusts us to keep her safe."

"And we do…we did. We can't stop what happens in her head. Post-traumatic stress is a tough thing to deal with. Poor girl."

They walked on, scanning the water for stragglers. Overhead, the sky was a black-purple and veined with lightning. Rain had begun to spit against their skin. Out over the ocean, the squall could be seen coming, wrapped in angry mounds of clouds, surf rising and falling in higher and higher walls. The easterly wind blowing from the inlands was colliding with its oppositional oceanic force, building a storm that would rage for supremacy and then diminish and move off as quickly as it had come in. Or it might battle into the night.

People were hastily collecting their beach chairs and towels, plucking umbrellas from the sand, retreating. Surfer crews headed for the beach road to beers and music, tacos and casados.

Hadley and Tiedemann spotted a lone man up ahead, leisurely strolling as if oblivious to the oncoming storm. His dark hair was pulled into a ponytail, and he wore a white tank top and tight black trunks that were like seal skin, sculpted around his firm buttocks.

"Excuse me, sir," Hadley said.

The man stopped in his tracks, turned around, his genitalia outlined by the clinging material. He smiled, lips parting to reveal ultra-white teeth. A gold chain hung around his neck, a gold loop pierced one earlobe. "Yes?" he asked.

"You need to get off the beach, there's a storm coming in."

"I see that," the man said. "Can you recommend a good place for dinner?"

34

THE TRUCK ROLLED INTO the refugee camp just as the sun was coming up behind the hills, a pale orange ball cloaked in the residual mist from the previous night's rain. The grasses and trees glistened in the expanding light, dirt road turned the color of nutmeg and sloshing beneath the weight of the Tata Motors six-wheeler. In spite of the early hour, its appearance drew streams of the ever-curious youngsters, followed by the more guardedly inquisitive adults. By the time Jake and his group had assembled, there was quite a crowd.

"Oh dear," Amelia Keogh lamented, "I was afraid of this. The thought of leaving even one person behind…" She averted her gaze from the faces of those encircling the truck, pressing the knuckles of a hand into her forehead. Her green eyes pooled with tears.

Her husband said, "We talked about this. You know we can only do so much. The important thing is that we keep trying to do more. We're doing what we can right now."

"I know," she said forlornly, swiping at her eyes.

Curran Niles burst forth, declaring, "I call shotgun!" Before anyone could counter his bid, in the way of explanation he said, "I'm injured."

Niles did, in fact, look like he'd been in a fight with a street gang, the bandaging over his nose and both eyes swollen nearly shut, the pouches of skin below and most of his face an ink wash of ugly bruises. His hair was loose, a light layer of blond stubble starting to become visible on his chin and jawbones.

Jake and Cyrus Keogh greeted Geoffrey Edgecombe who had taken the handoff from the truck driver. Simone Duvall and Dr. Nora Caron were nearby with the Keoghs' people, preparing them for their trip, Duvall checking each off a list and making sure they had supplies, Dr. Caron giving each a follow-up and any necessary medicines. She took her time, gazing intently into their faces, their eyes, making sure they were ready to make this transition. Camp staff were loading up jugs of water and cartons of fruit and snacks. Jake and Keogh followed Edgecombe as he walked around, inspecting the vehicle.

The Tata Motors cargo truck was a fairly new twenty-ton medium-duty class model with a thirty-two-foot ladder-sided metal deck. The overhead railings provided an ideal frame for a cover, which had been attached in the form of waterproof canvas, stretched across the top and tied at the corners, leaving the upper rails open for good ventilation. Outside of a bus—virtually impossible to find in these remote parts—it was as close to a dream scenario for this kind of passenger transport as one could ask for. At Dmello's request, Jake had asked Edgecombe to also inquire about fuel to top off their plane, and the abundantly resourceful Edgecombe had come through, procuring two fifty-gallon drums of A1 jet fuel, secured at the front of the deck along with boxes of medical supplies Dr. Caron had rounded up for them to take to Nakalé.

The rear drop-down panel was unlatched and those departing began to file aboard, placing their mats and bedrolls along the sides and settling in. Cyrus Keogh and Cameron McNamara stepped aside to make payment arrangements with the driver, and Jake addressed the rest.

"Get your weapons assembled and fire-ready," he instructed the four. "Two of you at the back and two to the front. And be sure your comms are on."

Niles, who hadn't really expected to ride in the cabin, asked, "You got another cold pack for me?"

"Yes, it's in my kit. Go ahead and get it before we set off."

Jake walked over to Duvall, Caron, and Edgecombe. Smiling, he said, "On behalf of us all, I want to thank you for your help and hospitality."

"It has been our pleasure," said Duvall. "I am just glad that I was here when you came. Another day or so and I would be gone. I will be leaving for Goma this afternoon. I have made it known that your visit here is to be kept in the strictest confidence so as not to reveal the whereabouts of the Keoghs."

"Appreciate that," Jake said, though he now believed their confidentiality had been compromised.

Keogh and McNamara rejoined them and Jake asked, "Everything set? How did you arrange for return?"

"No need, mate," Keogh smiled. "Hopefully we'll need 'er again on down the road."

"So...?"

"I bought it."

Jake looked at him for a moment without expression, then asked, "What about the driver?"

"Not part of the deal...he has to return to town."

"Do you know how to drive one of these trucks?"

Keogh grinned playfully. "Not particularly."

"And you didn't think to ask if I did?"

Keogh's grin widened, the corners of his eyes crinkling. "*Do* you?"

Jake continued to look at him, a smile pulling at his mouth.

"I will be in touch," Simone Duvall told the Keoghs, "and we will do everything we can to assist you in your rebuilding."

Beside her, Dr. Caron nodded. "You have our support as well and are welcome anytime you're in the neighborhood." She winked at Jake. "The gals here would certainly be glad to have you back...self included."

Hugs and handshakes were exchanged, Cameron McNamara squeezed into the sleeper compartment in back of the front seats, Jake got behind the wheel, and the Keoghs settled into the two seats beside him on the left. Both smiling, but feeling a gust of misgiving for what they had not been able to accomplish, a gutting loss for those they had not found.

The cabin was pleasantly modern, upholstery a smooth-woven fabric in a geometric design. The dash contained a straight-forward array of gauges and controls, and everything else was comfortably positioned. It had power steering, ABS, and air-conditioning, a panoramic windshield and a music system. Jake thought, *God bless Indian trucks*. After a quick comm check, he keyed the ignition, the four-cylinder Turbotronn engine responded with a healthy rumble, and he engaged the clutch and shifted into gear.

The assembled masses watched, most waving, and they began to move. Amelia Keogh, seated between Jake and Cyrus, looked because she had to. Took in the solemn faces. Prayed and made promises to herself that she knew she might not be able to keep. But felt an undeniable sense of elation for those they had recovered. She squeezed her husband's hand and dropped her head, not wanting to see any more. She knew he was right, they couldn't help all of them. It had to be enough to help some of them. The ones in the back of this truck were going to a new home and they would be taken care of. But the rest were still out there, somewhere, as was—she prayed—her child.

THE DISTANCE THEY WOULD be traveling, in any decent infrastructure, would have taken a couple of hours at the most, but this was the Congo. Roads—where they existed at all—were narrow and roughly rutted and cratered with holes the size of archeological digs, rocky and dusty in the best of conditions and slathered with mud and ponds of water in less optimal conditions, totally washed out in the worst. With a rest break or two, and the stop for the plane, Jake figured they should make it to Nakalé before dusk. The truck's five-liter 176-horsepower engine was grinding industriously onward, but until the sun began to bake into the mud, progress was going to be slow. As the morning light filtered through stretches of forest and spread over the savannas in golden layers, Jake became aware of Cyrus Keogh studying him keenly. He knew Keogh wanted to know what information had been imparted to him by Papa B, but Jake was still not inclined to share it just yet.

In between them, Amelia Keogh had fallen asleep, slumped against her husband's side. One of his hands was absently stroking her hair, which had a peachy cast in the sunlight beaming through the windshield. "Didn't get much sleep last night?" Jake asked.

"Yeah, I reckon a few of us were restless," Keogh replied, and looked at Jake.

Jake had also decided not to mention his evening foray into the woods, so he changed the subject, inquiring, "What was it that initially brought you to Africa? You mentioned The Sanctuary...but was there an interest before? Surfing, I'm guessing?"

"Yes, absolutely. We've both always loved the surf in the south… Jeffery's Bay, obviously, Cape Town, Durban…but we've also been to amazing surf spots in Morocco, like Anchor Point and Boilers, Dakar and N'Gor in Senegal, Tofinho and Ponta do Ouro in Mozambique, the Skeleton Coast in Namibia…" He gazed off, his face blissful in remembrance.

"I didn't realize you'd been to so many places in Africa," Jake said, genuinely surprised, as he'd not read any of that in his initial intel-mining on the couple.

"A few years before Sanctuary pursued us, we also did a safari."

"Really?" Jake was equally astounded that he'd not read about this, either, as it was the kind of publicity the wealthy tended to generate for positive buzz.

"Well," Keogh scoffed, "to be fair, it was not like this, being *in* the bush. This was one of those luxury deals with champagne and white-gloved world-class dining service and spas." His Australian brogue drew out the last word, pronouncing it *sp-ahhs*. "We saw some animals and then we retreated to our suite with all the amenities, the soft sheets and ice-cold bubbly, all that pampering that goes with being rich."

He continued, "Actually, we did two of those…one in Sabi Sands, which is at Kruger National Park in the south, and one in Madagascar. That one was a private island."

Jake laughed. "A safari on a private island? How does *that* work?"

"Quite bloody well, I assure you," Keogh chuckled. "Miavana was the place. It's also when we fell in love with the Seychelles, which is close by, and established our primary home there."

Jake shook his head. "Must be nice."

"Point is, we love all of Africa, and we've never done anything or anywhere in half measures. We're always all-in. Like the business, for instance. I didn't want to just do something connected to surfing. I wanted to do things that would elevate it and also somehow do good for others. The bud who runs my shipping and distribution is my best mate from school, Archer Judd. I'm an only child, so he's like a brother to me. In the research I'm sure you did on me, you probably know about the shark attack that lost him his leg and led to the technology that is at the core of our merchandise. But what's not usually highlighted in the media is that I designed a special line of boards and gear and courses for disabled surfers, all because I wanted Archie to still be able to do what brings him joy. So, no half measures."

He paused, his face turning solemn, placid blue eyes seeming to focus on something deeply and even more personally profound. "We experienced a real turning point while on a surfing trip to Mozambique. On the one hand, there's these gorgeous beaches, yeah? And then, we decide to take a spin around, and just a few miles in we came across this stretch of heartbreaking poverty and later learned that Mozambique is one of the poorest countries in Africa. We were gobsmacked. It's not like I was never aware of the rich and poor diversity that exists every-where in the world, but we were not expecting to find it there. We had been luxuriating in this beautiful place, as beautiful a place as God could create, and just a few miles away these people were struggling to sur-vive, eating rubbish and bathing in filthy water. Humanity…and humanity removed."

He peered out at the expanse of sprawling savanna, a skittish herd of duiker dashing off into the brush as they rode past. The incoming draft of air blew the blond waves of his hair around, an elbow propped on the open window frame. "The Sanctuary Initiative had been trying to en-gage us for a while, so at that point we decided to see what they were about. When we toured the Congo with them, that was it. We were in. We knew this was somewhere we could get a foothold and do a lot of good."

His gaze shifted to his dozing wife. "We always wanted kids, but found out early on that she's unable to get pregnant. We'd talked a bit about possibly adopting, but we travel so much and never really got down to it. Then, as fate would have it, as we were setting up our place here"—his voice shriveled into the back of his throat—"this precious lit-tle girl crawls up in Amelia's lap and looks at her with these big brown eyes…"

He stopped, again looking out his window, his face betraying the heartache he shielded from his wife.

Jake said, "Lula."

"Yeah," Keogh answered softly.

A few minutes lapsed, Jake's eyes watching the road through his sunglasses. He said, "I understand your connection with Africa. Mine is different and a lot more complicated, but it also stirs deep feelings in me." As rarely as Jake discussed his military experiences with others, given what Keogh had shared, he somehow felt compelled to do so now.

"A few years back, I had a contract to train soldiers in Uganda. This was with the State Department, endorsed by the UN and in coalition with the African Union. The Ugandan troops were preparing to join an international force deploying to Somalia to beat back al-Shabab. They're tied in with al-Qaeda and are especially active in East Africa. So we had classroom and field training, set up this boot camp complete with a mock city block, 'Little Mogadishu,' where we taught them the basics of urban warfare, weapon handling, roadside bombs, shit like that. As far as missions go, it was pretty satisfying and I felt like we accomplished our objective. But while I was there, I encountered something that will stay with me always."

He stared straight ahead, eyes hidden behind his Outlaw Fugitive sunglasses, face still. Finally, he said, "One night in our compound a group of boys were brought in. They had escaped from Joseph Kony and the LRA, where they had been held captive and brainwashed into child soldiers. Some of them were missing limbs—little kids with hands and arms and feet chopped off—all of them had terrible scars on their faces and bodies. Forced to take up guns and shoot people, forced to kill. They were like zombies, the indoctrination and trauma so embedded they could not even show relief or sadness or any emotions at all. Not at first, anyway. A local church took them in and an NGO began the rehabilitation process. I looked in on them several times while I was there, and the stories I heard about what they'd been through were beyond barbaric. Kony would capture or recruit these kids, manipulate and control them through dehumanization and fear. They were beaten, told they could never cry, regularly threatened with death. Any who did not obey were beaten or killed by other children—they made the children act on each other. They were also repeatedly told their families would never take them back."

Keogh had been listening, his mouth slack with horror. "God, that's sickening." An instant later, as if a hot light had blazed on in the back of his head, he said, "Oh Christ…you don't think…?"

"I don't know, Cyrus," Jake said gravely. "I fucking hope not."

An uneasy silence hung between them for a mile or so, the muddy road bumping unsteadily beneath the big truck's carriage. And then Jake said, "I put an extra Glock in the glove box. You know how to—"

Before he could finish the sentence, Keogh had popped the compartment open, reached for the handgun, dropped the mag out, released the slide to check the chamber, made sure the mag was fully loaded and popped it back in place, releasing the slide to load a round.

Jake managed a smile. "I guess that's a yes."

THEY WERE HALFWAY TO the plane when Keogh had cause to use the Glock.

The truck had hit a flooded section of road, its tires slogging through the water and mud, when a group of armed men stepped out from dense brush about thirty yards up ahead. Unlike the previous militia that had rousted them, these guys were all uniformly dressed in what looked like authentic FARDC attire—olive-and-tan camouflage fatigues, green berets, black combat boots—and carrying AKs.

"Probably just a checkpoint," Jake said tensely. "Amelia, get in back with Cameron." She climbed into the sleeper berth behind them, hunkering down with McNamara.

"Oh sweet Jesus," McNamara murmured, crouched and covering his head.

Through his comms, Jake said, "Listen up, we're about to be stopped. Pretty sure it's real military this time. Get everyone down, keep them calm and quiet. Weapons ready to go hot. Copy?"

Baladur, Dmello, Falcone and Niles all responded affirmatively and followed his instructions.

Jake hit the brakes and the truck lurched, settling into the sludge.

The camo-uniformed men, seven or eight by his count, shuffled slowly toward the truck, and Jake quickly thought about his options. Although it was not unusual for civilians to be armed in these parts, military guys would automatically assume they were mercenaries, which was a problem, especially with him being American. Even so, a calm explanation and satisfactory bribe might take care of that, and this time, unless it was totally ridiculous, he'd pay what they requested. Shooting at them was definitely a last resort, and with the mud they were trudging through, as rugged as this truck was, there was no hauling ass gear. Any aggressive action was not only risky but also came with higher stakes and more liability because not only was he the protector of his guys and the Keoghs, he had the additional responsibility for the precious cargo of their people. Not to mention he needed to keep this truck intact and running.

He watched the soldiers approach, all forming a staggered line in front of the truck, rifles held across their chests. At this proximity, he now noticed that although they were wearing the uniform, complete with the Congolese flag shoulder patches and Army insignias on their berets, the manner of wear was decidedly disheveled; collars were rumpled, shirt buttons half or all undone, shirts and pants soiled.

"Crikey, they're pissed!" Keogh said incredulously.

"Yeah, I'd say they've been hitting it pretty good...unfortunately, that makes them more unpredictable and therefore more dangerous."

One of them kept coming until he was adjacent to Jake and leered up to the driver side window, studying him without saying a word. Expecting to be asked for documents or given just a flat-out amount for payment, Jake waited. Instead, the soldier swaggered along the side of the truck, looking it up and down. His hand ran over the road-grimed white finish. He stuck a booted foot into the undercarriage railing, grabbed the top rail, and hoisted himself up.

In a low voice, Jake told Baladur, Dmello, Falcone and Niles to stay cool and, in his side mirror, saw the soldier stick his head under the canvas cover and look over the side. If he was at all concerned with the four armed guys stationed in each corner of the deck, he did not show it. He hopped to the ground and sidled back to Jake's window, head tilted up. Looked hard at Jake, but again, said nothing. He was not a big man, but his demeanor—even while intoxicated—gave him an air of brawn and self-importance. Not a good combination. He glared up at Jake, his eyes narrowing in thought and then, unexpectedly, strolled away from the truck, returning to the other men. They gathered around him and a discussion ensued.

"This is not good," Jake said. "I don't think they're after a bribe."

"Maybe they're deciding how much to ask for?" Keogh suggested.

"No, I don't think so. He saw what we've got. He wants the cargo."

"The cargo?"

"The supplies, whatever he thinks is in those drums…the women… probably the truck."

"Christ Almighty," Keogh muttered.

Jake said, "This is not going to end well."

BALADUR, DMELLO, FALCONE AND Niles listened to Jake through their comms, each syncing eyes with the others, and scrambled swiftly to the rear of the truck, fingers to their lips to silence the people they were stepping past. Women pulled children tightly to their bodies, all too familiar with the fear of what was to come.

Baladur unlatched the panel and the four dropped to the ground. Mud and water covered the tops of their boots and splashed up on their pants as they split off in pairs, two going left, two going right. Their rifles were raised, set on full auto. They stopped just short of each cabin door, their backs pressed against the sides of the truck and held up, sweat oozing, insects flying into their faces. Pulses pounded, Niles' whole face throbbed and he could feel his heart in his throat.

Up ahead, the FARDC soldiers were gathered in a tight huddle, heads turned inward in conference, their own weapons extended up, fingers on the grips and ready to fire.

Inside the truck's cabin, Jake said, "Go," and swung his door open, leaned over the window rim, his AK pointed dead center of the huddle. Keogh did the same on his side, the Glock gripped in both hands through the window opening. Baladur and Dmello and Falcone and Niles came up next to them on their respective sides, adrenaline flaring, ready to engage.

"Now!"

AKs, ARs, and Keogh's Glock fired in one massive onslaught, filling the air with raucous, rattling blasts that ripped through the soldiers like the S-blade of a food processor, flesh and blood exploding and splattering to the ground, dust swirling madly in the aftermath. All of them were obliterated, dead in a heap in the mud in a matter of seconds before even one could turn to aim their weapon.

For several charged seconds, no one moved or spoke, and then Jake removed his sunglasses, swabbed them against his shirt and said, "Load up."

35

THE REST OF THE trip to Nakalé was, thankfully, without conflict. With the exception of confronting several navigational challenges due to worsened road conditions—or tracts where the road ceased to exist at all—they got to the plane undeterred, and did not find any militant faction, official or otherwise, waiting for them by the dirt strip. And, given the near-catastrophic encounter with the FARDC, Jake got no resistance from the Keoghs when it came time to put them on the plane with Dmello; Cyrus Keogh spoke up before his wife could even try to make a case for staying with their people on the truck.

When Jake and the rest of them pulled into the village, its small multitude of hundreds, led by chief Gali Nsabimana, converged in exultant welcome, waving and clapping and chanting. With Dmello, McNamara, and the Keoghs arriving ahead of them, arrangements and accommodations were already well underway, women preparing a big evening meal while batches of others were setting up temporary spaces for the Keoghs' people to shelter until more permanent housing could be constructed.

As Jake stepped down from the driver's seat of the truck, stretching his sore muscles, Dmello approached with an American man in his thirties, clad in tactical wear similar to theirs, with short-cropped light brown hair, trimmed beard, and a fit build, introducing him as Kent Sanborn. A black holster strapped around one leg was packed with a Beretta.

Clasping Jake's hand firmly, Sanborn said, "Good to meet you, man."

"Remy got you here quicker than I expected. Sure am glad."

"He said to tell you he's still trying to break free and link up." He looked over to the Keoghs, who were surrounded by a mixture of children from the village and their own group of people. "I've met them and had some casual convo, great folks."

"They are," Jake agreed. "But be warned, they are a handful." He smiled wearily. "After we get some grub and settle in, you and I will talk."

Sanborn said, "Sounds good."

For the next few hours, as the daylight waned into the deeper end of dusk, the insurgence of people and activity slowed and settled, villagers retreating to their familiar routines and abodes and newcomers adjusting to their transitory placements. After what proved to be a satisfying and enjoyable dinner of roasted fish in a mango sauce, rice, and sweet potatoes, Cyrus Keogh paired off with Cameron McNamara to confer on business communications, Amelia checked in with all of their people to make sure they were comfortable, and Jake went over the security plan for the Keoghs with Kent Sanborn.

By nine o'clock, he was exhausted, and headed to the village church, which the chief and his wife had once again offered for the group's overnight stay. He selected a bench near the entrance, arranged his bedding and mosquito net, and fell asleep minutes after laying his head down.

BUT CALLIE WAS IN his dreaming mind, and he saw and felt her in a violent undercurrent that was taking her to a murky place, dragging her down as she called out for him. Deeper and deeper down, farther and farther away from him. He could hear a distant roar in the backdraft, and way back within it, a laugh that jarred every nerve in his body, penetrated his bones with fire and ice. And then he could no longer hear her, but he could see her eyes pleading, her face filled with pain and fear. He felt his heart ripped from his chest.

Oh God, please, I beg you, don't take her—

Jake came off the bench in a furor, clawing through the mosquito netting, his boots scuffling on the mud-brick floor, eyes bulging open.

Baladur, who was on watch near the door, got up from his bench and came over, pointing his flashlight in Jake's direction. "Everything all right?"

Jake wiped dust from his eyes and blinked into the beam, dazed as if he'd just been blinded by a smoke bomb. "Yeah, I just…" Shards of the dream were still real, still sharp, the desperation choking like vised hands around his neck.

"What?" Baladur asked, looking around.

"Nothing, all good." He stood. Reached for and felt the Glock tucked in the front of his pants, patted the sat phone in his pocket, and went outside. The night was cool, stars bright against a dark sky with only a slim comma of moon. He fought against a desire he could not control and, in truth, he did not want to. Checking his watch, he saw that it was after midnight—late afternoon in Costa Rica.

He took out his sat phone and called Callie.

This time, she answered, and he felt the tension in his body and the knots in his mind unwind, air flowing through his throat, the fog dissipating. Her voice, just the sound of her voice, took him apart from himself.

"Hi, angel. How are you? I heard you went to the beach yesterday. Did you enjoy it?"

He listened as she told him yes, she had, but her breath and tone seemed to shred and there was a pause before she finished by saying that she hadn't stayed long.

"Well, that's okay, love. It's good that you went even for a little while."

He talked with her for several more minutes but got a sense of building anxiety and a fragile dance around something she was not telling him. When the call was over, he dialed Jesse Segura.

"Hey, bud…how's it going?"

Segura assured him that everything was fine, Callie seemed to be having a good day, and he was about to finish his lifeguard shift and head to the villa. All *pura vida*. Jake asked him about Callie's time at the beach the day before. And, again, the pause.

"Something happen, Jesse?" Jake asked, his tension immediately returning.

Another, longer pause, and then Segura told him that it had been going well until Callie apparently saw someone who upset her. When Jake asked him to elaborate, Segura said they never figured out what had happened or who it was, but subsequent patrols of the beach did not turn up anyone questionable or shed any light on the episode.

Jake felt a prickly sensation around the base of his neck, a queasy ripple in his stomach. To Segura, he said, "Okay, no more beach. Good that you made the effort, but too much for now."

He stood outside for a while, trying to tamp down the turbulence that was bucking up inside him, rattled by the ominous dream he'd had before his phone calls. He reminded himself again to trust his home team; it was really all he could do in order to keep his focus on the mission. Even a split second off-game could cost dearly. But it was almost impossible not to worry about Callie and not to feel the entrenched guilt for leaving her.

IT WAS STILL DARK as they sat in the village communal area, drinking coffee that had been boiled in a big cauldron on a metal rack over the fire. The Keoghs watched and listened quietly while Jake finished reviewing maps and new satellite images that had come in from Kipnis, discussing the itinerary going forward. When he was done and Baladur and Dmello had ushered Falcone and Niles off to prepare for departure, Jake poured himself another cup of coffee, took the wooden crate he'd been sitting on, and went over to the Keoghs. Both looked sleepy and listless, and Jake surmised that the toll of the quest was finally catching up with them.

Dropping the crate, he sat and took a gulp of coffee. "All right," he said, his voice resolute. "We'll be wheels up very shortly and Kent will be in charge here. That means, whatever he says is law until I get back. I will keep in touch with him as often as possible and he will fill you in as necessary. What I am about to say, I cannot emphasize enough. You are to *stay here*." He looked from one to the other, gauging the extent to which his edict was taking hold. "I don't care if you get a message in the stars or smoke signals or someone comes into Nakalé with an urgent summons. You stay here. Am I clear on that?"

Both Keoghs nodded but said nothing.

"I need your word because I am responsible for whatever happens to you."

"We understand," Cyrus replied, his face empty of expression.

"You understand, and…?"

"Promise."

"Okay then," Jake said, and rose.

The Keoghs also rose and Cyrus said, "Just find them and bring them home."

Jake put a hand on each of their shoulders. "I hear you. I will do everything I can. You have *my* promise on that."

For the first time that morning, Keogh smiled, but the usual light that twinkled in his eyes was missing. He looked, Jake thought, like a man whose seemingly impervious bubble of sunny optimism was slowly sinking to the ground.

THE FIRST AMBER GLOW of sun was spreading through the clouds as the Cessna flew north, tracing the western side of Garamba National Park. Below, the terrain alternated between dense to scattered woodland and scrubby savanna gapped in wide stretches by open pelts of grass. The fine mist of dawn burned off to reveal a mosaic of green and gold, veined with the crooked brown tributaries from rivers and spotted randomly with ponds of bottle-glass water. They passed over the refugee camp which, from the air, looked both tiny and enormous with the thousands of individual tarps and huts squashed so closely together and reduced to miniscule proportions, the scope of its coverage like that of a small town.

After about two hours of flying, Dmello set the plane down on what looked like another rarely used dirt strip south of their targeted area, and everyone gathered the gear and supplies Jake had already instructed them to take: the last rations of fresh clothing, more MREs, water to refill their bottles and bags, ammunitions, and anything else that might be useful. Jake took all that and added a few more guns, a lot more ammunition, and some other incendiary apparatus.

The plane was secured, and the five of them set out, hiking through knee- and waist-high grasses, skin melting in the relentless heat and humidity, clothing heavy with sweat, insects clamoring in buzzing legions. By noon, they were all depleted, and came to a stop. Gathering beneath the wide umbrella of an acacia tree, they sunk to the ground, slipped off their packs, and dug out water bottles, drinking deeply.

Jake consulted his watch and said, "I know this is tough, but it's the only way we could do this. If we flew closer, there's a chance we'd be spotted. We have to keep the element of stealth. Any overflying of active mines would put their management or ownership on the defense."

"Yeah, I get that," Falcone mumbled, "but this sucks. It must be a hundred and twenty freaking degrees out here."

"At least," Niles agreed.

"I know, guys. I know. But we're close. Rest, hydrate, eat something. Then we'll move on."

Falcone grabbed his neck. "The damn bugs are driving me crazy."

"You have to keep reapplying the DEET, Eddie," Jake said. "It sweats off."

"No shit," Falcone grumbled.

"How's the nose?" Jake asked Niles, noting that the swelling and discoloration was worse today, due in large part to the heat.

"Still on my bloody face," he replied morosely.

They spent thirty minutes, imbibing water and eating bananas and protein bars. Jake rechecked his maps and the Garmin's navigational data from his watch, and got them begrudgingly on the move again. As was typically the case, they saw very few people along their route, just an occasional trickle of men and women transporting goods or a gang of kids who paused to watch them or sometimes tag along for a brief spell before slipping back through the grass. An hour into the afternoon portion of their trek, they were forced to wait while a few hundred head of cattle crossed, a mixture of white and brown and black that were headed southeast, herded by what appeared to be a couple of families.

"Whoa, look at those big-ass horns," Falcone observed, referring to the long, massive racks extending from the cattle's crowns.

"These are Mbororo," Baladur informed them. "They migrate, and usually, this time of year they would be going the other way, back to Sudan or the Central African Republic. It has been drier this year."

The Mbororo are Fulani nomad cattle herders who exist in the African region known as Sudano-Sahel, which cuts a wide swath across
north central Africa and runs through countries that include Senegal,
Guinea, Côte d'Ivoire, Togo, Burkina Faso, Benin, Ghana, Mauritania,
and Mali in the west; Ghana, Niger, Nigeria, Chad, and Cameroon in the
middle; CAR, Sudan and northern DRC in the east. They engage in what
is known as transhumance, the practice of seasonally moving livestock
in search of territory for fresh grazing and water sources, often with im-
punity into illegal or protected areas and causing chronic conflicts with
local farmers. Not only do the pastoralists infringe on land resources, the
meat and dairy they sell undercuts the prices in regional markets. Further complicating their blight on local farming communities are
alliances that often form between the Mbororo and opportunistic busi-
nessmen who, for a share of the profits, engage the protection of army,
police, or even militias, including the LRA.

Jake and his group stood watching as the men, some clad in white
robes and thick head wraps, strode alongside the long-horned Zebu cattle, prodding them with walking sticks. The women and children
followed, dressed in brighter garb, some of whom, like the men, had
tattoo-like markings on their faces.

When the herd had finally cleared their path, they resumed walking,
the sun high and hot, the ground here dry and dusty. Trees were widely
dispersed, so there was little or no shade, all of them perspiring profusely, sweat rolling from beneath their hats and caps. They had barely
gone a half mile before they were stopped once more, this time by the
distant peal of a gunshot. And then, a second and third.

Jake waited, listening. And felt a vibration beneath the soles of his
boots. He squatted and placed his hand on the ground, felt the tremor,
and stood, peering through his binoculars. Back in the direction they'd
just come, a reddish-brown cloud of dust was rising into the pale expanse
of sky, billowing out across the savanna.

"Run!" Jake commanded, and took off.

Baladur and Dmello reacted instantly and were right on his heels, but
Falcone and Niles were caught flat-footed, heads swiveling to look behind them, ignorant of the imminent peril.

Jake turned and yelled, "Move your goddamn asses!"

By now, the jeopardy they were facing had revealed itself as the two or three hundred bovines broke across the horizon, rumbling toward them, their hooves pounding and kicking up grass and dirt, bellowing emphatically.

"Oh shit!" Falcone exclaimed, running and looking over his shoulder. "What do we do?"

"You sure as hell can't outrun them," Jake shouted back. "We need to find a tree to climb if we can."

But there were no trees in sight, and the herd was quickly gaining on them, the ground shaking with the impact of their collective weight. Soon, all five men were enveloped in the mix and began jockeying wildly to remain upright as cows and bulls and calves bolted around them, bumping heavily against them and each other. The heat of the herd, mixed with the fecund stench of their panic, was forming a toxic vapor as the smog of dust filled their eyes and throats.

Jake was increasingly concerned about the real possibility of getting trampled underfoot, knowing that if that happened, they would most likely be stomped to death. Through his comms, he urged, "Try to work your way through them like you're swimming out of a riptide...keep moving with them but at an angle. I think I see a couple of trees up ahead...try to get to them!" He fervently hoped that they were *not* acacia trees, which were studded with vicious thorns. But, one thing at a time...they just had to survive the stampede first.

Jake got free of the herd, saw Baladur and Dmello find an opening and leap out, both turning to help Falcone and Niles. It took several attempts, reaching for flailing hands only to have them dragged back into the mass, but the two were finally extracted. When all of them had made it to the trees, which Jake noted with relief were thornless, he told them to climb up and lash in. Baladur, Dmello, and Falcone scaled one, Jake and Niles the other. Below, with the rampaging cattle thundering around and past the trees, they hugged the trunks and scrabbled amongst limbs, securing themselves with paracord from their packs.

Coughing and struggling to get a clear breath, Niles said, "I can't get a solid grip."

Above him, Jake said, "You got this, just get that cord wrapped and tied. Hopefully it will be over in a few minutes." He watched Niles fight to hold onto an armful of branches, looping his paracord around a strag-gly limb that Jake could tell was of questionable strength.

The boughs of the two trees, which Jake believed were jackalberries, swayed with the raucous passage of the herd, and below him, Niles con-tinued to waver. "Hold on, bud, almost over," Jake called to him.

The last of the herd galloped past, and they were beginning to untie and descend from the trees when Jake felt the trunk of his vibrate again. "Hold up!" he ordered, and looked through his binoculars, not believing what he was seeing. "Oh fuck."

"What? What is it?" Niles asked tremulously, bark crumbling from beneath his sliding feet. He pulled himself higher but only slid further down, unable to get purchase.

Through the lenses of his Steiners, Jake saw another massive cloud of dust, the ground—and trees—beginning to shake more markedly as hooves pummeled over the savanna, hooves that did not belong to cat-tle. When the mammoth shapes came into range, their large, distinctive heads and inwardly curving horns visible, Jake knew they were in trou-ble. "Everybody hold on tight, we've got buffalo!"

He heard Niles whimper in fear and assessed their relative positions, realizing that he was going to have to get closer to help him. But the sway of the trees, particularly in the crowns, made it risky to untie and move. The buffalo were closing in, almost directly below, and the branches around Niles were crackling. Jake unknotted and retied his par-acord to give him enough length to descend and started picking his way down. The buffalo were storming past now, but a few of them had bot-tlenecked at the base of the trees. *They can smell us*, Jake thought, and continued to maneuver toward Niles.

One of the buffalo, a russet-colored male easily weighing well over a thousand pounds, abruptly slammed the top of his head into the jack-alberry's trunk. The tree's girth was dense, but even so it rocked with the blow, which was followed by another and then another, and Jake watched in dread as Niles lost his grip, the limb he was tethered to com-pletely detaching, wood and paracord and Niles all crashing to the ground.

The buffalo froze momentarily, raised its head, nostrils working. Without seeming to acknowledge the presence of prey, it began to jab viciously at the ground with one of its thick hooves. Jabbing, huffing, and snorting. And then, charged on Niles, who screamed.

In a frenzied jumble of reaction and motion, Jake catapulted from the tree and, at the same time, heard Falcone yelling, Baladur and Dmello thrashing, all of which distracted the animal long enough for Jake to grab Niles and hoist him back into the jackalberry. He pushed him upward, using his shoulders to give Niles more leverage until he found sturdier limbs for anchorage. Jake got them both tied in, and they all waited for the buffalo to lose interest and move on.

Which it did about ten minutes later, giving them one final look before thumping off to rejoin its herd. Nobody moved from the trees until another ten minutes had passed and Jake gave them the all-clear. They climbed down from the jackalberries, glanced at each other in disbelief, and began walking across the savanna again, ground and grasses now still, dust settled and sky clear as if nothing had ever happened.

AFTER HOURS OF EXPOSURE to scorching sun in the open fields, they were all quietly elated to come upon a stretch of gallery forest with its towering trees, deeply green and rooted in rich, alluvial soil. The chatter of birds and monkeys echoed across the canopy, foliage alive with their movements. Flowering bromeliads and wild orchids splashed random color in the greenery, the fruit from plum and custard apple trees fermenting on the ground. They followed a path strewn with seed pods and decomposing dung, the biosphere layered with the cloying scents of resin and pollen, the dankness of fungus and lichen, and the pungency of animal musk and excreta. It wound through over a mile of woods, the silty, brackish smell of water becoming more pronounced and sunlight glinting in the gaps in increasingly wider apertures.

The nervous edge of endangerment had lessened with the time and distance, Falcone taking good-natured jabs at Niles. "That mofo wanted your skinny ass," he chided.

Dmello commented, "They like the white meat."

Baladur joined in, adding, "But it would have spit you out...too bland, no spice."

"I've got plenty of spice," Niles retorted.

"You must have something," Falcone said. "Everything goes after you…sharks…buffalo." He grabbed Niles and made a smooching noise into his neck. "Such a sweet thing."

Niles pulled away from him, made an insipid face. They all laughed.

Listening to their jocular banter as he walked in front of them, Jake shook his head but smiled, thinking he was glad to have these four guys by his side. Baladur and Dmello were pros and had the battleground resumes to prove it; Falcone and Niles were not, but they had gone balls-to-the-wall for him and had more than earned it. They were good and he was good with them.

He was ready to face whatever came next, but he worried that it might not yield the results the Keoghs hoped for. While he knew they wanted him to find more of their people, it was the child they hoped for most of all and, if he was being real—and that was his way—he did not see a good outcome. He wanted it just as badly for them…he knew what it was like to want and need something so much…but he did not think he could deliver it. And that notion flooded him with pervasive sadness, knowing how he would have felt, how he did feel, when he'd thought he might never have Callie again.

Jake walked on through the forest, embracing the sounds and smells and safety of its cover but looking to the light that was drawing them back to open terrain. The trees and brush parted, the sun flared, and a flurry of butterflies burst before him. He gazed out on the savanna and halted, everyone standing still behind him. They moved forward, apprehensive to see what held his attention. In front of them, Jake drew in a breath and gulped, his heart snared in his throat.

36

IN THE COURSE OF his many deployments and missions through the years, in all the countless places he'd set foot on the globe and situations he'd found himself in, there was not much Jake had not seen, so there was not much that caught him by surprise and even less that stunned him.

But the sight now before his eyes did.

He was stupefied, and for a long time did not so much as twitch, did not utter a word. He could hear himself breathing, feel his heart beating in his chest. It was as close to an out-of-body experience as he could have imagined, and he felt numb and electrically alive at the same time, transfixed as the massive wall of gray-brown moved slowly in front of him, so close he might have been able to reach out and touch it if he had leaned forward. In seconds that seemed to hang like drips of water clinging to the nozzle of a faucet, the clearing came into wide view, the passing mass shifting away from the opening at the forest edge, revealing the full splendor of the *bai*.

A mudflat ponded with tea-colored water, it extended a vast distance in every direction, trees surrounding it on all sides and, at this moment, teeming with wildlife—most prominently, elephants. The giant male that had passed mere feet in front of Jake was slogging his way toward a loose grouping of other males, some his size and some dwarfed versions of younger age. They were segregated from and disproportionately outnumbered by females who gathered in matriarch-reigned herds, socializing and playfully interacting as they dipped into and plopped through the mud and water. Both males and females sported straight, downward-pointing tusks, those of the males being longer and thicker. All of them flexed their big, rounded ears and swept their trunks in and out of the water, siphoning the rich minerals and salt from the mud, bubbles curdling around their submerged snouts, silt mushrooming to the surface in blooms from the bottom soil. Caravans of cows and off-spring formed and trotted along, tails flicking, as if they had somewhere important to go, but most wallowed in slow-motion, lumbering one way or the other, trunks raised in the air and then swinging below their imposing heads. While most of the bulls wandered about in isolation, some squared off in fraternal wrestling matches, interlocking tusks and entwining trunks, a few of which became slightly more combative duels for dominance. On the far side of the *bai*, red river hogs rolled content-edly in muddy pits and a herd of buffalo lay in the shallows of a deeper waterhole, birds picking over their backs, sandpipers and plovers and egrets poking about the papyrus marsh. Flocks of gray parrots and green pigeons flapped overhead, their formations parting to accommodate the flight of palm-nut vultures.

The late-afternoon sky was the blue of turquoise stone, meringued with frothy clouds, the twitter of birds effusive from the trees. It was a scene of such magical reverie, it felt of epic dimension and religious rev-erence, as if this were a page removed from Genesis, at the beginning of Earth and time from God's own hand. These magnificent descendants of prehistoric beasts, in their thick hides that were the color and texture of wet cement, etched with lines and sagging with wrinkles and set with eyes that seemed to gaze from a place of ancient wisdom, existing as pillars of eternity. It was as if they had always been and always would be, their size so immense, their movements so weighty and deliberate, their composition and countenance unlike any other creature. There was great strength but also a kind of vulnerability in their gentle spirits, and being in their presence was like a divine sanctity, the landscape they roamed an earthen Sistine Chapel set against the celestial backdrop of a Monet masterpiece.

It was simply a natural *bai* in a remote Congolese forest and savanna, but it was a sacred reminder that there were still places in the world untouched by time and consequence.

Or, so it would seem. Poaching over the years has decimated the hundreds of thousands of elephants by tens of thousands each year, with fewer than two thousand remaining in Garamba, which had twenty to thirty thousand in the 1960s and 70s. They are an endangered and vanishing species, any encounter in the wild such as this, increasingly rare.

But they were right here, right now. Jake felt an unspoken prayer stir inside, thought of Callie, wished she were here to witness this with him. And Remy. He bowed his head, pulled all of it within, and then looked out again. Realized the other four were watching him, waiting for him to react before they moved or spoke.

He swallowed and lightly cleared his throat. "We're actually not too far from where I'd hoped we'd be to set up camp for the night, but we'll have to go around the *bai*." He paused reflectively. "If you want to take some pictures, go ahead."

They did, and took out their phones, which he did as well.

They watched the elephants for several more minutes, mesmerized by the placid giants moving about in this real-life Jurassic Park, communing with each other by touch and rhythmic vibration, big ears flapping and long trunks waving and thick stump legs indenting the ground in boulder-size craters. Calves shadowed their mothers, clumsily trying to mimic each action, dunking and squirting, rambling and loitering, hoovering up dirt from the banks to throw over their backs.

Looking to the far side of the *bai*, Niles asked a little worriedly, "Are those buffalo going to come after us like the others?"

"No, they're chill," Jake reassured him. "The reason the others did was because they were spooked and riled up."

"The locals did that with the gunshots we heard," Baladur said. "To send the Mbororo and their herd away. It worked on the cattle, but also the buffalo. Most of the time, if we do not bother them, they do not bother us."

"Um, okay," Niles said uncertainly. He focused his phone's camera lens on the wildlife occupying the *bai* and, seconds later, a hearty cackle curled from his throat. "Look at the bloody cock on that bugger!"

"What, you jealous?" Falcone sneered, checking out the enormous genitalia dangling from the male elephant Niles was ogling, penis the length of a yardstick. "If you had a schlong like that you wouldn't know what to do with it."

"None of us would," Jake remarked, laughing at them. "Okay, let's get moving."

AFTER CIRCUMNAVIGATING THE *BAI*, they hiked a couple of miles through more forested terrain and were almost to Jake's targeted endpoint for the day when they came to a new clearing. At first glance, it appeared to be another mudflat, but there was no wildlife here, only birds flying overhead in wide, looping patterns. It was surrounded by a field of tall grass and scrub and, as Jake studied it through his binoculars, looked to be covered with rocks. Rocks and something else.

But, as it turned out, the field of mud was not covered with rocks, and the birds winging above were of the carrion variety.

When they made it to the periphery, each stood as equally dumbstruck as they'd been earlier at the edge of the beautiful *bai*. This time, not for such a blissfully transcendent scene—this time, for a shockingly gruesome one.

Scattered over the mud-and-grass field were thousands of bones, skeletonized corpses that had been disfigured and dismantled by scavenger birds and animals and insects. Jake knelt down, ran his hand reverently over one of the skulls. Looked at the hollowed orbital circles, the mandibles gaping open in some kind of stifled horror. What atrocity had happened here? Behind him, though it was blatantly obvious by the soiled and shredded fabrics mixed in with the bones, Falcone asked, "Are they…human?"

"Oh yeah," Jake replied, and felt every joyous ion from their previous stop evaporate.

"Could they be…oh God." Falcone dropped his head. Beside him, Niles looked like he was going to be sick.

Jake said nothing for a while, just began sifting carefully around the site. He crouched down in several spots and picked through the remnants of clothing that were stiff from being sticky with decomp and then rained on and ultimately plucked and gnawed. There were bits of faded color, yellows and reds and greens, the last clues to personalities taken from life, but no way of knowing why. This was obviously a fairly large body dump, and the fact that these poor souls had been callously discarded without any concern for dignity or discovery, suggested a lot of heinous scenarios. He studied random skulls and hip bones, which revealed the dead were predominantly male and of varying ages, mostly adults, but sadly, some children. The cause of death was evident in several—bullet holes, knife and machete cuts, possibly crush injuries—while on others, he could not make a determination.

Brushing dirt from his gloves, Jake said, "I didn't find anything in what's left of the clothing, but I don't think it's them. Given the degree of decomp, these bodies have probably been here a couple of weeks. It's been two weeks since the attack on the compound, so that would make it possible, but only if they were picked up and driven to this area. The people we found at the refugee camp had been on foot and only just got there. But no point in speculating." He looked from Baladur and Dmello, to Falcone and Niles.

They nodded soberly and followed Jake as he walked around the field of bones, all giving it one lingering look before putting it behind them.

IT WAS LATE IN the day and they were getting close to the mining territory, so they tacked on another mile and selected a campsite within the forested perimeter that encroached on the valley. As everyone was unloading their packs, Jake said, "Don't get too comfortable. We'll take a break and get some chow, but then I want to do an initial recce after the sun goes down. These mining operations will be crawling with people during the day, so we need to get whatever eyes on we can with night cover."

An hour later, as the sky was saturated with the deep red afterburn of the day's heat, the ground and trees tarnishing with darkness, they hiked to the edge of the woods into thick vegetation that abruptly dropped off, rolling downhill to a series of muddy ledges and slopes carved up with trenches and scooped out pits. Entrances to tunnels cored into the rises were crookedly squared by wooden frames, and rickety-timbered scaffolds and platforms stacked the sides, which also held a ramshackle assortment of thatched huts that looked as though they'd been slapped together time and again after any substantial rain. On the far side of the wide basin was a plateau illuminated by lights strung between wood beam poles, beyond which were more substantially constructed buildings, including a large open-sided one filling with people. Below, others were slowly making their way from various depths of the cavernous bowl up to the plateau.

Miners packing it in for the day.

Jake was taking this all in through his FLIR Recon thermal scope, crouched on the ledge overlooking the valley. Baladur and Dmello shared their handheld NVGs with Falcone and Niles, all surveying the scene but waiting for Jake's evaluation.

"This is a damned big operation," he said finally, lowering his scope to look at them. "We need to get to the other side where the camps are, also find out what's to the east and west of this basin. According to the sat images, there's a river on the west and a road to a village or town on the east. What we need to do tonight is one, find out if any of the Keoghs' folks are actually here—if not, no need to go any further—and, if affirmative, two, see what obstacles we're facing. An operation like this, there's going to be security, so we've got to do an assessment."

They all stood.

"Okay, let's move."

They took the western side first, following a scrubby path wide enough for a vehicle but full of the usual array of impediments that involved ruts and mud and water and trees. Soon, the terrain on their left began to slope down to the river, the sound of its currents rising up from a dam built into the rocky gorge. A wood-slat bridge creaked heavily underfoot as they crossed and gave a precarious view of both gorge and mining basin, which looked all the more immense from this height and angle. It took them close to twenty minutes to get to the north side where splinters of light slid through the trees, a mix of voices and music drifting from the plateau. They emerged from the wooded path and advanced cautiously into the open, walking a trail bordered by medium-high shrubs. Before they had ventured far, the scuffle of boots sent them scrambling for cover in the brush. They watched as a pair of men clad in khaki cargo pants and dark t-shirts approached the spot where they'd just been standing and glanced around. Both had AKs slung from their shoulders and two-way radios clipped to their belts.

Whether the men had heard them or were on casual patrol was not clear, but they stopped and one pointed a flashlight down the path and swept it across the shrubbery.

Squatting in front of the others, Jake nudged his rifle aside and drew his Glock, stiffening as the flashlight beam washed over the top of his boonie hat, the odor of masculine sweat and cigarette smoke wafting in front of him. Out of the corner of his eye, he saw Niles twitching his nose beneath the bandaging, fighting to quash an itch or worse, maybe a sneeze. The man knelt, inches away from them both, and tied the loosened laces of one of his boots. He spit on the ground and paused, as if sensing their presence, but then straightened and stood.

Seconds later, there was a muffled exchange between the two men and they retreated.

Jake saw that there was a narrow shelf behind the shrub line before the elevation sloped, so he warned them all to watch their steps and continued on the trail until they were parallel to the open-sided structure. The greasy smell of charred meat permeated the air, a rabble of voices mixing with the *soukous*-inspired Afropop playing from speakers set up on either side of a long, bricked grill, Koffi Olomide and Fally Ipupa and Roga Roga singing with an effervescence this crowd could hardly identify with or embrace given their circumstances. A few of them made a feeble effort, moving their heads to the beats.

Tables and chairs were filled with mostly men and boys, some women and smaller children, all plastered with dried mud and slouching with exhaustion. They dipped into bowls of food hungrily but without much enthusiasm.

Jake said, "Let's move on while they're occupied here, but Eddie and Curran, see if you recognize anybody as we go."

They went slowly by, Falcone and Niles using a pair of regular binoculars to pan through the miners dimly visible in the light cast from strung bulbs, not seeing anybody familiar. After they had moved past the dining structure, another large building came into view, this one enclosed. It was mud-bricked and metal-roofed, and a quick peek through a window opening revealed a barracks with rows of cots, all empty. They continued, now able to use the building for concealment from the occasional passage of one or more persons—and from the patrol of the camp's security team which, from Jake's observation, displayed the comportment of military training.

Tucked away in the northwest corner, shrouded by trees, was a structure made of thatch and wood, its window openings close to the roofline. It was also encaged with barbed wire. Jake crept around the side and spotted a stationary sentry in front. He slipped back behind the structure and whispered, "Our folks might be right here, inside."

"How can we find out?" Falcone asked.

"Luther, Kean, keep watch at the corners," Jake said, and clicked on his flashlight, aiming it at one of the window openings. When nothing happened, he flicked it away, then aimed it again, repeating the sequence several times. He was rewarded with the bobbing face of a young boy, probably straddling another's shoulders to reach the height of the window. Jake smiled and, to himself, said, "Son of a bitch." Through his comms, he said, "Jackpot."

"Oh my God!" Niles muttered softly. "It's Faustin! Eddie, look!"

The teenaged face of the boy caught in the 1800 lumens of Jake's Nitecore broke into an expression of astounded jubilation, his lips curled back from a dazzling mouthful of teeth.

Jake put a hand on Niles' shoulder to subdue his excitement. "Reach into my backpack and get a notepad and pen." Niles did so, and Jake flipped the pad open, printing in both English and French: *Keep quiet. We're coming for you soon.* He instructed Falcone and Niles to get him a tree branch long enough to reach the window opening, and when they had, he tore out the note and stuck it on one end of the stick, extending it over the barbed wire and up to the boy. Watched as the boy read it, grinning lips moving silently and then giving them a thumbs-up.

"When are we going to get them out?" Falcone asked.

"Not tonight," Jake replied. "We've got another half of this place to recon."

THEY WERE ABLE TO navigate the rear of the camp through trees stitched along the perimeter. The exterior revealed a staked stretch of land earmarked for expansion, lumped with hills, the valleys of which had been stripped of vegetation and crisscrossed with the treads of heavy vehicles. During their trek to the eastern side of the basin, they observed more armed personnel on patrol, and Jake noted that most of them were Anglo.

At the eastward turn, they found another layout similar to that on the western side, but with an adjunct section tiered with a network of long sluicing trenches for processing. On the rim above was a grouping of wood-and-thatch housing that most likely accommodated the mine's management, possibly buyers or brokers, and a heavier concentration of security that suggested it was also their on-site base of operations. Beyond that was a wire-gated entrance to the road Jake had seen on his sat images. This area was more well-lit than anywhere else in or around the basin, so Jake did not want to linger, but the shortest, most direct way back to their point of origin in the south brought a greater risk of exposure. To return the way they came was almost as risky because of the time it would take, which increased their odds of being seen. He decided to wait for an opportunity and take their exit the short way, even though they would be in plain sight for most of it.

The moment came with an unexpected and confounding bit of activity. Still concealed in the trees at the eastern corner, they watched as a dozen or so miners emerged from the western side into the dark pit, their path narrowly lit by plastic lights strapped to their heads. They were supervised by two Congolese men in clean shirts and slacks and trailed by a pair of security guys. The dots of headlamps bounced in the dark like meandering glowworms as the miners moved over and around piles of dirt, shovels and wheelbarrows, plastic and metal pans.

Security milling about in the complex of structures had shifted their attention to the procession below.

"Go," Jake said, and hustled the other four from the rear as they skirted the housing in a low crouch, making it to the southern rim where they had first surveilled the operation. They spread out and flattened themselves along the ledge.

Through his scope, Jake saw the miners going in and out of a low tunnel, retrieving sacks from the inside, carrying them up the slope, and then shoving them into the bed of an old Toyota pickup truck that had just come through the wired gate. Falcone and Niles were swapping the

NVGs between them, and it wasn't long before both spoke up in excited whispers, Falcone exclaiming, "That's them! That's more of them, going in and out of the tunnel."

When the pickup truck had been loaded, the miners retreated across the pit, climbed up the side, and were met at the top and led away. On the opposite bank, another vehicle had pulled up at the gate, its head-lights blazing. A man stepped out from the passenger side of a Range Rover and spoke with the driver of the pickup and then with the Congolese men and security guys.

Studying the profile of the Range Rover's passenger, for some reason Jake felt his skin tingle. *An American contractor.*

Minutes later, the man got back into the Range Rover, which accel-erated in reverse and U-turned. The pickup truck followed it through the entrance, heading down the night-darkened road. The gate was closed, secured, and the two Congolese men disappeared into one of the dwellings. The pair of security guys exchanged words and parted ways, one remaining by the gate and the other walking off in the direction of the north rim.

"What do you think, boss?" Dmello asked Jake.

Propped on his elbows, Jake did another pan with his thermal scope and then pushed up from the ground into a squat. "Well, we've found our folks and the intel was spot-on about them being used for slave la-bor, which necessitates a rescue plan. I'm not sure what was going on down there just now, but happening after dark makes it sketchy, as in maybe something off the books. I'm thinking tomorrow we'll do an-other recce from right here, see how the operation runs by day, get a better lay of the land, the numbers and movements. But I can tell you right now, security is going to be an issue."

He hoped it was not going to be an insurmountable one, and thought about the man from the Range Rover again, wondering why something had stirred in his gut.

THE RHYTHMIC PULSE OF a helicopter in the distance became louder until the rumble of its engines and thropping of blades could be heard as it passed low overhead, so low in fact that the belly could be seen, gleaming like a shark streaming across ocean depths. The roar diminished and then was absorbed into the black curtain of night, leaving a vacuous echo in its wake. Jake awakened with a start, swaying in his hammock, blinking through the gauze of sleep and wondering if he'd really heard and seen the bird or if it had been a dream. Looking at the canopy of trees, stenciled in opaque relief against the dark sky, he decided it must have been a dream. He reached for the bottle of water next to him, uncapped it and took a long swallow. Recapped it and slipped from the hammock to the ground, his boots thumping onto the damp forest mulch. He took a cursory glance around camp, noted Falcone and Niles and Baladur all tucked in and asleep, Niles snoring through his nose bandages, and walked over to Dmello, who was on watch.

"Hey, my man, how about I spell you?"

Dmello stretched, the muscles in his face straining to suppress a yawn. "You sure?"

"Yeah, I'm awake. Get some rack. You'll need it."

Dmello thanked him and headed for his hammock.

Jake took a slow stroll, gazing up to the sky again and seeing nothing but infinite darkness. The night was moonless and twenty degrees cooler than the day had been, but the humidity was still oppressive, his neck and armpits moist with sweat. Dawn was a few hours away, so the solitude would give him some time to think. But without more depth to his intel, Jake found it hard to even test-drive any kind of plan in his mind. So his thoughts shifted to the helicopter in his dream, how real it had seemed. He could identify almost any helo by sound, but this one was unfamiliar; then again, dreams were that way, splicing the real with the unreal. Militaristic themes were all-too-frequent nocturnal visions for him—helicopters and planes and diving out of them, guns and bullets and shooting them, hunting the enemy and being hunted, drawing blood and bleeding it—so this dream, by all accounts, was fairly normal. But it felt different for some reason, and he wondered if there was an element of portent to it.

He took out his sat phone, stared at it, and slid it back into his pocket. *Don't even think about it,* he told himself, *mind on the mission.* Mind on the mission always, and to allow anything outside of it to distract—especially anything of an emotional nature—was to invite vulnerability that could defeat you in a multitude of ways. His warrior mindset knew that if you allowed yourself to give in to that state when on mission, you could compromise yourself and others, but in his heart of hearts, he knew Callie was always going to be that vulnerability in him and he would have to find a way to lock it down before going to battle.

Right now, though, in these hours before daylight, wakeful and restless, his mind refused to go into emotional lockdown. Concern about her episode on the beach had been plaguing him ever since his conversation with Jesse Segura. He took his sat phone out again and made the call.

It was yesterday evening in Costa Rica, eight hours between them, and he figured she was in their bedroom with the lights on, dreading the night ahead or, hopefully, sitting on the terrace. Letting the ocean breeze riffle her curls and brush her skin, the salted air and floral scents from the garden tickle her nose…

Callie answered and the usual rush Jake felt swept through him with a ferocity that left him momentarily breathless.

"Hi, love. You doing okay?"

He could hear ambient rain and thunder in the background and her voice was tremulous as she spoke, saying, "It's storming…I wish you were here."

"I know, sweetie. I wish I was, too, but it will be all right." He told her about the elephants they'd encountered earlier, describing what a transformative experience it had been. This seemed to lessen her anxiety of the storm, even if only temporarily, which pleased him. He paused, not wanting to move off the pleasant subject, to ask what he needed to ask and upset her, but also knew he had to. "Callie, I talked to Jesse about what happened on the beach. He told me you saw someone."

She did not say anything for several moments, sounds of the storm and her uneven breathing filling his ear. He could feel the fear rising with each intake.

"Talk to me, love," he said. "Tell me what happened."

Finally, she stammered, "Jake, it was him…I saw *him*."

"Who? Who did you see?"

"*Him*." And she was sobbing.

He knew then who she meant, and felt as though his lungs had collapsed. Inhaling jaggedly, his grip on the sat phone tightened, his knuckles as hard as rocks. "Callie," he said as unemotionally as he could manage, "he's dead. I killed him."

"But it *was*…"

"No, baby," he insisted, his voice plaintive. "I promise you, it wasn't him. He's dead."

"Jake, I saw him," she whimpered, her voice small and eggshell-fragile, and all of it came crashing back, coming home to the empty house, hearing her tortured voice on the phone, the images of her in *his* house, finding her being violated after so much before. He felt a reflex of vile in his gut, in his throat. Living it all over again, just as she must every single day and night.

"Callie…love…he's really dead. It couldn't have been him."

Jake spent the next few minutes reassuring her, his heart flooding with anguish and an overpowering desire to turn heaven and earth to get to her. In the end, he continued to speak gently, coaxed her into bed and held on until the storm was receding and she was calming down. He told her he loved her and, with a pain that was like having his skin peeled away, he ended the call.

He raked a hand through his hair and squatted down, head bent, the pre-dawn quiet of the forest somehow excruciating. He let the emotion flow in the hope that he could flush it out of his system and gird himself, body and mind and heart, for what lay ahead. Because he had a feeling he was going to need every single ounce of focus and resolve to bring this mission in. He wanted, needed, to go home. But for now, he had a job to do.

37

A FEW HOURS LATER, as the sun rose over the eastern rim of the valley, slowly dissolving the earthen shadows in the basin below, Jake was in position with his Steiners trained on the movements of the camp perimeter, Baladur and Dmello on his right, Falcone and Niles on his left, all sitting on the ledge overlooking the mines. In the open-air dining structure on the plateau, miners were presumably having coffee and breakfast, though there was no smoke emanating from the bricked grills. The yellow orb on the opposite bank fully emerged, bright as a giant lemon drop and, as if they had punched a virtual time clock, the collective of miners dispersed en masse and began to trickle into the bowl below to start their long day's labor. Security personnel were conspicuous in the mix, some taking up stationary positions, some roaming, but at least one was posted at every mining shaft and several circulated about the panning and processing operations. By Jake's assessment, their presence was comprehensive, but there were always gaps to exploit if you looked closely enough, and one he noticed was their tendency to take breaks that overlapped so groups of them could smoke and shoot the breeze; he suspected that might be even more the case at night when they were not charged with covering ongoing operations.

By mid-morning, the broad strokes of those operations were beginning to coalesce.

The hundreds laboring in and out of the mines were comprised of not only men and boys, but women and children, all of whom were slimed in mud to the extent that their skin and clothing plastered into a kind of body paint that obscured distinguishing features. Even so, Falcone and Niles had quickly identified a multitude of individuals, all confined to one area and kept under constant supervision. This was encouraging to Jake because it probably meant they were also all housed together in the structure where they'd found the boy named Faustin. Shaft teams that worked inside the mines consisted of excavators and bag porters; the sluice team on the outside processed the ore brought out in hefty burlap sacks on the backs of the porters. Children gathered around mineshaft entrances, tying off the bags which were then hauled to the processing area where the contents were manually broken down with grinding stones against a rock slab. The grounds were mixed with water and run through the sluices to extract gold sediment. Water for the sluices was supplied by women who carried twenty-liter jugs of it up the slopes. Machinists, wearing unwieldy backpacks that resembled industrial leaf blowers with balloon tanks attached to the top, went from shaft to shaft connecting their machines to blue oxygen hoses that snaked into the mines, and a couple of construction maintenance technicians distributed pieces of timber and beams to shore up and extend the mine tunnels. Shaft managers supervised the workflow, making sure all the ore made it from mineshaft to the grinding pits to the sluices.

Jake noticed that the shaft managers were territorial, indicating they probably had some kind of stake in the mines they oversaw, each of them neatly dressed like the two Congolese men they'd seen last night. They got a little dusty, but for the most part were hands-off. The workers, on the other hand, wore threadbare jeans and tattered t-shirts, some with rubber boots and many more barefoot; none of them had helmets or any kind of protective gear.

Panning the upper banks through his binoculars, Jake saw minimal activity with most of the inhabitants at work below, but he glimpsed a few women starting to move about the open-sided dining structure, probably preparing to cook lunch. On the eastern side, perched on a ledge like a row of vultures sizing up prospective prey, was a group of young Congolese men talking or listening to music on their cell phones. They were flashily dressed in patterned button-up shirts and dress pants, small rolled-brim cowboy hats on their heads and leather briefcases by their sides. The on-site traders, Jake thought.

He continued to watch the toil of the miners, slogging into shafts that could collapse at any time, the porters hoisting bags of ore over their shoulders, those in the pits running their hands through the excavated sediment for glints of gold, none of which they would benefit from. The dredging went on, the curators in wait of their quarry, separated by dirt and sun and chiseled depths. Hands in the mud, foreheads creased in exertion, frames sunken in resignation.

After another hour of surveillance, Jake said, "Let's take a break and stretch our legs, hike into the village and see if we can pick up any intel from the locals."

ON THE ROADSIDE OF the mining enclave, just beyond the gated entrance, they passed a series of pop-up enterprises symbiotic to the operations: a stand that charged and repaired cell phones, peddlers of peanuts and fried beignets and sodas, a hut with a barber and hairstylist, stalls selling produce, and a woman brewing beer from maize called *mandale*. Her mudded thatch structure, with tarps of fermented corn kernels drying in the sun behind it, was a popular stop, and as they paused to watch the woman kneading flour in a big metal pot, several men came by with franc notes in hand to purchase some of her finished brew. A scrawny, gap-toothed man tilted a wooden bowl container to his mouth, took an enormous swallow and told them, "It gives strength and energy."

Niles nudged Falcone, smirking. "Fancy a pint of energy brew, mate?"

Falcone ignored him and they moved on.

The road to the village was lined with widely spread trees and palms and, once they'd put some distance behind them, not much else, the noon sun bearing down from a sky blanched with its heat. As they walked the mile stretch, Jake pondered his observations and thoughts about the gold mining operation. Conflict minerals were all too familiar to him from his time in Sierra Leone where the indigenous flavor was diamonds, and while he didn't know exactly what was at play beneath the surface here, he had a strong sense that something was, and the contractor had his hand in it—slave labor, at the very least. On the final approach to the village, an old Toyota pickup truck like the one seen coming and going from the complex the night before ambled past them. A pungent, gamey odor hung in the smoky trail of exhaust, causing them all to turn around and stare at its receding tailgate, which was streaked with red and brown.

"Bushmeat," Baladur said flatly.

"Yep," Jake agreed, his jaws tight. "Going to the camp."

Falcone and Niles made sour faces but offered no comment.

In anticipation of this excursion, Jake had suggested they put on a change of clothing that morning and had further instructed them to break down and stow their rifles in an effort to reflect a more civilian appearance, though Niles' bruised and bandaged face might throw some shade on that pretense. Wearing a sage-colored shirt tucked into his khaki cargo pants, Jake mopped perspiration from his face and neck, peering through his Outlaw TAC sunglasses at the edge of a settlement of thatched housing and wood-framed huts. Children and livestock spilled into the road and adults sat or strolled in customary languor, some already casting a quizzical eye toward them.

"We'll go with the geological surveying cover if it comes up," Jake reminded them.

They walked on, looking for a place to stop for lunch, not expecting to find a traditional eatery, but to their surprise, they were actually directed to one. Jake bent over to engage a bevy of kids, his charisma and the intriguing resonance of his voice beguiling them as he asked their names in French. When he inquired if they would like a snack, intending to dig into his backpack for the stash of candies he squirreled from MREs for just such occasions, several of the kids tugged him toward a large bricked building. It had the look of a typical small-town luncheonette, locals seated in plastic chairs out front, shelling peanuts and sipping from soda cans of Coke and Fanta. They stepped inside to a layout split between wooden tables and benches for dining and a grocery with shelves of basic goods and crates of produce.

An attractive young woman sat on a stool behind the plank counter, wearing a blue knit top collared with red and pink and yellow roses, her head wrapped in a red-and-yellow print scarf. She smiled in greeting, and

Jake asked, *"Quelque chose pour les enfants?"*

The woman looked around him and, seeing the string of kids, nodded and laughed, remarking in English, "They love the sweets we make." With an open palm, she indicated a platter stacked with some kind of snack bars and explained, "Coconut and peanuts and sugar."

Jake smiled back at her. "Okay, then, load 'em up."

The children tittered with delight as the woman handed out the treats. When she was done, she said, "Take a table and I will bring you our lunch servings."

"Thank you," Jake said, and the five of them slid onto benches around one of the tables. Most of the others were occupied by locals who had been watching them with growing interest.

It didn't take long for one to drift over, a pronounced limp to his gait. By way of introduction, he said, "That is my sister, Annet, and I am Felix Kambuyi. This is our place." He was tall and thin with an earnest face which, close up, looked older than his twenty-odd years, lines etched around his eyes and scars discoloring his forehead and cheeks. He wore gray pants and a blue-striped white shirt, rubber slides on his feet.

"Pleased to meet you, Felix," Jake replied. "Care to join us?"

The man retrieved a plastic chair from behind the counter and took a seat by their table. His sister led a procession of women with plates of *moambé* chicken, cassava leaves and rice, cobs of corn, and plantains. When everyone had been served, cans of soda and bottled water passed around, Felix Kambuyi skipped the preliminaries and abruptly asked, "Are you from the mines?"

Jake felt the eyes of the others on him as he finished chewing a piece of chicken, swallowed, and wiped his mouth with a paper napkin. "Why would you ask that?" He kept his face neutral, his posture relaxed.

Kambuyi was studying him hard, not in a hostile way, but clearly wary. "That is the only kind of outside people who come here," he stated simply, one of his eyes twitching.

Jake considered his response carefully and decided on measured candor. "As it happens, we are…but not *from* the mines. We're conducting a study."

Kambuyi leaned forward, his attention heightened. "What kind of study?"

On a developing hunch, Jake slightly changed his tact, replying, "To assess the working conditions, safety measures and—"

Kambuyi lurched back in his chair and started to say something but bit down on his lip.

Dmello, who was seated closest to him, asked, "Is everything all right?"

"No, it is not," snapped the young man, who stood up from his chair and hastily left the table, striding past the counter and disappearing into the adjoining kitchen.

"What the hell?" Falcone put down his ear of corn, kernels clinging to the stubble around his mouth.

"*That* hit a nerve," Jake said, and kept his eyes on the kitchen entrance as they ate in uneasy silence. But the food was exceptionally good and their hunger robust, so they cleaned their plates and thanked the women who returned to remove them.

Jake was counting out franc notes when Felix Kambuyi reappeared at their table, his head hung in penitence. "I must say I am sorry for my behavior."

Dmello gave him a reassuring smile and put a hand on his shoulder. "No worries, man."

"All good," Jake said.

Kambuyi sat down in his chair, hands folded in his lap. He seemed to be struggling with something, and after a few minutes of internal debate, decided to share it. "Most of my family has worked at the mines...until very recently. Our village and all the people in it once lived there."

"In the camp?" Jake asked.

"No," Kambuyi said. "Before the mining people came, our village was where it is. Then they came and forced us out. They promised to build us up here since they took everything, our homes, our livelihoods. We had good schools, a clinic, everything. But they have done nothing to help us." He looked away, trying to conceal his bitterness.

"You said your family members were working for the mines?" Jake prompted.

"Yes. They had to, because we lost everything and had to start over. And then some weeks ago, there was a collapse." His voice became brittle, his eye twitching again. "They had been telling the bosses they were going too deep in the hills, that it was not safe, but no one would listen. Many were trapped when it came down, some did not survive. The rest protested and were not going back, so they were shot."

"Jesus," Falcone said. "Killed?"

"Yes. My father and younger brother were killed because they did not want to go back and die in the mines." His eyes were glistening, and he swiped a hand across them.

"I'm so sorry," Jake said. "That's a horrible loss. Do you know anything about the people who run the mines?"

Felix Kambuyi looked up, confused. "I thought you said…"

"We *are* studying the mines, they just don't know it," Jake explained.

"I do not know the name of the company, but I have heard it is out of South Africa."

"You happen to know anything about the security outfit?"

"No." His face hardened. "But I know those men killed my father and brother." He paused, his throat working. "We never even got to bury them. They took all of the dead somewhere, to make it like it did not happen. But we know it did."

Jake exchanged penchant glances with Baladur and Dmello, then looked solemnly at Felix Kambuyi. "I think we know where you can find your father and brother."

BEFORE DEPARTING, JAKE HAD put the GPS coordinates for the bone field into Kambuyi's cell phone. Now that they were back on the southern rim surveilling the mining operations, he was ruminating over what they had learned. More of the sordid picture was coming into focus, but the objective of his mission had not changed and he still did not have a clear plan on how to accomplish it. There were two major obstacles: the density of people, even after dark, and the tight security. Often, and as he had deployed to rescue the Keoghs, a well-planned and –timed diversionary tactic was the best option, and he was inclined to go that way here. But the number of security personnel with their arms and training potentially lowered his odds of success and added the risk of being caught or killed. And he could not rationalize taking out an American security team.

They continued to watch the mine operations into the afternoon, with Jake giving each of the others a break to rest up for the night ahead. He himself opted not to take one, maintaining his vigil and looking for vulnerabilities in the security. So far, he was just not seeing much of significance. But watching the mud-slathered miners clumping onerously through the pits, others bent over and immersed up to their armpits, and the porters trudging up and down the slopes sagging under the weight of thirty-kilogram sacks of gold ore, was making him tired. He gave his eyes a rest, setting the binoculars down, and gazed into the harsh sun cast over the vast bowl of dirt and mud, all of it the color of ground cumin.

The unmistakable sound of a helicopter buzzing from the far side of the valley had him reaching for the binoculars again. Adjusting the focus, he scanned the distant sky until it came into view over the rise, a medium-size utility aircraft painted in green-and-tan camouflage. Maybe he *had* heard one last night, he thought, and as he was able to make out more detail, realized the reason he'd not recognized the engine sounds. It was an Atlas Oryx, a South African military bird, one he'd never heard before. He kept the Steiners trained on its flight path until it circled and decreased airspeed, descended and set down on what Jake could now see was a graded landing zone that he'd somehow missed. Through his lenses, he saw a male figure trot over to the Oryx and climb aboard. Minutes later, the helicopter lifted up, made a wide turn, and disappeared back over the rise to the north.

As he wondered about the bird and its passenger, he resumed his surveillance and, as the afternoon wore on, he still wasn't sure what he was going to do that night.

He did another pan around the rim of the mining basin, and this time picked up on new activity. At first he thought the security teams were changing shifts, handing over their posts to others who took their places. But then he noticed that the ones who'd left came back, so apparently they were covering for each other to take a break. He kept watching, following the comings and goings, and soon discovered what was taking place. Zooming in, he saw one of the men dragging a young girl into one of the huts. She was crying, pleading. The muscles in Jake's stomach clenched and he felt the skin of his face scald as if hit with boiling water.

Several minutes later, the man emerged from the hut, stuffing his t-shirt into the waistband of his khaki pants. Zipping them up, adjusting himself, and nodding to another from the security team who went inside.

"Fuckers," Jake muttered, and moved his binoculars to other huts in the complex, finding more of the same. All of the girls were young, all of the men were from the security team. He jerked the binoculars from his eyes and twisted away.

He knew what he was going to do tonight—and the rules of engagement had just changed.

38

WATCHING FROM THE SOUTHERN ledge as they waited for dusk to bleed off and night to infuse the valley, Jake went over the plan and made sure each fully grasped their parts. They had changed into black cargo pants, tees and shirts, and applied black camouflage to their faces. Weapons had been loaded and checked, extra ammunition packed into pockets. Jake had assembled his Colt M4A1 rifle—selected for its extended range and accuracy—fitting a FLIR ThermoSight in front of the day scope and a suppressor on the barrel, and was now working with Dmello to program several of the disposable cell phones that Dmello had purchased on their way back to the mining complex.

They kept up their vigil as the miners retired from the bowl to the western bank for their evening meal and then dispersed to camp lodging. They saw another group of Keoghs' people being accompanied down to the pits, in the same manner and at about the same time as the previous night, sent to retrieve bags from the mine they'd worked and load them into the same pickup truck. When the truck had departed and the Keoghs' people were returned to the structure of their imprisonment, they watched and waited for the security team to sift into their late-shift posts and patterns.

By 9 PM, it was full dark under the cloak of a new moon, the mining basin devoid of activity, the encampments and other housing above settled and quiet. Dmello led Falcone and Niles along the western rim while Jake and Baladur took a steep path straight down from their over-look. Nighttime security was concentrated on the perimeter with only an occasional sweep of a flashlight into the pits below, giving Jake and Baladur a mostly clear passage, although not without hazards. They had to climb around and over trenches and caverns and piles of excavated soil, maneuver through loose and sinking ground, sidestep sectors lit-tered with mining tools. As they meticulously made their way across the bottom of the bowl, the soft scrape of their tread near the eastern side drew a pair of beams from overhead, followed by an exchange of voices.

Jake and Baladur stopped, and Jake looked up through the scope of his M4. The two figures, squatting close to the edge and peering straight down, were lit up in the ThermoSight grayscale. Without a split sec-ond's hesitation, Jake pulled the trigger twice, the sound and flash of his rifle muted by the SOCOM suppressor. Even the best military-grade si-lencers on heavier guns typically reduced the percussive signature only slightly, but Kipnis had managed to engineer an even greater degree of containment, minimizing the M4's blast to the sharp pop and punch of a nail gun, the muzzle flash to a mere ember. The two men, struck cen-ter-mass, fell forward and dropped over the side, sliding to the bottom. Baladur scurried over and took their radios, and Jake said into his comms, "Two down, moving. Sitrep?"

Dmello responded, "Copy. All good this end…moving."

Jake and Baladur continued to a mineshaft about a third of the way down the eastern side. Jake handed his rifle to Baladur and removed his backpack, reaching inside for one of the bundles he'd prepared earlier. Leaving the backpack and gun with Baladur, he ducked into the shaft, clicked on his Nitecore headlamp, and began navigating through the tunnel.

The trapped air was damp and increasingly heavy, the odor both me-tallic and earthen, like that of an enclosed basement full of mold and corroded pipes. Without the free flow of oxygen in the narrowing space, it quickly became breathless. He was not particularly claustrophobic—it would have been near impossible to pass muster in any branch of the military unless you could withstand close-quarter confinement of every imaginable variety—but as the dirt barreled closer and closer around him and the oxygen volume diminished, he felt his pulse and heartbeat ramping up, sweat seeping from his body. He slowed his breathing and pushed on, until he got to a set of timbered joists well within the shaft.

With his gloved hands, he wedged the block of plastic explosive into a gap, making sure the blasting cap and wiring was secure, and made a mental note of which phone was attached. Then he backed carefully out of the tunnel until he was standing next to Baladur.

He clicked off his headlamp, exhaled and took a deep, purifying breath. "Any chatter or movements?" he asked.

"All quiet," Baladur told him.

"Okay, let's get this other one done and exfil."

The sound of several weapon pops came from above and, before he could inquire, Dmello's voice announced over the comms. "Two tangos down on this side, clear. Moving to target."

"Copy," Jake responded, and took his rifle from Baladur, checking the rim above through the thermal sight. Not seeing any figures or movement, they advanced to the mineshaft in the far corner.

The side of a wooden palette barricaded the entrance, across which was a length of heavy chain, each end anchored by large eyebolts that were screwed into the timbered frame, a padlock clamped in the middle. Bolt cutters or a sturdy wrench would have done the job, but in the absence of either, Jake dug his Swiss Army knife out of his pocket, manipulated the keyhole with a couple of tools, and unsnapped the lock in less than a minute.

Jake entered and clambered along the tunnel to the depth he sought, but this time he came to an intersection with multiple offshoots. The primary artery continued, but he could see that the adjacent veins had been cordoned off. He peered down one and immediately saw why. The secondary tunnels were occluded with rock and dirt. He ventured a few steps toward one and found himself staring at a partially skeletonized cadaver, insect masses present in and around whatever flesh and tissue remained, the foul odor of decay all the more concentrated in the enclosed area. He moved to the opposite side, and a quick glimpse revealed the existence of additional remains, though there had been an attempt to cover them, a crude cross made of sticks wedged in the mud. Was this the mine Felix Kambuyi's father and brother had been working in? It should have been closed off—the barricade giving that appearance—and yet the Keoghs' people had been forced to work in it. There must be a substantial volume of gold here, he thought, and he was betting the contractor was skimming it. Jake proceeded through the main tunnel and ran into a partially collapsed segment just ahead of the joists he was seeking. Already, he was snugly compressed with his arms and legs bent into contortionist positions. If he went much farther, he would almost certainly get stuck. The passage ahead was impossibly shrunken, the breadth of which would have challenged the tiniest gymnast. How in the hell, he wondered, did men fit and move around in here? His air was running out so he had to make a decision, which was to simply push the packaged C4 as far as he could—ultimately, placement in proximity to the joists versus in the joists themselves would hardly matter; the outcome would be much the same.

He backed up, reclined, slithered until he could half-stand, and retreated. Yards from the shaft entrance, Baladur's voice crackled over the comms. "Jake, we have chatter on the radios."

"Copy, I'm almost out. Just—"

The last part of his sentence was broken off by a small avalanche of rocks and mud chunks raining down on his head and shoulders, a fusillade of dirt hitting his back. He shoved against the ground and pushed himself backward, struggling for air and slimed in perspiration, muscles cramping in the compaction, and suddenly felt things unraveling. *Shit, shit, shit.* Willing himself to remain calm, he wriggled against the ground, using the weight above him as counter leverage, and when he had moved a few feet, felt Baladur's hands firmly grab his ankles and pull. Dirt and rubble fell away from him as Baladur helped him the rest of the way out.

Standing, Jake spit mud from his mouth and said, "Thank you, brother. Let's boogie."

He snuffed his light, slung his backpack and rifle, and started up the slope. Halfway, they heard the scuffle of boots just above them. They burrowed into an outgrowth of bushes and Jake took a quick look through his rifle scope. He gave Baladur a hand signal indicating three men. Seconds later, Jake took aim and shot from the right, Baladur from the left, and before the middle man could return fire, Jake had taken him out, too. The confiscated radios clipped to Baladur's belt were buzzing with talk, and Jake knew their window was closing.

He hoisted himself up to the ledge, extending a hand to Baladur, and looked toward the eastern housing complex. Security and occupants were stirring like disoriented and agitated ants from a disrupted colony.

Glancing at Baladur, Jake said through comms, "Okay, everybody, here we go."

AFTER KILLING THE PAIR of security men they encountered on the western rim, Dmello, Falcone and Niles had taken the path that ran behind the camp lodging. While Dmello descended a series of plank steps embedded in the far side of the river gorge, Falcone and Niles set up at the rear of the wire-encaged structure where the Keoghs' people were being kept. With the long tree limb Jake had used the night before, Niles tapped at the edges of the window opening. When Faustin's face eventually appeared, Niles aimed a flashlight on his own face and put a finger to his lips, signaling the boy to be quiet and hoping the message would be shared with everyone else inside.

Then, using the pair of cutters Jake had given them, Niles began to work on the barbed wire while Falcone kept an eye on both corners, AR-15 gripped anxiously in front of him. Dmello had just rejoined them when Jake's voice came over their comms.

JOGGING ACROSS THE SOUTHERN rim, Jake depressed the number 1 button on the keypad of the cell phone in his hand, triggering a concussive boom that shook the ground all the way to the ledge under their feet. They paused at the western corner and Jake aimed his M4 at the mine they'd just left, the image in his scope showing a thick column of dark smoke and a deep cavity in the slope, the borders of which were crumbling in widening waves on all sides. And, as anticipated, the chaos that followed was sending personnel running from their positions and those inside dwellings pouring out. Which was a good thing because when Jake thumbed the number 2 button, the mine closer to the swarm of activity blew up with an equally impressive and devastating effect.

They sprinted down the western rim, thumping over the wood-slat bridge and then along the shrub-lined path until they reached Dmello, Falcone and Niles.

"All set?" Jake asked Dmello, and got a thumbs-up.

Assessing the large opening Falcone and Niles had cut in the barbed wire, Jake signaled Baladur and the two of them went around the structure's sides to see if there was a security presence or any approaching from the periphery. But the detonations had accomplished exactly what Jake had intended; demolishing the two mines and pretty much everything in between and adjacent, the entire southeastern corner was a hive of pandemonium, and any personnel that had been patrolling in the west were now running to the scene. He also saw that the camp lodging nearby was rapidly emptying out as he had hoped, the miners spilling into the hills outside the basin.

Jake allowed himself a victorious smile.

He and Baladur went back around the enclosed structure where Dmello, Falcone and Niles had stepped through the opening in the barbed wire and breached the wood-framed thatch wall. When all of the occupants were out, Jake estimated there were at least a hundred men, women, and some children—no babies and no toddlers. Enthused nods from Falcone and Niles confirmed they were all, indeed, from the Keoghs' compound.

Addressing the assembly of people now under his care, Jake said, "Okay, folks, I need everybody to stay together and keep moving...as fast as you can. *Restes ensemble ... allons-y vite.* Anybody need medical attention? *Attention médicale?*"

Heads turned in different directions and there was a murmuring that suggested the affirmative but no one came forward.

"If it can wait," Jake suggested, "let's go."

With Jake and Baladur in the lead, Falcone and Niles along the line and Dmello at the rear, they hurried toward the northwestern corner and slowed to negotiate the plank steps. They were narrow, crooked, and not all firmly embedded, so it took a tedious amount of time to get everyone down. At the bottom, the air was cooler, river water gurgling against the dam. Jake had scouted the route earlier that afternoon, his sat images showing mostly forest extending from the banks for several miles, but they would eventually need to turn south and, with more mixed terrain, that was where it could get dicey.

Catching up to Jake, Falcone said, "They're saying we have all of them that were here."

"Good. Let's keep 'em moving."

Jake instructed Falcone and Niles to let those with headlamps use them, but as handhelds pointed toward the ground. He did not have to tell any of them to keep quiet; they were scared and more than anxious to make a clean getaway. About a half mile from the site, Dmello's voice crackled over the comms, warning of men coming up on their flank.

"Distance?" Jake asked.

"Five or six hundred meters."

"Standby to engage," Jake said, and told Falcone and Niles to keep the line moving while he and Baladur joined Dmello in the rear.

Raising his M4, butt against his shoulder and stock pressed firmly below his cheekbone, Jake peered through the thermal scope and visualized three armed men on the approach. He watched as one looked through a monocular and immediately reacted by aiming his rifle.

"Take cover!" Jake shouted, and the caravan at his back collectively dropped to the ground with scattered utterances of alarm.

The men opened up on them, an onslaught of semi-automatic fire peppering the space Jake, Baladur, and Dmello had just vacated. In the instant after the initial assault, the three of them took aim and squeezed off a couple of rounds each and, unlike their opponents, hit their marks as they were squaring off to launch another offensive. When the men dropped and did not get back up, Jake reached into a pocket for the cell phone he'd used earlier. Pressed the number 3 button.

A half mile behind them, the dam and bridge blew up.

THEY HIKED FOR A couple of hours into the night, pausing for a few brief breaks, all quiet after the fireworks except for the sound of the river's trickling waters and reptilian croaks. Jake wanted to get them as far from the mining site as possible while he had the cover of darkness and forest, but they would need to move away from the river soon, so he decided to stop for a more extended rest to take advantage of the water source. While Dmello began dipping up water to filter with the

Katadyn kit, filling everything they had, Falcone and Niles made sure everyone drank. Jake spent the time making a circuit to meet all of the people and inquire about medical needs, primarily finding topical wounds in various degrees of severity; scrapes and cuts, blisters and sores, bruises. A few were suffering from intestinal distress. But he found the most serious injuries on Yannick Libwatwani and Cédric Mbaya, the Keoghs' community director and security chief. Both had been beaten on their backs and were sporting vicious-looking abrasions and welts, bruising, and wounds on the verge of infection.

"What happened here?" Jake asked, his brow furrowed as Baladur lifted their shirts so he could examine them.

Mbaya said, "I tried to do my job to protect. The security men beat me with their guns. When Yannick tried to help me, they beat him, too."

"Damn," Baladur said.

Jake began cleaning and dressing the wounds, and listened to their story. Mbaya and Libwatwani gave an account similar to that of Beatrice Tshisungu, the woman who had opened up to Amelia Keogh at the refugee camp, telling of the night attack, the rampaging of the compound, the fire, and the fleeing. Where his rendition differed confirmed what Jake had suspected; the men were sought out and rounded up, thrown into trucks with whoever else had been unable to escape and transported to the mining operation. They were put to work on arrival, enduring grueling twelve-hour days with little or no breaks, given one meal after everyone else at the camp had eaten and, worst of all, indifferently endangered by being forced to labor in the unstable structure and depths of a mine that had recently collapsed.

"It was loaded with gold," Libwatwani said.

"What can you tell me about the security outfit?" Jake asked.

Mbaya winced as Jake applied antiseptic to his wounds. "Crooked!"

"Yeah, I got that," Jake remarked. "Do you know who they are?"

Mbaya shook his head. "Sorry, no. American and South African, well-trained."

"Ever see the head guy?"

"A couple of times, at a distance. He would meet the mining company people. Oh, and he is working with a rebel group…that is who took us."

"Okay, my man," Jake told Mbaya, "you're all set."

"Thank you, my friend."

Niles sidled up to them and Jake checked on his nose, satisfied that the bandaging was secure and the swelling no worse. While Jake was straightening his medical kit, Niles asked Mbaya and Libwatwani, "What happened to the doctors?" Jake glanced up, saw Niles toeing the ground, head averted. He looked, in that moment, like a little boy asking about a lost puppy.

Libwatwani shook his head sadly. "We are not certain, but we heard the rebels took them to their camp. We think they are LRA."

Jake tried to refrain from a response, clenched his jaw, hands planted on his hips. He paced away, head bent in thought. Then he clawed through his hair and said, "Damn."

Dmello trailed after him, saw him gaze up at the openings in the tree canopy, the dark beginning to take on a strange cast for this hour of night. "Thinking about the helicopter?" he asked.

Jake looked at him. "Yeah. If they have thermal, we're in trouble."

"Big heat signature," Dmello agreed.

Falcone was close by, helping with water distribution, and said, "Surely they won't bother coming after these people. I mean, that's kind of extreme, isn't it?"

"You're right," Jake replied. "But they sure as hell would want to come after whoever blew up their mines." *And maybe eliminate those who were privy to some of the big man's secrets,* he thought.

"You want to cover some more ground?" Dmello asked.

Jake surveyed the people, sitting in huddles, all watching him uneasily. "I do, but they've already put in a long, hard day's work. I don't know how much more we can push them." He unfolded a map from his pocket and studied it for several moments. "I think we're still too close to the mining territory. But to get to the next wooded area, we'll have to cross a big span of savanna. We'll be totally exposed to thermal or night vision from the air, but if we can get past it before daylight, we'll be in a much better position to turn back to the south." He looked at the people again, sighed. "I say we go."

*　*　*　*　*

THEY HAD TREKKED CLOSE to another mile when Jake detected the first distant vibration he had dreaded hearing. There were few trees, the sky above taking on a phosphorous blue that revealed a front of undulant clouds, a breeze beginning to stir through the tall grass. As the vibration became a more audible rumble, Jake shouted, "Everybody run as fast as you can! To the woods just ahead! *Allez vite vers les arbres!*"

The woods were about a hundred or so yards off, and not nearly dense enough to give them enough cover from the sky, but Jake thought they could make it and it was their only option. Everyone ran, some stumbling and being helped up by others, the sound of the helicopter's hum close enough to clarify into an air chop. They made it to the edge of the trees, Jake urgently spurring them on, just as the sky flashed bright with electricity followed by resonant volleys of thunder, and he thought: *God, we got to the trees only to be nailed by lightning.* But at the same time, he realized it was the caprice of weather that would give them what the sparsity of trees could not—a shield from the overhead surveillance, and a compelling incentive for its crew to return to base.

Addressing the now more critical situation, Jake called out, "Go to a tree cluster, the shorter the better…and squat down, head tucked. Stay as still as you can." Rain thrashed through the tree crowns and pounded the ground, lightning and thunder punctuating in rapid intervals. In the midst of it all, there was a solid strike somewhere within the woods, a strident clashing that was like heaven had dropped all of its orchestral cymbals. Or like gunfire, from above. Though Jake knew it was lightning, he could not help but lift his head and look up.

Thirty minutes later, the storm had passed, leaving the ground heavy and wet, the trees dripping, the sky clear and dark once more. Jake got everyone moving, taking them a half mile beyond the light vegetation and into a taller and thicker expanse of teak and mahogany. There, they took shelter for what remained of the night.

IN THE UNCOMFORTABLY WET hours before dawn, Jake managed to get an hour or so of rest—not sleep, because he was half-listening for a return of one or more helicopters but enough time to be alone with his thoughts and let his body recalibrate. He did not want to let this mission drag on any longer than necessary, but he had given the Keoghs his word that he would continue as long as he could justify doing so. Each phase of the operation had yielded a new lead, and he now had another with the contractor's ties to a rebel group. He knew there was a strong possibility that Libwatwani's theory about the Keoghs' medical staff being taken by the group was real—he'd been held captive himself on more than one occasion to medically treat militia and rebel groups—so he felt compelled to at least look into it. But this far in, he had to concede that the odds on locating the Keoghs' child were slim to none, and that had been the primary objective of his mission.

A fine mist fogged the treetops as Baladur and Dmello rose to help him find enough dry wood to make a fire for coffee and to allow everyone a chance to extract some of the dampness from their clothing. Jake took his cup and strolled around their camp, counting heads. It would be a packed load, he thought, but he doubted any of them would mind. He slid his sat phone from his pants pocket and selected one of the stored numbers.

"Got that truck fueled up?" he asked. "I've booked you a charter."

39

THEY HIKED SOUTH, STOPPING late in the afternoon to set up camp in a wooded area close to a washed out and overgrown road that, according to the maps, did not exist. But on sat imagery, it appeared to connect with the secondary road to Nakalé. When speaking with Cyrus Keogh that morning, Jake had asked him to pass the phone to Kent Sanborn, inquiring if Sanborn could find someone capable of driving the truck and, better yet, one or more others who could act as security; he knew there were several villagers who carried weapons and considered themselves the ad hoc defense force. Jake urged Sanborn to keep the Keoghs in the village preparing for the arrival of the influx of people.

Now, as they took shelter in the shade of the towering evergreens, Jake sent Sanborn a text with their GPS coordinates and joined the others in gathering limbs and brush. When everyone was settled and resting, he did an expanded perimeter check, taking another scan of the sky. He'd been keeping an eye out for any air traffic throughout the day, but thankfully, had not seen anything other than the feathered variety.

He glanced around once more to make sure all was well with the group and found a spot for himself, sitting beneath a guarea tree at an outer edge of camp. The densely crowned tree was well over a hundred feet tall and smelled pleasantly of cedar, the ground around it strewn with opened star-shaped seed pods. He set up his Goal Zero solar panels and connected his Iridium GO and iPhone, checking messages and email, and found one from Kipnis. In it, he learned that the mining company was Kaseme Mines out of Johannesburg, a relatively new enterprise with few verifiable details. Founded by Canadian business partners, Kaseme owned other mines in the DRC, most being in the Kivu region, and was estimated to export hundreds of millions in gold to countries that included the UAE, India, and China. They had been cited for various violations and investigated for trading improprieties. Kipnis added that this was pretty common in the mining industry no matter the scale or notoriety of the operations. He concluded by saying he did not as yet know anything about the security contract but was still digging.

Jake responded by asking Kipnis to also get anything he could on militias or rebel groups in the area with possible connections to the mining company or contractor.

Scrolling past most of his other emails, one from Callie snared Jake's attention. It was a sweet note from a few days ago, in which she simply said: *Missing and thinking of you. Love, Callie.* His instant reaction was one of piercing absence, wanting more words, more essence of her and home, just more. But he realized that she probably knew he tended to dislike lengthy emails and was honoring his predilection. High in the branches of the guarea, a black-and-white guereza colobus monkey was munching on seeds, the shells dropping to the ground in front of him. He tapped out a short response to her message and swiped through some images until he found a couple he'd taken of the elephants at the *bai*, attaching them to the email.

Baladur came over to take up watch for a while, and Jake let his eyes close, dozing lightly until an hour later when he was awakened by the approaching rumble of a heavy diesel engine.

DESPITE HIS EMPHATIC DIRECTIVE to Kent Sanborn, Jake was not the least bit surprised to see Cyrus and Amelia Keogh step from the passenger side of the Tata Motors truck, Cyrus beaming ear to ear with a bedazzling smile framed with dimples that could have chiseled ice. His wife's beatitude was more tempered but no less effusive, green eyes dancing with delight at the sight of their people rushing to greet them. Both were fresh and cooled from the truck's air conditioning, skin glowing, hair shining and neatly coiffed. Cyrus Keogh wore a Louis

Vuitton collared navy shirt exploding with white flowers loose over navy form-fitting Prada slacks and Brunello Cucinelli suede deck shoes without socks, a *Big Bluey* baseball cap snugged over his sandy blond waves. Amelia was dressed in a Veronica Beard white linen blouse and split-leg culottes patterned with lemons and limes, her radiant hair tied up in a wide yellow bow, ankle-strap flats on her feet. Both of them, as fashionably attired as they were, somehow managed to look casual and perfectly acclimated in the rough-hewn environment, as if the outbacks of the world adapted to them and not vice-versa.

Falcone and Niles worked their way through the excited throng of people until they were standing before the couple, all smiles. "God, you look as cool as an ice cream sundae," Niles quipped, hugging them both.

Falcone was shaking his head. "How is it even possible?"

Amelia Keogh laughed. "*Pfft*…These old things? Actually, we had one last good change of clothes stowed and were saving them for the right occasion. I'd say this fits the bill quite nicely, wouldn't you?"

"Jake, me ol' cobber!" Cyrus Keogh exclaimed, and moved to clasp his hand and then embrace. Amelia was right behind him, her gaze latching onto Jake's, her eyes a little too bright, her smile slipping almost imperceptibly.

But Jake saw it, and he knew she was going to make him say it. It wouldn't be real until he said it. He hugged her, stepped back, looked directly at her. "Amelia, I'm sorry."

She held the smile and did not respond.

He knew she was fighting to keep the joy afloat, surrounded by people she and her husband had come to love. A single tear formed but clung to her eyelid. She kept smiling and turned quickly, thrusting herself into the jubilant crowd, squeezing hands and hugging and kissing cheeks, her voice emoting with a happiness that was riddled with air bubbles rising to the surface, about to pop at any moment. He watched with doleful admiration as she squelched her inner despondency and gave everything she could draw from herself to celebrate those who had been found and returned.

She looked over her shoulder, reconnecting with Jake, and mouthed *thank you.*

Kent Sanborn came up to Jake, his arms spread in apology. "Sorry, man. You know how they are."

"Yes, yes, I do," Jake said. Watching the ongoing reunion between the Keoghs, Falcone and Niles, and people from their compound, Jake asked Sanborn, "What do you want to do? Overnight here or hit the road? Is it safe enough to travel after dark?"

"I think we could do it. We've got food and water for them, too."

"That's good," Jake said, "because they might be sitting ducks here with us. Okay, let me speak to them and then you can hit the road." Walking over to the Keoghs, Jake waited until the couple pulled away from the assemblage.

"We spoke with Yannick and Cédric," Cyrus Keogh said, his expression flattened. "Do you think you can find our medical staff?"

"I don't know," Jake replied evenly. "I need more intel, and we'd be going farther out." He paused, saw the expectancy in their eyes. "Get your people back to Nakalé, and I'll think on it. We need to get the plane."

"So...?" Amelia Keogh began, and bit her lip, willing herself to be stoic.

"I'll let you know, okay?"

Cyrus Keogh clamped a hand on Jake's shoulder, a smile reforming momentarily. Then he turned and, with his wife, began rounding up their people and arranging them in the truck's enclosed deck.

THE NIGHT PASSED UNEVENTFULLY, no helicopters in dreams or out, no driving rain or lightning storms, no armed marauders. Jake awoke on cue just before the dawn's first light filtered through the forest canopy, rested and ready to move on. He just didn't know yet what he was moving on to, or if he would soon be pulling up stakes, only part of his mission successful. It was not a feeling that sat well with him. Maybe some clarity would come on the way to the plane. But was there ever really any clarity when it came to lives sucked into the vortex of inhuman atrocity and depravity, blood lust and avarice, or the mechanisms of war? Still, he could not shake the instinct that had nestled in his gut, that there was something else going on behind all of it.

They broke down their camp, restoring the site to its previous natural state, and set off. Hours in, the sky yellowed with heat and steamed moisture from earth and flesh, the air smelling of the biologically piquant soil and the perspiration being emitted with each stride. As they approached the vicinity of the *bai* they had encountered en route to the mining territory, Jake found himself boyishly giddy at the prospect of seeing the elephants again. He knew there was a good chance they would not be present, but he was hopeful. With his iPhone fully charged, he wanted to take some video this time. Listening to Falcone and Niles' animated repartee as they hiked, Baladur and Dmello chiming in, he realized it was something they were all looking forward to. He smiled and savored the lush greenness of the savanna grasses, the iconic trees that spread and climbed overhead, the vibrant colors of birds flitting about in their branches. For some reason, the day had a sense of grandness, and again he felt an aura of transference to another era, one in which the earth was bathed in a golden light and men and women dined on columned verandas in the glow of tangerine sunsets through the twisting limbs of umbrella trees, the call of the wild beyond rolling hills. A *tink* of fine china, the sweet heat of vintage Napoleon brandy, mesquite smoke wafting in the air. Zebras and giraffes and lions and elephants, bestial exclamations in the night and carefully choreographed movements by day, poised and graceful and eternally present. The gilded dawn of rebirth over ancient valleys that slipped softly over the window sills of estates with billowing white curtains.

But the euphoric feeling was short-lived.

Within a half mile of the *bai*, Jake knew something was wrong, felt a sea change in the atmosphere that was palpable on a glandular level, like the tinnitus and vacuum that accompanied a drop in air pressure. The grass was now waist high, the ground becoming spongy underfoot as they crossed marshland, papyrus and reeds twisting around their legs. Just before they entered the stand of forest that surrounded the vast watering hole, all of their faces swung up to the sky where vultures gyrated in intersecting loops. Jake felt his stomach collapse, knowing without seeing, and quickly turned away and fought the first impulse to retch; it came not from physical revulsion or even the stench that hit his sinuses, but from a more deep seated emotional trigger.

With spiking dread they made their way through the trees and emerged at the edge of the *bai* and stood side by side in profound devastation and horror at the scene in front of them. There was a lapse of muted shock and then individual sputters and gulps and whimpers, none of them able to articulate a word or thought.

What had two days ago been an epically glorious experience was now one of unimaginable savagery.

Ten elephants lay dead in and beside the pond.

They were huddled together as they had been running to escape the attack of their predators, some felled on their sides, some upright with their feet splayed. Several had yawing holes where their heads had been, hacked flesh still dripping with blood and gore, others had their trunks chopped off. Genitals and tails had been butchered from their bodies and, where heads had remained attached, patches had been cut from their ears. Tusks had been extracted from all. The pond water was the color of old motor oil, viscous with blood and clotted with strings and hunks of bodily matter, thick hordes of flies swirling and buzzing. Overhead, the rank of carrion birds wheeled in ever-lowering circuits.

The five of them stood motionlessly staring until several backed up into the bush and vomited, the ghastly sight and smell and brutality just too much. Jake was battling it, almost gagging on the sourness rising and gripping his throat, stomach muscles wrenching. And then he saw movement on the far side of the huddled masses, heard a faint snorting.

Oh God.

He wiped his mouth with his cravat and stepped slowly along a mudflat, his boots squishing in the silt, circling the carnage until he was standing on the bank. And saw something that would be forever soldered into his brain and heart—a calf nudging the prone, lifeless body of its mother, again and again and again, snuffling noises coming from its trunk in an effort to trumpet. Jake's eyes were stinging, his throat raw. He went to the baby who was so confounded in its confusion and distress that it did not even attempt to flee. Bending down, Jake placed his hand gently on the calf's back. Looked with agonizing pain at the dead cow, on her chest and stomach, legs folded beneath her, then at the baby, eyes uncomprehending. Snuffling and pushing against its mother.

Oh God.

"Come on, baby," he said, trying to guide the animal's head away from the mother's body. The back of his throat was numb and, at the same time, on fire. "Let's get you into the woods. Your friends are in there somewhere."

But the juvenile would not budge from the mother's side, and after trying several more times, Jake reluctantly withdrew.

The others had joined him but were standing well back of the grisly mass. "Jake," Baladur said, stooping to pick something up from the mud.

Jake went over to him and Baladur put a bullet casing in his gloved hand. Rolling it around, Jake studied the etchings on the headstamp, and said, "Son of a bitch. This is the same type of casing we found at the compound. Same make." Fury began to bite into his anguish. He walked back to the carcasses and looked closer, now seeing the bullet holes in their backs, black holes riddling their tough hides. Shot from above…as in from a hovering Atlas Oryx. "Jesus Christ," he spat angrily.

"What is it?" Baladur asked.

Dmello answered for him. "They were shot from a helicopter."

Jake swallowed and looked away, then blew out a breath. "Luther, sorry to ask, but can you take some pictures?"

Baladur and Dmello gravely made their way around the elephants, Baladur holding out his phone to capture the horrific scene, using the zoom to avoid getting any closer than necessary. Several times, he had to pause, collect himself, and resume. Falcone and Niles had stumped to the opposite side and distanced themselves, dropping to the grass beyond the bank, knees drawn up and heads tucked. Once or twice each lurched into the woods, returning with heads averted. When Baladur had taken his last picture, he and Dmello trudged behind Jake to the tree line where Falcone and Niles were seated.

Before heading into the forest, Jake caught a last glimpse of the baby elephant frantically nuzzling its mother, and his hands balled into fists, nostrils flaring.

LESS THAN A HUNDRED yards from the *bai*, the sound of pained moaning came from the other side of a thicket of brush below a stand of terminalia mollis and sausage trees. They thrashed through the vegetation, snapping branches out of their way, and almost stumbled over the body of a man, face-down in the thatch where he had bled out from multiple gunshots perforating his camouflage shirt and pants, large blackened and bloody divots gouged from shoulders to waist. Another man was sprawled a few feet away with similar fatal wounds, a third and fourth several yards in front of them, also dead, one with his head pulped and half gone. A couple of bucket-style hats lay scattered on the ground. Jake noticed an embroidered patch that was visible on one of the men's shirts and leaned over to take a closer look. It bore the insignia of African Parks. They were rangers.

Jake pushed cautiously forward to the source of the moaning and found two more men, also clad in camouflage fatigues, slumped on the ground, their AKs beside them. One man was shot in the thigh, the other in the abdomen. Their shirt sleeves also displayed the parks' insignia. Kneeling to assess both, the man with the thigh wound murmured, "Thanks be to God...he sent you to save us."

"Okay, bud, we've got you." Jake took a quick glimpse around, looking for any movement in the brush. "How long ago?"

"Twenty, maybe thirty minutes..."

"What's your name?"

Face twisted in pain, the man winced, "Clement...Mbiyavanga." He gestured to the man next to him. "Michou Tshibanda. We are park rangers from Garamba." They were both in their early twenties and clearly shaken but trying to maintain a brave front.

Jake had already slipped off his backpack and Baladur dug into it for Jake's aid kit, taking out what he would need. Instructing Baladur to cut both men's clothing away from their wounds, Jake moved to Tshibanda and immediately saw the pink gleam of exposed bowel but, thankfully, not an excessive amount of bleeding. As he checked the man's pulse and looked into his face, gauging the pallor of his skin, he asked, "Were you guys shot by poachers? We just came from"—he grappled for a way to finish the sentence—"the elephants."

Tshibanda grimaced, trying to move, and Jake stopped him, elevating his knees. "Try to be still, I'm going to take care of you. You're going to be okay, Michou. Both of you are going to be okay." He palpated the area around the open wound and examined the bowel for lacerations, the man hissing through his teeth in intense discomfort. Addressing

Baladur, Jake said, "Saline on a sterile dressing, then cover all that with plastic…I've got some sheets in my bag."

Changing gloves, Jake returned his attention to Mbiyavanga, taking a distal pulse and checking the back of the man's thigh. Feeling another large wound, he knew the bullet had gone all the way through, which was usually the better scenario. As he prodded, he determined that the arteries had been missed but felt a nick on the femur. Applying pressure, he began stuffing QuikClot gauze into the cavity until it was completely packed, watched for seeping blood and, after keeping his fingers in place for a few minutes, wrapped the thigh with a pressure bandage. He rechecked Mbiyavanga's distal pulse, took off the boot from that foot and asked him to wiggle his toes.

Managing a smile as he was able to respond satisfactorily to Jake's instruction, Mbiyavanga said, "I guess I will live. How about Michou?"

"He will live, too," Jake assured him.

"The others?"

Jake shook his head. "Sorry, my man. We saw four dead."

Clement Mbiyavanga hung his head, a hand on his forehead. "We were on a patrol…and heard the poachers and their machetes, chopping off the ivory. We went after them, but they shot at us from the trees…" His voice trailed off, weakness settling in.

"Is anybody coming for you?" Jake asked him.

"I do not think so. Our radios are not working. The tower…"

Snapping off his nitrile gloves, slick with blood, Jake said, "Okay, well, you both *are* going to be fine. But we do need to get you more extensive medical care. Our plane is actually not far from here, so we'll evac you."

"Garamba base in Nagero," Mbiyavanga said, and closed his eyes.

While tending to the two men, Jake had sent Falcone and Niles to find timber from which to fashion stretchers. With Dmello following to cover them, they found bamboo stalks and tied their hammocks to make the carriers. When the men were loaded up, Jake noted the GPS coordinates so the deceased rangers could be located, and led the way to the plane, sweeping his rifle along both sides of the path as they went.

When they got to the plane, Jake administered morphine and got IVs going in both men, pumping up the pressure bags to quickly infuse the saline while he drew up ceftriaxone and metronidazole antibiotics. Dmello completed his pre-flight and entered the data for Nagero into his Garmin avionics, taking off into a sky mottled with clouds tinged with the brass of a descendant sun. As the Cessna leveled out on its course, Jake continued his care of the wounded rangers, listening to them mumble semi-coherently about the ambush under the cottony drift of the opioid easing their pain. Falcone and Niles and Baladur were staring straight ahead in their seats, none of them looking down until they were well past the *bai*.

THE NAGERO AIRFIELD, LIKE most in the region, is a single strip of dirt scraped through grass, in this case with a small cement outbuilding and A-framed open hangars attached on either side housing two small planes. Dmello had radioed ahead, and when their Cessna paralleled the Dungu River and scooted to a stop toward the end of the three-thousand-foot swath, a dark green Land Rover Defender with an African Parks logo painted on the sides was waiting. Dmello turned the Cessna and taxied until it was adjacent to the outbuilding, the Defender rolling to meet it. A tall, lanky man got out of the passenger seat and marched over to the plane. He was dressed in pressed khakis and a ball cap, arms crossed as he waited for the cargo door to open.

Falcone and Niles hopped out first, carefully guiding their makeshift stretchers, Jake and Baladur following at the ends, holding the IVs. A pair of medics from the Defender met them with gurneys and assisted with the transfers.

The man in khakis stepped up to Jake and extended a hand, keeping the other tucked beneath an armpit. He was mustached with thin, light brown hair and wore a solemn expression. "David Hannaford, general manager for the park," he said stiffly, his accent South African. "How're our boys?"

Wiping perspiration from his brow, Jake said, "They're stable, but honestly, they need a trauma hospital. Can you get them to one?"

"Yes, of course." Hannaford strode to the Defender and spoke to the driver. A moment later, the vehicle sped off down a dirt road that snaked behind the field's outbuilding. When he returned to Jake, he said,

"Thank you all for everything you've done. We are certainly in your debt."

"Glad we were there," Jake replied. He gave Hannaford a piece of paper with the GPS coordinates and was about to start a dialogue about the *bai* massacre when the general manager spoke up.

"We've had a terrible streak of poaching incidents just lately. Over the years, the bad actors have been from a variety of groups…the ethnic militias, the SPLA, LRA, Janjaweed…some coming from a thousand kilometers or more. But the past several months…" He looked off in the distance, his face clouding with the thoughts of a heavily burdened administrator. "Shooting from a helicopter, for God's sake."

"So you knew about that?" Jake asked, his eyes widening with focus.

"We'd received a report, which is why a team was out there. It's not the first time."

"Do you know of a mining operation in the north, Kaseme Mines?"

Hannaford scratched his chin, looking at Jake inscrutably. "I know of it, sure. Why?"

Jake started to elaborate, thought better of it, and said, "Your guys should be fine. Just get them to that hospital."

THEY TOOK A LITTLE time to clean up the plane, and then Dmello got them back in the air, the forests and savannas below coated in the golden hues of sunset. When he had reached a smooth cruising level and speed, Dmello asked Jake, "Where are we going?"

Slouched in his seat, sipping from a bottle of water and gazing absently out his window, Jake said, "I don't know. Just…fly west for now."

His mind had been wound as tight and tangled as a ball of rubber bands ever since they'd left the *bai,* and now that it was behind them and all was becalmed in the weightless cushion of flight, the tension should have started to lessen. Instead, he was unsettled, the synapses and neurons in his brain snapping, the uneasy feeling in his gut stirring again. Something just beneath the surface, just out of reach, that his mind kept dredging. It was like the splinter you never saw but could feel, so you just kept digging and picking, and when you gave up for a while you still felt it. There was something there, and he just couldn't pull it to the surface.

Jake rubbed his eyes wearily and looked out, heat lightning laced within the clouds as the sky's blues turned to mauves. Specks of rain streaked the windows, the steady hum of the Cessna's engine almost soothing. Baladur and Dmello were in subdued conversation in the cockpit, Falcone and Niles nearly in a stupor in the seats behind him. He reached for his Toughbook laptop, opened it and booted up. Checking his email, he found a reply from Callie, and read her jubilant reaction to the pictures he'd sent. And felt a stud of despair slam into his chest. He pressed his lips together and glanced away from the screen, his eyes moistening. He watched as the lightning rippled outside his window, heard the muted thunder, and the horrific images of the slaughtered elephants replayed in his head, the excruciating sight of the baby trying to rouse its mother from death. The tears came, his heart shuddering like rains over the Serengeti, a deep sense of desolation taking hold.

When he'd harnessed his emotions some minutes later, he exited Gmail and looked for the folder with all his satellite images, wanting to review those of the mining territory, and noticed a folder that he had not previously opened. It was the one sent from Cameron McNamara early on along with the information about the security team the Keoghs had employed. He scanned the documents inside, finding one titled SEC-CONBIDS. Curious, he clicked on it and saw a list of security contractors in consideration by them at the time, most of whom he was familiar with. There were notes under each, the one they'd chosen, Machai, bolded. Close to the bottom of the document, his eyes landed on a name that jolted him upright in his seat, pulse pounding in his head.

He dug his sat phone from the pocket of his cargo pants and saw that he'd received an SMS message. He remembered feeling the phone vibrate sometime during their evac of the rangers, but in the flurry of critical action, he had forgotten about it. He navigated to the text and read it. Kipnis, sharing the name of the security contractors for Kaseme. The elusive missing pieces materialized, tumblers shifted and interlocked.

"Fuck me," Jake muttered, and felt his blood pressure catapult. Felt an old, never-forgotten time flare from past to present.

"Kean," Jake said into his headset.

"Yes, boss?"

"Head north."

"Where are we going?"

"South Sudan."

Seeing the name in that document—the same one in the text from Kipnis—had just shot his mission into a whole other realm. One that had flipped his nuclear switch.

PART THREE

THE SHADOW WITH THE SPEAR

40

PADDY'S BAR WAS STARTING to fill up with the usual conflux of locals and a ragtag of expats and mercenaries and hustlers that included diamond dealers and *kolonkos*, women of the night trade. Located on the Aberdeen Peninsula along the shoreline between Pirate and Cockle bays, the watering hole had been one of few establishments of its kind to remain open in Freetown for the duration of the Sierra Leone civil war. Owned by a lanky Brit by the name of Paddy Warren, a balding and bespectacled expatriate of thirty-plus years, the dilapidated concrete block with white paint and blue trim faded by sea air and the sandblasting of war machinery clanking past or rumbling overhead wasn't much to look at on the outside or inside. WELCOME TO PADDY'S was scrolled in ragged cursive across the roofline, a graphic mural for Star beer on the front. Behind the slab structure was a large veranda with an exposed square-beam ceiling, a rectangular bamboo bar in the center, and plain wooden tables and plastic chairs. But in the late night and wee morning hours, the big open-air space would crowd with bodies moving in hedonistic liberation to a deejay's offerings and the not-so-subtle seduction of working women on the prowl for prospective marks.

As was the case on this particular night, which found Jake and Nash Remington—much younger versions—and a very much alive Haskell Delaney seated on stools at the bar of their frequent haunt, unwinding from a day of post-war soldiering. It had been several years since they'd all been there in the actual throes of battle when Freetown fell to politician and warlord Charles Taylor's Revolution United Front rebels. Brought in as part of the U.S.'s minimalist footprint to aid the Sierra Leone military in maintaining control of their country, Jake had managed a contract with the mandate of providing advice and military support. What transpired in the time he'd been on the ground and in the air had been nothing short of insane and utterly harrowing, fraught with the most gruesome of atrocities, violent armed clashes, death-defying confrontations, and blatant acts of betrayal. And miraculously, they had managed to get out of the country without the RUF rebel forces being able to cash in on the million-dollar bounty Taylor had pledged for the downing of their choppers or the fifty thousand per operator's head.

The war had eventually ended years later with the defeat of Taylor's forces under a renewed UN decree and Guinean air support of the ongoing British operations. It had come to be known as the Diamond War because a driving motivation for Charles Taylor's crusade was the massive wealth from the country's diamond mines. During their time spent in military support, Jake and his contingent were strictly warned to steer clear of anything even remotely associated with diamonds, so it struck him with great irony when he was offered a contract these years later to return to a Sierra Leone in peacetime to provide security for a magnate who was beginning to transition from the blood diamond trade to one that was conflict-free. They were now about to be, literally, up to their armpits in diamonds.

Remington sank a shot of whiskey and followed it with a gulp of beer. Without looking at Jake, he asked, "So why the hell are we here again?"

Jake took a swallow of his gin and tonic and said, "Yeah, yeah, I know. I said I'd never come back."

"And yet here we are."

"I guess I'm a sucker for giving back," he said, referring to the humanitarian part of their presence, for which he'd asked that the magnate sponsor the establishment of a medical clinic.

"You're a sucker all right," Delaney put in, ogling the women circling around them like a swarm of sharks.

"Well, the money's not bad," Remington conceded, adding lasciviously, "and neither is the pussy."

Jake cocked his head back and laughed robustly, but he, too, was keeping an interested eye on the local hospitality, in which he had partaken quite abundantly during his former days here. A tall and slender beauty was hovering, her long hair in tightly knotted ropes, cocoa-colored skin luminous in the mix of dim bar lighting and the moon's glow filtering in from the outside. She wore a black tube top plumped with breasts the size of navel oranges and a hip-hugging hot pink skirt that exposed her smooth stomach and stopped just below her pubis. She slid in next to him and brushed up against his thigh. He gave her a carnal grin and, in a low voice, said, "Find me in a little while."

She ran a finger along his arm and licked her glistening top lip in response, gliding away.

Remington and Delaney waited until she had moved off and leaned into each other, cackling. "You ol' stud daddy," Remington said.

Jake continued to grin, drained his drink and signaled for a replacement. The bartender brought another round and the trio turned on their stools to observe the night's crowd. Jake and Remington, with their masculine virility, thick, wavy locks and groomed beards drew copious attention; Delaney, sporting a buzz of hair on his egg-shaped head, was arguably even more of a magnet with his bold personality and shamelessly flirtatious conduct, gold chain looped around his neck and a permanent full-toothed smile on his face. But while the ladies and a fair amount of men were taking keen notice of them, another character had caught their eye.

A young man their age with brown hair cut Caesar-style and a heavy growth of facial whiskers, wearing jeans and a tan t-shirt, was swilling a beer and swaggering amidst a local group of militant types. His jeans were tight enough to show the bulge of his genitalia, chest and arms swelling in steroidal bulk against the shirt. He was pointing a finger into the shoulder of one of them, his stance and demeanor provocative.

Remington looked away with disgust. "How did that shitbag get on this gig?"

Jake shook his head woefully. "A favor for a friend."

"Yeah, well, that friend has some serious judgment issues." Watching the guy rock back on his heels as he bragged about his skill set and accomplishments, Remington commented, "What a fucking tool. He needs to keep his yap shut or it's going to get us all in trouble."

Jake sloshed the gin and ice in his glass, took a sip, and set it on the bar. He stood and walked over to the hotshot, placing a hand on his arm. A tattoo of a snake curled around an AK-type rifle was inked on the man's bicep. He flinched and pivoted, the grip on his beer bottle tightening, free hand reflexively clenching. When he recognized Jake, his defensive posture slackened, but only slightly.

"We don't advertise our profile, bud," Jake said evenly, but his expression was dark with warning.

That got a pompous sneer, but the man appeared to take his admonition, strolling to the bar for another beer, muttering something under his breath.

Delaney sidled up to the glowering man. "Better show some respect. He's your superior and your boss."

Jake took his seat next to Remington. "Yeah, he's a piece of work. We'll have to keep an eye on him."

The deejay's selections had begun to tip more toward the club beat, spinning American pop and hip hop and local favorites, at the moment a throwback mix of Sierra Leonean Steady Bongo. The three of them talked about the current op but mostly reminisced over their previous wartime experiences in-country, by an unspoken mutual accord avoiding those steeped in the horrors of dismemberment and rape and murder and child abuse that was so far off the scale it defied a category. After a while, Jake cast a glance across the jam of dancing bodies and caught sight of the woman who had approached him earlier. Felt his libido stir. Making his way to her, moving to the beat, he stepped close to her ear to be heard through the noise level of the music and asked, "What's your name, missy?"

"Isata. Can we dance?"

And so they did, until sometime later when Jake noticed for the first time that his dubitable man was no longer in view. He'd been having a good time with Isata, which included a few more drinks, but he had been keeping tabs on the guy who seemed to be quickly defining himself as an outcast with the members of Jake's team. Checking his watch and noting the late hour, Jake told the woman they'd be leaving momentarily and went to the bar. Remington and Delaney, also paired off with some *kolonkos*, were preparing to depart, fishing in their pockets for *leone* notes.

Jake waved them off, saying, "I've got it, gents." As the bartender took his money, he asked, "Do you know what happened to the American guy who was over there?"

"No, was he with you?"

"Um, yeah…"

"He did not pay his bill," he bartender said curtly.

"Okay, just add it to mine."

On his way out of Paddy's, Jake stopped by a table where the rest of his team were seated. "Hey, do any of you know what happened to—"

"The douchbag?" one of them smirked. "Oh, he went with some of the local boys to lose his shirt at the casino."

That revelation lodged renewed concern and Jake debated making a trip down the road toward the end of the peninsula to the hotel casino where, during the war, they had worked the women to gather intel on the rebels they were servicing. There might be nothing more to it than an appetite for gambling, but having one of his guys—and an unproven one at that—gallivanting with locals of unknown ethos and, possibly, machinations, was troublesome. Isata was tugging at his arm.

He turned back to her and smiled. They stepped into the night, and the scent of her perfume blurred with his light buzz erased the nibble of his misgivings, the sound of waves crashing against the rocks receding as they crossed the road and headed for her place on the other side.

SAMURA ENTERPRISES, THE COMPANY that had contracted Jake, was headquartered south of the Aberdeen Peninsula on the mainland, in a newly constructed complex that included multilevel office suites, a conference center, accommodations, and a canteen. When Jake convened his team in the lobby of their building the next morning, he did not see all of his guys. While he was conducting his briefing for the day, he sent Delaney off to round up those that were missing. Ten minutes later, Delaney returned with all but one.

"Sorry asshole says he's not gonna make it today," Delaney said disdainfully.

Jake looked at him over the rim of his coffee cup, and set it down.

"What?"

"Hungover as hell and says it's something he ate or some shit."

"Forget him," Jake snapped. "Probably just as well. Let's roll."

They collected their gear and piled into two Toyota LandCruisers that were waiting in front of their building, drivers heading north along Wilkinson Road into Murraytown, on the inland side of the Aberdeen estuary. It was here, on a plot of land secured by Samura, that the medical clinic had been set up in the form of several tents, each designated for different exigencies; one being for amputees, another for general medical needs, and a third for women and children. The sun was barely up when their freshly washed and waxed white SUVs pulled into the lot, but already the lines in front of each registration table extended well outside the lot perimeter, nearly every one of the men, women, and children missing one or more limbs from the machete-wielding RUF rebels that had shredded their country and their lives.

Not all of Jake's team were medically trained, but he kept everyone busy screening. Since they'd been chosen based on previous service in Sierra Leone, they had a working knowledge of Krio, the English-based creole *lingua franca*. Asking "What hurts?" would get a response of, *"Ah get pain na me... an."* Or *bak, bele, ed*...followed by, *"Aw fo du?"* What can you do about it? Which, in the case of the amputees, might not be much this day, but at Jake's request, Samura had also provided a prosthesis team to do initial assessments and take measurements with follow-ups for fittings. On his breaks, Jake watched as the clinicians delicately handled the stubbed limbs, many crudely misshapen and poorly healed. Phantom pain was a common source of additional suffrage and a cruel remnant of the mutilations inflicted. For this, medical pain management was configured, but they also tried psychological mirror therapy, which was fascinating to witness; a mirror was set up in the place of the missing limb in an effort to reimagine it by visualizing the reflection of the opposite one. The results were mixed, with some amputees confused or upset and others coming away with a new method of coping. But Jake wondered: where were they going to get their own mirrors to do it for themselves? As to the rest, general physicals were conducted, vaccinations and medications given. By midday, hundreds had been seen, and it was time to cede their involvement to the medical staff volunteers.

They were driven over the bridge, back to the peninsula and on to the helipad by the Mammy Yoko hotel, an aging white-walled building that had been commandeered by the UN during the war. Memories of the innumerable and, more often than not, perilous VIP and expat evacuations Jake had run from that helipad were still vivid in his mind. In fact, seeing the shelled out remains of the city stuck in a time-lock years later was haunting and not something he would have been doing had he not needed the job and the money. Still, he was glad for the opportunity to help these people, even on a small scale, and to now play a part in the process of making what had been the cause of so much destruction and suffering into a legitimate enterprise.

A Mil Mi-17 helicopter, just like the one Jake had flown in here before, sat on the pad. They were real warhorses of the skies and might have seemed extreme for their seven-man team, but also ideally suited for high and hot flight.

Haskell Delaney sprang from his seat next to Jake in the LandCruiser and sprinted for the bird, arms outspread, a look of unfettered infatuation beaming from his face. Painfully off-key, he sang, *"Time for me to flyyyyy...oh, I've got to set myself freeeee..."*

Remington groaned, "Jesus God."

Jake grinned at his friend's quirky exuberance and, when he caught up to Delaney, thumped him on the back. "All right, big man, giddy up."

AN HOUR'S FLYING TIME, following the road from Freetown into the eastern countryside, took them over wooded plateaus and rolling hills to the higher elevations of the Kono region where they landed at the Samura operations base just outside Kenema. During the flight, Jake inspected the route through binoculars, and by the time they arrived he had a good idea of where the potential trouble spots were. They would be taking a small convoy back to Freetown in a few days, but their first order of business was training the newly employed team made up of locals with police or military experience who would be providing the site and overland security going forward.

The Samura mining operation had existed prior to the war in a lawless vacuum and changed hands several times, but was now owned under the holdings of Ofek Tzur, a wealthy gem magnate in Tel Aviv. With the post-war establishment of the Kimberley Process Certification, in which participating countries are required to abide by the strict transparency provisions to authenticate conflict-free diamonds, Tzur had set forth a blueprint to bring Samura into compliance, a large part involving secure transport from the mines to the Government Diamond and Gold Office in Freetown where valuations and certifications would be done. From there, the diamond lots would be taken to Samura's holding facility for preparation to export.

As Jake's team unloaded gear and weapons from the helicopter, he strode over to greet the South African who was Samura's COO, Julius Sono. Though he'd never met Sono before, he knew him by background and reputation, which was somewhat controversial. Sono had been part of another mercenary group that served in Freetown and many other African conflicts, and his position with Samura was rumored to be one of the perks earned from his protection of the Kenema mines. Tall, broad-shouldered, and fit, though a little soft through the middle, his hair was cropped short and his face smooth-shaven. He wore creased tan slacks and a white collared shirt, the hand he extended sporting a large gold signet ring, a diamond-studded Audemars Piguet watch on his wrist that was almost feminine in its embellishment.

When Jake and his team had first arrived in Freetown for this contract and settled into the facilities at Samura's city headquarters, he'd been told that Sono was away on business and would join him at the mining site. Meeting the man now, within the first few minutes of their conversation it was clear Julius Sono had more or less fully detached himself from trench-level activity. A site manager was promptly introduced, Sono withdrew, and the group was taken on an orientation tour of the operations, concluding in a field that had been outfitted with tented barracks and a training ground.

Over the next week, the local recruits were evaluated for fitness, put through drills, and weapon trained. Jake passed the ones with potential and motivation and let the site manager know he was ready to deploy their final test, which happened to be an actual transport. The day prior, they had done a short dry-run to become familiar with the vehicles and protocols for various situations they might encounter. So far, everything was going smoothly and according to the plan and schedule Jake had submitted to Samura at the outset. If the transport was completed without incident—and he had no reason to think otherwise—the recruits would return to the mining operations and be formally hired.

On that final morning, Jake's team packed up their gear, the lots of diamonds were loaded, and the convoy set off for Freetown.

THE THREE BLACK LANDCRUISERS—a lead vehicle, the carrier, and trail vehicle—looked, for the most part, like any of the variations found traveling the roads throughout the country. But these Toyota 4x4s were actually 78 series troop carriers and armored to the teeth, with multilayered ballistic glass, reinforced suspensions, blast protection, and run-flat tires. Jake had divided his team and the recruits between the three vehicles, his in front. The route he'd mapped would take them along the Bo-Kenema highway into the southern province, then skirting north of Bo, which was the second largest city and a chokepoint to be avoided, and west on the Yonibana-Masiaka highway into Freetown. Not quite two hundred miles, he calculated the trip would take about six hours, much of the roads paved and in decent condition due to improvements made after the war; worst-case, they would arrive no later than mid-afternoon, make the drop, send the recruits on their merry way back to Kenema, have some dinner and drinks, and fly out of Sierra Leone the next morning.

They made good time, only hitting light traffic here and there as they passed through small and medium-size towns strung in between long spans of grass and trees or sprawls of rice fields and coffee and oil palm plantations. A few miles outside the town of Masiaka and roughly forty miles from Freetown, in a more heavily vegetated stretch where the road's surface was intermittently stripped for construction, they came up on a blockade. A thick log had been laid across wooden sawhorses, a detour sign in the middle with an arrow pointing to an obscured secondary road. On the other side of the barricade was an abandoned front-end loader, not unlike some they'd seen parked or moving along the construction zones. But this one seemed oddly out of place, no mounds of dirt or debris, no chasms in the road, nothing to indicate any kind of work in process. Jake was immediately suspicious and got out of his vehicle to investigate.

Speaking into his two-way radio, he said, "Let's check this out before we go any further. Everybody stay alert."

With Delaney covering him from behind and Remington standing beside the third LandCruiser, Jake walked cautiously around the curve to the adjoining road, clutching his AK-47 as he raised binoculars to look ahead. Seeing nothing but dirt road with trees on one side and tall grass on the other, he surveilled for several minutes and returned to his vehicle.

"What do you think?" Delaney asked him.

"I don't like it, but we need to keep moving."

They climbed back into their respective LandCruisers and the convoy turned off down the side road. A few minutes later, Jake thought he heard the throaty eruption and rattle of a heavy diesel engine coming from the highway, but then the noise stopped almost as soon as it had started and he wondered if he'd imagined it. The machine being moved? Or, maybe, it was a big truck backing away from the road block, not wanting to take the detour. They drove on.

Trees and brush and tall grass, nothing more. The LandCruiser's tires crunched over the dirt and grit, small rocks popping against the undercarriage.

And then, in the distance, a woman and two children appeared in the roadway, the woman frantically waving her arms. She was a diminutive peasant, dressed in tatters, the kids in wear-faded tees and shorts. As they got closer, Jake could see that the children were wailing. He told his recruit driver to slow down but not stop. All of his cautionary sensors were pulsing as he reassessed the detour and now the civilians in the road and instantly concluded they were heading right into an ambush.

Before he could react, his assumption bore out.

A mass of armed men, perhaps as many as twenty, poured from within the tall grass and onto the road, quickly surrounding their convoy. Bandanas were tied over the men's faces, their weapons aimed, including at least one Soviet-made RPG-7 fitted with a HEAT warhead—which could penetrate armor. At a glance, Jake saw that they were both outnumbered and outgunned. Into his radio, he said, "Nobody get out and be ready to roll hot. Wait for my command."

But the ambushing militia had another trick and played it brazenly, one of the men grabbing the woman and pushing the muzzle of his AK into her neck. She screamed. The children screamed.

"Stay put!" Jake ordered his team.

For several moments, nothing happened. The armed men held their positions, weapons unmoving. Jake was watching for an opening that could come and go in a fraction of a second. Delaney and Remington and the rest of his group sat tight and waited for Jake's next command.

There was no opening. The man with the AK on the woman pulled the trigger and she exploded like a smashed watermelon right in front of them, a spray of red-and-pink mist filling the air. The children let out blood-curdling shrieks and ran, but they were snatched up by two other men who then held them at gunpoint.

Behind Jake's vehicle, doors flew open and recruits jumped out, arms outstretched in surrender. "Goddammit, no!" Jake yelled, but it was over and he knew it. There was no way he was going to stand by and let two innocent children be executed.

Slowly, he opened his door and stepped from the LandCruiser, arms tense at his sides, AK clutched in his left hand, pointed down. He was ready to swing it up, bring his right hand to the trigger, and fire at one or both of the men with the children. Hit them direct and fast, one-two. But then a barrage of return fire would annihilate them all. And there was the problem of that RPG-7, which they might intend to use in any event.

"What do you want?" he demanded, trying and not succeeding in keeping hostility out of his face.

One of the men moved forward, and through the fabric of his bandana said, "You know what we want. Open the back of the truck with the diamonds. Open it now!" He came closer to Jake, his rifle raised and pointing to the middle LandCruiser. The man's accent and skin tone pegged him as a local.

Jake nodded to Delaney, who unlocked and popped open the double doors at the rear of the carrier he'd been riding in. When he did, he saw that two of the recruits had obeyed Jake's order and remained inside the vehicle, cowering in their seats. Delaney stood in front of the cargo bay to give them cover, hoping they would exit but, paralyzed by fear, they did not move. One of the bandits shoved Delaney aside and began removing and handing off the cases of diamonds, which were carried back through the grass.

Jake was seething with rage but also filled with dread over what appeared to be coming next, his mind racing with empty options. His eyes landed on the men holding the children captive. "You got what you came for," he said grittily. "Let those children go." When neither responded, he added, "Only cowards kill children."

The apparent leader gave a nod, and the two men released the children, two small boys under the age of six. They ran, terrified, into the brush.

Jake let out a breath, thinking maybe they would get out of this alive. The men surrounding them slowly began to peel away, walking backwards, their weapons still aimed. But Jake had also been watching the man with the rocket-propelled grenade launcher, and he had not retreated. Keeping his voice down, he asked Delaney, "Are there any guys still in the vehicles?"

Instantly, Delaney knew why he'd asked, and screamed to the two recruits, "Get out of the truck! Get out of the fucking truck!"

The RPG bucked on the shoulder of the shooter, there was a whisk, a cloud of smoke, and a boom, the cone-shaped warhead searing into the middle carrier vehicle. On impact, the LandCruiser lifted off the ground and imploded, the frame and glass remaining intact as it was designed to do, but fire consumed the interior, flames and black smoke billowing through the open doors.

There was no point in even attempting a rescue of the two recruits; they had been pretty much instantly incinerated.

When all of the armed men had dissolved into the grass, Jake stood motionless and speechless for several moments, processing what had happened. Distantly, he heard the start-up of engines, then the receding sound as the vehicles drove away with the unknown militants and the Samura diamonds.

IN THE AFTERMATH, AS Jake agonized over what, if anything, he could have done differently, they sent the recruits—including what remained of the two who perished—back to Kenema in the other two LandCruisers. Jake called Julius Sono and told him what had happened and, much to his surprise, the COO responded with an almost indifferent surety, as if it was a component factored into the cost of doing business. Sono even arranged for someone from Samura's Freetown headquarters to come for them. Undoubtedly, Samura was amply insured for such a considerable loss, but for Jake it was a loss he could not compensate on either a personal or professional level.

As the team shuffled listlessly into their accommodations at the Samura administrative complex that evening, Jake hung back in the lobby, gazing through the tinted floor-to-ceiling glass of the building, looking out at a city where he'd witnessed all those horrific things during the war—things he still relived in nightmares—only to see it fall to the rebels before having to bail out. And now, what was intended to be a financially lucrative and, he'd hoped, psychologically rehabilitative venture, had become a mortifying disaster he'd never live down. Nor should he. For the rest of his days, he would see that poor woman being shot, those now motherless children screaming and running for their lives, those two guys trusting his leadership being blown up. On the way back to Freetown, numb as he was, he had been rewinding and replaying everything that had happened and wondering how, why, and who. Who, because that ambush had obviously been planned and executed with precision timing. The militants had the right numbers, the weapons, knew the tactics that would get the job done. This was no generic guerilla gang. This had the earmarks of a military operative...or at least one who had access to intel.

Remington came up beside him and placed an arm on his shoulder. "You did everything I would have done."

"My hesitation got that woman killed," Jake said flatly.

"No. They were going to kill her no matter what you did."

"Those two guys, if I hadn't told them to stay—"

"Don't do that, brother. None of us knew what was going to happen. You just did what your gut told you."

"My goddamn gut should have known better," Jake said bitterly. He turned away from the windows and looked into space, a question twisting in his mind. "There's something that's been bothering me. The way it happened, that it happened at all, there had to be somebody…"

Delaney entered the lobby. "Oh yeah, there was somebody all right." He opened the palm of his hand and showed them a piece of notebook paper that had been balled up, scribbled on and apparently discarded. On it was a pencil-drawn route with mile designations—their route to and from the Samura mine site.

Jake stared at the crumpled piece of paper. "Where did you find that?"

Delaney's eyes lifted upward toward the lobby's high ceiling but seemed to be looking through it to the floors above. "Who was the only one of us not there?"

ARIS XAVIER OR, AS he preferred to be called, X.

When Jake and Remington had accompanied Delaney up to their floor and gone into Xavier's quarters, all of his gear had been cleared out. The room was disheveled, bed unmade, towels bunched about the bath vanity and tossed on the floor. The trashcan by the nightstand had been emptied, but the balled up piece of paper had rolled into a corner and was missed in haste, leaving the incriminating breadcrumb for Delaney to find.

And now, all these years later, Jake was staring at the name on the screens of his Toughbook laptop and Iridium sat phone. Aris Xavier, Spear-X International. His chest cavity tightened, his mind spiraling in furious incredulity. On his phone, he scrolled to the number for Cyrus Keogh, tapped, and waited for the call to connect.

"Talk to me about the security contractors you considered, your screening and bid process."

Keogh began to go through it, and when he got to the final part of his selection, mentioned Spear-X. Jake asked him to describe the entire transaction from start to finish with an emphasis on how the final interaction had transpired. Keogh imparted that there had been a few questionable things in the profile and they'd fallen short in some areas. When Jake inquired how the rejection had been handled, Keogh paused, as if seeing something insignificant in a strange new light. "Actually," he told Jake, "that bloke was quite pissed off and stormed out of the office.

He said some bizarre things as he left, but I don't quite recall what. Is there something—"

"Not right now. We'll talk more later. Just sit tight."

Jake disconnected and set the phone and laptop aside, gazing sightlessly through his darkened plane window, thoughts churning. Not long after the disastrous incident with Samura, he'd been livid to learn that Xavier had landed a new contract with them to run their security team. Jake managed to stave off his inclination to call Julius Sono, which took some mettle, especially with the hit his own reputation had taken as a result of their blown op. Ultimately, it didn't matter; Xavier's erratic temperament and glaring incompetence got him quickly ousted, starting a succession of career failures that were disseminated throughout the military community, making him a pariah within the ranks. Even so, Xavier proved to have a wily way of manipulating his Special Forces brethren and background, often using flagrant creative license or outright deception to reinvent himself for subsequent opportunities. But those who dared to deceive among the honorable had a tendency to eventually run head-first into the karma buzz saw, and a few years ago Xavier had done just that. Schmoozing his way into one of the top global security outfits active in Iraq and Afghanistan, he completed two cycles before the building blocks of his façade came crashing down when he was caught trafficking arms from stockpiles his unit was tasked with securing—the discovery coming to light during an investigation into the killings of civilians, in which weapons from the American warehouse were recovered. The incident boiled over into a scandal that defaced and dismantled the security company, Xavier summarily disgraced in the backlash and forced into the bowels of operational obscurity.

Until now. He had stealthily reemerged in yet another rebranding, this time at the helm of his own company, the one contracted by Kaseme Mines. And, he had been passed over by Cyrus Keogh for what would have been the security contract of his, or any other contractor's, lifetime.

Jake's reflection shifted to the nexus of events that had unspooled since he'd arrived in Africa, following the destruction of the Keoghs' compound: the surveillance of the couple in Kinshasa; the downing of the Keoghs' helicopter that Falcone and Niles were thought to be on; the sighting of Antoine in Nakalé, who Jake speculated was an "inside man" and who had later lured the Keoghs from the village to a remote location where they were held captive; the slaying of the Keoghs' security detail and, not long afterward, that of Antoine; the man dogging them at the refugee camp who was not a local and whose manner suggested a military background or training.

And then there were the events that occurred in the periphery: the armed assault on their campsite, the discovery of the ivory cache, the elephant massacre. On the surface, these events, which might also include the confrontation with militia at their plane, were unrelated, circumstantial. But there was one thing, when factored in, that potentially connected it all—the bullet casings found at the Keoghs' compound, the same ones found at the *bai* where the elephants had been shot from overhead, possibly from the helicopter he'd heard two nights prior. Again, theoretically, a random detail…except most poachers did not have access to a helicopter. The mining site wasn't far from the *bai* and had an LZ, where a helicopter landed and departed while they were there. A truckload of bushmeat had passed them on the road to the mines; maybe another inapplicable bit, but the meat had been fresh.

Finally, there was the one irrefutable piece, and it was a big one—the Keoghs' people they'd rescued from the mining site. By their telling, they had been abducted as they fled the attack on the Keoghs' compound, driven to the mines, held captive, and forced into labor. According to the intel Jake had just received from Kipnis, Xavier's company, Spear-X, had the security contract for Kaseme Mines. The gold skimming that appeared to be going on there, the slave labor, the sexual abuse, even the mass killing of the miners whose remains they'd come across in the field, all X's kind of fuckery. Was Xavier the man Jake had observed at the mine site's entrance and later, boarding the helicopter? The Atlas Oryx bird that could very well have been the one shooting down the elephants?

If Aris Xavier was behind the assault and destruction of the Keoghs' compound and the abduction of their people, Jake had been right about the Keoghs being targeted, and now he knew who was after them: a despicable man with no moral compass who would have no compunction whatsoever about harming or killing innocent people or animals. He'd done a lot of it before.

* * * * *

DMELLO'S VOICE CAME OVER Jake's headset, informing him that they were approaching the South Sudanese border. They had cleared the front of precipitation and the sky had lightened, but not by much, the sun having set an hour or so ago.

"Is there a strip close to the Congo side of the border?" Jake asked.

"Yes," Dmello replied. "Just ahead."

"Okay, let's put down there."

They found a lightly wooded spot near the airstrip and set up camp, gathering around the fire to eat and hydrate before turning in for the night. Jake had brought his Toughbook, hoping for new intel from Kipnis to help narrow down their search grid for the rebel camp. He was fairly certain it would not be far from the Kaseme mining site, but the disruption they'd caused might have put them on the run. The mind-blowing and deeply disturbing revelation about X had curtailed his appetite, but he assembled his MRE and drank the coffee while he waited for the pizza and cobbler to heat up. Falcone and Niles were well ahead of him, gobbling the rectangles of dough smeared with sauce and speckled with cheese and pepperoni.

Talking through packed cheeks, Falcone said, "It's not a slice at Joe's in the Village, but damn if it doesn't taste like heaven right now."

"The biscuit is even better, mate," Niles chirped, referring to the oatmeal cookie. "It's got cinnamon in it!"

Baladur came over and sat beside Jake. "Not hungry?" he asked, and eyed the screen of the open laptop where Jake was scrolling through his Gmail.

"Nah," Jake said absently and closed the Toughbook. "I'm just thinking about our next moves." And, in that moment, he realized the objective dictating his strategies was about to edge into mission creep, because now there was something—someone—of his own past intertwined like a dark and invasive malignancy, and he could never be unbiased when it came to Aris Xavier. Looking at the others, he said, "There's something I need to tell you."

For the next several minutes they listened as Jake shared his epiphany, providing a synopsis of his backstory with X. When he had concluded, all eyes were fixed on him with budding astonishment but lagging perception.

Falcone asked, "So you think this Xavier guy is behind everything...for what? Revenge against the Keoghs for not getting the security contract?"

"In part," Jake replied. "But I think it's more than that. If you look at the big picture...what has he accomplished with every incident? Wiping out their compound, taking their people, downing their helicopter, killing their security detail."

There were blank looks all around, no one else making the connection Jake had.

"He's made the security company they hired look grossly inadequate, like they can't handle the job."

"Oh, I get it, mate," Niles said. "So he can have another go at them for the contract."

"Exactly." Jake's expression hardened. "If you go even further into each incident that's occurred since the first with the compound, he's been isolating the Keoghs to make them even more vulnerable. I'm more convinced than ever that he ordered the helicopter to be shot down, not to take *them* out, but to take *you two* out. Because he has nothing to gain by killing the Keoghs."

Falcone and Niles blinked, staring at him speechlessly.

Jake went on, "I think Antoine was probably complicit—and there may have been others—but he was apparently tasked with luring the Keoghs away which, again, cast a bad light on the security detail and got them killed."

"If Antoine was working for X, why did he get killed?" Falcone asked.

"Well, he'd served his purpose, but he also might have started to waffle. By the time we got to the refugee camp and were close to the mines, X had one of his guys on us."

"The bloody arsehole that broke my nose," Niles sputtered, his gray eyes swimming with a humiliation that was still ripe.

"Yes."

"Do you think he knows that you are here, Jake?" Baladur asked.

"I'm not sure. I don't know what, if anything, the guy who tailed us at the refugee camp was able to find out. But I have no doubt X has been working his intel network since we came into the picture, especially now that we've blown up his shit. We crashed a wrecking ball through his legit livelihood and whatever shady ops he had going on the side. He'll be having to answer to Kaseme *and* his partners in crime, who are probably pretty gnarly characters."

"So, we best be on our big game," Dmello commented.

"Yeah, we best be," Jake said.

THE NEXT MORNING AS Jake was finishing his second cup of coffee, he heard the faint musical alert chime from his open Toughbook. It was email from Kipnis, with new satellite images and maps. He sat against the bent trunk of an ordeal tree chockful of pea-shape seed pods, studying the information and comparing various routes, settling on the one he felt was the least likely to present obstacles from border patrols, official or not. Border crossings in this part of the world were highly volatile, totally permeable in some places and, in others, rigidly, even contentiously controlled, subject to change at the whim, fate, or fortuity of those in territorial control. And while up-to-the-minute intel of the kind Jake was able to get from Kipnis was essential to find the gaps, there was no way of anticipating all the risks, particularly inanimate ones.

Rousing Falcone and Niles, Jake helped Baladur and Dmello pack up and clear camp, stowed his laptop on the plane and topped off supplies, and the five of them set off to the north. The sun had just dissolved the dawn's early mist and begun to flatten in the pale sky when they crossed the border in an isolated stretch of thick vegetation and tall grasses and encountered one of those hazards Jake had not accounted for.

They were hiking in what had become their standard formation— Jake leading the way, Baladur and Dmello bringing up the rear and Falcone and Niles sandwiched in the middle—the latter pair tending to revert to their civilian penchant for breaking that formation when structure became tedious and their spirits yearned for invigoration. Something small dashing through the bush captured their attention, its movements swishing the grass in the pasture, and they stepped off the line in curious investigation.

Jake glanced back, checking their position, and continued his steady but cautious advancement, panning the horizon through his Steiners at regular intervals. He had just removed the binoculars from his eyes when a spike of primal instinct compelled him to look down. The brush was thinning out, the clay soil visible in widening voids, the surface rutted and uneven. There were raised spots here and there, a few reflecting in the sun's light, suggesting uprooted rocks or metallic debris.

Looking several feet in front of him, Jake whipped his head to the side and saw Niles about to leap from the grass into an opening where a small- to medium-size animal had just darted. "Curran, stop!" he yelled.

Niles lost his footing and pitched forward, yelping, and Falcone grabbed him by the shirt and stopped him from falling. Both turned toward Jake as the animal, a long-eared gray-brown hare, scampered across the opening and into the brush on the other side. "What? What is it?" Falcone called over.

"Everybody stop and stand right where you are," Jake said tersely.

Each of them froze in place, heads swiveling in heightened alert, hands and fingers hastily finding the grips on their rifles. Only Baladur seemed to interpret Jake's cause for raising alarm and revealed it in one word. Pointing toward a heap of fur on the ground a few feet from where Jake stood, he said, "Landmines."

Decades of war have left South Sudan contaminated with nearly fifty million square miles of unexploded mines, munitions, and other incendiary devices, the inventory propagating during the recent civil wars. Their presence has been responsible for tens of thousands of deaths and injuries sustained by those trying to build homes and roads, plant and grow crops, and children at play. A growing campaign to remove them has engaged numerous NGOs, civil and government agencies, but the ordinances remain an omnipresent threat, especially in less-traveled stretches such as the one Jake had chosen.

The scorched fur, blackened now, had been that of a wild dog, its coat a bizarre mix of dark and light hairs with splotches of yellow, the animal's flesh blasted from the bones, many of which were broken apart. A charred radius extended out from the carcass, disrupted by rain but littered with telltale fragments of metal. Jake knelt down and visually examined the ground, then took out his knife and carved around the curved edge of an embedded object in slow and deliberate strokes, exposing a round shape the color of a rusted nail and the size of a barbell weight. He stood, wiped dirt from his knife, and stepped back.

"Safe to say this is one of the reasons there are no checkpoints in this area around here."

"Shit," Falcone muttered. "What do we do?"

Jake did not respond right away, lifting his binoculars to survey the surrounding terrain. As he swept his gaze to the east, he said finally, "That's our way."

"How can you tell, mate?" Niles asked.

Jake handed over the Steiners and showed him where to look. Through the lenses, Niles saw a large herd of tan animals moving en masse across a wide open field of green and gold, their migration smooth and graceful and nimble.

"That's kob antelope," he said. "If we can get around here to their path, we can use it to get us back to one of the wooded trails."

"But how do we get around here?" Falcone wanted to know.

His expression candid, Jake said, "Very carefully."

They reversed course and angled away from the direction they'd been heading. Walking slowly single file, each focusing on and following in Jake's footsteps, they made their way to an alternative route that appeared to be another path worn down by animals. A few yards in, Falcone paused to take a sip of water, inadvertently veering slightly off course, and let out an audible gasp, head and body and limbs seizing up as if suddenly injected with a paralytic.

Turning, Jake asked, "What's the matter, Eddie?"

Falcone's chin quivered, his eyes rolling downward. "I felt something move under my boot," he said shakily. "I think I stepped on..." He couldn't finish, his skin going clammy and breath wheezing.

Gaze dropping to Falcone's feet, Jake moved swiftly, taking out his machete and swiping it next to Falcone's leg so hard and fast that Falcone almost fell over.

"Be still," Jake said. "Don't move until I tell you to."

"What's happening? Shit, what's going on?" He was babbling now, his neck and shoulders shaking.

The others had gathered around him, staring tensely at the ground. Dmello echoed Jake's directive. "Do not move."

Jake jabbed his machete at the spot where Falcone had been standing, spearing the severed head of the snake he'd just cut in two. It had been unraveled on the sunny side of vegetation along their path, turgid with digesting prey and, fortunately for Falcone, a little slower on the draw as a result, which gave Jake the extra seconds he needed to react as the serpent furled around to attack. It was now coiled up like an old gray garden hose, about nine feet in length, but despite being decapitated, the head—even with Jake's machete impaling it—was roiling, mouth gaping open and ready to bite.

Seeing it, Falcone exclaimed, "God Almighty! That's what I stepped on?"

Jake drew his arm back and swung the fourteen-inch carbon steel blade in an arc, the snake head shish kabob jettisoning into the adjacent field. He then reached down and grabbed the still-wriggling rope of body in his gloved hand and flung it off in the same fashion. Its contact with the ground, compounded by the velocity of Jake's throw, triggered a blast that spewed dirt and smoke into the air.

Though most jumped at the landmine detonation, no one said anything for a moment until Jake broke the silence with an unexpected guffaw. Heads turned to look at him strangely, and then everyone else laughed, too, the tension of the preceding moments breaking like the snap and release of a slingshot.

THEY CONTINUED ALONG THE path, all a little more tentative in their strides, Falcone in particular, who was beginning to realize the gravity of what had almost happened.

"Are you sure I didn't get bit?" he asked Jake worriedly.

Glancing over his shoulder at Falcone, Jake gave him a reassuring but wry smile. "Do you *feel* like you've been bit? Believe me, you would know it, and you'd be close to dead by now."

"Was that a—"

"Mamba. Yep, sure was."

"Goddamn," Falcone muttered. "Bad enough we've gotta worry about being blown up...now friggin' snakes, too."

"There will *always* be snakes. And while we do need to be aware of mines as an ongoing risk, I think we'll be okay as we get farther away from the border."

When they were beside the field where the kob had crossed, a meandering dirt road took them in and out of copses of acacia and fruit trees and evergreen forests. They stopped shortly after noon to rest and top off their water at a stream, then waded across to traverse a span of savanna with only a smattering of trees and palms. During the respite, Jake had consulted his sat images and maps and GPS readings, determining that the location where he believed the rebels had their camp was somewhere within a dense cover of forest up ahead—so dense, in fact, that it really classified as jungle.

The savanna abruptly ended at the forest edge, which was packed with massive teaks and mahoganies and acacias and kapoks that towered high into a multitiered canopy. Initially, the lower vegetation was nearly impenetrable, requiring them to whack their way forward, machetes thrashing through brush and vines, but as they approached the area Jake was zeroed in on, they emerged onto a semi-cleared path. Looking ahead, the foliage thinned to form a cavern of hazy gray light. There was a trace of charcoal in the humidity trapped inside the layers of pine and peat and, as they got closer, the staleness of human sweat.

But there was no movement, the only sounds those of birds whistling and warbling from the ceiling of green overhead. Jake held up his hand in caution, leading them slowly forward. He was pausing with each step, looking all around, up and down and, at one interval, his eyes fell on a length of wire stretched across the path—a tripwire.

"Okay, whoa," he said. "We've got a booby trap."

He stepped back and bent over to examine it, following the wire from side to side. It ran up into the lower branches of a sycamore fig and, just within reach, were orange and green nodules of fruit growing in clusters from the bark, the wire disappearing within. Nudging some of the fruit aside he saw the mechanism he suspected was there, a pineapple-shell F1 frag grenade, the pin unbent and pulled almost all the way out. Tripping the wire would have disengaged it, sprung the handle and, after a few seconds' delay, set it off. He moved carefully around the tree trunk, another wire leading from the fruit cluster to an indented circle of dirt. A secondary detonation, he thought; most likely attached to a can of fuel with some kind of artillery around it. If the first one didn't kill the per-petrators, the next explosion in sequence definitely would.

Not wanting to take the chance of anybody touching the wire as they stepped over it, Jake led them around it. On the other side, they walked about the clearing, and it didn't take long to find remnants of a recent encampment; for all the security measures that had been taken—and Jake was relatively sure there were or had been additional ones—the in-habitants had been sloppy in their haste to depart. They had taken the fuel can and artillery from their two-stage booby trap, but there were ashes from a fire, just barely scraped over with dirt, some scattered pea-nut husks and cassava leaves, and a poorly maintained waste trench swarming with flies and reeking of urine and feces. Jake also found sev-eral bullet casings with the now-familiar Persian headstamp.

"Pretty sure these are our rebels," he announced.

While Falcone and Niles hovered skittishly by Jake's side, Baladur and Dmello had fanned out, canvassing the perimeter of the abandoned camp. Jake was collecting the spent cartridges when Dmello called out to him. He walked over to where Baladur and Dmello were standing, and looked down to see a large discolored section of ground. Behind him, Niles asked, "Is that what I think it is?"

Jake said, "Blood, and a lot of it."

42

THEY WERE WAITING FOR Jake to say something else, but he spent the next few minutes lost in thought, looking at the volume of blood, not quite dry, noting more of it speckling the surrounding brush and trailing away from the vacated campsite. Finally, his voice thick, he said, "This was a staging location, only a temporary waypoint. But I think a more permanent camp is probably close by."

"What about the blood?" Falcone asked.

"Could be human or animal, but either way, whatever the source, it's not alive anymore. My guess, it's animal." The words left a bitter aftertaste in Jake's mouth, visions of the slaughtered elephants haunting his mind, now conjoined with the specter of Aris Xavier. Checking the map he'd been using on his Garmin tactix watch, he said, "Let's move on."

They continued north through the jungle along what seemed to be a more defined path, the vegetation cut back, the trail tamped down. As a result, their progress was mostly unencumbered until they reached a stream. So far, they had forged across others without much difficulty, but the current in this one appeared to have more movement, froth bubbling around embedded rocks and logs. Stopping to assess their options, Jake said, "There's a pretty substantial river not far from here, so this must be coming from a tributary."

Baladur found a broken tree limb to use as a measuring stick and poked the depths as far as he could reach. Even an arm's length from the bank, it disappeared several feet below the stream's surface. He turned, looking at Jake in question.

"They wouldn't have crossed here," Jake said, "especially not if there were more than a few of them. Definitely not with captives. That means there must be a more favorable access further on."

Hiking a short distance along the stream, they discovered the means by which passage had been attained. But it was no longer available to them. The ends of a wooden bridge hung from the banks like an unstrung necklace, ropes severed and dripping splintered planks into the water. No one had to comment on why or how it had happened. The stream curved and graduated to a higher bank where the water braided off into shallow sections, the current throttled by outcroppings of rocks. Jake stopped, slipped off his pack and dug out a bundle of paracord, dispatching the others to find sturdy walking sticks. While they were doing so, he lithely clambered across the rocks, and made it to the other side. From there, he tied the paracord around the trunk of a mahogany and tossed the other end to Baladur. Each of them took turns crossing, holding onto the paracord and using their sticks as leverage. Only Niles slipped, but he used the tether to pull himself back up on the rocks and make it the rest of the way.

They hiked through more jungle and, an hour later, began to hear voices drifting through the trees.

JAKE PROVED TO BE right about the rebel camp; it had been established for some time, evidenced by the types of structures it comprised. Most were made of wood and thatch, some timbered, and there was one built with mud brick, which Jake guessed held weapons and ammunition. An open eating area was also timber-framed and outlined by stacked stone, a cooking pit in the center with a hulk of meat the size of a footlocker smoking over wood chips and charcoal, the scent oily and feral.

On picking up the initial vocals carrying back to their position, Jake had backtracked a considerable way to a place dense with lower-level trees and undergrowth, somewhere they had to put in extra work to create a shelter. He chose the spot for that very reason, knowing the rebels were familiar enough with the woods surrounding their base that the best concealment would be in an area without any clearings. By the time they got through building platforms in the trees and setting up a security perimeter with trimmings from thorn bush, the last light of day had melted away, bringing the chirr of insects and darker blues of evening. Jake had also ensured they were far enough removed that they could have a fire and get a meal in them, but as soon as they were done, it was extinguished and thoroughly covered over.

Now, as they got their weapons ready, checked their comms, and applied camo paint, Jake took a few minutes to discuss the situation. "This is going to be a whole different dynamic from the mining op," he explained. "And once we get the lay of the land, we won't be able to go in there guns blazing, either. At the mining camp, the Keoghs' people were separated, which allowed us to target the bad guys without putting the others at risk. With these rebels, whether they're LRA or not, they will have most likely put guns in their hands and be forcing them to fight. Some might just be porters, and whatever women or girls are there will be sex slaves."

Falcone and Niles both looked away, their faces drawn with revulsion.

"Sorry, that's just the fact of the matter," Jake said bluntly. "Point is, they will be integrated with the rebels who may even use them as human shields."

"The doctors, too?" Niles asked.

"I'm sure they're being put to use in their medical capacity, so they might be the only ones kept apart from the rest. We might be able to use that to our advantage. In any case, tonight we recon…probably tomorrow, too. We need to see what their routine is, find their vulnerabilities. We'll have to take extra care on stealth, too, because they probably know what went down at the mines and could very well be on the lookout for us. Needless to say, be vigilant for booby traps since we know they employ them."

They set out in the deepening twilight, pausing every fifty yards or so to look and listen. Most of the way, the normal sights and sounds of a forest shifting into night mode were all they saw and heard, but when they were within a few dozen yards of the camp, that all changed.

Chatter from the eating area wafted with the smells of food, occasional sallies of insouciant laughter rising and falling. After conducting an initial sweep of the periphery for security measures, they began their surveillance in a thicket of brush just beyond the dinner gathering. Watching through FLIR 51 night vision monoculars, they observed plates being scraped empty of rice and beans and whatever meat had been roasting. Some were drinking from plastic water bottles and tin cups, but many others were swigging from a jug that was being passed around. Chalk one up in the category of exploitable weaknesses, thought Jake. Then he noticed the jug being pressed on the younger members in the group, and that chink was counterbalanced; hooch for the adults might be a helpful impairment, but for the minors it would be a tranquilizer, only enhancing their submission. They could be drugged, too, a common practice in these groups, everything from stimulants and hallucinogens to hype them up for fighting to depressants and opioids to control them.

Taking inventory of those present, Jake numbered the ranks of domineering figures somewhere in the range of three to four dozen. Those dubbed subservient added again as many, if not more. Earlier, specific hand signals had been established for Falcone and Niles to communicate possible identification or absolute confirmation of people from the Keoghs' compound, and it wasn't long before the two of them were flashing to Jake in rapid bursts. They did not, however, see any sign of the doctors.

In the hours that followed dinner, the rebel clan broke off into batches of expected behavior: socialization that was varying degrees of tipsy frivolity or sated torpidity, retirement to sleeping arrangements, and the coordination of security details. Officers, dressed in either camouflage fatigues or modified military attire, were shadowed by personal bodyguards and an entourage of porters and young women and girls, all of whom had adopted the plodding postures and hollow expressions of the condemned. And, as far as Jake could tell, not a single one of those in captivity was without a rebel handler overseeing his or her every move. The security barrier was maintained with surprising discipline, though there were the typical lapses of boredom, during which cigarettes were lit, bladders or bowels emptied, vapid conversation exchanged. Despite these potential gaps, weapons were almost always slung with an arm draped over the receiver or a hand in the vicinity of the trigger. They communicated regularly with two-way radios and relieved each other often.

When it was obvious that the premises had buttoned down for the night, Jake signaled retreat and they returned to their own camp for a few hours' sleep.

THEY COMMENCED RECON BEFORE dawn and watched as the rebels and those in their dominion began the day. As with any communal conclave, there were chores to be done and, for a while, the only activities observed were those of washing, cleaning, and cooking for the women and girls, scavenging for the men. The latter seemed to be conducted on two fronts; one being the more obvious endeavor of hunting and fishing, the second of a more ambiguous nature in which a heavily armed troupe departed for parts unknown and later returned without any visible trappings. They were met by the uniformed man Jake had pegged as the most senior of the group, a lengthy interrogation taking place. The commander did not look pleased with the information they were providing and Jake wondered if they'd been dispatched to collect ivory from a cache and found none stored. Or maybe they had been sent on a patrol to look for the five of them. Whatever the objective, the results sent the commander stomping off, snatching the arm of a young girl and dragging her into one of the huts. She lolled in his grasp in the stumbling, flaccid way of a being stripped of all resistance, her face as molten as wax.

Before any of them could react emotionally, Jake redirected their focus, saying, "We need to look for those doctors. There's one larger structure on the back side of the compound with its own security crew. Let's check that out."

They took a wide lap around and set up behind the building, waiting until most of the camp had gravitated to the eating area for lunch. Two rebels were stationed by the hut's entrance, and there were no other openings for doors or windows. Studying the trees closest to the structure, Jake honed in on one with branches that extended over the thatched roof. Huddling with the others, he said, "You guys keep watch,

I'm going to climb up and see if I can find or make a hole." He paused. "If any of them approach, take off. I'll wait for an opportunity and exfil."

The tree was a teak, the lowest limbs just clearing the roof and making it easy for him to shimmy along one until he was above it. He wanted to avoid putting his weight on the thatch because he could not tell how much framing was supporting it. Instead, he straddled prone over the limb and used the tip of his machete to dig through the thatch. It was thickly layered and took some time and effort to get to the bottom, but when he did, the hole he'd made opened between timbers, allowing him to see all the way to the floor. The interior was dim in the shade of the forest, but he could make out figures moving inside. If any of them had heard his breach, they did not show it. Within a few minutes, he was certain that this was the building designated as the camp medical clinic, the moving figures attending to others. While he could not make out their features or clothing, he knew the choreography of their movements as they leaned over what appeared to be cots and went through the gestures associated with checking vitals and other medical administrations. He also thought he caught a glimpse of highlights in the hair of one, whose silhouette in shadow suggested a female, but in the absence of sunlight it was hard to tell.

He was debating whether to attempt signaling them in some way when Baladur's voice came over his comm. "Boss, the guards may have heard you. They are looking at the roof."

"Copy that," Jake replied. "On my way down."

As he maneuvered further back into the tree, Baladur reported, "Moving out," and Jake held his position up against the trunk, watching the ground. The two rebel guards approached and peered up at the hut's roofline, AK-47s clutched across their chests. Their gazes shifted to the crown of the tree, and Jake slowly reached for his Glock as they stared into foliage. For a moment, he was sure they had spotted him, one elbowing the other, but then they turned and strolled back to their post in front of the building.

Letting out a breath, Jake spoke softly into his comm to let the others know he was clear and climbed down from the tree, joining them several yards away. "Okay," he said, "I think I'm ready to make a plan."

* * * * *

THE FIRST CAPTURE CAME quickly. A pair consisting of two young males, both armed with AKs, had wandered away from the camp's perimeter, aimlessly poking through the brush. One was a rangy twenty-something, the other a scrawny teenager whose twitchy grip on his rifle and jittery gaze clearly revealed his abductee designation. The rebel wore dirty camo pants that sagged from his behind, a sweat-stained brown t-shirt faded nearly tan, and dusty rubber boots, his teenage draftee dressed in jeans and shirt so soiled they seemed part of his skin. As they shuffled along, the rebel repeatedly poked the teenager with the barrel of his rifle and, at one point, made him stop and aim his gun. The target was a little boy gathering branches for fire wood, aged somewhere between seven and nine. He stood, mouth open, mute and still with incomprehension. The branches he had collected slid from his arms.

The rebel gave the teenager an order, causing him to recoil in horror and lower his weapon. He pleaded, holding a hand out, his face averted, but the rebel pinned him against a tree, jabbering in a mocking tone. When the rebel stepped back, the teenager was shaking and sobbing, his jeans darkened in the crotch where he'd urinated on himself. The rebel raised his own rifle, the barrel touching the teen's head, then pivoted and aimed at the small boy. His finger flexed by the trigger, and then he laughed garishly, propping the rifle on his shoulder.

When they sidled past Baladur and Dmello, who were crouched and concealed in the brush, the two were snatched and restrained before they knew what was happening. Baladur and Dmello sprang up, each grabbing one, the teenager being yanked aside and easily disarmed, the rebel being immediately silenced by a strip of duct tape over his mouth, wrists restrained behind his back by 250-pound plastic zip-ties. Niles raced after and caught the little boy, taking him and the teenager to a heavily wooded area they'd set up as a temporary holding shelter; the rebel was marched off in the opposite direction to another just like it where Falcone was on guard duty. Jake's role in the snatch-and-grab was to communicate a heads-up and to jump in where necessary, ready to defend or launch an offensive. But for his plan to be the most effective, the captures needed to proceed covertly for as long as possible, at least until they had reduced the numbers in camp.

Everything went swimmingly for the first few hours, the holding areas filling with almost twenty heads each, but by then the remaining rebels had come to suspect something was afoot. Watching the camp through binoculars, Jake saw the commander bellow orders, his soldiers scrambling over each other to enjoin those in their charge. When they began fanning out, Jake called for Falcone and Niles to secure and leave their posts to pitch in on the captures. Niles came quickly, Falcone did not come at all.

EDDIE FALCONE STOOD OVER his prisoners, clumped together on the ground, wrists and ankles ligatured, mouths duct-taped. With his AR-15 fully loaded and now fairly comfortable in his hands, he felt confident in his ability to maintain control, but he was sweating like a frosty bottle of Coke fished from an ice-packed cooler on a triple-digit summer afternoon. Even though nearly every day here was sweltering and oppressively humid, he usually managed to stay hydrated enough to cope, but from the time he'd stirred this morning after getting maybe an hour of sleep, he'd felt weak and woozy, a dull ache ballooning in his head.

Wiping perspiration from his face and neck, he paced in front of the rebels, who were all watching him cagily, some wriggling in frustration. Or maybe, Falcone thought, they were scheming to escape. *Not gonna happen, shitheads.* Eying one of them, a solemn character who sat stiffly and stared straight ahead, Falcone knelt down and looked into his face. "Who are you guys?"

The man had no reaction.

"Are you LRA?"

The man still did not move, but his eyes blinked. A fly landed on his nose and Falcone flicked it away, waiting, as if somehow the man would speak through the tape on his mouth. Instead, he made a gurgling sound and Falcone reached for a bottle of water, peeled off the duct tape.

"LRA?" he asked again. "Kony?"

The man's eyes clung to the bottle of water then rolled up to Falcone.

Falcone held the bottle to the man's lips and, as he did, felt his rifle slide, the butt touching the ground beside his foot. Suddenly, the rebel lurched to his feet with a vitality that was astounding and swung his arms around, plastic zip-tie dangling from one wrist. He was brandishing a compact folding blade, blood trickling from where he'd sliced himself in the process of extrication. He seemed oblivious to the deep laceration, eyes that only moments ago were flat and deadpan now wild with drug-induced fervor. Flabbergasted, Falcone grappled for his AR-15, but the rebel was on him before he could get it in position, shoving Falcone down on his back and pushing the knife against his neck. He confiscated Falcone's rifle and pointed it at him, tossing the folder to another prisoner.

"Tie yourself!" the rebel ordered.

Falcone glared up at him, breathing hard.

The rebel clicked off the rifle's safety selector and repeated, "Tie yourself!"

Falcone jabbed a hand angrily into a pocket and took out a plastic cable and zipped it around his wrists.

A second rebel who had cut himself free with the knife joined the first and the two men jerked Falcone to his feet, dragging him away from the holding area. Falcone bucked and kicked and felt the ache in his head pulse, sparks of bright light behind his eyes. In his ear, he heard Jake calling for them all to come in.

WHEN FALCONE DID NOT appear or respond, Jake headed for the holding area, arriving just as Falcone was being hauled off. He ran around to their front, the rebel who had taken Falcone's gun holding it by his side as he pulled and dragged. Stepping directly into their path, Jake brought both of his arms up as if he were about to duck into a butterfly stroke, hooking the two heads of the rebels and slamming them together, the sound and impact like bowling balls striking. They dropped to the ground and Falcone clambered to his feet, wobbling unsteadily.

Jake regarded him with concern and asked, "You okay?" He extended his hand, which Falcone took to fully recover his balance.

"Yeah, yeah," Falcone blustered, "Sorry. Just pissed off that I let that happen. Bastards."

"It's okay," Jake said evenly, "let's just get back to it."

The two of them put new sets of zip-ties on the escaped rebels who were moaning and semi-conscious. Falcone recovered his rifle and tossed the knife to Jake. They walked back to the other captives, checked all of the ligatures and made sure there was no more missed contraband. When they were done, Jake took a longer look at Falcone, noting the flush in his face, the slight degree by which his focus seemed to be off, and asked again, "Okay?"

Falcone nodded and took a brisk sniff. "I'm good. Where do you want me?"

"Stay with them. The rest of us will get as many more as we can."

On return to Baladur and Dmello, Jake saw that they had caught another bunch with Niles' help. Glancing up as Jake approached, Niles asked, "Eddie all right?"

"For now," Jake said. "I'm estimating a couple dozen left. I'd like to get at least half of them taken off the board before we go into the camp."

Niles returned to the Keoghs' people while Jake, Baladur, and Dmello continued the roundup operation. The threesome spent the next couple of hours watching and waiting for their moments, changing positions in the bush as needed, and pouncing when the opportunities arose. Jake broke away periodically to check on Falcone and the detainees but did not find any more problems. For his part, Falcone seemed to have restored his self-possession and was holding court with unabashed machismo.

Dusk was creeping through the forest canopy when Jake summoned them all together. Addressing Falcone first, he asked, "Any problems?"

"No. It seems like they're resigned."

"Could be," Jake said. "You know, most of these guys were also abducted and forced into this life. They've been brainwashed over the years, and now they don't know a way out, don't know anything else."

"So what's going to happen?" Falcone asked.

"Hopefully, they'll surrender and begin the process of rehabilitation and reintegration. There are lots of success stories." Jake looked to Niles. "Curran, how are the Keoghs' people?"

"Well, it's taken them a while to realize they're being rescued from this hell, but most of them are starting to grasp it. They've…they've been through a bloody lot."

"I know," Jake said somberly. "Okay, next move. The remaining rebels in camp are now on heightened readiness and I'd be surprised if they didn't have a substantial stockade of weapons and ammunition in that armory. We can overtake them with the right execution, but I still want to avoid gunfire if possible. At this point, they will for sure be shielding themselves with abductees."

"What if they use the doctors?" Niles asked worriedly.

Jake said, "Actually, I'm kind of counting on that."

43

AS THEY MOVED THE prisoners and those they'd rescued farther away from the rebel camp, the sun slid from the sky and left an afterglow of heirloom tomato colors, full of orange-reds and plums and all the shades in between. The detainees were given water, their restraints checked and reapplied as necessary. The rescued, in a separate and well-concealed location, were evaluated for physical and mental stability; none were in great shape either way, but the objective was to single out a few who could be given some of the confiscated weapons for protection since Niles would not be staying with them. Jake needed all of the guys in action, but after the attempted escape earlier he decided to leave Falcone in place, not so much to guard the prisoners as to keep him out of the fray. He knew something was not right, but he'd just have to hope it wouldn't be an issue until this situation was resolved and he had time to find out what it was.

Before leaving Falcone to his post, Jake had looked him squarely in the eye and asked, "Are you sure you're up to this?"

Falcone flipped a hand through his dark hair and retorted irritably, "Jake, I swear to God, I am a hundred percent fine. I just got a little over-heated, all right?" Jake held his gaze until Falcone glanced away, blowing out an exasperated breath, muttering, "I'm good, I'm good."

With Niles, Baladur, and Dmello, Jake hiked back to the camp's perimeter, hunkering down in the woods in a position that gave them the best view of activity. The rebel commander was on his radio, undoubtedly trying to raise the missing members of his clan, pacing as he spoke heatedly into the handset. He clicked buttons and twisted dials, moving around and holding it above his head as if doing so might produce an improvement in reception, but reception was not the problem and he knew it. Disgusted, he snarled and yelled out to his subordinates, who came running with their subjugated entourage in tow. Minutes later, they spread out, patrolling the camp grounds. The commander retreated to his quarters.

This was when Niles and Dmello, in their part to launch phase one of the plan Jake had devised, took off in a brisk jog along one side of the compound. Keeping inside the trees, they fired their rifles in random directions as they continued their sprint to the opposite side where they did the same. The rebel soldiers responded exactly as anticipated, running amok in a frantic and confounded pursuit to find the source of the assault. Next, Baladur lured them in his direction, firing on full automatic toward the front of the camp. When they charged forward, returning fire, he simply watched from his perch high in a mahogany tree while Niles and Dmello came up on the side. As soon as the last pair of rebels had passed, with Dmello covering, Niles darted out from the bush and grabbed one of the Keogh abductees. The rebel paired with him was so wrapped up in tracking the enemy, he failed to notice the sudden absence of his conscripted sidekick.

Clamping a hand over the startled boy's mouth, Niles whispered, "Hey, it's okay, mate!" He wrapped him in a hug and said, "We've come for you, but I need you to do something for us. I'm going to let you go, and I want you to go back, get word to the others. Tell them as soon as they hear a big bang, they need to make a break and run as fast as they can." He turned the boy's head and pointed. "That way…until you get to the big tree split in the middle. Then stay there until we come. Can you do that?"

The boy, a twelve-year-old named Sebastien, nodded, and Niles reluctantly released him.

Dmello put a hand on Niles' shoulder. "I know you did not want to let him go, but it is so we can get the rest."

"Passing two," Niles relayed into his comms, letting the others know the second phase was successful. He hoisted his AR-15 and the two of them slipped back into the woods, shooting well beyond Baladur to draw the rebels out even further. They were actually being careful not to hit any as most were, true to Jake's prediction, holding the abductees close to them. Niles tried to keep his eye on Sebastien, saw him get the word to a couple of the Keoghs' people, but soon lost him in the escalating engagement and deepening darkness. Bullets were spraying through the forest, but they managed to stay out of range.

During the time his guys were moving the rebel combatants away from the camp, Jake had ventured inside it, working his way around the huts to find out who was still there. He now had his night vision monocular mounted on a Crye Precision head cap and was peering through the 51-degree lens, seeing everything in clear, green luminance. As he'd hoped, the camp's interior area had emptied—no one in the eating area and no roaming security patrols—but when he got within ten yards of the medical structure, he saw that the two-guard sentry had doubled to four. The good thing was, they were grouped at the hut's entry, which meant the medical staff was being held inside, integral to his plan. They also did not have NVGs. Jake moved on to the armory and found it surprisingly unattended. He reached into his backpack and took out two plastic green cylindrical objects the size of small juice cans and screwed them together.

Over comms, Jake said, "Executing three," pulled the ring from the top, and slung the joined components into the armory. He crouched down to take cover, and seconds later the structure burst apart in a concussive blast followed immediately by a succession of fireworks not unlike a battalion of machine guns, flames jumping and smoke billowing, the more than two hundred grams of explosives emitted by the Nammo HGO 115 scalable grenades blowing up the camp's artillery. He ran back to the medical hut where the guards had sprung into spastic action, rifles up, wheeling blindly in all directions. They impulsively started toward the burning armory and then, realizing it was a mistake, backpedaled to their posts. But Jake took advantage of the blunder and deployed a couple of smoke grenades, shrouding the rebels in a gray fog and allowing him the opening he needed to get inside the structure.

The night vision allowed him to see the entirety of the inside, where there were ten cots lined up on either side, about half filled with males of fighting age that Jake guessed were rebels; more than likely they would be the only ones permitted to be treated. He also saw the doctors. Noah Goossens and Julienne Baudin stood tightly together with several native Congolese, including a young man and woman and another female who was tall with a head full of winding braids. They were all clutching each other, their expressions tense with apprehension.

Jake said, "It's okay, it's okay...the Keoghs sent me."

He heard some gasps, coupled with, *"Mon Dieu!"* and *"Merci!"*

At least one of those in the cots sat up, trying to make him out in the darkness. Jake asked, "Are all the patients rebels?"

"Yes," Goossens said quickly, adding without hesitation, "leave them."

"Okay, let's get," Jake said. "Everybody behind me."

Grabbing some things, they followed Jake to the entrance, halting when he raised his rifle and popped off two rounds, then two more. When they emerged from the hut, the four rebel guards lay dead on the ground, one right at the doorway. They each stepped over the body and stuck close to Jake as he crossed the camp common, pausing near the rebel commander's hut. He had another grenade in a pocket of his cargo pants, really wanted to use it, but the possibility of a girl or woman also being in that hut made him averse.

"Status down and dirty, moving for exfil," he announced.

Jake turned and led the medical staff from the camp premises, ducking into the woods.

IT TOOK THEM FIFTEEN minutes to catch up with Baladur, Dmello, and Niles, who had been busy monitoring the flow of escapees while they laid down defensive fire to push the few scattered rebels back toward the camp, another ten minutes to reach the tree split by lightning that Niles had designated to Sebastien. They were met by him and an anxious cluster of kids who eagerly hopped up to go with them to the concealment where the rest were waiting.

Jake dug the Nalgene bottle from his pack, took a long swallow, and called to Falcone. "We're in the nest...sitrep?" He waited, got no response from comms, and repeated his query. Again got nothing, and frowned.

Before he could say anything, Niles darted off. Jake nodded to Baladur, and the three hurried to the prisoner staging area a few hundred yards away. Even before they got there, Jake felt dread humming in his chest, instantly second-guessing his decision to leave Falcone behind. The first thing he noticed as they approached was the lineup of prisoners—there were empty spots where some had been. Then he saw Falcone sprawled face-down on the ground.

"Oh God, Eddie!" Niles cried, and ran to him, dropping to a knee and leaning over his motionless body.

Baladur began a survey of the prisoners, reporting, "There are three missing."

Jake knelt beside Niles, gripping him by the shoulders to move him aside. He turned Falcone over on his back and looked at his face. Falcone's eyes were closed, skin reddened and slick with perspiration. After trying to rouse him, Jake took his pulse and, detecting a weak thread, vigorously rubbed Falcone's sternum with his knuckles. That elicited a moan and a blink of eyelids. Jake exhaled with relief and said, "Okay, bud, I got you." Already lifting his shirt and moving him around, he asked, "Did you get shot? Cut?" He finished checking him over, not finding any wounds.

Falcone mumbled something unintelligible and fell unconscious again. Niles glanced anxiously at Jake. "What's wrong with him?"

"I have my suspicions, but right now we need to get him up and moving…and that isn't going to be easy." Addressing Baladur, Jake asked, "They still zipped up?"

"Yes," Baladur replied. "They are not talking much, but one says Eddie cut some loose."

"Why the bloody hell would he do that?" Niles asked.

Baladur replied, "They said after he let them go, he dropped."

Jake blew out a breath, shook his head. "Okay, guys. Let's get him up, try to get some water in him, and head back. We don't know where those rebels went, if they returned to the camp, and we didn't get all of the rest."

He thought: *And I didn't get the man in command.*

*   *   *   *   *

WHEN THEY RETURNED TO the others, the doctors were making rounds among the escapees and tending to whatever they could with the belongings they'd grabbed on the way out. They had some bottles of water, though not nearly enough, and some medical supplies. Dr. Baudin saw Baladur and Niles propping Falcone up and came over to assist, asking, "What is going on with Eddie?"

Jake said, "Pretty sure it's malaria. I thought he looked off earlier…I shouldn't have left him, but I didn't want him in the fight."

Baladur and Niles eased Falcone to the ground, and Dr. Baudin squatted in front of him, studying his face. She placed a hand on his cheek and forehead. "He is burning up."

Jake slipped off his pack and took out his aid bag. "I've got a malaria kit and Malarone," he said, and rooted around until he found both. He snapped on some gloves and ripped opened the kit, swabbed one of Falcone's fingers with an alcohol wipe and pricked it with a lancet. Using a pipette to extract a drop of blood, he deposited the sample in a slot on the test kit and squeezed on the reagent, adding a drop to the glucometer strip.

Looking at Falcone, who was going in and out, eyelashes flickering, Jake said, "Hey, bud. Have you been taking your malaria meds?"

Falcone grinned lopsidedly, saliva drooling from his lips. "Wha…gah, lookit…" His eyes seemed to be seeing something in the ethers, rolling back in the sockets.

While they waited the five minutes for the results, Jake read the glucometer. "A hundred…that's okay, but he's going to need ORS soon." He pulled out his BP cuff, snugged it on Falcone's arm, pumped the bulb and listened with his stethoscope. "One hundred over seventy. A little low, but holding." He removed the stethoscope from his ears, draping it around his neck, and glanced at Dr. Baudin.

Extending her hand, she said, "Julienne Baudin, by the way."

Jake gave her an easy smile and formally introduced himself, returning his gaze to Falcone. Baudin's seemed to linger on him. Holding the rapid test strip under the beam of his flashlight, Jake saw the lines appear by both the control and test markers, indicating a positive. He popped four of the dark pink tablets from a blister pack of Malarone and slipped an arm under Falcone to prop him up. "All right, big guy, let's get these pills down." He tipped a water bottle into Falcone's mouth, making sure he swallowed all of the tablets, then passed it to Baudin.

She fished out a handkerchief from her things and moistened it, dabbing Falcone's hot forehead. "Do you have any Paracetamol? We can put the ORS in the water bottle."

Jake said, "Yes and yes, but we've been here longer than we should. We need to move out."

TRYING TO CROSS THE stream was not an option, not with all these people and certainly not at night. So Jake took them parallel to it, going west. It was going to put them farther out from their point of origin where the plane was, but he really did not see a choice. And, Falcone's declining condition notwithstanding, he also knew he could not keep them mobile for very long, so as they made the trek, he was keeping an eye out for a good place to stop. The pale slice of moon had disappeared behind slowly sifting clouds, the humidity rising, which gave the search for a campsite an even greater sense of expediency; rain was probably on the way.

Thankfully, there had been no indication of rebel pursuit in their wake, but Jake knew better than to interpret that as game over. The ones they had vanquished might be motivated to reorganize—or ordered to do so by their commander—and there was also the possibility that other outposts in the region would be rallied to join in the initiative. But for right now, Jake had to get everyone sheltered to rest, protect them through the night, and take care of Falcone.

A few miles downstream, Jake spotted a slope that overlooked the water and the ground they'd just hiked and led the group uphill to a lushly forested plateau of tall, abundantly crowned trees. Baladur, Dmello, and Niles had been taking turns walking with Falcone draped between them, and now Baladur hoisted him over his shoulder, trudging up the incline. Jake issued instructions and a shelter was assembled, fire built, water filtered and distributed, a night watch rotation set.

When all were settled, Jake joined Niles and Dr. Baudin who were seated beside Falcone, the doctor focused on her patient and Niles, on her. Jake could see why, noting the classic Gallic sophistication in Baudin's facial features, the smooth nose and cheeks, full coral-tinted lips, light brown hooded eyes that were almost amber. It had been her hair, he realized, that he'd seen through the opening in the medical hut's roof, the caramel-colored tresses falling out of a scrunchie-style band.

Touching Niles on the shoulder, Jake said, "Curran, we'll stay with him. Why don't you go get some rest while you can?"

Sheepish by the exposure of his preoccupation, Niles got to his feet and reluctantly walked off.

Taking the space Niles had occupied, Jake placed the back of his hand against Falcone's cheek, the heat from his skin like a lightbulb.

"I just checked his temperature," Baudin commented. "Quite high. One-oh-four."

"Fluids?"

"Some. He has vomited a bit."

Jake checked his watch ponderously and studied their position on the tactix's maps, speculating about the viability of getting a medevac for Falcone through Keogh or Remington. He decided they could reach the plane in the time it would take to make that happen, and malaria often got better quickly in healthy people with appropriate treatment. When they got to the plane, if need be Dmello could fly Falcone and Dr. Baudin, the rest of them hiking on to meet up with the Keoghs' transport truck. It was late, after eleven o-clock, so he would call Kent Sanborn in the morning.

They sat in reflective silence for a while and then Baudin said, "I cannot begin to thank you, and the Keoghs of course, for coming after us. I have been through some things, but nothing like that."

Jake said, "Glad we got to you. Tell me what happened."

Baudin's response was lean and devoid of much inflection at first as she described the night the Keoghs' complex was overrun and how they were taken. Her French accent was genteel and yet at the same time, clinical and aloof. The account she related aligned with what Jake had already heard from the others until she got to a new part. She told him she had known with utter certainty that she would be raped and possibly killed. With that statement, she stole a look at him and was taken aback by the onset of emotion that shone in his eyes, but she sensed it was emotion triggered by something other than what she'd just shared. She stopped speaking, and watched Jake curiously.

He looked up abruptly, his expression unreadable.

She continued, "They knew we were doctors and set us apart, Noah and I. When they were about to take us away, I told them we had to have our staff. I pointed out two of our nurses who were with us at the time, Honorine and Patrice…and Betty, Betty Ndongala." She paused. "Betty is my best friend here. She is a teacher. But I told them she was a nurse. I knew if they took her with the other women and girls—" She stopped again, looked up to the treetops, black silhouettes whose canopy merged with the sky. Her profile was strong, determined, but the ordeal had thrown her a nasty curveball.

"Why don't you get some rest, too?" Jake suggested, casting a protective glance over Falcone. "I've got him."

"Very well," Dr. Baudin said, stood, stretched her arms, and walked back to where the others were sleeping. Or trying to.

Looking at the batch of rescued souls huddled together in the dark forest, Jake took a moment to reflect on the near-impossible feat that had been accomplished in the two weeks since he'd been here, these, for all intents and purposes being the last of the Keoghs' missing people. He felt a wave of exhaustion roll over him, and with it, a tiny ripple of dismay for what he had *not* accomplished, the primary goal of his mission: finding and returning Lula.

He could conclude it now, he was *ready* to end it now. Just the thought of getting on a plane and flying back home to Dominical and Callie sent a rush of exhilaration through him. So why couldn't he let it go? Had he done everything he could? He thought so. But the momentum that had been building did not seem to be diminishing or letting him detach, the way gravity and adrenaline kept pulling and pushing you when there was still some other obstacle in your path.

His mind still wrestling with the decision he needed to make, Jake got up and strung his and Falcone's hammocks in the trees, covering both with their rain ponchos and mosquito netting. Then he gathered wood and made a fire. He lifted Falcone in his arms and put him in the hammock, droplets of rain beginning to fall. So much for the fire, he thought.

Falcone groaned with the transition, mumbling restlessly.

"It's okay, bud," Jake said calmly. "You're okay. Go back to sleep."

Falcone continued to squirm, eyes closed. "Let 'em go," he slurred.

"Let who go?"

"…to piss…"

"You have to piss?"

"No, no, no…let 'em go…"

Jake's brow creased in puzzlement, elucidation coming a few seconds later. "Oh…the prisoners had to piss and you let them go. Is that it? Okay…well, it's all right. We're good. Get some rest."

But Falcone's feverish rant continued. "X…exes…"

Jake eyes widened. "What?"

"X…Xbox…" Falcone groaned again, this time his body spasmed and he rolled and threw up over the side of his hammock. "Oh God, oh God, I'm sorry…" Then, feebly, "Don't go."

Jake got some water and wiped his mouth and chin. "Don't worry, I'm right here."

He leaned back against the tree Falcone's hammock was tethered to, spittles of rain peppering his face. Was Falcone's blubbering just hallucinatory gibberish or was it a message from on high, an omen to his quandary? Maybe, he thought, it was his own conscience communicating the truth that was staring him down.

Aris Xavier was at the center of everything that had happened to the Keoghs, and he was still out there.

44

THE MORNING COULD NOT come soon enough for Jake, who was anxious to get everyone to Nakalé safe and sound, but for Eddie Falcone, it was like being emptied out of the back of a dump truck full of boulders with him on the bottom. Once he'd been taken by the sleep that carried him through the rest of the night, it was as if he'd been adrift in a psychedelic meadow filled with butterflies that looked like vividly colored and kaleidoscopically ornate Chinese dragons and candy cane poles of musical calliope horses, his mind floating somewhere far away from his body. Sunshine pattered down in balloon raindrops and warmed and cooled like a Caribbean breeze that tasted of rum and fruit and exotic flowers.

And then, pain and nausea and dizziness and a hot and cold that was not as pleasant as balmy tropical breezes. Not even remotely. His teeth and eardrums ached and there was an incessant buzzing in his head that made him think an insect was trapped somewhere inside. His skin felt like it was melting from his bones.

"Eddie."

Jake squeezed his arm again, saw Falcone's eyelids twitch. On the opposite side of his hammock, Dr. Baudin stood waiting to take his temperature and give him another round of medication.

Falcone squinted at them, a low moan curling up the back of his throat. He tried to speak but only huffs of breath came out.

"All right," Jake said, "give it a few minutes, then we'll talk." He checked Falcone's blood pressure and listened to his heart and chest, nodding to Dr. Baudin. "Good."

Reading the thermometer after she plucked it from Falcone's mouth, she said, "One-oh-two," and added, "I will get his ORS going."

Tossing her a full bottle of water, Jake looked at Falcone. "How you feeling, buddy?"

Falcone seemed to consider his answer carefully, the way a child does when making a gambit on what his parent needs to hear to choose reward over punishment. But he also knew he could not fool Jake, a skilled interrogator who could see a lie through metal. "Um...like shit," he croaked, "but I can make it." He took delicate sips from the bottle of water, wary of the queasiness coiled in his stomach.

"Yeah...you're gonna be in the hurt box for a few days. If we need to, I can get you evaced, but it might take a day or so."

That got Falcone struggling to sit up in the hammock. "Oh no...hell, no," he protested, bobbling the water bottle and lunging to grab it. In the process, his equilibrium exhumed his innards through his eyeballs and every gastro-elimination function misfired at once, threatening to erupt, the top of his skull slamming down on his brain.

Jake clasped both of his arms and eased him back. "Slow down. Drink, get yourself acclimated. Then we'll see. Okay?"

Niles approached and said he would stay with Falcone, so Jake went to check on everyone else. It was still dark in the forest, the sun veiled in mist, ground and foliage wet from the rain. The others were mostly awake, physically uncomfortable in their damp clothing but visibly relieved in the freedom from captivity. Baladur and Dmello joined Jake near the edge of the ridge, the stream below a colorless undulating vein in the pre-dawn opacity.

"How is Eddie?" Dmello asked.

"I think he'll live," Jake said dryly and, seeing the sobriety of their expressions, grinned. "You know how he is. He's chomping at the bit, but it's going to be rough for him for a while. I'm giving him a minute. Hopefully he'll be able to hit the trail." He took out his sat phone. "I need to call Kent, get him heading our way with the transport truck, and then we need to get out of here."

Baladur held out a radio he had swiped from one of the rebels. "We never heard anything and now it is out of range."

"Okay," Jake said. He gazed down at the stream. "We need to cross as soon as we can and start back in the other direction toward the plane. Get everybody ready to go."

Jake tried for several minutes but could not get a signal on his sat phone, so he put it in his pocket and returned to see how Falcone was faring. He wasn't surprised in the least to find him standing, fussing with Niles as they stumbled around each other untying and rolling up Falcone's hammock. Falcone was unsteady on his legs, but seemed determined to stay upright and push past his debilitation and discomfort.

Sunlight began to seep through the trees, moisture dripping and glistening like icicles.

HIKING A MILE FARTHER west along the stream brought them to shallows they could cross without much difficulty, except for Falcone who had to be helped, something which both humbled and frustrated him. On the other side, Jake led them back to the east and toward the field where they had traversed behind the migration of kob. After the previous night's rain, the heavens had delivered a beautiful, nearly cloudless morning, but the sun without filter was already cooking past eighty degrees, necessitating a slower pace and more frequent stops. And Falcone, despite his insistence to the contrary, was struggling, and the fact that he was not sweating as much as the others was of concern because it indicated a losing battle with dehydration.

Resting in the shade of some mango trees, Jake was about to try Sanborn again when he heard something from across the savanna that resonated in the pit of his stomach. At first it was a muted thudding, like the sound of another herd of animals moving through the forest just ahead—the one where Falcone had narrowly escaped being bitten by the mamba. But soon, there was no mistaking what was making the sound as the thudding became more distinctive and was accompanied by a call like no other. Trumpeting. As the elephants got closer to breaking through the edge of the trees and emerging into the savanna, their exclamations took on a frantic pitch, the reason for which required no speculation on Jake's part.

Into his comms, Jake said, "Get everybody moving *now*! Away from the trees, but as wide as we can from those mines."

As they hurried back through the field, the elephants thundered out of the forest, wailing as they ran in a pack of a dozen or more. Behind them, automatic gunfire popped. With the elephants coming up fast and the poachers right behind them, Jake scanned the landscape ahead for a course of evasion and just did not see one. If it had been just the five of them, he would have been all over launching an offensive, probably no matter the size of the rebel troops, but he knew he could not jeopardize the lives of all the people in his protection, so there was a decision to be made.

Glancing over his shoulder, he saw Niles and Dr. Goossens lifting a flailing Falcone off the ground. The panicked elephants were less than fifty yards away and closing, their human predators now clearing the trees in a rattling line, muzzles flashing.

Just as Jake was sure they were going to be seen and become part of the rebel poachers' assault, in an ironic twist of déjà vu, a moving sea of white came into view from the southwest. Fulani cattle stood rooted in place, placid but lowing in alarm of the frenzied flight and pursuit so close by, the collection of their long, lyre-shaped horns giving them the look of a stalwart army of Vikings. Kakwa herders appeared from within the throng and began corralling the animals. Despite the shooting, growing louder with the advancement, the cattle moved off slowly without any sign of bolting.

Drawing his group together, Jake lowered his voice and said, "Stay calm and weave your way into the herd. Don't spook them. This is the only cover I can see, so we need to make it count." To his guys, he added, "Keep your weapons down. We don't want the herd or herders to feel threatened."

"Do you think these are the same rebels?" Baladur asked him.

"Quite possibly," Jake replied. "Okay, let's go."

Spreading out, they all eased up on the retreating cattle and began to maneuver in between them. When the herders spotted them, they did not react, monitoring as silent sentinels. Exceedingly tall and thin, they wore long, flowing patterned cloths draped from the shoulder, their faces smudged with ash and bare skin pocked with tribal scarification.

Jake hung back, hunched low beside an umbrella thorn tree, its trunk not wide enough to completely conceal him. The elephants pounded past, poachers quickly gaining on them. There were at least ten men, reloading from packed ammo vests and lengthy bandolier belts.

Jake's mind was in a maelstrom of deliberation, weighing pros and cons, advantages and disadvantages, odds and risks. Many herdsmen had weapons to defend themselves against marauders and militias, but these did not appear to have any, so no help there. He had warned his guys off to stay with the group—were they back far enough to be safe if he engaged? His warrior mindset was always ready and willing to take on any enemy in most any situation, and he trusted his skills and ability to target and maneuver and overpower. But making potentially life-or-death tactical decisions became complicated when the lives and fates of others were in the mix. Still, he rarely, if ever, capitulated.

At that moment, he heard his iPhone ring. *What the hell?* He'd not been able to get a signal for his sat phone all morning and now, in the middle of nowhere, he was getting one for his cell phone? Impulsively, he slipped his hand into the pocket of his pants and took it out, too late to catch the call. Glanced at the display and saw two notifications.

Missed call and *Voicemail*. Both Callie.

In a blinding flash, his heart imploded and his mind jumped track. A flurry of anxiety-riddled thoughts spiked. Why had she called? Was something wrong? What time was it in Costa Rica…early morning?

His focus U-turned to the situation at hand. Odds and risks…

He fought to contain his fury, the compulsion to charge forward and shred the men to pieces so all-consuming he had to look away and loosen his grip on his rifle to leverage more self-control. Letting them go went against everything in his code of conduct, and it broke him in every other conceivable way. The sudden, excruciating shriek from one of the elephants snapped his head around and he saw a gigantean bull crash to the ground, bleeding from multiple bullet wounds, the rebel poachers gathering around, excited in their conquest. God, it would be so easy to take them out right now, he thought, agonizing, his gloved finger tight against the trigger of his M4. But in a split second, his odds for success dwindled as several of the men took up defensive positions, AKs pointed in every direction, including his.

One of the men produced a machete and marched to the front of the magnificent animal, still alive and now quiet as if steeling itself to die with dignity.

Jake could not watch, did not have to see the act to know that, like the *bai* massacre, he would see it and carry it with him forever.

Out of the corner of his eye Jake saw Falcone staggering toward him, a glazed expression of zombielike fixation, AR-15 pointed in front of him. Niles and Dmello were wrestling with him, trying without success to rein him in.

Jake turned and grabbed the end of Falcone's rifle, pushing it down. "Hey, what are you doing? Get back…come on, we're moving out."

"What?" Slack-jawed, Falcone looked incredulous. "No! Gotta get these fuckers!"

"I know," Jake said jaggedly, feeling as if he'd swallowed a mouthful of grit and glass. "Just not this time."

THEY HIKED A COUPLE of miles before taking another break, which became their stop for the day. It was early afternoon, the temperature hitting a torrid ninety degrees, and between the heat and the duress of their encounter with the rebel poachers, everyone was stressed and fatigued. Off their original course, if they continued it would be past dark by the time they reached the plane, and Jake just didn't think Falcone had it in him to keep going—not to mention the hallucinations he was experiencing. They were in a good place to make camp, with trees for shelter and another stream for water supply. Jake also knew he needed to get some food in the group, but hunting and cooking game would take too much time and effort. Fishing in a stream was ideal, so after announcing his decision to put down stakes, he dispatched some to see what they could catch. As it turned out, the Keoghs' people were quite adept with primitive fishing methods and did not need Jake to show them how to make hooks out of thorns and weave grasses and vines for lines and set up traps in the water.

After a satisfying meal of catfish and tilapia that had been wrapped in leaves and smoked over a big fire, Jake spent some time talking with individuals in the group to see what information he could glean about the rebels. He didn't learn anything actionable, but most agreed they were LRA, a few even saying they'd heard Joseph Kony mentioned. No one seemed to know anything about an American security contractor, but the general impression was that the rebel commander did have another affiliation more salient than Kony and with whom he was in a more engaged capacity. Jake asked about ivory and was told tusks had been brought into the camp but quickly disappeared. He delicately broached the subject of abuse, confirming what he'd already surmised; they had all suffered it in one form or another. Finally, he asked about the younger children and babies who had not yet been found. None had an answer. Aside from the accounts of abuse and unknown whereabouts of the youngest, the most chilling thing he heard was that the rebels had been on the verge of transferring the abductees to another camp in Kafia Kingi at the border of South Sudan and CAR; if Jake had come a day or so later, they would have all been gone.

Now, as he sat reviewing what had been shared, a rustling nearby brought him out of his rumination.

Niles plopped beside him with a sulky frown.

"What's wrong?" Jake asked him.

Nodding toward Falcone, who was stretched out on his hammock with Dr. Baudin mopping and fanning his face, Niles sniffed, "Lucky bastard. Why couldn't that be me?" He made a disgruntled noise. "Just not bloody fair."

"You crushing on her?" Jake shook his head and grinned. "Oh, bud. And trust me, you don't want malaria. It's not the flu. Are *you* taking your antimalarials?"

"Yeah." Niles sighed.

"Your nose is looking better," Jake offered.

Niles fingered it. "Well, thanks for that, for all the good it does." He went quiet, brushing dirt from his pants, and then said, "You know, Eddie says he doesn't remember letting those guys go free."

"I'm not surprised. Malaria often does a real number on the head…I'm sure you've noticed his altered behavior. The rebels we captured probably picked up on it and took advantage."

"Oh, okay, that makes more sense now. So what comes next?"

"We get everybody to Nakalé. After that, I don't know."

*   *   *   *   *

JAKE SAT GAZING WISTFULLY at the champagne-colored moon, barely showing, the night sky bright with stars. Somewhere in the trees, an owl hooted in the stillness and a frog croaked as if in reply. He had just completed a patrol, found everyone resting or asleep, and was about to take out his Iridium sat phone when Julienne Baudin came over.

"Mind if I join you?" she asked, smiling.

"Sure," he said, and made room for her at the base of the tree where he sat. He noticed that she had cleaned up, brushed her hair, applied some kind of lip gloss. The doctors apparently kept a change of clothing in their bags because she had also switched the soiled jeans and t-shirt she'd been wearing for a clean pair of khaki slacks and a sleeveless white linen blouse. The cleft between her ample breasts glistened with perspiration.

She took a seat next to him and exhaled. "That was something today." When Jake did not reply, she asked, "Did they get any of the elephants?"

"They did," Jake said flatly.

"*Ils sont très vils*," she said, her jaw tight.

"They are."

She looked at him, her eyes filling with interest. "You know French."

"I know a few languages," he said. "It's a Special Forces thing."

"I am not surprised that you have that background," she remarked, sliding a finger beneath her hair and lifting it away from her neck. "So the Keoghs hired you to find and rescue us?"

"Yes, but also their child."

"Lula…such a beautiful little girl. It is so sad. I do not think you will find her."

"No, it's not looking that way," he said dolefully.

She took a deep breath. "It feels so good to be outside, in the fresh air, even if it is hot. Being kept in that hut for days was not pleasant, but it could have been worse."

They sat in silence for a while, the buzz and whine of insects rising and falling. Dr. Baudin placed her hand on Jake's thigh without looking at him.

He did not move, pretending not to notice.

A moment passed and she slid her hand further toward his groin, fingers stretching into his inseam. Now she was looking at him, waiting, her lips parted.

Jake rolled on his haunches as if he was going to reach into a pocket of his cargo pants and she removed her hand. Unruffled, she asked, "No?"

"No," he answered. "I'm flattered, but no." He looked back at her and forced a smile. "You're lovely, really. But I have someone."

She was undeterred. "So? This is just now. A moment. *Il n'y a pas de mal.*"

"Sorry, no," he said a little more stiffly.

She seemed amused. "I always thought you military types were…on the edge, in the moment."

He said nothing.

She stood, her air of detachment returning, grasping and releasing the bottom section of her hair. It swished back over the nape of her neck. "Okay," she said lightly. "All good. See you in the morning."

He watched her saunter away, hips swaying back and forth, the fabric of her slacks conforming to her buttocks, thinking that in another time it would have gone a very different way. Just as his deliberation over going after the rebel poachers, and the ultimate decision about not doing so, also would have.

He acknowledged that this was his new reality, and again thought about the vulnerability he was not accustomed to and now had to own and learn to negotiate every time he was in a precarious situation. Today, he could have been killed—he could have been many times over in the days since his arrival in Africa. But he went into every mission knowing and accepting that. The day he could not do that was the day he would have to step away permanently. And, indecision in the moment was deadly. Was this the cost of love?

He took out his iPhone and replayed the message from Callie he'd listened to earlier. In the hesitant, endearingly timid voice, she said, *"Hi…I…I knew you probably wouldn't be able to talk. I just…I just wanted to hear your voice."* Long pause, then tremulously, *"I hope you're okay. Miss you."*

Soon, baby, soon, he thought.

He played it again, eyes welling, desire and yearning trenching deep into his gut. There was no cost he would not pay for that. God, he wanted to go home. Maybe tomorrow. As soon as he made the linkup with Sanborn and put the last of the Keoghs' people on the truck.

Wiping his eyes, he took out his sat phone and got a signal. There was a text message from Kent Sanborn. It read: *Call me asap. Urgent!*

He stood and placed the call.

Sanborn answered immediately. He said, "Jake, we've got a problem."

45

THE BEDROOM WAS STILL in shadow, but the sun was bright beyond the terrace, arcing toward its pinnacle over the Pacific, a golden beacon to the tropical greens and blues sparkling outside the open French doors. Callie lay in the big bed, feeling small in its emptiness and depleted from the hours of night that always passed so endlessly, especially without Jake. This time of morning, when the shade of dawn drew up to give daylight its first full reveal, was a tough negotiation. With darkness lifted and its apparitions driven back into the realm in which they existed, the relief for having made it through another night was so consummate that her mind and body let go of the tightly strung bindings of fearfulness and actually relaxed. The feeling was so fleeting that she lingered in it for as long as she could, the warmth of day swirling around the corners of the breezy vortex created by the ceiling fan turning overhead. The psychological bargaining would commence, a feeble inner voice invoking courage and campaigning for forward momentum, a much more desperate one pushing back with an entreaty to cling to the cocoon of calm that descended over the bed in the absence of night, and in that daylight embrace of comfort, she felt closer to Jake.

As she lay nestled in the pillows and sheets, holding onto the ethereal essence of him for those precious few moments, she experienced a profound pang of loneliness and wondered if he was safe, wondered if he was missing her the same way she missed him, wondered if he would be back soon. And just wanted, so badly, to hear his voice.

It had been about a week since she'd accompanied Jesse Segura to the beach and seen the man—at least she thought she had. Jesse Segura and Jerry Hadley had not seen him, and Jake emphatically assured her he was dead. Since then, she had repeatedly questioned the credibility of what her eyes had sighted on. Had the nighttime apparitions of that vile man now crossed over into the days? She needed to hear Jake telling her, again, that the monster no longer existed. Because the nightmares continued to be very real, and so had the daytime vision seemed.

She pulled up images of Jake on her phone and listened to the message he'd left before departing for Africa, but it was just not the same as hearing his voice live. As much as she wanted to talk to him, she did not want to bother him and always deferred to waiting for him to call her. But this particular morning, as she looked through the images on her iPhone, the yearning to hear his voice would not let go.

She tapped his contact and waited nervously for the connection to go through.

When his voicemail picked up, her heart pounded and she almost disconnected. She stammered something, seconds later not even remembering what, and was off the phone so quickly it was as if she'd not even placed the call. But the brief sound of his voice in her ear was as exhilarating as it was soothing, and it gave her the impetus to get out of bed and face the day.

CALLIE TOOK HER COFFEE onto the patio and sat watching as Ramón Cárdenas performed his daily pool maintenance, the pair of gardeners, Estabon Mina and Mauricio Leguizano, moving around the property putting out mulch and fertilizing and trimming. Cárdenas, listening to music through his earbuds, pointed to his head and gestured to her in question. Callie nodded, so he redirected his stream and Emmanuel Jal and Xavier Rudd's island-flavored *Be the Love* flowed from the patio's Bluetooth speaker.

"I like that," Callie told him, smiling.

Pleased, Cárdenas grinned and went back to work, kneeling to clean insects and leaves and flower petals out of the skimmer basket. "Already hot today," he observed. He finished, fit the lid on, and stood. "You should take a dip, *chica.*"

Hesitantly, she answered, "Maybe." But with the suggestion, temptation began to nibble, and she thought how rejuvenating and refreshing the water would feel. As the sun began to bake her skin, drawing perspiration and pink splotches of color, she went back inside and up to the bedroom to exchange her shorts and blouse for a swimsuit. She returned to the patio a few minutes later, wearing a floral-printed two-piece tankini under a crocheted white cover-up. She sat on one of the wicker chaises and squeezed sunscreen into the palms of her hands, applying it to her face and arms and legs, thinking about Jake's hands doing that, which spontaneously triggered the memory of their stay at the Tabacón spa resort in Arenal. They had only just met and, at his insistence, she'd donned a bikini and joined him in the luxuriant hot springs under a night sky of sparkling stars and floating volcanic embers, overwhelmed by a riotous deluge of never-experienced sensuality.

Feeling giddy with the memory, Callie fanned herself and started at the sudden presence of Camilla standing beside her. "Oh," she said, "I'm sorry, I didn't see you there."

The housekeeper smiled, recognizing the flush in Callie's face, one she had only seen when Jake was around. "Ah, *mija,* you must be thinking nice thoughts," she remarked. "Good, very good." Her cheerful demeanor was replaced by a flicker of reluctance. "I need to pick up some groceries in town at the Super."

"Okay," Callie replied, not quite concealing the look of unease that involuntarily arose. Attempting to suppress it, she said, "Take your time, do something nice for *you*...go to the hair salon if you'd like or buy something new to wear?"

Camilla glanced down at her dress, an attractive orange shift patterned with white orchids. "Oh, I have plenty of—" she began.

"I just meant as a treat," Callie clarified. "Treat yourself, you deserve it. You take such good care of me. Please?"

The housekeeper beamed and leaned down to kiss Callie's cheek. "*Mi preciosa niña,*" she uttered affectionly. "*Gracias,* Miss Callie, I will see, but probably just the groceries. Just...you, no too much sun." She wagged her finger.

Callie watched Camilla go over to Ramón Cárdenas and say

something to him, both glancing back at her. Camilla retreated and Cárdenas returned to his task of sweeping the patio.

Not long after Jake had left, it occurred to Callie that, as much work as a residence this size required, particularly given the pool and land-scaped grounds, it hardly constituted a seven-day-week presence by all involved. When Jake had told her there would always be someone around, it was because he'd arranging for the staff to be here, necessary or not, and yet none took advantage of the arrangement. They were always doing something productive while also keeping an eye on her, which went a long way toward making her feel more secure in Jake's absence. Still, especially since seeing—or imagining—the man at the beach, she would often experience a wave of raw vulnerability that came out of nowhere.

With a little quiver, she removed her wrap and padded to the pool. Dipped a toe in and felt the water, warm but cooler than the air. She sat down on the stone pavement and twisted around, slipping her legs into the pool and gazing out over the curved infinity edge, marveling at the breathtaking view. From this perspective, the turquoise ocean appeared to abut right up against the treetops and stretch boundlessly below a sky of nearly the same hue, delineated by a pale stripe of light, giving the illusion of being steps away instead of across the low-cut grass and down the slope of rainforest. She eased onto the inner ledge, submerging her hips, and sat like that for a little while as Cárdenas cleaned the tables and chairs, spraying and wiping, moving with the music of Michael Castro and singing along with *Be Happy Be Free*. To her right, Mina and Legui-zano were clearing old mulch and shoveling new from a wheelbarrow, smoothing it with rakes around the bases of trees and in the borders of shrubs and flowerbeds bursting with bright color. Even with the faint tinge of chlorine in the air, she could smell the rich earthiness of the mulch. Tilting her head, she peered up at the royal palms that towered past the roof of the villa, somehow feeling reassured by their tall, an-chored presence and the fullness of their cascading fronds.

Eventually, Callie slid fully into the water, wading out until it came up to her collarbone, closing her eyes in enjoyment of the weightless envelopment that seemed to untether her from everything. Since Jake had been gone, the extent of her pool time was cautiously limited to shallow dips and relaxing on a lounge chair. But this morning, after a few moments, she found herself drifting further toward the deep side in the curve, and slipped beneath the surface.

When she emerged, she thought she heard the distant gurgle of a vehicle's motor turning off. Cárdenas was still working on the patio furniture, the gardeners still mulching in the gardens. She submerged again, this time spreading her arms and paddling her feet, beginning to let go, the depths of the pool like the aqua sky, light and expansive and serene. And then something wrinkled over the water above her and she rose, breaking the surface. Wiping her eyes, she squinted blurrily, and found Cárdenas squatting at the edge.

Water clogged her ears, but his mouth was moving and she brokenly heard, "...front...right back..."

Cárdenas stood and walked away, striding across the grass. From the gardens, Mina and Leguizano had set their shovels and rakes aside and were following him, removing their gloves and wiping sweat from their faces.

Callie propped her arms on the pool's edge and watched as they disappeared and then returned, a uniformed man trailing behind them wheeling a hand truck piled high with big plastic buckets and hefty sacks of pool and gardening supplies. They all disappeared around the far lower side of the villa where the storage area was. Several minutes went by and Callie swished back into the water, gliding with her head above the surface. Finally, she dropped below again, moving gracefully from one end of the pool to the other, the sun shimmering in fractals of light overhead.

For a moment, that prickly sense of vulnerability, a kind of foreboding, shimmied through her, and she glanced up. Diamonds of sunlight danced in the crystal clear water.

She was about to ascend when a dark figure materialized above, truncated and indistinguishable. She paused, thinking it did not look like Ramón Cárdenas, but she could not tell who it did look like; from this depth, anyone or anything overhead was a wash of skewed shapes and achromatic shadows. She felt a pinch of anxiety as she floated up, lifted her head from the water, and gripped the curved infinity side of the pool. Blinked. Details came in and out of focus and, as her eyes cleared, a scream dry-heaved up her throat.

The figure looming over her displayed a fixed, open grin, eyes hidden behind wraparound Locs. His Gucci leather-thonged feet were splayed at forty-five-degree angles in his crouch, hands clasped between his knees, the nails of both hands and feet impeccably manicured and buffed to a sheen. A Hawaiian-style shirt open to mid-chest hung loose over tight denim shorts, a gold chain dangling from his neck. His hair was dark and slicked back, twisted into a knot behind his head.

But the only thing Callie registered was a composite of the grin, the gleaming white teeth, and the sunglasses. Receptors of fear and panic collided in a frenzy of overclocked reaction, her heart exploding inside her chest.

Her hands released from the pool rim and she slid thrashing below the water.

SHE WAS BEING LIFTED up, water sluicing from her arms and legs and torso, streaming from her hair and dripping from her feet. Sunlight was white and blinding, dizzying, her head heavy. She felt her body quaking, unable to see through the haze or to speak through the thickness in her mouth and throat. Her breath seemed to come from behind a concrete wall.

"Miss Callie…hey, *oye ven aquí*…"

Her eyelids fluttered, focus slowly returning. Three heads hovering over her all exhaled at once, exchanging rapid Spanish between them and murmuring, "*Ay, ay, ay*," and "*gracias a Dios*."

"Hey, what happened, *querida*? Huh?"

Callie recognized Ramón Cárdenas, Estabon Mina and Mauricio Leguizano standing behind him, their swarthy faces furrowed with puzzlement and concern. "I…I don't know," she finally said.

"You think you might have hit your head?" Cárdenas speculated.

Callie was mentally struggling to find the threads to pull her thoughts together when her mind was blasted by a harsh flash that was like the ultraviolet light in the blackness of a nightclub.

Punctuated in the flash, she saw his face…it was him, again.

"That man…" she stammered, her lips trembling.

"What man?" Cárdenas asked.

"Here...the pool," she said weakly.

The three men huddled around her looked at each other, nonplussed.

"You see a man? Here at the pool?" Cárdenas glanced over both shoulders, as if someone might be loitering at the corners of the villa, and then his posture relaxed and he smiled lightly. "Ah, the truck driver for our delivery. He came to the pool?" He reconsidered that. "No, I see him leave."

"No," Callie said, and felt the heaviness again, the sun hurting her eyes and making her even more dizzy. "The man I saw...the beach..."

"Okay," Cárdenas said, "we go inside." He helped her up from the chaise and walked with her into the villa.

CAMILLA PULLED INTO THE driveway in her gray SUV and switched the ignition off, touching the dashboard with reverence, a rosary hanging from the mirror. The music from 88 Stereo continued playing until she opened the door. She was still getting acquainted with the brand new Toyota RAV4 Jake had gifted her with all its techno gadgetry, her previous car a rusting, over-heating compact that she had driven on nearly bald tires. Rising from the driver's seat, she instinctively listened but heard nothing out of the ordinary.

She walked around to the rear and opened the trunk, extracting canvas grocery bags and hooking them onto her arms. Though tempted, she'd passed on the hair salon and clothes shopping, unable to free herself from worry over being gone too long. Striding toward the front door of the villa, one of the canvas bags slipped and she stopped to adjust it. As she did, another bag tipped and several avocados popped out, rolling into the grass below a cluster of areca palms.

"Ay," she muttered, and started toward the spot to retrieve them.

To her surprise, a man in a tropical-patterned shirt and denim Bermuda shorts appeared, bent down, collected the avocados, and handed them to her with a dazzling smile. As gallant as he was, and certainly striking in physical attributes, there was something about him that made Camilla inwardly recoil.

She tucked the avocados back into the bag and stepped closer to her

SUV. *"Gracias, Señor,"* she said, and quickly strode to the front door of the villa, jiggling her key in the lock. Glancing over her shoulder as the lock's tumblers turned, she saw that the man was gone.

Pushing the front door open, she found Cárdenas with Callie, the two gardeners behind him. They hurried over to take the groceries from her.

Looking at Callie, Camilla asked, *"Que esta pasando?"*

"I am not sure," Cárdenas said. "Maybe too much sun."

46

AFTER THE SECOND NIGHT with the last of the Keoghs' people, Jake and Dmello were flying, not to Nakalé with an afflicted Eddie Falcone aboard, but to Kenya. Earlier in the day he'd met Kent Sanborn to make the handoff, then he and Dmello had boarded the Cessna, notifying Nash Remington they would be making a stop at Nairobi's Wilson Airport to refuel. Remington let Jake know he would be there with a restock of supplies and as much up-to-the-minute intel as Kipnis could gather. When Jake informed Baladur and Niles that he was making the trip solo with only Dmello flying him, both were somewhat stunned and lobbied fervently, but Jake insisted they stay to help Sanborn with security detail in Nakalé.

During the flight to Nairobi, Jake spent the first couple of hours on his Toughbook researching what he could, but with the signal cutting in and out he eventually gave up and dozed intermittently. He'd not gotten any sleep the previous night and, after his thoughts of going home had been so abruptly derailed by Sanborn's upending call in the wee morning hours, his mind had been spinning in full-tilt impending disaster mode, so he forced himself to rest while he had the chance; he'd have to hit the ground running as soon as they made the second landing. It was just after three o'clock when Dmello put the plane down at Wilson and taxied to their hangar. Jake saw Remington standing with Kipnis, both wearing grim expressions. Dmello brought the Cessna to a stop, and Jake climbed out, striding over to them.

"No good news, I'm guessing," he said.

"No. Sorry, brother," Remington replied tersely. "And I've got to run in a minute…but I wanted to be here when you landed. Wish I wasn't committed and could go with."

Jake crossed his arms and gripped his biceps, blowing out a breath. "Me, too, but I understand." His gaze shifted to Kipnis. "You have anything for me?"

"It's all on here," Kipnis said, and handed him a thumb drive. "There's some sat images with coordinates, but things being in flux, I'll keep monitoring and text you any updates."

"You have any idea what you're going to do when you get there?" Remington asked.

"Not really," Jake said, "but I guess there aren't many options."

"Are you sure you don't want me to notify anybody?"

"No, I think it's gonna have to be off the radar. But if you pick up any chatter, let me know."

"I will," Kipnis said.

A strained look of chagrin creased Remington's forehead. "Maybe I should blow my gig. I don't feel good about you doing this without some kind of support."

Jake thumped him on the shoulder and met eyes that were the color of cactus and every bit as sharp. "It's all good, Remy. Stick to your commitments. I'll manage. I almost think for this, you either go in with an army or an army of one."

Remington held Jake's eyes, trying to measure his level of confidence.

"Really, Remy. I'll be fine."

After several more minutes of conversation about what lay ahead for Jake, they parted ways, Remington and Kipnis in the Range Rover with Jimiyu Chilemba grinning and waving from behind the wheel. Jake and Dmello reboarded the Cessna and got ready for takeoff.

They sped down runway 14 and lifted into a sky layered with ashen clouds, flying over the Southern Bypass and the sprawl of Nairobi National Park and then bearing southeast toward Tsavo and Mount Kilimanjaro. Watching the changing landscape through his passenger seat window, Jake felt a trickle of ambivalence and wondered if he should have agreed to more help. But his gut instinct told him to go dark.

One thing was for sure—this was about as hairy an undertaking as he could ever have imagined.

CYRUS KEOGH HAD BEEN fondly watching his wife teach a circle of children how to recite English phrases when Cameron McNamara came running up to him waving the sat phone. Keogh's expression of pleasure lingered as he had turned to greet his assistant, expecting the call to be from Jake with the good news that more of their people had been found and rescued, but his smile quickly deflated when he'd seen the blanched look of shock on McNamara's face. "What is it, mate?"

McNamara motioned him out of earshot from Amelia Keogh and, in a lowered voice, said, "It's from Archer."

Smile recovering, Keogh took the sat phone and spoke brightly. "Archie! I reckon you're about ready to blow that big tinny to tip a cold one, yeah?"

But it had not been his friend Archer Rudd on the phone and, after listening for a few moments, all lightness had drained from Keogh. "Who is this?" A minute later, he said tightly, "Yes, I've got it. You have my word. I'm on my way. Yes, I understand."

Before the call disconnected, he'd heard Rudd yell, "Don't bloody do it, Cy!"

Now, as he lay next to Amelia on one of two cots pushed together in their hut, he listened to her breathing to make sure she was sound asleep. Leaning over, he brushed strands of russet hair from her cheek and touched his lips to her skin, whispering, "I love you, my darling," and then got quietly to his feet. Earlier, while she was still occupied with the children, he had stuffed some things into his backpack and issued instructions to McNamara, one of which was to keep everything to himself as long as possible. Another was to arrange for a helicopter to wait in the clearing outside of the village. He hated not telling Amelia, but she would probably have tried to stop him, and Sanborn most certainly would. He'd left a note for Amelia with McNamara in which he explained what was happening.

He took one last look at his sleeping wife, inhaled deeply, and peeked through the fabric hung over the hut's entrance. When Kent Sanborn strolled in the opposite direction, Keogh darted out and headed for the trees, advancing furtively until he reached the field and saw the helicopter, waning moonlight glinting on the metal shell. He trotted to it, hopped aboard, and minutes later it was winding up for liftoff.

The Airbus H125, engaged from the same company as the Eurocopter, one he'd been using for years, delivered him to Bunia in just over an hour. From there, he boarded a King Air 350, also from the charter previously used, and was flown another two and a half hours.

As a brilliant sunburst of pink and orange lit up the horizon, he landed at the airport on Manda Island in the Lamu Archipelago off the Kenyan coast, one hundred fifty miles from Mombasa. Manda town, once a trade route for ivory, is now a locale of historical and archaeological significance and of exclusive resorts. But when Keogh stepped off the plane, a surly man was waiting for him with his name scrawled on a sign, definitely not an employee from one of those resorts. The man was tall and lean and spoke no English. After being roughly patted down, Keogh was led past the modest arrival and departures structure to a jetty at the water's edge and prodded onto a small boat with an outboard motor. Next to them, a larger boat destined for Lamu, which was across from Manda, was being filled with chattering tourists.

The man yanked the engine to sputtering life and they motored into the inlet between islands. The sky above and water below were among the most spectacular shades of blue Cyrus Keogh had ever seen, like ancient Persian pottery. But the waves looked like they could cut glass. The spray generated by the boat's speed blew through his hair and he glanced back at the shrinking shoreline with the sinking feeling that maybe he should have called Jake after all and at least asked him what to do. But it was too late now.

The boat's motor buzzed raucously and the chop of its bow splashed over the sides as they ploughed out into the Indian Ocean.

JAKE SPENT MOST OF the second leg of the flight going over the intel on the thumb drive Kipnis had provided, but there wasn't much. A series of sat images, a range of coordinates, local information. Then he sorted what he would need and packed it into a Watershed drybag, putting his radio and phones into Ziplocs for extra protection. When they reached the coast of Mombasa, Jake relayed the coordinates from the intel and Dmello flew out over the ocean, descending to two thousand feet for surveillance. With his binoculars trained on the water, Jake searched as Dmello flew south and then looped back and headed north. Where the waters within fifty miles of the big port city were heavily congested, the farther they got beyond that radius, the more scattered the traffic became. A few minutes along the northern trajectory and Jake said, "I've got it."

Flying inland, they passed over a long strip of uninhabited beach.

Kipini is a small fishing village located near the estuary of the Tana River, a major artery that flows over five hundred miles from Mount Kenya. It is comprised of thick mangrove forests and vegetation that terminates at the river and ocean shore with steep white sand dunes and rocky cliffs, seagrasses, and offshore coral reefs. Most times, it appears to be untouched by humanity, as it was today. It was near here Dmello landed, on a dirt strip about a mile inland. There was nothing around it but forest.

Standing beside the plane, Dmello watched solemnly as Jake gave his pockets and drybag a last check to make sure he had everything. His normally jolly face was filled with concerned intensity and evolving doubt. He asked, "Are you sure you do not want me to come with you?"

"No, Kean, you stay here with the plane. Just be prepared for a hot exfil. I'll stay on comms as much as I can, and if I lose contact I'll try to reestablish on my way back."

"I have contacts with the Coast Guard here...you do not want to involve them?"

Jake gave him a contemplative look. "It's a tough call, but no."

Dmello sighed. "Okay, boss. Godspeed."

Jake nodded and headed into the mangroves.

It took him about twenty minutes to reach the river, the forest clamoring with the undulations and shrieks of primates, the whistles and squawks of birds, and the whine of insects. It was steamy and smelled of brackish organics and spawning fish and algae, the ground squishing underfoot. Walking along the river's edge, he heard the grunts and groans and splashes of crocodiles and occasionally spotted the bobbing heads of hippos. Emerging from the trees, the river's muddy silt turned the color of rust in the light of a retreating sun. He followed the shore for a couple more miles past the river's mouth, winding up on a stretch of empty beach. But at this hour of the day, with dusk approaching, he was counting on the return of local fishermen. He sat down on the sand, took out a bottle of water, drank thirstily, and waited.

As the sun lowered to meet the water, coating it with a glimmer that was like hammered bronze, haggard men and boys in dilapidated wooden boats flowed in with the tide, hopping into the surf and dragging their crafts onto the beach. Jake watched as they plopped slabs of fish by their feet, eying him curiously. He continued waiting and watching until finally he heard the drone of a motor and saw the boat it propelled come into view. A single fisherman killed the outboard and began collecting his fish and gear.

Kipnis had included a deflated RIB with the restocked supplies, but finding a boat locally was a better option than hauling it from the plane, so he was encouraged by his luck.

Jake approached the fisherman casually with a friendly smile. *"Hujambo,"* he said.

The man turned and gaped at Jake, his face gaunt and frame emaciated. Despite the boat's outboard motor, which would have enabled him to venture into the more plenteous sea depths, there were none of the big game fish in his catch, no tuna or swordfish or marlin, only some snapper and mackerel. He continued cleaning out his boat, keeping a wary eye on Jake.

"Can I use your boat?" Jake asked, pointing to the weather-beaten skiff. When the man did not respond, Jake said, *"Mashua"* and took out some Kenyan shilling notes from his pants pocket, fanning the bills for him to see.

This stopped the man who stared at the money as if Jake had presented the keys to some otherworldly kingdom which, in a way, he had. He suspected the fisherman had a destitute family, and his offer of twenty thousand shillings, though modest at the equivalent of just under two hundred dollars, would afford them many days of sustenance. Extending his bony palm, the man said, *"Asante."*

As an afterthought, Jake tried to convey in what limited Swahili he knew that he would try to return the boat, but he didn't think the man understood, so he peeled off several more bills and put them in his hand. The man's eyes grew big and he broke out in a jagged-toothed grin, repeating, *"Asante,"* and adding, *"Mungu akubariki."*

"You're welcome," Jake said. He watched the man gather his belongings and drag the sachel containing his catch, plodding barefoot across the sand and disappearing over the dunes.

IT TOOK CONSIDERABLE TIME and skill to maneuver the boat past the offshore fringe of coral reefs and beds of seagrass, but Jake did so by using the oars. A little over a mile out, he felt a tidal surge—a convergence of the East African Coastal and Somali currents—and started the motor. The Chinese-made outboard appeared to have been extensively jerry-rigged and, with the added impairment of corrosion from the marine elements, took several tries to engage. But once it did, coughing up an initial puff of black smoke, the horsepower was surprisingly robust, pitching the boat forward in a bow-tipping lurch. When the boat's ride leveled, Jake checked the compass and GPS on his tactix watch and steered accordingly, heading southeast out of Ungwana Bay where the Indian Ocean depths dropped to more than two miles.

The moon was barely visible in the twilight, which would be a disadvantage for him, but it did help navigation, illuminating the water in a silvery sheen. As he motored on, he began to notice moving clouds blotting out the light in intervals and knew a storm was brewing. It wasn't long before filaments of lightning began crawling across the sky. He was also seeing a difference in the water, swells rising and falling and capping with curls of foam, spraying him from both sides of the boat. Consulting his watch, he saw that he was ten miles out and getting close to the targeted coordinates.

Fifteen minutes later, he could just make out an elongated shape in the distance, stamped against the darkness like a stencil in the cloud-filtered moonlight. He peered through his FLIR Recon thermal scope, zoomed in, and the silhouette became dimensional in the form of a container ship—all six hundred-plus feet and a minimum of twenty-five thousand tons—where, according to the note Keogh had left, his best friend and partner, Archer Rudd, and the ship's captain and crew were being held hostage by pirates. And, probably by now, so was Cyrus Keogh.

Jake got within a few hundred yards and killed the motor. Being downwind, he doubted he would be heard, but he didn't want to take any chances. With his motor off, he could hear faint clanking from the ship, which was not moving. International Maritime laws require directional lighting consisting of green on the starboard side, red on the port side, and white on the stern in both directions, but it had gone completely dark. Panning the ship's length with his scope, he was able to pick out several human figures in the vicinity of the stern, which confirmed the situation, because with the high definition 640x480 thermal sensor, he could clearly see the rifles they carried.

As he began rowing the rest of the way to the ship, rain started to fleck against his face.

THAT MORNING, WHEN CYRUS Keogh was picked up in Manda, he'd thought perhaps he would be taken to another coastal location and was therefore surprised when the motorboat sped farther and farther out to sea, the shore soon gone from view. They had moved at a pretty swift clip, completing the trip in about thirty minutes and coming to a stop by the side of a vessel he recognized all too well. With a midnight-blue hull, massive containers stacked like Legos on the deck, and the Liberian flag that looked like an American knockoff with its red-and-white stripes, navy square and white star, he knew it was his. But the space on the middle of the upper hull where the name *Empowered* should have been was painted over, conspicuous by the mismatch of shades, though it might not be noticeable from a distance and that was all that mattered.

One of the ship's ladders was extended over the side and he was ordered to climb. Which he did. At the top, he was pulled onto the deck, facing two dark-skinned men with hostile expressions and AK-47s aimed at him. Forcing a grin, Keogh had said, "It's all right, mates. No need to point those at me. I've got an invitation, don't I?"

They shoved him around and poked him in the back with the muzzles of their rifles.

Walking, he said, "Hey, it's my boat, I know where we're going."

When they reached the stern of the ship, one of the men opened the door for the stairs leading to the bridge and pushed Keogh into the corridor. They ascended several flights to the top and entered the wheelhouse. Inside was a console that spanned much of the spacious suite, around which was a wall of window panels affording a clear view from port to starboard. A steering wheel platform centered a complex layout of gauges and dials and knobs and buttons and screens and keyboards—the brains of the ship with electronic navigation and radar charts, engine controls and communications. Separated by a row of cabinets and storage lockers were chart tables and a radio station.

Seated against the row of lockers behind the console, legs stretched straight out in front of them, were the captain, his first mate, and one other crewman. Their wrists and ankles were bound with duct tape, their mouths taped as well. When they saw Keogh, their eyes went wide with reactions that were a mixture of hope and despair.

Had they been able to talk, they would have told Keogh that the ship had been cruising smoothly at nineteen knots and was on schedule for their approach to Mombasa when a small craft appeared on the radar, racing their way. They had immediately begun evasive measures, which included altering their course and increasing speed, but once the pirates had closed the gap, they had no choice but to surrender; an RPG flew over the bow and a fusillade of automatic gunfire sealed the deal. On the decrease in recent years, most incidents of piracy occurred farther north in Somali waters, and even though drills were a part of their ongoing training, an attack such as this was not something they anticipated. In the hours that followed the boarding, they had been forced to divert north, some one hundred miles from Mombasa, and then shut the engines down.

Peering down at the captain and two crewmates, Keogh chuckled nervously and quipped, "Boys, I don't pay you to be mucking about." He winked at them and turned to face the man who seemed to be in charge, holding court from the captain's chair.

"Mr. Keogh," the man said, pronouncing the name *Kee-yo*. "You got our instructions. Where is the money?" Like the pair of men that had marched Keogh from the main deck to the bridge, he was dark in complexion and hair and could have been native Kenyan or Somali or Arabic or some other regional ethnicity, but what he did not look like was what Keogh would have envisioned as a pirate. He was a little older, maybe early thirties, and neatly dressed in a freshly laundered pinstriped shirt, pressed beige slacks, and brown stitched-leather cowboy boots. His accented English was good, his tone all-business.

"Let's take it down a notch, yeah?" Keogh asked calmly. "First things first. Who am I dealing with? What is your name?"

The man did not reply.

"Look, you know my name. Just give me something to call you."

The man glared at Keogh for several seconds, finally replying, "Mr. Dhahar." He stuck his chin out, hands clasped in his lap. "The money."

Keogh glanced around the wheelhouse, abandoning his cooperative air. "I don't see Archer."

"And you will not," Dhahar said bluntly. "Until we have the money."

Keogh thought about his dilemma for several moments as Dhahar and his two comrades all stared at him. "All right, I have your money, and you will get it. But I need some time to put things in motion."

"No. You have already had plenty of time."

Keogh had looked at Dhahar then, realizing that he'd badly misjudged his ability to control the situation. These were not desperate, hyped up locals—no, there was something else going on here. But he could not let them dictate the terms if he was to have any chance of emerging from this successfully, and success for him had nothing to do with the ship and everything to do with the lives of its crew and his best friend, Archer Rudd.

"You want that money, you will get it. But I won't start the process until I see Archer."

"No," Dhahar said again. "Five million is the price. You get nothing until you pay."

Keogh crossed his arms defiantly. "I will start the process, but I will not complete it until Archer is right here next to me." Again, Dhahar did not respond, so Keogh tried another tact. "You know, it would be best if we concluded our business sooner rather than later. This ship is equipped with automatic tracking, and certainly by daylight—"

Dhahar sneered and glanced at his lap, as if humored by some private joke. "You mean the AIS," he said, referring to the Automatic Identification System installed onboard that was closely monitored by the Coast Guard and local authorities. "That would be true except the device from your ship is back near Mombasa."

Keogh looked at him in disbelief, said nothing.

Dhahar added with relish, "Moving around slowly in one of *our* boats."

Minutes later, after making a call to Cameron McNamara, Cyrus Keogh had been taped up and seated beside the captain of his ship.

The man named Dhahar had not made a move to produce Archer Rudd.

JAKE STOPPED PADDLING WITHIN twenty yards of the container ship and conducted another surveillance with his scope, finding the same number of figures in basically the same positions. That was good and indicated to him that the hijack team probably had assigned places on the ship, which he surmised would make it easier for him to move around. He took up the oars and resumed his advancement, rain coming down with a little more persistence, wetting his face and dripping into his eyes. He debated slipping on the rain poncho in his pack but decided he'd trade off getting wetter with more freedom of movement. He paddled all the way to the ship, astounded at the immensity of it once he was alongside it. Digging out a suction tether he'd put in one of his pockets, he attached the boat's line to the metal hull.

Glancing up, he estimated the distance to the deck to be at least forty feet, and extracted the grappling hook he had configured while sitting on the beach. The hook was attached to Teflon rope with Prusiks for hand-holds. Pulling on his MTP gloves, he stood up in the skiff and tried to balance, which wasn't easy in the pitching water. When he was as set as he could be, he leaned back and tossed the hook into the air and hoped it would catch on the first try. With the dark and the wind and the rain, his aim was off, and the hook clinked against the side. The sound barely registered, so he recovered it, steadied himself again, and made another throw. This time, the hook caught. He tugged hard to make sure it was secure, and then hoisted himself up and began his ascent.

It was a tough climb, wind-driven rain pelting his face and little or no traction against the ship's side, but he made it to the top, and grabbed the base of a railing. He looked right and left, saw no one, and pushed himself up onto the deck.

AS THE HOURS HAD passed, Cyrus Keogh had been increasingly convinced he'd made a huge mistake. When he had spoken to Cameron McNamara on the phone, he'd instructed him to slow-walk the transaction process by using a code word they had worked out before his departure. Once the hijackers, whoever they were, had the ransom, there would be no more leverage on his end, and they knew Keogh's incentive was the well-being of his friend. They were obviously going to use that until he came through with the money. So, while it was a game of chicken, they had all the road. Why should they release Rudd or, really, any of them?

God, he had been such a fool.

Keogh turned to look at the captain and two crew. He'd met them on previous visits to the ship when it had been in port in the Seychelles. He knew their names—Captain Aiden Byrne, First Mate Toby McInnes, and Jackson Farrugia—but not a whole lot more, like if they had kids or dogs or were zealous football fans. His thoughts turned to Rudd, the one person other than his wife that he would do anything for. Like this, which he'd done without question.

But was getting these guys the money going to be enough?

He glanced through the window panels beyond the wheelhouse command center and saw Dhahar talking on a sat phone, nodding. *He's talking to whoever is orchestrating this*, Keogh thought. Is he telling the boss that it's going well, that it's going according to plan, or is he expressing skepticism and frustration? Closing his eyes, Keogh reflected on the day Archer had lost his leg—a day that had changed both of their lives.

They'd been surfing in Jeffrey's Bay and having a blast of a time. It was coming up on sunset and Rudd had been telling him they needed to pack it in. But Keogh had been watching the waves grow bigger and bigger and wanted one last ride. Rudd indulged him and joined in, both catching a monumental swell that wrapped around them in a barrel, a condition all skilled surfers lusted for. Rudd had wiped out early on, but Keogh had ridden it all the way and was euphoric at the conclusion. But when he looked for his friend, he saw no sign of him. And then he noticed people on the beach pointing and yelling, saw lifeguards racing into the water. He'd instinctively raced in after them, a dread seizing him like he'd never experienced before, somehow already knowing.

There had been so much blood, the crystal blue water turning bright red in an expanding wash that seemed the size of a small oil slick, and when Rudd was pulled out, his lips were purple, his skin the color of a raw oyster, and he wasn't breathing. Keogh had not even noticed the severed leg, had only focused on the lifeguards trying to resuscitate Rudd. He remembered praying more than he'd ever prayed in his life, making promises to any higher power that existed. And then, miraculously, Rudd had been revived.

Later, when Rudd had been released from the hospital, the first thing he wanted to do was go surfing, but of course that was next to impossible with only one leg. Keogh made it his mission to find his friend the best prosthetic available, but even when it was fitted and Rudd had put in the torturous work required in physical therapy, the surfing was resoundingly subpar. That was when the two of them brainstormed and came up with the seeds of technology and the product line that launched the foundation division of Blue Aurora dubbed Empowered Breaks, *Empowered* ultimately adopted as the name for their first ship.

Keogh's thoughts broke off with the return of Dhahar. He jerked Keogh to his feet, and stepped close to his face. "I have waited long enough. There has been no contact, no transaction activity. You are fucking with me, so you will see what that gets you."

Before Keogh could even register the words, Archer Rudd was marched through the door, tall, tanned, fuzz of blond-brown hair, his bionic synthetic leg concealed by relaxed-fit stonewashed jeans. He was similarly taped, his eyes steely with courage and determination. When his gaze landed on Keogh, the slack in his facial muscles suggested a smile.

And then Dhahar had put a handgun to Rudd's temple and pulled the trigger.

47

JAKE STOOD ON THE deck near the bow where he had boarded and made his way slowly toward the stern. Kipnis had included detailed blueprints of Keogh's ship on the thumb drive, so he already had something of an orientation. He was pretty sure the leader of the group would be stationed on the navigation bridge of the ship's accommodations tower and was probably holding Rudd and Keogh there. The multi-decked tower contained staterooms for the ship's officers and crew, mess halls and galley, pantries and cold storage, offices and lounges and recreational areas, an infirmary and gym, laundry and fire locker, and engine control. Much of the rest of the ship's real estate was taken up by cargo, and lots of it, a mix of twenty- and forty-foot metal containers numbering about twenty-five hundred and stacked in columns that rose at least sixty feet above deck, filling another twenty-four below, rows spanning most of the one hundred feet between port and starboard. Ships such as this one carried everything from electronics and goods for big-box stores to cars and industrial machinery, and Keogh's typically transported inventory for his many distribution centers, but these containers also held the replacement components of infrastructure and humanitarian aid the Keoghs had used to build up the village compound that had been destroyed: bricks and lumber, construction tools and materials, solar panels and generators, satellites and water systems, clothing and personal supplies, food and medicine.

The rain was moderate but steady, pinging on the metal railings and blowing into the covered passageway, lightning coming more frequently and thunder drumming in the muted fashion that leads up to a more dramatic salvo. As he approached the accommodations tower, Jake saw a pair of armed men standing by the entrance and ducked down a narrow gap between the last row of containers and crossed to the other side. He peered around the end and spotted another man who was standing by the starboard entrance, his back turned.

Jake slipped up behind him, pulled out his Spartan Horkos knife and, clamping a hand over his mouth, thrust the blade into his head through the right ear. He eased the man's lifeless weight to the deck and bent to drag him away from the tower. One down, but how many more? The two he'd seen on the port side, the leader on the bridge, probably one or more guarding the crew. That would be five or six. Had they come in one boat or two? Since he'd not seen any on his approach, they must have attacked from this side.

He stepped into the passageway and looked out to the water through his scope, and saw two motorboats bobbing in the choppy sea, lines tied to something below. Two boats could mean ten or twelve men. *Shit.* Where were they all?

Going back to the tower, he waited at the end of the container row, watching to make sure there were no others by the starboard side entrance. Then he went to the door, opened it, light spilling out, and paused. He was sure there would be one or more pirates at the top of the stairwell and, depending on where the crew was being held, maybe a landing before the top. Walking around to the stern deck, he saw a metal staircase on the outside of the tower, and chose it instead.

He climbed each of the six flights, his hair and shirt damp from rain, and came to the bridge wings that extended out from the wheelhouse and stopped. If there were men up here on the outside, he'd probably have to shoot them and that would stir up a hornet's nest in a hurry. Again, he waited and watched. Saw nobody moving, at least not on this side. Crouching down, he walked around the platform until he came to the paneled windows and carefully peered inside the dimly lit space.

He saw the man whose posture and mannerisms marked him as the leader, pacing restlessly but affecting a confident swagger. He put the thermal scope to his eye and scanned the interior but saw no one else.

The captain and crew could be any number of places on this massive ship. But he had expected to see Keogh up here. Where was he?

AT THE SIGHT OF his best friend, Keogh's spontaneous reaction had been one of overwhelming relief and gratitude, but in an instant, as Dhahar put the gun to Rudd's head and pulled the trigger, his brain froze up and then broke apart like ice cracked by a mallet.

Behind the duct tape over his mouth, he screamed, "Nooooooo!" And looked away just as Dhahar pulled the trigger. But instead of a bang, he heard a click. Shakily, he turned his head. Archer Rudd was still there, still standing, still breathing. Not bleeding. Keogh sagged and sobs convulsed in his chest.

Dhahar's eyes flashed angrily at Keogh and he declared, "No more stalling! There will be a bullet next time." He made a show of removing the 9mm's empty magazine, digging into his pants pocket and coming up with a loaded one, snapping the clip in place, and pulling the slide to load a round. He gestured to the man holding Rudd and he was put on the floor next to Keogh. His eyes fell on the captain, first mate, and crewman. "Take them below with the others."

The three were pulled up, tape cut between their ankles to allow movement, and paraded from the wheelhouse.

Dhahar squatted in front of Keogh and Rudd, gripping the handgun and coddling the barrel with his free hand. "Okay," he said sharply. "That is your one pass. You got what you asked for, now I get what I asked for." He ripped the tape from Keogh's face.

Working his mouth and wetting his lips, Keogh could not find his voice, could not look at Rudd. He tried to steady his breathing, murmuring, "Water."

Dhahar raised his arm, wiggled his fingers, and a bottle was put in his hand. He reached over, also pulling the tape from Rudd's mouth, and tipped water into it, most dripping down his chin. Then he gave a few mouthfuls to Keogh, capped the bottle and set it aside. He twisted Keogh's hand and put a cell phone in his palm. "Make your call."

Keogh tapped the number for Cameron McNamara, but with his hands bound could do little else. Dhahar took the phone from him and put it on speaker, but the call went straight to voicemail. Keogh heard McNamara's solicitous voice on the message and was not sure whether to be glad or distressed, but he'd called the number because he knew it would go unanswered; it was the spare phone McNamara kept as a backup. But he had not expected any call to go through, given the lack of cellular reception in Nakalé.

"No signal, mate," Keogh said quietly.

Dhahar looked at the number Keogh had dialed and threw the cell phone, which clattered across the floor. Then he jerked Keogh to his feet, sliced the tape binding his ankles, and shoved him past the navigation console and out through one of the doors to the bridge wing. "Call the correct number," he growled, and handed Keogh a sat phone.

Keogh realized there was no reason to stall at this point. Rudd was alive and with him. Either he transferred the money and they were released or...or what? He could not bring himself to see the other side of that equation. He tapped the numbers to the sat phone he'd called earlier, the one McNamara had answered.

As he'd waited for the connection, he had gazed out over the ocean, the sun's parting signature a ribbon of candy stripes in tangerine and raspberry. Just above, the sky was taking on the color of an old washtub, clouds flowing like the soap suds poured from its rim, foamy and gray.

JAKE WATCHED THE PIRATE leader pacing inside the wheelhouse, then pulled back, debating what to do next. He stole another quick look with his scope, realizing he could not see everywhere inside. But the fact that the leader was here tended to indicate he still had an expectation of ransom, so Keogh and Rudd must be just out of sight or somewhere else on the ship. Should he breach right now? There were other armed pirates on the bridge with this guy, of that he was certain. One, two, more? He glanced below and retreated to the next landing, slowly opening the door. The directional plaque inside the stairwell said: F Deck, and listed Chief Engineer, Pilot, Battery Room, C.G. Locker, Toilet, Captain, Administrative Office. The corridor was empty as far as he could see, so he cautiously proceeded, looking in where doors were opened, listening by those that were not. The floors were spotless and waxed to a shine devoid of marks, the walls a shade of cream that looked newly painted with framed images of the ship and tasteful artwork and safety notices. There were navigational signs hung overhead in spaced intervals, and metallic plates on the doors identified each room. On his way back through the corridors, he opened the doors that were closed, Glock in hand.

He found nobody in any of the rooms, the lack of personnel and activity making it truly seem like a ghost ship.

When he returned to the landing, he scanned the directory. There were five more decks, the main deck, and the areas below. Knowing it would take him considerable time to search every deck with all the staterooms for officers and crews, he contemplated the most likely places and decided to check the mess and recreational rooms, the engine room and its machinery spaces.

The mess rooms for officers and crew were on opposite sides of the galley, and both were empty. The chairs were neatly ordered, tables covered in tablecloths and set with turntables full of condiments. The galley was also unoccupied, every stainless steel appliance gleaming, all food prep surfaces clean, pots and pans hanging in their designated spots. Of course, this made sense for the most part, as the ship had been taken at night. He descended the stairs past the remaining decks until he got to the sub-level and came to the engine room.

Here, he stopped and listened. With the ship's engines shut down, it was quieter than normal, but there were still sounds of water and steam in pipes and hoses and air in ductwork, generators purring and mechanical components whirring and grinding and clanking—ventilation fans, blowers, hydraulic pumps, electrical power. He crept down the metal stair rungs, stopping again, peering into the dimly lit abyss. It was a labyrinth of machinery—the behemoth MAN B&W engine that was multiple levels tall, encircled by platforms and occupying some six hundred square feet and the many generators, the water pumps and air compressors, the feed and fuel pumps—with hundreds of niches that would be perfect for hiding if the crew had holed up in here. But it was also a good place to keep a crew captive.

He went a little further down and the tops of three heads came into view and, with them, the extended barrels of their three automatic rifles.

✳   ✳   ✳   ✳   ✳

AFTER KEOGH HAD MADE the call and spoken to McNamara, Dhahar had taken him back to sit beside Rudd. The tape had been reattached over their mouths, but as soon as Dhahar wandered off to confer with his men on one of the bridge wings, Keogh lifted his hands and peeled a corner away from his lips.

"God, I'm so sorry, mate," he told Rudd, his eyes forlorn, skin gray and creased below them.

"Shh," Rudd hissed. "We shouldn't be talking."

Disregarding the admonition, Keogh said, "Listen, I think Cam was trying to tell me that Jake's on his way. Not sure, but he said, 'this is badass,' and I've never heard him use that word, so if we can just hold on a little bit longer…"

"I told you not to come! How could you leave Amelia like that?"

"I know…but you're my brother. I could never—" He stopped, emotion clogging his throat.

Beside him, Rudd turned his head, his eyes wet.

"This will be over soon," Keogh said, but he was not sure that it would be; something about the hijacking and these pirates seemed skewed to him. But maybe that bode well; pirates were reputed to be brutal and, like the other kinds of bad guys he'd encountered recently, had little or no regard for human life. If this group had a different agenda, maybe things would turn out for the better.

Both looked up as Dhahar stood over them in the semi-darkness now dousing the room. His face was bladed with anger. He started to say something but then just bent down and slapped his hand over the tape on Keogh's mouth, doing the same to Rudd's.

He gave them one last glare and stalked off.

Keogh felt his hope for a good outcome wither away.

JAKE THOUGHT ABOUT SHOOTING the men, had his Glock aimed at one of their heads and knew he could take them out in quick succession, but decided not to risk it. He wasn't sure if shots could be heard on the main deck above and, if he missed one, his presence would undoubtedly be broadcast over their radios, so instead he retreated up the stairs, keeping his eye on the three men until they were out of sight, and crossed toward the accommodations tower. Even though he'd not laid eyes on them, he was inclined to believe that Keogh and Rudd would be close to the leader. He needed to find a way to get into the wheelhouse that would not put their lives in jeopardy. When he was approaching the port side of the ship and saw the two men still standing by the tower entrance, he watched them for a moment and, as their conversation broke into laughter, made his move.

He grabbed the first man around the arms and knifed him in the neck, pivoting to the second man, prepared to do the same. But the guy reacted with a swiftness and dexterity Jake had not expected, bringing up his rifle. Swinging around with a high leg kick, Jake knocked him down and was about to stomp him when he heard shouts and the sound of running feet. He took off down the passageway, his boots splashing in the rain that had blown in, wind roaring in his ears as he ran. Midway, he ducked out and shot through a gap between container rows. He could still hear footfalls behind him, so he looked for cover and found it below a lashing bridge, remaining there until he no longer heard anything. He waited several more minutes for good measure and emerged guardedly. He continued by alternating passageways, cutting across the deck wherever he found an opening wide enough for him to fit and was emerging from one when he was jumped by a man who had been on top of the containers.

Jake was slammed hard against the metal deck, the wind practically knocked out of him by the force of the man's weight from the height he'd dropped. Pinned down, a second man and then a third quickly piled on. Jake managed to wrestle his way free at one point and landed some solid blows to his attackers, clocking one in the T of his face and drawing a geyser of blood, and kicking another in the groin. The one he'd kicked in the nuts was momentarily incapacitated, hunched over and keening in agony, but the face bleeder was still charging and pummeling and the guy who had initiated the take-down smacked Jake against the side of his head with the butt of his AK-47. Jake was stricken with excruciating pain that blared through his head like the turbine of a jumbo jet, flooding his senses with a blast of white-hot light and sound that blinded and deafened him. It was only a few seconds, but in that few seconds, Jake's wrists were zipped in plastic cuffs and he was wheeled around with a rifle at his back, being jabbed toward the accommodations tower.

He was going to get his entrance—just not in the way he'd wanted.

AS SOON AS HE was brought into the wheelhouse, Jake saw Keogh and Rudd seated together on the floor, and realized why he had not been able to see them from the outside. They were in a blind spot, only visible from the opposite side. In the minimal light, he met their eyes and tried to mentally transmit calm confidence, but the fact that he was cuffed at gunpoint and his head was probably swelling and coloring up like an eggplant did nothing to instill reassurance. Seeing him, both sat up straighter and stared with expressions of alarm.

Dhahar motioned to his men, and Jake was slung into one of the two swivel chairs at the navigation console. His drybag was dropped on an end of the nav station, Glock and Horkos knife laid down beside it. Eying Jake inquisitively, Dhahar asked, "And who are you?"

Jake did not reply.

Dhahar's gaze flicked to Keogh, saw the intensity in his face, and looked back at Jake. "Mr. Keogh certainly seems to know you. I am guessing you came to his rescue, yes? Did not quite turn out the way you expected."

Rain was drumming heavily on the bridge and streaming down the window panels, thunder reverberating through metal.

An alert tone sounded from an open laptop close to Dhahar and he moved over to check it. He studied the screen and frowned. Pressed a key and clicked the trackpad, pursing his lips. Turning, he stepped to Keogh, leaned down, and peeled the tape from his mouth.

"The transaction is still pending," he snapped. "Why is that?"

"I told you, it takes time to process that kind of amount," Keogh said.

Dhahar straightened up and went quiet, thinking.

Keogh stole a glance at Jake, mouthing *I'm sorry*, not sure if Jake could read his lips in the semi-gloom. While the rest of the ship's interiors were normally lit, the pirates had turned off the primary lights in the wheelhouse. Periodically, lightning flashed the space, highlighting all of the faces in stark reveal before casting them back in shadow.

Dhahar reaffixed the tape over Keogh's mouth and returned his attention to Jake, sizing him up, taking in his fit physique, muscular arms and chest, dark and unwavering countenance. He asked again, "Who are you?"

Jake remained silent, keeping his expression completely neutral. Once the reality of his capture had sunk in, he had contemplated negotiation with the pirate leader—Special Forces were all about hearts and minds, but that ideology did not apply in all situations, and as soon as he got his instant-read of Dhahar, he knew this was one of those where it definitely did not.

"Tough bastard, huh? Okay, let me see for myself," Dhahar said, and tugged Jake's Watershed drybag toward him.

Watching Jake with the morbid fascination Dexter might have shown while assessing a new victim, Dhahar opened the bag—having some difficulty figuring out the ZipTight closure at first—and began to rummage through its contents. The man who had frisked Jake and emptied his pockets had placed the FLIR thermal scope, Leatherman tool and Swiss Army knife, an Ocean Guardian eSpear, extra loaded clips for the Glock, and other items inside the top. Dhahar handled each with cool detachment but piquing interest, particularly for the eSpear, which he held up and rotated, trying to decipher its function. Below these things were the rope and grappling hook, a small aid kit, Federal Premium 147 Grain HST bullets, Ziplocs containing Jake's radio and spare comms, his Iridium and iPhone.

When Dhahar got to the iPhone, he grinned.

Jake clenched his jaw, a sensation that was like an electrical impulse piercing his ear canals and running down the base of his neck.

Holding the slim silver phone in his hand, Dhahar tapped the surface and the lock screen appeared. Cutting his eyes to Jake to gauge a reaction and getting none, he teased, "I bet I can find out," and thrust the phone, screen forward, into Jake's face. Drawing it back and seeing the unlocked icon, his grin widened in sadistic delight. "Now look at that…the wonder of technology."

Jake continued to show no emotion, but inside he was struggling mightily, his mind spinning in frantic gyrations to come up with a plan that just didn't seem to exist. His hands were cuffed, his weapons were out of reach, and there were several armed men standing around that he had badly battered, waiting for an excuse to unload their AKs on him. He'd been in some pretty grim situations before and endured many forms of torture, but this was about to go to a whole new level.

He used Signal encryption for his calls and texts and much of his images, but what would hurt him the most was right there for prying eyes to see.

Dhahar was tapping and scrolling, murmuring to himself, and then his face lit up when he found it. "Ah, look here," he said, smirking. He gave Jake a wink and emitted a low whistle. "What a beauty! Why don't I just give her a call, see how she answers…" He swiped and scrolled and tapped. "Ah, it's ringing, let's see if she—"

Dhahar never got the rest out, because at the discovery and mention of Callie, Jake's rage had erupted and sent adrenaline surging, launching him from the chair and onto Dhahar, his body as rigid and hard as a battering ram busting through a steel door. The phone was ejected from the pirate's hands and fell to the floor. Jake raised his foot and smashed it with the heel of his boot. Stunned, Dhahar shoved Jake back, impulsively reaching for the gun in his waistband, but at the same instant, Keogh and Rudd somehow managed to rise to their feet and lurch forward, faces florid with valiant intention.

Which, in turn, drew a reflexive response from the three other pirates who raised their rifles and fired. Jake's head jerked toward Keogh and Rudd— and saw their heads explode, flesh and blood and bone splattering and bodies collapsing—and yelled out in fury and anguish.

Dhahar was also screaming, hands flailing in the air. "No, no, no, no, no! *Hooyadiis wase!*"

But Jake did not hear him or see him, everything at that moment a blur of black primal reaction. His eyes saw, his brain registered the demise, his senses shredded apart. And then he raised his hands over his head and whipped them down, snapping the plastic cuffs, reached for his gun and knife, grabbed his drybag, and raced for the door to the bridge wing, shooting his Glock and ducking the fire of the pursuing pirates.

Leaving behind Cyrus Keogh and Archer Rudd, because there was nothing he could do for them now, anymore, or ever.

* * * * *

JAKE KNEW HE HAD one chance taking this way. Descending the stairs to the main deck would have probably been the better choice as far as putting distance, and obstacles, between him and Dhahar's men. But exiting via the bridge wing was the quickest and, if he made it, cleanest exit. Almost as soon as he cranked the door handle and stepped onto the exterior deck, they were on top of him. He spun around and got off a succession of shots that drove them back inside the wheelhouse and, in the moments they took cover from his fire, he snugged the drybag on and trotted to the surrounding side wall, blinking to see through the rain buffeting his face. He flipped over to the outside, clinging to the railing on top, trying to keep his footing on the narrow outer ledge as the rain drove relentlessly and the wind lashed. The pirates came charging from the wheelhouse, AKs rattling, rounds striking all around him and not missing by much.

Crouching on the other side of the wall to evade their fire, he secured his Glock and knife, pulled the straps tight on his pack, and looked down. A serendipitous flash of lightning gave him a brief spotlight on the thrashing waves below, but it was all he needed.

He stood, raised his arms over his head, arched his back, and leapt into the darkness, diving the seventy-five to eighty feet from the bridge wing into the ocean.

48

JAKE HIT THE WATER with his fists, which minimized the impact, but at a speed of close to sixty miles an hour, his skull and spine felt as though he'd shattered the glass pane of a tank of mad hornets, his bones shrieking and skin buzzing. He'd made several successful dives from comparable heights over the years, but he did not remember them being so brutal. The kick start of his flight instinct propelled him past the pain, and he ascended to the surface. Amazingly, his drybag was still on but had loosened and shifted, so he adjusted it and, after getting his bearings, began swimming alongside the container ship's hull toward the bow. The fisherman's skiff was about midway of the six-hundred-foot vessel, banging against the side.

Almost immediately, artillery rained down from the deck, pelting the water like lead-weighted raindrops mingled with the thunderous downpour from the heavens. To evade the gunfire, he swam below the surface most of the way until he reached the small boat, grabbed the side and rolled into it, several inches of rainwater sloshing in the bottom. He remembered seeing a bucket and groped in the darkness until his hands found it, hurriedly scooping and dumping and then tossing it aside to work on starting the outboard motor.

It did not so much as sputter, the cord whisking impotently as he pulled it from the engine. *Come on, come on, no time to be coy*, he thought. Distantly, he heard the motor of at least one boat from the far side of the container ship and renewed his efforts, hastily checking the connections and praying there wasn't a leak in the fuel line or some other problem that he could not instantly resolve—because, judging from the now indisputable sound of a motorboat much more robust than this one growling from around the tip of the big ship's bow, he had seconds to get this thing going.

Jake gave the starter cord another hard yank, hearing the slightest tick, and glanced up to see the murky shape of the oncoming boat bouncing toward him in the water. He yanked the starter cord again, and this time he was rewarded with the stuttering vibration of engagement, followed by a regulation in tone that signified commitment. He detached his tether from the ship's hull, took the tiller in hand, and plunged forward at the highest speed he could coax from the outboard, gripping the side of the skiff as it chopped up and down in the pitching sea, rain and spume already replacing what he'd bailed out. In his wake, in a boat much more substantial in build than this one and, just by the sound of its motor, significantly faster, its occupants had begun shooting again. He moved the tiller back and forth to zigzag his course, but bullets were hitting the water around him, a few landing in the boat—which meant that some might be hitting it.

And then there was the storm which, incredibly, had intensified in the past few minutes. The torrential rain proved to be both a godsend, greatly hampering the progress of the pirates' boat in pursuit, and an escalating crisis for him. With one hand on the tiller, he had to use his other to bail water from the shallow shell of his skiff as he fought to keep from being slung out of it.

It wasn't long before he lost the battle.

As a result of water coming over the sides or seeping in through bullet holes or a combination of both, the dilapidated boat and its straining motor surrendered to the sea, capsizing and dumping him into the violently tossing waves, breaking into pieces that either floated away or were swallowed up by the ocean. Treading in the water, he watched lightning ripping down from the black sky as if tearing seams in the universe, absently aware that electrical storms were exponentially more intense over water, thunder exploding in sequences of elevating decibels like a fireworks display approaching a grand finale.

Peering into the rain, he no longer saw or heard the pirates' boat, but at this point, that was almost an afterthought as he realized the challenge he now faced.

JAKE ALLOWED HIMSELF A moment to let it sink in how truly and completely fucked he was, and then recalibrated his mind to survival mode. Squinting to see the face of his waterproof Garmin tactix watch, he got a fix on his position and felt the air go out of his rallying determination; if the reading was accurate, he was miles from shore. He knew he could do two miles in normal conditions, possibly a little more, but these were far from normal conditions, not to mention the blow to the head he'd sustained. He didn't think he had a concussion, but he could not be sure; symptoms often did not manifest for hours or even longer.

Doesn't matter, he told himself, just get going.

As he swam, fighting against the current, he tried to hone every thought in his mind to the task of forward movement, nothing more, blocking out all emotions and reflections, all misjudgments and recriminations. He focused on each stroke of his arms, each kick of his legs, constructing a visualization of the beach and the mangroves beyond it, of the river through the forest to the plane. Just the singleness of purpose, each stroke bringing him closer to the finish line, imagining that the powerful ocean swells were actually working with him and not against him, convincing himself that the storm was beginning to abate.

As worrisome as the prospect of getting struck by lightning was, it occurred to him that the storm did potentially provide protection from another danger; during atmospheric turbulence, transmitted by falling barometric pressure, fish—including the predatory ones—gravitated to deeper and calmer depths. Even so, he was glad to have the eSpear. How ironic was it, he thought, that a Shark Shield technology product similar to this one had saved the lives of Falcone and Niles off the coast of Cartagena? Breaking his rhythm, he slipped his drybag off and, holding it above the water, dug out the device and its holster. He resealed his bag, slipped it back on, and fit the holster around his thigh. There were other things he contemplated taking out, like his radio and comms, but he knew there was almost no chance he would be able to establish a connection with Dmello in this storm and probably not from this

distance. He was also thirsty and really wanted a swig of water. But neither of those were worth the effort right now. What was worth it, was
what he did next. Going under, he untied his boots and strung them to
a belt loop on the waist of his cargo pants. When he came up and started
swimming again, he could feel a difference in the decreased drag and felt
a sliver of optimism.

After what seemed like an extended period of time, Jake checked his
watch again and instantly lost any sense of accomplishment he'd been
building. Not only was his timing off, so was his direction; the currents
had pulled him so far off course he had actually gone backward. Despite
his will to remain positive and the confidence in his ability to endure,
knowing that all the effort put forth since escaping from the ship had
been the equivalent of running a treadmill—putting in the time and energy and accumulating the distance but with nothing quantitative to
show for it—was acutely dispiriting.

With the physical setback came the psychological regression, and his
mind began to drift in the monotony and exertion of righting his course
and duplicating the strokes and kicks and, hopefully, gaining forward
momentum.

He saw Keogh and Rudd getting killed all over again, in even more
graphic detail now that he was not caught up in the blitz of the crazed
chaos of the moment. He saw the disintegration of their lives by a hail
of bullets, their breaths and humanity and hearts and souls just ended in
an instant, there and gone. And taken as they were selflessly acting in
support of him. Jake's head began to throb, his chest ached, and his body
felt so heavy he feared he was going under. And then, while the aching
intensified, he felt the weight lighten as if he'd been lifted out of himself
and he realized it was because of the profound sense of loss overtaking
him. Cyrus Keogh had not only garnered his respect, but had become
someone with whom Jake had expected to have an abiding friendship.
Amelia sprang to mind and the leadenness returned at the thought of
having to tell her...*oh God*.

He also thought of the ship's crew he'd abandoned. Maybe he should
have stayed onboard and gone back to free them. But the hard truth was,
his only real objective had been to rescue Keogh, and he'd failed.
Awfully, horribly, miserably. And he'd almost caused Callie to be put

through yet another trauma, then almost been killed himself. Almost, the word for hanging over a cliff and not falling…but also the word for failure and defeat that could have gone another way.

Idly, he wondered what would happen now…would the transaction go through or would the pirates continue to hold the ship for ransom? Would they release the crew? Kill them? Abandon the undertaking? Who were they affiliated with? Had Keogh's ship been a random target or was the hijacking part of the ongoing campaign to kneecap him?

Damn you, Cyrus, why couldn't you have just called me? But he really could not bring himself to blame Keogh for responding the way he did, for taking on the responsibility of dealing with the hijackers to defend his best friend. After all, he had done the very same for Falcone and Niles—and would do it again.

But…fuck, Cyrus…*fuck.*

So caught up in the spin of his emotions and speculations, Jake had not noticed the changing conditions. When he broke from his immersion and realized the rain was finally slackening, he felt the tide turning, literally. The seas were settling down and a check of his watch showed he had made some progress.

But the shore was still a long, long way off.

IT WAS IN THE earliest hours before dawn, the moon reappearing in a sky that was still dark and brooding with lingering clouds. Jake was scissoring through the water in smooth, even strokes, but he was growing increasingly tired. Even though the eighty-degree water was comfortable, he was beginning to feel numbness creeping through his limbs. He thought he might be past his two-mile threshold, but he was not sure. The throbbing in his head came and went and he was beginning to feel a fuzziness that made him lethargic, sleepy. Several times he caught himself slipping below the water's surface in a dreamy trance, jerking to alertness just as his nostrils filled.

Hours in, he started to feel the inexorable draw of letting go. In those moments, he saw Callie. She was waiting for him, she needed him, she was just out of reach but on the other side of whether he made it or whether he did not. He could not, would not, let her go. He pushed himself past each of the persuasions to fold. He was going to survive this. He was going to get back to her.

Images of their time together floated through his mind: the first time he'd held her in his arms and kissed her, the purity of her awe of Costa Rica's natural wonders, the blush of sunset on her cheeks as they watched the sun pool into the ocean from the deck of a sailboat—the rapture of being inside her and losing himself to that feeling forever. And more…feeling her lose herself to him.

CALLIE HAD BEEN DOZING, not because she wanted to, but because she'd not slept since the day before when she had seen the man at the pool. Everyone was deeply concerned about her, but she could tell that none of them really believed she *had* seen the man, at the beach or at home. And, she conceded, they were probably right, but she could not free her mind of the vision, if that's what it was. It triggered every horror she had been through in Colombia, even the physical internal pain.

She awoke, laying on their bed, the French doors open with a breeze tickling in. Through the bedroom's windows, palm fronds swished and birds flitted about in the foliage. Her eyes closed again and she was floating off to sleep when the ringing of her phone pulled her back with a jolt. Snatching it from the bedside table, she looked at the screen and saw Jake's smiling face, happily swiping the *slide to answer* and putting the phone to her ear. But instead of hearing his voice, there was the *beep-beep-beep* of disconnection. Her heart sank in disappointment.

Must have been a dropped call from the loss of a signal. He had told her the reception would be almost non-existent where he was. But what if he was calling and something had happened to him in the process? No, don't think like that, she told herself. He would be okay, he would be coming home.

Sighing, she got up from the bed and walked out onto the terrace. Ominous-looking clouds the color of stone were beginning to gather over the ocean, waves beyond the beach tossing and capping with white peaks.

Another afternoon storm was brewing.

*   *   *   *   *

IN HIS MIND JAKE was holding Callie, so absorbed in the vision that he did not see the dorsal fin approaching until almost the last second. The sky had lightened enough for him to make out the streamlined torpedo shape, the triangular rather than hooked fin, ruling out a dolphin. Great Whites were not common here, but another deadly species—the bull shark—was. He reached for his eSpear, fingered the release lever, and the electrode wand sprang out and activated, emitting a three-dimensional electronic field that would cause the shark to have muscle spasms. The best part was the device did not hurt the shark, it merely repelled it, which is what happened. As soon as the eSpear was deployed, the dorsal fin above water and the form below it did a swift one-eighty, speeding away.

Jake exhaled and swam on, the adrenaline spike giving his metabolism a much-needed boost of invigoration, which helped to drive him another hundred yards or so, but that energy soon began to wane. The time and GPS on his watch told him that he had already surpassed the two-mile mark, so if the shore was much farther, he honestly did not know if he could make it, and that reality flooded him with emotions so strong he felt his eyes welling with tears. Not for himself, but for Callie, and he could not bear the thought of that loss. He knew that his will to survive was as strong as any human could possibly possess, but as the minutes continued to mount and the movements of his arms and legs grew increasingly weaker, he felt his physical core starting to shut down even as his emotional one was desperately clawing to remain in this world to get back to what he could not leave behind.

In the aftermath of the storm, the air was clear and the ocean calm, cobalt sky sprinkled with fading stars. The moon was low and ghostly white and looked as though it was about to drop into the water, its beams glimmering across the surface like a liquid path to the edge of the horizon. Jake's head was throbbing again, every muscle aching, his lungs burning, but he had to keep going. Arm over arm over arm into the water, legs barely paddling, the pack on his back and boots tied to his waist feeling as heavy as concrete blocks. Several times, he very nearly jettisoned them, but reminded himself that he needed the contents of the bag, not to mention the boots for the coral reefs awaiting him at the shore.

Oh God, the shore…where had it gone? What if his GPS was wrong? What if he was actually many miles out instead of a few?

The throbbing in his head blurred to a dull ache, the ache in his muscles and the burn in his lungs to a radiating pain that seemed fused to bone, and now gravity was drawing him down like a magnet. His arms and legs would go limp and he would sink until the water started to invade his sinuses and he'd thrust himself up and scream inside his head: *NO, you are not giving up!* And then he would think of Callie again…and again…and again. Holding onto her like a life preserver.

But when he was under, the world turned into a beautiful blue paradise, so peaceful, so soothing, where everything was shimmering in such a beautiful, beautiful blue…and he started to see her there, pale blond hair fanned out in the water, her brown eyes plaintive…and he wanted nothing more in the entire world than to go to her, to hold her, to kiss her. But he could not reach her.

Suddenly, something massive lifted him up, up, up, and he broke the surface and slid over the side of whatever the enormous thing was. He was startled to hear a jet of air expelled, followed by a fountain of hot spray that came down on his head. He twisted and looked, saw the mass just beside him, and realized in dazed astonishment that it was a whale.

In the summer months, as in Costa Rica, humpbacks migrate from Antarctica to the warm waters of the Indian Ocean off the coast of Kenya to congregate and breed, and the gargantuan mammal that had apparently nudged him up to the surface was the size of a bus; they are, in fact, typically up to sixty feet long, weighing roughly forty tons. Noting the black dorsal coloring, actually feeling the knobby tubercles on its head and the vertical grooves on its body, Jake knew the kind it was, and while humpbacks are intentionally benign to humans as long as they don't feel threatened, one powerful hit by a fin or tail could be fatal. With that in mind, he began to slowly move away from the whale. But the humpback was not ready to leave and brushed up against him again, this time emerging high enough to expose an eye.

It looked directly at him, eye wide and wet and bright with

intelligence, communicating something at a visceral level, and Jake felt it. It was telling him to live.

SOMETIME LATER, HE HAD no idea how much later, the horizon was another degree lighter and the shore came into view.

Elation bloomed inside him and he swam with inspired vigor until his bare feet started hitting the coral reefs and pain shot through him like hot rivets and the translucent water filled with swirls of his blood. He fumbled for his boots, tugged them on, and continued. The last few yards seemed to take forever, but he could see the mangroves and he now knew he would make it.

And then he was trudging through the beds of seagrass, never so happy to be tangled up in muck and bloody from the lacerations on his feet and scrapes on his legs. He turned and gazed out to the ocean, looking for the humpback whale that had stayed with him until the last stretch. But he saw nothing more than waves rolling in to shore below the pre-dawn sky where the moon was gone and the sun had not yet appeared. He concluded that the whale was probably a hallucination, but it had gotten him to shore.

He staggered shakily to the beach and dropped to his knees, head bowed. He stayed like that for a few minutes, thanking God for his survival and then pulling his pack off in a flurry of urgency, as if suddenly remembering his raging thirst. He dug out his water bottle, uncapped it, and swilled until it was empty and held it to his lips several moments longer to milk every drop. He put the bottle back in his pack and twisted around, sitting on his haunches. Inhaled the briny air.

He stood, and was about to head down the beach when he heard a splashing sound that made him look around—just in time to see the humpback whale make a majestic leap into the air, arched backward with its white underbelly on top, and then fall into the ocean, its fluked tail the last thing visible before it fully submerged and disappeared.

JAKE TOOK OUT HIS radio and Invisio comms which, like everything else in the Watershed bag were, incredibly, dry. He wasn't sure hauling the pack on his back through miles of ocean was worth it, but nonetheless he was glad to have it now. He was also exceedingly grateful for the ripstop fabric of his clothing and waterproof boots, knowing it would not be long before they were also dry. Inspecting the lacerations on his legs and feet, he took out the bag's aid kit and applied antiseptic and bandages. Then, he connected his radio and control unit, inserted the earbuds, and tried to raise Dmello but got only static; he'd have to get closer to be in range. Orienting his position by his watch's GPS, he noted with dismay that he was at least a mile from where he had departed in the fisherman's boat.

His legs were still rubbery, but he wasted no time getting underway. The dunes along this section of the shore, stacked by wind-blown sand composed of carbonate coral skeletons, algae, and shells, were immense, and he did not want to deplete what minimal energy he had scaling them, so he hiked farther down the beach in search of an opening. It was still too early for even the fishermen, seabirds his only company, terns and boobies and gulls wheeling overhead. He found a breach in the wall of dunes and crossed into a lagoon wreathed by shaggy doum palms and broccoli-crowned baobab trees, storks and ibis poking through the shallows for small fish and crustaceans. Entering the mangroves, the first pink flushes of dawn began to tease through the leaves and branches as he made his way to the Tana riverbank, periodically attempting to get Dmello on his radio. Near the edge, he spotted a fishing camp up ahead, dugout canoes lined up and ready to launch, the smell of smoking fish wafting from fires within a small group of thatched huts.

He walked on, taking in the riverine biodiversity and listening to the sounds of its inhabitants stirring in the last moments before sunrise, feeling a sense of tranquility that he should not be feeling. But it was borne more out of exhaustion than peace, which was something he would not—could not—feel after what had happened.

He had been weaving through a stand of looking glass trees, the tall, spreading buttresses of which curled like the rolls of Christmas ribbon candy, when he came to a thicket of bushy lola palms and caught his breath. Gnashing around in the greenery was a quartet of elephants, feeding on the palm fronds, munching contentedly. They seemed to take no notice of him, so he stepped back and took a moment to enjoy the sight. At the same time, he felt the well of associated grief rippling just below the surface.

He watched them for a while and then, checking coordinates, made a turn from the river and hiked another half mile and heard his radio crackle.

49

JAKE TRIED DMELLO AGAIN and this time got a response.

"Jake!" The voice on the other end was cheerful but tense. "Do you copy? Are you close? Something is going on here."

"Read you loud and clear, brother, and I am. Sitrep?"

"It has been quiet, no one around the whole time, but I heard some voices just now and took cover away from the plane. Some men appeared and walked around it. They had AKs and were speaking Somali."

Picking up his pace, Jake asked, "Are they still there?"

"I do not know where they went," Dmello replied.

"Okay, sit tight, I'm about a klick from you."

Shit, Jake thought.

Two possibilities came immediately to mind—with the elephants nearby, local poachers…or more pirates—and he was pretty sure he knew which was the most likely of the two. Pirate teams usually had a land crew, and certainly word of the botched hijacking had been relayed to them by now. They were probably out searching for him and looking for anything out of the ordinary; a plane sitting on a dirt strip would definitely fall into that category.

He found Dmello hunkered down at the edge of the forest surrounding the dirt strip. Seeing Jake, Dmello's face cracked a smile, but it quickly disappeared when he saw Jake's disheveled appearance.

"Are you okay?" he asked, his eyes dropping to Jake's bloodied pants legs. His concern mounted with the realization that Jake was alone.

"Where is Cyrus?"

"Not with me," Jake replied tersely. "I'll fill you in later. But right now, we need to get out of here. Fast."

Dmello had brought Jake's AK-47 and handed it to him, his own slung over his shoulder. They emerged from the bush and cautiously approached the dirt strip, each with their rifles pointed in front of them as they scanned the perimeter. Dmello had turned the Cessna around to face north in preparation for takeoff, so the plane was at the near end of the strip but still about fifty yards away.

Jake walked slowly, listening keenly, his eyes darting from side to side monitoring the tree lines. All was still, but almost too much so. The birds and monkeys and other small animals in the bush had gone quiet or gone altogether, and that always ticked his alert level way up.

They were within twenty yards when shots rang out.

Both ducked low and retreated to the trees, firing in the direction of the shots. A handful of militia spilled from the bush, heads and faces swathed in black wraps, belts of ammunition looped over their chests, rifles blasting.

"Let's draw them as far away from the plane as we can," Jake said, elbows and boots crashing through the forest, pivoting, aiming, and shooting. Tree bark and branches became flying projectiles as bullets ricocheted behind them.

"Then what?" Dmello asked as they ran.

Jake did not answer because he wasn't sure. It was the two of them versus who knew how many, or if militia backup was coming. At one point, they ran into a thatch of brush with no clear trail out. They took what cover they could, pushing back into the vegetation, and waited. Elevated voices were approaching from adjacent angles, Somali queries and responses.

Dmello whispered, "Who are these guys?"

"I think they're part of the pirate crew."

Seconds later, three men converged into the same dead end, standing directly in front of them. Jake and Dmello charged from the thatch, dropping all three. Knowing there would be more on their flank, Jake grabbed the men's rifles, tossed one to Dmello, and the two came out of the wooded skein firing their own AKs and those of the fallen militia men. Here, accuracy didn't matter as much as creating a wall of artillery.

Their strategy proved effective. Shooting their way back to the strip, they stepped over a couple of bodies along the trail they'd forged in the forest and, when they came to the edge, saw several more dead in the dirt, dust swirling from the heavy shelling.

"Okay, let's go!" Jake shouted, and ran to the plane, glancing over his shoulder to make sure Dmello was with him. But before they made it, another round of gunfire rattled, close but not as prolific. Maybe one or two shooters, Jake thought. He reached up, cranked the Cessna's door open, unfolded the metal stepladder, and climbed aboard. Dmello's steps thunked behind him.

"Jake," he heard Dmello say.

He turned. Dmello stood just inside the entry hatch, the door still open. His shirt was saturated with blood at the shoulder, rapidly oozing from a hole in the fabric.

Jake stepped over and reached around him, pulled the ladder up and secured the door. He was looking through the cockpit window glass, back at Dmello's stunned face, and then at his gunshot wound. "Okay, bud, just get in here and we'll deal." He peeled off the unbuttoned shirt he wore over his tee and handed it to Dmello. "Put this around you and pull it as tight as you can."

Jake held Dmello's eyes for a moment, beginning to realize the implication both medically and operationally. The problem was, they needed to get the plane off the ground and out of here, Dmello was clearly incapacitated, and he was no pilot.

Dmello took his place in the pilot's seat, wincing from pain, and paused. His face was full of conflict and worry. Jake sat in the co-pilot's seat, still dividing his attention between Dmello and the strip he could see from the windows. "You tell me what to do to get this bird in the air and I'll get you fixed up, okay?"

"Jake, I can do it," Dmello said, but his voice lacked conviction, the muscles in his cheeks twitching.

"We will do this together. But we gotta boogie. They're still coming for us."

As if on cue, a pair of militants were closing in on the plane. One shot in the right place could end it right here. A tire, the windscreen, the fuel tank. The men fired and bullets pinged and whanged against the Cessna's metal frame.

"Tell me what to do," Jake said, trying to keep the urgency out of his voice but feeling it rising in his chest. Gazing at all the screens and dials and switches in front and overhead, he was momentarily overwhelmed but quickly recovered, manifesting confidence he hoped would reassure Dmello.

Dmello started to reach to the console, grimacing and sucking air through his teeth, and Jake quickly stopped him. "Hey, don't move. Let me do it."

"These toggles on my left—"

Jake reached around him.

"—flip the battery switch on…fuel boost pump, starter…"

The Cessna's Pratt & Whitney 867-horsepower engine came to life, revving smoothly, filling the cockpit with a comforting thrum that elevated to a high whine, the propeller spinning.

"Okay," Dmello continued, "fuel in, gas generator speed passing twelve percent…fifty-two percent, low idle…and…starter off."

At this point, the Garmin avionics flashed on, three screens with flight instrumentation, navigation, weather, terrain, and engine data on high-resolution displays, some of which Jake could interpret.

The two men were still firing on the plane.

Dmello told Jake, "Push the power lever forward and keep your hands on the control wheel. Pull it back easy until I say stop. Ready?"

"Yeah, we've got to go…now."

The plane began to move, trees at the end of the strip coming closer. Quickly. Dmello said, "Good…go for a hundred, hundred ten…"

The plane's nose pitched up, the trees disappearing below it and, at a thousand feet per minute, lifted into the sky.

When the plane reached cruising altitude, Jake asked, "It's what, two hours to Nairobi? Is there somewhere closer we can put down, get you to a hospital?"

"No, I would like to just go to Nairobi," Dmello replied.

"You sure?"

"Yes. I already had it programmed in, so autopilot will get us there." He smiled weakly. "I will just have to school you on the landing."

When autopilot was engaged, Jake freed himself from his seatbelt harness and turned to assess Dmello. Blood was dribbling through the fingers of Dmello's left hand which he had pressed firmly against his right shoulder, and for the first time Jake also noticed the considerable amount of blood on the back of Dmello's seat.

"Okay, my man, let's see what we've got. I already have some good news for you," he said as he reached for his Voodoo backpack in the seat behind him and extracted his aid kit.

"What is that? I am alive?" Dmello tried to laugh but could only manage a wince.

"Well, hell, yeah." Jake gave him a grin, snapped on gloves, and lifted Dmello's shirt in front. When he did, a dark flower of blood spread wetly from a wound the size of a half-dollar coin. "But what I was going to say is, the fact that you're sitting here and able to tell me how to fly this thing lets me know that the bullet missed your lungs. So it could be worse. Still, it is serious and I *know* it's painful."

Jake had Dmello lean forward so he could see both the front and back of his shoulder. "It went through, but I think it might have cracked the scapula, which means there might be some bone fragments. That can be an issue, so you need to go easy on movement. For the time being, I'll wrap it and get you some pain relief. Okay?"

"That would be good," Dmello said. "You save me now, but Remy will kill me for bleeding all over his plane."

Jake laughed heartily and took out an H&H dressing, which was actually four yards of gauze compressed and sealed in a small airtight square, and pressed it in the posterior wound, instructing Dmello to lean back against the seat. Then he packed the front with QuikClot gauze and, after applying pressure, began wrapping elasticized Coban. While Dmello held that, Jake swapped the blood-soaked H&H for QuikClot and continued winding the Coban around Dmello's shoulder and chest over the packed entrance and exit wounds.

Glancing at the blood on the cockpit's seats, upholstery, and console, Jake shook his head. "You might be right about Remy, but we'll deal with him when the time comes." He dug into his aid bag and took out a foil packet and extracted a swab-like stick. "This is a fentanyl pop. It will handle your pain, but it can also knock you out, so if you want to help me keep us flying and then land, I strongly suggest just a brief hit. Okay?"

Dmello nodded, put the stick in his mouth for a moment and took it out. He scanned the cockpit, checking all the gauges and Garmin data and, satisfied with the autopilot operation, looked solemnly at Jake. "What happened with Cyrus? Why did he not come with you? I thought—"

Jake heaved a heavy sigh. "He didn't come because he's dead, Kean." He started to say more, but his throat dried up as if a wad of his gauze had lodged inside. He reached between their seats and plucked two bottles of water, handed one to Dmello, and drank half of his in one long swallow.

Dmello drank more slowly, eyes moistening. "He is dead?" he asked, voice raspy. "No...no..." He glanced away, wiped at his eyes.

Jake cleared his throat. "His friend Archer, too. I...it's a lot to tell. Later, okay?"

"Certainly." Dmello bowed his head, mumbling something in Swahili. When he looked up, he asked, "Should we notify..." but was unable to finish.

"No, I need to be there. She needs to hear it from me." Something suddenly occurring to him, he said, "With all the shooting, I didn't get a chance to say, we *should* notify those contacts of yours with the Coast Guard."

"What do I say?"

Jake toggled screens on his tactix watch and read off coordinates he'd managed to input. "Tell them to look for the ship in that vicinity. Hopefully the crew is still alive."

WITH THE CESSNA CRUISING smoothly at 175 knots and just under nine thousand feet, Dmello and Jake were relaxed in the cockpit, Dmello from the fentanyl buzz and Jake, for the time being emancipated from flying the plane, finally decompressing. Autopilot was a wondrous thing. Jake got Remington on his sat phone and informed him of Dmello's gunshot wound, also giving him a bare-bones account of what had happened to Cyrus Keogh. He left out the part involving his oceanic marathon, and when Remington pressed him for more details about

Keogh, Jake wrapped up the call. He just could not talk about it now.

But he did get Dmello talking to keep him from nodding off. He had put an oximeter on one of Dmello's index fingers so he could monitor his oxygen level; with a narcotic as strong as fentanyl and the area of his wounds in proximity to the chest, it was an added measure for his own assurance. He also kept a check on his heart and lungs, and so far, so good.

Through the cockpit glass, the sky was a placid blue with tufts of clouds drifting by, the plane's engine droning steadily. As they winged their way back to Nairobi, Jake was in turmoil over what to do next. His mission was over—failed, but over—and he wanted to go home as much as he wanted his next breath. But he could not get past the feeling that it wasn't truly finished. He knew why he felt that way, but he needed to look past the reason, past the person, past the shadow.

Studying the Garmin displays, he determined that they were approaching their destination. He glanced at Dmello. His eyes were closed, his face slack. Jake reached over and gave him a light shake, checking the oximeter on his finger. His O2 reading had dropped but was still in an acceptable range.

"Hey, bud. Time to get this baby on the ground."

Dmello did not respond.

Jake shook him again, a little more vigorously. "Hey, come on. I need you."

Dmello's eyelids fluttered and he murmured. "What? I am here. Is it time to land?"

"Yeah, getting close."

"Okay." Dmello straightened up in his seat, but just as soon as he did, his eyes closed again. Dreamily, he said, "Disengage the autopilot and take the controls."

Jake did so and felt himself tense; taking off into a boundless sky with no ceiling to hit was one thing, but coming down onto a solid and unforgiving strip of tarmac was another thing altogether.

"Maybe I should do it," Dmello said, but his arms remained listless, hands folded in his lap.

"No, I can do it. Just tell me step by step like you did when we took off."

"Okay, push the prop control forward." Dmello took him through the maneuvers of trim and power and flap extensions, and everything appeared to be going routinely.

"Wilson Tower, good morning…Caravan five Yankee kilo tango Oscar," Jake said.

"Caravan five Yankee kilo tango Oscar, good morning, go ahead."

"Kilo tango Oscar approaching your station, estimate in"—Jake glanced to Dmello, who extended the fingers of both hands, still in his lap—"ten minutes. Request landing instructions for full stop." As the verbiage slipped from his tongue, Jake realized that he'd apparently absorbed a good bit of secondhand knowledge from all the combat flying he'd done as a passenger. Out of the corner of his eye, he caught Dmello smiling lopsidedly at him.

"Kilo tango Oscar, join long final 32, you're number two for landing qnh 1013."

"Kilo tango Oscar, qnh 1013 long final 32, number two…on final 32."

Jake could see the runway in the distance, but the blue skies had been infiltrated by ugly-looking gray clouds, a storm building to the northwest.

"Kilo tango Oscar, still number two…Fokker on short, continue final. Expect late landing clearance."

Late landing clearance? Jake shot another glance at Dmello, but his head was back, eyes closed. Peering through the windscreen, he saw the Fokker 50 ahead and below.

"Kilo tango Oscar, visual on number one. Continuing final," Jake said.

"Kilo tango Oscar, you're cleared for landing, winds variable five knots."

Just as they had descended to the five-hundred-foot threshold and were almost to the runway, the Cessna lifted and dropped and veered side to side, the controls jerking in Jake's hands. Another powerful surge seemed to push up one of the wings and the plane canted sideways forty-five degrees, threatening to roll.

Dmello snapped to attention as if cold water had been thrown in his face. He sat forward and grasped his controls, leveling the plane, setting full throttle, and broadcasting, "Tower, this is kilo tango Oscar. Going around due to wake turbulence."

There was a burst of static from the tower radio, possibly covering something muttered by the traffic controller, followed by, *"Kilo tango Oscar, confirm intentions."*

"Kilo tango Oscar...stand by, tower..."

In the next few minutes, Dmello took over, grunting through renewed pain, ascending as though from takeoff to a thousand feet and then banking 180 degrees in ninety-degree turns, setting the flaps to 20. He told Jake, "This is like a do-over, and hopefully the turbulence will be gone on the second try."

He began reducing speed and making the second flap adjustment, descending. "Kilo tango Oscar request left hand circuit for full stop."

"Kilo tango Oscar, roger, join left hand downwind runway 32...you're number one. Report on final 32."

With the runway in front of them again, Dmello slumped back into his seat, fatigued by his efforts. "Jake," he huffed, "do you think you can do it? I—"

The rest of his sentence was truncated by a groan.

"No worries, bud, I got this," Jake said in the most stalwart voice he could manage.

But did he? If there was no turbulence, he felt like he could do it. If there was a repeat of the turbulence, he would just do exactly what Dmello had done. And was Dmello okay? Was he just folding under the pillow of the medication or was he in worse shape than Jake had thought? God, he could not lose another person in all this. He just could not.

As the Cessna coasted down on its glide path to the runway, the Garmin avionics mechanical voice announced: *"Five hundred."* Jake felt his muscles tense, sensing a moment of truth or dare coming. Below them, the green and gold sprawl of Nairobi National Park came and went and they were about to cross the Southern Bypass, streaming with traffic. Same as they had moments earlier. Jake's palms were sweaty on the control yoke. He could hang halfway out of a helicopter with few, if any, qualms, but he was out of his element here, literally flying by the seat of his pants.

Jake said, "Kilo tango Oscar, on final 32."

"Kilo tango Oscar, cleared to land 32."

The plane was drifting down, down, down…the runway was coming…the wings wobbling ever so slightly at the last moment, causing Jake's stomach to flip. Continue? Abort and ascend again?

And then they bumped on the tarmac, hard, Jake and Dmello bouncing up from their seats, the plane rumbling up and down and then just racing forward. Racing and then finally decelerating and stopping.

Jake exhaled.

"Fuck," he muttered, and glanced to Dmello.

Whose eyes were closed again, but this time he was conscious and murmuring another prayer of some kind—not for the dead but for the living.

ALMOST STUMBLING OFF THE ladder as they deplaned, Dmello said, "Well done, boss."

Jake did not know what to say. His nerves were still trilling. In the past twenty-four hours, he had almost been shot numerous times, had almost drowned—or been eaten by a shark had it not been for his eSpear—and just now, weathered an incident with the plane that could very well have resulted in a crash. His feet felt as if they were not quite touching the ground.

Remington strode over, removed his sunglasses, and gave Jake and Dmello a full, unfiltered assessment, and whistled. "Now you boys have been having a little too much fun."

"You saw the landing?" Jake asked.

"I did," Remington said. "Mellie, that was some mighty fine handling you did there."

"It was not me," Dmello said.

"*What?*" Remington's brows hitched up and he gaped at Jake. "You?"

"I just did what Kean told me."

"You might have missed your calling." Remington was giving Jake a closer look, taking in the bruised and swollen side of his face, the torn and blood-stained pants, the sea- and sand-ravaged hair. "Kean looks pretty rough, but shit…you look like *hell*, brother."

Jake shook his head wearily. "I feel like it, too."

"Well, let's get this guy to the hospital and we'll head to the ranch and toast a few to living another day."

"There's nothing I'd like more, Remy," Jake said sadly. "But if you can get me another ride, I need to go straight on to Nakalé."

Remington nodded. "Okay, yeah, I guess you do." He put his hand on Jake's shoulder. "I'm so sorry, man. If anybody could have pulled it off, it was you."

But Jake wondered, *was it*? Or had he actually gotten Cyrus Keogh killed?

50

THE PURPLE SKY WAS ablaze with vermillion fire, a backdrop that would have been breathtakingly exquisite were it not for what Jake was seeing on the ground below, a scene that made what he had to do even more dreadful. Remington had put him in another Cessna and provided him with another pilot and now, as they descended to the field cast in the scarlet glow of that sunset, enthusiastic villagers were, unsurprisingly, rushing to greet them. The prominent female figure amongst them, whose shimmering hair was the color of flame in the vintage light, was peering upward, a hand shielding her eyes, and in minutes he would be yet again shattering the world of that lovely, vibrant soul. For her, an exciting new journey had begun on these soils, bringing new hope and new life for so many, but it would also be the place on earth that had taken the most precious life away.

As the plane landed and rolled to a stop in the grass, he felt nauseated in the pit of his stomach, his throat so dry he couldn't swallow, his head pulsing with pressure bands. Through the plane's windows he saw Amelia Keogh stop, and even from this distance, could make out the look of puzzlement on her face. She had no doubt noticed that the pilot was not African; he was light-skinned and therefore not Keanjaho Dmello.

Jake opened the co-pilot's door, unfolded the ladder, and stepped down. He removed his sunglasses and stuck them on his head. Walked woodenly toward the awaiting flock, toward Amelia Keogh. Falcone and Niles had joined her, Luther Baladur, Kent Sanborn, and Cameron

McNamara not far behind. Jake could see Amelia staring at the empty wake between him and the plane, her brain probably jumbled with disconnected thoughts and a tide of emotion that was already beginning to roll. Falcone and Niles seemed to have grasped the strings of impending tragedy, their faces stricken.

Amelia Keogh was still staring behind Jake as he came to her and stood, arms at his sides. He wanted to embrace her, look into her beseeching green eyes and fill them with every ounce of comfort he could impart because for this, there would be no words that could make any of it conceivable or less devastating.

When she finally looked directly into his face, it was as if a single bubble was trapped beneath the surface of a frozen lake, suspended just below a tiny crack that was about to spread and then split apart.

Before he could speak, Amelia asked, "Where's Cy?" She sidestepped him and started for the plane, but he extended an arm and intercepted her, drew her back.

"Amelia," he said softly, "let's go and sit." He tried to walk with his arm around her, but she resisted, her feet planted.

"Where is he?" she asked hollowly, her expression glazing with shock, all color ebbing from her face.

"Let's go sit," Jake said again, the words thick on his tongue, wanting to be anywhere but here and in this moment. He got her almost to the trees bordering the village when she stopped once more, turned, and looked back across the field where the pilot who was not Dmello strode from the plane. Like Cyrus Keogh, he was tall and tanned and blond, but that was the extent of the similarity; there was a stiff carriage in his gait, no wave in his hair and no perennial grin on his face.

Amelia seemed to be measuring every step the pilot took, breathing in sync with his cadence until one particular footfall snapped something inside her and she broke, a cry erupting from her belly and shrilling through her mouth and nose. Jake pulled her against him and steered her through the woods to the village commons, a perplexed and worried procession of men, women, and children behind them. Chief Nsabimana and his wife moved everyone away, giving them privacy. While Baladur, Sanborn, and McNamara hovered nearby, Jake eased Amelia down to a carved log bench by the fire, Falcone and Niles taking a seat on either side. He pulled over a plastic chair, sat, and faced her.

Falcone and Niles each put an arm around Amelia as she sobbed deeply, bent forward, her head almost in her lap. When the sobs became gulps and the convulsions of her body lessened, she let both of them hug and hold her for a few minutes and then she wiped her eyes and gazed at Jake.

She shook her head several times, glanced away, looked back, and shook her head again. Finally she said, "It can't be true…please, Jake, tell me. It can't be true. It can't." Tears sprung anew and continued to flow.

Jake reached for her hands and held them. "I'm so sorry, Amelia."

She withdrew her hands from his and pushed them out in front of her. "I can't. I just can't." She sprang from the bench and hurried away.

Fingers pressed into his temples, Jake muttered, "God." His chest felt like an animal was clawing into the flesh.

Fighting to hold back his own tears, Niles asked, "Where's Kean? Did he—?"

"No, but he got shot. He's okay, in Nairobi." Jake lifted his head, studying Falcone. "How're you doing, bud?"

Falcone looked at him incomprehensibly, his face frozen with the shock they were all reeling from. When he realized what Jake was asking, he said, "Oh…uh…a lot better. Thought I was going to die a couple of times, but the docs and those drugs got me through."

"Good, glad."

"Christ, Jake," Falcone said, "What the hell happened?"

"Eddie, I really don't want to talk about it right now. Okay? I will, but I just need a little more time." His voice was as brittle as gravel, his posture slumped with exhaustion.

"Yeah, okay," Falcone said and, with Niles, drifted off.

Everyone left him alone and, as the dusk gave way to evening dark, Jake sat by the fire holding his head, which was as heavy as his heart. Feeling so very tired and so very done.

THE NEXT MORNING, HE was making coffee over the fire when Falcone and Niles approached, sullen and tentative. Glancing at them, he said, "Grab some joe and we'll talk."

They filled their cups and drank.

As Jake related what had happened on the ship, they listened in stunned silence and, when he had finished, Niles asked, "So what happens now?"

Jake's eyes lifted skyward. "Honestly, I don't know. I'm certainly ready to go home."

Falcone put his cup down and reached into a pants pocket. "I need to show you something."

Holding his phone, he tapped and scrolled and then presented it to Jake. Jake took it and zoomed in on an image using his thumb and index finger. He looked sharply at Falcone. "This is Aris Xavier. Where did this come from?"

"While I was laid up with the malaria, I got my phone charged and was going through some photos on it…this was one that came from social media."

Jake's forehead wrinkled. "Social media? Like Facebook or Instagram? What do you mean? Whose social media?"

Falcone glanced away uneasily. "Iris's."

"*What?*" Jake's eyes widened, his face reddening. "The woman from Sanctuary Initiative that you—"

"Yeah," Falcone said dully. "That was in her photos."

"And you still haven't been able to reach her?" Jake asked.

"Nope. Not since they left."

"Which you told me was right after you guys and the Keoghs went to Kinshasa."

"We don't know if they made it out or if they were still at the compound when it was attacked," Niles reminded him.

"Well, I think they would have been considered high-value hostages," Jake said, his agitation showing. "So either they made it out or they would have been held along with the others."

"Do you think…?" Falcone began, but didn't know how to finish the sentence or the thought.

"What I *don't* think is that it's a coincidence," Jake said. "I've always believed there was a so-called 'inside man'." He looked at the image on Falcone's phone again. Iris Margolis, wearing tight designer jeans and a sleeveless knit top that more than accentuated her assets, was seated at a bar next to a smirking Aris Xavier and another man who was vaguely familiar. It took Jake a few moments, but then he recalled why; he had seen him not quite a week ago—as part of the security team at the mining operation.

Flustered, Falcone said, "I don't understand. How could Iris be involved with him?"

"Not sure about the involvement part, and meeting and inviting you here might be a coincidence, but I don't believe her connection with X is." He tapped the screen of Falcone's phone with his finger. "She is, or was, most likely the primary source of his intel on the Keoghs and their movements. The inside woman."

AMELIA KEOGH DID NOT make it to breakfast, which was eggs, mangos, and oil-fried dough balls called *makati*, but when the villagers gathered in the thatched dwelling that was their church, she emerged from the medical hut and slowly made her way to them. Dr. Julienne Baudin and Betty Ndongala bracketed her, their arms linked at the elbows, both watching her with acute sadness. She was wearing one of her husband's button-up shirts, a cream-colored Ferragamo patterned in beige paisley, tan capris, and flat-heeled rope sandals embellished with beads. Her hair was loose, her face free of makeup and as pale as candle wax. She walked, trancelike, her gaze fixed somewhere on a horizon visible only to her.

The little church was packed to its modest capacity, an overflow outside that comprised most, if not all, of the other villagers, their voices raised in song that seemed much too bright to be that of spiritual condolence. When word circulated that Amelia was approaching, the singing dwindled to a stop and heads turned, worshipful eyes focused on her in sorrow.

She gave them a wan smile, hands clasped as if in prayer. "No, no, *mes amis, continuez, s'il vous plaît. Gardez-le heureux.* Keep it happy...it's the only way he would have it. *Continuez!*"

The congregation resumed singing and she sat listening, lost in thoughts that rode on the blissful waves of happier times in the surf and the sun and in a life of promised years, twisting the wedding band on her ring finger and running her hands over the front of Cyrus' shirt. As the voices blended in a multilayered harmony that was as naturally harmonious as birds in a meadow, their spirituality unexpectedly lightened her heart to the point that it ached with a happiness she should not have been feeling.

When the church gathering dispersed, Amelia assured Baudin and Ndongala that she would be all right and strolled to the common area where Jake and the others were cleaning up.

Seeing her, Jake drew up a pair of plastic chairs and motioned her to sit. Before she did, she gave him a hug which, from her height, required leaning down. "Thank you," she said softly. "I know how hard this has been for you, and no matter what happened, I have no doubt that you did everything you possibly could."

Jake sat and eyed her closely. "How are you feeling? Physically, I mean…did you get any rest?"

"Oh yes, Julienne made sure of that. She gave me something, so I did sleep."

"That's good." He placed his hands on his thighs, palms down, fingers splayed. "Okay, I will tell you anything you want to know. But first, know this…I came to accept that Cyrus did everything from his heart, and I know his impulses were always driven by protecting those he loved. He had one of the purest, most generous and joyful spirits of anyone I've ever had the pleasure to know. I consider him a brother and I will mourn and miss him."

Amelia bent forward, put her hands over Jake's and, through a film of tears, said, "Thank you. He was extremely fond of you, had so much respect for you, so that means a lot to me."

Jake's face clouded and he shifted uncomfortably. "I also need to tell you…in all honesty, I don't know if my intervention or my actions got him killed."

"I could never blame you, Jake. As you probably know by now, I can be quite tempestuous, but I don't do blame. Cyrus doesn't—*didn't*—either." She brushed strands of hair back from her face, the flaxen light of the morning making her freckles look like fine flecks of dust. "I also don't want you to feel like you failed in your efforts to find Lula. That was an impossible task, and what you accomplished in finding so many of our people is nothing short of incredible. I will be eternally grateful to you and to everyone with you."

Jake could not bring himself to smile. "Well, I appreciate the kind words, but I do hold myself responsible in everything I undertake and I try to never leave a mission unfinished or anyone behind. Just so you know, Remy is working on"—he hesitated—"recovery."

Amelia nodded, sniffling. "Do I...should I go there?"

"To Mombasa? No. It will be handled and we'll be notified. Then you can make whatever arrangements you want."

She was thoughtful for several moments, then said, "I don't know what to do. Cyrus and I did everything in life together. I am lost. I feel like just floating away somewhere." She glanced around, her eyes following the people moving about in their daily routines, the children at play. Tears rolled again. "But I don't want to leave them..."

"Give yourself time, Amelia," Jake said. "You will find your way and know what to do. And whatever that is, I will make sure you have the best security. You *will* go on."

"What about you? Are you going home?"

He paused, felt the draft and draw of a doorway opening at the universe's threshold of innermost desires, there for him to step through to the other side.

But he said, "Well...there are some things I want to pursue before putting it all to bed."

"What kind of things?"

"Not for you to concern yourself with."

"All right." She took a deep breath and blew it out. "Tell me what happened to Cy."

He held her eyes, their green today the shade of seawater, and said, "He died about as bravely as a man can, coming to my defense."

"Tell me," she said.

JAKE DIDN'T KNOW IF seeing the image of Aris Xavier was what pulled him back from the threshold or if it was the aggregate sum of everything Xavier had machinated in the Keoghs' world, but while he did not, as yet, have any direct evidence, there was no doubt in his mind that Xavier had been behind the hijacking of their ship. Jake knew his fierce instinct to protect Callie had caused the reaction in Keogh that resulted in his death but, ultimately, X was the man responsible—Aris Xavier had murdered Cyrus Keogh. Also on the indictment of his egregious vendetta was the exploitation and violation of many innocent people, including children, the deaths of two men charged with protecting the Keoghs, the collateral death of Keogh's best friend Archer Rudd, the failed attempt to kill Falcone and Niles, the captivity and victimization of hundreds, and the slaughter of magnificent and increasingly endangered animals.

No, his mission was not over, but it was time to change the mission objective. Time to bring X and his spear out of the shadows and into the hard light of reckoning.

I'm coming for you, motherfucker.

51

SHORTLY AFTER NOON, JAKE received a call from Kipnis, who let him know that the Kenyan Coast Guard had located and boarded Keogh's ship and found the captain and crew alive, the pirates gone. The bodies of Cyrus Keogh and Archer Rudd had been recovered and were in transit to the prestigious Lee Funeral Home in Nairobi, renowned for its handling of foreign nationals and country dignitaries. Remington was going to personally oversee their admission and coordinate further arrangements with Cameron McNamara. Kipnis also told Jake that he had spoken with the brigadier in Mombasa, the highest-ranking official in the coast guard and, while he was assured the full resources of all law enforcement organizations would be brought to bear, the identities and affiliations of the hijackers were, as yet, unknown.

After a slightly contentious debate, wherein Jake wanted Falcone and Niles to stay behind and they would hear nothing of it, the duo joined Jake and Baladur on the plane, which was now headed toward the border. The pilot, Steve Haggis, got them in the vicinity in just under thirty minutes. Overflying the mining territory, he circled the Cessna in gradually decreasing altitudes until they were low enough to confirm that the site—or what was left of it—was deserted. They set down in the landing zone just beyond the north end of the basin. Haggis stayed with the plane, and the rest hiked to the rim.

So much of the site had been destroyed by the explosives Jake detonated that it was difficult to maneuver, their boots slipping and sliding in the loose soil, but they made it around to the entrance gate which was still intact. Everything it had been attached to was not. The housing for the site's management and security was leveled and, on sifting through the remains, it appeared that anything of significance had been removed. There were mud-caked garments and rubber boots and blankets twisted in the mire, but not much more. They continued along the southern ledge, looking into the cavern where mining activity had been going on just a week ago, everything buried in mounds of rubble and red dirt. The western side was the least damaged, which had been by design, and Jake prayed that all of the workers got out. The ledge above the dam had collapsed, so they scuttled down to the river bank and peered up where the huts incarcerating the Keoghs' people had been.

"So we put them out of business?" Falcone asked. He was sweating heavily from the exertion, still weak from his sickness. His face was boiled and bloated in the heat.

"No, I'm sure we didn't," Jake answered. "They've just gone some-where else to regroup." He was thinking of Kaseme but also of Aris Xavier and Spear-X, wondering how the demise of this mining operation had impacted Xavier's contract. He also realized that the hijacking of Keogh's ship had probably been in the works by that time. Distracted by his thoughts, he looked at Falcone with exasperation. "You should *not* have come."

"I'm okay," Falcone insisted. He fumbled in his pack for a bottle of water, dug one out, and twisted off the cap. Guzzled from it and sighed with relief. Wiping his mouth, he blathered, "I just can't believe…Iris…"

Jake said nothing.

"I mean, what would be her motivation?"

"People do things for all kinds of reasons, Eddie," Jake said crisply.

"I can't believe I got played. I mean, she seemed…we were…"

"Eddie, we don't know what she did, and whatever you had with her could very well have been totally legit."

"But you said…"

"I know, but just because I think something doesn't mean it's true."

Falcone scowled. "You're almost never wrong."

"You think they're coming back here?" Niles asked.

"Maybe," Jake replied. "But my guess is probably not." He glanced up at the sun's harsh midday glare and thought of all the hours people had slaved in this pit, others furrowing deep into airless tunnels that could cave in on them at any moment. He also thought of the bone field where those who lost their lives trying to escape that fate had died at the directive—and hands—of X. "Okay, nothing more to see here. Let's head to the poacher's camp."

IN AN EFFORT TO avoid navigating the field of ordinances and crossing the stream they'd dealt with before, Jake had studied his sat images and found a savanna on the South Sudanese side of the border that Haggis deemed open and flat enough in which to land, so within fifteen minutes of takeoff from the mining site, they were back on the ground, hiking toward the jungle terrain that encompassed the rebels' base camp. Jake doubted they were still there, but he thought they might not be far; they would want to keep the cover of jungle and be close to any caches of ivory they were maintaining. Then again, after coming under their attack and subsequently being captured, the rebels could have unearthed the ivory and relocated it elsewhere. In the couple of days since, they'd had enough time to log some miles.

As it turned out, Jake's secondary supposition was the correct one; both the staging and base camp areas were abandoned. Giving everyone time to rest and hydrate, Jake reviewed his maps and intel, realizing that whatever direction they took from here would be speculative at best. Going over all the options, he chose northwest based on the known trafficking corridor, which angled up toward the border of CAR. He didn't want to get too far out of range from Haggis and the plane, but he felt it was too risky to fly farther into South Sudan without encountering some kind of local challenge to their presence, so he relayed their current coordinates and intended route to the pilot over comms with instructions to stay put, and they hiked on.

The afternoon in the jungle was steamy, their progress hindered by overgrowth that had probably never seen the blade of a machete, and Jake was beginning to think he'd made the wrong choice when they came to a trail that was the approximate width of an elephant's body. Baladur and Niles were drenched in perspiration, their exposed skin daubed with dirt and plastered with particles from wood and leaves, but Falcone looked to be an inch away from passing out, lagging well behind the other two.

Stopping to wait for him to catch up, Jake tried to conceal his irritability, hands on his hips.

Wheezing between breaths, Falcone held up his hand. "I know, I know…shouldn't have come." He bent over, fists on his knees. "I just…I have to be part of this…for Cyrus."

Frowning, Jake said, "I understand, but it's really too soon for you to be putting yourself through this. Just keep drinking your water."

They continued for another hour and the jungle began to fill with more light as the dense vegetation thinned and the gaps in the canopy widened, strobing white bursts of sun. They emerged into a clearing that stretched a short distance to a dirt road. Jake wasn't keen on being exposed, but trekking through the bush was not only taking its toll on them physically, it was slowing them considerably. Glancing at his watch and the position of the sun in the sky, he knew they didn't have many hours of daylight left. Cautioning everyone to be alert and keep their weapons ready, Jake led them down the dirt road.

They had gone about a half mile when the outskirts of a village came into view, the road bisecting a series of scattered mud-and-thatch *tukuls*. But there was something peculiar about the settlement, and it didn't take them long to grasp what it was.

There were no people or animals milling about and, after observing for several minutes, no one materialized or exited any of the dwellings. Jake immediately felt a sense of wariness come over him, a kind of Twilight Zone eeriness, as he surveyed the empty village.

"Looks like these people have been run off," Baladur commented.

"It does," Jake agreed, "but none of the structures are damaged in the usual way when a place is looted."

They walked past each *tukul*, Baladur calling out in Zande and Jake trying Arabic, but there was no response. With his AK-47 pointed in front of him, Jake stuck his head in one, then another, and another, finding each uninhabited. There were no traces of any belongings, no remnants of food and, perhaps more telling, no waste from any animals; given that the vacant abodes offered shelter from the elements, he would have expected that. Gazing toward the last of the huts, he saw clusters of doum nut palms, a stand of baobab trees, and the start of another forest behind them, tall and thick with eucalyptus, teak, and mahogany. The sun was now a wash of orange sinking below the treetops, which were utterly still.

Jake stopped, a tingling sensation at the base of his spine, his pulse percolating. The grip on his rifle tightened.

Beside him, Baladur asked, "What is it, boss?"

"Something doesn't feel right. Let's move out."

They had reversed and begun retreating when a loud crack split the quiet, something thudding heavily into the dirt inches from Jake. He pivoted, rifle snapping up, and caught the glint of metal high in one of the hardwoods.

"Go!" he yelled, and the four of them ran.

"Where did that come from?" Niles shouted.

"Sniper in the trees!" Jake exclaimed.

"What?"

Jake did not need to respond as a hailstorm of bullets pounded around them, kicking up a cloud of dust that made it impossible to see how many were behind them or how close. When they made it to the woods, each scrambled into position and began firing. But for every round of theirs, many more were returned.

"Is it the poachers?" Niles asked.

"Don't know, but it's a shitload of weaponry." Jake kept shooting but took a moment to look through his FLIR Recon monocular and could not believe what he saw. Not poachers. The attack force was mostly Caucasian, lots of them, wearing tactical camo and packing serious hardware. "Fuck," he said, firing until his mag was empty, releasing it, and snapping another in. To everyone, Jake said, "These guys are mercs...possibly X's guys from the mine site. Keep laying it down, but draw back!"

They fell into a rhythm of aggressive fire, gnashing their way through the jungle, and then finding a new position to dig in and continue their defense. But Jake knew this was not something they could sustain for long and, with darkness coming, if the mercs had night vision—and he had to believe they did—their ability to evade would become increasingly more difficult. With running, he also had the concern of Falcone's weakened condition.

Looking at Baladur, Jake asked, "Do you remember that bluff we passed? I think it's close. It looked pretty steep and I don't know what's below, but if we can manage, maybe we can get out of this or at least get more distance between us and them."

"That is a good idea," Baladur said.

Jake led them to the ridge and stopped, looking down. The slope dropped with almost no graduation, well over a hundred feet, snarled with roots and vines, and terminating somewhere out of view. It was a risk he would normally never have entertained, even in full daylight, and in the expanding dusk, it was especially treacherous. There was no time to set up for rappelling, but right now he was about out of options.

"Okay, hold onto whatever you can, and stay close to each other."

"Shit!" Falcone blustered, peering over the edge "You can't be serious!"

Gunfire hammered behind them, loud and close.

"You got a better idea?" Jake asked.

They started down, boot treads jabbing for purchase and hands grabbing whatever they could, the sound of artillery beginning to fade as their descent took them out of one forest and into another. The final forty feet was virtually a freefall, each landing in a nest of thorn bush at the bottom. When they got to their feet, they moved swiftly through the trees and found a large stream—or, rather, a small river—and with it, hopefully a way to escape from the firefight Jake didn't think they had any chance of winning.

DESPITE THE PAIN OF thorns on landing, none paused to remove them. Jake ran alongside the river, the rest following, and did not look back until they could no longer hear any gunfire. When they finally did stop, he took out his thermal scope and panned the landscape around them, relieved to not pick up any heat signatures.

"Reload quickly and let's move," he said.

Minutes later, they resumed their course parallel to the river. After nearly an hour without seeing or hearing anything to suggest pursuit,

Jake allowed himself to feel optimistic, thinking that the killing squad might have decided they weren't worth further effort. But deep down, he conceded he didn't really believe that. He was certain they were X's security team from the mines and had probably cleared out that village for their own use, maybe even anticipating Jake's return to hunt the poachers. A lookout had spotted them approaching, the men had taken to the trees, and Jake had walked right into their ambush.

Goddamn, he muttered to himself. He heard a wince and turned to see Niles limping. "What's wrong?" he asked.

"Dunno…just started hurting."

"Let me take a look."

Niles sat on the ground, pointing to his left leg, and Jake worked his fingers over the bones and muscles and tendons, Niles grimacing when he found the spot at the calf.

"Yeah," Jake sighed. "It's a strain, but at least it's not your ankle." He took out a roll of Ace bandage and wrapped it around Niles' leg below the knee. "Ideally you need to keep weight off it, but we gotta keep moving."

"I know, mate."

Jake dug out a bottle of ibuprofen and dumped a couple of tablets in his hand. "This will help some."

"How much farther?" Falcone asked breathlessly, his face deeply flushed.

"Enough to make sure we're in the clear, and right now, I'm not sure we are."

Which was when he heard the thrum of rotors and the whine of a familiar engine, distant but headed their way.

"Shit. Okay, let's go."

With a fatigued Falcone helping Niles, they followed Jake away from the river, but the tree coverage here was scant with the high umbrella crowns of acacias taking the place of the copious networks of limbs and leaves afforded by the giant canopy trees in the forest. Out here, they would be easy to pick off, Jake thought, and made the only decision he could.

"We're going to have to get back to those woods, there's just not enough cover here," he said grimly. He peered through his scope, and pointed. "That way…it's near where we were, but hopefully they're expecting us to keep moving in the direction we were going by the river."

It was almost full dark, so they donned their Crye Precision mesh caps fit with FLIR night vision monoculars and began the hike across the open terrain, going from one acacia to the next, checking the ground and sky as they went. The sound of the helicopter was louder, its two turboshaft engines, at over 1900-horsepower each, conspicuously noisy. His sense of urgency to get them under the cover of woods kicked into overdrive. The tree line was in sight when the Atlas Oryx suddenly loomed directly overhead, outlined in the moonlight and, even at five hundred feet, Jake could see the gunner perched in its open door, 7.62 machine gun aimed in their direction.

The gunner unloaded, artillery blasting down. With a velocity of 2800 feet per second, it could shred them like smoked pork. "To the trees!" Jake shouted.

They ran with bullets pummeling the ground and made it into the forest. But just as Jake thought they might have bought some time, there was a strident rattling in front of them, wood splinters exploding. Through his night vision, he saw the green-lit shapes of men converging on them.

"Luther, you got any big bang?" Jake asked.

"I have one," Baladur replied, and Jake saw him dig a frag grenade out of his pack.

"And I've got one," Jake said. "Let's toss 'em."

Jake threw first, aiming for the middle of the lineup. It landed within ten yards of them, exploded, and sent a few flying. The rest scattered sideways, which was when Baladur flung his to the right. Through the smoke, Jake could not tell how many of the men they had taken out, but he could still hear the heavy automatic fire reverberating overhead.

They all watched tensely, eyes honed on the attack zone, waiting for the air to clear. When it did, there were survivors, still too many of them, and they were marching forward, spraying bullets.

Holy fuck, Jake thought desperately, *we're done.*

They fired into the oncoming squad, slowing the advancement but not by much. As Jake and Baladur and Falcone and Niles gave it everything they had, Jake caught flashes of their faces, intense and grated with fear. There was a smear of blood below Falcone's bottom lip where he'd bitten it. Niles' longish blond locks were whipping wildly about his head as the recoil of his AR-15 rocked his shoulders. Baladur's focus was as fervent as a hunter, locked in and oblivious to even his own breathing.

In the next few moments, in the vacuum of his ears, Jake heard a declaration from each of them, announcing, "I'm out."

He shoved the last magazine into his AK-47 and raked his barrel from left to right, teeth gritted, willing some of it to matter. And then, all the bullets spent, he pressed himself against the ground, smelling the teak resin and decomposed matter and dirt and praying they were not about to die here.

"Hold on," he murmured, to himself and to the others. "Hold on…just…hold on." But there was nothing left to use in defense, nothing left at all, and the assault continued. Jake clutched his emptied rifle tightly, listened to the bombardment drawing closer, rounds whistling over him and striking the ground like a meteor shower, and waited for the inevitable.

ANOTHER ONSLAUGHT THAT WAS raucous and sharp rattled from what seemed like a new dimension. It was as if it was coming from nowhere and everywhere. There were outbursts and screams. The ground tremored, the trees shook. The brush crashed with the boots of warriors in victorious conquest, the air permeated by gunpowder and the musk of sweat and testosterone. Jake braced, inhaled and prayed, his final thoughts of Callie's touch, her soft breath on his skin, the throb of her heart against his chest.

God, don't take me from her now…but if it's my time…oh God.

His heart was flooded with anguish and anger and despair and prayers for deliverance. All around him, the world was still exploding, from the air and on the ground.

He felt his scalp tingle, his testicles knot up, the tip of a boot by his head.

52

THE IMPRESSION IN THE soil was unmistakable. It had not rained the night before, and the tread was cleanly defined, embedded between rows of the rosebushes. It might have escaped her notice were it not for the emergence of newly opened blooms on several of the bushes, Archduke Charles being on the end of a row where she had bent forward to cup one of the lovely roses in her hands, taking in the creamy pink center edged in crimson and reveling in its velvety texture and light fragrance. Before she straightened up, she saw the indentation in the ground next to the bush and, taking a closer look, spotted another just outside the row.

Callie felt unease fall over her, her heart tripping as she glimpsed around the garden, across the grass, and back toward the pool. No one was anywhere in sight, but she knew Estabon Mina and Mauricio Leguizano were working at the front of the villa and Ramón Cárdenas was cleaning windows and tile inside the patio portico, so he was nearby. She also knew these imprints did not belong to any of them. Watching the three work as much as she did, she knew they took great care around the plantings, particularly the flowers, and now, especially the roses.

She was staring at the two prints when a voice behind her asked, "*Qué es eso?*"

Cárdenas startled her, but she blew out a breath and said, "Oh, no, it's nothing." She brushed at her pink-and-white gingham seersucker capris, even though there wasn't a speck of dirt on them.

Cárdenas leaned down and peered at the soil. "*Ay, ay, ay,* that is not me...I know better."

She smiled and said quickly, "No, of course not, Ramón."

His forehead creased in perplexity, and she knew he also did not believe the prints belonged to either Mina or Leguizano but didn't say it. "I will get Esta and Maurice."

The tread pattern of the impressions was unusual, waffles of isosceles trapezoid shapes: raised ones around the edges, scooped ones at the heel, a couple of hollowed ones in the middle of the top, and a large solid one in the center with some kind of insignia that resembled a yin and yang or a pair of opposing C's, or maybe G's. Not the tread of a work boot, but possibly that of a pricey athletic shoe.

She looked up to see the anxious faces of the gardeners. She stepped aside to let them look and they both took a few moments to scrutinize the treads. She saw them exchange fretful glances, then an accord seemed to pass between them.

"*Lo siento,* Miss Callie," Mina said, bowing his head. "I was putting the fertilizer and my foot slip." He corrected himself. "Feet...my feet, they slip." He shot another sideways glance to Leguizano, flexing the fingers inside his thick leather gardening gloves. It was as if they were both waiting for her vindication.

"It's okay, Estabon," Callie said. "Really, don't worry at all."

They nodded contritely and backed away, their eyes holding hers. Cárdenas stood with her for another few minutes and then asked, "Okay?"

"Yes," Callie answered, and watched as he, too, returned to his work.

Her gaze lingered on the impressions, and another thought drifted over her like a graying storm cloud in transition. In a flickering visual, she saw the thong sandals that had been pointed at her face when she'd broken the water's surface in the pool several days ago—the thong sandals on the feet of the man no one else saw.

Callie became aware of Camilla approaching with a tumbler of lemonade. "Here, *mija,*" she said cheerfully, handing her the iced beverage. Seeing the haunted look on Callie's face, Camilla's smile drooped. "*Qué?*"

"Thank you," Callie said, and sipped from the lemonade.

The housekeeper's eyes went to the spot on which Callie had been fixated. She tried to stifle a reaction, but there was a twitch in her cheek, a pull of breath, and then she said, *"Esa soy yo,"* adding, "I could not help me…I touch and smell…*muy hermosa."*

Callie regarded her doubtfully. "You? But—" She glanced off toward the villa.

It took her a moment to comprehend, but when Camilla figured it out, she said, "They just take the blame," and rolled her eyes to further sell it. "I will have lunch ready soon, *mija."*

When she was alone again, Callie stepped to the end of the row of roses, looked down at the treads in the soil. And saw the feet in the thong sandals, the striped straps. The swarthy face obscured behind the hearse-black wraparound sunglasses, the teeth like white tombstones, the gold chain…the same man she had seen at the beach.

The same man at the beach had been poolside at the home where she and Jake lived. Not just any man…*that* man.

Though it did not rain last night, it *had* rained since the day she'd seen him at the edge of the pool. The impressions in the rose garden, if they were made by those thong sandals, meant he had been back after that. How many times? Once? Twice? More? Was he watching her right now? Suddenly the serenity and beauty of the garden and the tropical rainforest beyond it morphed into the jungle of her nightmares and she fled to the villa, scrambling up the stairs to the bedroom.

She crawled onto the bed and pulled pillows around her, trying not to hear footfalls thudding on each step.

PRONE ON THE GROUND, Jake saw the tip of the boot by his head and a frenzied swarm of thoughts cut through his mind like razor wire, all too fast to seize one with which to launch a response. But he just knew he did not want to go down like this, he could not go down without a fight. Maybe in some other time, maybe in some other place, but he had a reason to fight, to do whatever he could do until the very last second, just as he had done in the ocean when he didn't think he could make it another inch, let alone another mile.

And then, he felt a moist puff of air at his ear followed by a soft snuffling. Turned his head a few degrees further and saw a wet black nose.

He jumped to his feet, incredulous.

"Mother—"

"Anybody order some biscuits and gravy?" Quipped in the familiar Tennessee twang.

Nash Remington stood, dressed in tactical wear and strapped with an M4, night vision goggles flipped back from his eyes. The Belgian Malinois, one of which had nosed Jake, sat at his side like a pair of Lladró statuettes.

Jake jabbed him in the upper arm, hard, and let out a husky laugh. "Son of a bitch…about time you showed up!" He felt the tension go out of his body, the release of adrenaline momentarily making his knees go weak. "We could have shot you."

Tapping the comm in his ear, Remington said, "I heard you were out of ammo."

"How'd you find us?"

"Brother…Kip could find your ass on the moon if he had to." He glanced around. "We'll have our tea party later. Right now, looks like we've still got some bad guys to deal with."

Surrounding Remington were Efron Kipnis and several other armed men, Kipnis clutching a Barrett M82 fitted with a FLIR ThermoSight HISS-XLR scope, the others firing at the scattered group of mercs still engaging. Kipnis slipped off his backpack and dropped it to the ground, telling Baladur, Falcone, and Niles, "There's loaded clips in there."

While they collected magazines to reload and rejoin the fray, Remington tossed another M4 to Jake and, with Kipnis, they focused their attention on the Atlas Oryx still making passes and shelling from overhead. Finding a spot with a clear line of sight through the treetops, Kipnis set up in the V of a bifurcated mahogany, peering through the scope and making his adjustments. When he had lined up his spot, he waited for the Oryx to drift into it, sighted on the door gunner, and pulled the trigger. The .50-caliber BMG round tore into space, hitting the target nearly instantaneously, the gunner heaving backwards, his 7.62 swinging. Seconds later, the helicopter banked sharply and flew off.

Jake stared at Kipnis with unabashed awe.

"Pick your jaw up," Remington chided. "That's a shot he makes all day long."

They spent the next twenty minutes or so pushing off the last of the merc squad, which continued to be stubbornly determined and seemingly supplied by some limitless ammunition depot dispensing bullets like gumballs from a bubbletop machine. Kipnis had traded his sniper rifle for a Galil and all of them together were able to force their attackers into defensive shooting. But just when Jake felt like they had gained the advantage, he thought he heard the turbine growl of the helicopter from somewhere behind the enemy line, the noise of something heavy crashing through the trees.

"What the hell?" he asked out loud. They soon found out as one of the mercs emerged with a grenade launcher hoisted on his shoulder.

"RPG!" Jake shouted. "Take cover!"

Everyone dropped to the ground, rolling away from the trajectory of the weapon, its propellant landing in the space they'd just cleared, blasting into the ground, spraying grass and roots and dirt.

"Enough of this shit," Jake sputtered, and stood, shouldering his M4. "Cover me." Watching through his rifle scope, he saw the merc with the RPG launcher reloading and moved from tree to tree until he was within range. When he had the guy in his crosshairs, from about five hundred yards, Jake took the shot and saw his target fly backwards, the launcher firing up into the air, scattering the squad around him.

Remington and the rest of their guys advanced to Jake's position and, with sustained fire that lasted several more minutes, it was over.

THE DECISION WAS MADE to hike a few miles from the area and set up overnight camp, and an hour later they found a location with ample tree cover near a tributary from the river Jake had followed earlier. With a fire going, MREs digesting, and most either working on their shelters or settling into them, Jake and Remington sat sharing some coffee in their first one-on-one time since reuniting.

"Have to tell you, man," Jake said, "You saved our asses. I really thought we were done."

"Yeah, we cut it a little close. I'm just glad we made it."

"How did you get to us?"

"Mellie actually flew us. Thanks to you, he's already back in the fight. He wanted to come all the way, but I made him stay with the plane. He's back at the strip where you landed with Haggis." He paused, stroking the whiskers under his mouth. "Kip has been working intel for your op pretty near twenty-four seven."

Jake glanced in the direction of the man who, to the unknowing eye, looked so much more the reserved nerd scientist than a self-assured tech genius and Mossad-trained specialist. He was disassembling and cleaning his Barrett M82 with the care of a museum curator handling a centuries-old antiquity. Jake said, "I know, and he's been indispensable. Not to mention amazing."

"Well, he got something on the pirates. They are, in fact, Somalis, and…there are connections to the ivory syndicate I've been pursuing."

Jake's dark eyes flashed in the firelight. "What?"

"I couldn't believe it, either."

Jake shook his head. "Damn. I was so sure Xavier was behind the hijacking of Keogh's ship."

Remington set his cup down, leaned forward, and clasped his hands between his knees, peering at Jake over the fire. "I'm not saying that he isn't."

"How do you mean? What do you know?"

"Nothing for certain yet, but there are some overlaps in associations."

"There seem to be a lot of overlaps with that son of a bitch," Jake said with disgust. "I know he's behind everything that happened to the Keoghs. We know about his contract with the mines where a lot of the Keoghs' people were being held, and while I can't definitively prove his direct involvement in poaching operations, there is a lot to suggest that he is up to his ass in that. There's the bullet casings from the Keoghs' compound matching the ones from the poachers' camp…and the mercs we just fought off are his guys, from the same outfit doing security at the mining site. I saw the Oryx helo at the LZ there, too. It could have been for management or owners, but now I'm sure it was his or at least being used by him."

Jake glanced away, a clot forming in his throat. When he looked back at Remington, he said, "I just know he took an extraordinary man out of this world."

Neither spoke for a few moments, letting that avowal resonate, and then Remington said, "Knowing that despicable piece of shit is in play in my backyard, I want to take him out like the nasty vermin he is." He inhaled deeply as if to re-center himself. "But...no matter whether he's tied to the poaching directly or not, I also want to annihilate *them*."

Jake pressed his lips together, his jaw tight. "I do, too. Remy, you can't imagine just how much I do."

"I think I can. I've been fighting this for a while. And you're on to a really good lead here, so I've cleared my schedule and I'm all in for the rest of the haul, wherever it takes us. I brought my dogs because this is one of the things they're trained for. On the way here, we stopped at the poachers' camp you found, and they got good sensory exposure." His gaze cut to Kipnis. "And he's got the tech. We're going to get these bastards, Jake."

JAKE AWOKE TO BARKS. With the successive accumulation of ordeals he'd endured in the past few days, let alone the past few weeks, he had slept like the dead. Now, from his hammock, he opened his eyes to see Falcone and Niles playing with Remington's dogs, tossing sticks for them to chase. Luna and Solis dutifully ran them down and brought them back, time after time.

"Hey," Jake said, swinging his boots to the ground, "that's enough. Don't tire them. They've got hard work ahead." At the sound of his voice, both dogs trotted over to him, hind ends and tails wagging, ears pinned back against their heads as they nuzzled in for his affection. He knelt, pet and rubbed and scratched, then dismissed them so he could pack up his hammock.

After an MRE breakfast of hash browns with bacon, peppers, and onions, granola with blueberries and an apple turnover, the camp was broken down and cleansed of their presence. By the time the sun had spread its yellow glow across the ground and through the trees, they were already underway, back on the northwesterly route, traversing alternating terrains of savanna grasslands and forests.

Walking alongside Jake, Remington clutched the leashes of Luna and

Solis, which were attached to K9 Storm tactical harnesses made of Kevlar-lined 1000 Denier Cordura and replete with a host of technology that included EO/IR cameras and video; illuminators and beacons; audio and two-way radios; GPS and Doppler radar; and an assortment of clips and rings and buckles and tie-downs.

They had barely hiked an hour when the dogs, with noses ten thousand times more sensitive than those of humans, picked up a scent that energized their pace and heightened their senses. Remington let them lead the way, which took the group through swaths of woods, papyrus marshes, and across vast fields of waist-high grass. Several times, the dogs abruptly changed course and took off in another direction, but their enthusiasm and certainty never wavered. The trek took them to a savanna dotted with acacia and sausage trees and surrounded by forest, where both dogs paused and paced, noses sniffing the ground and the air. They ventured down a worn path in the grass and looked back at Remington expectantly. He went to see what they had found and called to Jake.

"Look here." He pointed to a cluster of coconut-sized elephant dung, and said, "We're tracking...the poachers have probably been through here."

Jake took out his Steiner binoculars and panned the horizon in every direction, seeing nothing but bird activity—carmine bee-eaters bright against the deep green trees, hawks and eagles and hornbills winging across a powder blue sky feathered with clouds, ibis and francolin plundering in shorter, lime-colored grass—and the dogs meandering in the quest of a new lead. Organic smells of any kind were always of interest to them, the more fecund or feculent the better, but they were in the singular pursuit of one thing—ivory—and, therefore, on-mission.

Remington took them off leash to work more freely and it wasn't long before both alerted him with a sharp bark. The Malinois had stopped in an area where the grass appeared to have been dug up and replaced. They were panting and whining excitedly, circling the spot.

"Good dogs!" Remington praised, giving them both a robust pat on the head.

With shovel tools from their packs, Jake and Remington started digging and prodding at the edges and several large intact sections of the grass came up. There was an enormous grave-size hole below, but it was empty.

"This was a cache," Remington said, wiping sweat from his forehead.

"Seems to be fresh," Jake remarked. "Like maybe it hasn't been dug up long."

Remington turned and gestured to Kipnis who had remained with the others, cooling themselves in the shade at the edge of the savanna. In his comms, he said, "Let's deploy the drone." To Luna and Solis, he commanded, *"Hier, rechts."* In response, the Malinois obediently heeled by his right side.

Kipnis retrieved a rucksack from one of their guys and began extracting components that he quickly assembled into something that resembled a giant four-legged spider with propellers. He snapped in the battery panels and affixed an HD Zoom camera. Next, he set up the base module and powered up the touchpad tablet.

Noticing Jake's inquisitive observation, Kipnis explained, "This will save us a lot of mileage or show us where to go."

Remington added, "Since we know they were here, we can take the search aerial and see if they're nearby."

Kipnis deployed the SkyRaider drone, sending it high into the sky, tapping the touchpad to map and follow its navigation in real time. With a speed of up to thirty miles an hour and a duration of forty minutes, it was able to provide a wide zone of surveillance in a short span, and the results were everything they could have hoped. The camera relayed images of a group of men just a few miles away and, after hovering the drone overhead for several minutes and zooming in, Jake and Remington were able to get confirmation; not only had the rebel poachers set up a new camp amidst a light forest, there were stacked bundles of tusks visible at the site.

Looking at the image on the touchpad Kipnis held, Remington smiled. "We got you."

Jake smiled, too. He saw someone he recognized—the man in command that had eluded them during their rescue operation.

BEFORE THEY LEFT THE area, Kipnis set up a half-dozen motion-sensitive cameras powered by AI. Not much bigger than a pencil, the TrailGuard devices—created by a coalition that includes Resolve, Intel, the National Geographic Society, and the Leonardo DiCaprio Foundation—were a strategy Remington had recently begun employing in his consultations with various parks and animal reserves throughout Kenya. After nesting the small units in the trees fringing the savanna, Kipnis told them, "I'll monitor these just in case we have any action here."

"Good," Remington said. "Might as well cover our bases."

With renewed motivation, they hit the trail and made good time, approaching the rebel camp in under an hour. It was late afternoon, the sun and heat peaking with merciless intensity, the ground baking and the brush crisping. Stopping at the last stretch of woods before the camp, Remington asked Jake, "How do you want to do this?"

"They are well-armed and fight aggressively and still have a good number. Last time, we executed a divide-and-conquer strategy. This time, I'm thinking we get them when they're concentrated together." He glanced at his watch. "Another hour or so will be dinnertime."

"Works for me," Remington said.

They took turns surveilling the rebel camp, the others taking advantage of the time to rest and hydrate. Kipnis checked his iPad for transmissions from the TrailGuard cameras, but nothing had been captured, meaning no humans or vehicles had triggered the sensors; the algorithm in the devices had been refined to disregard the movements of birds and animals and natural elements, such as wind or rain. When Jake announced that it was time to go, Kipnis took another quick look at the tablet and got a fleeting glimpse of images that had just popped up, quite a few of them. But there was no time to study them, so he slipped the iPad into his pack and fell in behind Remington.

The plan was to surround the camp and call out for a surrender. No one expected the rebels to comply, and they would all be ready to fire when the men went for their guns. Stalking through the trees, they got into position, fanning around the assembled men, and waited for Jake's command. In the center of the camp, a fire was going, some kind of animal skewered and roasting over it. It was blackened and dripping grease, the flames sputtering and smoke puffing. There were some adolescent boys and a few women, but most of the thirty-odd were men, rifles either slung behind their backs or on the ground beside them. They were totally at ease and oblivious in their anticipation of repast, talking and laughing, some smoking cigarettes.

Remington and everyone else raised their rifles, and Jake yelled, *"Tout le monde à terre!* Everyone on the ground, now!"

Baladur repeated the order in Zande.

There was a brief moment of stunned inaction, followed by a disorderly scramble, and then men were clutching their weapons and veering in every direction. As expected, no one was getting down on the ground. They began to fire their AKs and, in some cases, Lee Enfields and G3s.

Jake, Remington, and the rest returned fire, and it became a volley of artillery from both sides. A few of the rebels were hit and fell, but most were managing to evade, ducking behind the trees or shooting to hold off their attackers. Jake had made it known before the op that he wanted to capture some, if possible, so they could be interrogated, but it did not appear that this was going to happen. And, twenty minutes into the fight, another element came into play, one that posed an imminent threat to both sides.

In between the piercing individual rifle reports and rattling automatic bursts, they began to hear a muffled rumble that grew more pronounced as the source drew closer. And then, through the trees, a cloud of dust spilled across the open terrain in the distance. Both sides continued moving and shooting, but the attention of all was distracted by what was oncoming.

Jake recognized them first, shouting, "Janjaweed!" Then: "Fall back! Fall back!"

Men on horseback broke through the dust storm generated by the pounding hooves of their mounts, all armed with automatic rifles and bandoliers of ammunition looped over their chests and the necks of their horses. Their heads were turbaned, the lower part of their faces covered.

The Janjaweed which, in Arabic, translates as "a man with a gun on a horse" or "devils on horseback" are militiamen from nomadic Arab tribes whose early clashes were with farmers in Darfur over grazing land. Through the years they have become a fierce armed force, rumored to be abetted by the Sudanese government and involved in more consequential conflicts, many stemming from ethnic bias. They are among those who compete with the LRA for poaching domains.

Falcone and Niles, both with Jake, froze, Niles muttering, "Oh my God!"

Jake grabbed them by the arms, spurring them to move.

As they all withdrew further into the trees, the horsemen began firing on the rebels and, with their defense already weakened, the rebels were quickly dropping. Jake and Remington had instructed their guys to avoid shooting the women and boys, but the Janjaweed militia had no such constraint and they were included in the casualties.

Through comms, Kipnis summoned the pair of guys who had been tasked with carrying the heavy Barrett, and they brought the gun to him. While the Janjaweed were occupied targeting the rebels, Jake, Remington, and Kipnis spread out around the back side of the fight and lined up their shots, aiming to start taking out the horsemen. There were at least a dozen, so they knew their offensive would need to be accurate and swift. Jake and Remington each hit a rider, and Kipnis followed up with a third. Becoming the new enemy now brought the focus of the Janjaweed on them, so while the others sprayed fire, Jake, Remington, and Kipnis lined up three more target-specific shots, all hitting their marks. Jake managed to take out two with one round that cored the first guy and struck the rider beside him.

Through it all, horses were whinnying and bucking, some rearing up, which made it more difficult to lock in on the riders, and the additional time and effort provided the remaining rebels a diversion with which to flee the battle. Noticing this, Remington yelled, "We've got rabbits!" Whistling to his dogs, he commanded, *"Voriut! Stellen!"*

Luna and Solis took off running, and Remington watched tensely through the scope of his rifle, ready to fire on any who turned their guns on the dogs. But most people who run from a dog don't stop long enough to shoot at them, not when the dog's speed can top thirty-five miles an hour, so the Malinois easily caught up to their deserters, taking two down with momentum-charged leaps and powerful bites. Remington took the rebels' weapons and zip-tied their hands, dispatching the dogs to find and run down any others.

In the end, there were only three rebels left standing, or rather sitting on the ground in their custody. The remaining, and their Janjaweed counterparts, were either dead or departed on foot or horseback. One of those seated on the ground, zip-cuffed, and bound to a tree, was the rebel commander.

Jake knelt in front of the man and asked, "Do you speak English?"

The man, who wore the same pseudo military uniform he'd had on when Jake and his guys had attacked their former camp, said nothing.

"I'm thinking you do," Jake persisted. "You're done. Not just for now, because we're not releasing you to recruit another army, but *done*." He looked over his shoulder and craned his neck toward Remington, who was on his sat phone with the Garamba ranger headquarters. Because they were in South Sudan, their captives would have to be handled by the SPLA—South Sudan People's Defense Forces—but Jake intended to be long gone by the time they came on the scene, and he knew the Garamba rangers would return the favor for Jake coming to the aid of their wounded with discretion in relaying the report.

Jake placed a boot on the commander's thigh, which had a bullet hole in it; fortunately for the rebel, it had exited and missed anything vital. Jake pressed the sole into the man's flesh until he cried out in spite of his bravado. "If I had my way," Jake growled, "I would rip your skin off one piece at a time…anyone who brutalizes animals the way you and your men have deserve to die in the same kind of agony you inflict. Are you LRA?"

The man gave a subtle nod, his face quivering with anger and pain.

"With Kony?" Jake asked, veins cording in his neck.

That got a hard look but no response.

Jake pressed his boot down again, but the man still said nothing.

"Okay, one more question…and you *will* give me an answer." When the man met his eyes, Jake said, "Aris Xavier."

To his astonishment, the rebel commander spoke, but the words out of his mouth were not what Jake wanted to hear. He said, "I have never seen him."

53

JAKE AND REMINGTON STOOD gazing at the bundles of ivory, piled in a big stack below a pair of mango trees, both together but distant in their thoughts as they quantified what it all represented. There were several huge tusks, including four that were probably a hundred pounds each and many others five and six feet in length and weighing fifty to seventy pounds. The rest were slightly smaller, enough to fill the trunk of a car. All in all, a substantial lot. Remington was keeping some of the smaller pieces with the intention of passing them on to a biology professor with whom he consulted at the University of Nairobi, but the remaining haul was collectively too much for them to transport.

"What did Garamba say about the ivory?" Jake asked.

"They're going to contact Lantoto, which is the closest South Sudanese park. Hopefully, the SPLA will let them handle custody."

"Because the SPLA isn't the most trustworthy," Jake said.

"No."

Jake sighed sadly. "Honestly, I wish we could burn it, but unless we had some highly combustible fuel to add to the fire, that would be futile. Even then, it would take days."

Remington nodded and said, "That doesn't mean we can't at least pay homage. What do you say?"

"Let's do it."

As dusk drew down, dusting gold and bronze over the landscape, a bigger fire was built from the one the rebels had been cooking over, the

largest tusks arranged around the outside of the pit. When the flames of
the fire fully encompassed and consumed the wood, licking up toward
the gilded sky, all of them gathered and bowed their heads.

There was a long silence and then, in a solemn voice, Remington
said: "May the grace of God be with you in your sacrifice." Taking a peek
at Jake's face, he caught his friend fighting emotion, eyes moist.

Amens were uttered and, as everyone dispersed to prepare for departure, Kipnis came up to Jake and Remington, iPad in hand. Holding it
out, he said, "Take a look."

The images captured by the TrailGuard cameras just as they had
been engaging the rebels showed a sequence of the Janjaweed in the
monitored zone, removing the grass clods and finding the hole empty.
Jake and Remy stared at the tablet, their expressions reflecting the confusion they shared.

"I don't know what I'm looking at," Jake said. "If this was the cache
site for these poachers, why are the Janjaweed there?"

"I guess there are some possible scenarios," Remington replied.
"Maybe these guys stole the ivory…or maybe it *was* their ivory and the
Janjaweed were going to steal it from them."

Jake put his hands on his hips. "Damn," he muttered petulantly. "I
feel like we haven't really gotten anywhere with this."

"Sure we have," Remington said. "We've taken out a sizable poaching cell, maybe even LRA. That's big."

"But I'm nowhere closer to making solid poaching connections to X,
and I know he's involved in it. I *know* he is."

"Hey, you can't go by what that son of a whore rebel said. Whether
he's seen X in the flesh or not, he didn't exactly deny knowing him, did
he?" He put a hand on Jake's shoulder, looked him in the eyes. "We're
going to get him…I promise you that, brother. Now let's get these po-
nies on the trail."

HAVING HORSES TO RIDE back was a fortuitous bonus and, after
corralling the spooked animals and checking each for wounds or any
sign of lameness, the group loaded up. But not everyone was embracing
the upgrade. Unsurprisingly, Falcone and Niles had never ridden

before—Falcone had never even been near a horse—and both were shuffling nervously while trying not to appear intimidated. Remington approached them with a look of amusement. "You boys need to chill. Horseback riding is as old as time and just a natural thing. Nothing to it."

"I don't know how to…steer it," Falcone stammered, his eyes sliding up the arched neck of the chestnut-colored stallion next to him, which was walleyed with anxiety.

"I don't think I can do this, mate," Niles chimed in shakily. "They're right large buggers."

Jake came up beside Remington. Speaking to Falcone and Niles in a coddling voice and tone that sounded as if he were reasoning with children in a squabble, he said, "Just get up in the saddle, take the reins, and we'll lead the way. You will be fine. The key is to be calm and confident and they will respond in kind."

Jake and Remington each gave them a lift up to their mounts, made sure their feet were in the stirrups, reins in hand, and chuckled as they made their way to the pair of horses in front. They got into the saddles, did a comm check, and set off. Glancing back at Falcone and Niles, both hugging the necks of their horses, Jake spoke into his comms, "Sit up straight, take the reins, and just let them go."

"Let them go where?" Falcone asked, his voice riddled with trepidation.

"Eddie, Curran…trust me. Just let them go."

Fifteen minutes into the ride, Falcone and Niles were still trying to relax in the saddle, but watching the Belgian Malinois dogs trotting happily alongside Remington seemed to bolster their courage. With the return trip expedited by the increase in pace on horseback, Jake and Remington had calculated they could make it to the planes without stopping, so they rode on as darkness descended, the land turning a lunar blue in the light of a half moon. A quiet serenity settled over the caravan, the steady thump of hooves creating a comforting rhythm and, after the energy expelled during the course of all-out battle, many found themselves drifting into a soporific lull.

The lull was broken in dramatic fashion, horses suddenly bucking and pulling at their reins as if a ripcord had been yanked through them, releasing their hold on the ground. Experienced riders struggled to stay upright; Falcone and Niles were bent over their horses' necks, holding on for dear life.

And then the dogs were barking furiously, running in intersecting circles in front of Jake and Remington's horses. As the two men fought to maintain control, issuing reassurances to their mounts, the dogs' level of alarm and the pitch of their bark was escalating. Before either could dismount to see what was causing the ruckus, Solis let out an ear-splitting yelp of distress and seemed to tumble off into the grass, rolling with legs pumping helplessly in the air, her cries becoming a long, shrill wail.

Seeing the grotesquely long and thick shape moving in the grass, Remington realized what was happening just as Luna leaped to Solis' defense, biting into the mass and viciously shaking. Remington screamed, "No, Luna! *Nee! Loslaten!*" But Luna was doing something neither dog ever did when Remington issued a command—disobeying—his inbred instinct to save his canine partner and his human overriding all rules of behavior.

"No, Luna, no!" Remington shouted again, now plunging into the grass.

The massive snake, an African rock python, writhed and released Solis who darted off, still yelping, and turned its attack on Luna, striking and then wrapping its body around the dog, constricting. Remington grabbed the snake and tugged, the firm muscles in his arms expanding like inflating balloons straining to the point before busting.

"Christ Jesus," he exclaimed, sweat streaming down the sides of his reddened face.

Beside him now, Jake jabbed his Horkos knife into the snake's body, which had the girth of a distended fire hose and looked to be fifteen to twenty feet long, but the reptile only seemed to tighten its grip.

"Motherfucker," Remington swore, pulling with all the strength he could muster, his eyes on Luna's terrified face, jaws open and gasping for breath.

Jake raked the knife through scales and skin, splitting the snake open and finally causing it to unfurl. Remington grabbed Luna, lifting the dog in his arms, and dashed away from the snake. Jake watched as the tan-and-brown reptile slithered into the brush, and went after Solis. He found her shaking and whining under an acacia tree.

Off their horses, Falcone and Niles stood, watching in horror, Falcone muttering, "Oh God, is it gone? Did you see it go? Are the dogs all right?"

Noting the shock and consternation on everyone's faces, Jake said, "It's handled. Calm your horses." He carried Solis to the spot on the ground where Remington had put Luna and set her down. She immediately transformed from quavering in fear to wiggling in unbridled joy, licking Remington's face and then prancing around Luna, whimpering.

Baladur handed Jake a vet med kit from Remington's gear and stepped over to assist. Despite the protection afforded by the K9 Storm harness, Luna had been bitten in two places, on the neck and the leg; Solis, because of Luna's intervention, had not sustained any bites and was just badly bruised and shaken. Jake instructed Baladur to monitor and comfort her while he began to examine Luna.

"Thank God that bad boy—or girl—was of the non-venomous variety," Jake said, running gloved hands through Luna's fur, exposing the bite wounds and checking for others. "Even so, we got to it just in time—they will consume anything." He let Luna lap his face, and made soothing noises as he poured bottled water to irrigate the punctures and then cleaned them out with alcohol. With the application of an antimicrobial spray, a swallow of antibiotic tablets, and dressings on the wounds, Luna stood, shook, and rejoined Solis, both engaging in earnest face-licking, sniffing, and sashaying around together.

"If I could only blow off a snakebite like that," Falcone remarked.

"You couldn't even blow off not-a-snakebite like that," Jake said sardonically. "We could learn a lot from the resilience of animals."

"Yeah, I guess we could," Falcone conceded.

Remington gave his dogs water, watched them for a few minutes, and asked, "Think we're good to go?"

"Yeah." Jake consulted his tactix watch. "Just a couple of klicks and we'll be at the planes."

AFTER MAKING A BRIEF stop to retrieve the TrailGuard devices, they made it to the parked Cessnas, where Dmello and Haggis were waiting.

As Remington's men led the horses away from the planes and gave their rumps a smack to send them off, Jake stood with Falcone and Niles.

The duo, who had been so afraid of their four-legged transports before, were now concerned about their fate. Falcone inquired, "Who's going to take care of them after we leave?"

"They're rugged and used to this environment, they'll be okay," Jake assured him. "What do you guys want to do? I'm going with Remy to Nairobi. You can come with us, but I think you might want to go back to Nakalé. Remy is sending another guy to join Kent."

"Amelia's probably gone to Nairobi, too, by now…don't you think?" Falcone asked.

"To see to arrangements for Cyrus, yeah, probably," Jake said. "But I have a feeling she'll be returning to Nakalé sooner rather than later, and when she does…" He didn't have to finish.

"She's going to need the support of some friends," Niles said.

"If she doesn't return or, if by the time I'm headed back you want to leave, give me a shout." He looked from one to the other, managing a wan smile. "Okay?"

Their faces were gloomy in the moonlight, tired and conflicted and sad. They watched as Remington lifted his Belgian Malinois dogs into one of the two Cessnas and climbed in after them.

"Yeah, okay," Falcone said without enthusiasm.

Jake said, "Take care…I'll see you, guys."

They headed for the plane Steve Haggis was piloting, turning to wave before boarding. Jake saw them in and then walked to the other Cessna, climbed the ladder, and took a seat behind Dmello and Remington. Minutes later, both planes were airborne, one heading south, the other bearing east.

REMINGTON'S PLANE LANDED IN Nairobi late, and Jake hardly remembered crawling into bed, his exhaustion so complete, but when sunlight streamed in through the window the next day, he was ready to get moving—at least his mind was, his body not so much. While he had the chance, he wanted to call Callie, let her know he would be home soon, but squinting at his watch and foggily doing the math, that notion was dismissed as it was almost midnight in Costa Rica. Glancing at the nightstand, he was also reminded that he didn't have his iPhone anymore. As he lay in the comfort of the big four-poster with its sheer billowing drapes, all he wanted was to have her here in his arms. Inhaling deeply, he marshalled himself back to reality and rolled out of bed, stretching his sore muscles.

Three weeks—he had been in Africa three weeks—and it seemed like a lifetime. Again, he wondered what had he really accomplished? Yes, he had found and recovered most of the Keoghs' people, but in the process Amelia Keogh had lost her husband and Jake had been unable to find the child they cherished and were adopting. How did you measure any kind of gain at the cost of such a devastating loss?

He'd showered before bed to defoliate the grunge of the bush, but indulged in another wash now to invigorate. He pulled on a pair of dark G-Star Raw D-staq jeans and a slate blue Banana Republic t-shirt, shaved, ran a comb through his wet hair, and brushed his teeth. Felt like a new man. Almost. The mirror showed the reminder of his ordeal in Mombasa, the bruising on his face fading but still visible, the scars from the death of Cyrus Keogh permanently embedded beneath. His arms were etched with scratches, one lacerated where a bullet had glazed.

He found Nash Remington on the patio, drinking coffee from his *Habari* mug. The dogs were romping in the grass beyond. Pouring himself a cup and savoring the first few sips, he asked, "How's Luna?"

Remington turned, greeting him with a smile, and said, "Feisty as hell. I've had to fix the bandages three times already, but just seeing him out there like that…" He swung his gaze to the two canines, racing and dodging and pouncing on one another, the morning sun bright over the emerald grass. "It's all good."

"I'll check his wounds and re-dress in a bit." Jake took a seat across from him and Remington's houseman, Issa Lusalah, set platters of steak and eggs in front of both. Looking at the plate with relish, Jake asked, "When was the last time we ate?"

As they dug in, Remington said, "I just got off the phone with the guy I was telling you about, biology professor at UON." He shoveled a chunk of steak into his mouth, chewed, and stuffed roasted potatoes in after it. "I told him I had some ivory for him to test and he said he thinks he has something for us."

"Really? Like what?" Jake felt a nudge by his elbow and found both Malinois avidly eying his plate. He laughed. "Okay, I feel for you two, but I am hungry…you'll have to get your own."

"Issa, get these guys some breakfast," Remington called, and told the dogs, "*Loslaten.*" Unlike the last time he'd used the command, they obeyed, and went into the house. To Jake, he replied, "He just said he was in the process of analyzing something that I would be interested in." He wiped his mouth on a napkin and reached into the pocket of his Levi's, producing an iPhone. Placing it on the table, he said, "Kip set it up for you, uploaded your data from the Cloud. He also added some much better encryption."

"When did he have time to do that?" Jake asked in amazement.

Remington shrugged. "Shit if I know. That man is spooky good."

Jake took the phone, unlocked it with Face ID, and glanced at Remington. "It still opens with—"

"See what happens the next time a bad guy tries."

"I don't intend for there to be a next time," Jake said tightly.

"We never do," Remington answered.

JIMIYU CHILEMBA WAS HURTLING along Ngong Road in the sage green Range Rover, traffic at the mid-morning hour not nearly as bad in the outskirts of the city center. They passed through Karen and the Ngong Forest, heading east from the Southern Bypass with the Motorsports tracks and Telcom Sporting Grounds on their right, the Junction Mall coming up on their left. The sound system in the Range Rover wasn't up to par with that of the Rubicon, but Remington had Toto streaming from the speakers and was drumming to Jeff Porcaro's beats in *Africa*.

They were seated next to each other behind Chilemba, and when the song ended, Jake said, "Tell me about this guy."

Gesturing for Chilemba to turn the sound down, Remington replied, "I met him a few years ago while I was pursuing some leads on the syndicate. The leads went nowhere, but he was working with the investigators in trying to establish the origination of ivory they had confiscated. I was intrigued and spent some time with him, but at that point, he was still a few years from perfecting his system."

"His system?"

"He can extract DNA from tusks and match it to elephants specific to territory."

"Okay, but I'm not sure I see…" Jake began.

"Just wait. You will."

Approaching Kilimani, they were starting to hit the more typical inner-city congestion, which only increased as they proceeded. The route took them onto Valley Road past Nairobi Hospital and east onto Kenyatta Avenue where traffic slowed even more and eventually snarled before moving again. They merged onto Uhuru Highway, with the greenery of Central Park on the left, banks and shops and hotels on the right. After the University Way roundabout, the university's main property came into view and they made a left across from it, passing through a gate where signage indicated they were entering the University of Nairobi College of Biological and Physical Sciences, Chiromo campus. They rode past sporting fields and the graduation grounds and then entered a wooded stretch, glimpsing slivers of the Nairobi River on the right. Emerging at a junction, they took a left and Chilemba drove to a three-story building made of stone and stucco with latticed upper floors and pulled into a parking slot in front. Jake and Remington got out of the Range Rover and walked to the entrance, Remington carrying a box with a few small tusks and a sample he'd taken from the elephant dung they'd come across on the way to the rebel poachers.

Noting the lack of other vehicles, Remington explained, "They're in between semesters, so the place is mostly empty."

They were met in the lobby by a man in his late fifties, medium brown hair starting to gray and worn collar-length with a beard. He was dressed in loose-fitting jeans, a blue plaid button-front shirt, and Adidas sneakers, browline-style glasses framing his eyes. "Hey Nash," he said pleasantly, and extended his hand to Jake, saying, "Tom Janney." His accent was American, of indeterminate origin.

They walked a short distance down a hallway, their footsteps echoing in the emptiness, and entered a large office with a desk and seating on one side, two long tables pushed together in the middle, and a wall of bookcases and cabinets on the other. The bookcases were crammed full of scientific texts and journals and references, the back-to-back tables covered with notebooks and papers and maps.

When they were all seated by the desk, Remington said, "Before you tell us what you've got, can you give Jake some background? I thought you could explain it a lot better than I could."

"Sure, sure," Janney said. "I got my education and degrees in the U.S.—I'm from Kansas, but I went to the University of California—and always wanted to travel, so while I was doing grad work on conservation, I accepted offers to intern with animal sanctuaries in Uganda and Tanzania. The more I researched, the more aware I became of the declining numbers of wildlife, particularly elephants. To make a long story shorter, when a professorship opened up here and they encouraged me to continue with my research, it was my best-case scenario. I was able to teach my passion but also do something that will hopefully help to preserve endangered animals."

He rose from his chair and strolled to a giant map of Africa on the wall behind his desk. It was plastered with small sticky tabs, thumbtacks, Post-It notes, and strung with colored strings. "Others who do this kind of work were already using DNA from animal feces, but it took perfecting the extraction of DNA from the ivory to begin this mapping project. By matching the DNA from the seizures of illegal ivory shipments to the DNA from dung collected from various elephant herds, we can determine provenance within several hundred kilometers. The majority of trafficked ivory actually originates from only a few places and we're working our way toward pinpointing it to specific brokers and cartels."

Remington placed the box he'd been holding on Dr. Janney's desk. "This is from what we got yesterday."

"Great, I will get it analyzed." Janney paused, his expression keen with the anticipation of someone about to reveal the killer in a murder mystery. "Now…for what I have."

Jake and Remington leaned forward in their seats, their attention riveted, but Remington's gaze drifted to the map behind Janney, his eyes honed in on one particular Post-It. He leapt from his chair, exclaiming, "Holy shit, Tom! Have you found Zhuang?"

Janney grinned but looked a little disappointed for being deprived his

moment of revelation. "Well, not exactly. But that's why I called you."
He picked up a laminated binder and said, "This report just came to me,
and the samples taken from a small seizure are a match to a previous
one thought to be tied to that syndicate."

Remington's excitement deflated slightly. "Okay, well, that's a new
lead, at least."

Janney's eyes illuminated behind his glasses. "There's more, Nash."
He turned and poked a finger on the wall. "This is where the DNA mapping puts the source of origin."

Jake stood and joined Remington beside Dr. Janney at the map. Janney's finger was on a spot almost exactly where Jake had come upon the
bai massacre.

54

DMELLO GOT THEM TO Mombasa just before 3 PM, landing the Cessna at Moi International Airport, where they picked up a bronze Toyota Prado rental, loaded the Malinois in the rear, and headed out on Port Reitz Road. Remington sat in front giving Dmello navigational instructions to the port. "Just don't tell Chile I let you drive, I'll never hear the end of it," he said, plucking the fabric of his t-shirt away from his skin and savoring the SUV's air-conditioning.

They rode along the two-lane, which began as a rural route lined with trees and hedges of white and fuchsia bougainvillea and became more industrialized, first with small businesses and then with the steady trundle of big trucks, the buildings becoming increasingly dilapidated and dingy. The Indian Ocean could be seen in random bits of blue-green on the right and, as they looped around to a highway that paralleled the port, yards stacked high with colored metal containers brought the whole ship hijacking experience back to Jake in a queasy ripple.

Though they were all wearing sunglasses making eyes unreadable, Remington caught the pinch in Jake's cheeks, the poached hue of his tanned skin, and said, "Bad vibes, I know."

Jake did not respond, and took a swig from a bottle of water as if he could somehow wash the malaise of the memory away, but every time he gazed out toward the sea and the containers and ships and cranes that climbed high over the yards, his temples throbbed and he felt sick to his stomach, still seeing the image of Cyrus Keogh in the instants before he died.

They passed through several checkpoints, Remington handing his ID over and, moments later, they were waved on. "I've been out here a few times and I also called ahead," he explained. They drove past one terminal after another, bypassing a complex of ports authority offices and crossing a causeway that took them to Mombasa Island, the road curving south on the other side. Cargo ships of various kinds were berthed in the water, warehouses and cylindrical storage tanks crowding the inland industrial area. Remington instructed Dmello to turn into one of the large container terminals where they pulled in next to a grouping of trees, beneath which was a nondescript trailer.

Jake and Remington got out of the Prado and went inside. A few men were seated or moving about, most wearing white uniform shirts with the Kenya Ports Authority emblem over the pocket and some also donning orange safety vests and white hard hats. One man, whose shirt was adorned with gold-striped epaulets, looked up when they entered and came over with a cordial smile and an outstretched hand. He was of small stature but with the posture and grooming of a punctilious officiant.

"Mr. Remington, nice to see you again," he said, his eyes moving to Jake. "You must be Mr. Tyler."

Jake shook his hand, and Remington said, "This is Captain Darius Ikinya, he's the general manager of operations and harbor master." To Ikinya, he added, "I appreciate you agreeing to meet us down here and sorry to disrupt your weekend."

"No matter," Ikinya replied, "I work all week a lot of the time and am on call all of the time." He indicated a desk where they sat, Ikinya with hands folded in front of him. "So...you are here about the ivory that was intercepted last week." He flecked an invisible piece of lint from his shirt.

"Yes," Remington said. "What can you tell us about it?"

"Well, it was intercepted here at Kilindini in a container going on a ship bound for Dubai, and—"

Remington's brows hitched upward in question. "Wait, what? Dubai? That's not usually one of the trafficking destinations."

Ikinya looked momentarily confused, then continued, "It was

actually a very small shipment mixed in with other exports, so we think it might have been meant for another container, perhaps one going to a different ship. With another destination perhaps?"

It was Remington's turn to look confused. "What did the rest of the container have in it?"

Ikinya glanced at a clipboard on the desk. "Handbags and women's apparel." He quickly added, "All of it was checked and cleared."

Remington did not comment on that, but he and Jake both knew being "checked and cleared" meant nothing; ivory and other illegally trafficked commodities were typically moved in that very manner with corrupt and complicit clearing agents at the ports. He said, "Captain, the ivory from that shipment was sampled for DNA and matched ivory tied to someone we're tracking. With your permission, I'd like to take my dogs around the vicinity, see if we can pick up anything. I'd also like to know the source for the apparel."

A flicker of disinclination appeared on Ikinya's face. "We have already conducted our investigation, and like I said, the exporter has been cleared. A search of their storage facility near here was also done and no ivory or anything irregular was found."

In an effort to placate the captain's defensiveness, Remington said, "I have no doubt the investigation was very thorough. This would just be really helpful to us."

"All right then," Ikinya said stiffly, and stood. "I will get you clearance."

ONE OF THE KPA'S agents accompanied them as Remington let the Malinois follow their noses around the terminal yard. They got briefly interested circling the container where the ivory shipment had been discovered but did not hit on anything beyond it. Next, with the name and location of the container storage facility associated with the apparel, they drove from the port terminal to a yard further down the road. It was hot and humid, despite the ashen clouds lining the sky, an occasional breeze kicking up enough dust to tinge the sea air with a vaguely chemical smell.

They were walking the perimeter of metal storage buildings when the dogs became animated, their heads snapping one way and then another, nostrils twitching. Both halted by one of the units and sat, looking at Remington.

"Good dogs!" he proclaimed.

Skeptical, Jake asked, "Can they really detect through galvanized metal?"

"Probably not, but if ivory was handled or exposed on the outside, they'd pick up that."

Jake glanced around the premises, which were vacant except for them. Each unit was secured by electronic keypad combination locks, the one on this door appearing to be brand new, not a scratch or smudge on it. "We going to breach it?" he asked Remington.

"Hell, yeah. You know the old saying about asking for forgiveness and begging permission later. Looks like they've replaced the lock, so I'm betting they didn't ask for permission, either."

Jake grinned. "Got some kind of gadget from Kip?"

Remington was already reaching into his backpack. "You know it." He took out a small rectangular case and sprung the cover, revealing a black block inset with a microchip. "I don't begin to know how he made this, but it works on the same principles as a rare earth magnet." He left the block in the case and held it against the unit's metal, sliding it around the lock until a light beep sounded, followed by a click.

Both wearing gloves, they leaned down and tugged the door up. It rolled easily, and as soon as the space was opened, the Malinois began whining excitedly. Remington let them go, and within minutes the pair were sitting by a metal crate toward the rear. It was secured by padlocks, so Remington sent Dmello to the rental in search of a jack. When he came back with one, the padlocks were broken with single, heavy blows.

Inside the container were boxes nested in packing straw, the labels reading: ARCANA TRADING. Each of them took a box, sliced it open, and examined the contents. Since they were expecting ivory or something that could conceal ivory, they set aside the handbags and scarves and hats and belts and kept going through boxes. When they were halfway into the container, they gazed at each other in disappointment and vexation.

"Could Luna and Solis be wrong?" Jake asked.

"Doubtful." Remington whistled, commanding, *"Reveiren!"*

The dogs stuck their heads inside the container and immediately both pawed at the bottom and barked. Remington pulled them back and scraped straw away with his boot, finding a wooden pallet platform. Using the jack, he pried several boards loose and then pulled them up. Beneath the wood were sections of particle board. Even before he lifted those, they knew what they would find.

"Fucking-A!" Remington exclaimed, peering down at layers of tusks, knitted to evenly fit in the compartment.

Jake was speechless for several moments, a swirl of mixed emotions cycling through him, victorious but sad and angry at the same time. "What now?" he asked hollowly.

"Almost wish I didn't have to," Remington said, "but I'm obligated to notify KPA."

Jake was sifting through the other contents of the container, picking up and looking at the items of apparel. Holding a handbag, something caught his eye and he gave it closer scrutiny. The bag was scallop-shaped and intricately beaded in a colorful and sparkly design of flowers and butterflies. There was also a lot of gold beading, but the beads were not consistent with the colored ones. He took out his Swiss Army knife and, using a couple of tools, loosened and popped one of the beads off the bag. It was about five millimeters in diameter, the approximate size of a peppercorn. He dropped it into his water bottle and watched it sink directly to the bottom.

"Remy."

Turning, Remington saw him gazing at the bottle. "What are you doing?"

Quietly, Jake said, "I think we might have our connection to X."

IT WAS NEAR DARK by the time they boarded the plane and took off from Moi, Mombasa thankfully in their rearview. They had spent several hours with Captain Ikinya and a host of other Kenya Ports Authority personnel, local law enforcement, and customs agents, their unauthorized breach omitted from the captain's report in light of a yield that would garner him plenty of praise from the upper hierarchy. Jake and

Remington kept the discovery in the apparel to themselves, stashing a couple of the handbags in their backpacks.

As Dmello flew over the lower plains of the east toward the elevations of the Rift Valley, Jake said, "I guess I'm jumping to conclusions. We don't know for sure if it's actual gold, but it didn't float in the water like almost any bead would have…and the Dubai destination is a good indicator."

"Easy enough to find out," Remington said, holding a cold bottle of water against his neck, head tilted back and eyes closed. "Kip will test it."

Jake sighed. "Well, we have no idea where X is, either."

"That's true. But this puts his feet in the fire, brother."

Jake sank back in his seat and tried to let the tension in his thoughts dissipate, but he could not shake the feeling that he was standing on the edge of something he had not realized just how badly he wanted. And it was a lot like reaching for a trapeze bar in midair—close wasn't good enough.

AFTER A LATE DINNER back at Remington's Ngong Hills ranch house, Jake retired to his bedroom to begin packing for home, organizing the clothing Issa Lusalah had laundered for him, folding and placing it in one of his duffels. He kept glancing at the new iPhone on the bed, planning to call Callie as soon as he was done. But just as he was about to pick it up, Remington's big frame filled the doorway, his eyes dancing with titillation.

"Put on your boogie shoes, my man, we're going clubbing!"

Jake looked at him blankly, unable to program his mind to process that blithe announcement. "Remy, I—"

Remington blurted, "I just talked to Kip. X has been spotted!"

Jake felt his pulse spike. "Where?"

"Right here in Nairobi!"

"Shit…are you serious?"

"As a nun's rosary on Sunday. Ever since you first shared your suspicions about him, I've had Kip doing a deep dive and he got intel that put X here at various times, but nothing specific. One thing he heard, was that whenever X was in Nairobi, he hit the club scene pretty hard. So Kip's been keeping tabs with a couple of bartenders that know me, and one just called him. X is there…right now."

Jake did not need any coaxing. He rummaged through his neatly ordered duffel and pulled out black slacks and shirt—Armani gabardine chinos and a silk tee—and, from another bag, black Palladium Pampa high-top boots. He looked at Remington. "Hey, don't just stand there…get dressed!"

Fifteen minutes later they were in Remington's Rubicon, speeding down Ngong Road, headed for the city. At this hour, what should have taken forty-five minutes on a speed-limit drive took under thirty, with Remington screeching into the parking lot of Galana Plaza in Kilimani shortly before 10 PM. The S-curved nine-story building's turquoise glass glimmered darkly in the night, the club entrance teeming with bedazzled and gaudy revelers.

The Billionaire Club or, as it's more commonly known, B-Club, was established in 2016 by flashy Rwandan tycoon Barry Ndengeyingoma, and is considered by many to be the premiere nightclub of Nairobi, hosting extravagant parties and special events and frequented by the famous and infamous alike. Celebrities and politicians are among the many who run up exorbitant tabs of a million or more shillings, some of it shooting bills into the air with the cash canon or washing hands and other body parts in Moet.

Jake and Remington strolled through the decadent red-carpeted lobby, where a white hubless Tron bike was on display behind velvet ropes and below the gold-glitter "b" logo. From there, it was into a blitzkrieg of light and sound—fluorescent pinks and purples and greens and the pulsing beats of artists like Meddy and Davido and Iyanya—and a hive of bodies bumping and gyrating and twerking. Attractive cocktail waitresses slithered through the crowd in skin-tight black cutout dresses, trays of drinks or champagne sparklers held over their heads. The décor was futuristic-modern, much of the seating resembling marshmallows, white and overstuffed with hot pink cushions. Other sectioned lounges were couched in black leather with art deco and mirrors, the open overhead gridded with white metal beams.

Catching a glimpse of his friend's face, which looked dazed in the sensory overload, Remington asked, "When was the last time you had a wild one, man?" He had to shout for his words to be heard, let alone understood.

Jake did not respond, his eyes starting to scan the sea of heads jostling around him. It was not long before schools of women were wiggling their way toward them, circling like hammerheads in a Caribbean reef. While Remington enjoyed the lascivious attention, Jake was locked into an impermeable zone of single-mindedness.

Laughing, Remington commented, "Whoa, buddy, you *are* gone. Gotta get you back home to that pretty little thang."

Ignoring him, Jake asked, "How the hell are we going to find him in this place? It's a madhouse."

"I'm headed to the bartender who Kip spoke with."

A pair of tall and curvaceous Kenyan women wormed in front of them, both with long braids piled on their heads, exotically lined eyes and brightly glossed lips, filling out clinging dresses that revealed more flesh than they covered. One sidled brazenly up to Jake and murmured Swahili in his ear, "*Unasura nzuri sana…Sisi tunafaa kuwa pamoja,*" telling him how handsome he was and that they should be together. Jake gave her a thin smile and kept moving.

Remington led them to a bar where a young man in a black collared shirt was juggling multiple bottles, flipping and swinging and pouring into cocktail glasses and tumblers. His hair was cornrowed and he wore silver-framed glasses, rings on almost every finger of each hand. When he saw Remington, he grinned and flashed an extended thumb and fore-finger shaka gesture.

"Hey Panya, how's it going?"

"Nash, my man!" The bartender's eyes slid to Jake. "A friend?"

"Oh no, man…this is my brother of many years."

"Very nice to meet you," Panya said to Jake, rattling a shakerful of mojito ingredients.

Jake gave Remington a sidelong glance piqued with impatience, so Remington got on with it. "You told Kip that the guy we're looking for is here tonight?"

The bartender shook his head. "He *was* here. Maybe ten or fifteen minutes ago?"

Jake and Remington both looked dumbfounded and bereft. "Shit," Remington muttered. "And you're sure it was him? How do you know he left?"

"Oh yeah, he is known around here. Only started coming in recently, but he likes to flash the money."

"Most people in here do," Remington pointed out.

"Yes, but he talks the big talk, you know?"

Oh yeah, we know, Jake thought.

"About all the wars he has fought in, the big fighter stud," Panya said, his tone tipped in sarcasm.

Jake felt his stomach knot up in revulsion and he had to work to keep his expression neutral. Remington's hand closed around Jake's arm and he repeated, "How do you know he left?"

"He paid his tab," Panya said. "From what I hear, he likes to club hop."

"Like where? Westlands? CBD?"

The bartender shrugged. "I would try the ones in Westlands first."

"Okay," Remington said, "Thanks, buddy. *Haya, baadaye.*"

Jake and Remington were making their way out when yet another woman approached, sheathed in a black leather dress, her feet stacked in Goliath-style stilettos. Her hair was long and sleek and she threw it back with a wave of her hand, the other striking Remington on the cheek, hard enough to make a *thwapping* sound. She shrilled something close to his ear and sashayed off into the crowd.

"What was *that?*" Jake asked, watching her shapely ass and swishing hair in retreat.

Remington grinned sheepishly, touching the spot on his face that was already as red as a rare steak. "A small misunderstanding."

Jake crooked his head at him. "Uh-huh." Then he said, "God, I can't believe we just missed the son of a bitch."

Remington stroked his mustache and beard, his gray-green eyes shadowed like mist over a bog. "Well, let's see if we can catch up to him."

REMINGTON DROVE NORTH ON various roads, beyond Waiyaki Way and into Westlands. Then, for the next two hours, they stopped in a mix of nightclubs, all of them dungeon-dark with flashing neon lighting and deafening music that throbbed and drove the beat into bone, the passion into the uninhibited movement of bodies and spirits relinquished to some existential power. They went to Hypnotica, Havana, K1, 40Forty, Club City Space, and Tribeka; they also checked the strip clubs, such as Small World Water, Liddos, Tahiti, and XS Millionaires. In places where X was acknowledged as a recent frequent flyer, they were either told he'd not been seen this night or had come and gone. They heard similar characterizations as those imparted by the bartender at the B Club, but in the strip clubs they heard something else: he was also known for his mean treatment of the women. When they got to XS Millionaires, one of the servers who was waiting for her drink orders overheard Remington's inquiry and said, "Oh yes, he was here just now, actually."

"Damn it," Remington fumed. "Well, there's Mordern and Monte Carlo near here. We can try those."

"I can save you the trouble," the waitress said, puckering her lips and pouting at Jake. "But then you would leave."

Jake indulged her with a smile in return, hoping to entice an answer. "You know where he was going next?" he asked.

"I told him he was looking very fly tonight and he said he was on his way to a VIP grand opening."

"Did he say what grand opening?" Jake asked, trying to curb his excitement.

"Not exactly. Just said it was some big deal."

Jake and Remington stared at each other, Jake reaching into his pocket for his iPhone. He opened a browser search and typed in a few words. An instant later, he declared, "Oh my God, are you fucking kidding me?"

He showed the screen to Remington.

As they dashed from the club and sprinted for the Rubicon, Jake said, "Got you, motherfucker."

55

THERE WERE FEW CARS along the street so they easily found an isolated space in which to park the Rubicon. They both got out of the Jeep,
making sure their handguns and radios were concealed beneath the
black button-up shirts they were wearing over their tees, and strode
briskly toward the building that, tonight, was illuminated by alternating
sweeps of gold and silver-white spotlights. A sign implanted in the
smooth carpet of manicured sod had a new message added to an older
one, the top reading: VIP GRAND OPENING TONIGHT. Beneath that
was a graphic showcasing an elegant lounge set against the backdrop of
a Nairobi skyline at sunset, insouciantly affluent people sharing drinks
and, perhaps, bragging on their latest investments. The familiar tagline
below read: NOW LEASING THE LUXURY YOU DESERVE.

The fountain that ran the full length of the porte cochere, glimmering
with glass and brass and marble, was spraying jets of water into the air
as cars pulled up and frenetic valets darted around each other to open
their doors. Bespoke-suited men and women in glamorous evening
dress stepped from Porsches and Mercedes and Ferraris and proceeded
through the lobby entrance.

Almost three weeks to the day, they were standing on the site where
Jake had taken part in an impromptu op that had, at the time, seemed
completely extraneous to his presence and purpose in Africa.

"How can we know he's here?" Jake asked as they walked past the
front of Angani Place, finished and immaculate, all construction debris

gone.

"I guess we don't," Remington replied, "but somehow this all seems—"

"Like kismet?"

"Something like that. But that feeling you get in your gut…"

"Yeah, I'm feeling it, too. If he *is* here, he's got to be tied to Zhuang."

"I would say so," Remington agreed, adding, "but unless we can put Zhuang here himself, I don't know. We were never able to get enough detail from that screen cap we got. Kip ran it through everything. The bugs I planted got nothing more than housekeeping and maintenance people jabbering in Swahili. Investigating ownership of the penthouse unit came up equally nil, everything tracing back to numerous shell companies."

"Well, that in itself tells us we had him, and might yet. So what's our approach?"

Remington reached into a pocket of his pants and produced the access card they'd used before. "This should still work…Kip says there's a service entrance and elevator on the back side. With all the valets coming and going in that parking bay tonight, this is the better choice."

They continued around the side of the building, and were momentarily stymied by the unforeseen amount of activity they found there. Food service trucks, florists' vans, a linen service and, worst of all, the rigs of several news crews.

"Shit," Jake muttered. "This is not ideal."

"Actually," Remington mused, "maybe it is. There's so much going on, we should be able to slide in, but let's see if we can get that service elevator to ourselves."

They struck a casual gait, walking past people milling about, including some building staff on smoke breaks, and entered through a pair of doors already propped open for deliveries. Inside, they went straight to the elevator and Remington tapped the UP button. No one else was waiting and, when the bell chimed and the elevator doors opened, no one emerged. They stepped inside and Remington held his cloned access card in front of the RFID reader in the digital touchpad, the red light turning green. The doors closed with a light bump.

Jake and Remington exchanged a relieved glance and Remington depressed the button marked LOUNGE. Blowing out a breath, he said, "Here we go."

WHEN THEY EXITED THE elevator, they found themselves in a marble-tiled corridor just off the main hallway of the floor, the sound of a live band playing Sauti Sol's *Melanin* coming from that direction. Turning the corner, they saw the lounge just beyond a recessed reception desk, the concierge and attendants occupied with guests to an extent that allowed Jake and Remington to merge into the flow of people without any particular notice. The hall ceiling lighting was artistically baffled white panels framed in wood, which was replicated in columns separating sections of the lounge's glass. On the other side, people like the ones represented in the exterior sign were mingling with drinks in hand, some swaying to the music. Impeccably tailored suits, sequined couture dresses, gold and diamonds, Italian shoes. Male and female servers circulated with trays of drinks, the men in pressed long-sleeved white shirts, black vests and bowties, and the women in form-fitting black cowl-neck dresses with side slits.

Jake and Remington eased inside, taking in the layout and scanning faces. On one side was a bar with a white pleated base trimmed in black and topped in black granite, black-and-white checkered tile floor below and track lighting above. The mid-century modern bar stools were all filled, another layer of people crowded in behind. Small round white tables and chairs dotted the rest of the side, a buffet table set up with a line of silver chafing pans brimming with hors d'oeuvres: spicy chicken wings and dips, *samosas* and *bhajiyas*, spring rolls and sushi, kebabs and prawns. The other side of the lounge was carpeted in pale gray, furnished with caramel leather sofas and scooped gray fabric chairs grouped around low tables, the ceiling above paneled in wood beams and lit with intersecting circle fixtures. There were abstract sculptures and pottery randomly scattered, but few paintings or prints because there was almost no wall space, the hallway wall being glass and the exterior, full-view windows.

They took their time combing through the guests, but it did not take long to come to the conclusion that X was not here. "This just doesn't strike me as his kind of scene," Remington observed.

"No," Jake sighed. "It doesn't."

A female server took notice of their inquisition and stopped by them. "Can I help you gentlemen?" she asked, batting her eyelashes. She canted a hip and steadied the tray she carried.

"We're looking for someone," Jake began. "Are there any other gatherings in the building for the grand opening?"

"Oh yes, quite a few," she answered. "In the lower level restaurant… but it is getting late so probably wrapping up. Some private ones, but the most lively one is around the corner from here."

"Around the corner?" Jake asked.

"On the other side of this floor. That is where the pool party is going on."

Jake and Remington left the lounge and went to the end of the hallway and, sure enough, on the other side was a pool, glassed on the exterior and overhead, bouncing with bikinis and beach balls and showered in a rainbow of oscillating lights, the music spun by a deejay whose taste ran a lot more electronic, and louder. They stood surveying for several moments and then Jake snagged a young server strutting by with the hands of both fingers clutching bottles of Tusker and Heineken.

"Yes?" she asked.

Jake had taken out his iPhone and scrolled to an image he'd pulled from the Spear-X website. He held it out for her. "Have you seen this guy tonight?"

She glanced at the phone and beamed in recognition. "Oh yes! That is Aris!" Pronouncing it 'R-E.' "He was here just a little while ago with Mr. Zee!"

Jake and Remington seemed to suck in their breath at the same time, Remington responding first. "Mr. Z?"

"I think they went up to his penthouse," she said. "The owners just sent some Dom champagne up there."

TAKING THE ELEVATOR TO the forty-fourth floor, Remington said, "No rappelling tonight and we don't have the cameras to check the hall, but we know there's security. Any thoughts on how to deal with them?"

"Preferably no shooting, either," Jake replied, "although, with the noise and inebriation, it might not be noticed. I guess, depending on how many, some kind of distraction could work."

When the elevator doors parted, both had their Glocks out but were concealing them behind their backs. Instead of cautiously leaning out to see how many men were there, they sprang into the hallway.

"Hey! Come quick!" Remington yelled. "Mr. Z's niece…she's bleeding in the elevator! We need all the help we can get! Hurry!"

There were three men, clad in suits which they solidly filled out, and all of them looked totally flummoxed, first glancing uncertainly at each other, then back to Jake and Remington, animal reflexes in conflict over urgency versus caution.

Before they could choose a reaction, Jake shouted, "Now!"

Heightening the effect, Remington bemoaned, "Oh, Jesus, the blood!"

That got all three running to the elevator, handguns drawn. When they were almost to the doors, which had closed, Jake and Remington each stepped toward a man and gripped the back of their gun hands, bending the wrists and twisting them down and into their hips, guns dropping to the floor in the process. With the men's elbows flared out, Jake and Remington reached through the open space, grabbed the back of their triceps and pulled their arms across. Then, stepping between their legs, they swung around behind the men and latched onto their hipbones, finishing with control that allowed them to restrain with Zipties. But while the first two were being taken out of commission with the arm-drag maneuver, the third guy had reassessed the situation and was waiting to get a clear shot at Jake or Remington.

Signaling his move to Remington, Jake used the man he had restrained as a shield and rammed the third man as Remington cut wide to the right and, in the time it took the man to adjust his aim, Jake had pinned him on the ground. Remington summoned the elevator, and they dragged the three cuffed men into the carriage.

"Okay," Jake said, catching his breath, "prime time."

Remington used his access card on the door entry, halfway expecting it not to work on the penthouse, but it did, so Jake turned the knob and they quietly slipped inside the foyer. They could hear a conversational exchange going on between two people and, taking a quick peek, Remington raised two fingers to confirm it, gesturing that he would go right and Jake would go left. With Glocks aimed, they continued along the short foyer, stopped at the end, and waited for their moment.

It came within minutes.

Inside the living room, the two men were at ease, seated on opposite ends of the sectional couch, lifting champagne glasses in a toast. Which was when Jake and Remington stormed into the room.

"What the fuck?" the younger man sputtered, hand still clasped around his flute of champagne.

The older man, aged in his mid-forties, was frozen in place but had dropped his glass, which caught the edge of an area rug and rolled, spilling vintage Dom Pérignon in a fizzy puddle. He wore a black silk suit with a red-and-black pinstriped tie, his features vaguely Oriental—narrow eyes, short, dark hair, thin mustache.

The younger man, roughly the same age as Jake and Remington, was Aris Xavier. His "fly" look for the evening consisted of a Tom Ford charcoal sharkskin suit, a Haynes patterned shirt open at the collar, and Magnanni gray suede shoes, all of which were as out of character and class on him as The Rock in a princess dress. Recent years had taken away the lean, adding some padding to his frame, but left no less of the mean, his face set in a deviant glower. He had kept the Caesar haircut and beard.

"What the fuck?" he repeated, mouth agape, spilling his own champagne as he set his glass down on the coffee table with a solid thunk.

"You tell me," Jake said dryly. "Apparently you need better intel, asswipe—security, too. Where'd you get them? Mercs 'r' us?"

Xavier lunged from the couch, but dropped back onto it as Jake moved closer, his Glock out in front of him and pointed at Xavier's center mass. Next to him, the older man flipped over the side of the couch and scrambled to his feet, running for the kitchen, the other side of which had a secondary access door to the exterior hall. Jake's focus flickered for a split second, making eye contact with Remington. When he did, Xavier leapt up and took off for the balcony.

"I've got this," Remington shouted. "Go get that son of a bitch!"

Jake went after Xavier, stepping onto the balcony just in time to see him straddling the safety glass and latching onto the corner beam. Jake watched as X clambered down and swung into the balcony of the unit below. From somewhere overhead, Jake thought he heard the sound of helicopter rotors. He ducked back inside the penthouse, raced through to the hall and into the stairwell. Listening, he heard the heavy thunk of feet on stairs just above him.

He's going to the roof, Jake thought. *Helicopter.*

When Jake reached the stairwell landing, he pulled the door open and stepped outside. It was cool at this height with a brisk breeze, the night lit by a nearly full moon. Another set of stairs, enclosed by grating, led to the raised platform where a bird was, in fact, parked, rotors turning. Jake climbed up to the pad and saw that the helicopter was not the Atlas Oryx but an Airbus, probably waiting to pick up one or more VIP guests. But Xavier was about to appropriate it, running for the open passenger door, the tails of his suit coat flipped up on his back. Aiming for the interior of the helo, knowing that would rattle the pilot, Jake began firing his Glock, some of his rounds pinging against metal and others making contact somewhere inside. X reached for the handle, but the pilot was not taking any chances, spooling up from the pad. X's hand caught the skid. He swung his other arm up and got a two-handed hold, his legs swinging as he dangled. For a moment, the helicopter paused its ascent, as if the pilot was debating what to do.

Jake ended the deliberation, grabbing X around the legs and yanking him down. The Airbus rose and peeled off, its downdraft blowing fine concrete dust and grit on top of them.

X jumped to his feet and charged Jake, his face ugly with fury. Jake came up with his Glock, but X hit him in the chest before he could aim. The force took them both to the helipad stairs, Jake's back against the railing. Three stories below was the top of the penthouse.

Pressing his full weight to keep Jake pinned, his face inches from Jake's, Aris Xavier snarled, "You fucking maniac. It's been *you* blowing up my shit, hasn't it? You!"

Jake smirked. "You didn't know that? You're more of dumbass than I even knew."

"Fuck you!" X barked, spittle spraying from his mouth and hitting Jake's face.

Jake rubbed the saliva off on the fabric of X's jacket. "You had your dirty little hands in just about every kind of pie out here, didn't you? Ivory, gold, trafficking…a real one-stop shop." Feeling his wrath ignite like a flamethrower, he asked, "What I want to know is why Keogh?"

"Oh, I'm sure you've got it all figured out," X replied acidly, breathing over Jake's nose. "But Keogh getting whacked was not part of the plan. If the arrogant bastard had just done the fucking contract…"

Jake was listening, but his mind was devising strategy, his hands working. His Glock had somehow dislodged from his grip. *Where's my gun? Got to get the gun.*

Aware of Jake wriggling his hands underneath him, X pressed down harder and pushed so that Jake was bent backwards over the railing, his feet leaving the ground. Jake felt his equilibrium flip and a rush of dizziness, his eyes sliding to the side. Seeing the distance below the railing. If he couldn't hold on, if he slipped, if he was pushed…would he fall to the top of the penthouse or pitch farther out and plummet the full forty-seven stories? Either way, he'd be dead. Just like that, dead and gone. No will to live, no fight for survival. Just dead.

Not gonna happen.

Summoning all his inner strength and years of disciplined physical regimes, Jake heaved upward and drove his body into X, the man's eyes bulging in their sockets as his breath was pushed forcefully through his rib cage and trapped in his windpipe. Jake kept driving until they were all the way to the other side of the helipad and it was X who was pinned down, flat on the ground. Only here, as was the case all the way around the pad, there was no ledge or railing, just a slightly elevated lip. And on this side, the ground below was the full forty-seven stories.

All or nothing, motherfucker. All or nothing.

When Xavier was inhaling and exhaling again, wheezing and glancing down over the edge, his face went pasty white. "Hey…hey…look. I wasn't going to push you. That's not me."

"That's not you?" Jake gave a hideous laugh. "That's not you? Oh, that's a good one. Remember who you're talking to, asshole. I know where all your bodies are buried. Literally."

"That was me when I was younger, a blowhard, you know." X was blabbering now, perspiration slick on his face. "This is not the way…"

"No? Tell me why. Give me a reason." Jake shoved a knee into X's throat, causing him to gag, his head dipping over the side.

X squeezed his eyes shut, gulping for breath, and then, unexpectedly, Jake removed his knee and stood. X rolled to get his balance and was pulling himself up when he swayed—drunkenly, too much celebratory drinks and champagne. A foot skidded over the lip of the helipad and he dropped, a hand grappling for and clamping the pavement. He quickly brought up his other hand and held on. Jake bent down and grasped both of X's wrists, and paused.

"Goddammit, pull me up! Shit, Jake, pull me up. I'm sorry, okay?" He sniveled for several moments and then, as if his psyche had switched channels, his eyes hardened and he grew stonily composed. "Go ahead, just do it. I know you want to. Let go. Are you too much of a pussy to do it? Go on, do it."

"Oh, believe me, nothing would give me greater pleasure," Jake assured him. But then you'd miss out on the fun of the War Crimes Tribunal. That wouldn't be very sporting of me."

"You're one to talk," X hissed.

"Everything I have done can be justified," Jake bristled. "Sure can't say the same about you."

He waited another few seconds and then hauled Aris Xavier up to the helipad, spun him around and ligatured his hands behind his back. He retrieved his Glock from the pavement by the stair railing and shoved X down the steps.

WHEN HE'D UPDATED HIS status to Remington on the way down, Jake learned that Zhuang was in Remington's custody and Baladur and Kipnis had arrived in case they were needed for backup. It was approaching 1 AM and the VIP grand opening was still going strong in extravagant oblivion. Jake marched X to the Rubicon where Remington had stashed Zhuang in the backseat.

"Ah, we meet again, scumbag," Remington gloated.

X had gone quiet, but he twisted so Remington could see his middle-finger salute.

"What are we doing?" Jake asked Remington.

"Waiting for all the alphabet soup of law enforcement."

"You got a smoke?" X asked off-handedly.

"No," Jake said.

"Water then…can I get some water?"

Jake reached into the front seat of the Rubicon for his backpack and, in an instant, X stuck his hand into the pocket of Jake's chinos and found his Swiss Army knife, flipping a blade out and cutting through his plastic cuffs. Then, he was off and running into the night.

"Fuck!" Jake screamed, and ran after him.

But behind him, Kipnis was yelling, "No, Jake, stop!"

Remington caught up to Jake, grabbing him around the torso, saying, "Let him go."

Jake looked at Remington in crazed disbelief. "*What?* What are you talking about? He's getting away!" He wrestled to free himself from Remington's hold, but his friend's arms were like a vise.

In the distance, silhouetted by the streetlights, Aris Xavier got into a low-slung sports car and slammed the door.

Jake was furious now, his eyes blazing, boring into Remington's face. "What the hell? Remy? I could have got him…why didn't you let—"

And then an explosion rocked the night, lifting vehicles from the street, setting off their alarms, sending a firebomb high into the dark sky. Jake stared, reeling in shock. Turned his face to Remington and, a few seconds later, to Kipnis. "What did you do? What did you *do?*"

Kipnis, cool and detached, his eyes as glazed as a fish, said, "I identified his car and set up a contingency."

"You set up a—"

Remington said stoically, "Jake…he got what he gave…an eye for an eye. For those guys in Sierra Leone. Among others. *Many* others."

Jake was still battling his anger, but he had nothing to say to that. Nothing at all.

56

JAKE STOOD BENEATH A giant acacia tree, the reach of its wide dome giving ample shade from the hot sun, watching as the villagers surrounded Amelia Keogh at the conclusion of the memorial service for her husband. There were hugs and kisses and clasped hands, tears and smiles. It had been beautiful and poignant and indelibly inspirational. It also hurt his heart but, as he studied the valiant grace in her face, he knew hers was hurting a lot more. *This is Africa*, he thought somberly. It gives you beauty and strength and it kills you along the way.

Following the op at Angani Place, much of the day before had been spent with a team from Interpol, which had taken custody of the man presumed to be their Red Notice, Bái Zhuang. He was not talking but, with his image and fingerprints being put into wide circulation, investigators felt it was only a matter of time before links and affiliations would be established, associates would emerge to negotiate immunity deals, and evidence would be linked. Dr. Janney had called to let Remington know that the tusks they'd brought him to test, despite having been recovered in South Sudan, were a DNA match to others originating from the *bai* massacre in DRC. Kipnis had also confirmed that the gold beads from the handbags in Mombasa were, in fact, authentic gold and, as a result, Interpol was also launching investigations into Arcana Trading, Kaseme Mines, and Spear-X.

The Somali pirates suspected in the hijacking of the Keoghs' ship and the killings of Cyrus Keogh and Archer Rudd remained at large, but the local case had been turned over to the CTF 150, a multinational coalition of combined maritime forces based in Bahrain. As Kipnis had discovered, there were connections to Daahir Aljabarti and the ivory trafficking syndicate and, by extension, Spear-X and Aris Xavier.

Due to the presence of media at the Angani Place grand opening, the aftermath of the car bomb in the street adjacent to the high-rise had been widely reported but was being characterized as a "random act of terrorism," a conclusion that was not likely to be challenged given the frequency of such incidents in Kenya—also because Kipnis never left any traces.

Kipnis had been in communication with the legal authorities and advocacy agencies working with the rebels that had either surrendered or been captured, many admitting to an alliance with "an American contractor" in which they were facilitated with obtaining slave labor and arms in exchange for protected territory. So far, none had confessed to being involved in either the gold mining or poaching operations, but the accumulation of evidence was beginning to thread that needle, and while the attack on the Keoghs' compound could not yet be tied to a specific group of rebels, the bullet casings Jake found at the site and the *bai* massacre and the basecamp had been linked to a faction of known LRA rebels integrated with those in custody. Kipnis had also been told that the advocacy agencies involved were optimistic for the successful rehabilitation and community reintegration of many.

In the hours following the previous night's op, Jake had a difficult time resolving his fury for being denied formal justice of Aris Xavier who would have most certainly been a solid candidate for war crimes, but he conceded that it was also possible Xavier could have somehow been acquitted. And, ultimately, he could not regret—not for one instant—the fate that had been delivered to X. All of the souls, human and animal, that had been used and abused or tortured and killed at his hand, now had salvation. Furthermore, whether or not all of the connections were eventually made for his atrocities, Jake knew he was guilty.

The sound of a helicopter drew Jake's gaze to the field where Remington's Cessna was parked. He joined the stream of people, which included Falcone and Niles, heading over to greet its arrival. Three figures stepped from the cabin, all young and male, clad in jeans and slinging backpacks. When Jake caught up to Falcone and Niles, the three young men were extending their hands and introducing themselves.

"...and we're with The Sanctuary Initiative," one was saying.

Falcone and Niles were both staring speechlessly.

Remington and Kipnis came up beside them. "Eddie, Curran, these guys are actually with Sanctuary," Remington said. "I hate to tell you this, but Iris Margolis and the two with her were not. When Kip found out, we got in touch."

One of the new arrivals said, "We're so sorry for the deception—well, it's fraud, really—and when we heard, we wanted to apologize in person." He was tall and fair in a Nordic way, and had introduced himself as Gunner Hagland.

Falcone stammered, "I...I don't understand. You mean Iris really wasn't...she was part of...you mean I..." His voice died and, for a moment, he looked like he was going to be sick. He raked at his thick, unruly hair. "Oh God."

Jake put a hand on his shoulder. "Hey, bud...you did nothing wrong. Nothing at all. But damn, I'm sorry."

Hagland went on, "Now that we're here, let's see what we can do to help this community."

Amelia Keogh had joined them, and offered a slim smile. "We'd love to show you around, get your thoughts and ideas."

She stepped over to Jake as the others began to walk toward the village. Turning the mesmerizing focus of her expressive green eyes on him, her smile broadened. Today she wore a midi-length denim skirt, embroidered at the hem, with a simple white cotton shirt, her vibrant red hair tied in the high-ponytail style she favored.

"How are you doing?" Jake asked.

"Oh...you know..." Her head tilted to the sky, which was as starkly blue as a sky could ever be, dolloped with clouds that looked as light and fluffy as whipped cream. "God, what a shade of blue," she remarked wistfully. "Just so excruciatingly beautiful, but it's hard to be happy for it. But *he* would be. I can just see him now, kicking the soccer ball around the field with the kids."

She smiled again and bit her lip, eyes moistening.

"Hold on to those moments, those images." Jake twitched as his sat phone rang. He answered, listened, and said, "Okay, I'll be there as quickly as I can."

"What's wrong, Jake?" Amelia asked.

"I don't know," he said vaguely. "But I need to get Kean to fly me." He left her standing in the field, hastening off to find Dmello. She watched him worriedly, wondering what else could possibly be happening.

THE SUN WAS JUST a dark red ember in the sky by the time Jake returned hours later. He'd called ahead to fill Remington in, but not Amelia. Now, as he strode toward the village with Dmello by his side, those sitting around the fire with Amelia noticed that Jake was carrying something. Remington nudged her and, seeing Jake's approach, she stood, arms clasped in front of her as if she were cold, even though it was still well into the eighties.

When Amelia made out what Jake had, her hands flew to her mouth and she gasped for breath, her knees buckling.

On the other side of her, Niles reached out to give her support, but before he could, she bolted for Jake.

The bundle in his arms stirred and, seeing Amelia running toward Jake, began to cry, arms outstretched.

"Lula!" Amelia shouted, and stumbled into Jake, her arms enveloping and lifting the little girl to her. Tears came in an unrelenting torrent as she held the child tightly, swaying back and forth, murmuring, "Oh my God, oh my God...our little girl..." And, then, quietly, "*My* little girl."

Finally turning to look at Jake, she asked, "How on earth did you find her after all this?"

"Well, I can't take credit for this miracle," he said, shaking his head in wonder. "The call I got was from Dr. Caron at the refugee camp. They were being inundated with wounded from a village that had been attacked, and the village had an orphanage. There was so much chaos, the only thing I could make out was, 'come as soon as you can, it's urgent'. When I got up there, things had calmed down and she had Lula sitting there, waiting for me."

"Jake, there are just no words," Amelia said, cradling the child in her arms. The little girl was now visibly content, her eyelids drooping in sleepiness.

Gazing at the child, Jake thought about the way her traumatic world had forever changed when Cyrus and Amelia Keogh first laid eyes on her, and now, the way she would continue to change Amelia's.

"No words needed," Jake said. He looked at Remington. "You about ready to go?"

"Jake, wait," Amelia said, and carefully handed Lula to Betty Ndongala, who was standing behind her. "I was about to show you something earlier when you took off." She nodded to Remington, Falcone and Niles, and several of the others, leading them all through the village to the far side, beyond which was a savanna dotted with acacia and palm trees almost to the horizon and then fringed with forest.

She stopped by what appeared to be a small monument of carefully stacked stones, the top of which displayed a bronze plaque. The daylight was all but gone, but Jake could just make out the engraving, and felt a lump swell in his throat as he read: FUTURE SITE OF THE CYRUS KEOGH WILDLIFE RESERVE. Below that was: MADE POSSIBLE BY AND WITH GRATITUDE TO JAKE TYLER AND FRIENDS.

Jake swallowed hard and looked at her.

"I know what you're thinking," she said softly. "It's only been a couple of days. But Cy and I had already been planning this before…" She paused, blinking. "I had the plaque made while I was in Nairobi."

"Amelia…you have no idea what this means to me," Jake said, awed, adding, "to all of us."

"Well, it can't possibly mean more than what you've done for me." She inhaled and glanced around at the trees darkly silhouetted against the evening sky. "And you're right, Jake. I will go on."

BEFORE THEY DEPARTED FOR Nairobi, Jake spent some time with Falcone and Niles. Seated together in Nakalé's communal area as the village prepared dinner over the fire, Falcone and Niles watched as Remington, Kipnis, Baladur, and Dmello gathered their gear. Jake had packed up and was ready to go.

"So," he asked them, "what have you decided to do?"

"We're staying," Falcone said. "At least for a while."

"Amelia will be going to Australia for Cy's funeral, of course," Niles said. "But we want to finish the documentary, also help her here for a bit."

Jake smiled. "That's wonderful. Remy just told me he's going to hire and train some more guys for a security team he's putting together for her. He's also going to set up monitoring for the village and new compound as well as the wildlife reserve." Standing, he said, "Okay, guys, I've got to go. Take care of yourselves."

"Yeah, okay," Falcone said, and stepped forward, giving Jake a solid hug. When he withdrew, he looked like he wanted to say something but could not find the right words.

Jake said lightly, "I know."

Niles hugged him even harder, wiping at his eyes on release. "Take care, mate. And please, give our love to Callie."

"I will." Grinning crookedly, Jake wagged his finger. "Don't get into any more trouble."

Niles feigned astonishment. "Us get into trouble?"

AFTER THE FLIGHT FROM Nakalé, which got them back to Nairobi around midnight, Remington had crashed but Jake got almost no sleep, anxious for the early-morning flight out. He could have departed any-time he chose, but he did not want to stay another minute in Africa. It was finally time to go home.

They rolled into terminal 2 at Jomo Kenyatta before dawn, Jimiyu Chilemba turning Jake's baggage over to the FBO handlers while Re-mington walked with his friend through the private departure lounge. The Gulfstream 650ER waiting on the tarmac was one of the Keoghs' actual planes, and the captain was waiting to personally escort Jake aboard. Indicating to the pilot that he would join him momentarily, Jake turned to Remington and sighed.

"Couldn't have done it without you," he said, a tired smile tugging at his mouth. "And those guys of yours...they are some of the best I've ever worked with."

"Well, the way they feel about you, I just hope they never vacation in Costa Rica. I might not get them back," Remington chuckled. "And I am indebted to you for enabling me to get a guy I've had a hard-on for just about as long as I've been here in Nairobi…might very well unravel that whole syndicate."

"I'm sorry I got so bent out of shape about X."

Remington shook his head. "Don't be. It's going to take some time to process, but I don't have any regrets. Do you?"

"Not a one," Jake said without hesitation.

"I'll look after Amelia and help in any other way I can, and I'll also keep tabs on those two guys of yours. I can see how you got so attached to them. What they lack in combat virility, they more than make up for in ferocity of heart."

"Yeah, they do."

"And they're hilarious as hell."

Jake's smile widened.

"All right…get on board that dream machine and go home to your sweet little honey. Rest well and be happy, my brother…you've more than earned it."

They embraced and Jake started for the door to the tarmac, but Remington clutched his arm, his expression serious. "Hey, I almost forgot—I'm still half asleep—did you know there's a hit out on you?"

Jake looked at him unflinchingly.

"A hit, a contract."

"What else is new," Jake remarked blandly. "There was one on me the whole time I was operating in Colombia. Where'd you hear about it?"

"No, I'm pretty sure this is something else," Remington replied.

"What do you mean?"

"Kip ran across it on the Dark Web yesterday and wanted me to be sure and tell you. It's just been posted within the past few weeks."

AS THE GULFSTREAM CLIMBED into the sky over Nairobi, the sun was dispelling the last vestiges of darkness with deep pink and orange layers that spread like watercolors and, relaxing in the whisper-luxury of the plane's interior, Jake could feel the tension draining from him in waves. Gazing through the window by his seat, the city began to recede, replaced by the tans and browns and golds and greens of savannas and forests that went on for endless miles until a small settlement here and there wove into that earthen tapestry or a river stitched across it like a jagged seam. Before the jet had reached its cruising altitude, Jake watched the land flow below, his eyelids heavy, and then he honed in on something that made him catch his breath—a herd of elephants moving through a sea of tall grass, isolated in a vast field as if they were the only creatures on earth.

Watching the elephants, Jake felt emotion and pride swelling inside him and, for the first time, realized he really had accomplished something here besides part of his mission objective. He had made a difference in the ecosystem; he had thwarted predators and extended life for some of the most endangered species on the planet. Maybe not many, but some...and some was good. More than good. But he hoped, devoutly hoped, that there would be many more coming behind him to continue the fight. He watched the magnificent beasts plodding forth across the savanna, becoming smaller and more distant as the jet continued its ascent. It was a glorious sight to behold and one he would long remember.

Baby, wherever you are, I hope you found your family.

He leaned back and closed his eyes, reflective of what he had experienced here, what he had done, and what he hoped for the soul of Africa.

57

AFTER CROSSING EIGHT TIME zones and arriving in Costa Rica at sundown of the day before, Jake was halfway through the drive from San José to Dominical when his cell phone rang. He'd already called Callie, whose palpable excitement for his homecoming had blasted his heart with a crescendo of happiness that strummed inside like the rich vibrations of taut guitar strings, a song of exhilaration playing through him from head to toe. His touchscreen showed Jesse Segura, returning his earlier call. Tapping the button on his steering wheel, Jake said, "Hey, Jesse, I just wanted to let you know I'm on my way home. I spoke with Callie a little while ago and she sounded good…how is everything?"

Jake listened as Segura slowly related the events that had occurred in his absence, his jaw tightening as a mixture of disbelief and dismay mounted with each revelation. Finally, to allay Segura's contrition, he said, "Okay, all good, Jesse. I understand why you didn't tell me—I can appreciate and respect that—and it sounds like you guys handled everything perfectly. I'm beyond thankful for the care all of you have been providing. We'll talk more later, okay?"

Segura told him there was one more thing, and recounted Callie's episode at the pool. Jake felt a constricting sharpness in his neck as if a fishbone had impaled his throat.

"Nobody else saw a guy? You're sure?"

Segura said no one had but then added the detail about the shoe prints in the rose beds. When the call was concluded, Jake's high spirits had all but evaporated, his mind descending into a space his lifestyle forced him to revisit all too often, that of situational awareness and defensive readiness. And, once again, he began a bleak inner dialogue that was unsettlingly familiar; when he'd returned home to Callie the first time, from Colombia, he had debated whether he should continue the relationship, not because of any equivocation of his feelings for her, but because of the jeopardy his life would put her in—which had proved to be a concern of real portent—and, in the aftermath, he'd vowed to never let anyone or anything hurt her again.

He thought about his reassurances to Callie that the man she'd seen on the beach was not Adonís Valentín, returned from the dead. But had she really seen *a* man? At the beach and at their home? Had an assassin accepted the contract and found out where they lived and been stalking Callie? *Oh God…oh Jesus God.*

His foot pressed down on the accelerator and he sped down the Costanera Sur Pacific coastal highway as darkness fell, silently urging the Jeep to get him home quicker, the full moon shining overhead like an admonitory beacon.

HE PULLED HIS JEEP into the driveway, crushed shells crackling beneath the tires. The villa's lighting illuminated the exterior with a combination of low upward beams and roofline downward-angled ones, providing good coverage of the grounds. Instead of going directly through the front door, he walked around the side, his eyes combing the periphery. The somnolent chorus of insects and crickets, with an occasional wisp of breeze through the trees and palms, and the distant ocean waves rolling in to shore were the only sounds he heard. In back, the pool was bathed in aqua stillness, the lighting in the villa dimmed. He was walking toward the garden when he heard the French doors open. Camilla stepped out, her arms extended in welcome, a broad smile on her face.

"*Señor* Jake," she said warmly. "*Bienvenida a casa.*"

"Thank you, Camilla…it's good to be home."

Before he could ask, she said, "Miss Callie…she is upstairs. So happy, waiting for you."

"Good, good. I'm going to speak to Jesse then I'll be coming in. But you should go home now…it's late."

"*Si*, I was just waiting until you come."

She retreated and Jake crossed the patio, walking around to the other side of the villa, to the space that had been converted for Jesse Segura. Hearing Jake, Segura had emerged and was standing on the grass by the gardens. The two clasped hands and Segura said, "Good to have you home again."

Jake nodded, and said, "So, all good tonight?"

"Yes, all good."

"And…nothing since that pool episode? Any more footprints or anything else?"

"Nada…is all okay." Segura smiled.

"Thank you, Jesse. *Mañana, mi amigo*." When Segura had gone back inside his quarters, Jake took another look around, looked at the gardens, looked at the surrounding rainforest, his senses on heightened alert. But all seemed calm and safe and secure. He inhaled and exhaled, felt his blood pressure slowing, his guard relaxing. Watched, listened, waited a few minutes more. He padded over to the roses, knelt, and admired them. Almost colorless in the moonlight but subtly fragrant, their petals were like tissue. He stood and strode to the French doors and entered the villa.

The quiet inside sent a shiver of déjà vu through him, thinking of when he had returned to the empty house before, when he'd gone up the stairs and expected to find Callie, only to find her gone, taken.

As he ascended to the top floor, he started to call out to her but something stopped him, an irrational voice asking: *What if she didn't respond? What if she wasn't there?* He moved quicker, almost bounding to their bedroom, and stepped into the doorway. Stopped. His eyes lasered to the bed.

She lay on top, her eyes closed, the room's nightlights and moonbeams casting a soft radiance that glowed on her skin and made her silky curls glimmer like white gold. She was wearing a white cotton cami top and bottom, trimmed in eyelet, and the sight of her made his heart trip and flutter so fast he thought it might arrest. Was this a dream? She *looked* like a dream, like something that could not possibly be real. Like something that could not possibly have ever been hurt or in danger or here for him after everything he'd just been through. Had any of it really happened? He knew it had, but seeing her in this moment was like the elixir of everything bad breaking back to good. Yes, he knew it had been real, remembered her pulling him back in his darkest moments, giving him life when he thought he could not go on.

He didn't know how long he stood staring at her, transfixed by the swirls of her hair, the parted lips that were softer and lovelier than the roses, the gentle rise and fall of her chest, but at some point he began peeling his clothes off—boots, shirt, pants, underwear. Shucked and dropped on the floor. He climbed gingerly onto the bed, part of him not wanting to wake her, wanting just to gaze at her...but another, more insistent part wanting to touch and feel and melt into her eyes.

God, God, God...

She stirred, her eyelids flickering open, momentarily disoriented but quickly realizing and reacting with a flood of euphoria.

"Jake! Oh...I can't believe I fell asleep...I was waiting for you!"

Everything inside him collapsed and slid like candlewax, hot and liquid. Breath could not seem to escape his lungs.

"Angel," he rasped, and took her in his arms, shuddering inside. He lifted her face to his, and kissed her, at first lightly, delicately, as if he was afraid of cracking eggshell. And then, still carefully but more deeply, hungrily. Craving, wanting, every tissue and muscle and chamber of his body aching.

She was touching his face, his cheeks, his chest, his arms, the touch like electric lace. "Oh, Jake...you're..."

Knowing what she was seeing—the fading bruises, the lacerations—he said, "I'm okay, baby, I'm fine. How about you? How are you feeling? However you feel, it's okay. I promise you, it's okay, love." He wanted her so badly, but more than his desire, he wanted and needed for her to not be hurting, to not be afraid, to fully trust him not hurt her.

Her eyes met his, something there he hadn't seen before. "I...I'm...Jake, I..."

She could not tell him, but somehow he knew. Her eyes told him. He slipped off her cotton bottoms and rolled over. Stroked the softness of her thighs, inhaled her ambrosial essence, his fingertips caressing her breasts. Touched her gently, felt her gasping, felt her opening to him, and eased inside her. She was warm, oh so warm and, after a brief tenseness, took him and he was gone, so gone. All of the brutality of battle, all of the doubts and fears and anguish and uncertainties dissolved into a cloud of blissful white light, every energy fusing and boiling and exploding in a stream of lava that flowed from a deep, deep core. Again and again, he plunged into a cavern of pinkness that bloomed like a red hibiscus flaring to sunshine, falling through a beautiful blue grotto where the water and the sky seemed to meet in one perfect place and then roll out in a wave capped by a breeze on a sunlit beach where palm trees arched and seabirds sailed high above.

Later, cradling her in his arms, feeling the sweet blow of her breath on his skin, he knew he would do anything to hold onto this love, to her, whatever it took to protect her and this life. Anything.

The French doors to the terrace were open, and he heard the sound of the breeze, the ocean, the light clang of the chimes, all the sounds of tranquility and home. A home he could embrace forever.

In that moment, he knew what he was going to do next.

Below the balcony, a broken tree branch skittered across the pavement, stifling a scuffle. Jake heard it, felt his pulse quicken, and then drew Callie closer, his heart, mind, and body, at peace. His last waking thought was that nothing, no one, could take this away from him.

www.ingramcontent.com/pod-product-compliance
Lightning Source LLC
Chambersburg PA
CBHW022358110726
47903CB00004B/1045